*Five Times Maigret*

# Five
# Times
# Maigret

## GEORGES SIMENON

MAIGRET RIGHT AND WRONG
(MAIGRET IN MONTMARTRE & MAIGRET'S MISTAKE)
MAIGRET HAS SCRUPLES
MAIGRET AND THE RELUCTANT WITNESSES
MAIGRET GOES TO SCHOOL

2475

*A Helen and Kurt Wolff Book*
*Harcourt, Brace & World, Inc.*
*New York*

# Contents

# MAIGRET RIGHT AND WRONG

*comprising*

## MAIGRET IN MONTMARTRE

*and*

## MAIGRET'S MISTAKE

# MAIGRET IN MONTMARTRE

## I

FOR Jussiaume, the policeman, who passed the same spots on his beat
at practically the same time every night, comings and goings of this kind
were so commonplace that his mind registered them automatically,
rather in the way that people living near a railway station notice the
trains pulling in and out.

Sleet was falling, and Jussiaume had stepped into a doorway at the
corner of the Rue Fontaine and the Rue Pigalle, to shelter for a moment.
The red sign of Picratt's was one of the few still alight round there, and
its reflected glow looked like splashes of blood on the wet cobblestones.

It was a Monday, when business is always slack in Montmartre.
Jussiaume could have listed the order in which most of the night-clubs
had closed. Now he saw Picratt's neon sign go out in its turn; the proprietor, a short, fat man who had put on a beige raincoat over his
evening clothes, came outside to wind down the shutters.

A figure—it looked like a small boy—slipped out of the door and
glided off down the Rue Pigalle, towards the Rue Blanche, keeping
close to the wall. Two men emerged next, one of them with a saxophone
case under his arm; they turned in the direction of the Place Clichy.

Almost immediately afterwards another man came out, and set off
down the Rue Notre-Dame de Lorette; the collar of his coat was
turned up.

Jussiaume did not know the names of these people; in fact he scarcely
knew their faces; but like hundreds of others, they had a meaning for
him.

He knew that the next to come out would be a woman wearing a very
short, light-coloured fur coat and perched on exaggeratedly high heels
—walking very fast, as though she were scared at being out alone at
four in the morning. She lived only a hundred yards away. She had to
ring the bell, because the house door was shut at this hour.

Then came the last two—women, together, as usual. They walked,
talking in undertones, to the street corner a few feet away from where
Jussiaume was standing, and there they parted. The older and taller
of the two lounged away up the Rue Pigalle. She would be going to the
Rue Lepic, where he had sometimes seen her enter a house. The other
woman hesitated, glanced at him as though about to say something;

9

and then, instead of turning down the Rue Notre-Dame de Lorette, as she usually did, moved off towards the *tabac* at the corner of the Rue de Douai, which was still lit up.

She seemed to have been drinking. She wore no hat, and her fair hair shone when she passed beneath a lamp. She walked slowly, stopping now and then as though talking to herself.

'Coffee, Arlette?' asked the owner of the *tabac*, an old acquaintance.

'Laced,' she replied.

And a few seconds later the familiar smell of rum warmed up in coffee was wafted on the air. Two or three men were standing drinking at the bar, but she took no notice of them.

'She looked very tired,' the proprietor declared later.

That was probably why she had another coffee, laced with a double portion of rum—after which she fumbled rather clumsily to get money out of her bag, and paid.

'Good night.'

'Good night.'

Jussiaume, the policeman, saw her coming back down the street, walking even more hesitantly than on the way up. As she drew level, she caught sight of him through the darkness, turned to face him, and said:

'I want to make a statement at the police station.'

'That's easy,' he replied. 'You know where it is.'

It was almost opposite, behind Picratt's, as it were—in the Rue de La Rochefoucauld. From where they were standing they could both see the blue lantern above the door, and the cycle patrol's bicycles propped against the wall.

At first he thought she wouldn't go. Then he saw her crossing the road, and she vanished into the building.

It was half past four when she walked into the ill-lit office, where Sergeant Simon was alone except for one young policeman. She said again:

'I want to make a statement.'

'Go ahead,' replied Simon good-naturedly. He had been twenty years in the district and was used to this kind of thing.

The girl was heavily made-up, and the various ingredients had run into each other a bit. She wore a black satin dress under her imitation mink coat. She swayed slightly as she stood clutching the bar which separated the policemen from the public part of the office.

'It's about a crime.'

'There's been a crime committed?'

There was a big electric clock on the wall, and she looked at it as though the position of the hands might be significant.

'I don't know whether it's *been* committed.'

'Then it isn't a crime,' said the sergeant, with a wink at his subordinate.

'But it probably will be committed. In fact it's certain to be.'

'Who told you?'

She seemed to be laboriously following some train of thought.

'The two men, just now.'

'What two men?'

'Clients. I work at Picratt's.'

'I knew I'd seen you somewhere. You do the nude act, don't you?'

The sergeant had never set foot inside Picratt's, but he went past the place every morning and every evening, and he had noticed an enlarged photograph of this girl displayed outside, with smaller photos of the other two.

'So some clients have been talking to you about a crime—just like that?'

'Not to me.'

'Who to, then?'

'They were discussing it together.'

'And you were listening?'

'Yes. I didn't hear it all. They were on the other side of a partition.'

Sergeant Simon understood this point, too. When he went past the place while the cleaners were at work, the door would be open, and he could see a dark room with red curtains and upholstery, a gleaming dance-floor, and all along the walls, tables separated by partitions.

'Go on. When was this?'

'Tonight. About two hours ago. Yes, it must have been two o'clock. I'd only been on once for my act.'

'What did the two visitors say?'

'The oldest said he was going to kill the Countess.'

'What Countess?'

'I don't know.'

'When?'

'Probably today.'

'Weren't they afraid you'd overhear them?'

'They didn't know I was there.'

'Were you alone?'

'No. With another client.'

'Someone you know?'

'Yes.'

'Who?'

'His first name's Albert: I don't know his surname.'

'Did he hear them too?'

'I don't think so.'

'Why shouldn't he have heard?'

'Because he was holding my hands and talking to me.'

'Making love?'

'Yes.'

'While you listened to what was being said on the other side of the partition? Can you remember the actual words?'

'Not exactly.'

'Are you drunk?'

'I've had a drop, but I know what I'm saying.'

'Do you drink like this every night?'

'Not so much.'

'Were you drinking with Albert?'

'We had just one bottle of champagne. I didn't want to let him in for a lot of expense.'

'He isn't rich, then?'

'He's only young.'

'In love with you?'

'Yes. Wants me to throw up the job.'

'So you were with him when the two chaps came in and sat down in the next box?'

'That's right.'

'You didn't get a look at them?'

'I saw them from behind, later on, as they were leaving.'

'Did they stay long?'

'About half an hour.'

'Did they drink champagne with the other girls?'

'No. I think they ordered brandy.'

'And they began at once to talk about the Countess?'

'Not at once. I wasn't paying attention, to begin with. The first thing I heard was something like this:

' "You see, she's still got most of her jewellery, but at the rate she's going it won't last long." '

'What was the voice like?'

'A man's voice. A middle-aged man. When they went out I saw one of them was short, stumpy and grey-haired. It must have been him.'

'Why?'

'Because the other was younger, and it wasn't a young man's voice.'

'How was he dressed?'

'I didn't notice. I think he had a dark suit—black, perhaps.'

'They'd left their overcoats in the cloakroom?'

'I suppose so.'

'So he said the Countess still had some of her jewels, but at the rate she was going they wouldn't last long?'

'That's right.'

'What did he say about killing her?'

The girl was really very young, though she did her best to seem a lot older than her real age. Sometimes, for an instant, she looked like a little girl on the verge of panic. At such moments, she fixed her eyes on the clock, as though that helped her to think. She was swaying to and fro, almost imperceptibly. She must be very tired. The sergeant noticed a slight smell of perspiration from her armpits, mingling with the scent of cosmetics.

'What did he say about killing her?' he asked again.

'I can't remember. Don't rush me. I wasn't alone. I couldn't listen all the time.'

'Albert was cuddling you?'

'No, just holding my hands. The older man said something like: "I've decided to finish it tonight." '

'That doesn't mean he's going to kill her, though. It might mean he's going to steal her jewels. Or perhaps she owes him money and he's decided to have her up.'

'No,' said the girl stubbornly.

'How can you tell?'

'Because that's not it.'

'He definitely spoke of killing her?'

'I'm certain that's what he meant to do. I don't remember the exact words.'

'You couldn't possibly have misunderstood?'

'No.'

'And that was two hours ago?'

'A little more.'

'And knowing a man was going to commit a crime, you waited all this time to come and tell us about it?'

'I was upset. I couldn't leave Picratt's before it closed. Alfonsi's very strict about that.'

'Even if you'd explained why?'

'He'd only have told me to mind my own business, I expect.'

'Try to remember just what was said.'

'They didn't say much, and I couldn't hear it all. There was music going on. And then Tania came to do her act.'

For the last few minutes the sergeant had been making notes—but in an offhand way, as though not really convinced.

'Do you know any Countess?'

'I don't think so.'

'Is there one who comes to the joint?'

'Not many women come. I never heard it said that one of them was a Countess.'

'You didn't manage to get a proper look at the men?'

'I didn't dare. I was scared.'

'Scared of what?'

'That they'd guess I'd overheard them.'

'What names did they call each other by?'

'I didn't notice. I think one of them was called Oscar, but I'm not sure. I think I've had too much to drink. My head aches. I'd like to go to bed now. If I'd known you weren't going to believe me, I wouldn't have come.'

'Go and sit down.'

'Mayn't I go home?'

'Not yet.'

He pointed to a bench that stood against the wall, below the black and white sheets of official announcements.

Then, at once, he called her back.

'What's your name?'

'Arlette.'

'I mean your real name. Got your identity card?'

She took the card out of her bag and handed it to him. He read aloud: 'Jeanne-Marie-Marcelle Leleu, aged 24, born at Moulins, dancer, 42 ter., Rue Notre-Dame de Lorette, Paris.'

'So your name isn't Arlette?'

'That's my stage name.'

'Ever been on the stage?'

'Not in a proper theatre.'

He shrugged his shoulders and gave her back her card, after copying out the particulars.

'Go and sit down.'

Then, murmuring to his subordinate to keep an eye on her, he went into the next room, where he could telephone without being over-heard, and rang up the central emergency service.

'That you, Louis? This is Simon, at La Rochefoucauld Station. There hasn't been a Countess murdered tonight, by any chance?'

'Why a Countess?'

'I don't know. It's probably a cock-and-bull story. The girl seems a bit cracked, and in any case she's as tight as they come. Makes out she heard two chaps planning to bump off a Countess—a Countess who has jewels.'

'News to me. Nothing's come in.'

'If anything of the kind turns up, let me know.'

They chatted on for a time about this and that. When Simon got back to the outer office, Arlette had fallen asleep, as though in a station waiting-room. The resemblance was so striking that he even glanced automatically down at the floor, looking for a suitcase beside her feet.

\*

At seven o'clock, when Jacquart arrived to take over from Sergeant Simon, Arlette was still asleep, and Simon explained the situation to his colleague. He noticed she was waking up just as he left, but he preferred not to wait.

She stared in astonishment at the newcomer, who had a black moustache. Then she glanced uneasily at the clock and leapt to her feet.

'I've got to go!' she exclaimed.

'Just a minute, please,' said Jacquart.

'What do you want now?'

'Perhaps the nap has refreshed your memory?'

She looked sulky now, and her face was shiny, especially along the line of her plucked eyebrows.

'I don't know anything more. I've got to go home.'

'What did Oscar look like?'

'Oscar who?'

The policeman was glancing through the report Simon had made out while she was asleep.

'The one who meant to murder the Countess.'

'I never said his name was Oscar.'

'What was it, then?'

'I don't know. I don't remember what I said last night. I was tight.'

'So you made up the whole story?'

'I don't say that. I did hear two men talking on the other side of the partition, but I could only catch a few words here and there. Perhaps I got it wrong.'

'Well then, why did you come here?'

'I tell you, I was tight. When you're tight things seem different and you're apt to get excited about nothing.'

'No one said anything about the Countess?'

'Oh, yes. . . . I think so. . . .'

'And about her jewels?'

'There was something about jewels.'

'And about finishing with her?'

'That's what I thought at the time. I was already sozzled by then.'

'Who had you been drinking with?'

'With several clients.'

'And with this chap Albert?'

'Yes. I don't know him either. I only know people by sight.'

'Such as Oscar?'

'Why are you always dragging in that name?'

'Would you know him again?'

'I've only seen his back.'

'Backs are quite easy to recognize.'

'I'm not sure. Perhaps.'

Struck by a sudden thought, she asked a question in her turn:

'Has anyone been killed?'

When he did not answer, she became very agitated. No doubt she had a terrific hangover. Her blue eyes were pale and washed-out, and her lipstick had spread, making her mouth look disproportionately large.

'Can't I go home?'

'Not just yet.'

'I've not done anything wrong.'

By this time there were several policemen in the room, working or swapping stories. Jacquart rang up the emergency service, where there was still no news of the death of a Countess; and then, to be on the safe side, telephoned to police headquarters at the Quai des Orfèvres.

The telephone was answered by Lucas, who had just come on duty and was still half asleep.

'Send her over to me,' he replied on the spur of the moment.

After which he thought no more about it. Maigret arrived a few minutes later, and glanced through the night's reports before taking off his hat and coat.

It was still raining. Clammy weather. Most people were bad-tempered that morning.

Just after nine o'clock, a policeman from the IXth *arrondissement* appeared at the Quai des Orfèvres with Arlette. He was a new man who did not know the building very well, and he knocked on several wrong doors, Arlette following him all the time.

Finally he happened on the inspectors' room, where young Lapointe was sitting on the edge of a table, smoking a cigarette.

'Sergeant Lucas's office, please?'

He did not notice that Lapointe and Arlette were staring hard at each other, and on being told that Lucas was in the next room, he shut the door again.

'Sit down,' said Lucas to the girl.

Maigret, as usual, was making a quick round of the offices before the new report came in, and happened to be there at the moment, standing by the fireplace and filling his pipe.

Lucas explained to him: 'This girl says she heard two men plotting to murder a Countess.'

'I never said that,' she retorted, in a manner which had entirely altered—it was now assured, almost aggressive.

'You said you'd heard two men. . . .'

'I was tight.'

'And you made up the whole thing?'

'Yes.'

'Why?'

'I don't know. I'd got the blues. I didn't feel like going home and I just sort of drifted into the police station.'

Maigret threw her a fleeting, speculative glance and then went back to his papers.

'So there was no truth in all that Countess story?'

'No. . . .'

'None at all?'

'I may perhaps have heard something about a Countess. You know how you sometimes catch a stray word and it sticks in your mind.'

'Last night?'

'Very likely.'

'And you built up your whole story on that?'

'Do *you* always remember what you said when you'd been drinking?'

Maigret smiled. Lucas looked annoyed.

'Do you realize that's a legal offence?'

'What is?'

'Making a false statement. You may find yourself in the dock on a charge of . . .'

'I don't care if I do. All I care about is getting home to bed.'

'Do you live alone?'

'You bet I do!'

Maigret smiled again.

'And you can't remember the client with whom you drank a bottle of champagne and who held your hands—the fellow called Albert?'

'I can hardly remember anything. How many more times have I got to tell you that? Everyone at Picratt's knows I was plastered.'

'How long had you been that way?'

'If you must know, it began yesterday evening.'

'Who were you with?'

'I was by myself.'

'Where?'

'All over the place. In different bars. You've never lived alone, or you'd understand.'

That sounded funny, addressed to young Lucas, who always tried so hard to look dignified.

The rain seemed to have set in; it would go on all day—a cold, steady drizzle from a lowering sky; the lights would be burning in all the offices, and there would be wet patches on the floors.

Lucas had another job on hand, a burglary in a warehouse on the Quai de Javel, and was in a hurry to get there. He looked at Maigret and raised his eyebrows, as though asking:

'What am I to do with her?'

Just at that moment the telephone rang. It was to summon Maigret for the report, and he turned away with a shrug which meant:

'That's your affair.'

'Are you on the telephone?' the sergeant asked Arlette.

'The concierge is.'

'Do you live in a hotel?'

'No, I have a flat of my own.'

'Alone?'

'I've told you so already.'

'You're not afraid of running into Oscar, if I let you go?'

'I want to go home.'

They couldn't keep her indefinitely, simply because she had told some yarn to her local police.

'Ring me up if anything else happens,' said Lucas as he rose to his feet. 'You won't be leaving Paris, I suppose?'

'No. Why?'

He opened the door for her and watched her as she walked away down the long, broad corridor and paused uncertainly at the top of the stairs. People turned to look at her as she went by. She obviously belonged to a different world, the world of night, and it gave one a kind of shock to see her in this harsh winter daylight.

In his office, Lucas was conscious of the atmosphere she had left behind her: the place smelt of woman, almost of bed. He rang up the emergency service again:

'No Countess?'

'Nothing to report.'

Then he opened the door of the inspectors' office.

'Lapointe,' he called, without looking in.

Another man's voice replied:

'He's just gone out.'

'Didn't he say where he was going?'

'He said he'd be back at once.'

'Tell him I want him. Not about Arlette or the Countess. I want him to come to Javel with me.'

Lapointe came back a quarter of an hour later. The two men put on their coats and hats and set out for the Châtelet Metro station.

When Maigret returned from the Chief's office, where the daily report had been delivered, he lit his pipe and sat down to look through a pile of records, vowing that he would not let himself be interrupted before lunch-time.

It must have been about half past nine when Arlette left the Quai des Orfèvres. It never occurred to anyone to inquire whether she was going home by bus or by Metro. She may have stopped in a bar for a cup of coffee and a *croissant*.

Her concierge did not see her come in, but that was natural, because the house—just off the Place St. Georges—was a big place, humming with activity.

It was nearly eleven o'clock when the concierge started to sweep the staircase of Building B, and noticed with surprise that Arlette's door was ajar.

Lapointe, at the Quai de Javel, seemed absent-minded and preoccupied. Lucas thought he looked off-colour and asked him if he felt all right.

'I think I've got a cold coming on,' replied Lapointe.

The two of them were still questioning the people who lived near the burgled warehouse, when the telephone rang in Maigret's office.

'This is the Chief Inspector, St. Georges district.'

It was from the station in the Rue de La Rochefoucauld where Arlette had gone about half past four that morning, and where she had fallen asleep on a bench.

'My secretary tells me that Jeanne Leleu, alias Arlette—the girl who said she'd overheard some talk about murdering a Countess—was brought round to you this morning.'

'I know more or less what you mean,' said Maigret, frowning. 'Is she dead?'

'Yes. She's just been found strangled, in her room.'

'In bed?'

'No.'

'Dressed?'

'Yes.'

'With her coat on?'

'No. She was wearing a black silk dress. At least, so my men have just told me. I've not been round there yet. Thought I'd better ring you first. It looks as though she'd been talking sense.'

'She was undoubtedly talking sense.'

'Still no news of any Countess?'

'Nothing so far. It may take time.'

'Will you see about informing the finger-print people, and so on?'

'I'll ring them up and then go straight to the house.'

'I think that's the best thing. Strange business, isn't it? The sergeant on night duty here didn't take her too seriously, because she was drunk. See you in a few minutes.'

'Right you are.'

Maigret decided to take Lucas with him, but found his office empty and remembered about the Javel affair. Lapointe wasn't there either. Janvier had come in that moment, and had not even had time to get out of his cold, wet raincoat.

'Come along with me!'

As usual, Maigret put a couple of pipes in his pocket.

## II

JANVIER brought the little police car to a stop beside the pavement, and the two men, after craning their heads simultaneously to check the house number, looked at each other in surprise. There was no crowd outside, no one under the arched entrance or in the courtyard. A policeman had been sent from the station, as a matter of routine, to keep order; but he was merely strolling up and down at a little distance.

They soon discovered the reason for this unusual calm. Monsieur Beulant, the local inspector, came out of the concierge's quarters to greet them, bringing with him the concierge herself, a large, placid, intelligent-looking woman.

'This is Madame Boué,' he said. 'She's the wife of one of our sergeants. When she found the body, she locked the door with her passkey and came down here to telephone me. No one else in the building knows anything about it yet.'

Madame Boué bowed slightly, as though acknowledging a compliment.

'So there's nobody up there?' asked Maigret.

'Inspector Lognon's gone up with the police doctor. I myself have been having a long talk with Madame Boué—we've been trying to think what Countess the girl could have been speaking of.'

'I can't think of any Countess around here,' put in Madame Boué.

It was obvious from her manner, her voice and her way of speaking, that she was determined to be the perfect witness.

'The girl was harmless enough, poor thing. I didn't see much of her, because she didn't get home till the small hours and was asleep most of the day.'

'Had she been living here long?'

'Two years. She had a two-room flat in Building B, at the far end of the courtyard.'

'Did she have a great many visitors?'

'Hardly any.'

'Any men?'

'If any came I never saw them. Except at the very beginning. When she moved in, and her furniture was being delivered, I once or twice saw an elderly man. I thought at first he might be her father—short and very broad-shouldered, he was. He never spoke to me. So far as I know, he's never been back since then. But a great many people come here, especially as Building A is full of offices, so one doesn't notice them all.'

'I shall probably be back in a few minutes for another word with you,' said Maigret.

The house was old and shabby. Two dark staircases led off under the archway, one on either side, with imitation marble plates announcing a ladies' hairdresser on the *entresol*, a masseuse on the first floor, an artificial flower workroom on the second, a solicitor, and even a fortune-teller. The cobbled paving of the courtyard was glistening with rain, and at the far side, straight ahead of them, Maigret and Janvier saw a door surmounted by a large B in black paint.

They went up three flights of stairs, leaving muddy footprints all the way, and only one door opened as they passed—to reveal a fat woman, her sparse locks twisted into curlers, who stared at them in astonishment, stepped back and locked herself in.

They were met by Inspector Lognon, of the St. Georges district. He was as glum as usual, and the eye he turned upon Maigret said plainly: 'This would have to happen!'

The inevitability attached, not to the strangling of a young woman, but to the fact that, a crime having been committed in the district and Lognon sent to investigate, Maigret had immediately arrived in person, to take matters out of his hands.

'I haven't disturbed anything,' he said in his most official tone. 'The doctor's still in the bedroom.'

No rooms would have looked cheerful in weather like this. It was one of those gloomy days that make you wonder why you came into the world and why you take so much trouble to stay in it.

The first room was a kind of sitting-room—pleasantly furnished, spotlessly clean, and, contrary to what might have been expected, perfectly tidy. The first thing Maigret noticed was the floor—the parquet was as well polished as if it had been in a convent, and there was an agreeable smell of beeswax. He must remember to ask the concierge, on the way out, whether Arlette did her own housework.

Through the half-open door of the bedroom they could see Dr. Pasquier putting on his overcoat and arranging his instruments in their case. On the white goatskin rug at the foot of the bed (which had not been disturbed) lay a body in a black satin dress: all they could see was one very white arm and a mass of shining, copper-coloured hair.

The most pathetic impression always comes from some absurdly trivial detail, and when, this time, Maigret felt a slight lump in his throat, it was because, while one of the girl's feet was still wearing its high-heeled shoe, the other was unshod, the toes showing through a mud-spattered stocking in which a ladder started from the heel and ran up beyond the knee.

'Dead, of course,' said the doctor. 'The fellow who did it held on to her until he'd made sure of that.'

'Can you say when it happened?'

'Not more than an hour and a half ago. There's no sign of stiffness yet.'

Maigret noticed behind the door, near the bed, an open cupboard in which dresses were hanging—nearly all evening dresses, most of them black.

'Do you think he caught her from behind?'

'Probably; I found no trace of a struggle. I send my report to you, I suppose, Monsieur Maigret?'

'If you please.'

The bedroom was neat and bright, not at all suggestive of a night-club dancer's room. Here, again, everything was in order, except that Arlette's imitation mink coat was flung untidily on the bed, and her handbag lay on an armchair.

Maigret explained:

'She left the Quai des Orfèvres about half past nine. If she took a taxi she must have got here about ten o'clock. If she came by bus or Metro it would be a little later, of course. She must have been attacked at once.'

He went over to the cupboard and looked carefully at the floor inside.

'Someone was waiting for her, hiding in here. He must have grabbed her by the throat the moment she'd taken her coat off.'

It had happened such a short time ago: the police were not often called in so promptly to the scene of a crime.

'You don't need me any longer, I suppose?' inquired the doctor.

The local inspector asked, in his turn, whether he need wait till the photographers and other experts arrived, and was glad to get back to his office, which was only a few yards away. As for Lognon, he stood in a corner looking sulky, expecting to be told that he, too, was no longer needed.

'You haven't found anything?' Maigret asked him as he filled his pipe.

'I had a look in the drawers. See what's in the left-hand one in the chest of drawers over there.'

It was full of photographs, all of Arlette. Some of them were for publicity, including those which were displayed outside Picratt's. These showed her in a black silk dress—not the day dress she had on now, but a skin-tight evening dress.

'You belong to this district, Lognon; did you ever see her turn?'

'I never saw it myself, but I know what she had to do. As you can see from these photos at the top of the pile, her "dancing" consisted of wriggling about, more or less in time to the music, while she gradually took off her dress—the only thing she had on. By the end of her act she was stark naked.'

Lognon's long, bulbous nose twitched and almost seemed to be blushing.

'Seems that's what they do in America—strip-tease, they call it over there. Just as the last stitch dropped off her, the light would go out.'

He hesitated, and then went on:

'Have a look under her dress.'

Seeing that Maigret, surprised, was waiting for more, he added:

'The doctor who examined her called me and showed me. She's completely shaved. And even out of doors she had nothing on beneath the dress.'

Why did they all three feel embarrassed? By tacit agreement they avoided looking at the body, which still had something wanton in its appearance, as it lay outstretched on the goatskin rug. Maigret only glanced at the remaining photographs, which were smaller—probably taken with an ordinary camera—and showed the girl naked, in the most erotic poses.

'Try to find me an envelope,' he said.

At which Lognon, the damn' fool, gave a silent sneer, as though he suspected his superior of taking the things away to gloat over privately in his office.

Janvier, meanwhile, had begun an inch-by-inch inspection of the other room, and this called further attention to a kind of discrepancy between the place and the photographs—between Arlette's home and her work.

In a cupboard they found a little oil stove, two very clean saucepans, plates, cups and cutlery, which showed that she used to cook at least some of her own meals. In a meat safe that hung outside the window, above the courtyard, there were eggs, butter, celery and two lamb chops.

Another cupboard was full of brooms, dusters and tins of polish. From all this, in fact, anyone would have imagined the place to belong to some elderly, respectable, even rather fussy housewife.

They looked in vain for letters or private papers. There were a few magazines lying about, but no books, except a cookery book and a French-English dictionary. And no photos of parents, of other girls or of boy-friends, such as most young women display in their rooms.

There were a great many pairs of shoes, with exaggeratedly high heels—most of them almost new. Arlette must have had a passion for shoes, or else her feet were sensitive and she had difficulty in fitting them comfortably.

Her handbag contained a powder-compact, an identity card and an unmarked handkerchief. Maigret slipped the identity card into his pocket. Then, as though he felt ill at ease in the two small rooms, where the central heating was turned full on, he said to Janvier:

'You wait here for the experts. I'll probably be back before long, but they'll be arriving any minute now.'

No envelope had been found, so he pushed the photos into the pocket of his overcoat, smiled at Lognon, known to his colleagues as 'the churl'—and made for the stairs.

There would be a long, tedious business to be gone through in the house: all the tenants would have to be questioned, including the fat woman with her hair in curlers, who seemed to take an interest in passers-by and might have caught sight of the murderer on his way up or down.

Maigret stopped at the concierge's room and asked her if he might use the telephone, which stood beside the bed, with a photo of her husband, in uniform, hanging above it.

'Lucas isn't back yet, I suppose?' he inquired when he got through to the Quai des Orfèvres.

He dictated to another inspector the particulars entered on the identity card, and went on:

'Get into touch with Moulins. Try to find out whether she has any relations left there. There should be people who knew her, anyhow. If her parents are still alive, have them informed: I expect they'll come straight up to Paris.'

He was walking along the street towards the Rue Pigalle when he heard a car pull up. It was the photographers. The finger-print people and the rest would be arriving too, and he was anxious to be out of the way while some twenty people bustled about in the two small rooms where the body was still lying as it had fallen.

\*

To the left of Picratt's was a baker's shop and to the right a wine merchant's. At night the place showed up clearly, of course, with its neon-lighted sign standing out against the dark fronts of the neighbouring houses. But in the daytime anyone might walk past without even noticing that it was a night-club.

The façade was narrow, just a door and a window; and in the chilly light of this wet morning the photographs in the show-case looked melancholy and rather suggestive.

It was past noon by now. To Maigret's surprise, the door was open. One electric lamp was burning inside, and a woman was sweeping the floor between the tables.

'Is the proprietor here?' inquired Maigret.

The woman paused in her work and looked at him calmly.

'Why do you want to know?' she asked.

'I'd like to have a word with him.'

'He's asleep. I'm his wife.'

She must be over fifty—nearly sixty, perhaps. She was stout, but still alert, with fine brown eyes in a plump face.

'I am Inspector Maigret, of the Judicial Police.'

Even at this she showed no uneasiness.

'Please sit down.'

It was dark inside, and the red walls and hangings looked almost black. Only the bottles behind the bar, just inside the open door, caught some gleams of daylight.

The room was long and narrow, with a low ceiling. There was a small platform for the musicians, on which stood a piano and an accordion in its case; and on either side of the dance floor the walls were divided, by partitions about five feet high, into boxes where clients could sit in comparative privacy.

'Must I really wake Fred?' asked the woman. She was wearing

bedroom slippers and an old dress with a grey apron over it, and she
had not yet washed or done her hair.

'Are you here at night?'

'I look after the cloakrooms and do the cooking if clients want a
meal,' she explained.

'Do you live in this house?'

'Yes, on the *entresol*. There's a staircase at the back, leading from the
kitchen to our own rooms. But we have a house at Bougival where we
go on closing days.'

She seemed quite unperturbed. Her curiosity must have been stirred
by the arrival of such an important member of the police force. But
she was used to seeing all kinds of people, and she waited patiently
for an explanation.

'Have you had this place for long?'

'It'll be eleven years next month.'

'Do you get a lot of clients?'

'It varies.'

Maigret caught sight of a card on which was printed, in English:

> *Finish the night at Picratt's,*
> *The hottest spot in Paris.*

He had forgotten most of his English, but realized that 'hottest' in this
sense must mean exciting—or, on second thoughts, something a bit
stronger and more precise than that.

The woman was still gazing calmly at him.

'Won't you have something to drink?'

She obviously knew that he would refuse.

'What do you do with these cards?'

'Give them to the porters at the big hotels, who pass them on to
visitors—especially Americans. And at night, late, when the foreigners
are beginning to get bored with the larger night-spots and don't know
where to go next, the Grasshopper strolls about outside and hands
cards to them. And he drops them into cars and taxis. We do our real
business after the other places close. You understand?'

He understood. Most people, by the time they got here, had been
wandering round Montmartre for some time without finding what they
wanted, and this was their last shot.

'I suppose most of your clients are half drunk when they come in
here?'

'Yes, of course.'

'Did you have many people last night?'

'It was Monday. There's never a crowd on Mondays.'

'From where you stand, can you see what goes on in this part of the
place?'

She pointed down the room: at the far end, to the left of the musicians' platform, was a door marked 'Toilet'. To the right was another door, with no inscription.

'I'm nearly always there. We aren't keen on serving meals, but sometimes people ask for onion soup, *foie gras* or cold lobster. And then I go off to the kitchen for a few minutes.'

'Otherwise you stay in this room?'

'Most of the time. I keep an eye on the women, and at the right moment I come along with a box of chocolates, or some flowers or one of those satin dolls. You know how it's done, I expect.'

She was not putting on any airs. By this time she had sat down, with a sigh of relief, and now she shook the slipper off one swollen, shapeless foot.

'What are you trying to get at? I don't want to hurry you, but it'll soon be time for me to go and wake Fred. He's a man and he needs more sleep than I do.'

'What time did you get to bed?'

'About five o'clock. Sometimes I don't get upstairs till seven.'

'And when did you get up?'

'An hour ago. As you see, I'd finished sweeping.'

'Did your husband go to bed at the same time as you?'

'He went upstairs five minutes before me.'

'Has he been out of doors this morning?'

'He hasn't been out of his bed.'

This insistence on her husband's doings was making her a little uneasy at last.

'It's not him you're after, is it?'

'Not specially. But I'm after two men who came here last night, about two o'clock, and sat in one of the boxes. Do you remember them?'

'Two men?'

She looked round at each table in turn, as though searching her memory.

'Do you remember where Arlette was before her turn came round for the second time?'

'Yes, she was with her young man. I even told her she was wasting her time.'

'Does he often come here?'

'He's been two or three times lately. Every now and then a man does stray in like that and fall in love with one of the girls. As I always tell them, it's all right for once, but they mustn't let it keep on happening. They were both here, in the third box as you look in from the street— No. 6. I could see them from where I stood. He was holding her hands all the time, and talking away to her with the soppy expression they all get when they're in that mood.'

'And who was in the next box?'

'I didn't see anyone.'

'Not at any time in the evening?'

'You can easily make sure. The tables haven't been wiped yet. If there was anybody at that one there'll be cigar or cigarette ends in the ash-tray, and the marks left by glasses on the table itself.'

She sat still, leaving him to go and look.

'I don't see anything.'

'If it had been any other day I wouldn't be so positive; but Mondays are so slack, we sometimes think it isn't worth opening. I wouldn't mind betting we didn't have a dozen clients in all. My husband will be able to tell you exactly.'

'Do you know Oscar?' he asked point-blank.

She didn't jump, but he had the impression that she became a little reticent.

'Oscar who?'

'An elderly man—short, square-shouldered, grey-haired.'

'I can't think of anyone like that. The butcher's name is Oscar, but he's tall and dark, with a moustache. Perhaps my husband . . .'

'Go and fetch him, if you don't mind.'

Maigret sat still, in the dark red tunnel of a room with the light grey rectangle of the open door at its far end, like a cinema screen with the dim figures of some old news-reel flickering to and fro across it.

On the wall opposite him was a photograph of Arlette, in the inevitable black dress which clung to her body so tightly that she seemed more naked than in the indecent photos he had put in his pocket.

That morning in Lucas's office, he had paid scarcely any attention to her. She was just one of the little night-birds of which Paris held so many. All the same, he had noticed how young she was, and felt that there was something wrong somewhere. He could still hear her weary voice—the voice they all have at daybreak, after drinking and smoking too much. He remembered her anxious eyes; he remembered how he had glanced automatically at her breast; and above all he remembered the smell of human female that emanated from her—almost the smell of a warm bed.

He had seldom met a woman who gave such a strong impression of sensuality: and that was out of keeping with her worried, childish face and still more out of keeping with the rooms he had just left—with the polished floor, the broom-cupboard and the meat safe.

'Fred will be down in a minute.'

'Did you tell him what I wanted to know?'

'I asked him if he'd noticed two men. He doesn't remember them. In fact he feels sure there weren't two men at that table. It's No. 4. We always refer to the tables by their numbers. At No. 5 there was an American who drank almost a whole bottle of whisky, and at No. 11

there was a whole party, with women. Désiré, the waiter, will tell you about that, this evening.'

'Where does he live?'

'In the suburbs. I don't know where exactly. He goes home by train every morning from the Gare St. Lazare.'

'What other employees have you?'

'The Grasshopper, who opens car doors, runs errands, and now and then hands out cards. And the musicians and the girls.'

'How many girls?'

'Apart from Arlette there's Betty Bruce. She's the one in the left-hand photo. She does acrobatic dances. And Tania, who plays the piano when she's not dancing. That's all, at present. Other girls come in, of course, for a drink in the hope of picking up someone; but they don't belong to the place. We like to keep it small, Fred and me—we're not ambitious, and when we've saved enough money we shall retire and settle down to a quiet life at Bougival. Ah, here he comes. . . .'

A man of about fifty—short, sturdy, very well preserved, his hair still black except for a touch of grey at the temples—came out of the kitchen, pulling on a jacket over his collarless shirt. He must have snatched up the first clothes that came to hand, for he was wearing his evening trousers and had bedroom slippers on his bare feet.

He, too, was quite calm—even calmer than his wife. He must have known Maigret by name, but it was the first time he had actually set eyes on him, and he came forward slowly, so as to observe him at leisure.

'I'm Fred Alfonsi,' he announced, extending his hand. 'Didn't my wife ask you to have a drink?'

As though to confirm something of which he was already sure, he went to No. 4 table and rubbed the flat of his hand across it.

'You really won't have anything? Do you mind if Rose gets me a cup of coffee?'

At this, his wife went off to the kitchen and disappeared. The man sat down opposite Maigret, his elbows on the table, and waited.

'You're sure there were no clients at that table last night?'

'Now see here, Inspector. I know who you are, but you don't know me. Perhaps before coming here you made inquiries from your colleague in the *brigade mondaine*. His men drop in on me from time to time—it's their job and they've been doing it for years now. They'll tell you, if they haven't already done so, that there's never been any funny business at my place, and that I'm quite a harmless chap.'

Maigret was amused at the contrast between the man's words and his appearance, for he had the broken nose and cauliflower ears of an ex-boxer.

'So when I say there was nobody at that table, you can be sure it's true. This is a small place, there are only a few of us to run it, and I keep an eye on everything, the whole time. I could tell you exactly how many people came in last night. I've only got to look at the tickets on the cash desk; they're numbered according to the tables.'

'It was at No. 5, wasn't it, that Arlette sat with her young man?'

'No—at No. 6. The even numbers—2, 4, 6, 8, 10 and 12—are all on the right. The odd numbers are on the left.'

'Who was at the next table?'

'No. 8? Two couples came in at about four o'clock—Parisians who'd never been here before, who'd come because they didn't know where else to go, and who soon decided it wasn't their kind of place. They had just one bottle of champagne and then left. We closed almost directly afterwards.'

'And you never saw, either at that table or any other, two men by themselves, one of them elderly and, judging by the description, rather like you in appearance?'

Fred Alfonsi, who must have heard this sort of talk before, smiled and rejoined:

'If you'd spill the beans I might be able to help you. Don't you think this cat and mouse game has been going on long enough?'

'Arlette is dead.'

'What?'

The man gave a violent start. He got up agitatedly, and shouted down the room:

'Rose! . . . Rose?'

'Coming in a minute. . . .'

'Arlette's dead!'

'*What* did you say?'

She came rushing out at an amazing speed for one so fat.

'Arlette?' she echoed.

'She was strangled this morning, in her bedroom,' went on Maigret, watching them closely.

'Well, I'll be . . . Who was the bastard who . . .'

'That's what I'm trying to find out.'

Rose blew her nose and was obviously on the verge of tears. She was staring hard at the photograph on the wall.

'How did it happen?' asked Fred, going over to the bar.

Carefully selecting a bottle, he filled three glasses and came over to give the first one to his wife. It was old brandy, and he put one of the other glasses, without comment, on the table in front of Maigret, who finally took a sip of it.

'She overheard a conversation here, last night, between two men who were talking about a Countess.'

'What Countess?'

'I don't know. One of the men seems to have been called Oscar.'

There was no reaction to this.

'When she left here she went to the local police station to report what she'd heard, and they took her to the Quai des Orfèvres.'

'And that's why she was bumped off?'

'Probably.'

'What about you, Rose—did you notice any two men together?'

She said she had not. Both she and he seemed genuinely amazed and distressed.

'I can assure you, Inspector, that if there had been two men here I should know and I'd tell you. We can speak quite straight to each other. You know how this kind of joint works. People don't come here to see first-class turns or dance to a good band. And it's no fancy drawing-room either. You've read our announcement. They go first of all to other places, looking for a thrill. If they pick up some girl there, then they don't get this far. But if they don't find what they want, they end up here more often than not, and by that time they've had about as much as is good for them.

'I'm in with most of the night taxi-drivers and I give them good tips. And the doormen at some of the big night-clubs whisper this address to clients when they show them out.

'We mostly get foreigners, who imagine they're going to see something sensational.

'The only sensational thing was Arlette undressing herself. For about a quarter of a second, when her dress slipped right down to her feet, they saw her absolutely naked. To avoid trouble, I asked her to shave herself—that's supposed to look less shocking.

'After that she'd nearly always be asked over to one of the tables.'

'Did she go to bed with clients?' asked Maigret deliberately.

'Not here, in any case. And not in working hours. I don't let them go out before we close. They keep the men here as long as possible by encouraging them to drink and I suppose they promise to meet them when they come out.'

'And do they?'

'What d'you think?'

'Did Arlette, too?'

'She must have, now and then.'

'With the young man who was here last night?'

'No, not with him, I'm sure. He was there from the purest motives, you might say. He came in one evening by chance, with a friend, and fell in love with Arlette at first sight. He came again several times, but never waited till we closed. He probably had to get up early and go to work.'

'Had she any other regulars?'

'Hardly any of our clients are regulars, you must surely have realized that. They're birds of passage. They're all alike, of course, but they're always different.'

'Hadn't she any men friends?'

'I know nothing about that,' replied Fred rather stiffly.

Maigret glanced at Rose and said, a little hesitantly:

'I suppose you yourself never . . .'

'Oh, go ahead—Rose isn't jealous and she got over that a long time ago. Yes, if you must know, I did.'

'In her flat?'

'I never set foot in the place. Here, in the kitchen.'

'It's always that way with him,' observed Rose. 'You hardly notice he's gone, before he's back again. And then the woman comes in, shaking herself like a ruffled hen.'

She laughed at the thought.

'You don't know anything about the Countess?'

'What Countess?'

'Oh, never mind. Can you give me the Grasshopper's address? What's his real name?'

'Thomas. . . . He hasn't any other. He was a foundling. I can't tell you where he sleeps, but you'll find him at the races this afternoon. That's the only thing he cares about. Some more brandy?'

'No thank you.'

'Do you suppose the journalists will be coming round?'

'Most likely. When they get wind of what's happened.'

It was difficult to make out whether Fred was delighted or annoyed at the publicity he was liable to receive.

'Anyhow, I'll do all I can to help you. I suppose I'd better open as usual this evening? If you like to drop in, you can question all the others.'

When Maigret got back to the Rue Notre-Dame de Lorette, the police car was no longer there, and an ambulance was just taking away the girl's body. A few idlers were hanging round the door, but not as many as he had expected.

Janvier was in the concierge's lodge, making a telephone call. He rang off just as Maigret came in, and said:

'The report from Moulins has come through already. The Leleu couple—father and mother—are still living there, with their son who's a bank clerk. As for Jeanne Leleu, their daughter, she's small, snub-nosed, dark-haired, left home three years ago and hasn't given a sign of life since. Her parents aren't in the least interested.'

'The description doesn't fit at a single point, does it?'

'No. She's two inches shorter than Arlette, and she isn't likely to have had her nose straightened.'

'No phone calls about the Countess?'

'Nothing at all. I've questioned all the tenants in Building B. There are a great many of them. The fat, fair-haired woman who watched us go upstairs is cloakroom attendant in a theatre. She makes out she isn't interested in what goes on in the house, but she did hear someone go past a few minutes before the girl got home.'

'So she heard the girl go up? How did she know who it was?'

'Says she recognized the footstep. In actual fact she spends her time peering through the crack of her door.'

'Did she see the man?'

'She says she didn't, but that he came upstairs slowly, as though he were very heavy or had a weak heart.'

'She didn't hear him go down again?'

'No.'

'She's quite sure it wasn't one of the tenants from higher up the house?'

'She knows the step of all the tenants. I saw Arlette's neighbour, too —a waitress: I had to wake her up, and she hadn't heard a thing.'

'Is that all?'

'Lucas phoned to say he was back in the office, waiting for instructions.'

'Finger-prints?'

'Only ours and Arlette's. You'll get the report sometime this evening.'

'You haven't got an Oscar among your tenants?' Maigret asked the concierge, on the off chance.

'No, Inspector. But once, a long time ago, I took a telephone message for Arlette. It was a man speaking, with a provincial accent, and he said, "Will you tell her Oscar is waiting for her at the usual place".'

'About how long ago was that?'

'A month or two after she came to live here. It struck me particularly, because it was the only message that ever came for her.'

'Did she get any letters?'

'One from Brussels, now and then.'

'A man's writing?'

'No, a woman's. And not an educated one.'

Half an hour later, Maigret and Janvier were on their way upstairs at the Quai des Orfèvres, after stopping for a pint at the Brasserie Dauphine.

Maigret was hardly inside his office when young Lapointe rushed in, red-eyed and agitated.

'I've got to speak to you at once, sir.'

Turning away from the cupboard where he had been hanging up his coat and hat, Maigret looked at the young man and saw that he was biting his lips and clenching his fists, to keep himself from bursting into tears.

# III

HE spoke between clenched teeth, with his back to Maigret and his face almost pressed against the window-pane.

'When I saw her here this morning, I wondered why she'd been brought in. Sergeant Lucas told me the story while we were on our way to Javel. And now I get back to the office, only to hear that she's dead.'

Maigret, who had sat down, said slowly:

'I'd forgotten for the moment that your name was Albert.'

'After what she'd told him, Sergeant Lucas ought not to have let her go off by herself, without any protection at all.'

He spoke like a small, sulky boy, and Maigret smiled.

'Come over here and sit down,' he said.

Lapointe hesitated, as though he felt resentful towards Maigret too. Then, reluctantly, he came and sat down on the chair opposite his chief's desk. He still hung his head, staring at the floor, while Maigret sat gravely puffing at his pipe. The two looked rather like a father and son in solemn colloquy.

'You've not been here very long yet, but you must have realized by now that if we had to give police protection to everyone who comes to us with an accusation, you'd often have no time for sleep or even to swallow a sandwich. Isn't that so?'

'Yes, sir. But . . .'

'But what?'

'She was different.'

'Why?'

'Well, you can see she wasn't just talking for the sake of talking.'

'Tell me about it, now you're feeling a bit calmer.'

'Tell you about what?'

'Everything.'

'How I got to know her?'

'Yes. Begin at the beginning.'

'I was with a chap from Meulan, an old school-friend who's not often been to Paris. First of all we went out with my sister, then we took her home and went up to Montmartre together, just the two of us. You know the sort of thing. We went into two or three joints and had a drink in each, and as we came out of the last of them, a kind of gnome pushed a card at us.'

'Why do you call him a kind of gnome?'

'Because he looks about fourteen years old, but his face is all wrinkled in fine lines—the face of a man who's past his youth. At a short distance you'd take him for a little street arab, and I suppose that's why they call him the Grasshopper. My friend had been disappointed with the places we'd tried so far, and I thought he might get more of a kick out of Picratt's; so we went there.'

'How long ago was this?'

He thought for a moment and seemed quite astonished and rather upset by what his memory told him; but he was forced to admit:

'Three weeks.'

'And that was how you met Arlette?'

'She came to sit at our table. My friend, who isn't used to that kind of thing, took her for a tart. We had a row when we got outside.'

'About her?'

'Yes. I'd realized at once that she was different from the others.'

Maigret let this pass without a smile; he was cleaning one of his pipes with the greatest care.

'And you went back there the following night?'

'Yes—to apologize for the way my friend had spoken to her.'

'What had he actually said?'

'He'd offered her money to sleep with him.'

'And she refused?'

'Of course. I got there early, to make sure of finding the place more or less empty, and she allowed me to stand her a drink.'

'A drink, or a bottle?'

'A bottle. The proprietor won't let them sit down at a table if they're only offered a drink. It has to be champagne.'

'I see.'

'I know what you're thinking. All the same, she came and told the police what she knew, and she's been strangled.'

'Did she say anything to you about being in danger?'

'Not in so many words. But I knew there were some mysteries in her life.'

'Such as?'

'It's difficult to explain, and no one will believe me, because I was in love with her.'

He spoke the last few words in a lower voice, raising his head and looking his chief straight in the face—ready to take offence at the slightest suggestion of irony.

'I wanted to get her to drop the life she was leading.'

'You wanted to marry her?'

Lapointe hesitated; he was visibly embarrassed.

'I hadn't thought about that. I don't suppose I'd have married her right away.'

'But you wanted her to stop showing herself naked in a cabaret?'

'I know it made her miserable.'

'Did she tell you so?'

'It wasn't as simple as that, sir. Of course I understand it looks different from your point of view: I know what sort of women one generally meets in places like that.

'But for one thing it was very difficult to tell what she was really thinking, because she used to drink. Usually, as you know, they don't drink. They pretend to, so as to encourage the clients, but all they really take is some syrup or other, served in a little glass so that it looks like a liqueur. Isn't that so?'

'Nearly always.'

'Arlette used to drink because she *had* to. Nearly every evening. So much so, that before she went on for her act, Mr. Fred, the proprietor, had to come round and make sure she could still stand up.'

Lapointe had become so much at home at Picratt's that he spoke of 'Mr. Fred', just as the employees no doubt did.

'You never stayed till closing time?'

'She wouldn't let me.'

'Why not?'

'Because I'd let out that I had to get up early and go to work.'

'Did you tell her you were in the police?'

The young man blushed again.

'No. I told her I lived with my sister, and it was she who told me to go home. I never gave her any money. She wouldn't have accepted it. She would never let me order more than one bottle of champagne, and she always chose the least expensive kind.'

'Do you think she was in love with you?'

'Last night I felt sure she was.'

'Why? What did you talk about?'

'The same as usual—about her and me.'

'Did she tell you who she was and what her parents did in the world?'

'She admitted she had a false identity card, and said it would be terrible if her real name were found out.'

'Was she well educated?'

'I don't know. She certainly wasn't made for that job. She never told me about her past life. She only referred to some man she said she'd never be able to shake off—adding that it was her own fault, that it was too late now, and that I must stop coming to see her because it only made her unhappy to no purpose. That's what makes me think she was beginning to love me. She was clutching my hands hard, all the time she was talking.'

'Was she already drunk?'

'Perhaps. She'd certainly been drinking, but she was quite clear-headed. She was like that nearly every time I saw her—all strung up, with an expression either of grief or of hectic gaiety in her eyes.'

'Did you ever go to bed with her?'

Lapointe glared almost with hatred at his chief.

'No!'

'Didn't you ever ask her?'

'No.'

'And she never suggested it?'

'Never.'

'Did she kid you into believing she was a virgin?'

'She'd been forced to submit to several men. She hated men.'

'Why?'

'Because of that.'

'Because of what?'

'Because of what they did to her. It had happened when she was almost a child—I don't know the details—and it left its mark on her. She was haunted by the memory of it. She was always talking about some man she was terrified of.'

'Oscar?'

'She didn't mention his name. I suppose you think she was fooling me and that I'm a simpleton. I don't care if you do. She's dead, and that at least proves she was right to be afraid.'

'Didn't you ever want to go to bed with her?'

'Once I did,' he admitted, 'the first evening, when I was with my friend. Did you ever see her alive? Yes, of course—but only for a few minutes, this morning, when she was worn out. If you'd seen her as she usually was, you'd understand. . . . No other woman . . .'

'No other woman . . . ?'

'It's too difficult to explain. All the men who went there were wild to have her. When she did her act . . .'

'Did she go to bed with Fred?'

'She'd had to submit to him, the same as to the others.'

Maigret was trying to discover how much Arlette had given away.

'Where?'

'In the kitchen. Rose knew. She didn't dare to make a fuss, because she's so afraid of losing her husband. Have you ever seen her?'

Maigret nodded.

'Did she tell you her age?'

'I suppose she must be over fifty.'

'She's nearly seventy. Fred's twenty years younger than she is. It seems she was one of the most beautiful women of her day, and was kept by some very wealthy man. She's really in love with her husband. So she daren't show any sign of jealousy, and she tries to fix things so that everything happens in her own house. She feels it's less dangerous that way—you understand?'

'I understand.'

'She was more scared about Arlette than about any of the others, and she'd hardly let her out of her sight. But it was Arlette who practically kept the place going. Without her, they won't get a soul. The other girls are just the commonplace type you find in every cabaret in Montmartre.'

'What happened last night?'

'Did she say anything about it?'

'She told Lucas you were with her, but she only mentioned your Christian name.'

'I stayed till half past two.'

'At what table?'

'Number six.'

He spoke like one who was at home in the place—almost as though he belonged there.

'Was there anybody in the next box?'

'Not in number four. A whole crowd came in to number eight—men and women, a very noisy lot.'

'So if there had been anyone in number four you wouldn't have noticed?'

'Oh yes, I should. I didn't want anyone to hear what I was saying, so I got up every now and then and looked over the partition.'

'You didn't see, at any table, a short, thick-set, middle-aged man with grey hair?'

'No.'

'And while you were talking to Arlette, she didn't seem as though she were listening to any other conversation?'

'I'm certain she wasn't. Why?'

'Would you like to go on working on the case, with me?'

The young man looked at Maigret, first in surprise and then with a sudden flush of gratitude.

'You'll really let me, although . . .'

'Now listen—this is important. When she left Picratt's at four o'clock this morning, Arlette went to the police station in the Rue de La Rochefoucauld. The sergeant who took down her statement says she was very strung up, and not too steady on her feet.

'She talked to him about two men who came in and sat down at number four table while she was at number six with you, and said she had overheard part of their conversation.'

'Why on earth did she say that?'

'That's what I want to find out. When we know that, we shall probably be a lot further on than we are at present. And that's not all. The men were talking about some Countess that one of them was planning to murder. Arlette said that when they left she got a clear view of them from behind, and that one of them was middle-aged, shortish, broad-shouldered and grey-haired. And that during the conversation she caught the name "Oscar", which seemed to be addressed to this man.'

'But I'm pretty sure I should have heard. . . .'

'I've been along to see Fred and his wife. They say the same—that table number four wasn't occupied at all last night, and that nobody corresponding to that description came into Picratt's. So Arlette must have had some information and wouldn't or couldn't confess how she'd come across it. She was drunk—you said so yourself. She didn't think the police would bother to check where the clients had sat during the evening. You see what I mean?'

'Yes. And what made her mention a name?'

'Exactly. She wasn't asked for one. There was no need for her to do it. So she must have had some good reason. She must have been giving us a clue. And that isn't all. At the police station she seemed very sure of herself; but when she got here, after the effect of the champagne had worn off, she was much less talkative, and Lucas had the impression she'd have been glad to withdraw everything she'd said. And yet, as we know now, she hadn't made it all up.'

'I'm certain she hadn't.'

'She went home, and was strangled by someone who was waiting for her, hidden in her bedroom cupboard. Someone who must have known her very well, known his way about her flat, and probably had a key to it.'

'What about the Countess?'

'No news so far. Either she hasn't been killed, or no one has found the body yet—it might be that. Did she ever say anything to you about a Countess?'

'Never.'

Lapointe stared down at the desk for a moment and then asked, in an altered voice:

'Do you think she suffered much?'

'Not for long. The murderer was very strong, and she didn't even struggle.'

'Is she still in her room?'

'She's just been taken to the mortuary.'

'May I go and see her?'

'When you've had something to eat.'

'What shall I do after that?'

'Go to her flat in the Rue Notre-Dame de Lorette. Ask Janvier for the key. We've already been over the place, but you, who knew her, may find a meaning in some detail that escaped us.'

'Thank you,' said the young man eagerly; he was convinced that Maigret was giving him this task solely as a favour.

Maigret took care not to mention the photographs, whose corners were sticking out from under a file that lay on his desk.

Someone came to tell him that five or six journalists were waiting in the corridor, clamouring for news. He had them brought in, told them only part of the story, but gave each of them one of the photographs— those which showed Arlette in her black silk dress.

'And you might mention,' he added, 'that we should be glad if a certain Jeanne Leleu, who must be going by another name now, would come forward. We promise her there'll be no publicity, and we haven't the slightest wish to make trouble for her.'

*

He lunched late, at home, and had time to read through Fred Alfonsi's file when he got back to the office. Paris still looked ghostly in the fine, misty drizzle, and the people in the streets seemed as though they were moving through a kind of aquarium, and hurrying to get out.

The proprietor of Picratt's had a bulky police file, but there was hardly any significant information in it. When he was twenty years old he had done his military service in the penal *Bataillons d'Afrique*—for at that time he was being kept by a prostitute who lived in the Boulevard Sébastopol, and had already been arrested twice for assault and battery.

Then, after an interval of several years, he turned up in Marseilles, where he was recruiting girls for several brothels in the South of France. He was twenty-eight years old by that time. He was not yet a leading light in the underworld, but he was already too big a man to soil his hands in fights in the bars of the Vieux Port.

He had no prison sentences during that period, though there was one narrow escape over a girl of only seventeen whom he had prematurely 'placed', with forged identity papers, in Le Paradis, an establishment at Béziers.

Then came another gap. All that was known was that he had gone to Panama with a cargo of women, five or six of them, aboard an Italian boat, and had gained a certain notoriety over there.

At the age of forty he was back in Paris, living with Rosalie Dumont, alias La Rose, a woman well into middle-age, who had a beauty parlour in the Rue des Martyrs. He was a keen race-goer and boxing enthusiast, and was thought to take bets as a sideline.

After a time he had married Rose, and together they had opened Picratt's, which was originally no more than a small bar with its own group of regular customers.

*

Janvier had gone back after lunch to the Rue Notre-Dame de Lorette He was not in Arlette's flat, as he was still questioning the neighbours—not only the other tenants in the building, but the nearby shopkeepers and everyone else who might have any information.

As for Lucas, he was left alone to clear up the Javel burglary, and was thoroughly disgruntled about it.

It was ten minutes to five, and darkness had fallen long ago, when the telephone rang in Maigret's office, and he heard what he had been expecting all day.

'This is the Emergency Centre.'

'Is it about the Countess?' he asked.

'It's *a* Countess, at any rate. I don't know if she's the one you're after. We've just had a call from the Rue Victor-Massé. A few minutes ago the concierge discovered that one of her tenants had been murdered, probably last night. . . .'

'A Countess?'

'Countess von Farnheim.'

'Shot?'

'No, strangled. That's all we know so far. The local police are on the spot.'

A few moments later, Maigret jumped into a taxi, which took an endless time to get through the centre of Paris. Going along the Rue Notre-Dame de Lorette, he caught sight of Janvier coming out of a greengrocer's shop, so he stopped the cab and called to him:

'Jump in. The Countess is dead!'

'A real Countess?'

'I don't know. It's quite near here. The whole business is happening in this district.'

For Picratt's, in the Rue Pigalle, was scarcely five hundred yards from Arlette's flat, and about the same distance from the Rue Victor-Massé.

On this new occasion the scene was different from that of the morning, for a score of inquisitive idlers were hanging round the door of the comfortable, respectable-looking house.

'Is the Chief Inspector there?'

'He wasn't at the station. It's Inspector Lognon who . . .'

Poor Lognon! He was so eager to distinguish himself, and every time he started on a case he seemed fated to have it taken out of his hands by Maigret.

The concierge was not in her quarters. The walls of the staircase were painted to imitate marble, and there was a dark red stair-carpet held in place by brass rods. The atmosphere was rather stuffy, as though all the tenants were old people who never opened their windows; and the place was strangely silent—not one door so much as quivered while Maigret and Janvier were on their way up. On reaching the fourth floor, however, they heard sounds, and a door opened to reveal the long, lugubrious face of Lognon, who was talking to a very short, very fat woman with a tight bun of hair on the top of her head.

They went into the room, which was dimly lit by a standard lamp with a parchment shade. The atmosphere here was more oppressive than in the rest of the house. They suddenly felt, without quite knowing why, as if they were far removed from Paris, from the outside world, from the damp streets with their crowded pavements, the screeching taxis, the hurtling buses with their abruptly grinding brakes.

The place was so hot that Maigret took off his overcoat at once.
'Where is she?'
'In the bedroom.'
The first room was a kind of drawing-room, or had been—but in these surroundings the usual names didn't seem to fit. The whole place looked, somehow, as though it had been put ready for an auction sale, with all the furniture in unaccustomed places.

There were bottles lying round everywhere, and Maigret noticed that they had all contained red wine—the coarse red wine that navvies drink straight from the bottle, to wash down their lunch-time sausage as they sit by the roadside. There was sausage too—not on a plate, but on a piece of greasy paper, mixed up with scraps of chicken; and chicken bones were strewn on the carpet.

The carpet itself was threadbare and incredibly dirty, and the rest of the furniture was no better—there was a chair with a broken leg, a sofa with tufts of horsehair escaping from it, and the parchment shade on the lamp was singed brown with long use, and quite shapeless.

Next door, in the bedroom, on a bed which had no sheets and had not been made for several days, lay a half-naked body—exactly half-naked, for the upper part was more or less covered by a bodice, while from waist to feet the puffy, livid flesh was bare.

Maigret's first glance took in the little blue specks on the thighs and told him that he would find a syringe somewhere at hand. He found two—one with a broken needle—on what served as a bedside table.

The dead woman appeared to be at least sixty, but it was difficult to judge. No one had touched the body as yet. The doctor had not arrived. But she had obviously been dead for a long time.

The cover of the mattress on which she lay had a long slit in it, and some of the stuffing had been pulled out.

There were bottles in this room, too, and scraps of food; and, right in the middle of the floor, a chamber-pot with urine in it.

'Did she live by herself?' asked Maigret, turning to the concierge.

The woman nodded, with pursed lips.

'Did she have many visitors?'

'If she had, she'd probably have kept the place a bit cleaner, wouldn't she?' retorted the woman—adding, as though she felt the need to defend herself:

'I've not set foot in here for at least three years, until today.'

'Wouldn't she let you in?'

'I didn't want to come.'

'Had she no servant or charwoman?'

'Nobody. Only a woman friend, as crazy as herself, who used to look in now and then.'

'Do you know her?'

'Not by name, but I see her sometimes in the streets round here. She's not quite so far gone yet. That's to say she wasn't when I last saw her, which was some little time ago.'

'Did you know your tenant was a drug addict?'

'I knew she was half crazy.'

'Were you concierge here when she took the flat?'

'I'd have taken care she didn't. It's only three years since we came to the house, my husband and I, and she's been here for at least eight. I've done my best to get rid of her.'

'Is she really a Countess?'

'So it seems. At any rate she was married to a Count; but before that she can't have been any great shakes.'

'Was she well off?'

'I suppose so, for it wasn't starvation she died of.'

'You didn't see anyone going up to her flat?'

'When?'

'Last night or this morning.'

'No. Her woman friend didn't come. Neither did the young man.'

'What young man?'

'A nice-mannered, sickly-looking boy with long hair, who used to visit her and called her "Aunt".'

'You don't know his name?'

'I never concerned myself with her affairs. The rest of the house is quiet enough. The first-floor tenants are nearly always away, and on the second floor is a retired General. You see the style of the place. This woman was so filthy that I used to hold my nose as I went past the door.'

'Did she never have a doctor in?'

'I should think she did! About twice a week. Whenever she was really drunk, on wine or whatever it was, she'd imagine she was dying and ring up her doctor. He knew her, and was never in a hurry to come.'

'A local man, was he?'

'Yes—Dr. Bloch, who lives three houses further down the street.'

'Was it he you rang up when you found the body?'

'No. That wasn't my business. I got on to the police at once. First the inspector came, and then you.'

'Would you try to get Dr. Bloch on the phone, Janvier? Ask him to come along as soon as he can.'

Janvier began a search for the telephone, which he finally discovered in another, smaller room, where it was on the floor, surrounded by old magazines and tattered books.

Maigret continued to question the concierge.

'Is it easy for anyone to get into the house without your seeing them?'

'Same as in any other house, what?' came the sharp retort. 'I do my job as well as any other concierge—better than most—and you won't find a speck of dust on the staircase.'

'Are those the only stairs?'

'There's a service flight, but hardly anybody uses it. And if they do, they still have to come past my door.'

'Are you there all the time?'

'Except when I'm out shopping: even a concierge has to eat.'

'What time do you do your shopping?'

'About half past eight in the morning, as soon as the postman has been round and I've taken up the letters.'

'Did the Countess get many letters?'

'Only circulars. From shops that must have seen her name in the directory and got excited because she had a title.'

'Do you know Monsieur Oscar?'

'Oscar who?'

'Any Oscar.'

'Well, there's my son.'

'How old is he?'

'Seventeen. He's apprenticed to a carpenter in the Boulevard Barbès.'

'Does he live here with you?'

'Of course.'

Janvier, having made his call, came in to report:

'The doctor's at home. He has two more patients to see and then he'll come at once.'

Inspector Lognon was keeping ostentatiously aloof all this time—touching nothing and pretending not to listen to what the concierge was saying.

'Did the Countess ever get any letters with a bank address on them?'

'Never.'

'Did she go out much?'

'She sometimes stayed in for ten or twelve days at a stretch—in fact I used to wonder if she wasn't dead, for there wouldn't be a sound out of her. She must have been lying in a stupor on that filthy bed. Then she'd dress up, put on a hat and gloves, and one would almost have taken her for a lady, except that she always had a kind of wild look on her face.'

'Did she stay out long, at such times?'

'It varied. Sometimes for only a few minutes, sometimes for the whole day. She'd come back loaded with parcels. Wine was delivered to her by the case. It was always that cheap red stuff—she bought it from the grocer in the Rue Condorcet.'

'Did the delivery man come into the flat?'

'He used to leave the case outside the door. I had words with him because he wouldn't use the back stairs—said they were too dark and he didn't want to fall on his nose.'

'How did you come to hear she was dead?'

'I didn't hear she was dead.'

'But you opened her door?'

'I didn't have to take the trouble—and I wouldn't have taken it.'

'What do you mean?'

'This is the fourth floor. On the fifth there's an old gentleman, partly paralysed, and I do his housework and take him up his meals. He used to be in the Inland Revenue. He's been living in the same flat for years and years, and he lost his wife six months ago. You may have read about it in the papers; she was run over by a bus one morning at ten o'clock, when she was crossing the Place Blanche on her way to the market in the Rue Lepic.'

'What time do you go up to do his housework?'

'About ten o'clock every morning. On my way down I sweep the stairs.'

'Did you sweep them this morning?'

'Why wouldn't I have?'

'You go up once before that, with the letters?'

'Not right up to the fifth floor—the old gentleman doesn't get many letters and he's in no hurry to read them. The third-floor people both go out to work and leave early, about half past eight, so they pick up their letters as they go past my lodge.'

'Even if you're not there?'

'Even if I'm out shopping—yes. I never lock the door. I do all my marketing in this street, and I keep an eye on the house while I'm about it. Do you mind if I open the window?'

Everyone was hot. They had all moved back into the first room—except Janvier, who was searching through drawers and cupboards as he had done in the morning at Arlette's flat.

'So you only bring the letters up as far as the second floor?'

'That's right.'

'And this morning about ten o'clock, you passed by this door on your way up to the fifth floor?'

'Yes, and I noticed it was a crack open. That surprised me a bit, but not much. On my way down I didn't think to look. I'd put everything ready for my old gentleman, and I didn't need to go up again till half past four—that's when I take him up his supper. On the way down I noticed this door was still a crack open, and without thinking, I called out—not loudly:

' "*Madame la comtesse!*"

'Because that's what everybody called her. She had a foreign name, difficult to pronounce. It was quicker to say "Countess".

'There was no answer.'

'Was there a light on in the flat?'

'Yes. I haven't touched anything. That lamp over there was burning.'

'And the one in the bedroom?'

'Must have been, mustn't it, seeing it's on now and I didn't lay a finger on the switch? I don't know why, but I felt there was something wrong. I put my head through the door and called again. Then I went in, though I wasn't keen—being very sensitive to bad smells. I peeped into the bedroom and then I saw . . .

'So I ran down to call the police. There was no one else in the house, except the old gentleman, so I went and told the concierge next door, who's an old friend of mine; because I didn't fancy being alone. Some people asked us what was the matter; and there were several of us round the door when the inspector there turned up.'

'Thank you, Madame——?'

'Aubain.'

'Thank you, Madame Aubain. You may go back to your lodge now. I can hear someone coming upstairs, and I expect it's the doctor.'

It was not Dr. Bloch as yet, but the medical examiner—the same one who had examined Arlette's body that morning.

As he came through into the bedroom, after shaking hands with Maigret and nodding in a vaguely gracious manner to Lognon, he gave an involuntary exclamation:

'What—again!'

The Countess's bruised throat showed clearly how she had been killed. And the blue specks on her thighs showed equally clearly that she was hopelessly addicted to drugs. He sniffed one of the syringes and said with a shrug:

'Morphia, of course!'

'Did you know her?'

'Never set eyes on her before. But I know a good few of her sort, in this district. I say—looks as though theft had been the motive, doesn't it?'

He pointed to the slit in the mattress, where the horsehair was hanging out.

'Was she well off?'

'We don't know yet,' replied Maigret.

Janvier, who for some minutes had been picking at the lock of a drawer with his penknife, announced at this point:

'This drawer's full of papers.'

Someone with a young, light step came quickly upstairs and into the room. It was Dr. Bloch.

Maigret noticed that the medical examiner greeted the newcomer with no more than a curt nod, pointedly refraining from extending his hand, as he normally would do to a colleague.

## IV

Dr. Bloch's skin was too sallow, his eyes too bright, his hair black and oily. He had apparently not paused on his way to listen to the gossipers in the street or to speak to the concierge. Janvier on the telephone had not told him the Countess had been murdered—only that she was dead and that the inspector wanted to speak to him.

He had rushed upstairs, four steps at a time, and now stood looking uneasily about him. Possibly he had given himself an injection before leaving his surgery. He did not seem surprised at being snubbed by the other doctor, and made no protest. His manner suggested that he was expecting trouble.

Yet the moment he stepped into the bedroom, he showed relief. The Countess had been strangled, so her death was nothing to do with him.

In less than half a minute he had recovered his self-assurance and was even inclined to be bad-tempered and insolent.

'Why did you send for me rather than for some other doctor?' he began, as though feeling his way.

'Because the concierge told us this woman was your patient.'

'I only saw her a few times.'

'What illness were you treating her for?'

Bloch turned towards the other doctor, as though to indicate that he must know perfectly well.

'You've surely realized that she was a drug addict? When she'd overdone it she'd have a fit of depression—it's frequent with such cases—work herself into a panic, and send for me. She was terrified of dying.'

'Have you known her long?'

'It's only three years since I took over this practice.'

He could hardly be more than thirty years old. Maigret would have been ready to bet that he was a bachelor and had become addicted to morphia as soon as he set up in practice—perhaps even before he qualified. He must have had his reasons for settling in Montmartre, and it was easy to guess what type of patients he attracted.

He wouldn't last long, that was obvious. His goose was cooked already.

'What do you know about her?'

'Her name and address, which are on my register. And the fact that she'd been taking drugs for fifteen years.'

'How old was she?'

'Forty-eight or forty-nine.'

Looking at the emaciated body on the bed, at the thin, colourless hair on the head, it was difficult to believe that she had been no older.

'Isn't it rather unusual for a morphia addict to drink to excess as well?'

'It happens sometimes.'

The doctor's hands were slightly shaky, as a drunkard's are apt to be in the morning, and one side of his mouth twitched every now and then.

'I suppose you tried to cure her?'

'At first, yes. It was a pretty hopeless case, I made no headway. She would let weeks go by without sending for me.'

'Didn't she ever send for you because she'd run out of the stuff and had to get hold of some at all costs?'

Bloch glanced at the other doctor. No use lying about it—the answer was written, as it were, on the body and all over the flat.

'There's no need, I imagine, for me to give you a lecture on the subject. An addict who has got beyond a certain point simply cannot, without serious danger, be cut off from the drug. I don't know where she obtained her supply. I never asked her. Twice, so far as I can remember, I arrived here to find her almost crazy because it hadn't turned up and I gave her an injection.'

'Did she ever tell you anything about her past life—her family, her background?'

'All I know is that she really was married to a certain Count von Farnheim—I understand he was an Austrian and a great deal older than she. They lived together in a big house on the Riviera; she mentioned that once or twice.'

'One more question, doctor: did she pay you by cheque?'

'No—in cash.'

'And you know nothing about her friends, her relations, or her sources of supply?'

'Nothing whatever.'

Maigret let it go at that.

'Thank you,' he said, 'that is all.'

Once again he felt disinclined to wait until the technical people arrived, and still more reluctant to answer the questions of the journalists who would soon be thronging in: he wanted to escape from this stifling, depressing atmosphere.

He gave some instructions to Janvier and went off in a taxi to the Quai des Orfèvres, where he found a message asking him to ring up Dr. Paul, the official pathologist.

'I'm just writing my report, which will be with you tomorrow morning,' said the doctor—all unaware that he would have another post-mortem to carry out before his day's work was over. 'But I thought I'd better tell you right away about two points that may have a bearing on your inquiries. The first is that in all probability the girl wasn't as old as her record makes out. She's supposed to be twenty-four, but according to the medical evidence she can't be a day over twenty.'

'You're sure of that?'

'Practically certain. And the second point is that she'd had a child. That's all I can say. And the person who killed her must have been very strong.'

'Could it have been a woman?'

'I don't think so. If it was, she must have had the strength of a man.'

'Haven't you heard about the second crime yet? You'll be wanted any moment in the Rue Victor-Massé.'

Dr. Paul grumbled something about a dinner engagement, and the two men rang off.

The early editions of the evening papers had printed Arlette's photograph, and as usual several telephone calls had been received. Two or three people were waiting in the ante-room. An inspector was attending to them, and Maigret went home to dinner. His wife, having seen the newspapers, was not expecting him.

It was still raining. He was wet, and went to change his clothes.

'Are you going out again?'

'I shall probably be out for part of the night.'

'Have they found the Countess?'

(The papers had said nothing as yet about the murder in the Rue Victor-Massé.)

'Yes. Strangled.'

'Well, don't catch cold. According to the wireless, it's going to freeze and there'll probably be ice on the roads tomorrow morning.'

He took a small glass of brandy before leaving, and went on foot as far as the Place de la République, to get a breath of fresh air.

His first idea had been to let young Lapointe deal with Arlette's case; but on second thought he felt that would be cruel in the circumstances, and decided to leave it to Janvier.

Janvier would be hard at it now. Armed with a photo of Arlette, he would be making the round of all the cheap hotels and lodging-houses in Montmartre, with special attention to the small places that let rooms by the hour.

Fred, of Picratt's, had hinted that Arlette, like the other women, sometimes went off with a client at closing time. The concierge of her house had been positive that she never brought anyone home with her. But it was unlikely that she went far. And if she had a permanent lover, perhaps she met him at some hotel.

Maigret had told Janvier to take the opportunity of inquiring about a man called Oscar, about whom the police had no information and whose name the girl had only mentioned once. Why had she—apparently—regretted her mention of him and lapsed into silence afterwards?

Being short-handed, Maigret had left Inspector Lognon in the Rue Victor-Massé, where the photographers would have finished their work by now; probably the body had been removed while he was at dinner.

When he reached the Quai des Orfèvres, the lights were out in most of the offices. Young Lapointe was in the inspectors' room, going through the papers found in the Countess's drawer, which he had been told to examine.

'Found anything, my boy?'

'I haven't finished yet. All this stuff is in confusion and it's difficult to sort it out. Besides, I'm checking everything as I go along. I've made several phone calls already, and I'm expecting several others—including one from the flying squad at Nice.'

He held up a postcard photograph of a big, opulent-looking place overlooking the Baie des Anges. The house was built in the worst sham-oriental style, complete with minaret, and the name, The Oasis, was printed in one corner of the card.

'According to these papers, she was living here with her husband fifteen years ago.'

'She'd have been under thirty-five then.'

'Here's a photo of the two of them, taken at that time.'

It was an amateur snapshot, showing the couple standing at the front door of the villa; the woman had two huge borzois on a leash.

Count von Farnheim was a small, dried-up man with a little white beard; he was well-dressed and wore a monocle. The woman was buxom and good-looking—the type that men would turn to stare at.

'Do you know where the marriage took place?'

'At Capri, three years before this photo was taken.'

'How old was the Count?'

'Sixty-five at the time of the marriage. It only lasted three years. He bought The Oasis as soon as they got back from Italy.'

The papers were a jumble of bills, yellow with age, much-stamped passports, cards of admittance to the casinos at Nice and Cannes, and even a bundle of letters. Lapointe had not had time to look at these; they were written in an angular, rather Germanic script, and signed 'Hans'.

'Do you know what her maiden name was?'

'Madeleine Lalande. She was born at La Roche-sur-Yon, Vendée, and at one time she was in the chorus at the Casino de Paris.'

Lapointe seemed to look upon his present job as almost a penance.

'Nothing's turned up, I suppose?' he inquired after a pause. He was obviously thinking of Arlette.

'Janvier's seeing to it. I shall be taking a hand too.'

'Are you going to Picratt's?'

Maigret nodded, and walked away to his office next door, where he found the inspector who was dealing with telephone calls and visitors who claimed to identify Arlette.

'Nothing reliable so far. One old woman seemed so sure of herself that I took her to the mortuary. Even when she was faced with the body she swore it was her daughter. But the chap on duty put me wise. She's cracked. She's been claiming to recognize every woman who's been brought in there for the last ten years or more.'

The weather forecast might have been right for once, because when Maigret left the office it was colder, as cold as winter, and he turned up the collar of his overcoat. He reach Montmartre too early: it was only just after eleven, and the night life had not begun—people were still packed together in theatres and cinemas, the neon lights of the cabarets were being turned on one by one, and the uniformed doormen were not yet at their posts.

Maigret went first of all to the *tabac* at the corner of the Rue de Douai, where he had been scores of times and was recognized. The proprietor had only just come in, for he too was a night bird. In the daytime his wife ran the bar, with a team of waiters, and he took over from her in the late evening, so they only met in passing.

'What will you have, Inspector?'

Maigret had already caught sight of a figure to which the proprietor, with a sidelong glance, now seemed to be directing his attention. It could only be the Grasshopper. His head scarcely topped the bar at which he was standing, drinking a *menthe à l'eau*. He, for his part, had recognized Maigret, but was pretending to be absorbed in his racing paper, on which he was making pencil notes.

He might easily have been taken for a jockey—he was just the right size. It was uncanny to discover, on looking closely, that with his childish body went a wrinkled, grey-skinned face with sharp, darting eyes which seemed to take in everything, like the eyes of some restless animal.

He was not in uniform, but wore a dark suit which gave him the appearance of a small boy in his first long trousers.

'Was it you who were here this morning, about four o'clock?' Maigret asked the proprietor, after ordering a glass of *calvados*.

'Yes, as usual. I saw her. I know what's happened—it was in the evening paper.'

These people would make no difficulties. A few musicians were there, taking a *café-crème* before going off to their work. And there were two or three shady characters whom Maigret knew and who put on innocent expressions.

'What was she like?'

'Same as she always was at that time of night.'

'Did she come every night?'

'No, only now and then. When she thought she hadn't had enough. She'd drink a glass or two of something strong and then go off to bed—she never stayed long.'

'Not even last night?'

'She seemed rather on edge, but she said nothing to me. I don't think she spoke to anyone, except to give her order.'

'Did there happen to be a middle-aged man in the bar, short and thickset, with grey hair?'

Maigret had deliberately refrained from mentioning Oscar to the journalists, so there had been nothing about him in the papers. But he had questioned Fred on the subject, and Fred might have repeated his questions to the Grasshopper, who . . .

'I didn't see anyone like that,' replied the proprietor—a little too emphatically, perhaps.

'You don't happen to know a man called Oscar?'

'There must be any number of Oscars in the district, but I can't think of one who fits your description.'

Maigret edged along a couple of paces, to stand beside the Grasshopper.

'Anything to tell me?'

'Nothing in particular, Inspector.'

'Were you at the door of Picratt's all last night?'

'More or less. I went a little way up the Rue Pigalle once or twice, to hand out cards. And I came here once, to get some cigarettes for an American.'

'You don't know Oscar?'

'Never heard of him.'

The Grasshopper was not the type to be overawed by the police, or by anyone else. His common accent and street arab manner were no doubt assumed, because they amused the clients.

'You don't know Arlette's lover, either?'

'Did she have one? First I've heard of it.'

'You never saw anyone waiting outside for her?'

'Sometimes. Clients.'

'Did she go with them?'

'Not always. Sometimes they were hard to shake off and she had to come here to get rid of them.'

The proprietor, who was quite frankly listening, confirmed this with a nod.

'Did you ever come across her in the daytime?'

'In the morning I'm asleep, and in the afternoon I'm at the races.'

'Had she any woman friends?'

'She got on all right with Betty and Tania, but they weren't close friends. I don't think she and Tania hit it off too well.'

'Did she ever ask you to get drugs for her?'

'What for?'

'For herself.'

'Not she. She was fond of a glass, and even of several, but I don't think she ever took drugs.'

'In fact you know nothing about her.'

'Except that she was the most beautiful girl I've ever seen.'

Maigret hesitated, sweeping the grotesque creature from head to foot with an involuntary glance.

'Ever have a date with her?'

'Why not? I've got off with plenty of others—clients, some of them, in the mink, not only local tarts.'

'That's perfectly true,' interrupted the proprietor. 'I don't know what gets 'em, but they swarm round him like flies. I've known some—and they weren't old or ugly either—who've come here well into the night and hung about waiting for him for an hour and more.'

The gnome's wide, rubbery mouth stretched in a complacent, sardonic grin.

'Maybe they've their reasons,' he said with a lewd gesture.

'So you went to bed with Arlette?'

'Shouldn't have said so if I hadn't.'

'Often?'

'Once, anyhow.'

'Was it her suggestion?'

'She saw I wanted to.'

'Where did it happen?'

'Not at Picratt's, of course. D'you know the Moderne, in the Rue Blanche?'

This was a house of call with which the police were well acquainted.

'Well, that was where.'

'Was she good?'

'She knew her stuff.'

'Did she enjoy it?'

The Grasshopper shrugged. 'Even when a woman doesn't enjoy it she pretends to,' he observed, 'and the less she's enjoying herself, the more she feels obliged to pile it on.'

'Was she drunk that night?'

'She was the same as usual.'

'And with the boss?'

'With Fred? Did he tell you about that?'

The gnome paused for thought, and gravely drained his glass.

'That's no business of mine,' he replied at last.

'Do you think the boss fell for her?'

'Everyone fell for her.'

'You too?'

'I've told you all I had to say. D'you want me to set it to music?' inquired the Grasshopper mockingly. 'Are you going to Picratt's?' he added.

Maigret went, without waiting for the Grasshopper, who would soon be at his post. The red sign of the night-club was already alight. The photos of Arlette were still in the showcase. The door and window were curtained, and there was no sound of music.

He walked in, and found Fred, in a dinner-jacket, arranging bottles behind the bar.

'I thought you'd be round,' he said. 'Is it true that a Countess has been found strangled?'

It was not surprising that he should have heard, since the thing had happened in his district. Besides, the news might have come over the wireless by now.

Two musicians—one a very young man with shiny black hair and the other, about forty years old, who looked sad and unhealthy—were seated on the platform, tuning their instruments. A waiter was putting final touches to the room. There was no sign of Rose; she must be in the kitchen, or perhaps still upstairs.

The walls were painted red, the lighting was bright pink, and things and people looked rather unreal in the atmosphere thus created. Maigret felt as though he were in a photographer's dark room. It took him a little time to get used to the place. People's eyes seemed darker and more gleaming, while the outline of their lips disappeared, the colour sucked out of them by the pink light.

'If you're staying on, give your coat and hat to my wife. You'll find her at the far end,' said Fred. 'Rose!' he called.

She came out of the kitchen; she was wearing a black satin dress with a little embroidered apron over it. She took away Maigret's coat and hat.

'You don't want to sit down yet, do you?'

'Are the women here?'

'They'll be down any minute. They're changing. We have no dressing-rooms, so they use our bedroom and wash-place. You know, I've been thinking carefully about what you asked me this morning. Rose and I have talked it over. We both feel certain that it wasn't by listening to clients that Arlette got her information. Come here, Désiré.'

This was the waiter, who was bald except for a ring of hair that encircled his head, and closely resembled the waiter on the poster advertising a well-known brand of *apéritif*. He was no doubt aware of the resemblance and did his best to foster it: he had even grown side-whiskers for the purpose.

'You can talk quite frankly to Inspector Maigret. Were there any clients at table four last night?'

'No, sir.'

'Did you see two men come in together and stay for some time—one of them short, middle-aged and' (with a glance at Maigret) 'rather like me?'

'No, sir.'

'Who did Arlette talk to?'

'She was quite a long time with her young man. Then she had a few drinks with the Americans at their table. That's all. Towards closing time she and Betty sat down together and ordered brandy. It's entered to her account—you can see for yourself. She had two glasses.'

A dark-haired woman now emerged from the kitchen, looked with a professional eye round the empty room, where Maigret was the only stranger to be seen, went over to the platform, sat down at the piano and began talking in a low voice to the two musicians. They all three looked across at Maigret. Then she struck an introductory chord, the younger man blew a few notes on his saxophone, the other sat down to the percussion instruments, and a moment later a jazz tune burst upon the air.

'It's important for people to hear music as they go past the door,' explained Fred. 'It'll probably be at least half an hour before anyone comes in, but when they do they mustn't find the place silent, or the men and girls sitting round like wax dummies. What can I offer you? If you're going to take a table, I'd rather make it a bottle of champagne.'

'I'd prefer a glass of brandy.'

'I'll give you brandy in your glass and put the champagne bottle on the table. You see, as a general rule, especially at the beginning of the evening, we only serve champagne.'

He took evident pleasure in his work, as though it were his life's dream come true. Nothing escaped his attention. His wife was already seated on a chair at the far end of the room, behind the musicians, and she, too, seemed to be enjoying herself. They must have looked forward for a long time to setting up on their own, and it was still a kind of game for them.

'I know—I'll put you at number six, where Arlette and her boyfriend were sitting. If you want to talk to Tania, wait till they play a rumba. Then Jean-Jean takes his accordion and she can leave the piano. We used to have a pianist, but when we took her on and I discovered she could play, I thought we might as well cut down expenses by using her in the orchestra.'

'There's Betty coming down. Shall I introduce her?'

Maigret had already taken his seat in the box, like an ordinary client, and Fred now brought over a sandy-haired young woman in a blue shot-silk dress with spangles.

'This is Inspector Maigret, who's investigating the murder of Arlette. You needn't be frightened. He's O.K.'

The girl might have been pretty if she had not been as tough and muscular as a man. She looked almost like a young man in woman's dress—so much so that it was embarrassing. Even her voice added to the impression—it was deep and rather hoarse.

'Do you want me to sit here?'

'I should be glad if you would. Will you have something to drink?'

'I'd rather not just yet. Désiré will put a glass in front of me. That's all that's needed.'

She seemed tired and worried. It was hard to realize that she was there to attract men, and she did not appear to have much illusion on the point.

'Are you Belgian?' he asked, because of her accent.

'Yes—from Anderlecht, near Brussels. Before I came here I was with a team of acrobats. I began when I was only a kid—my father belonged to a circus.'

'What is your age?'

'Twenty-eight. I got too rusty for that line of work, so I took up dancing.'

'Are you married?'

'I was, to a juggler. He walked out on me.'

'Was it with you that Arlette left here last night?'

'Yes, as usual. Tania lives near the Gare St. Lazare, so she goes down the Rue Pigalle. She's always ready before us. I live practically next door, and Arlette and I used to walk together to the corner of the Rue Notre-Dame de Lorette.'

'She didn't go straight home?'

'No. That happened sometimes. She'd pretend to turn to the right and then, as soon as I was round the corner, I'd hear her walking on up the street, to get a drink at the *tabac* in the Rue de Douai.'

'Why didn't she do it openly?'

'People who drink don't usually like to be seen hurrying off for a last glass.'

'Did she drink a great deal?'

'She had two glasses of brandy with me before we left, and she'd already had a lot of champagne. And I'm pretty sure she'd been drinking even before she got here.'

'Was she unhappy?'

'If so, she never told me about it. I think she was just disgusted with herself.'

Betty was perhaps in the same state of mind, for she said this with a dreary expression, in a flat, indifferent voice.

'What do you know about her?'

Two clients, a man and a woman, had just come in, and Désiré was trying to steer them to a table. Seeing the place was empty, they looked at each other hesitantly, and finally the man said, with an air of embarrassment:

'We'll come back later.'

'They've come to the wrong address,' remarked Betty calmly. 'This isn't the place for them.'

She made an effort to smile.

'It'll be a good hour before we get going. Sometimes we begin our programme with only three people watching.'

'Why did Arlette take up this job?'

Betty gave him a long look, and then murmured: 'That's what I often asked her. I don't know. Perhaps she enjoyed it.'

She glanced at the photos on the wall.

'You know what she had to do in her act? They're not likely to find anyone who can carry it off so well. It looks easy, but we've all tried it and I can assure you it takes a bit of doing. Because if it's done just anyhow, it looks indecent at once. It really has to be done as though one were enjoying it.'

'Did Arlette do it like that?'

'I sometimes wondered whether she didn't do it because of that! I don't mean because she wanted the men—very likely she didn't. But she had to feel she was exciting them, keeping them on tenterhooks. When it was over and she went off into the kitchen—that's the "wings" of this place, we go through there on our way upstairs to change— she'd open the door a crack and peep out to see what effect she'd produced—just the way actors peep through the hole in the curtain.'

'She wasn't in love with anyone?'

There was quite a long silence before Betty replied: 'Perhaps she was. Yesterday morning I'd have said no. But last night, after her young man left, she seemed upset. She told me she thought she was a fool. I asked her why. She said that if she chose, things could be quite different.

' "What things?" I asked her.

' "Everything! I'm fed up."

' "Do you want to leave this place?"

'We were talking quietly, so Fred shouldn't hear us.

' "It's not only this place," she said.

'I knew she'd been drinking, but I'm certain she meant it.

' "Has he offered to keep you?" I asked.

'She shrugged her shoulders, and muttered:

' "It's no use, you wouldn't understand."

'We nearly quarrelled, and I told her I wasn't so dumb as she seemed to think—I'd been through that kind of thing too.'

At this moment the Grasshopper, with a triumphant expression, ushered in some worthwhile clients—three men and a woman. The men were obviously foreigners; they must be in Paris on business or for a conference, for they looked like important people. As for the woman, they had picked her up goodness knows where—probably on the terrace of a café—and she looked rather uncomfortable.

With a wink at Maigret, Fred settled them at number four table, and handed them an enormous wine-list on which every imaginable variety of champagne was set forth. Hardly a quarter of it could have

actually been in the cellar, and Fred recommended a completely unknown brand which doubtless showed him a profit of about three
hundred per cent.

'I must go and get ready for my act,' sighed Betty. 'Don't expect
anything wonderful. It's good enough for that lot, anyhow—all they
want is to look at legs!'

The orchestra had started a rumba, and Maigret beckoned to Tania,
who had come down from the platform. Fred nodded to her to accept
the invitation.

'You want to speak to me?'

In spite of her name she had no trace of a Russian accent, and
Maigret soon discovered that she had been born in the Rue Mouffetard.

'Sit down and tell me what you know about Arlette.'

'We weren't particularly friendly.'

'Why not?'

'Because she put on airs and I didn't like it.'

The words came out with decision. This was a girl with a very good
opinion of herself, and she was not in the least intimidated by Maigret.

'Did you quarrel?'

'We did even go that far.'

'Did you never speak to each other?'

'As seldom as possible. She was jealous.'

'Of what?'

'Of me. She couldn't admit that anyone else could be in the very
least interesting. She thought she was the only person in the world. I
don't like that sort of thing. She couldn't even dance—never had a
lesson in her life. All she could do was take her clothes off, and if she
hadn't shown them everything she had to show, her act would have had
nothing to it at all.'

'You're a dancer?'

'I was taking ballet lessons before I was twelve.'

'And is that the kind of dancing you do here?'

'No. Here I do Russian folk dances.'

'Did Arlette have a lover?'

'Certainly she did; but she must have felt he was nothing to be
proud of, so she never mentioned him. All I know is, he was old.'

'How do you know that?'

'We all undress together, upstairs. Several times I've seen bruises
on her. She'd try to hide them with a coat of cream, but I have sharp
eyes.'

'Did you ask her about them?'

'Once. She told me she'd fallen downstairs. But she can't have fallen
downstairs every week. And when I noticed the position of the bruises,
I understood. Only old men have those nasty habits.'

'When did you first notice this?'

'At least six months ago, almost as soon as I began to work here.'

'And it went on?'

'I didn't look at her every night, but I often noticed bruises. Anything else you want to ask me? It's time I went back to the piano.'

As soon as she had taken her seat again, the lights went out, a spotlight was turned on the dance-floor, and Betty Bruce bounded into the middle of it. Behind him, Maigret could hear men's voices trying to speak French, and a woman's voice teaching them how to say '*Voulez-vous coucher avec moi?*' They were laughing and repeating, one after another, '*Vo-lez vo* . . .'

Fred came across without a word, his shirt-front glimmering through the darkness, and sat down opposite Maigret. Betty Bruce, keeping approximate time to the music, stretched one leg straight in the air and hopped about on the other foot, her tights clinging closely to her body and a strained smile on her face. Then she let herself fall to the floor, doing the splits.

# V

WHEN his wife woke him with his morning coffee, Maigret's first thought was that he had not had enough sleep and that his head was aching. Then, opening his eyes wide, he wondered why his wife was looking so brisk, as though she had a delightful surprise for him.

'Look!' she said, as soon as his rather shaky hands had grasped the cup.

She drew back the curtain, and he saw that it was snowing outside.

He was pleased, of course; but there was a muddy taste in his mouth which indicated that he must have had more to drink than he had realized at the time. That was probably because Désiré, the waiter, had opened the bottle of champagne that was only supposed to be there for show, and he had poured himself some, without thinking, between two glasses of brandy.

'I don't know if it will settle, but anyhow it's more cheerful than the rain.'

Maigret didn't very much care whether it settled or not. He liked every kind of weather—especially the extreme kinds, which were reported in the papers next day—torrential rain, hurricanes, bitter cold or scorching heat. He liked snow, too, because it reminded him of his childhood; but he wondered how his wife could find it cheerful in Paris —especially that morning. The sky was even heavier than on the previous day, and against the white snow, the black, shiny roofs looked still blacker, the houses still more drab and dirty, and the curtains at most of the windows still dingier than usual.

It took him some time, while eating his breakfast and getting dressed, to sort out his memories of the night before. He had not had much sleep. He had stayed at Picratt's till it closed—that was at least half past four—and then he had felt he ought to imitate Arlette by calling at the *tabac* in the Rue de Douai for a final glass.

He would have been hard put to it to give a brief summary of what he had found out. For long periods he had sat alone in his box, puffing slowly at his pipe and gazing at the dance-floor or the clients, in that strange light which made everything look unreal.

As a matter of fact, he reflected, he could have left earlier: he had stayed on, partly out of indolence and partly because it amused him to watch the people, and the behaviour of Fred, Rose and the girls.

They made up a little world of their own, seeing practically nothing of the life that ordinary people lived. Désiré, the two musicians and the rest of them went to bed just as the alarm clocks were beginning to ring in most houses, and they slept through the greater part of the day. Arlette had led that life, not really waking up till she came into the reddish glow of Picratt's lamps, and seeing hardly anyone except the men who came here, who had had too much to drink and been brought in by the Grasshopper as they left other joints.

Maigret had watched Betty who, aware of his attention, responded by showing off her whole bag of tricks—with a sly wink at him every now and then.

Two clients had come in about three o'clock, when she had finished her act and gone upstairs to dress. They were already well lit up, and as the place was rather too quiet at the moment, Fred had vanished into the kitchen—evidently to call Betty back at once.

She had gone through her dance again—this time entirely for the benefit of the newcomers, waving her leg in the air right in front of their noses and ending up with a kiss on the bald pate of one of them. Before going away to change she sat on the other man's knee and took a sip of champagne from his glass.

Was that how Arlette went on? She was probably more subtle in her methods.

The men spoke a little French, but not much. Betty kept repeating to them: '*Cinq minutes. . . . Cinq minutes. . . . Moi revenir . . .*' and holding up the fingers of one hand. She did come back a few minutes later, wearing her spangled dress, and called to Désiré of her own accord to bring another bottle.

Tania, meanwhile, was busy with a solitary client whose gloom deepened as he drank; he held her by one bare knee and was no doubt confiding his conjugal misfortunes to her at great length.

The two Dutchmen's hands moved to and fro, but never let go of

Betty. They were laughing loudly, their faces growing gradually redder, and bottles were arriving at their table in rapid succession. Once emptied, these bottles were put under the table, and Maigret finally realized that some of them had already been empty when they were brought. That was the trick—as Fred's glance admitted.

Maigret had got up once and gone to the cloakroom. There was a lobby here, with brushes, combs, and powder and rouge laid out on a shelf, and Rose had followed him in.

'I've remembered something that may perhaps help you,' she said. 'It was seeing you come in here that reminded me. It's usually here that the girls get talking to me, while they're doing themselves up. Arlette was no chatterbox, but she did tell me a few things about herself, and I guessed others.'

She offered him soap and a clean towel.

'She certainly didn't come from the same class as the rest of us. She never talked about her family to me, or to anyone else so far as I know but she several times mentioned the convent where she had been to school.'

'Do you remember what she said?'

'If anyone spoke about some woman being harsh and unkind—especially about the sort of woman who puts on a good-natured air to cover her mean ways, Arlette would say softly:

' "*That's like Mother Eudice.*"

'And one could tell she spoke from unhappy memories. I asked her who Mother Eudice was, and she said she was the person she hated most in all the world, and she had done her the most harm. She was the Mother Superior of the convent, and she'd taken a dislike to Arlette. I remember the girl once said:

' "*I'd have gone to the bad if it was only to spite her.*" '

'She never told you what convent it was?'

'No, but it can't have been far from the sea, because she often talked in a way that showed she'd lived by the seaside as a child.'

Funnily enough, all the time she was talking, Rose was treating Maigret like a client, automatically brushing his coat-collar and shoulders.

'I believe she hated her mother, too. That was less definite, but it's the sort of thing a woman notices. One evening there were some real swells here, doing the rounds in style—including a Cabinet Minister's wife who really did look like a great lady. She seemed depressed and absentminded; took no interest in the show, drank very little, and hardly listened to what the others were saying.

'I knew all about her, and I said to Arlette—in here, as usual, while she was doing up her face:

' "It's brave of her to go about like this—she's been having all kinds of trouble lately."

'At which Arlette said, with a sneer:

' "I distrust people who've had troubles, especially women. They make that an excuse for trampling on other people."

'It's only a hunch, but I'd swear she was thinking of her mother. She never spoke of her father—if that subject came up, she'd turn her head away.

'That's all I can tell you. I always thought she was a girl from a good family, who'd kicked over the traces. They're the worst of all, that kind, and that would explain a lot that seems mysterious.'

'You mean her obsession about attracting men?'

'Yes. And the way she set about it. I'm no infant in arms myself. I did the same job at one time, and worse, as you probably know. But not the way she did. That's why there's nobody to take her place. The genuine ones, the professionals, never put so much energy into it. Look at them. Even when they let themselves go you can feel they're not really enjoying it.'

Fred came across to Maigret's table every now and then and sat down for a few words with him. On each of these occasions Désiré brought them glasses of brandy and water, but Maigret noticed that the liquid in Fred's glass was always the paler of the two. As he drank his own he thought of Arlette and Lapointe, sitting together in this same box on the previous evening.

Inspector Lognon would deal with the Countess, in whom Maigret felt little or no interest. He had known too many women of that kind— middle-aged, nearly always on their own, nearly always with a brilliant past life, who took to drugs and sank rapidly into utter degradation. There were probably a couple of hundred of them in Montmartre, and several dozen, slightly higher in the social scale, in comfortable flats in Passy and Auteuil.

It was Arlette who interested him, because he had not yet managed to place her, or to understand her completely.

'Hot stuff, was she?' he asked Fred at one moment.

Fred replied, with a shrug:

'Oh, I don't bother much about the girls, you know. It's quite true what my wife told you yesterday. I go to join them in the kitchen, or upstairs while they're changing. I don't ask them what they think about it, and the whole thing passes over very quickly.'

'You never met her outside this place?'

'In the street?'

'No. I mean, did you never make a date with her?'

He had the impression that Fred hesitated, glancing towards the far end of the room, where his wife was sitting.

'No,' he said at last.

He was lying. That was the first thing Maigret discovered on arriving at the Quai des Orfèvres next morning (he was late and missed the report). The atmosphere in the inspectors' office was lively. Maigret began by telephoning to the Chief, to apologize and to say that he would come along as soon as he had heard what his men had to say.

When he rang, Janvier and young Lapointe came hurrying to his door in a neck-and-neck race.

'Janvier first,' he decided. 'I'll call you presently, Lapointe.'

Janvier looked as knocked-up as Maigret himself, and had obviously spent part of the night in the streets.

'I was rather expecting you to look in on me at Picratt's.'

'I meant to. But the further I went, the busier I got. In fact I haven't been to bed at all.'

'Found Oscar?'

Janvier took from his pocket a paper covered with notes.

'I don't know. I don't think so. I called at practically every small hotel between the Rue Châteaudun and the Montmartre boulevards, and showed the girl's photograph in all of them. Some of the proprietors pretended not to recognize her, or tried to dodge the question.'

'And the result?'

'She was known at at least ten of these hotels.'

'Did you try to find out whether she'd often been there with the same man?'

'That was the point I pushed hardest of all. Apparently she hadn't. It was usually about four or five o'clock in the morning when she turned up, and the men she brought were well loaded—probably clients from Picratt's.'

'Used she to stay long with them?'

'Never more than an hour or two.'

'Did you discover whether she took money from them?'

'When I asked that, the hotel-keepers looked at me as though I was cracked. She went twice to the Moderne with a greasy-haired young man who was carrying a saxophone case.'

'That'd be Jean-Jean, the musician from the night-club.'

'Perhaps. Last time was about a fortnight ago. You know the Hôtel du Berry, in the Rue Blanche? It's not far from Picratt's or from the Rue Notre-Dame de Lorette. She went there often. The proprietress was very talkative, because she's already had trouble with us about girls who were under age, and wants to put herself right. Arlette came there a few weeks ago with a short, broad-shouldered man whose hair was going grey at the temples.'

'Didn't the proprietress know him?'

'She thought she'd seen him about, but she didn't know who he was. She makes out he must be a Montmartre man. They stayed in their room until nine in the evening. That struck her particularly, because Arlette hardly ever used to come during the day or the evening, and usually went away again almost at once.'

'Get hold of a photo of Fred Alfonsi and show her that.'

Janvier, who had not met the proprietor of Picratt's frowned at this name.

'If it was him, Arlette met him somewhere else as well. Wait a minute while I look up my list. At the Hôtel Lepic, in the Rue Lepic. It was a man I saw there—a fellow who's lost one leg and spends the night reading novels; says he can't sleep because his leg hurts him. He recognized her. She went there several times—usually, he told me, with a man he often sees in the Lepic market, but doesn't know by name. A small, thickset chap, who generally goes shopping late in the morning—without bothering to put on a collar, as though he'd just got up. Sounds rather the type, doesn't it?'

'Maybe. You'll have to make your round again, with a photo of Alfonsi. There's one in his file, but it's too old.'

'Will it do for me to ask him for one?'

'Ask him for his identity card, as though you were making a check-up, and get the photo copied upstairs.'

The office boy came in to say that a lady would like to speak to Maigret.

'Ask her to wait. I'll see her presently.'

Janvier went on: 'Marcoussis is going through the mail. He says there are a whole lot of letters about Arlette's identity. And he's had about twenty phone calls already this morning. Everything's being checked, but I don't think there's anything reliable yet.'

'Did you ask everybody about Oscar?'

'Yes. None of 'em turned a hair. Sometimes they described some local Oscar, but it never sounded like our man.'

'Send Lapointe in.'

Lapointe arrived, looking worried. He knew his superiors must have been talking about Arlette, and wondered why he hadn't been called to join in their discussion, as usual. He gave an almost imploring look of inquiry at the inspector.

'Sit down, my boy. If there'd been anything fresh, I would have told you. We've not got much further since yesterday.'

'Did you spend the night up there, sir?'

'Yes, at the table you had the evening before. By the way, did she never tell you anything about her family?'

'All I know is that she ran away from home.'

'She didn't tell you why?'

'She told me she loathed humbug, and that she'd felt stifled all through her childhood.'

'Tell me frankly—did she treat you nicely?'

'What exactly do you mean by that?'

'Did she treat you like a friend—talk to you quite sincerely?'

'At times, I think. It's difficult to explain.'

'Did you begin making love to her right away?'

'I told her I loved her.'

'The first evening?'

'No. The first evening my friend was there, and I hardly opened my mouth. It was when I went back there by myself.'

'And what did she say?'

'She tried to make out I was only a kid, but I told her I was twenty-four—older than she was.

' "*It isn't age that matters, my child,*" she retorted. "*I'm ever so much older than you!*"

'You see, she was very unhappy—in fact, desperate. I think that was why I fell in love with her. She'd laugh and joke, but she was bitter all the time. And sometimes . . .'

'Go on.'

'I know you think she was fooling me. . . . She'd try to make me stop loving her—she'd talk in a vulgar way on purpose, and use coarse words.

' "*Why can't you just get into bed with me, like the rest of them? Leave you cold, do I? I could teach you a lot more than other women. I bet there's not one that has my experience and knows her stuff like I do. . . .*"

'Oh, I've just remembered, she added: "*I got my training in the right school.*" '

'Were you never tempted to try?'

'I wanted her. I could have screamed, sometimes. But I didn't want her like that. It would have spoilt everything, you understand?'

'I understand. And what did she say when you urged her to drop that kind of life?'

'She'd laugh, call me her little shrimp and begin to drink harder than ever, and I'm sure it was because she was desperate. You haven't found the man?'

'What man?'

'The one she called Oscar.'

'We haven't found anything at all so far. Now tell me what you did last night.'

Lapointe had brought in a thick file. It contained the papers found in the Countess's flat, which he had carefully sorted out; and he had written several pages of notes.

'I've managed to trace practically the whole story of the Countess,' he said. 'I had a telephone report from the Nice police first thing this morning.'

'Tell me about it.'

'To begin with, I know her real name—Madeleine Lalande.'

'I saw that yesterday on her marriage certificate.'

'Oh yes—I'm sorry. She was born at La Roche-sur-Yon, where her mother was a charwoman. Father unknown. She came to Paris to go into service, but within a few months she'd found a man to keep her. She changed lovers several times, doing a bit better with each one, and fifteen years ago she was one of the most beautiful women on the Riviera.'

'Was she already taking drugs?'

'I don't know, but there's nothing to suggest it. She was gambling, always in the casinos. Then she met Count von Farnheim, who came of an old Austrian family and was sixty-five years old at the time. Here are the letters he wrote her; I've arranged them according to date.'

'Have you read them all?'

'Yes. He was passionately in love with her.'

Lapointe blushed as though they were the kind of letters he himself might have written.

'They're very touching letters. He never forgot he was an old man, and almost infirm. At first they're full of respect. He calls her *Madame*, and later on *dear friend*, and finally *my dearest little girl*; he implores her to stay near him, never to leave him alone: he keeps on saying she's all he has in the world and he can't bear the thought of living his last years without her.'

'Did she become his mistress at once?'

'No. It took months. He fell ill, in a furnished house where he lived before buying The Oasis, and persuaded her to come there as a guest and spend a few hours with him every day. You can feel in every line that he's sincere, that he's clinging desperately to her, ready to do anything rather than lose her. He writes bitterly about the difference in their ages, and says he realizes he can't offer her a very pleasant life.

'*But it won't last long,* he writes in one letter. *I'm old and sick. In a few years you'll be free, little girl; you'll still be beautiful, and if you wish you'll be rich. . . .*

'He wrote to her every day—sometimes just short notes, like a schoolboy in love: "*I love you! I love you! I love you!*"

'And then, all of a sudden, he bursts into a kind of Song of Songs, in an entirely different tone—speaking of her body, with a mixture of passion and a kind of reverence:

'*I can hardly believe that your body has lain in my arms—that those breasts, those thighs. . . .*'

Maigret gazed thoughtfully at Lapointe, without a smile.

'From that moment, he's haunted by the fear of losing her. And tortured by jealousy. He implores her to tell him everything, even if it gives him pain. He asks what she was doing the day before, what men she met. There's a lot about one of the musicians at the Casino, whom he thinks handsome and is terribly afraid of. He wants to know about her past life, too:

'*I have to have you "all complete".* . . .

'And he ends by begging her to marry him.

'I've no letters from her. It looks as though she never wrote to him—just came to see him, or telephoned. In one of his last letters, writing again about his age, he says:

'*I ought to have understood that that beautiful body of yours has cravings that I cannot satisfy. The thought is agony to me; whenever it comes into my mind, I feel as if I should die of torment. But I would rather share you than do without you altogether. I swear I will never blame you, or make scenes. You shall be as free as you are now, and your old husband will sit quietly in his corner, waiting for you to bring him a little happiness.*'

Lapointe blew his nose.

'They went to Capri to get married, I don't know why. There was no marriage settlement, but they had a joint bank account. For a few months they travelled about, visiting Constantinople and Cairo; then they spent some weeks at a big hotel in the Champs-Elysées—I came across the hotel bills.'

'When did he die?'

'The police at Nice were able to give me all the particulars. It was barely three years after the marriage. They had been living at The Oasis for several months. They used to be seen driving in a big closed car with a chauffeur, going to the Casinos of Monte Carlo, Cannes and Juan-les-Pins. She was magnificently dressed and covered with jewels. They caused a sensation wherever they went, for she could hardly fail to attract attention and she always had her husband in tow—a small, shrivelled man with a little white beard and a monocle. People used to call him "the rat".

'She gambled heavily, flirted openly, and was thought to have several love-affairs.

'He would wait, like her shadow, till the early hours of the morning, with a resigned smile.'

'How did he die?'

'Nice is sending you the report by post, for there was an inquest. The Oasis stands on the Corniche, and has a terrace, fringed with palms, below which there's a sheer drop of about three hundred feet. Most of the places round there are like that.

'The Count's body was found one morning, lying at the foot of the precipice.'

'Had he been drinking?'

'He was on a diet. His doctor said he was apt to get fits of dizziness, because of some medicines he had to take.'

'Did he and his wife share a room?'

'No, they had separate suites. The previous evening they'd been to the Casino, as usual, getting back about three in the morning, which was unusually early for them. The Countess was tired. She explained frankly to the police that it was the bad time of the month for her, and she used to have a lot of pain. She went to bed at once.

The Count, according to the chauffeur, went first of all to the library, which had a french window opening on to the terrace. He used to do that when he couldn't sleep—he was a bad sleeper. The theory was that he'd gone outside for air, and sat down on the stone balustrade of the terrace. It was his favourite place, because there's a view from there of the Baie des Anges, the lights of Nice and a long stretch of coast.

'There were no signs of violence on the body when it was found, and no trace of poison was discovered at the autopsy.'

'What happened to her after that?'

'She had to cope with a young nephew who turned up from Austria to dispute the will, and it was nearly two years before she won the case. She went on living at Nice, at The Oasis. She entertained a great deal —the house was very gay, and drinking went on till all hours. Very often the guests slept there, and the fun began again as soon as they woke up.

'The local police say she had several gigolos, one after another, and they got away with a good deal of her money. I asked if that was when she began taking drugs, but there was no information about that. The police will try to find out, but it's a long time ago. The only report they've found so far is very scrappy, and they aren't sure they can lay their hands on the file.

'What they do know is that she drank and gambled. When she was well under way, she'd collect a bunch of people and take them home with her. So you can see there must be plenty of her crazy kind in that part of the world. She must have lost a lot of money at roulette; sometimes she'd stick obstinately to the same number for hours on end.

'Four years after her husband's death she sold The Oasis. That was in the middle of the slump, so she got very little for it. I think it's a sanatorium now, or a nursing-home. Anyway, it's no longer a private house.

'That's all that's known at Nice. After the house was sold the Countess disappeared, and she's never been seen again on the Riviera.'

'You'd better go and look in on the gambling-licence office,' advised Maigret. 'And the narcotics squad might have some news for you too.'

'Aren't I to deal with Arlette?'

'Not for the moment. I'd like you to ring through to Nice again, as well. They may be able to give you a list of the people who were living at The Oasis when the Count died. Don't forget the servants. I know it's fifteen years ago, but we may be able to trace some of them.'

It was still snowing, fairly hard; but the flakes were so light and feathery that they melted as soon as they touched a wall or the ground.

'Is that all, sir?'

'That's all for now. Leave the file with me.'

'You don't want me to write up my report?'

'Not till it's all finished. Off you go.'

Maigret got up: the heat of the office made him feel drowsy, and he still had a nasty taste in his mouth and a dull ache at the back of his head. He remembered there was a lady waiting for him in the ante-room, and decided to fetch her himself for the sake of walking a few yards. If there had been time he would have gone to the Brasserie Dauphine for a glass of beer to freshen him up.

There were several people in the glass-partitioned waiting-room, where the green of the armchairs looked harsher than usual, and an umbrella was standing in a corner, surrounded by a pool of melted snow. Looking round for his visitor, Maigret saw an elderly woman in black sitting bolt upright on a chair. She got up as he came in—she had probably seen his photo in the papers.

Lognon was there too, but made no move to rise; he just looked at the inspector and sighed. That was his way. He had a positive need to feel wronged, unlucky, a victim of circumstances. He had been working all night, trailing round the wet streets while hundreds of thousands of Parisians were asleep. The case was out of his hands now, since head-quarters had taken it over. But he had done his best, knowing that the credit would go to others; and he had made a discovery.

He had been sitting in the waiting-room for the last half-hour, to-gether with a strange young man with long hair, a pale face and a thin nose, who stared straight ahead of him as though about to faint.

And naturally nobody paid any attention to him. They just left him to kick his heels. They didn't even ask who he'd brought with him, or what he'd found out. Maigret merely murmured: 'See you in a minute, Lognon!' as he showed the lady out.

Maigret opened the door of his office and stood back, saying: 'Please sit down.'

He soon realized he had made a mistake. Because of what Rose had said, and because of his visitor's respectable, rather prim appearance, her black clothes and stiff manner, he had assumed it was Arlette's mother, who had recognized her daughter's photograph in the papers.

Her first words did not correct this impression. 'I live at Lisieux,' she said, 'and I came up by the first train this morning.'

Lisieux was not far from the sea, and he seemed to remember that there was a convent there.

'I saw the paper yesterday evening and recognized the photograph at once.'

She put on a distressed expression, because she felt that would be expected; but she was not in the least upset. There was even a gleam of triumph in her little black eyes.

'Naturally, the girl has altered in the last four years, and that style of hairdressing makes her look different. But I have no doubt whatever that it is she. I would have gone to see my sister-in-law, but we have not spoken to each other for years now, and it is not for me to make the first advance. You understand?'

'I understand,' said Maigret gravely, with a little puff at his pipe.

'The name was different too, of course. But living the life she did, it was only natural she could have changed her name. However, I was puzzled to learn that she called herself Arlette and had an identity card in the name of Jeanne Leleu. The strange thing is that I used to know the Leleu family. . . .'

He waited patiently, watching the falling snow.

'Anyhow, I showed the photograph to three different people, reliable people who had known Anne-Marie well, and they all agreed that it was undoubtedly she—the daughter of my brother and sister-in-law.'

'Is your brother still alive?'

'He died when the child was only two. He was killed in a railway accident—you remember it, perhaps, the famous Rouen catastrophe. I'd warned him. . . .'

'Your sister-in-law lives at Lisieux?'

'Never left the place. But as I told you, we are quite out of touch. It would take too long to explain why. I am sure you will agree that there are some people with whom it is quite impossible to remain on friendly terms. Let us leave it at that!'

'Let us leave it at that!' he repeated.

Then he asked: 'What was your brother's name, by the way?'

'Trochain, Gaston Trochain. Ours is a large family, probably the largest in Lisieux, and one of the oldest. I don't know whether you are acquainted with the place. . . .'

'No, Madame. I have only passed through.'

'But you doubtless noticed the statue of General Trochain in the principal square. He was our great-grandfather. And the château with the slate-tiled roof that you see on your right as you go towards Caen, was our family property. It no longer belongs to us. It was bought by some *nouveaux riches* after the 1914 war. But my brother was comfortably off.'

'Would it be indiscreet to ask you what he did?'

'He was an Inspector in the Department of Civil Engineering. My sister-in-law was the daughter of an ironmonger who had made a little money, from whom she inherited nine or ten houses and a couple of farms. While my brother was alive she was accepted in society for his sake. But as soon as she was widowed, people began to realize that she had married above her, and now she is left practically alone in her big house.'

'Do you think she will have seen the newspaper?'

'Undoubtedly. The photograph was on the front page of the local paper that everyone sees.'

'Don't you find it strange that she has not got into touch with us?'

'Not in the least. She will certainly not do so. She is too proud. In fact I am convinced that if she were confronted with the body she would swear it was not her daughter. I know she had heard nothing from the girl for the last four years. Nobody had, at Lisieux. And she's not upset about her daughter—only about what people are thinking.'

'Do you know why the girl left home?'

'I should say nobody could stay under the same roof as that woman. But there was another reason. I don't know where the child inherited her character from; it was not from my brother, everyone will tell you that. But when she was fifteen, she was expelled from her convent-school. And after that, if I happened to go out in the evening, I never dared look at dark doorways, for fear of seeing her there with a man. Even married men, there were. My sister-in-law thought fit to lock her up, which has never been a wise method, and it only made her worse. People say she climbed out of the window once without her shoes, and was seen like that in the street.'

'Is there any distinguishing mark by which you would be sure of recognizing her?'

'Yes, Inspector.'

'What is it?'

'I have not been blessed with children myself. My husband was never very strong, and he has been an invalid for years now. When my niece was a little girl, her mother and I were still on friendly terms. As the child's aunt I often took care of her, and I remember she had a birth-mark under her left heel—a small port wine mark that never faded out.'

Maigret picked up the telephone and asked for the police mortuary.

'Hello? This is the Judicial Police. Will you please look at the left foot of the young woman who was brought in yesterday? Yes. . . . I'll hold on. Tell me if you find any distinguishing point. . . .'

The woman waited with the complete self-assurance of one to whom misgivings were unknown—sitting very straight on her chair, her hands folded over the silver clasp of her handbag. One could imagine her sitting like that in church, listening to the sermon, with that same hard, secretive face.

'Hello? Yes. . . . That's all. . . . Thank you. Someone will be coming along to identify the body. . . .'

He turned to the lady from Lisieux.

'You're not afraid to go, I take it?'

'It is my duty,' she replied.

He had not the heart to keep poor Lognon waiting any longer: besides, he felt no wish to escort his visitor to the morgue. He went over and looked into the next-door office.

'Are you free, Lucas?'

'I've just finished my report on the Javel business.'

'Would you take this lady round to the mortuary?'

She was taller than Sergeant Lucas, and very stiff, and as she marched ahead of him down the corridor, she looked rather as though she were leading him on a string.

# VI

LOGNON came in, driving his prisoner in front of him. Maigret noticed that the young man's hair was so long that it made a kind of pad at the back of his neck, and that he was carrying a heavy brown canvas hold-all, clumsily mended with string, its weight pulling him to one side as he walked.

Opening the door that led to the inspectors' office, the inspector signed to the young man to go in there.

'See what's inside that,' he said to his waiting subordinates, pointing to the hold-all.

About to close the door, he had a second thought.

'Make him let his trousers down, to see if he's got needlemarks.'

Alone with the gloomy Lognon, he turned and looked at him benevolently. He was not disturbed by the man's bad temper, and knew his wife did not lead him a very pleasant life. Some of the other men had tried to be friendly with Lognon. But he was too much for them. The mere sight of his glum face, with its perpetual air of foreseeing disaster, was enough to provoke a shrug or a grin.

Maigret rather suspected that he had developed a taste for bad luck and ill-temper and adopted them as his pet vices—gloating over them just as some old men gloat over their chronic bronchitis and the sympathy it earns for them.

'Well, old chap?'

'Well, here I am.'

That meant that Lognon was ready to answer questions, since he was a mere underling, but that he thought it outrageous to have to present a report—he, who would have led the investigation if it hadn't been for the Judicial Police—he, who knew his district inside out and had not allowed himself a moment's rest since the previous day.

His pursed lips said more clearly than words: 'I know what will happen. It's always like this. You'll pick my brains, and tomorrow or next day the papers will announce that Inspector Maigret has cleared up the crime. With the usual talk about his unerring instinct and his methods.'

Lognon, in fact, didn't believe in all that, and this probably accounted for his attitude. If Maigret was an inspector, and the other fellows here were in the Special Branch instead of kicking their heels in a district police station, it was only because they'd been lucky, or pulled strings, or knew how to make anything of themselves.

In his opinion, he was as good as the best of them.

'Where did you pick up that lad?'

'At the Gare du Nord.'

'When?'

'This morning, at half past six. Before it was light.'

'Do you know his name?'

'I've known it for ages. This is the eighth time I've arrested him. He's best known by his first name, Philippe. His full name is Philippe Mortemart, and his father is a professor at Nancy University.'

It was unusual for Lognon to provide so much information in one breath. His shoes were muddy, and as they were old they must have let the water in; his trousers were damp up to the knees, and his eyes were red-rimmed and weary.

'You realized at once who it was when the concierge mentioned a long-haired young man?'

'I know the district.'

Which amounted to a hint that Maigret and his men had no need to interfere.

'Did you go to his home? Where does he live?'

'In an attic, at the top of a block of flats in the Boulevard Roche-chouart. He wasn't there.'

'What time was that?'

'Six o'clock yesterday evening.'

'Had he already taken away his bag?'

'Not yet.'

It had to be admitted that Lognon was the most persistent of blood-hounds. He had gone off on a trail, not even sure that it was the right one, and had followed it up without losing heart for a moment.

'You were looking for him from six o'clock yesterday until this morning?'

'I know his haunts. He needed money to get away, and he was looking for someone to borrow from. It wasn't till he'd got the money that he went to fetch his bag.'

'How did you find out he was at the Gare du Nord?'

'From a woman who'd seen him take the first bus at the Square d'Anvers. I found him in the waiting-room.'

'And what have you been doing with him since?'

'I took him to the Station to question him.'

'And . . . ?'

'He either knows nothing or won't say anything.'

Maigret had a curious impression that the inspector was in a hurry to get away, and that it wasn't because he wanted to go to bed.

'I suppose I'm to leave him with you?'

'Have you made your report?'

'I'll give it to my inspector this evening.'

'Was it Philippe who supplied the Countess with drugs?'

'Unless it was she who kept him supplied. Anyhow, they were often seen together.'

'Had that been going on long?'

'Several months. If you don't need me any more . . .'

He obviously had something on his mind. Either Philippe had
dropped some remark that had set him thinking, or else, during his all-
night search, he had come across a clue that he was eager to follow up
before other people got on the same track.

Maigret, too, knew the district, and could imagine how Philippe and
the Inspector had spent the night. In order to get money, the young
man must have been looking up everybody he knew, and he would be
looking among the drug addicts. He would have asked the prostitutes
lurking at the doors of shady hotels; he would have asked café waiters
and night-club porters. Then, as the streets emptied, he would have
knocked on the doors of hovels inhabited by degenerates like himself,
as seedy and penniless as he was.

Had he succeeded in getting a supply of the drug he wanted? If not,
he would fall completely to pieces before long.

'Can I go now?'

'Thank you. You've done a good job.'

'I'm not suggesting he killed the old woman.'

'Neither am I.'

'You're going to hold him?'

'Perhaps.'

Lognon went off, and Maigret opened the door of the inspectors'
office. The hold-all was lying on the floor, open. Philippe's face had
the colour and general appearance of melted tallow, and whenever
anyone moved he raised his arm, as though afraid of being hit.

Not one of the men showed the least pity for him—disgust was
written clearly on all their faces.

The bag held only some shabby underwear, a pair of socks, some
bottles of medicine—Maigret sniffed at them to make sure they didn't
contain heroin—and a few notebooks. He flicked over the pages. They
were filled with poems, or to be more exact, with disjointed phrases
inspired by the delirium of a drug addict.

'Come in here!' he said.

Philippe slid past him in the attitude of one who expects a kick in the
pants. He must be accustomed to them. Even in Montmartre there are
people who can't see a fellow like that without hitting him.

Maigret sat down, and left the young man to stand up, sniffing all
the time with a dry, exasperating twitch of his nostrils.

'Was the Countess your mistress?'

'She was my protectress,' came the reply, in the mincing tones of a
homosexual.

'In other words, you didn't go to bed with her?'

'She was interested in my writing.'

'And gave you money?'

'She helped me to get along.'

'Did she give you a lot?'

'She wasn't rich.'

This was confirmed by the state of his suit, which, though well-cut, was completely threadbare—a blue, double-breasted suit. His shoes must have been given to him, for they were patent leather shoes, more appropriate to evening clothes than to the dirty raincoat he was wearing.

'Why did you try to run away to Belgium?'

The lad did not answer at once, but looked at the door leading into the next office, as though dreading that Maigret would call two tough inspectors to beat him up. Perhaps that had happened to him on previous occasions when he was arrested.

'I've done no harm. I don't understand why I've been arrested.'

'You go with men?'

In his heart of hearts he was proud of it, like all pansies, and an involuntary smile crossed his unnaturally red lips. Maybe he even got a thrill from being pushed about by real men!

'So you won't answer?'

'I have some men friends.'

'But you have women friends too. . . .'

'That's not the same thing.'

'Am I right in supposing that the men provide you with enjoyment and the old ladies with cash?'

'They appreciate my company.'

'Do you know many?'

'Three or four.'

'And they're all your protectresses?'

It took some self-control to speak of such things in an ordinary voice and to look at the lad as though he were a human being.

'They help me sometimes.'

'Do they all take drugs?'

Seeing him turn away his head without replying, Maigret lost his temper. He did not get up, seize the fellow by the filthy collar of his raincoat and shake him; but he rapped out his next words in a metallic voice.

'Listen! I'm not feeling very patient today, and I'm not Lognon. Either you answer my questions at once, or else I'll put you in the cooler for a nice long time. And my inspectors can have a turn at you first.'

'You mean they'll hit me?'

'They'll do whatever they like.'

'They've no right to.'

'And you've no right to hang around spoiling the view. Now, try to answer me. How long had you known the Countess?'

'About six months.'

'Where did you meet her?'
'In a little bar in the Rue Victor-Massé, almost opposite her house.'
'Did you realize at once that she took drugs?'
'It was easy to see.'
'So you sucked up to her?'
'I asked her to give me a little.'
'Had she got any?'
'Yes.'
'A lot?'
'She hardly ever ran short.'
'Do you know how she got it?'
'She didn't tell me.'
'Answer my question. Do you know?'
'I think so.'
'How?'
'From a doctor.'
'A doctor who takes dope himself?'
'Yes.'
'Dr. Bloch?'
'I don't know his name.'
'That's a lie. Ever been to see him?'
'A few times.'
'Why?'
'To get him to give me some.'
'And did he?'
'Only once.'
'Because you threatened to give him away?'
'I had to have some at once. I'd been without for three days. He gave me an injection—just one.'
'Where used you to meet the Countess?'
'In the little bar and at her flat.'
'Why did she give you morphine and money?'
'Because she took an interest in me.'
'I've already warned you that you'd better answer my questions.'
'She was lonely.'
'Hadn't she any friends?'
'She was always alone.'
'You made love to her?'
'I tried to give her pleasure.'
'In her flat?'
'Yes.'
'And you both used to drink red wine?'
'It made me quite sick.'
'And you fell asleep on her bed. Did you ever spend the night there?'
'I stayed as much as two days there.'

'Without ever pulling back the curtains, I bet. Without knowing when it was day and when it was night. Isn't that so?'

After which he doubtless roamed about the streets like a sleep-walker, in a world to which he no longer belonged, looking for another opportunity.

'How old are you?'

'Twenty-eight.'

'When did you begin?'

'Three or four years ago.'

'Why?'

'I don't know.'

'Are you still in touch with your parents?'

'My father washed his hands of me long ago.'

'And your mother?'

'She smuggles a money-order to me now and then.'

'Tell me about the Countess.'

'I don't know anything.'

'Tell me what you do know.'

'She used to be very rich. She was married to a man she didn't love, an old fellow who never gave her a moment's peace and had her trailed by a private detective.'

'Is that what she told you?'

'Yes. He used to get a report every day, describing all she'd said and done, almost minute by minute.'

'Was she already doping herself?'

'No. I don't think so. He died, and everybody tried to grab the money he'd left her.'

'Who was "everybody"?'

'All the gigolos on the Riviera, the professional gamblers, her women friends. . . .'

'Did she never mention any names?'

'I don't remember any. You know what it's like. When you've got your load, you talk in a different way. . . .'

Maigret knew this only by hearsay, having never given it a trial.

'She still had some money?'

'Not much. I think she was gradually selling her jewels.'

'Did you ever see them?'

'No.'

'Didn't she trust you?'

'I don't know.'

He was swaying on his legs—they must be skeleton-thin under those loose trousers—to such an extent that Maigret motioned to him to sit down.

'Was there anyone else in Paris besides yourself who was still trying to get money out of her?'

'She never spoke to me about anyone.'

'You never saw anybody in her flat, or talking to her in the street or in a bar?'

Maigret noticed a perceptible hesitation.

'N . . . no!'

He looked sternly at the lad.

'You haven't forgotten what I told you?'

But Philippe had pulled himself together.

'I never saw anyone with her.'

'Neither a man nor a woman?'

'Nobody.'

'Did you ever hear the name "Oscar" mentioned?'

'I don't know anybody of that name.'

'She never seemed to be afraid of anyone?'

'She was only afraid of dying all alone.'

'Did she ever have rows with you?'

The lad's face was too pasty to blush, but a faint pink tinge appeared at the tips of his ears.

'How did you guess?'

He added, with a knowing, slightly contemptuous smile:

'It always ends like that.'

'Explain.'

'Anybody will tell you so.'

That meant, 'anybody who takes drugs.'

Then he added in a dreary tone, as though realizing that he would not be understood:

'When she'd run out of dope and couldn't find any more at once, she'd turn on me, accusing me of having wheedled the stuff out of her, or even of having stolen it—swearing there'd been six or a dozen phials left in the drawer the night before.'

'Had you a key to her flat?'

'No.'

'Did you never go there when she was out?'

'She was hardly ever out. Sometimes she stayed in her room for a week or more on end.'

'Answer my question, yes or no. Did you never go into her flat when she was out?'

Another almost imperceptible hesitation.

'No.'

Maigret muttered as though to himself, without persisting:

'Liar!'

Because of this Philippe, the atmosphere of his own office had become almost as stifling and unreal as that of the flat in the Rue Victor-Massé.

Maigret knew enough about drug addicts to feel certain that now and then, when he was short of dope, Philippe must have tried to get

some at all costs. In such a case he would do what he had done the
night before, when he was trying to find the money to leave Paris—he
would go the round of all his acquaintances, begging shamelessly, all
self-respect abandoned.

On the low level where he lived, it must be difficult at times. So he
would surely remember that the Countess nearly always had a supply
in her drawer, and that if for once she should be reluctant to part
with it, he need only wait for her to go out?

This was only a hunch, but it was a logical one.

These people spy on one another, envy one another, steal from one
another and sometimes inform on one another. The police are always
getting anonymous telephone calls from vengeful characters.

'When did you last see her?'

'The day before yesterday, in the morning.'

'Sure it wasn't yesterday morning?'

'Yesterday morning I was ill and stayed in bed.'

'What was the matter with you?'

'I'd been out of dope for two days.'

'Wouldn't she give you any?'

'She swore she hadn't any, and that the doctor hadn't been able to
supply her.'

'Did you quarrel?'

'We were both in a bad temper.'

'Did you believe what she said?'

'She showed me the empty drawer.'

'When did she expect the doctor to come?'

'She didn't know. She'd rung him up and he'd promised to come.'

'You haven't been back there since?'

'No.'

'Now listen. The Countess's body was found yesterday afternoon,
about five o'clock. The evening papers were out already. So the news
didn't appear till this morning. But you spent the night looking for
money so you could get away to Belgium. How did you know the
Countess was dead?'

He was obviously about to say:

'I didn't know.'

But the inspector's stony stare made him change his mind.

'I went along the street and saw a crowd on the pavement.'

'What time was that?'

'About half past six.'

Maigret had been in the flat then, and it was true that a policeman
had been left at the door to keep out inquisitive idlers.

'Turn out your pockets.'

'Inspector Lognon has made me do that already.'

'Do it again.'

He brought out a dirty handkerchief, two keys on a ring—one was the key of his bag—a penknife, a purse, a little box containing pills, a pocket-book, a notebook, and a hypodermic syringe in its case.

Maigret took the notebook, which was an old one with yellowed pages, full of addresses and telephone numbers. There were hardly any surnames, only initials or Christian names. No mention of an Oscar.

'When you heard the Countess had been strangled, you thought you would be suspected?'

'It's always like that.'

'So you decided to go to Belgium. Do you know anybody there?'

'I've been to Brussels several times.'

'Who gave you the money?'

'A friend—a man.'

'Who?'

'I don't know his name.'

'You'd better tell me.'

'The doctor.'

'Dr. Bloch?'

'Yes. I hadn't found anything. It was three o'clock in the morning and I was beginning to feel scared. Finally I rang him up from a bar in the Rue Caulaincourt.'

'What did you say to him?'

'That I was a friend of the Countess, and that I must have money right away.'

'And he let you have it?'

'I also said that if I were arrested it might be unpleasant for him.'

'In other words, you blackmailed him. Did he tell you to come to his flat?'

'He said if I came to the Rue Victor-Massé, where he lives, he'd be waiting on the pavement.'

'Was that all you asked him for?'

'He gave me a phial of morphine too.'

'And I suppose you gave yourself a shot at once, in some doorway? Is that all you've got to tell me?'

'That's all I know.'

'Is the doctor a homo, too?'

'No.'

'How do you know?'

Philippe shrugged his shoulders, as though the question were too childish to answer.

'Are you hungry?'

'No.'

'Are you thirsty?'

The young man's lips quivered, but it was not food or drink that he needed.

Maigret got up, almost with an effort, and again opened the door into the next office. Torrence happened to be there—a tall, powerful fellow with great beefy hands. Suspects who were interrogated by him would have been surprised to learn that he had a soft heart.

'Come here,' said the inspector. 'You're to shut yourself up with this chap, and not let him out till he's come clean. I don't care whether it takes twenty-four hours or three days. When you're tired, hand over to someone else.'

Philippe protested, wild-eyed.

'I've told you all I know. This is a mean trick. . . .'

Then, shrill-voiced as an angry woman:

'You're a brute! . . . You're horrid! . . . You . . . you . . .'

Maigret stood aside to let him pass, and exchanged a wink with the burly Torrence. The two men went through the inspectors' big office and into a room which was jokingly known as 'the confessional'.

'Have some beer and sandwiches sent up for me!' called Torrence to Lapointe as he went by.

Alone with his assistants, Maigret stretched, shook himself, and refrained with some difficulty from flinging open the window.

'Well, boys?'

Then he noticed that Lucas was back already.

'She's here again, sir, waiting to speak to you '

'The aunt from Lisieux? Oh yes—how did she behave?'

'Like an old woman who enjoys nothing so much as a funeral. No vinegar or smelling-salts needed. She inspected the body calmly from head to foot. Half-way through, she jumped and asked me:

' "Why have they shaved her?"

'I explained that it wasn't us, and she nearly choked. She showed me the birthmark on the sole of the girl's foot, and said: "You see! But I should have recognized her even without that."

'Then, as we were leaving, she announced, without consulting me: "I'm going back with you. I have something else to say to the inspector."

'She's in the waiting-room, and I don't think it'll be easy to get rid of her.'

Young Lapointe had just picked up the telephone, and the line seemed to be bad.

'Is that Nice?'

He nodded. Janvier wasn't there. Maigret went back to his office and rang for the usher to bring in the old lady from Lisieux.

'I understand you have something to tell me?'

'I don't know if it will interest you. I was thinking, as I went along. You know how it is. One remembers things, without meaning to. I should not like to be suspected of ill-natured gossiping.'

'Go on, please.'

'It is about Anne-Marie. I told you this morning that she left Lisieux five years ago and that her mother had made no attempt to find out what had become of her—which, between you and me, is a disgraceful way for a mother to behave.'

He would just have to wait; it was no use trying to hurry her.

'There was a lot of talk, of course. Lisieux is a small town, and things always get around in the end. A woman in whom I have every confidence, and who goes once a week to Caen, where she is part owner of a shop, swore to me on her husband's life that not long before Anne-Marie left home she met her at Caen, just going into a doctor's house.'

She paused with a smug expression on her face, and seemed surprised when Maigret asked no question. Then she continued, with a sigh:

'Not just an ordinary doctor—she was going to see Dr. Potut, the gynaecologist.'

'In other words, you suspect your niece of having left the town because she was pregnant?'

'That was the rumour, and people wondered who the father could be.'

'Did they find out?'

'Plenty of names were suggested. But I had my own idea, all along, and that's why I came back to see you. It is my duty to help you discover the truth, is it not?'

She was beginning to feel that the police were not as inquisitive as people made out; for Maigret wasn't helping her at all. Far from urging her to speak, he was listening as indifferently as an old father-confessor, dozing behind the latticed partition of his box.

She went on, as though making a most important disclosure:

'Anne-Marie's throat was always weak. She used to get tonsillitis at least once every winter, and when her tonsils were removed it made no difference. That year, I remember, my sister-in-law had decided to take her to La Bourboule for treatment—that's the great place for throat illnesses.'

Maigret remembered that Arlette's voice had been slightly hoarse; he had put it down to drink, smoking, and sleepless nights.

'When she left Lisieux she can't have been pregnant for more than three or four months, because it didn't show. That's the utmost it can have been, especially as she always wore very tight-fitting dresses. Well, that exactly fits in with her visit to La Bourboule! I am perfectly certain it was there that she met the man by whom she became pregnant, and she most likely went off to join him. If it had been a Lisieux man, he would either have arranged for an abortion or gone away with her.'

Maigret slowly lit his pipe. He was aching all over, as though from a long tramp; but it was disgust that caused it. He was tempted to go and open the window, just as when Philippe had been there.

'You're going back to Lisieux, I suppose?'

'Not today. I have friends in Paris and shall probably spend a few days with them. I will leave you their address.'

The friends lived near the Boulevard Pasteur. She had already written out the address, on the back of one of her visiting cards, and added the telephone number.

'Don't hesitate to ring up if you need me.'

'Thank you.'

'I shall always be ready to help.'

'I am sure you will.'

He conducted her to the door, without a smile, closed it slowly behind her, stretched himself and rubbed his head with both hands, groaning in a low voice:

'What a filthy lot!'

'May I come in, sir?'

It was Lapointe. He had a sheet of paper in his hand and looked much excited.

'Did you phone for beer?'

'The waiter from the Brasserie Dauphine has just come up with the tray.'

The beer had not yet been taken to Torrence in his retreat, and Maigret, seizing the glass, swallowed its cool, frothy contents in one long draught.

'Ring up and tell them to send round some more!'

# VII

LAPOINTE said, not without a faint touch of jealousy in his voice:

'I'm beginning by giving you "best regards from little Julien". I was told you'd understand.'

'Is he at Nice?'

'He was moved there from Limoges a few weeks ago.'

Julien was the son of an old inspector who had worked with Maigret for a long time and gone to live on the Riviera when he retired. As luck would have it, Maigret had hardly seen the boy since the days when he used to give him rides on his knee.

'It was he who spoke to me on the telephone yesterday,' went on Lapointe, 'and I've been in touch with him ever since. When he knew it was you who'd told me to ring up, and that it was really you he was to work for, he got tremendously excited and went all out at the job. He's been spending hours in an attic at the police station, hunting through old records. It seems there are any number of parcels, full of reports on cases everybody's completely forgotten. They're thrown about in an awful mess, and the pile nearly reaches the ceiling.'

'Did he find the report on the Farnheim business?'

'He's just been giving me the list of the witnesses who were questioned after the Count's death. I'd asked him to make a special effort to find the names of the servants who were employed at The Oasis. Here they are:

'*Antoinette Méjat, aged nineteen, housemaid,*

'*Rosalie Moncoeur, aged forty-two, cook,*

'*Maria Pinaco, aged twenty-three, kitchen-maid,*

'*Angelino Luppin, aged thirty-eight, butler.*'

Maigret waited, standing by the window of his office, watching the snow, which was falling less thickly now. Lapointe continued, after a dramatic pause:

'*Oscar Bonvoisin, aged thirty-five, valet-chauffeur.*'

'An Oscar!' observed the inspector. 'I suppose nobody knows what's become of all these people?'

'Well, Inspector Julien had an idea. It isn't long since he came to Nice, and he'd been struck by the number of wealthy foreigners who come to spend a few months there, rent biggish houses and do a lot of entertaining. It occurred to him that they must need servants at very short notice. And he found an employment bureau which specializes in staffing big houses.

'It's kept by an old lady who's been there for over twenty years. She doesn't remember Count von Farnheim, or the Countess, or Oscar Bonvoisin: but not more than a year ago she found a job for Rosalie Moncoeur, the cook who's one of her regulars, with some South Americans who have a villa at Nice and spend part of the year in Paris. I have their address—132, Avenue d'Iéna. The old lady thought they were in Paris now.'

'Anything known about the others?'

'Julien's still following that up. Shall I go and see her, sir?'

Maigret almost agreed, to please Lapointe, who was burning with eagerness to question the Farnheims' ex-cook. But he finally declared that he would go himself—chiefly, to be quite honest, because he wanted to get some fresh air, have another beer on his way, and escape from his office, where he felt stifled that morning.

'Meantime, you look through the registers and see if there's anything under "Bonvoisin". You'll have to hunt through the police forms of the lodging-houses too. And ring up all the town halls and police stations in Paris.'

'Very well, sir.'

Poor Lapointe! Maigret felt sorry for him, but not to the extent of giving up his outing.

Before he left, he looked into the little room where Torrence and Philippe were shut up together. Torrence had taken his coat off, but even so there were beads of sweat on his forehead. Philippe, perched on the edge of a chair, was as white as a sheet and appeared likely to faint at any moment.

Maigret had no need to ask any questions. He knew Torrence would never give up—that he would go on with the little game till night came—and right through the night if necessary.

Less than half an hour later, a taxi pulled up outside a solemn-looking building in the Avenue d'Iéna, and the inspector walked into a marble-pillared hall, where he was greeted by a porter in a dark uniform.

He explained his identity, asked whether Rosalie Moncoeur was still working in the house, and was directed towards the back-stairs.

'It's on the third floor.'

He had drunk two more beers on his way and got rid of his head-ache. The staircase was a narrow, spiral one, and he counted the floors in an undertone as he went up. He rang the bell at a brown-painted door. A stout, white-haired woman opened it and looked at him in astonishment.

'Madame Moncoeur?'

'What do you want with her?'

'To speak to her.'

'It's me.'

She was busy at her stove, and a swarthy little girl was putting a delicious-smelling mixture through a sieve.

'I believe you worked at one time for Count and Countess von Farnheim?'

'Who are you?'

'I come from the Judicial Police.'

'You don't mean to tell me you're digging up that old story?'

'Not exactly. Did you know the Countess was dead?'

'It happens to everyone. No, I didn't know.'

'It was in the papers this morning.'

'Do you suppose I read the papers! With fifteen or twenty people coming to dinner here almost every day!'

'She was murdered.'

'That's funny.'

'Why does it strike you as funny?'

She had not asked him to sit down, and now went on with her work, talking to him as she might to a tradesman. She was obviously a woman of experience, not easily impressed.

'I don't know what made me say that. Who killed her?'

'We don't know yet, and that's what I'm trying to find out. Did you keep on working for her after her husband's death?'

'Only for a couple of weeks. We didn't get on.'

'Why not?'

Rosalie looked to see how the kitchen-maid was managing, and then opened the oven to baste a fowl.

'Because it wasn't the kind of work for me.'

'You mean it wasn't a respectable house?'

'Put it that way if you like. I'm fond of my work, and I expect people to come to meals at the right time and in a state to know more or less what they're eating. That'll do, Irma. Take the hard-boiled eggs out of the refrigerator and separate the yolks from the whites.'

She opened a bottle of Madeira and poured a liberal quantity into a sauce which she was stirring slowly with a wooden spoon.

'You remember Oscar Bonvoisin?'

She looked at him then, as though on the point of saying:

'So that's what you were getting at!'

But she remained silent.

'You heard what I asked?'

'I'm not deaf.'

'What kind of man was he?'

'A valet.'

As Maigret looked surprised at her tone, she added:

'I don't like valets. They're all bone-idle. Specially when they're chauffeurs as well. They think they're cock of the roost, and put on worse airs than the master and mistress.'

'Was Bonvoisin like that?'

'I don't remember his surname. He was always called Oscar.'

'What did he look like?'

'He was a good-looking fellow, and knew it. At least, some women admire that sort. I don't myself, and I let him know it.'

'He made love to you?'

'In his way.'

'Meaning——?'

'Why are you asking me all this?'

'Because I need to know.'

'You think he may have killed the Countess?'

'It's possible.'

Irma was more excited by this conversation than either of the participants—she was so thrilled at being almost mixed up in a real crime that she had quite forgotten what she was supposed to be doing.

'Well, Irma? What about mashing up those yolks?'

'Can you give me a description of him?'

'As he was in those days, yes. But I don't know what he looks like now.'

At that moment Maigret saw a gleam in her eyes, and he said quickly:

'Are you sure? You've never seen him since?'

'That's just what I was wondering. I'm not sure. A few weeks ago

I went to see my brother, who has a small café, and in the street I met a man I thought I knew. He looked hard at me, too, as though he was searching his memory. And then, suddenly, I had the impression he'd begun to walk very fast, turning away his face.'

'And you thought it was Oscar?'

'Not at the moment. Later on I had the vague idea, and now I'd almost swear it was him.'

'Where's your brother's café?'

'In the Rue Caulaincourt.'

'And it was in Montmartre that you met this man you thought you recognized?'

'Just at the corner of the Place Clichy.'

'Now try to tell me what kind of man he was.'

'I don't like giving people away.'

'You'd rather let a murderer go free?'

'If he's only killed the Countess he's done no great harm.'

'If he's killed her, he's killed at least one other woman and there's no reason to suppose that he'll stop there.'

She shrugged her shoulders.

'Oh well, it's his look-out, after all. He wasn't tall. Rather on the small side. It made him so cross that he used to wear high heels, like a woman, to make himself look taller. I used to tease him about it, and he'd scowl at me without saying a word.'

'He wasn't very talkative?'

'He was as close as any oyster—never said what he was doing or what he thought. He was very dark, with hair that grew thick down to a low forehead, and bushy black eyebrows. Some women thought his eyes had an irresistible expression. Not me. He'd stare at you, looking as pleased with himself as if he'd been the only man in the world, and you were just dirt.'

'Go on.'

Now that she was launched, she showed no hesitation. All the time she talked, she was bustling about the kitchen, which was full of delicious smells, juggling deftly, as it were, with pans and gadgets, and glancing every few minutes at the electric clock.

'Antoinette fell for him—she was crazy about him. So was Maria.'

'You mean the housemaid and the kitchen-maid?'

'Yes. And others who worked there before them. Servants never stayed long in that house. You never knew whether to take your orders from the old man or from the Countess. You see what I mean? Oscar didn't make love to the servants, as you said a minute ago. As soon as he saw a new one, he just stared at her as though he was taking possession of her.

'Then, the first evening, he'd go upstairs and into her room as though it was all arranged beforehand.'

'Some men are like that—they believe no woman can resist them.'
'Antoinette cried her eyes out.'
'Why?'
'Because she was really in love with him, and hoped for a time that he'd marry her. But once he'd had enough he'd go away without a word. And after that he'd take no more notice of them. Never say anything pleasant or pay them the slightest attention. Until he was in the mood again, and then back he'd go to one of their rooms.
'Anyhow, he had all the women he wanted, and not only servants.'
'You think he had an affair with the Countess?'
'Before the Count had been dead two days.'
'How do you know?'
'Because I saw him come out of her room at six in the morning. That was partly why I left. When the servants begin to share the best bedroom, it's the last straw.'
'Was he getting above himself?'
'He was doing just as he liked. You could feel there was nobody giving him orders any more.'
'Did it never occur to you that the Count might have been murdered?'
'It was none of my business.'
'But it did occur to you?'
'It occurred to the police too, didn't it? Else why did they ask us all those questions?'
'It might have been Oscar?'
'I don't say that. She was probably just as capable of doing it herself.'
'Did you go on working at Nice?'
'At Nice and Monte Carlo. I like the climate down there, and I've only come to Paris accidentally, to please my employers.'
'You never heard any more about the Countess?'
'I saw her go past once or twice, but we didn't lead the same kind of life.'
'And Oscar?'
'I never saw him again in those parts. I don't think he stayed on the Riviera.'
'But you think you caught sight of him a few weeks ago. What did he look like?'
'All you policemen seem to think that whenever one passes a man in the street one notices everything about him.'
'Had he aged much?'
'He's like me—fifteen years older than he was.'
'That means he's in his fifties.'
'I'm nearly ten years older than he is. Another three or four years in service, and then I'll retire to a little house I've bought at Cagnes and cook only for myself. Fried eggs and cutlets.'
'You don't remember how he was dressed?'

'In the Place Clichy?'

'Yes.'

'In rather dark clothes. I don't say black, but dark. He had a heavy overcoat on, and gloves. I noticed the gloves. He was very smart.'

'What about his hair?'

'A man doesn't go round carrying his hat, in the middle of winter.'

'Was it grey at the temples?'

'I think so. But that wasn't what struck me.'

'What did?'

'He'd got fatter. He was always broad-shouldered. Used to go around naked to the waist whenever he could, because he had tremendous muscles, and some women found that attractive. He didn't look so powerful when he had his clothes on. Now—if it was him I met —he looks rather like a bull. His neck's thicker, and he seems even shorter than he used to.'

'You never heard any more of Antoinette?'

'She died. Not long afterwards.'

'What of?'

'A miscarriage. At least that's what I was told.'

'And Maria Pinaco?'

'I don't know if she's still at it, but last time I saw her she had her stretch on the Cours Albert-Premier, at Nice.'

'Was that long ago?'

'Two years, or a bit more.'

She did have the curiosity to ask him:

'How was the Countess killed?'

'Strangled.'

She made no comment, but looked as though she thought that sounded quite like Oscar's way.

'And who was the other woman?'

'A girl you're not likely to have known—she was only twenty years old.'

'Nice of you to remind me that I'm an old woman.'

'That's not what I meant. She came from Lisieux, and there's nothing to suggest that she ever lived on the Riviera. All I know is that she once visited La Bourboule.'

'Near Le Mont-Dore?'

'In Auvergne—yes.'

She looked at Maigret with thoughtful eyes.

'Well, once I've begun to give him away . . .' she muttered. 'Oscar came from the Auvergne,' she went on. 'I don't know exactly what part, but he had a bit of an accent, and when I wanted to annoy him I'd imitate it. He'd go pale with rage. And now, if you'll excuse me, I'll ask you to clear out, because it's only half an hour to lunch-time, and I need the kitchen to myself.'

'I may be back to see you again.'

'Well, so long as you give no more trouble than you have to-day. . .! What's your name?'

'Maigret.'

The kitchen-maid jumped—evidently she read the papers—but the cook had obviously never heard of him.

'I shall remember that, because it means "thin" and you're rather on the fat side. Now I come to think of it, Oscar's about your build, these days, but a head shorter. You see what I mean?'

'Thank you very much.'

'Not at all. Only if you arrest him, I'd prefer not to be called as a witness. Never does you any good, when you're in service. Besides, those lawyers ask a lot of questions to try and make a fool of you. It happened to me once, and I swore it shouldn't happen again. So don't count on me.'

She showed him calmly out of the door, and he had to walk the whole length of the Avenue before finding a taxi. Instead of going to the Quai des Orfèvres, he went home to lunch. He got back to the office about half past two; the snow had quite stopped by then, and the streets were covered with a thin layer of blackish, greasy mud.

When he opened the door of the 'confessional' he found it was blue with smoke, and there were about twenty cigarette-ends in the ashtray. It was Torrence who had smoked them, for Philippe was not a smoker. There was a tray there too, with the remains of some sandwiches, and five empty beer glasses.

'Would you come outside for a moment?'

Emerging into the outer office, Torrence mopped his forehead and relaxed, sighing:

'That chap's wearing me out. He's like a wet rag—nothing to get hold of. Twice I thought he was going to come clean. I'm sure he's got something to say. He seems to be at the end of his tether—looks at you with imploring eyes—and then, at the last second, he changes his mind and swears he doesn't know a thing. It makes me sick. Just now he drove me so far that I slapped him in the face with the flat of my hand. Do you know what he did?'

Maigret said nothing.

'He put his hand to his cheek and began snivelling, as though he was talking to another pansy like himself: "You're very unkind!" I mustn't do that again, because I bet it gives him a thrill.'

Maigret couldn't help smiling.

'Am I to go on?'

'Have another shot. We'll try something else presently, perhaps. Has he had anything to eat?'

'He nibbled daintily at a sandwich, with his little finger crooked in the air. You can see he's missing his dope. If I promised him some, he

might begin to talk. The narcotics people must have some, don't you
think?'

'I'll mention it to the Chief. But don't do anything about it yet. Just
keep on with your questions.'

Torrence gave a glance round at his familiar surroundings, drew a
deep breath of air, and went back again into the depressing atmosphere
of the 'confessional'.

'Anything fresh, Lapointe?' asked Maigret.

Lapointe had hardly put down the telephone since his arrival that
morning and, like Torrence, had lunched on a sandwich and a glass
of beer.

'About a dozen Bonvoisins, but not one of them's an Oscar.'

'Try to get a call through to La Bourboule. You may have better
luck there.'

'Have you got a tip?'

'Perhaps.'

'From the cook?'

'She thinks she met him quite lately in Paris—and better still, in
Montmartre.'

'Why La Bourboule?'

'For one thing, he comes from that district, and for another thing,
Arlette seems to have had an eventful meeting with someone or other
down there, five years ago.'

Maigret spoke without much conviction.

'No news of Lognon?' he went on.

He rang up the police station in the Rue de La Rochefoucauld himself,
but was told that Inspector Lognon had only looked in for a moment.

'He said he was working for you and would be out all day.'

For the next fifteen minutes, Maigret paced to and fro in his office,
smoking his pipe. Then he seemed to reach a decision, and went for an
interview with his chief.

'What's the news, Maigret?' he was asked. 'Why weren't you in to
hear the report this morning?'

'I was asleep,' he confessed frankly.

'Have you seen the afternoon papers?'

Maigret indicated by a gesture that these did not interest him.

'They're wondering whether any more women are going to be
strangled.'

'I don't think so.'

'Why not?'

'Because the man who killed the Countess and Arlette isn't a lunatic.
On the contrary, he knows exactly what he's about.'

'Have you identified him?'

'Perhaps. Probably, in fact.'

'D'you expect to arrest him today?'

'We have to discover where he hangs out, and I haven't the faintest idea about that, except that it's more than likely to be in Montmartre. There's only one circumstance in which there might be another victim?'

'What's that?'

'If Arlette talked to anybody else—for instance, to Betty or Tania, the other women at Picratt's.'

'Have you asked them?'

'They don't say a word. Neither does Fred, the proprietor, neither does the Grasshopper. And neither does that unhealthy worm, Philippe, although he's been questioned all morning. And he, at least, knows something, I'll be bound. He used to be always seeing the Countess. It was she who supplied him with morphine.'

'Where did she get it?'

'Through her doctor.'

'You've arrested him?'

'Not yet. That's a job for the narcotics people. I've been wondering for the last hour whether I ought to take a risk, or not.'

'What risk?'

'The risk of being landed with another corpse. That's what I want your advice about. It's more than probable that this chap Bonvoisin killed both women, and I've no doubt we can lay hands on him by routine methods. But that may take days, or weeks. It's largely a matter of luck. And unless I'm much mistaken, he's no fool. Before we catch him he may bump off someone else—or several other people —for knowing too much.'

'What's the risk you want to take?'

'I didn't say I wanted to.'

The Chief smiled.

'Explain, please.'

'If Philippe knows something, as I'm convinced he does, Oscar must be feeling very uneasy. I need only tell the Press that Philippe has been questioned for several hours with no result, and then let him go.'

'I'm beginning to understand.'

'The first possibility is that Philippe will go straight to Oscar, but I'm not really counting on that. Unless it's his only way of getting dope—he's beginning to need it very badly.'

'And the other possibility?'

The Chief had already guessed what it was.

'You see the notion. A drug addict can't be trusted. Philippe's said nothing yet, but that doesn't mean he'll keep quiet for ever, and Oscar knows it.'

'So he'll try to get rid of him.'

'That's it! I didn't want to make the experiment without consulting you.'

'D'you think you can prevent him from killing the boy?'

'I shall take every precaution. Bonvoisin isn't the man to use a gun. Guns make too much noise, and he doesn't seem to like noise.'

'When do you propose to let your witness go?'

'At dusk. It'll be easier to keep a discreet watch over him then. I'll put as many men as necessary on his tail. And after all, if there should be an accident I don't feel it would be any great loss.'

'I'd rather there wasn't one.'

'So would I.'

There was a moment's silence, and then the Chief said with a sigh: 'I leave it to you, Maigret. Good luck.'

*

'You were quite right, sir.'

'About what?'

Lapointe was so glad to be playing an important part in an investigation, that he had almost forgotten Arlette's death.

'I got the information at once. Oscar Bonvoisin was born at Le Mont-Dore, where his father was a hotel porter and his mother a chambermaid in the same hotel. He had his first job there, as a page boy. Then he left the district and didn't come back till about ten years ago—when he bought a house, not at Le Mont-Dore, but nearby, outside La Bourboule.'

'Does he usually live there?'

'No. He spends part of the summer there, and sometimes a few days in the winter.'

'He isn't married?'

'No—a bachelor. His mother's still alive.'

'Living in his house?'

'No. She has a small flat in the town. It's thought that he supports her. He's supposed to have made a good deal of money and to be doing some very big business in Paris.'

'The description?'

'Fits with what we've got.'

'Would you like to take on a confidential job?'

'You know I would, sir.'

'Even if it's pretty risky and means a lot of responsibility?'

His love for Arlette must have come surging back, for he said a little too ardently:

'I don't care if I'm killed.'

'Right! It's not a question of being killed, but of seeing that someone else isn't. And it's essential for you not to look like a police inspector.'

'You think I generally look like one?'

'Go to the wardrobe room and pick yourself out something suitable for an unemployed man who's looking for work and hoping not to find any. Take a cap rather than a hat. And be careful not to overdo it.'

Janvier was back, and Maigret gave him very similar instructions.

'You're to look like a clerk going home from work.'

Then he chose two inspectors whom Philippe had never seen.

He called the four men into his office, spread out a plan of Montmartre, and explained what they were to do.

Dusk was falling fast. The lamps on the quay and up the Boulevard Saint-Michel were already lit.

Maigret was reluctant to wait for complete darkness, but it would be more difficult to follow Philippe without attracting his attention—and Bonvoisin's, which was more important—in the deserted streets, before the night life of Montmartre began.

'Would you come here for a moment, Torrence?'

Torrence emerged, to declare furiously:

'I give it up! He makes me spew, that lad does! Anyone else can try who's got a strong stomach, but as for me . . .'

'You'll have finished in five minutes.'

'We're to let him go?'

'As soon as the last edition of the evening papers is out.'

'What have the papers got to do with him?'

'They'll announce that he's been questioned for hours, with no result.'

'I see.'

'Go and shake him up a bit more. Then put his hat on his head and push him out, telling him he'd better behave himself.'

'Do I give him back his syringe?'

'His syringe and his money.'

Torrence looked at the four waiting inspectors.

'Is that why they're all dolled up for a fancy-dress ball?'

One of the four went to look for a taxi, in which he was to wait quietly near the entrance to police headquarters. The others set out for certain strategic points.

Meanwhile, Maigret had found time to ring up the 'narcotics squad' and the police station in the Rue de La Rochefoucauld.

Torrence had purposely left the door of the 'confessional' ajar, and his thunderous voice could be heard at full pitch, as he told Philippe exactly what he thought of him.

'I wouldn't even touch you with a barge-pole, d'you understand?' he roared. 'I'd be afraid of giving you the wrong idea. And now it's time I had this office disinfected. Take what you call your overcoat. Put your hat on.'

'You mean I can go?'

'I mean I'm sick of the sight of you—we all are. You're more than we can stand—is that clear? Pick up your rubbish and get out, you filthy rat!'

'There's no need to jostle me.'

'I'm not jostling you.'

'You're shouting at me. . . .'

'Get out!'

'I'm going. . . . I'm going. . . . Thank you.'

A door opened, and banged shut. At this hour the corridor was deserted, and only two or three people were waiting in the badly-lit ante-room.

Philippe made his way down the long, dusty passage, where he looked like an insect hunting for its way out.

Maigret, who was watching him through the crack of his own door, saw him at last reach the stairs and begin to descend.

All the same, he felt a little remorseful. He shut the door and looked at Torrence, who was stretching himself like an actor who has just got back to his dressing-room. Torrence could see that he was worried and thoughtful.

'You think he'll get himself bumped off?'

'What I'm hoping is that the attempt will be made, but won't succeed.'

'The first thing he'll do will be to rush to where he thinks he can find morphia.'

'Yes.'

'Do you know where?'

'To Dr. Bloch.'

'Will he give him any?'

'I sent him a message to forbid him to, and he won't dare.'

'So what?'

'I don't know. I'm going up to Montmartre. The men know where to find me. You stay here. If anything turns up, phone me at Picratt's.'

'That means more delicious sandwiches for me. Never mind—I shan't be sharing them with that pansy this time!'

Maigret put on his hat and coat, chose two empty pipes from the selection on his desk and put them in his pockets.

Before taking a taxi to the Rue Pigalle, he called in at the Brasserie Dauphine for a brandy. He had lost his hangover, but began to suspect that he was in for another next morning.


# VIII

ARLETTE's photographs had at last been removed from the show-case. Instead, there were those of another girl, who had taken her place and was to do the same act, perhaps even in the same dress. But Betty was right, it was a difficult business. The girl was young and plump, probably pretty; but even in the photo, her gesture of beginning to

undress had a provocative vulgarity which was reminiscent of an indecent postcard, or of one of the clumsily-painted nudes that undulate
on the canvas-sided booths of fairgrounds.

The door opened at a push and Maigret went in. A lamp was burning above the bar and another at the far end of the room, with a long
stretch of dimness between the two. Right at the back of the room was
Fred, in a white, polo-necked sweater, with big horn spectacles on his
nose, reading the evening paper.

The Alfonsis' upstairs quarters were so cramped that in the daytime they probably used the cabaret as a dining-room and sitting-room.
Very likely some of the regular customers, who were more like personal
friends, came in for a drink at the bar at *apéritif* time.

Fred looked across the top of his glasses at Maigret advancing towards him and, without getting up, held out a fat hand and motioned
him to sit down.

'I was expecting you,' he said.

He didn't explain why, and Maigret didn't ask. Fred finished reading his article on the case, took off his spectacles, and inquired:

'What will you take? A brandy?'

He went to the bar, poured out two glasses, and returned to his seat
with the contented sigh of a man glad to be at home. Steps could be
heard overhead.

'Is your wife up there?' asked the inspector.

'Yes—giving a lesson to the new girl.'

Maigret repressed a smile at the thought of fat Rose giving a lesson
in the art of strip-tease.

'Doesn't it interest you?' he asked Fred, who answered with a shrug:

'She's a pretty kid. Her breasts are better than Arlette's and her
skin's clearer. But it's not the same thing.'

'Why did you make out to me that you'd never been with Arlette
except in the kitchen?'

Fred showed no embarrassment.

'You've been questioning the hotel-keepers? I had to tell you that,
because of my wife. No sense in hurting her feelings unnecessarily. She's
always afraid I'll leave her one day for a younger woman.'

'You wouldn't have left her for Arlette?'

Fred looked Maigret straight in the eyes.

'For her, yes, if she'd asked me to.'

'You'd really fallen for her?'

'Call it how you like. I've had hundreds of women in my life, probably thousands. I've never bothered to count 'em. But I've never
known another like her.'

'Did you suggest she should settle down with you?'

'I gave her to understand that it wouldn't displease me, and that
she'd do quite well out of it.'

'And she refused?'

Fred sighed, raised his glass, gazed through it for a moment and then took a sip.

'If she hadn't refused, she'd probably be alive now. You know as well as I do that she had a man somewhere. How he kept his hold on her, I never found out.'

'You tried?'

'I even trailed her sometimes.'

'With no result?'

'She was too smart for me. What's your game with the pansy?'

'You know Philippe?'

'No. But I know others like him. Now and then one of 'em ventures in here, but I don't encourage them. D'you suppose it'll lead to anything?'

It was Maigret's turn to reply by silence. Fred had understood, of course. He was practically in the same line of business—the two of them worked with much the same material, only in a different way and for different reasons.

'There are certain things you didn't tell me about Arlette,' remarked the inspector gently.

Fred gave a slight smile.

'You've guessed what they were?' he inquired.

'I've guessed what kind they were.'

'May as well take the opportunity, while my wife's still upstairs. Although the kid's dead, I prefer not to talk too much about her in front of Rose. Between you and me, I'll probably never leave the old girl. We're so used to each other, I couldn't get along without her. Even if I'd gone away with Arlette I'd most likely have come back.'

The telephone began to ring. There was no call-box—the instrument was in the cloakroom, and Maigret went towards it, saying:

'That'll be for me.'

He was right. It was Lapointe.

'It's just as you said, sir. He went straight to Dr. Bloch's house, by bus. He was only in there for a very few minutes and when he came out he was a bit paler than before. Now he's making for the Place Blanche.'

'Everything all right?'

'Everything's all right. Don't worry.'

Maigret went back to his seat, and Fred asked no questions.

'You were telling me about Arlette.'

'I'd always thought she was a girl from a good family, who'd left home for some whim. Matter of fact, it was Rose who called my attention to some points I hadn't noticed. And I rather think she was younger than she made out. She'd probably swapped identity cards with an older friend.'

Fred spoke slowly, like a man pondering over pleasant memories, while Maigret's gaze followed his, down the long dusky funnel of the narrow room, to where the polished mahogany of the bar beside the door gleamed in the lamplight.

'It's hard to explain what I mean. Some girls have an instinct for love-making, and I've come across virgins who were hotter than any old pro. But Arlette was different.

'I don't know the fellow who taught her her stuff, but I take off my hat to him. As I told you before, I'm an authority on the subject, but I assure you I've never come across a woman who was her equal. He'd not only taught her as much as I knew, but some tricks I didn't know as well. At my age, just imagine! And with the life I've led! I was staggered.

'And she enjoyed doing it, that I'd swear. Not only going to bed with anybody and everybody, but even her act; such a pity you didn't see that.

'I've known women of thirty-five or forty, most of them a bit cracked, who found it amusing to lead men on. I've known young girls who liked playing with fire. But they were never like her—they never went at it so purposefully.

'I know I'm not explaining it properly, but I can't describe exactly what I mean.

'You asked me about a fellow called Oscar. I don't know if there is such a person, or who he is. But what's certain is that Arlette was in somebody's hands, and that he had a firm hold on her. Do you suppose she suddenly felt sick of him and decided to give him away?'

'When she went to the police station in the Rue La Rochefoucauld at four o'clock yesterday morning, she knew a crime was to be committed, and that it involved a Countess.'

'But why did she pretend she'd found it out here, by listening to a conversation between two men?'

'To begin with, she was drunk. That was probably what made her decide to take the step.'

'Unless she drank to screw up her courage to the right point?'

'I wonder,' murmured Maigret, 'if the way she behaved with young Albert . . .'

'Oh, by the way, I've discovered he's one of your inspectors!'

'I didn't know it myself at first. He was genuinely in love.'

'I noticed that.'

'There's a romantic streak in every woman. He was urging her to change her way of life. She could have had a husband if she wanted.'

'And you think that made her fed up with Oscar?'

'At any rate she felt restive at one moment, and went to the police station. But even then she didn't want to say too much. She left him a chance to get away with it, by giving only a vague description and a Christian name.'

'A mean trick all the same, don't you think?'

'Once faced with the police, she may have regretted her idea. She was surprised at being kept there, and at being sent to the Quai des Orfèvres, and she'd had time to sleep off her champagne. So then she was much less definite—came near to declaring she'd made it all up.'

'That's just like a woman,' nodded Fred. 'What puzzles me is how the chap found out. Because he was already waiting for her when she got back home.'

Maigret stared silently at his pipe.

'I bet you thought I knew him and wouldn't admit it,' went on Fred.

'Perhaps.'

'At one moment you even thought it might be me.'

It was Maigret's turn to smile at this.

'In fact I've been wondering,' continued the other, 'whether it wasn't on purpose that she gave a description that sounded a bit like me—just because her man is quite different.'

'No. The description was correct.'

'D'you know the fellow?'

'His name's Oscar Bonvoisin.'

Fred showed no reaction. The name was evidently unknown to him.

'Well, he's no fool!' he exclaimed. 'Whoever he may be, I take off my hat to him. I thought I knew Montmartre inside out. I've talked it over with the Grasshopper, who's always rooting about in corners. Arlette had been working here for two years. She lived only a few hundred yards away. As I've told you, I followed her more than once, because I was curious. So don't you find it extraordinary that we should know nothing about this fellow?'

He flicked at the paper spread out on the table.

'What's more, he was in with that crazy old Countess. Women like that don't go around unnoticed. They belong to a separate world, where everybody knows everybody, more or less. And yet your men seem to be as much in the dark as I am. Lognon dropped in a while ago and tried to pick my brains, but there weren't any pickings.'

The telephone rang again.

'Is that you, sir? I'm speaking from the Boulevard de Clichy. He's just gone into the restaurant at the corner of the Rue Lepic and been round to all the tables, as though looking for someone. He looked disappointed. There's another restaurant next door, and he began by pressing his nose against the window. Then he went in, and through to the cloakroom. Janvier went in afterwards, and questioned the attendant. She said he'd asked whether a man called Bernard had left a message for him.'

'Did she say who Bernard was?'

'She made out she didn't know.'

He must be a drug-peddler, of course.

'Philippe's going towards the Place Clichy now.'

Maigret had scarcely hung up when the phone rang again, and this time it was Torrence.

'I say, sir, when I went back to the "confessional" to open the window, I fell over young Philippe's bag. We forgot to give it back to him. Do you suppose he'll come to fetch it?'

'Not before he's found some dope.'

Returning to the main room, Maigret found Madame Rose and Arlette's successor both there, on the dance-floor. Fred had moved into one of the boxes, and was sitting there like a customer. He signed to Maigret to do the same.

'Rehearsal!' he announced with a wink.

The girl was very young, with fair, fuzzy hair and the pink complexion of a baby or a country lass—whose firm limbs and artless expression she had as well.

'Shall I begin?' she asked.

There was no music and no spotlight. Fred merely switched on one more lamp, above the dance-floor, and began to hum the tune that usually went with Arlette's act, beating time with his hand.

Rose, after greeting Maigret, started gesticulating at the girl, to show her what she had to do.

The newcomer broke awkwardly into what was intended as a dance step, swaying her hips as much as possible; and then began, slowly, as she had been taught, to undo the hooks on the long black sheath she was wearing, which had been let out to fit her.

Fred cast an eloquent glance at the inspector. Neither of them laughed, though they could hardly keep from smiling. The girl's shoulders were revealed, and then one breast, which, in this humdrum atmosphere, caused a kind of surprise.

Rose held up her hand for a pause at this point, and the girl stared fixedly at it.

'Go right round the floor now,' said Fred, resuming his humming at once. 'Not so quick. . . . Tra-la-la-la. . . . . Good! . . .'

And Rose's hand indicated:

'The other breast. . . .'

Her nipples were large and pink. The dress slid slowly down, the shadow of the navel appeared, and finally the girl, with a clumsy gesture, let it fall right to the ground and stood there on the dance-floor, hands clasped over her nakedness.

'That'll do for today,' sighed Fred. 'You can go and put your clothes on again, my child.'

The girl picked up the dress and went off to the kitchen. Rose came to sit with the men for a moment.

'They'll have to be satisfied with that! It's the best I can get out of her. She does it the way she'd drink a cup of coffee. It's nice of you to come and see us, Inspector.'

She meant it, she really was pleased to see him.

'Do you think you'll find the murderer?'

'Monsieur Maigret hopes to catch him tonight,' said her husband.

She glanced from one to the other, decided she was in the way, and went off to the kitchen in her turn, announcing:

'I'm going to get some food ready. You'll have something with us, Inspector?'

He did not refuse. He didn't know yet whether he would. He had chosen Picratt's as a strategic point and also, a little, because he liked being there. He wondered whether it wasn't the atmosphere of the place that had made young Lapointe fall in love with Arlette.

Fred went to turn off the lamps over the dance-floor. They heard the girl walking about overhead. Then she came down and joined Rose in the kitchen.

'What were we saying?'

'We were talking about Oscar.'

'I suppose you've made inquiries in all the cheap hotels?'

The question was not worth an answer.

'And he never went to Arlette's place either?'

They had reached the same point, because they both knew the district and the kind of life that went on there.

If Oscar and Arlette had been on intimate terms, they obviously must have had some meeting-place.

'Did no one ever ring her up here?' asked Maigret.

'I didn't pay attention, but if it had happened often I should have noticed.'

And she had no telephone in her flat. According to the concierge, no men ever came there—and that concierge was reliable, not like the one in the Countess's house.

Lapointe had been all through the registration slips of the cheap hotels. Janvier had been the round of the places themselves, and done it thoroughly, for he'd come across Fred's traces.

It was more than twenty-four hours since Arlette's photo had appeared in the papers, and nobody had so far reported having seen her go regularly into any particular place.

'I tell you again, he's no fool, that chap!'

Fred frowned as he spoke. He was obviously thinking the same thing as the inspector—that this Oscar was something out of the ordinary. Ten to one he lived in the district, but he didn't share in its life. One couldn't place him, or imagine what his existence must be. To all appearances he played a lone hand—that was what chiefly struck them both.

'Do you think he'll try to get rid of Philippe?'

'We shall know before morning.'

'I went into the tobacconist's in the Rue de Douai just now. They're old pals of mine. I don't think anyone knows the district better than they do. They get every possible type of customer, according to the time of day. And yet they're completely fogged, too.'

'All the same, Arlette must have been meeting him somewhere.'

'At his own home, perhaps?'

Maigret would have sworn that wasn't it. Which was possibly rather absurd. Because practically nothing was known about him, Oscar was taking on terrifying proportions. In the long run one began to be influenced in spite of oneself, by the mystery that surrounded him, and perhaps to credit him with more brains than he really had.

He was like a shadow—always more impressive than the solid object that casts it.

After all he was only a man, a flesh-and-blood man, who'd worked as valet and chauffeur and always been keen on women.

The last time he'd been seen in his true light had been at Nice. He was probably responsible for the pregnancy of little Antoinette Méjat, who'd died of it; Maria Pinaco had been his mistress too, and now she was a prostitute.

Then, a few years later, he'd bought a house near the place where he was born—typical of a self-made man who'd suddenly got hold of money. He went back to parade his new fortune in front of those who had seen him in his days of poverty.

'Is that you, sir?'

The telephone again, with the standard opening. Lapointe's job was to report progress.

'I'm speaking from a little bar in the Place Constantin-Pecqueur He went into a house in the Rue Caulaincourt, and up to the fifth floor. He knocked on a door there, but nobody answered.'

'What does the concierge say?'

'That a painter lives there, a Bohemian type. She doesn't know whether he takes drugs, but says he often looks strange. She's seen Philippe go up there before. Sometimes he's spent the night there.'

'Is the painter a homo?'

'Probably. She doesn't believe there are such people; but she's never seen him with a woman.'

'What's Philippe doing now?'

'He's turned to the right, towards the Sacré-Cœur.'

'Nobody seems to be following him?'

'Nobody except us. Everything's O.K. It's begun to rain and it's damn' cold. If I'd known, I'd have put on a sweater.'

Madame Rose had covered the table with a red-checked cloth, and placed a steaming soup-tureen in the middle. Four places were laid: Arlette's successor, who had got back into a navy-blue suit in which she looked like a well brought-up young girl, was helping to serve, and it was hard to realize that only a few minutes earlier she had been standing naked in the middle of the dance-floor.

'I'd be surprised if he never came here,' said Maigret.

'To see her?'

'Well, she was his pupil. I wonder if he was jealous.'

That was a question to which Fred would certainly know the answer; for Fred, too, had had women who went to bed with other men—he even forced them to do so—and must know how a man felt in such circumstances.

'He'd never be jealous of the men she met here,' he said.

'Are you sure?'

'Well, he must have been so self-confident. He was convinced he'd got a firm hold and that she'd never escape.'

Was it the Countess who had pushed her old husband over the precipice, from the terrace of The Oasis? Most likely. If Oscar had done it, he wouldn't have had such a hold over her. Even if he'd been an accomplice.

There was a certain irony in the whole story. The poor Count had been crazy about his wife, putting up with all her whims and humbly begging her to keep a little corner for him in her shadow. If he had not loved her so much, she might have put up with him. It was the very intensity of his adoration that she had found intolerable.

Had Oscar foreseen that that would happen one day? Had he been spying on her? Very probably.

It was easy to imagine the scene. The couple had gone out on to the terrace when they got back from the Casino, and the Countess had had no difficulty in leading the old man to the edge of the precipice and then pushing him over.

When she turned round, she must have been terrified to see that the chauffeur had been watching, and was now staring silently at her.

What had passed between them? What agreement had they reached?

In any case, it was not the gigolos who had squandered all her money—a good share of it must have gone to Oscar.

He was too shrewd to stay with her. He had disappeared, and waited for several years before buying that house near his birthplace.

He had done nothing to attract attention, he hadn't started throwing money about.

Maigret always found himself back at the same point: the man was a lone wolf, and he had learnt that lone wolves were not to be trusted.

Bonvoisin was known to have a taste for women—the old cook's description had been revealing. Before meeting Arlette at La Bourboule, he must have had other women.

Had he trained them in the same way? Kept as firm a hold over them? There had never been a scandal to call attention to him.

The Countess had begun to go downhill, and nobody spoke of him. She used to give him money. He must live not far off, somewhere in the district; yet a man like Fred, who had been employing Arlette for two years, had never been able to find out anything about him.

And now, perhaps, it was his turn to be trapped as the Count had been. Wasn't it quite likely that Arlette had been trying to get rid of him? In fact she *had* tried at least once—after that impassioned discussion with Lapointe.

'What I can't understand,' said Fred—as though Maigret had been uttering his thoughts aloud, while he ate his soup—'is why he killed that crazy old woman. He's supposed to have been after the jewels she kept hidden in her mattress. It's possible he was—in fact it's certain. But he had a hold over her, and he could have got them some other way.'

'There's no saying she'd have let them go so easily,' objected Rose. 'They were all she had left, and she must have been trying to make them last. Besides, remember, she doped, and those people are apt to talk too much.'

Arlette's successor understood not a word of this, and sat staring curiously at each of them in turn. Fred had found her in a little theatre where she had a walking-on part. She was very proud of being promoted to a solo act, but one could feel she was rather afraid of meeting the same fate as Arlette.

'Will you be staying on this evening?' she asked Maigret.

'Perhaps. I don't know.'

'The inspector may leave in two minutes' time, or he may stay till tomorrow morning,' said Fred with a sly smile.

'If you ask me,' remarked Rose, 'Arlette was fed up with him, and he knew it. A man can hold a woman like that for a time, especially when she's very young. But she'd met other men. . . .'

She stared rather hard at her husband.

'Hadn't she, Fred? They'd made offers to her. And it isn't only women who can feel that kind of thing coming. I wouldn't be surprised if he'd decided to get hold of a lot of money at one stroke, and take her away to live somewhere else. Only he made the mistake of being too sure of himself, and told her about his plans. He's not the first to have been ruined that way.'

All this was still rather confused, of course; but the truth was beginning to take shape, in a way which shed a clearer light on the sinister figure of Oscar.

Again the telephone rang, but when Maigret went he found the call was not for him, but for Fred—who took the receiver, and courteously refrained from shutting the cloakroom door.

'Hello?' they heard him say, 'Yes. . . . What? . . . . What are you doing there? Yes. . . . Yes, he's here. . . . Don't shout so loud, you're deafening me. . . . O.K. . . . Yes, I know. . . . Why? . . . But that's idiotic. . . . You'd better speak to him yourself. . . . All right. . . . I don't know what he'll decide to do. . . . Stay where you are. . . . Probably he'll come along and join you. . . .'

He came back to the table looking rather worried.

'That was the Grasshopper,' he murmured, as though to himself.

He sat down, but did not go on with his meal at once.

'I wonder what's at the back of his mind. He's been working for me for five years, but I never know what he's thinking. He's never even told me where he lives. For all I can tell, he may have a wife and family.'

'Where is he now?' inquired Maigret.

'Up at the top of the *Butte*, at Chez Francis, the little restaurant at the corner, where there's always a bearded fellow telling fortunes. You know where I mean?'

Fred pondered, searching for an explanation.

'The funny thing is that Inspector Lognon is walking up and down just opposite.'

'What's the Grasshopper doing up there?'

'He didn't tell me exactly. I gathered it was something to do with that chap Philippe. The Grasshopper knows every pansy in Montmartre—in fact I used to wonder if he wasn't one himself. And between ourselves, it's possible he does a bit of drug-peddling at odd moments. I know you won't take advantage of that, and I promise you there's never any brought in here.'

'Is Chez Francis one of Philippe's hang-outs?'

'So it would seem. The Grasshopper may know more about that.'

'That doesn't explain why he went there.'

'Very well—I'll tell you, if you haven't already guessed! But please understand that it's his own idea. He thinks we might just as well tip you the wink, because you'll bear it in mind and give us the benefit of the doubt if we should ever need it. In this line of business we have to keep on the right side of the police. Anyhow, he's probably not the only one who's on to this idea, since Lognon is already prowling around there.'

Seeing that Maigret did not move, Fred exclaimed in astonishment:

'Aren't you going up there?' Then he added:

'Oh, of course—you can't leave here, in case your inspectors ring up.'

All the same, Maigret went to the telephone.

'Torrence? Have you any men to spare? Three? Good! Send them up to the Place du Tertre and tell them to keep an eye on Chez Francis, the *bistrot* at the corner. Ring the district police too, and tell them to send some of their men up that way. No, I don't know exactly. I'm staying here.'

He was rather sorry, now, to have made Picratt's his headquarters, but didn't quite feel he ought to go up to the *Butte*.

The telephone rang. It was Lapointe again.

'I don't know what he's playing at, sir. For the last half-hour he's been weaving to and fro around Montmartre. I wonder if he suspects he's being followed, and is trying to shake us off. He went into a café in the Rue Lepic, and then down again to the Place Blanche, where he took a turn round the same two restaurants. Then he turned back up the Rue Lepic and branched into the Rue Tholozé, where he went into a house where there's a studio at the far end of the courtyard. An old woman lives there who used to be a *café-concert* singer.'

'Does she take drugs?'

'Yes. Jacquin went in to question her as soon as Philippe left. She's a kind of scruffier version of the Countess. She was tight. She started laughing, and swore she hadn't been able to give him what he wanted. "I haven't even got any for myself!" she said.'

'Where is he now?'

'Eating hard-boiled eggs in a bar in the Rue Tholozé. It's raining cats and dogs. Everything's all right.'

'He'll probably go up to the Place du Tertre.'

'We nearly got that far just now, but he suddenly turned back. I wish he'd make up his mind. My feet are frozen.'

Rose and the new girl were clearing the table. Fred had fetched the brandy and was pouring some into the two balloon-glasses, while waiting for coffee.

'I shall soon have to go up and change,' he announced. 'That's not a hint for you to leave. Stay as long as you like. Here's how!'

'Do you suppose the Grasshopper knows Oscar?'

'Funny! That's just what I was thinking.'

'He goes to the races every afternoon, doesn't he?'

'Yes—and you mean the chances are that a man like Oscar, with nothing to do, will spend part of his time there too?'

He drained his glass, wiped his mouth, looked at the girl, who was wondering what to do next, and winked at Maigret.

'I'm going upstairs to change,' he announced. 'Come up for a minute, kid, I want to talk to you about your act.'

He winked at Maigret again, and added in an undertone:

'Helps to pass the time, you know!'

Maigret was left alone in the cabaret.

# IX

'HE went up to the Place du Tertre, sir, and nearly ran into Inspector Lognon, who just had time to jump back into the shadow.'

'You're sure he didn't see him?'

'Quite sure. He went and looked in at the window of Chez Francis.

In this weather there's hardly anyone there. A few regular customers, sitting gloomily over their drinks. He didn't go in. Then he turned into the Rue du Mont-Cenis and went down the steps to the Place Constantin-Pecqueur, where he stopped outside another café. There's a big stove in the middle of the floor, sawdust sprinkled around, marble-topped tables, and the *patron* is playing cards with some friends.'

The new girl at Picratt's came downstairs again, looking slightly embarrassed, and not knowing what to do with herself, came and sat beside Maigret. Perhaps so as not to leave him all alone. She had already put on the black silk dress that had belonged to Arlette.

'What's your name?'

'Geneviève. They're going to call me Dolly. I'm to be photographed tomorrow in this dress.'

'How old are you?'

'Twenty-three. Did you ever see Arlette do her act? Is it true she was so awfully good? I'm a bit awkward, aren't I?'

Next time Lapointe rang up, he sounded depressed.

'He's going round and round like a circus horse. We're following, and it's still raining cats and dogs. We've been back through the Place Clichy, and then to the Place Blanche, where he went round the same two restaurants again. As he's got no morphia, he's beginning to take a drink here and there. He hasn't found what he wants, and he's walking more slowly now, keeping in the shadow of the houses.'

'He still has no suspicions?'

'No. Janvier's had a chat with Inspector Lognon. Lognon went back to all the places Philippe visited last night, and that's how he came to hear of Chez Francis. He was just told that Philippe went there now and again, and that probably someone supplied him with dope.'

'Is the Grasshopper still there?'

'No, he left a few minutes ago. At the moment, Philippe is on his way down the steps in the Rue du Mont-Cenis again, most likely to have another look in the café in the Place Constantin-Pecqueur.'

Tania and the Grasshopper came in together. It was still too early to turn on Picratt's neon sign, but evidently they were all in the habit of arriving in good time. Everybody seemed pretty much at home. Rose put her head round the door before going upstairs to change. She was still holding a dishcloth.

'Oh, there you are!' she said to the new girl.

Then, looking her up and down, she added:

'Another evening, don't put your dress on so soon. It wears it out unnecessarily.'

And to Maigret she said, in conclusion:

'Help yourself, Inspector. That's what the bottle's for.'

Tania seemed to be in a bad temper. She stared at Arlette's successor and gave a slight shrug.

'Move up a bit, I want to sit down,' she told the girl.

She stared hard at Maigret, and then inquired:

'You haven't caught him yet?'

'I expect to catch him tonight.'

'You don't think it's occurred to him to cut and run?'

She knew something, too. In fact everybody had some scrap of knowledge. He'd had the same impression the night before. And now Tania was wondering whether she wouldn't be wise to tell what she knew.

'Did you ever meet him with Arlette?'

'I don't even know who he is or what he looks like.'

'But you know he exists?'

'I've a shrewd suspicion.'

'What else do you know?'

'Where he hangs out, perhaps.'

Helpfulness was not her habit, and she spoke sulkily, as though it went against the grain.

'My dressmaker lives in the Rue Caulaincourt, just opposite the Place Constantin-Pecqueur. I'm asleep most of the day, so I usually go there about five o'clock in the afternoon. Twice, I've seen Arlette get off a bus at the corner of the *place* and walk across it.'

'In what direction?'

'Towards the steps.'

'It didn't occur to you to follow her?'

'Why should I have followed her?'

That was a lie. She was inquisitive. By the time she got to the foot of the steps, Arlette had presumably vanished.

'Is that all you know?'

'That's all. He must live somewhere there.'

Maigret had poured himself a glass of brandy, and was in no hurry to get up when the telephone rang again.

'He's still at the same game, sir.'

'Hanging round the café in the Place Constantin-Pecqueur?'

'Yes. The only places where he stops now are there, at the two restaurants in the Place Blanche, and outside Chez Francis.'

'Is Lognon still up there?'

'Yes. I just caught a glimpse of him as I went past.'

'Ask him from me to go down to the Place Constantin-Pecqueur and have a word with the proprietor. Not in front of the customers, if he can avoid it. Tell him to ask whether he knows Oscar Bonvoisin— and if not, to give a description of him, because he may be known there by some other name.'

'Right away?'

'Yes. He'll have the time, while Philippe's on his round. Tell him to ring me up as soon as he's done it.'

When he went back into the cabaret, the Grasshopper was there, pouring himself a drink at the bar.

'Not caught him yet?'

'How did you get the tip about Chez Francis?'

'From some pansies. They all know one another, in that bunch. First they told me about a bar in the Rue Caulaincourt where Philippe goes from time to time, and then about Chez Francis, where he sometimes looks in late at night.'

'Do they know Oscar?'

'Yes.'

'Bonvoisin?'

'They don't know his surname. They told me he's a local man who comes in now and again for a glass of white wine before bedtime.'

'Does he know Philippe?'

'Everyone's on speaking terms in that place; he behaves like the rest of them. You can't say I haven't helped you.'

'Has he been seen today?'

'No. Nor yesterday.'

'Did they tell you where he lives?'

'Somewhere in the neighbourhood.'

Time was dragging now, and one began to feel as though nothing would ever happen. Jean-Jean, the accordionist, came in and went to the cloakroom to wipe his muddy shoes and comb his hair.

'Not got Arlette's murderer yet?' he inquired.

Then came another telephone call from Lapointe.

'I passed on your instructions to Inspector Lognon. He's gone to the Place Constantin-Pecqueur. Philippe's just gone into Chez Francis and is having a drink, but there's no one there who answers to the description of Oscar. Lognon will ring you. I told him where you were. Was that right?'

Lapointe's voice didn't sound the same as at the beginning of the evening. Every time he wanted to telephone, he had to go into some bar or other. This was his umpteenth phone call; and no doubt he had a drop of something on each occasion, to warm himself.

Fred came downstairs, resplendent in his dinner-jacket, with an imitation diamond in his starched shirt-front, and his freshly-shaven face a pleasant shade of pink.

'Get along up and change now,' he said to Tania.

Then he went to turn on the lights and straighten the rows of bottles behind the bar.

The second musician, Monsieur Dupeu, had just arrived in his turn when Lognon at last rang up.

'Where are you speaking from?' inquired Maigret.

'From Chez Manière, in the Rue Caulaincourt. I've been to the Place Constantin-Pecqueur and I've got the address!'

He was in a state of great excitement.

'Did they give it to you without any fuss?'

'The *patron* didn't suspect anything. I didn't tell him I was a police-man. I pretended I was up from the country, and looking for a friend.'

'Do they call him by name?'

'They call him Monsieur Oscar.'

'Where does he live?'

'Above the steps, on the right, in a little house with a plot of garden in front. There's a wall all round—the house can't be seen from the street.'

'He's not been to the Place Constantin-Pecqueur today?'

'No. They waited for him to begin their game, for he's usually punctual. That was why the proprietor was playing, instead of him.'

'What has he told them he does in life?'

'Nothing. He doesn't talk much. They think he has private means—seems comfortably off. He's a very good *belote* player. He often drops in during the morning, about eleven, for a glass of white wine before doing his shopping.'

'He does his own shopping? Hasn't he got a servant?'

'No. And no charwoman. They think he's a bit eccentric.'

'Wait for me somewhere near the steps.'

Maigret finished his brandy and went to the cloakroom to fetch his heavy overcoat, which was still damp; the two musicians began to play a few notes, as though to warm themselves up.

'In the bag?' inquired Fred from behind the bar.

'Soon will be, perhaps.'

'Come back here, won't you? We'll have a bottle of champagne on it.'

The Grasshopper called a taxi. As he was shutting the door, he said below his breath:

'If it's the chap I've heard some vague talk about, you'd best take care. He's a tough customer.'

Water was streaming down the windows of the taxi, and the lights of the town could be seen only through a close-striped curtain of rain. Philippe must be splashing through that, somewhere, with the inspectors following him in the shadows.

Maigret got out and walked across the Place Constantin-Pecqueur, where he found Lognon flattened against a wall.

'I've identified the house.'

'Any light showing?'

'I looked over the wall. Nothing to be seen. I suppose the pansy doesn't know the address. What do we do now?'

'Is there any way out at the back?'

'No. This is the only door.'

'We're going in. You've got a gun?'

Lognon merely pointed to his pocket. There was a dilapidated wall, like that of a country garden, overhung by branches of trees. Lognon set to work on the lock, and it took him several minutes, while the inspector stood on guard.

Once the door opened, they found themselves looking across a small garden towards one of those small, low houses of which a few are still hidden in the byways of Montmartre. It was in complete darkness.

'Go and get the front door open, and then come back here,' said Maigret—who, despite skilled tuition, was a poor hand at picking a lock.

'Wait for me outside the gate, and when the others come past, tell Lapointe or Janvier I'm here, and that they're to keep on trailing Philippe.'

Inside the house there was not a sound, not a sign of life. But Maigret kept his revolver in his hand. The passage was warm and had a countrified smell: Bonvoisin must use wood for heating. It was a damp house. He hesitated for a moment and then, with a shrug, turned the electric switch he had just found on his right.

To his surprise, the place was very clean; it did not have the dejected and rather grubby appearance of most bachelors' homes. The passage was lit by a lantern with coloured glass panes. Maigret opened the right-hand door and found himself in a drawing-room of the type to be seen in the windows of furniture emporiums—in deplorable taste, but prosperous-looking, with everything made of the heaviest available wood. Next came a dining-room, furnished from the same source in an imitation Provençal style, with plastic fruit on a silver dish.

There was not a speck of dust to be seen, and he found the same spotless cleanliness in the kitchen. The fire was not yet out in the stove, and there was warm water in the kettle. Opening cupboards, he saw bread, meat, butter and eggs, and there was a bin containing carrots, turnips and a cauliflower. The house evidently had no cellar, for there was a cask of wine, too, with a glass turned upside-down on the bung, as though it were in frequent use.

There was one more room on the ground floor—across the corridor, opposite the drawing-room. It was a biggish bedroom, with silk-shaded lamps that gave a very feminine touch, and a satin eiderdown on the bed. It had a profusion of mirrors too, reminding Maigret of certain brothels, and there were almost as many in the bathroom next door.

Except for the food in the kitchen, the cask of wine, and the embers in the stove, there was not a sign of life. Nothing was out of place, as happens even in the best-run house. There were no ashes in the ashtrays. No dirty linen or shabby clothes in the cupboards.

He understood why, when he went upstairs and opened the two landing doors—not without apprehension, for the silence, broken only by the rain drumming on the roof, was rather nerve-racking.

There was nobody there.

The room on the left was Oscar Bonvoisin's real bedroom, where he spent his solitary nights. Here the bed was an iron one, covered with thick red blankets; it had not been made, and the sheets were none too clean; on the bedside table lay some fruit, including an apple which had been bitten into, its flesh already brown.

There was a pair of muddy shoes on the floor, two or three packets of cigarettes, and a liberal scattering of cigarette-ends.

Though there was a proper bathroom downstairs, this upper floor had nothing but a handbasin in the corner of the bedroom, with one tap, and a few dirty towels lying around. A pair of trousers hung from a hook.

Maigret sought in vain for papers. The drawers yielded a mixed harvest, including cartridges for an automatic pistol, but not a single letter or document.

Going downstairs again, however, he found a drawer full of photographs in the bedroom chest of drawers. The films were there too, together with the camera and a flash-lamp.

Not all the photos were of Arlette. At least twenty women, all young and shapely, had posed for Bonvoisin in the same erotic attitudes. Some of the photographs had been enlarged. Looking for the dark-room, Maigret found it upstairs; there was a red electric lamp hanging above a sink, and a great many little bottles of chemicals.

He was on his way down when he heard steps outside, and flattened himself against the wall, pointing his revolver at the door.

'It's me, sir,' said a voice.

Janvier stood there, water streaming off him, his hat soaked out of all shape.

'Have you found anything?' he asked.

'What's Philippe doing?'

'Still going round in circles. I don't know how he manages to stand up by now. He had a squabble with a flower-seller opposite the Moulin Rouge—he'd asked her for dope. She told me about it afterwards. She knows him by sight. He implored her to tell him where he could find some. Then he went into a telephone-box and rang up Dr. Bloch, saying that he was at the end of his tether, and making all kinds of threats. If it goes on much longer he'll throw a fit in the middle of the street.'

Janvier looked round at the empty house, where lights were burning in every room.

'You don't suppose the bird has flown?'

His breath smelt of alcohol, and his lips were twisted in a slight, tense smile that Maigret knew well.

'Aren't you having the railway people warned?'

'Judging by the fire in the stove, he left the house at least three or four hours ago. In other words, if he means to run away he'll have got on a train long ago. He had plenty to choose from.'

'Still, we could warn the frontier stations.'

Strangely enough, Maigret felt not the slightest inclination to set the cumbersome police mechanism in motion. True, it was only a hunch; but he felt certain the affair was going to be settled in Montmartre, where everything had happened so far.

'You think he's watching for Philippe somewhere?' asked Janvier.

The inspector shrugged his shoulders. He had no idea. He went outside and found Lognon, flat against the garden wall.

'You'd better put out the lights and stay here to keep watch,' he said.

'Do you think he'll come back?'

He thought nothing at all.

'I say, Lognon, what were the addresses where Philippe went last night?'

The inspector had made a note of them all. Since his release, the young man had been back to every one of them, in vain.

'You're sure you haven't left any out?'

Lognon was offended.

'I've told you all I know. There's only one other address and that's his own, in the Boulevard Rochechouart.'

Maigret said nothing, but he lit his pipe with an air of quiet satisfaction.

'Good. Stay here, just in case. Janvier, you come with me.'

'Have you had an idea?'

'I think I know where we shall find him.'

They walked, with coat-collars turned up and hands thrust deep in their pockets. It wasn't worth taking a taxi.

As they reached the Place Blanche they caught sight of Philippe in the distance, coming out of one of the two restaurants. A little way behind him was young Lapointe, still wearing his cap; he made them a slight sign.

The others were not far off, still keeping watch on Philippe.

'You come with us,' said Maigret to Lapointe.

They had only five hundred yards still to go, along the almost deserted Boulevard. The night-clubs, whose neon lights were gleaming through the rain, couldn't be doing much business in weather like this, and the doorkeepers in their gold-braided uniforms were keeping under shelter, ready to open their big red umbrellas.

'Where are we going?' asked Lapointe.

'To Philippe's house.'

For the Countess had been killed in her own flat. And the murderer had been waiting for Arlette at her home in the Rue Notre-Dame de Lorette.

It was an old building. Above the shuttered ground-floor windows was a book-binder's sign, and, to the right of the entrance, that of a bookseller. They were obliged to ring for the *cordon* to be pulled. The door opened silently, the three men stepped into a dimly-lit corridor, and Maigret signed to the others to make as little noise as possible. As they went past the concierge's door he growled out an indistinguishable name, and then they began to climb the uncarpeted stairs.

On the first floor one of the door-mats was wet, and a ray of light could be seen under the door. From there until they reached the sixth floor, they were in pitch darkness, for the *minuterie* had gone out.

'Let me go first, sir,' whispered Lapointe, trying to slip past between Maigret and the wall.

The inspector pushed him back with a firm hand. He knew from Lognon that Philippe's attic was the third room on the left on this top floor. His electric torch showed him that the narrow corridor, with its yellowing walls, was empty; he pressed the button of the *minuterie* and the light came on again.

He placed one of his men to either side of the third door, and took hold of the door handle, his revolver ready in the other hand. The handle turned. The door was not locked.

He pushed it with his toe and then stood motionless, listening. As in the house he had just left, he could hear nothing but the rain beating on the roof and water flowing through the drainpipes. It seemed to him that he could hear his companions' hearts beating as well; his own too, perhaps.

He put out his hand and found the electric light switch, just inside the door.

There was nobody in the room. There was no cupboard to hide in. Bonvoisin's room—the upstairs one—had been luxurious compared to this. There were no sheets on the bed. There was a chamber-pot that had not been emptied. There were dirty clothes on the floor.

Lapointe bent down and looked under the bed. No use. Not a soul in the place. The room stank.

Suddenly, Maigret had the impression of a movement behind him. To the stupefaction of the two inspectors, he bounded backwards, gave a half-turn, and heaved vigorously with his shoulder against the opposite door.

The door yielded. It was not shut. There was someone behind it, someone who had been watching them, and it was the faintest movement of the door which had caught Maigret's attention.

He had thrust so hard across the passage that he was flung forward into the room, and was saved from falling only because he collided with a man almost as heavy as himself.

The room was in darkness, and it was Janvier who had the sense to turn on the light.

'Look out, sir. . . .'

Maigret had already been butted in the chest. He reeled, but saved himself from falling by clutching at something that pitched over with a crash—a bedside table with some china object on it.

He grabbed his revolver by the barrel and tried to strike a blow with the butt. He didn't know the elusive Oscar, but he had recognized him—this was the man described to him, the man he had been seeing all this time in his imagination. The fellow had bent double again and was charging at the two inspectors who were barring his way.

Lapointe clutched automatically at his jacket, while Janvier tried to get a grip on his body.

They had no time to look at one another. There was a body lying on the bed, but they could pay no attention to that.

Janvier was knocked down, Lapointe was left with the jacket in his hands, and a figure was darting down the corridor, when a shot rang out. For a moment they didn't realize who had fired. It was Lapointe, who was too frightened to look in the direction of the fugitive, and was staring at his revolver with a kind of bewildered astonishment.

Bonvoisin staggered on for a few paces, bending forward, and finally collapsed on the floor.

'Take care, Janvier. . . .'

He had an automatic pistol in his hand. The barrel was moving. Then, slowly, the fingers opened and the weapon fell to the ground.

'D'you think I've killed him, sir?'

Lapointe's eyes were starting from his head, and his lips quivering. He couldn't believe it was he who had done such a thing, and he looked again at his revolver, in respectful astonishment.

'I've killed him!' he repeated, still not daring to look at the body.

Janvier was bending over it.

'He's dead. You got him full in the chest.'

Maigret thought for a moment that Lapointe was going to faint. He laid a hand on his shoulder.

'Your first, is he?' he asked gently.

Then, to cheer the lad up, he added:

'Don't forget he killed Arlette.'

'So he did. . . .'

It was amusing to see the childish expression on Lapointe's face; he didn't know whether to laugh or cry.

Cautious steps were heard on the stairs. A voice asked:

'Has anyone been hurt?'

'Don't let them come up,' said Maigret to Janvier.

He turned to attend to the human figure he had seen for a second on the bed. It was a girl of sixteen or seventeen—the bookseller's servant. She was not dead, but a towel had been tied over her face to keep her from shouting. Her hands were tied behind her back and her slip was pushed right up to her armpits.

'Go down and ring up headquarters,' said Maigret to Lapointe. 'If you can find a *bistrot* that's still open, have a drink while you're about it.'

'Oh—do you think . . . ?'

'It's an order.'

It was some little time before the girl could speak. She had come up to her room about half past ten, after a visit to the cinema. Before she had even had time to turn on the light, she had been seized by an unknown man who had been waiting for her in the dark, and he had tied the towel tightly over her mouth. Then he had bound her hands and thrown her on the bed.

After that he had paid no attention to her for a time. He was listening to the sounds in the house; and every now and then he opened the door a crack. He was waiting for Philippe, but he was suspicious, and that was why he did not wait in the young man's own room. He had no doubt inspected it before crossing to the maid's attic, and that explained why the door had been open.

'What happened after that?'

'He took my clothes off—and he had to tear them, because of my hands being tied.'

'Did he rape you?'

She nodded, and began to cry. Then, picking up a heap of light-coloured material from the floor, she said:

'My dress is ruined. . . .'

She didn't realize what a narrow escape she had had. It was most unlikely that Bonvoisin would have left her behind him, alive. She had seen him, just as Philippe had seen him. If he had not strangled her at once, like the other two, it was no doubt because he planned to have a little more fun with her while waiting for the young man to arrive.

\*

By three o'clock in the morning, Oscar Bonvoisin's body was lying in one of the metal drawers at the mortuary, not far from those of Arlette and the Countess.

Philippe, after a row with a customer at Chez Francis, where he had finally gone in, had been taken to the local police station by a uniformed policeman. Torrence had gone to bed. The inspectors who had been going the round from the Place Blanche to the Place du Tertre and from there to the Place Constantin-Pecqueur, had gone home too.

Leaving police headquarters on the Quai des Orfèvres with Lapointe and Janvier, Maigret had suggested, after a moment's hesitation:

'What about a bottle of champagne?'

'Where?'

'At Picratt's.'

'Not for me,' said Janvier. 'My wife will be waiting for me, and the baby wakes us early.'

Lapointe said nothing. But he followed Maigret into the taxi.

They reached the Rue Pigalle just in time to see the new girl do her act. Fred came to meet them as they went in.

'In the bag?' he inquired.

Maigret nodded; and a few moments later a bucket with a bottle of champagne appeared on their table—which, as it so happened, was number six. The black dress was slipping slowly down over the white body of the girl, who was gazing at them with a scared expression, she was reluctant to uncover her belly and as soon as her nakedness was revealed she put both hands to cover it, as she had done at the evening rehearsal.

Did Fred do it on purpose? At that precise moment he should have turned off the spotlight and left the room in darkness, giving the dancer time to pick up her dress and hold it in front of her. But the spotlight did not go out, and the poor girl, completely at a loss, decided, after a long pause, to scuttle off to the kitchen—thus displaying a round, white behind.

The few clients in the place burst out laughing. Maigret thought Lapointe was laughing too; but looking more closely, he saw that tears were running down the inspector's cheeks.

'I beg your pardon,' he stammered. 'I ought not to. . . . I know it's stupid. But you see I . . . I loved her!'

He was even more ashamed when he woke up next morning, for he had no notion whatever of how he had got home.

His sister, who seemed to be in a particularly cheerful mood—Maigret had had a word with her—greeted him, as she drew back the curtains, with:

'A fine idea, having yourself put to bed by the inspector!'

That night, Lapointe had buried his first love. And killed his first man. As for Lognon, nobody had thought to release him from his watch, and he was still shivering on the steps above the Place Constantin-Pecqueur.

# MAIGRET'S MISTAKE

---

## I

It was eight-twenty-five in the morning when Maigret rose from the breakfast-table still drinking his last cup of coffee. Though it was only November, the lights were on. At the window, Madame Maigret was peering through the fog at the passers-by, who were hurrying to work, shoulders hunched and hands in pockets.

'You'd better put on your heavy overcoat,' she said.

For it was by watching people in the street that she decided what the weather was like. This morning, everyone was walking fast and many wore scarves; they had a particular way of stamping along the pavement to warm their feet, and she had noticed several blowing their noses.

'I'll go and get it for you.'

He was still holding his cup in his hand when the telephone bell echoed through the house. Picking up the receiver, he too looked outside; the houses opposite were almost hidden by the yellowish mist that had overnight filled the streets.

'Hello! Inspector Maigret? . . . Dupeu speaking from the Quartier des Ternes. . . .'

It was odd that it should be Inspector Dupeu, for he was the man who probably had most in common with the atmosphere of that day. Dupeu was Inspector of Police in the Rue d'Etoile. He squinted. His wife squinted. And it was said that all three of his daughters, whom Maigret had never seen, squinted too. He was a conscientious official, so bothered about doing his best that he practically made himself ill by it. Even inanimate objects seemed peculiarly dreary when he was present, and in spite of the fact that he was the best fellow in the world, one could not help trying to avoid him. Besides, summer and winter, he had a perpetual cold.

'Sorry to trouble you at home. I thought you wouldn't have left yet, and so I said to myself . . .'

There was nothing to do but be patient. Dupeu had to explain himself. Invariably he felt obliged to recount at length why he did this or that, as if he were in the wrong.

'. . . I know you like to be on the spot in person. I may be mistaken, but I have an idea that we are on to a pretty interesting affair.

117

Bear in mind that I don't know anything yet, or hardly anything. I
have only just arrived.'

Madame Maigret was waiting with the overcoat in her arms, and,
so that she would not grow impatient, her husband whispered to her:
'Dupeu!'

Meanwhile Dupeu droned on.

'As I usually do, I reached the office at eight o'clock and I was looking through the first post, when at eight-seven I had a telephone call
from the charwoman. It was she who found the body when she entered
the flat in the Avenue Carnot. As it's almost next door, I hurried
round with my secretary.'

'Murder?'

'Strictly, it could be suicide, but I'm convinced it's murder.'

'Who is it?'

'A certain Louise Filon. I've never heard of her. A young woman.'

'I'll be along.'

Dupeu started speaking again, but Maigret, pretending not to
notice, had already hung up. Before leaving, he called the Quai des
Orfèvres and had himself put through to the *Identité Judiciaire*.

'Is Moers there? Yes, call him to the telephone. Hello! Is that you,
Moers? Will you come along with your men to the Avenue Carnot?
. . . Murder . . . I shall be there. . . .'

He gave him the number of the block, put on his coat, and, a few
seconds later, one more dim outline was hastening through the fog.
Not until the corner of the Boulevard Voltaire did he find a taxi.

Around the Etoile, the avenues were almost deserted. Men were
collecting dustbins. For the most part, curtains were still drawn, and
only in a few windows was a light to be seen.

In the Avenue Carnot, a policeman in a cape was standing on the
pavement, but there were no onlookers and no crowd.

'What floor?' Maigret asked.

'The third.'

He went through the main door, ornamented with highly polished
brass knobs. In the porter's lodge, where the lights were on, the concierge was eating breakfast. She watched him through the window, but
did not get up. The lift worked noiselessly, as in every well-kept house.
The carpets, on the waxed oak of the staircase, were of a deep red.

On the third floor he was confronted with three doors; as he paused,
the one on the left opened. Dupeu was there, his nose red, as Maigret
had expected.

'Come in. I decided not to touch anything while I was waiting for
you. I haven't even questioned the charwoman.'

Crossing the hall, which contained only a coat-rack and two chairs,
they entered the sitting-room, where the lights were on.

'The charwoman was at once struck by the lights being on.'

In the corner of a yellow sofa sprawled a young woman with brown hair, curiously doubled over herself. A big dark red stain marked her dressing-gown.

'She was hit by a bullet in the head. It seems to have been fired from behind, and from very close quarters. As you can see, she didn't fall down.'

She had simply collapsed to the right, and her head hung down, the hair almost touching the carpet.

'Where is the charwoman?'

'In the kitchen. She asked permission to make a cup of coffee. According to her, she arrived at eight, as she does every morning. She has a key to the flat. She came in, saw the body, claims that she touched nothing and telephoned me at once.'

Only then did Maigret appreciate what had struck him as so odd when he had first arrived. Generally on the pavement he would have had to make his way through a row of spectators. Usually, too, the other tenants are on the look-out on the landings. But here, all was as quiet as if nothing had happened.

'Is the kitchen this way?'

He found it at the end of a corridor. The door was open. A woman in a black dress, and with dark hair and eyes, was sitting near the gas stove, drinking a cup of coffee and blowing on it to cool it.

Maigret had an idea that he had seen her before. He observed her, frowning, while she steadily returned his gaze, still drinking coffee. She was very small. Sitting down, she could scarcely touch the floor with her feet; she was wearing shoes too big for her and her dress was too full and too long.

'I think we have met before,' he said.

Self-possessed, she replied:

'It's very likely.'

'What is your name?'

'Désirée Brault.'

The Christian name gave him a clue.

'Weren't you once arrested for shoplifting in one of the big stores?'

'That among other things.'

'What else?'

'I've been arrested so many times!'

Her face showed no fear. In fact, it showed nothing. She looked at him. She answered him. But what she was thinking it was impossible to guess.

'You've done time?'

'You'll find all that in my record.'

'Prostitution?'

'Why not?'

A long time ago, obviously. Now she would be fifty or sixty. She was wizened. Her hair had not turned white or even grey, but it was sparse, and through it you could see her scalp.

'There was a time when I was as good as the next girl!'

'How long have you been working in this flat?'

'A year next month. I began in December, not long before the holidays.'

'Do you work here all day?'

'Only from eight till twelve.'

The coffee smelt so good that Maigret helped himself to a cup. Inspector Dupeu was standing timidly in the doorway.

'Would you like a cup, Dupeu?'

'No, thank you. I had breakfast less than half an hour ago.'

Désirée Brault got up to pour a second cup for herself as well, and her dress hung loosely round her. She could not have weighed more than a little girl of fourteen.

'You have other jobs?'

'Three or four. It depends on the weeks.'

'You live alone?'

'With my husband.'

'Has he done time, too?'

'Not likely! He keeps to the drink.'

'Has he no job?'

'He's never done a stroke of work in fifteen years, not even to hammer a nail in the wall.'

She spoke without bitterness, in level tones in which it was hard to detect any irony.

'What happened this morning?'

She nodded at Dupeu.

'Didn't he tell you? All right. I got here at eight o'clock.'

'Where do you live?'

'Near the Place Clichy. I took the Metro. I opened the door with my key and I noticed a light in the sitting-room.'

'The sitting-room door was open?'

'No.'

'Is your employer usually up by the time you arrive in the morning?'

'She didn't get up till about ten, and sometimes later.'

'What did she do?'

'Nothing.'

'Go on.'

'I opened the sitting-room door and I saw her.'

'You didn't touch her?'

'I didn't need to, to see that she was dead. Have you ever seen any-one walking about with half her face blown off?'

'And then?'

'I called the police.'

'Without arousing the neighbours, or the concierge?'

She shrugged her shoulders.

'Why should I?'

'But after you telephoned?'

'I waited.'

'Doing what?'

'Doing nothing.'

It was astonishing, this artlessness. She had simply stayed there, waiting until someone rang the door-bell, perhaps gazing at the corpse.

'You're sure you didn't touch anything?'

'Of course I didn't.'

'Did you find a revolver?'

'I found nothing at all.'

Inspector Dupeu interrupted:

'We have looked everywhere for the weapon, but without success.'

'Did Louise Filon own a revolver?'

'If she did, I never saw it.'

'Is any of the furniture kept locked up?'

'No.'

'I suppose you know what these cupboards contain?'

'Yes.'

'And you have never seen a gun?'

'Never.'

'Tell me, did your employer know that you had been in prison?'

'I told her everything.'

'It didn't frighten her?'

'It amused her. I don't know whether she had done time, too, but she might have.'

'What do you mean?'

'That before she came to live here she was on the streets.'

'How do you know?'

'Because she told me. And even if she hadn't . . .'

Footsteps were heard on the landing and Dupeu went to open the door. It was Moers and his men with their gear. Maigret said to Moers:

'Don't begin just yet. And while you're waiting for me, telephone the Public Prosecutor.'

He was fascinated by Désirée Brault and by everything he guessed to lie behind her words. He took off his overcoat, for it was warm, sat down and sipped his coffee.

'Sit down.'

'Kind of you. It's not often charwomen have that said to them.'

And for once she almost smiled.

'Have you any idea who might have killed your employer?'

'Certainly not.'

'Did she have many callers?'

'I never saw anyone, except the local doctor once when she had bronchitis. But of course I leave at twelve o'clock.'

'You don't know if she had any friends?'

'All I know is that there are some men's slippers and a man's dressing-gown in a wardrobe. Also a box of cigars. She didn't smoke cigars.'

'You've no idea who the man was?'

'I've never seen him.'

'You don't know his name? He never telephoned when you were here?'

'That did happen.'

'What did she call him?'

'Pierrot.'

'Somebody kept her?'

'I suppose somebody had to pay the rent, and all the rest of it, don't you?'

Maigret got to his feet, set down his cup and filled his pipe.

'What do you want me to do?' she asked.

'Nothing. You just wait.'

He returned to the sitting-room where the men of the *Identité Judiciaire* were waiting for his orders before falling to work. The room was perfectly tidy. In an ash-tray near the sofa was some cigarette-ash, and the butts of three cigarettes, two of them marked with lip-stick.

A half-open door led into the bedroom where Maigret noted with some surprise that the bed was unmade, the pillow dented as if someone had slept there.

'Hasn't the doctor come?'

'He wasn't at home. His wife is trying to reach him at the homes of patients he is to see this morning.'

He opened a number of cupboards and drawers. Clothes and underclothes were those of a girl who dressed with rather poor taste and not those one expected to find in a flat in the Avenue Carnot.

'Look after the fingerprints and the rest of it, Moers. I am going down to talk to the concierge.'

Inspector Dupeu asked him:

'Do you need me any more?'

'No, thank you. Send me your report in the course of the day. It's been very kind of you, Dupeu.'

'Well, I thought at once that this would interest you. If there had been a weapon near the sofa, I should have concluded that it was suicide, for the shot seems to have been fired point-blank. Although women of this sort generally kill themselves with veronal. It's at least five years since I have known any woman in this district kill herself with a revolver. Therefore, as long as there was no weapon . . .'

'Dupeu, you've done a fine job. . . .'

'I try to the best of my ability to. . . .'

He talked on all the way down the staircase. Maigret left him on the mat outside the porter's lodge, and went in.

'Good morning, madame.'

'Good morning, Inspector.'

'You know who I am?'

She nodded that she did.

'You are aware of what has happened?'

'I asked the policeman on duty on the pavement. He told me that Mademoiselle Louise is dead.'

The porter's lodge had the middle-class look of all the lodges in the district. The concierge, who was only in her forties, was well dressed, and even smartly so. She was rather attractive, though her features were slightly overblown.

'Has she been murdered?' she asked, as Maigret sat down near the window.

'Why do you think that?'

'I suppose if she'd died a natural death, the police wouldn't be here.'

'She might have committed suicide.'

'That wouldn't have been like her.'

'You knew her well?'

'Not very well. She never spent much time down here. She just opened the door to ask for her mail. She never felt herself at home, you know, in this house.'

'You mean to say that she wasn't of the same class as the other tenants?'

'Yes.'

'What class do you think she belonged to?'

'I don't quite know. I've no reason to run her down. She was a quiet creature, and didn't give herself airs.'

'Her charwoman never said anything?'

'Madame Brault and I don't speak to each other.'

'But you know her?'

'I don't care to. I've seen her come and go. That is enough.'

'Was Louise Filon a kept woman?'

'It could be. But, in any case, she paid her rent regularly.'

'Did she have visitors?'

'From time to time.'

'Not regularly?'

'No, it couldn't be called regularly.'

Maigret thought he sensed a reticence. Unlike Madame Brault, the concierge was nervous, and now and again she cast a quick glance through the glass door. It was she who observed:

'The doctor's going up.'

'Tell me, Madame . . . by the way, what is your name?'

'Cornet.'

'Tell me, Madame Cornet, is there something you'd like to keep from me?'

She did her best to look him straight in the eye.

'Why do you ask that?'

'No reason. I just like to know. Was it always the same man who came to see Louise Filon?'

'It was always the same one I saw.'

'What sort of a man?'

'A musician.'

'How do you know he was a musician?'

'Because once or twice I saw him carrying a saxophone-case.'

'Did he call yesterday evening?'

'About ten o'clock, yes.'

'Did you let him in and out?'

'No. Until I go to bed, about eleven, I leave the door open.'

'But you can see who is passing through the hall?'

'Mostly, yes. The tenants are a quiet lot. Nearly all are people of standing.'

'You say that this musician went upstairs about ten o'clock?'

'Yes. He didn't stay more than ten minutes. When he left he seemed to be in a great hurry, and I heard him rushing towards the Etoile.'

'Did you notice his expression? Did he seem excited? . . .'

'No.'

'That night did Louise Filon have any other visitors?'

'No.'

'So that if the doctor finds that the crime was committed between ten o'clock and eleven, it is almost certain that . . .'

'I didn't say that. I only said that he was her only visitor.'

'According to you, the musician was her lover?'

She did not at once reply. Eventually she muttered:

'I don't know.'

'What do you mean?'

'Nothing. I was just thinking about the rent of the flat.'

'I see. He wasn't the kind of musician who could keep a girl-friend in a flat like that?'

'That's it.'

'You don't seem to be surprised, Madame Cornet, that your tenant should have been murdered.'

'It's not a thing I expected, but I'm not much surprised either.'

'Why not?'

'For no real reason. I rather think that women of this sort run greater risks than others. At any rate, that's the idea you get from reading the newspapers.'

'I should like to ask you for a list of all the tenants who came in or went out after nine o'clock yesterday evening. I shall pick it up when I go.'

'Very good.'

When he left the lodge he met the prosecutor and his deputy getting out of their car, along with their clerk. All three seemed to be feeling the cold. The fog had not yet dispersed, and the steam of their breath was blowing into it.

They shook hands, and took the lift. With the exception of the third floor, the whole block was as quiet as when Maigret had arrived. People here were not the sort to spy on comings and goings through half-open doors, nor to gather in a crowd on the landings because a woman had been murdered.

Almost all over the flat, Moers and his men had set up their technical apparatus, and the doctor had finished examining the body. He clasped Maigret's hand.

'About what time?' the inspector asked.

'At first sight, between nine in the evening and midnight. Eleven o'clock, perhaps, rather than midnight.'

'I suppose death was instantaneous?'

'You've seen the body. The shot was fired point-blank.'

'From behind?'

'From behind, but a little from one side.'

Moers interrupted:

'At that moment she must have been smoking a cigarette, which fell on the carpet and burnt itself out. It was lucky that the carpet didn't catch fire.'

'What exactly is the case?' asked the deputy prosecutor, who was still in the dark.

'I don't know. It may be a commonplace murder. But that would surprise me.'

'You have a clue?'

'None at all. I am going to talk to the charwoman again.'

Before making for the kitchen, he telephoned the Quai des Orfèvres, and asked Lucas, who was on duty, to join him at once. After that, he took no further notice of the prosecutor and his staff, nor of the police technicians who were carrying on with their usual jobs.

Madame Brault was sitting in the same place. She had stopped drinking coffee, but was smoking a cigarette, which went oddly with her tiny figure.

'I suppose I may?' she asked, following Maigret's glance.

He sat down facing her.

'Out with it.'

'Out with what?'

'Everything you know.'

'I've told you already.'

'How did Louise Filon spend her time?'

'I can only speak for what she did in the mornings. She got up at about ten o'clock, or rather she woke then, but didn't get up at once. I used to bring her coffee and she drank it in bed while she read and smoked.'

'What did she read?'

'Magazines and novels. She also often listened to the radio. You must have noticed that there's a set on the bedside table.'

'She didn't telephone anyone?'

'About eleven.'

'Every day?'

'Nearly every day.'

'Pierrot?'

'Yes. Sometimes about noon she dressed to go out and eat, but that wasn't very often. Most days she sent me down to the delicatessen to fetch cold meat and made-up dishes.'

'You don't know what she did with her afternoons?'

'I suppose she went out. She must have done, because every morning her shoes were dirty. I expect she hung around the shops as all women do.'

'She didn't have dinner at home?'

'There were seldom any dirty dishes.'

'She went out to meet Pierrot?'

'Him or somebody else.'

'You're sure you've never seen him?'

'Quite sure.'

'You've never seen any other man here either?'

'Only the gas-man or a delivery boy.'

'How long is it since you came out of prison?'

'Six years.'

'Have you lost the itch to go shoplifting?'

'I don't have the right looks any more. . . . They're just taking the body away.'

A noise could be heard in the sitting-room, and it was in fact the men from the *Institut Médico-Légal*.

'She didn't enjoy it for long!'

'What do you mean?'

'She had a wretched life until she was twenty-four, and then she hardly had more than two years in the good.'

'She confided in you?'

'We talked like human beings.'

'Did she tell you where she came from?'

'She was born in the XVIIIth *arrondissement*, practically in the gutter. She spent most of her life in the Chapelle district. When she moved in here, she thought she was in for a lovely life.'

'She wasn't happy?'

The charwoman shrugged her shoulders and gave Maigret a pitying glance, as if she were surprised to find him so lacking in understanding.

'Do you think it was fun for her to live in a house like this, where people wouldn't condescend to look at her when they passed her on the stairs?'

'Why did she come here?'

'She must have had her reasons.'

'Was it her musician who kept her?'

'Who's been talking about a musician?'

'Never mind. Pierrot is a saxophonist?'

'I think so. I know that he plays in a dance-hall.'

She said only what she chose to tell. Now that Maigret had a slightly clearer idea of the sort of girl Louise Filon was, he was convinced that the two women had spent their mornings chattering freely to one another.

'I do not think,' he said, 'that a dance-band musician could have been in a position to pay the rent of a flat like this.'

'Nor do I.'

'So?'

'So there must have been someone else,' she admitted calmly.

'Pierrot came to see her yesterday evening.'

She showed no surprise, but kept looking him straight in the eye.

'I suppose you decided straight off that it was he who killed her? There's only one thing I can tell you: they were very much in love.'

'She told you so?'

'Not only were they in love, but their one thought was to get married.'

'Why didn't they?'

'Perhaps because they had no money. Perhaps because the other one wouldn't let her go.'

'The other one?'

'You know as well as I do that I mean the man who paid the rent. Do I have to draw a diagram?'

A thought came to Maigret and he went into the bedroom and opened the cupboard. He pulled out a pair of men's slippers in glacé kid, made to measure by a boot-maker in the Rue Saint-Honoré who was one of the most exclusive in Paris. Taking the heavy silk dressing-gown down from the peg, he observed the label of a shirt-maker in the Rue de Rivoli.

Moers's men had already left. Moers himself was waiting for Maigret in the sitting-room.

'What have you discovered?'

'Finger-prints, of course, both old and new.'

'A man's?'

'One man's, at least. We shall have them developed within the hour.'

'Send them to the Index Office. You may take away these slippers and the dressing-gown. At the Quai, hand them over to Janvier or Torrence. I should like them to be shown to the shops where they were bought.'

'The slippers will be easy, I think; they're marked with the maker's number.'

Once more quiet enveloped the flat, and Maigret went to look for the charwoman in the kitchen.

'You needn't stay any longer.'

'Can I clean up?'

'Not today.'

'What shall I do?'

'You may go home. But you are forbidden to leave Paris. It may be . . .'

'I understand.'

'You're sure you've nothing more to tell me?'

'If I remember anything else, I'll let you know.'

'One more question. You're sure that from the moment you found the body to the moment the police arrived, you never left the flat?'

'I'll take my oath.'

'And nobody called?'

'Not even a cat.'

She unhooked her shopping bag, which she probably always carried with her, and Maigret made certain that it held no revolver.

'You can search me, if you wish.'

He did not search her, but for conscience' sake, and not without feeling embarrassed by it, he ran his hands over her baggy dress.

'Once upon a time you might have enjoyed doing that!'

She took her leave, and on the stairs must have passed Lucas, whose hat and coat were wet.

'Raining?'

'For the past ten minutes. What shall I do, Chief?'

'I don't know exactly. I should like you to stay here. If anyone telephones, try to find out where the call is coming from. It may be that someone will ring at about eleven. Tell the office to tap the wire. As for the rest, just make a thorough search. It's been done already, but one never knows.'

'What's it all about exactly?'

'A prostitute who had her beat in the Barbès district. Someone set her up here. So far as we can tell, she had a dance-band player for a steady lover.'

'Did he kill her?'

'He came to see her last night. The concierge declares that nobody else went up.'

'Have you a description of him?'

'I am just going down to interview the concierge again.'

The concierge was busily sorting out the second post. According to her, Pierrot was a young man of about thirty, fair and thickset, who looked more like a butcher's apprentice than a musician.

'You've nothing else to tell me?'

'Nothing, Monsieur Maigret. If I remember anything I shall let you know.'

It was strange. Almost the same reply as the charwoman had given. Maigret was certain that both of them, doubtless for different reasons, were trying to avoid telling him all they knew.

As he would indubitably have to walk as far as the Etoile before finding a taxi, he put up his overcoat collar and set off, hands in pockets, just like the people whom Madame Maigret had watched from the window that morning. The fog had turned into a fine cold rain which put him in mind of a cold in the head, and at the corner of the street he stopped at a bar to drink a hot toddy.

## II

JANVIER was the one who checked up on the man named Pierrot, and reconstructed his actions and movements up to the moment when the musician had chosen to vanish.

A little before eleven-thirty, Lucas, who was quietly ferreting about in the flat in the Avenue Carnot, had at last heard the telephone ring. He lifted the receiver, taking care to say nothing. At the other end a man's voice had murmured:

'Is that you?'

Before he grew suspicious of the silence that greeted him, Pierrot had added:

'You aren't alone?'

And then anxiously:

'Hello! Is that Carnot 22–35?'

'Carnot 22–35. Yes.'

Over the telephone Lucas could hear the man's breathing. He was calling from a public booth, probably in a bar, for there had been the characteristic noise of a telephone-token falling in the metal box.

After a moment, the musician hung up. Lucas had merely to wait for a call from the official at the switch-board. This took hardly a couple of minutes.

'Lucas? Your man was calling from a *bistrot* on the Boulevard

Rochechouart, at the corner of the Rue Riquet. Its name is Chez Léon.'

Lucas immediately telephoned the police station in the Goutte d'Or district, a few steps from the Boulevard Rochechouart.

'May I speak to Inspector Janin?'

As it happened, he was in the office. Lucas gave him a rough description of Pierrot and told him the name of the bar.

'Don't do anything until Janvier joins you.'

Then he got Janvier on the line. Meanwhile the rain was still falling on a world of brick, stone and concrete, through which dark shadows with umbrellas flitted by. Maigret was in his office, his collar undone and four stuffed pipes set before him, finishing off an administrative report that had to be delivered by midday. Janvier pushed the office door half-open.

'He's telephoned, sir. We know where he is. Lucas has warned the Goutte d'Or district and Janin ought to be on the spot already. I'm pushing down there now. What shall I do with him?'

The inspector looked up with heavy tired eyes.

'Bring him to me, gently.'

'Are you going out to lunch?'

'I shall have sandwiches sent up.'

Janvier used one of the little black P.J. cars which he stopped some distance away from the bar. The *bistrot* was long and narrow, with so much steam on the windows that it was impossible to see inside. When he opened the door, he saw Janin waiting for him, drinking a *vermouth-cassis*. There were only four other customers. The tiled floor was covered with sawdust, the walls were a dirty yellow, and the telephone booth stood by the wash-rooms.

'Has he gone?'

Janin, as he shook hands, nodded yes. The proprietor, who must have known the local policeman, asked Janvier in slightly ironical tones:

'Have a drink?'

'A *bock*.'

The customers were watching them. Janin must have already interrogated them.

'It's safe to talk,' he said in a low voice. 'He came in at ten-forty-five, as he usually does.'

'Does the proprietor know his name?'

'He only knows that he's called Pierrot; that he's a musician and must live in the neighbourhood. Every morning he comes in here at ten-forty-five to have his coffee. Generally, at eleven o'clock he has a telephone call. This morning nobody called him. He waited half an hour and then went into the booth. When he came out he looked worried. He paused for a moment at the bar; then he paid and left.'

'Do they know where he has his lunch?'

'The proprietor claims he doesn't know. Do you need me any more?'

'I don't know. Let's go.'

Outside, Janvier glanced up the Rue Riquet; it was a very short street in which hung signs of two hotels that probably let rooms by the hour.

If it was Pierrot's habit to take his morning coffee in this bar, it was likely that he lived just round the corner.

'Shall we go and see?'

The first lodging-house was called the Hotel du Var. To the right of the corridor was an office, and in it an old woman.

'Is Pierrot in?'

Janin, who would be well known to her, took care not to show himself and Janvier, of all the officers in the P.J., looked least like a policeman.

'It's more than an hour since he went out.'

'You're sure he hasn't come back?'

'Quite sure. I haven't stirred from the office. Besides, his key's on the rack.'

Suddenly she caught sight of Janin who had stepped forward a few paces.

'Oh! That's it, is it? What do you want with the boy?'

'Hand me the register. How long has he been living here?'

'More than a year. He rents a room by the month.'

She reached for the register and turned over the pages.

'Look. This house is above board.'

Pierrot's real name was Pierre Eyraud; he was twenty-nine and born in Paris.

'What time does he usually come in?'

'Sometimes he comes back in the early afternoon. Sometimes not.'

'Does he bring women in with him?'

'They all do.'

'Always the same girl?'

She did not hold back for long. She knew that if she did not toe the line, Janin would find a hundred opportunities for making trouble for her.

'You must know her, Monsieur Janin. She hung about this district long enough. It's Lulu.'

'Lulu who?'

'I don't know. I've always called her Lulu. A nice girl, and she's struck it lucky. Now she has fur coats and all, and comes in a taxi.'

Janvier inquired:

'Did you see her yesterday?'

'No, not yesterday; the day before. That was Sunday, wasn't it? She arrived just before midday with some small parcels and they had lunch upstairs. Later they went out arm in arm—to the cinema, I suppose.'

'Give me the key.'

She shrugged her shoulders. Refusing would do no good.

'Do your best so that he won't notice you've searched his room. He'd blame it on me.'

By way of precaution, Janin stayed downstairs; among other things, to stop the old woman from telephoning Pierre Eyraud and giving him the news. All the doors were open on the first floor, which contained the rooms hired for an hour or for less. Higher up, the weekly and monthly tenants lived, and various noises could be heard from behind their doors; evidently there was another musician in the hotel, for someone was playing an accordion.

Janvier reached number 53, which looked out on the courtyard. The bed was an iron one, and the rug worn and faded, as was the table-cover. On the wash-stand lay a toothbrush, a tube of toothpaste, a comb, a shaving-brush and a razor. A large, unlocked suitcase in a corner served as a receptacle for dirty linen.

In the cupboard Janvier found only one suit, an old pair of trousers, a grey felt hat and a cap. As for Pierrot's linen, it consisted solely of three or four shirts, some pairs of socks and underpants. Another drawer was filled with sheets of music. From the lower shelf of the bedside-table he unearthed a pair of women's bedroom slippers, and, hanging behind the door, a dressing-gown in salmon-pink crêpe-de-chine.

By the time he came downstairs, Janin had had a chat with the landlady.

'I've got the address of two or three restaurants where he usually eats his lunch, sometimes in one, sometimes in another.'

Janvier took no notice until they were in the street.

'You had better stay here,' he told Janin. 'When the evening papers are on the streets, he will find out what has happened to his girl-friend, if he doesn't know it already. Perhaps he will drop in at the hotel.'

'You think he did it?'

'The boss has told me nothing.'

Janvier set off first for an Italian restaurant on the Boulevard Rochechouart; a quiet comfortable place which smelt of highly seasoned cooking. Two waitresses in black·and white hustled around the tables, but nobody answered to Pierrot's description.

'Have you seen Pierre Eyraud?'

'The musician? No. He hasn't appeared. What day is it? Tuesday? I should be surprised if he did come; it isn't his day.'

The second restaurant on the list was a brasserie near the Barbès crossroads; nobody there had seen Pierrot, either.

The last chance remained; it was a drivers' café, painted yellow outside, and with a bill of fare chalked on a slate hanging on the door. The proprietor was behind the counter, pouring out wine. One young girl, tall and thin, was the only waitress, and the proprietor's wife could be seen in the kitchen.

Janvier approached the zinc-topped bar and asked for a *bock*; the customers must all have been regulars, for they watched him with curiosity.

'I have no draught beer,' the proprietor said. 'Won't you have a glass of Beaujolais?'

Janvier nodded, and paused a few moments before he asked:

'Has Pierrot been in?'

'The musician?'

'Yes. He made an appointment with me here for twelve-fifteen.'

It was twelve-forty-five.

'If you'd come at twelve-fifteen, you would have found him.'

They were unsuspecting; for Janvier's attitude seemed quite straightforward.

'He didn't wait for me?'

'To tell you the truth, he didn't even finish his lunch.'

'Someone came to fetch him?'

'No. He left suddenly, saying he was in a hurry.'

'What time was that?'

'About a quarter of an hour ago.'

Janvier, who was glancing round the tables, noticed that two of the customers were reading the afternoon papers over their lunch. One table near the window had not yet been cleared. There, by the side of a plate of veal stew, a paper lay spread out.

'He was sitting there?'

'Yes.'

Janvier had some two hundred yards to walk through the rain in order to join Janin, who was on duty in the Rue Riquet.

'Has he returned?'

'I've seen no one.'

'Less than half an hour ago, he was sitting in a little restaurant. A newspaper-seller passed by, and as soon as he caught a glimpse of the front page, he rushed away. I had better telephone the boss.'

At the Quai des Orfèvres, a tray stood on Maigret's desk bearing two huge sandwiches and two bottles of beer. The inspector listened to Janvier's report.

'Try to find out the name of the dance-hall where he works. His landlady probably knows it. It must be somewhere in the district. Tell Janin to continue watching the hotel.'

Maigret was right. The landlady knew. She, too, had a newspaper in her office but she had not connected the Louise Filon of the headlines with the Lulu whom she knew. In any case, all the paper said in its first edition was:

*A certain Louise Filon, of no profession, was found dead this morning by her charwoman in a flat in the Avenue Carnot. She had been killed by a revolver bullet fired at point-blank range, probably yesterday evening. Robbery does not seem to have been the motive for the murder. Inspector Maigret is personally conducting the investigation, and we understand that he is already following a promising line of inquiry.*

Pierrot worked at the Grelot, a dance-hall in the Rue Charbonnière, almost on the corner of the Boulevard de la Chapelle. It was in the same district, but in the least savoury part of it. As soon as he reached the Boulevard de la Chapelle, Janvier came upon Arabs wandering about in the rain, looking as if they had nothing to do. Besides the Arabs, there were other men, and women too, hanging about in broad daylight and, in spite of the regulations, waiting to pick up customers on the steps of the hotels.

The front of the Grelot was painted mauve, and in the evenings its lighting was evidently also mauve. At this time of day, no one was to be seen inside except the proprietor, engaged at lunch with a middle-aged woman who may have been his wife. He scrutinized Janvier, who had shut the door behind him, and Janvier sensed that the man at first glance had guessed his profession.

'What do you want? The bar doesn't open until five.'

Janvier displayed his badge, and the proprietor didn't move a muscle. He was short and broad, with the nose and ears of an ex-boxer. Above the dance-floor there hung from the wall a sort of balcony to which the band had to climb by a ladder.

'Well, then?'

'Is Pierrot here?'

The proprietor gazed round the empty room, and said no more than:

'Can you see him?'

'He hasn't been here today?'

'He doesn't start work in the evenings until seven o'clock. Sometimes he looks in at four or five o'clock for a game of *belote*.'

'Was he at work yesterday?'

Janvier at once saw that he was on to something, for the man and woman had exchanged glances.

'What has he done?' the proprietor cautiously asked.

'Perhaps nothing. I just have one or two questions to put to him.'

'Why?'

The inspector staked all on one throw.

'Because Lulu is dead.'

'What? What are you saying?'

He was genuinely surprised. And there was no newspaper in sight.

'When did she die?'

'Last night.'

'What happened to her?'

'Did you know her?'

'There was a time when she used to be a regular. She was here nearly every night. I mean about two years ago.'

'But since then?'

'She came from time to time, for a drink and to listen to the band.'

'What time yesterday evening did Pierrot take time off?'

'Who told you he'd taken time off?'

'The concierge at the Avenue Carnot, who knows him well, saw him enter the block, and leave again a quarter of an hour later.'

The proprietor was silent for a full minute, making up his mind what line to take. He, too, was at the mercy of the police.

'Tell me first what happened to Lulu.'

'She's been murdered.'

'Not by Pierrot!' he retorted emphatically.

'I didn't say it was by Pierrot.'

'Then what do you want with him?'

'I need certain information. You maintain that he worked here last night?'

'I maintain nothing. It's the truth. At seven o'clock he was up there playing his saxophone.'

With a glance he indicated the hanging platform.

'But about nine o'clock he left?'

'He had a telephone call. It was nine-twenty.'

'From Lulu?'

'I don't know, but very likely.'

'I do know,' his wife said. 'I was near the telephone.'

The telephone was not in a booth, but in a recess in the wall, next to the wash-room door.

'He told her:

' "I'll be round at once."

'Then he turned to me:

' "Mélanie, I simply must slip round there."

'I asked him:

' "Something wrong?"

'He answered:

' "It seems so."

'And he climbed up to speak to the rest of the band before rushing out.'

'What time did he come back?'

It was the man's turn to reply:

'A little before eleven.'

'Did he seem excited?'

'I didn't notice. He apologized for his absence and went back to his place. He played until one in the morning. Then, as usual after closing-time, he had a drink with us. If he had known that Lulu was dead, he would never have had the nerve to do that. He was crazy about her. And it didn't date from yesterday. Many a time I've told him:

' "Pierrot, my boy, you're making a mistake. You have to take women for what they're worth and . . ." '

His wife interrupted him dryly:

'Thanks?'

'Ah, that's not the same thing at all.'

'Lulu wasn't in love with him?'

'Of course she was.'

'But she had another man, too?'

'A saxophonist couldn't keep her in a flat in the Etoile district.'

'Do you know who he was?'

'She never told me, nor did Pierrot. All I know is that her life changed after her operation.'

'What operation?'

'Two years ago she was taken very ill. She lived round here then.'

'She walked the streets?'

The man shrugged his shoulders:

'What else do they do round here?'

'Go on.'

'She was taken to hospital, and when Pierrot came back from seeing her, he said there was no hope. It was something to do with her head, I don't know what. Two days later, they took her to another hospital on the Left Bank. They performed God knows what operation on her, and in a few weeks she was cured. Only she never came back to these parts afterwards, except on a visit.'

'So she set up immediately in the Avenue Carnot?'

'Can you remember?' the proprietor asked his wife.

'Yes, I do. At first she had a flat in the Rue La Fayette.'

When Janvier returned to the Quai des Orfèvres, about three o'clock, he knew nothing more. Maigret was still in his office, in his shirt-sleeves, for the room was over-heated and the air blue with tobacco-smoke.

'Sit down. Tell me everything.'

Janvier recounted what he had done and what he had discovered.

'I have ordered the stations to be watched,' the inspector said, when Janvier had finished. 'Up to now, Pierrot has not tried to catch a train.'

He showed him an identification card on which there were full-face and profile photographs of a man who did not look thirty, but much younger.

'Is that Pierrot?'

'Yes. He was first arrested when he was twenty for assault and battery during a brawl in a bar in the Rue de Flandre. The second time, a year and a half later, he was suspected of being an accomplice in the robbery of a client, committed by a prostitute with whom he was living, but nothing was proved. He was last arrested when he was twenty-four for living on immoral earnings. At that time he had no job and was dependent on a girl named Ernestine. Since then, there has been nothing against him. I have circulated his description to all police stations. Is Janin still watching the hotel?'

'Yes, I thought it wise.'

'Well done. I don't think he will go back there for some time to come, but we mustn't take risks. On the other hand, I need Janin. I am going to send young Lapointe to relieve him. You see, I should be surprised if Pierrot did try to leave Paris. He has spent his entire life in a district he knows like the back of his hand, and it is easy for him to vanish in it. Janin is more at home in that district than we are. Get Lapointe.'

Lapointe listened to his instructions and rushed out into the street as eagerly as if the whole investigation rested with him.

'I have also looked up Louise Filon's file.

'Between the ages of fifteen and twenty-four she was picked up more than a hundred times by the Black Maria, taken to the station, examined, placed under observation and for the most part released again within a few days.

'That's all,' Maigret said with a sigh, knocking out his pipe on his heel. 'Or rather it is not quite all, but the rest is more indefinite.'

Perhaps he was really talking to himself, to sort out his ideas, but Janvier was none the less flattered at being taken into his confidence.

'Somewhere there lives the man who set Lulu up in the Avenue Carnot flat. First thing this morning, it bothered me to find a girl like her living in that house. You know what I mean?'

'Yes.'

It was not the kind of block of flats in which kept women are usually found. It was not even the right district. The house in the Avenue Carnot smelt of the respectable, well-to-do middle-classes, and it was surprising that the proprietor or manager should have accepted a prostitute as a tenant.

'It first occurred to me that if her lover installed here there, it was to keep her near his own home. Now the fact is that, if the concierge is telling the truth, Lulu received no callers except for Pierrot. Nor did she go out regularly, and it sometimes happened that she stayed at home for a whole week on end.'

'I think I understand.'

'Understand what?'

Janvier confessed with a blush:

'I don't know.'

'Nor do I. I am only making assumptions. The man's slippers and dressing-gown found in the cupboard certainly did not belong to the saxophonist. At the shirt-makers in the Rue de Rivoli they cannot say who bought the dressing-gown. They have hundreds of customers and don't record the names of cash customers. As for the shoe-maker, he's a real character who claims that he has no time to examine his books at present, but promises to do so one of these days. The fact remains that some man other than Pierrot used to call on her, and was sufficiently intimate with her to wear his dressing-gown and slippers. If the concierge never caught sight of him . . .'

'Then he must have lived in the same block?'

'That's the logical explanation.'

'Have you a list of the tenants?'

'Lucas has just let me have it by telephone.'

Janvier wondered why his chief had assumed his cross-tempered look, as if something in this case displeased him.

'What you have told me about Lulu's illness and her operation might provide a clue, and in that event . . .'

He paused to light his pipe, and bent over the list of names on his desk.

'Do you know who lives immediately above her flat? Professor Gouin, the surgeon, who, as it happens, is the greatest specialist in brain operations.'

Janvier's reaction was to ask:

'Is he married?'

'Yes, he's married, and his wife lives with him.'

'What are you going to do?'

'First, have a talk with the concierge. Even if she did tell me the truth this morning, she certainly didn't tell me the whole truth. Perhaps I shall also go to see Madame Brault, who's probably in the same boat.'

'What do you want me to do?'

'Stay here. When Janin telephones, ask him to start a search for Pierrot in his district. Send a photograph over to him.'

It was five o'clock, and night was falling as Maigret crossed town in a police car. That morning, when his wife was looking out of the window to see how people were dressed, an odd idea had crossed his mind. It had occurred to him that the day exactly fulfilled his general conception of what a 'working day' should be like. Those two words had entered his head quite irrationally, as one suddenly recalls the refrain of a song. It was a day on which it was unthinkable that people should go out of doors for pleasure, or that they should find any place at all in which to enjoy themselves; it was a day in which to be busy, to do grimly what had to be done, splashing through the rain into

Metro stations, shops and offices, surrounded by damp monotonous greyness.

So had passed his own working day; his office was as warm as an oven, and he could work up little interest in the event when he once more arrived in the Avenue Carnot, where the huge stone block of flats seemed totally devoid of attraction. That fine fellow, Lucas, was still there, in the third-floor flat, and Maigret observed him from below, parting the curtains and gazing gloomily into the street.

Sitting in front of the round table in the lodge, the concierge was busily mending sheets. Wearing her spectacles, she looked older. It was warm in here too, and peaceful, with an old clock ticking, and the gas-stove in the kitchen hissing.

'Don't worry. I've just come in to have a little chat.'

'Are you sure that she was murdered?' she asked as he was taking off his overcoat and sitting down, familiarly, facing her.

'Unless someone removed the gun after she died, which seems unlikely. The charwoman was only a few minutes alone up there, and before she left I made sure that she was taking nothing away with her. Of course, I did not put her through a thorough search. What are you thinking about, Madame Cornet?'

'Nothing in particular. Just about that poor girl.'

'You're sure you told me this morning everything you know?'

He saw her blush, and bend her head over her needle-work. A few moments went by before she said:

'Why do you ask me that?'

'Because I have an idea that you know the man who set up Louise Filon in this house. Was it you who let him the flat?'

'No. It was the manager.'

'I shall go and see him; no doubt he'll be better informed. I think I shall also go up to the fourth floor where I have some inquiries to make.'

At this she quickly looked up.

'To the fourth floor?'

'That's Professor Gouin's flat, isn't it? I understand his wife and he occupy the whole floor.'

'Yes.'

She had recovered her composure. He went on:

'In any case, I can ask them if they heard anything yesterday evening. Were they in?'

'Madame Gouin was.'

'All day?'

'Yes. Her sister came to see her and stayed till eleven-thirty.'

'And the Professor?'

'He left for the hospital at eight o'clock.'

'When did he return?'

'About eleven-fifteen. A little after that, his sister-in-law left.'

'Does the Professor often visit the hospital at night?'

'Not very often. Only when there is an emergency case.'

'Is he upstairs at present?'

'No. He hardly ever comes home before dinner-time. He has an office in his flat, but he doesn't receive patients here save in exceptional circumstances.'

'I shall go and speak to his wife.'

She watched him rise and walk to the chair on which he had placed his overcoat. He was about to open the door when she murmured:

'Monsieur Maigret!'

He had been rather expecting this, and turned round, smiling slightly. While she was groping for words, with an almost pleading expression, he observed:

'So he's the one?'

She misunderstood him.

'You don't mean to say it was the Professor who . . . ?'

'Certainly not. That's not what I meant. What I am almost sure about is that the Professor introduced Louise Filon into this house.'

Reluctantly she nodded.

'Why didn't you tell me?'

'You did not ask me.'

'I asked you if you knew the man who . . .'

'No. You asked me whether I sometimes saw anyone else go up to the flat besides the musician.'

Discussion was useless.

'Has the Professor asked you to keep mum?'

'No. It doesn't matter to him.'

'How do you know?'

'Because he is never secretive.'

'Then why didn't you tell me? . . .'

'I don't know. I didn't think there was any point in implicating him. He saved my son's life. He operated on him free of charge, and treated him for over two years.'

'Where is your son?'

'In the army. In Indo-China.'

'Does Madame Gouin know the truth?'

'Yes. She's not jealous; she's used to it.'

'In short, the whole house knew that Lulu was the Professor's mistress?'

'If they didn't know, it was because they didn't care to. The tenants here don't bother about one another's affairs. He often went down to the third floor wearing pyjamas and a dressing-gown.'

'What sort of a man is he?'

'Don't you know him?'

She looked at Maigret with a disappointed air. The inspector had often seen Gouin's picture in the papers but had never had occasion to meet him personally.

'He must be nearly sixty, isn't he?'

'Sixty-two. He doesn't look it. Besides for men like him, age doesn't matter.'

Maigret dimly remembered a powerful head, with a strong nose and determined chin, but with cheeks a little sunken and bags under the eyes. It was amusing to see the concierge speaking of him as enthusiastically as a young girl might about her piano-teacher.

'You don't know whether he saw her yesterday before he left for the hospital?'

'I told you that it was only eight o'clock, and the young man came in later.'

All that interested her was to keep Gouin out of it.

'But after he returned?'

She was obviously groping for the best reply.

'Certainly not.'

'Why?'

'Because his sister-in-law came down some minutes after he went up.'

'You think that he met his sister-in-law?'

'I expect she was waiting for him to arrive before she left.'

'You're warmly defending him, Madame Cornet.'

'I am only telling the truth.'

'As Madame Gouin is in the know, there's no reason why I shouldn't go to see her.'

'Do you think that's tactful?'

'Perhaps not. You're right.'

Nevertheless, he started for the door.

'Where are you going?'

'Upstairs. I shall leave the door half-open, and when the Professor comes in I shall ask him for a moment's interview.'

'I suppose you must.'

'Thank you.'

He thought her likeable. Now the door was shut, he turned round to look at her through the glass. She had risen, and seeing him, seemed to regret having moved so quickly. She entered the kitchen as if she had something urgent to do, but he was convinced it was not to the kitchen she had meant to run; much more likely, it was to the table near the window where the telephone stood.

'WHERE did you find it?' Maigret asked Lucas.

'On the top shelf in the kitchen cupboard.'

It was a white cardboard shoe-box, and Lucas had left on the table the red string with which it had been tied when he found it. Its contents reminded Maigret of other 'treasures' that he had so often come across in the country or among poor people—the marriage lines, a few yellowing letters, perhaps a pawnbroker's receipt—not always kept in a box, but sometimes in the best soup-tureen or fruit-dish.

Louise Filon's treasures were not so very different from these. They contained no marriage lines, but a birth certificate issued at the town hall in the XVIIIth *arrondissement*, stating that the said Louise Marie Josephine Filon was born in Paris, the daughter of a certain Louis Filon, tripe-seller, resident in the Rue de Cambrai, near the slaughterhouses of La Vilette, and of Philippine Le Flem, washerwoman.

The photograph, taken by a local photographer, was probably of the mother. The traditional backcloth displayed a park with a balustrade in the foreground. The woman, who must have been about thirty when the picture was taken, had not managed to summon up a smile at the photographer's command, and she stared straight ahead. She must have borne several other children besides Louise, for her figure was gross and her breasts hung flabbily in her bodice.

Lucas had seated himself in the armchair he had been occupying before opening the door for the inspector. The latter could not help smiling when he came in, for lying open, near the cigarette burning in an ash-tray, was one of Lulu's pot-boilers which the sergeant must have picked up out of boredom, and nearly half of which he had read.

'She died,' Lucas said, pointing to the photograph, 'seven years ago.'

He handed his chief an old newspaper cutting from the births, deaths and marriages column, listing the persons deceased on that day; among them was the name of Philippine Filon, née Le Flem.

The two men had left the door half-open, and Maigret had an ear cocked for the sound of the lift. The only time that it had been used, it had stopped at the second floor.

'What about her father?'

'Only this letter.'

It was written in pencil on cheap paper, and the handwriting was of someone who had not had much schooling.

'*My dear Louise,*
*This is just to say that I am in hospital again and in a very bad way. Perhaps you will be kind enough to send me a little tobacco money. They say that*

*it is not good for me to eat and they are letting me die of hunger. I am sending this letter to a bar where someone here says he saw you. I expect they will know you there. I shan't make old bones.*

*Father.*

At the top was the name of a hospital at Béziers in Hérault. As there was no date, it was impossible to tell when the letter had been written, though to judge by the yellowing paper, it must have been two or three years ago.

Had Louise Filon received any other letters? Why had she kept only this one? Was it because her father had died shortly afterwards?

'You can find out from Béziers.'

'Very good, Chief.'

Maigret discovered no more letters, only photographs, most of them taken at fairs, some showing Louise alone, and others accompanied by Pierrot. There were also identity pictures of the girl, taken by automatic machines.

The rest consisted of small odds and ends, won at the fair—a china dog, an ash-tray, an elephant in spun glass, and even some paper flowers.

It would have been quite natural to have unearthed such petty treasures in the Barbès district or around the Boulevard de la Chapelle. Here in an Avenue Carnot flat the cardboard box became almost tragic.

'Nothing else?'

As Lucas was about to reply, they were startled by the ringing of the telephone. Maigret quickly lifted the receiver.

'Hello!' he said.

'Is Monsieur Maigret there?' said a woman's voice.

'Speaking.'

'I am sorry to trouble you, Inspector. I spoke to your office and they told me that you were probably here or on your way. This is Madame Gouin speaking.'

'Yes, madame.'

'May I come down and have a talk with you?'

'Wouldn't it be easier if I came up to you?'

The voice was firm. It continued so as she replied:

'I'd rather come down, so that my husband won't find you in our flat when he returns.'

'As you wish.'

'I'll come at once.'

Maigret had time to breathe a word to Lucas:

'It's Professor Gouin's wife, who lives on the next floor.'

A few seconds later they heard steps on the staircase, then someone passed through the front door, which was open, and shut it. There was a knock on the half-open vestibule door and Maigret stepped forward, saying:

'Come in, madame.'

She did so with poise, as she might have entered any other flat, and, without looking round the room, fixed her eyes at once on Maigret.

'May I introduce Sergeant Lucas. If you would like to sit down?'

'Thank you.'

She was tall and well-made, without being stout. If Gouin was sixty-two, she was probably forty-five, and scarcely looked it.

'I suppose you were rather expecting me to call,' she said with the hint of a smile.

'The concierge warned you?'

She hesitated a moment, her eyes on his, and her smile became more pronounced.

'Yes, she did. She has just telephoned me.'

'Then you knew I was here. If you telephoned my office, it was merely to make your actions seem spontaneous.'

She blushed faintly, and lost none of her self-possession.

'I should have suspected that you'd guess. But, believe me, I would have got into touch with you anyway. Ever since this morning, when I heard what had happened here, I've been meaning to talk to you.'

'Why didn't you do so?'

'Perhaps because I'd have preferred my husband to be kept out of this business.'

Maigret had not ceased observing her. He noted that she had not spared a glance for their surroundings, nor shown any sign of curiosity.

'When were you last in this flat, madame?'

Once more there was a slight blush on her cheeks, but she parried gamely.

'Ah! so you know that too? Yet nobody could have told you. Not even Madame Cornet.'

She thought for a moment, but did not take long to find an answer to the riddle.

'I probably didn't behave like someone entering a flat for the first time, especially a flat that has been the scene of a murder.'

Lucas was now sitting on the sofa, almost on the spot occupied that morning by Louise Filon's corpse. Madame Gouin had settled into an armchair, and Maigret was standing, his back to the fireplace, which was filled with sham logs.

'In any case, I will tell you. One night, seven or eight months ago, the person who lived here called me, in a state of panic, because my husband had just suffered a heart attack.'

'Was he in the bedroom?'

'Yes, I came down and gave him first aid.'

'You've studied medicine?'

'Before we married I was a nurse.'

Ever since she had appeared, Maigret had been wondering what class she belonged to, without being able to find the answer. Now he had a better understanding of her kind of self-possession.

'Go on.'

'That's almost all. I was going to telephone one of our doctor friends, when Etienne came to and forbade me to call anyone.'

'Was he surprised to find you at his bedside?'

'No. He always kept me informed. He never kept anything from me. That night he came upstairs with me and finally went peacefully to sleep.'

'Was that his first attack?'

'He had had a milder one three years earlier.'

She was composed and self-possessed, as if she were still in nurse's uniform and at a patient's bedside. Lucas was the one who was astonished; he was not up to date on the situation, and did not understand how a wife could speak so calmly about her husband's mistress.

'Why,' Maigret asked, 'did you want to talk to me tonight?'

'The concierge told me that you intend to question my husband. I wondered whether this could be avoided, and whether you might not get the information you want by interviewing me. Do you know the Professor?'

'Only by repute.'

'He is an outstanding man; there are only one or two like him in each generation.'

The inspector nodded in agreement.

'He dedicates his whole life to his work which is a real mission for him. Besides his lectures and consultations at the Cochin Hospital, it often happens that he performs three or four operations a day, and, as I expect you know, they are extremely delicate operations. You can't be surprised that I do my utmost to spare him any worry.'

'Have you seen your husband since Louise Filon's death?'

'He came in to lunch. This morning, when he left, there was already some activity in the flat, but we knew nothing then.'

'What was his attitude at lunch?'

'It has been a blow for him.'

'He was in love with her?'

She looked at him for an instant without replying. Then she glanced at Lucas whose presence she seemed to find irksome.

'From what I have heard of you, Monsieur Maigret, I think you are a man of understanding. It is precisely because other people wouldn't understand that I wanted to prevent the news of this affair from spreading. The Professor is a man who ought not to be subject to ill-natured gossip, and his work is too precious for everybody to run the risk of reducing its value by causing him unnecessary worry.'

In spite of himself, the inspector glanced at the spot where Lulu's corpse had lain that morning, as if in commentary on the words 'unnecessary worry.'

'May I try to give you a sketch of his character?'

'Please do.'

'You probably know that he was born into a poor peasant family in the Cevennes?'

'I knew he came from peasant stock.'

'What he has achieved, he has done by sheer will-power. It might be said, almost without exaggerating, that he never had a childhood, nor a youth. You follow what I mean?'

'Indeed I do.'

'He is a kind of force of nature. Although I am his wife, I may add that he is a man of genius, for other people have said so before me, and they will go on saying so.'

Maigret again agreed.

'People in general have a curious attitude towards geniuses. They are quite prepared to admit that they are different from others where intelligence and professional activity are concerned. Any patient will think it normal that Gouin should get up at two in the morning to perform an urgent operation which he alone can carry out, and at nine o'clock be in the hospital attending to his other cases. Yet these same patients would be shocked to learn that in other ways, too, he is different from them.'

Maigret could guess what was to follow, but he preferred to let her talk. Besides, she was doing so with a convincing calmness.

'Etienne has never bothered with the minor pleasures of life. He has, as it were, no friends. I do not remember him taking a real holiday. The energy he uses up is unbelievable. And the only way in which he has ever been able to relax is with women.'

She glanced at Lucas, and turned back to Maigret.

'I hope I haven't shocked you?'

'Not at all.'

'You do know what I mean? He isn't a man who would pay court to women. He hasn't the patience, nor the inclination. What he wants from them is a brutal release, and I do not think he has ever been really in love in his life.'

'Not even with you?'

'I've often wondered. I don't know. We have been married now for twenty-two years. At that time, he was a bachelor living with an old housekeeper.'

'In this house?'

'Yes. He took the lease of our flat by chance when he was thirty and he has never thought of moving since, even when he was appointed to Cochin which is at the other end of the town.'

'Did you work for him?'

'Yes. I suppose I can speak freely.'

The presence of Lucas was still embarrassing her, and Lucas, who kenw it, was ill at ease, crossing and uncrossing his short legs.

'For months he paid no attention to me. Like everyone in the hospital, I knew that most of the nurses went through it some day or other, and that it was of no consequence. The next day he didn't even seem to remember. One night when I was on duty, and we had to wait for the result of a three-hour operation, he took me, without a word.'

'Were you in love with him?'

'I think I was. In any case, I admired him. A few days later I was astonished when he invited me to lunch in a restaurant in the Faubourg Saint-Jacques. He asked me whether I was married. Up to then he hadn't troubled about it. He inquired who my parents were and I told him my father was a fisherman in Brittany. Am I boring you?'

'Not at all.'

'I so much want you to understand him.'

'Are you afraid that he'll come home and be surprised not to find you?'

'Before I came down, I spoke to the Saint-Joseph Clinic, where he is operating at the moment, and I know he won't be back before half past seven.'

It was a quarter past six.

'What was I saying? Oh yes. We were lunching together and he wanted to know what my father did. Now, things get more difficult. Especially since I shouldn't like you to misunderstand. What most people don't know is that he is terribly timid, I might say morbidly timid, but only in relation to people belonging to a different social class. I suppose it was because of this that at the age of forty he was still unmarried and had never moved in what is called society. All the girls he took came from the lower classes.'

'I see.'

'With any other kind of girl I wonder whether he could have . . .'

She blushed at the words, giving them a precise meaning.

'He got used to me, while still carrying on with the others as he always had done. Then one fine day, almost absent-mindedly, he asked me to marry him. That's the whole of our story. I came to live here. I kept house for him.'

'The housekeeper left?'

'A week after our wedding. There's no need to add that I am not jealous. That would be absurd on my part.'

Maigret could not recall ever having studied someone quite so intently as he was studying this woman; she knew it, and was not intimidated; on the contrary she appeared to understand the kind of interest he was taking in her.

She was trying to tell him everything, leaving no trait of her great man's character unilluminated.

'He has gone on sleeping with the nurses, with his successive assistants, and, in fact, with every girl who comes to hand and who is not likely to complicate his life. Perhaps that is the main point. Nothing in the world would induce him to start an affair that might lose him time that he considers sacred to his work.'

'Lulu?'

'You already know she was called Lulu? I'm coming to that. You'll see that it's just as simple as the rest of it. May I fetch a glass of water?'

Lucas was about to get up, but she had already passed through the kitchen door and they could hear the tap running. When she sat down again, her lips were damp and a drop of water clung to her chin.

She was not pretty in the ordinary sense of the word, nor beautiful, in spite of her regular features. But she was attractive to look at. There was a sort of soothing influence about her. As a patient, Maigret would have enjoyed being nursed by her. She was also the kind of woman with whom one could go out lunching or dining without troubling to keep the conversation going. A girl friend, in fact, who would understand everything, and never be surprised nor shocked nor angry.

'I suppose you know how old he is?'

'Sixty-two.'

'Yes. Mind you he has lost none of his vigour. And I use the word in its fullest sense. I think, however, that all men of a certain age are terrified by the idea of losing their virility.'

While she was speaking she recollected that Maigret himself was over fifty, and suddenly stammered:

'I beg your pardon.'

'Not at all.'

For the first time they smiled at each other.

'I suppose it is the same with other men. I don't know. But the fact is that Etienne put more furious energy than ever into his sexual activities. I hope I'm not shocking you?'

'By no means.'

'About two years ago, he had a young patient, Louise Filon, whose life he quite miraculously saved. I suppose you already know what her life had been? She came from as near the gutter as anyone can, and that is probably what interested my husband.'

Maigret nodded agreement, for everything she said sounded true, and had the simplicity of a police report.

'It must have started at the hospital, when she was convalescent. Later, he set her up in a flat in the Rue La Fayette, after mentioning it to me incidentally. He never went into details. He was very reserved about such things, and still is. Unexpectedly over a meal he'd tell me what he had done or what he meant to do. I never asked him questions. And then we never spoke of it again.'

'Was it you who suggested that she should come and live in this block?'

She seemed pleased that Maigret should have guessed.

'To help you grasp it, I must give you a few more details. I apologize for taking so long. But it all hangs together. At one time Etienne used to drive his own car. Then, some years ago, four to be exact, he had a slight accident in the Place de la Concorde. He knocked down a woman, passing by, who luckily suffered nothing more than contusions. Nevertheless, he was much upset. For some months we had a chauffeur, but Etienne could never get used to it. It shocked him that a man in the prime of his life should have nothing to do but wait for him by the kerb for hours at a time. I suggested that I should drive, but that wasn't practical either, and he fell into the habit of taking taxis. The car stayed in the garage for several months and in the end we sold it.

'It is always the same taxi that comes to fetch him in the morning and does a part of his rounds with him. It is some way from here to the Faubourg Saint-Jacques. He also has patients at Neuilly, and often in the other city hospitals. To have to go to the Rue La Fayette in addition . . .'

Maigret was still nodding assent, while Lucas seemed to be dozing.

'Quite by chance, a flat fell vacant in this house.'

'One moment. Did your husband often stay the night at the Rue La Fayette?'

'Only part of the night. He insisted on being here in the morning when his assistant who acts as his secretary arrives.'

She gave a little laugh.

'In a way domestic complications brought about everything. I asked why he didn't set the girl up here.'

'You knew who she was?'

'I knew all about her, including the fact that she had a lover named Pierrot.'

'Your husband knew, too?'

'Yes. He wasn't jealous. Probably he wouldn't have liked to find him with Lulu, but so long as things happened without his knowing . . .'

'Go on. He accepted your proposal. What about her?'

'It seems that she held off for a while.'

'What in your opinion were Louise Filon's feelings for the Professor?'

Maigret was automatically beginning to speak in the same tones as Madame Gouin about this man whom he had never seen, but who seemed to be almost present in the room.

'Shall I be frank?'

'Please do.'

'In the first place, like all women who meet him, she fell under his influence. You may be thinking that this is a curious kind of pride on my part, but though he isn't what might be called handsome, and he's far from young, I knew few women who have resisted him. Instinctively, women feel his strength and . . .'

This time she could not find the words that she wanted.

'At any rate, it's a fact, and I don't think that anyone you question will deny it. It was the same with this girl as with the others. Furthermore, he had saved her life and had treated her in a way she wasn't used to being treated.'

It was all straightforward and logical.

'I am convinced, to be completely frank, that the question of money played its part. If not the money itself, at least the prospect of a certain security, of a life free from worry.'

'Did she ever speak of leaving him to follow her lover?'

'Not to my knowledge.'

'Have you ever seen this man?'

'I have passed him in the entrance-hall.'

'Did he come often?'

'In general, no. She used to meet him in the afternoons, I don't know where. But on occasion it happened that he came to see her.'

'Did your husband know?'

'He may have.'

'Would it have annoyed him?'

'Possibly, though not because of jealousy. It is hard to explain.'

'Was your husband greatly attached to this girl?'

'She owed him everything. He had practically created her, since without him she would have been dead. Perhaps he was thinking of the day when there would be no more girls for him? Then again, though this is only an assumption, with her he was ashamed of nothing.'

'And with you?'

For a moment she glanced away at the carpet.

'After all, I am a woman.'

He almost retorted:

'Whereas she was nothing!'

For that was indeed the thought she had in mind, and perhaps the Professor shared it?

He decided to say nothing. All three of them remained silent for a moment. The rain outside was still falling noiselessly. In the house opposite the windows were lit up, and a shadow moved behind the cream curtains in one of the flats.

'Tell me about yesterday evening,' Maigret eventually suggested, adding, as he held out his pipe which he had just filled:

'May I?'

'Please do.'

Up till then he had been so interested in Madame Gouin that he had not thought about smoking.

'What would you like me to tell you?'

'To begin with, a detail. Was your husband in the habit of spending the night with her?'

'Very rarely. Up above we occupy the whole floor. On the left is what we call the flat. On the right, my husband has a bedroom and bathroom, a library, another where he stacks scientific publications, on every square inch of space, finally his office and his secretary's office.'

'You sleep in separate bedrooms?'

'We always have. Our rooms are separated only by a dressing-room.'

'May I ask you an indiscreet question?'

'You are fully entitled to do so.'

'Do you still have marital relations with your husband?'

She glanced once more at poor Lucas who felt he was one too many, and did not know what to do with himself.

'Seldom.'

'You mean practically never?'

'Yes.'

'Since when?'

'For years.'

'You don't miss it?'

She was not startled, smiled, and shook her head.

'It is a confession you're asking of me, and I am ready to answer as frankly as I can. Let us say that I do miss it a bit.'

'You don't let him see that?'

'Certainly not.'

'Have you a lover?'

'The idea has never occurred to me.'

She paused, her eyes on his.

'You do believe me?'

'Yes.'

'Thank you. People don't always accept the truth. When one lives with a man like Gouin, one is prepared to make some sacrifices.'

'He used to come down to her and then go up again?'

'Yes.'

'Did he do so yesterday?'

'No. It didn't happen every day. Sometimes a few minutes' visit satisfied him for nearly a week. It depended on his work. Probably it depended, too, on what opportunities he found elsewhere.'

'He didn't stop having relations with other women?'

'The kind of relations I have described.'

'And yesterday . . . ?'

'He saw her for a few minutes after dinner. I know because he didn't take the lift when he left, which is a sure sign.'

'How can you be certain that he only stayed a few minutes?'

'Because I heard him come out of this flat and ring for the lift.'

'You were spying on him?'

'You are a terror, Monsieur Maigret. Yes, I was spying on him, as I always do, not because of jealousy, but . . . How shall I explain without seeming conceited? Because I consider it my duty to protect him, to know everything he does, where he is, and to follow him in my thoughts.'

'What time was it?'

'About eight o'clock. We had eaten dinner quickly, because he had to spend the evening at Cochin. He was anxious about the results of an operation he had performed that afternoon and he wanted to be within reach of the patient.'

'So he spent some minutes in this flat and then took the lift?'

'Yes. His assistant, Mademoiselle Decaux, was waiting for him downstairs, as she does when he is returning at night to the hospital. She lives round the corner, in the Rue des Acacias, and they always make the journey together.'

'She, too?' he asked, giving an obvious meaning to the words.

'She, too, occasionally. Does it seem preposterous to you?'

'No.'

'Where was I? My sister arrived at half past eight.'

'Does she live in Paris.'

'In the Boulevard Saint-Michel, opposite the School of Mining. Antoinette is five years older than I am and has never married. She works in a municipal library and is a typical old maid.'

'Does she know about the life your husband leads?'

'She doesn't know everything. But from what she has found out, she hates him and despises him deeply.'

'They do not get on?'

'She never exchanges a word with him. My sister is still a great Catholic, and for her Gouin is the devil himself.'

'And how does he treat her?'

'He ignores her. She seldom calls here, and then only when I'm alone in the house.'

'She avoids him?'

'As often as she can.'

'Yesterday, however . . .'

'I see that the concierge has told you everything. It is true that yesterday they did meet. I wasn't expecting my husband before midnight at the earliest. And my sister and I were chatting.'

'About what?'

'Nothing in particular.'

'Did you discuss Lulu?'

'I don't think so.'

'But you're not sure?'

'In fact, I am. I don't know why I answered evasively. We talked about our parents.'

'Are they dead?'

'My mother is dead, but my father is still alive in Finistère. We have some other sisters down there, too. We were six girls and two boys.'

'Do any of them live in Paris?'

'Only Antoinette and I. At half past eleven, or a little earlier, we were surprised to hear the door opening and to see Etienne coming in. All he did was nod. Antoinette said good-bye and left almost immediately.'

'Your husband did not go downstairs?'

'No. He was tired and anxious about his patient whose condition was not so satisfactory as he would have wished.'

'I suppose he had a key to this flat?'

'Of course.'

'During the evening, did anything unusual happen? Did you or your sister hear any noises?'

'In these old stone houses you can hear nothing between one flat and another, still less between one floor and another.'

She looked at her wrist-watch and showed signs of impatience.

'Forgive me, but it's time I went upstairs. Etienne may be coming in at any minute. Have you any further questions?'

'None at the moment.'

'Do you think you will be able to avoid questioning him?'

'It is impossible to make any promise, but I shall only trouble your husband if I consider it essential.'

'What do you feel about it at present?'

'At present I do not think it essential.'

She rose and held out her hand, as a man might have done, still looking him in the eye.

'Thank you, Monsieur Maigret.'

As she turned, her glance fell on the cardboard box and on the photographs, but the inspector could not see the expression on her face.

'I am at home all day. You may come when my husband is out. And I mention that, of course, not as an order but as an entreaty.'

'I gathered that instantly.'

She repeated:

'Thank you.'

So she went out, shutting the two doors behind her, while little Lucas looked at the inspector with the air of a man who has just been hit on the head. He was so afraid of saying something stupid that he remained silent, watching Maigret's face in the hope of being able to read on it what he should think.


# IV

ODDLY enough, in the car taking him back to the P.J. Maigret was thinking not about Professor Gouin, nor his wife, but, almost half-consciously, about Louise Filon. Before leaving he had slipped into his wallet the photographs of her taken at the fair.

Even though these pictures had been taken on evenings when she should have been enjoying herself, there was no happiness in her face. Maigret had known many girls like her, born in the same surroundings and who had experienced more or less the same kind of childhood and life. Some of them had possessed a crude noisy cheerfulness that could at a moment's notice give way to tears or rebellion. Others, like Désirée Brault, especially as they grew older, became hard and cynical.

It was difficult to define the expression he observed in Lulu's pictures, and which she must have worn all through her life. It was not a question of melancholy, but rather the sulky look of a little girl who stands apart in the school-yard watching her companions at play.

He would have been hard put to it to explain why she had been attractive, but he sensed it, and it had often happened, in spite of himself, that he had been more gentle than with others, in questioning girls like this.

They were young and still gifted with a certain bloom; in some respects, they seemed hardly to have emerged from childhood, and yet they had lived through much and there were already too many loathsome memories in their eyes, which no longer sparkled, and their bodies had the unhealthy charm of a thing about to wither, or half withered already.

He pictured her in the hotel room in the Rue Riquet, or in any other room in the Barbès district, spending her days reading on the bed, sleeping, or gazing out of the greenish windows. He pictured her sitting for hours in one of the cafés of the XVIIIth *arrondissement*, while Pierrot and three friends played *belote*. He could see her also, serious-looking and almost transfigured, dancing in a cheap dive. And he pictured her, planted on a street corner watching for the lurking shadows of men, never taking the trouble to smile, and, later, climbing up the stairs of a lodging-house ahead of them, calling out her name to the landlady.

For more than a year she had lived in the imposing stone block in the Avenue Carnot, in a flat that seemed too big and chill for her; and that was where he had difficulty in picturing her; in front of a man like Etienne Gouin.

Most of the lights at the Quai des Orfèvres had been switched off. Slowly he climbed the stairs, still soiled with the footprints of damp soles, and opened his office door. Janvier was waiting for him. It was the time of year when the contrast is most marked between the cold outside and the warmth of buildings, which seem so overheated that at first entry the blood rushes to the head.

'Anything new?'

The whole machinery of the police was busy with Pierre Eyraud. In the railway stations, inspectors were stopping travellers whose descriptions tallied with his. And at the airfields, too. The lodging-house squad would also be on the job, sifting through the hotels and furnished rooms of the XVIIIth *arrondissement*.

Ever since early afternoon, young Lapointe had been kicking his heels in the Rue Riquet outside the Hotel du Var, around which, now that night had fallen, the girls were on the prowl.

As for Inspector Janin, the local man, he was devoting himself to more specialized inquiries. . . . That north-east corner of Paris is a real jungle of stone, in which a man could disappear for months, and where often a crime never comes to light until months after it has been committed; thousands of people, men and women, live on the edge of the law in a world where they find as many hiding places and accomplices as they can wish; and where, from time to time, the police throw out a dragnet, and by accident they fish up someone for whom they are looking, but they rely much more upon a telephone call from a jealous prostitute or an informer.

'Gastine-Renette called an hour ago.'

The ballistics expert.

'What did he say?'

'You will have his written report tomorrow morning. The bullet that killed Louise Filon was fired from a .25 automatic.'

At the P.J. they called it an amateur's weapon. Hoodlums, who really intend to kill, use more impressive guns.

'Dr. Paul also called. He asks you to get in touch with him.'

Janvier looked at the clock. It was a little after seven-fifteen.

'He should have arrived at the restaurant La Pérouse where he is taking the chair at a dinner.'

Maigret called the restaurant. A few minutes later he had the medical examiner on the line.

'I have carried out the autopsy on the girl you sent me. If I'm not mistaken, I think I have seen her before.'

'She's been under arrest several times.'

The doctor had certainly not recognized Lulu's face, disfigured as it was by the revolver shot, but her body.

'Of course the shot was fired point-blank. One does not need to be an expert to perceive that. I reckon the distance to have been between twelve and fifteen inches, not more.'

'I suppose death was instantaneous?'

'Absolutely instantaneous. The stomach still contained undigested food, lobster among other things.'

Maigret recalled seeing in the kitchen garbage-pail an empty lobster tin.

'She drank white wine with her meal. Are you interested in that.'

Maigret did not know. At this stage of the investigation, it was impossible to tell what might become important.

'I discovered something else which may surprise you. Did you know the girl was pregnant?'

Maigret was indeed surprised, so much so that he was silent for a moment.

'How many months?' he eventually asked.

'About six weeks. Very likely she didn't know it. If she did, it can't have been for long.'

'I suppose this is definite?'

'Absolutely. You will see the technical details in my report.'

Maigret hung up, and said to Janvier who was standing waiting in the office:

'She was pregnant.'

But Janvier, who knew only the broad outlines of the case, remained unmoved.

'What shall we do with Lapointe?'

'Quite so. We must send someone to relieve him.'

'There is Lober, who is doing nothing in particular.'

'We must also relieve Lucas. It probably won't serve any purpose, but I should prefer to go on having the flat guarded.'

'If I can take time for a bite, I'll go myself. Would it be in order to sleep on the job?'

'I see no reason against it.'

Maigret glanced through the latest editions of the newspapers. There was still no picture of Pierrot. Presumably it had arrived too late for the news-editors, but they had published a full description:

'*The police are searching for the lover of the Filon girl, a musician in a dance-band, named Pierre Eyraud, known as Pierrot. He was her last caller yesterday evening.* . . .

'*Pierre Eyraud, who has had several convictions, has disappeared, and it is presumed that he is hiding in the La Chapelle district which he knows well.*'

Maigret shrugged his shoulders, rose, and paused before going to the door.

'If there is anything new, shall I call you at home?'

He said yes. There was no reason to stay in the office. He was driven back home in one of the cars and, as usual, Madame Maigret opened the door of the flat before he had turned the knob. She did not tell him that he was late. Dinner was ready.

'You didn't catch cold?'

'I don't think so.'

'You ought to change your shoes.'

'My feet aren't wet.'

Which was true, for he had not done any walking during the day. He saw on a chair the same newspaper he had been looking at in the P.J. His wife must know about the case, but she asked no questions.

She knew that he meant to go out again, for he had not taken off his tie as he nearly always did. Dinner over, she followed him with her eyes as he opened the sideboard cupboard to pour himself a glass of *prunelle*.

'You're going out?'

A moment earlier, he had not been sure. In fact, he had been half expecting Professor Gouin to telephone him. This was not founded on anything definite. But would it not occur to Gouin that the police would like to question him? Surely he would be surprised at not being approached, when so many people knew about his relations with Louise Filon.

He called Louise Filon's flat. Janvier had just settled in.

'Anything new?'

'Nothing, Chief. I have warned my wife. I am quite happy. I shall spend the night on this wonderful sofa.'

'Do you know if the Professor has returned?'

'Lucas told me he went up at seven-thirty. I haven't heard him go out.'

'Good night.'

Had Gouin guessed that his wife would speak to Maigret? Was she capable of not letting on? What had they talked about between themselves while they were dining alone together? When dinner was over did the Professor generally withdraw into his office?

Maigret helped himself to a second glass which he drank standing next to the sideboard, then he went to the coat-rack and took down his heavy overcoat.

'Better take a scarf. Do you expect to be out long?'

'An hour or two.'

He had to walk as far as the Boulevard Voltaire before finding a taxi, to which he gave the address of the Grelot. There was not much life in the streets, except round the Gare de l'Est and the Gare du Nord, and the latter always reminded Maigret of his early years in the police force.

In the Boulevard de la Chapelle, beneath the elevated Metro, the familiar shadows were in their place, the same as on every night, and if it was easy to understand what the women were doing there, and what they were waiting for, it was much more difficult to work out what reasons some men could have for hanging about, doing nothing, in the darkness and cold. They were not all looking for temporary company. Nor had they all got appointments. Among them were men of all races and all ages, who emerged in the evenings, like rats from a hole, to make bold on the fringe of their territories.

The neon sign of the Grelot shed a violet light on a strip of pavement, and from the taxi Maigret could hear muffled music, or rather rhythmic sounds accompanied by a low stamping noise. A short distance away two policemen in uniform were on duty under a lamp post, and at the door, apparently taking the air, was a midget who shot inside as soon as Maigret stepped out of his cab.

In such places it is always like that. The inspector had not yet made his entrance when two men rushed out, and, jostling past him, made off for the darker depths of the district. At the bar, others turned away their heads as he passed, in the hope of not being recognized, and as soon as his back was turned, slipped out also.

Short and thickset, the proprietor came forward.

'If it is Pierrot you are looking for, Inspector . . .'

He was talking loudly on purpose, emphasizing the word inspector, in order to warn everyone in the room. Here too the lighting was violet, and it was hard to make out the customers seated at the tables and in the boxes, for only the dance-floor was illuminated; the faces were lit only by the reflection of the spotlights, which gave them a ghostly appearance.

The band went on playing, the couples dancing, but talk had stopped and all eyes were turned upon the bulky outlines of Maigret who was looking round for a table.

'You would like a seat?'

'Yes.'

'This way, Inspector.'

In saying this, the proprietor had the air of a huckster putting across his patter in front of the painted canvas of his booth at a fair.

'What will you have? It's my round.'

Maigret had expected all this, as he came in. He was used to it.

'A marc.'

'An old marc for Inspector Maigret!'

On their hanging platform, the four members of the band were dressed in black trousers and dark red silk shirts with long flowing sleeves. They had managed to replace Pierrot, for someone was playing the saxophone, doubling with the accordion.

'Do you want to talk to me?'

Maigret shook his head and pointed to the platform.

'The band?'

'The one who knows Pierrot best.'

'In that case, it's Louis, the accordionist. He's the conductor. In a quarter of an hour's time there's an interval, so he could join you shortly. I suppose you're not in a hurry?'

Five or six persons, including one of the dancers, found it necessary to seek some fresh air. Calmly looking about him, Maigret paid no attention to them, and gradually people began to resume their conversations.

He recognized a number of girls, but they had not come here to pick up customers. They came to dance, mostly with their steadies, and they were wholly rapt up in the dancing, which was for them like a holy rite. Some of them had their eyes closed, as if in ecstasy, others were dancing cheek to cheek with their partners, but with their bodies hardly touching.

There were typists and shop-girls, as well, who had come simply to listen to the band and to dance, and no sightseers were to be seen, nor, as in most night-clubs, couples on the spree, slumming amid the mob.

In the whole of Paris there were not more than two or three dance-halls like this, generally frequented only by regulars, and where much more lemonade was drunk than alcohol.

The four members of the band, up above, looked down upon Maigret with inscrutable expressions; it was impossible to guess their thoughts. The accordionist was a handsome dark young fellow of about thirty who looked like a film star, and who had grown Spanish-style side-whiskers.

A man with a large bag attached to his apron was collecting bills.

Couples waited on the floor. There was one more dance, this time a tango, for which the spotlights changed from violet to red, fading out the girls' make-up and dimming the musicians' shirts; eventually the band put down their instruments and the proprietor, from below, said a few words to the accordionist named Louis.

The latter glanced once more at Maigret's table and decided to come down the ladder.

'You may sit down,' said the inspector.

'We start again in ten minutes.'

'That will be long enough. What will you have?'

'Nothing.'

Silence ensued. From the other tables people were watching them. The bar was crowded, for the most part with men. In some boxes only the girls remained, re-touching their make-up.

Louis spoke first.

'You're barking up the wrong tree,' he observed with bitterness.

'About Pierrot?'

'Pierrot didn't kill Lulu. But it's always the same old thing.'

'Why did he disappear?'

'He's no more a fool than the next man. He knows that he's bound to catch it. How would you like to be arrested?'

'He's a friend of yours?'

'A friend of mine, yes. Probably I know him better than anyone.'

'Perhaps you know where he is?'

'If I knew, I wouldn't say.'

'Do you know?'

'No. I haven't had news of him since we shut down last night. You've seen the papers?'

Louis's voice shook with repressed anger.

'People imagine that because a chap plays in a band he must be a hoodlum. Perhaps you think that, too?'

'No.'

'You see that big fair fellow who plays the drums? Believe it or not, he's taken his *bachot* and even been to the university. His parents are well-off. He's here because he likes it, and next week he's getting married to a girl who's studying medicine. I'm married, too, in case you're interested; I have two children, my wife is expecting a third, and we live in a four-room flat in the Boulevard Voltaire.'

Maigret knew it was true. Louis was forgetting that the inspector knew his kind of people almost as well as he did.

'Why didn't Pierrot get married?' he asked in lowered tones.

'That's another story.'

'Lulu didn't want to?'

'I didn't say so.'

'Some years ago Pierrot was arrested for being a pimp.'

'I know.'

'Well?'

'I tell you again, that's another story.'

'What story?'

'You wouldn't understand. In the first place, he comes from a public orphanage. Does that mean anything to you?'

'Certainly.'

'When he was sixteen, they slung him out on the streets, and he did the best he could. In his place I might have done worse things. As for me, I had my parents, like most people, and I still have.'

He was proud of being a man like any other, but at the same time he felt the need to defend those on the other side of the fence, and Maigret could not help smiling in sympathy.

'What are you smiling at?'

'Because I know all that.'

'If you knew Pierrot, you wouldn't be setting all your cops on his heels.'

'How do you know that the police are after him?'

'The papers don't invent from nothing what they print. And you can feel the backwash in the district. When you see certain faces, you know what that means.'

Louis did not like the police. He did not conceal it.

'There was a time when Pierrot acted the tough,' he went on.

'But he wasn't one?'

'Would you believe me, if I swore he is shy and romantic? Yes, it's a fact.'

'He was in love with Lulu?'

'Yes.'

'He knew her when she was on the streets?'

'Yes.'

'And he let her stay on the streets.'

'What else could he have done? I told you that you wouldn't understand!'

'Then he allowed her to take a steady lover and be kept by him?'

'That's different.'

'Why?'

'Do you need telling how little he had to offer her? Do you imagine he could make a living for her on what he earns here?'

'You keep your family, don't you?'

'Wrong again! My wife is a seamstress; she works ten hours a day and looks after the children, too. What you don't understand is that if you're born in the district and have never known any other . . .'

He broke off.

'Only four minutes left.'

The other members of the band watched them closely from up above, their faces expressionless.

'What I do know is that he didn't kill her. And if he didn't take her away from the claws of her doctor . . .'

'So you know who Lulu's steady lover was?'

'So what?'

'Was it Pierrot who told you?'

'Everybody knows it started in the hospital. Now I'm going to tell you what Pierrot's view was. She had the chance to escape once and for all, to have an easy life and be sure of tomorrow. That's why he said nothing.'

'And Lulu?'

'She must have had her reasons.'

'What reasons?'

'That's no business of mine.'

'What sort of a girl was she?'

Louis looked at the women around them with an expression that suggested that she was no different from the rest.

'She had had a hard life,' he remarked as if that explained everything. 'She wasn't happy down there.'

By 'down there' he evidently meant the far-off Etoile district, which seen from here seemed another world.

'Now and again she came dancing here.'

'Did she look sad?'

Louis shrugged his shoulders. Could the word have any meaning in the La Chapelle district? Were there any really happy girls around them? Even the shop-girls, as they danced, wore a melancholy air and requested plaintive tunes.

'We have a minute left. After that, if you still need me, you will have to wait half an hour.'

'Did Pierrot say anything to you when he came back from the Avenue Carnot last night?'

'He apologized, and spoke of important news, without saying what it was.'

'Was he gloomy?'

'He's always gloomy.'

'Did you know that Lulu was pregnant?'

Louis looked at him hard, at first unbelieving, then astonished, and finally solemn.

'You're sure of that?'

'The medical examiner who performed the autopsy could not have made a mistake.'

'How many months?'

'Six weeks.'

This sank in, perhaps because he had children, and his wife was expecting another. He beckoned to the waiter who stood near them trying to overhear what they were saying.

'Fetch me a drink, Ernest. Anything will do.'

He had forgotten that the minute was up. From the bar the proprietor was observing them.

'I hadn't expected that.'

'Nor had I,' Maigret admitted.

'I suppose the Professor is too old?'

'Men have had children at the age of eighty.'

'If what you say is true, that's another reason why he couldn't have killed her.'

'Listen to me, Louis.'

The latter looked at him with some suspicion still, but he was no longer aggressive.

'It may happen that you will get word of Pierrot. In one way or another. I am not asking you to "finger" him. Only to tell him that I should like to talk to him, wherever he wants and whenever he wants. You understand?'

'And you'll let him go?'

'I am not saying I'm going to call off the inquiries. All I promise is that he'll leave me freely.'

'What do you want to ask him?'

'I don't know yet.'

'You still think he killed Lulu?'

'I have no opinion.'

'I don't think he will send word to me.'

'But if he does. . . .'

'I'll pass on your message. Now, if you'll excuse me. . . .'

Draining his glass at one gulp, he climbed up to the platform and buckled the accordion straps round his waist and shoulders. The men in the band asked no questions. He bent over them but it was only to give them the title of the next number. From the bar the men were looking over the girls who were sitting out, and making up their minds which to pick as partners.

'Waiter!'

'There's nothing to pay. It's on the house.'

It was no use arguing. He rose and made for the door.

'Have you found out anything new?'

There was a touch of irony in the proprietor's voice.

'Thank you for the *marc*.'

It was useless to look for a taxi in the neighbourhood, and Maigret reached the Boulevard de la Chapelle, brushing aside the girls who did not recognize him and were trying to pick him up. Three hundred yards away shone the lights of the Barbès crossroads. A fog like the morning's began to fall over the city, and car lights were encircled with a halo.

The Rue Riquet was a few steps farther. He was not long turning into it, where he found Inspector Lober, a man of nearly his own age but who had never been promoted, leaning against a wall smoking a cigarette.

'Anything fresh?'

'Plenty of couples go in and come out, but I haven't seen him.'

Maigret wanted to send Lober home to bed. He also could have telephoned Janvier and told him to go home. And called off the watch in the stations, for he was convinced that Pierrot would not try to leave Paris. But he was compelled to follow routine. He had no right to run any risks.

'You aren't cold?'

Lober already smelt of rum. So long as the *bistrot* on the corner stayed open, he wouldn't do badly. That, indeed, was the reason why all his life he would remain a plain detective.

'Good night, old man. If anything happens, telephone me at home.'

It was eleven o'clock. The crowds were beginning to pour out of the cinemas. Couples on the pavement were walking arm in arm, some women clasping their companion's waist; in corners and doorways some pairs stood clinging together, others were running to catch their bus.

Behind the lighted Boulevards, each side street had its own mystery and its shadows; each one, too, had somewhere or other the yellowing signs of a hotel or two.

It was for the lights that he was making, and at the Barbès crossing he entered a brilliantly illuminated bar where some fifty people were crowded round a huge copper counter.

Though he had meant to order a rum, he said automatically, because of what he had drunk at the Grelot:

'A *marc.*'

Lulu had hung about here, as other girls hung about now, on the look-out for a man's glance.

He walked to the telephone booth, slipped a counter into the instrument and dialled the number of the Quai des Orfèvres. He did not know who was on duty, but recognized the voice of one Lucien, a new man, who had taken his training very seriously and was already preparing for his examinations in order to qualify for promotion.

'Maigret here. Anything new?'

'No, sir. Only that two Arabs have just had a fight with knives in the Rue de la Goutte d'Or. One of them died the minute he was placed on a stretcher. The other, who was wounded, managed to get away.'

It was no more than three hundred yards from where he stood. It had happened hardly twenty minutes ago, probably while he was walking along the Boulevard de la Chapelle. He had known nothing about it, had heard nothing. The murderer might have passed him by. Before the night ended, other dramas would be played out in the district, one or two of which would come to the notice of the police, but others for long afterwards would remain undetected.

Pierrot, too, was holed up somewhere between Barbès and La Villette.

Did he know that Lulu was pregnant? Was it to tell him about it that she had called the Grelot to ask him out to see her?

Dr. Paul had said six weeks. That meant that for some days past she must have had her suspicions.

Had she disclosed them to Etienne Gouin?

It was possible, but not probable. She was more the kind of girl who would consult a local doctor or a midwife.

Maigret could only go by guess-work. Back at the flat she must have waited a while before making up her mind. According to Madame Gouin, the Professor had looked in on Lulu after dinner but had stayed only a few minutes.

Going back to the bar, Maigret ordered another drink. He had no desire to leave just yet. This seemed to him the best spot in which to think about Lulu and Pierrot.

'She didn't talk to Gouin,' he murmured.

Pierre Eyraud was the one she would have confided in, which explained his hurried visit.

In that case, would he have killed her?

First, one had to be sure that she knew about her condition. Had she been living in a different district, he would have been positive that she had seen a local doctor. At the Etoile, where she remained a stranger, it was less likely.

Next morning he would have to circulate a notice to all the doctors and midwives in Paris. This seemed most important. Since Dr. Paul's telephone call, he was convinced that Lulu's pregnancy was the key to the affair.

Would Gouin be peacefully asleep? Or was he taking advantage of an evening off to work on some article of surgery?

It was too late to go and see the charwoman, Madame Brault, who lived not far away in the neighbourhood of the Place Clichy. Why had she not mentioned the Professor? Spending as she did every morning in the flat, was it credible that she should be unaware of the identity of Lulu's lover?

They exchanged gossip. In the whole house Madame Brault was the only person who could have understood the secrets of a Louise Filon.

The concierge, to begin with, had kept silent because she owed a debt of gratitude to the Professor and because she must be more or less consciously in love with him.

In fact, it might be said that all the women were striving to protect him, and not the least interesting feature of the case was the power exercised over them by this man of sixty-two.

He made no attempt to charm them. He merely made use of them, almost absent-mindedly, for the sake of physical release, and not one of them bore him a grudge for his cynicism.

Maigret would have to interview the woman assistant, Lucile Decaux. And also, perhaps, Madame Gouin's sister, who was the only one the Professor had apparently failed to captivate.

'How much?'

He took the first taxi.

'Boulevard Richard Lenoir.'

'I know, Monsieur Maigret.'

That reminded him to inquire for the taxi in which Gouin had driven home last evening from the hospital.

He felt sluggish, heavy with the *marc* he had drunk, and he half-closed his eyes as the lights flashed by on both sides of the cab.

He kept coming back to Lulu, and in the darkness of the taxi he pulled his wallet out of his pocket in order to look at her photographs. Her mother had not smiled, either, when she went to have her picture taken.

## V

NEXT morning he had an unpleasant aftertaste of *marc* in his mouth. When, in conference at about nine-fifteen, he was told he was wanted on the telephone, he was under the impression that his breath still smelt of stale alcohol and he tried not to talk too closely to his colleagues.

As on every morning, the departmental heads were present, in the office of the P.J.'s Director, whose windows looked out on the Seine; all of them were clutching pretty bulky files. It was a grey day, the river was a dirty colour, and people were walking fast, as on the day before, especially when crossing the windswept Pont Saint-Michel, where men lifted their arms to hold on to their hats, and women reached down to hold in their skirts.

'You can take the call in here.'

'I am afraid it will be a long one, sir. I had better go back to my office.'

Though the others had probably not drunk *marc* the night before, they looked no better than he did, and everyone seemed to be in a bad temper. It must have been the effect of the light.

'Is that you, Chief?' Janvier asked in a voice in which Maigret detected a note of excitement.

'What's happened?'

'He's just come by. Shall I give it you in detail?'

Probably Janvier, too, who had slept on the sofa in Lulu's flat, was looking tired and ill.

'Go on.'

'Here it is. It was a few minutes ago, ten at the most. I was in the kitchen, drinking some coffee I'd made. I had my coat and tie off. I ought to say that it was very late last night before I managed to go to sleep.'

'Did you have a quiet night?'

'I didn't hear anything. It was just that I couldn't sleep.'

'Proceed.'

'You will see, it's quite simple. So simple that I can't quite get over it. I heard a slight noise, a key turning in the lock. I stood still, in a position from which I could observe the sitting-room. Someone entered the vestibule, crossed it and opened the inner door. It was the Professor, who is taller and thinner than I had expected. He was wearing a long dark overcoat, a woollen scarf round his neck, hat on head, and gloves in hand.'

'What did he do?'

'Exactly. That's what I was coming to. He did nothing. He walked forward a few paces, slowly, like a man entering his home. I wondered for a moment what he was gazing at so intently, and I realized it was at my shoes which I had left on the carpet. Turning his head, he saw me and frowned. Just slightly. He wasn't startled. He didn't seem to be either embarrassed or alarmed.

'He looked at me like someone whose thoughts are elsewhere and who needs a moment to return to reality. Eventually, without raising his voice, he asked:

' "You're from the police?"

'I was so surprised by his appearance, and by the way in which he was taking things, that all I could do was nod.

'For a whole minute both of us were silent, and by the way in which he looked at my stockinged feet I got the impression that he was annoyed by my casualness. But that is only an impression. He may not have noticed my feet.

'I finally said:

' "What were you going to do, Professor?"

' "So you know who I am?"

'That man makes you feel as if you don't exist, and even when he fixes his eyes on you that you have no more importance for him than the pattern on the wallpaper.

' "I was going to do nothing in particular," he muttered. "Just have a look around."

'And he did look around, observing the sofa where the pillow and quilt were lying which I had used, and sniffing the smell of coffee.

'In an impersonal voice, he went on:

' "I am surprised that your chief has not had the curiosity to interview me. You may tell him, young man, that I am at his service. I am now going to Cochin where I shall remain until eleven o'clock. Before returning for lunch I shall visit the Saint-Joseph clinic, and this afternoon I have an important operation at the American Hospital at Neuilly."

'He took one more look around, turned and went out, shutting both doors behind him.

'I opened the window to watch him leave. A taxi was parked outside the house, and on the pavement a young woman with a black brief-case under her arm was waiting for him. She opened the cab-door and got in after him.

'I suppose that when she calls for him in the morning, she telephones from the lodge to say that she is down below.

'That's all, Chief.'

'Thank you very much.'

'Do you think he is well off?'

'He is reported to make a lot of money. He operates free on poor patients, but when he asks a fee it is a stiff one. Why do you ask?'

'Because last night, when I couldn't sleep, I made an inventory of the young woman's effects. It was not what I expected to find. There are indeed two fur coats, but second-rate and one of them sheep-skin. Not a single item, from lingerie to shoes, came from a first-class shop. They aren't, of course, the kind of clothes she used to wear in the Barbès district, but no more are they the clothes you expect to find in the home of a woman kept by a wealthy man. I didn't find a cheque book, nor any document indicating that she had a bank account. Yet, there are only a few thousand-franc notes in her handbag and two more in the drawer of the bedside table.'

'I think you can come back. Have you a key?'

'I saw one in her handbag.'

'Close the door. Fix a thread, or something, across it so that we shall know if it has been opened. Has the charwoman turned up?'

The night before he had not told her whether or not she should come in to clean the flat. No one had considered that she had not been paid her wages.

It was not worth going back to the Director's room, where the conference was over. Lober, in the Rue Riquet, would be tired and perished with cold; probably, since the *bistrots* had opened, he would have warmed himself with a few rums.

Maigret called the Goutte d'Or station.

'Is Janin there? Not in yet? Maigret here. Would you send someone to the Rue Riquet where they will find one of my men, Lober. Tell him that unless there's been a new development he is to telephone his report and get some sleep.'

He did his best to recall the various things that on his way back from Barbès last night he had decided to do this morning. He telephoned Lucas.

'How are things?'

'All right, Chief. At one time last night two patrolling police on bikes in the XXth *arrondissement* thought they had laid hands on Pierrot. They took the man to the station. He wasn't Pierrot, but a young man much like him, and who, as it happens, is also a musician, in a brasserie in the Place Blanche.'

'I should like you to telephone Béziers. Try to find out whether a certain Ernest Filon, who was in the town hospital some years ago, is still living in the district.'

'Very good.'

'I also want to have the taxi-drivers questioned who generally park in the evenings around Cochin. One of them, the day before yesterday, must have driven the Professor home.'

'Anything else?'

'That's all for now.'

All this was part of the routine. On his desk a large pile of papers was awaiting his signature, besides the reports of the medical examiner and of Gastine-Renette which he ought to pass on to the coroner's court.

He broke off work to ask for the number of his friend Pardon, who was a doctor, and whom he saw pretty regularly once a month.

'Busy?'

'Four or five patients in the waiting-room. Fewer than usual at this time of year.'

'Do you know Professor Gouin?'

'He has operated on several patients of mine, and I have been present at the operations.'

'What is your view of him?'

'He is one of the greatest of doctors, not only that we now have, but that we have ever had. Unlike many surgeons, he is not merely a hand, but a brain; and we owe him a number of discoveries that are very important, and always will be.'

'But as a man?'

'What do you want to know, exactly?'

'Your opinion.'

'It is hard to say. He is pretty stand-offish, especially with small local doctors such as myself. It seems he keeps his distance with the others too.'

'He's not liked?'

'People are rather afraid of him. He has a certain way of replying to the questions that people are bold enough to put to him. Apparently he's tougher still with some of his patients. There's a story of an extremely rich old lady who begged him to operate on her, offering him a small fortune to do so. Do you know what he answered?

' "The operation would give you an extra fortnight, perhaps a month. The time that I spent on it might save the whole life of another patient." '

'Then again, the staff at Cochin worship him.'

'Especially the women?'

'You've heard about that? Apparently in that direction he's almost a case. Sometimes immediately after an operation, he . . . You follow?'

'Yes. Is that all?'

'He's none the less a great and fine man.'

'Thanks, old chap.'

Without quite knowing why, he wanted to have a chat with Désirée Brault. He could have summoned her to him or had her fetched. That is the way in which most of the departmental heads did their work, some of them never leaving the office throughout the day.

He looked in on Lucas, who was busy telephoning.

'I am going out for an hour or two.'

He took one of the official cars and had himself driven to the Rue Nollet, behind the Place Clichy, where Lulu's charwoman lived. It was a dilapidated block, that had not seen a coat of paint in twenty years, and the families packed into it brimmed over on to the landings and on to the staircase, where the children were playing.

Madame Brault lived on the fourth floor, on the courtyard side. There was no lift, the stairs were steep, and Maigret had to stop several times on his way up, sniffing more or less unpleasant odours.

'What is it?' a voice shouted when he knocked. 'Come in. I can't get to the door.'

She was in the kitchen, in her underclothes, with bare feet, washing laundry in a galvanized iron basin. The sight of the inspector did not seem to surprise her. She offered no greeting and waited for him to speak.

'I just looked in as I was passing by.'

'I bet you did!'

Because of the washing, steam covered the windows, through which nothing outside was visible. Sounds of snoring could be heard from the next room, where Maigret caught a glimpse of the foot of a bed; Madame Brault shut the door.

'My husband's asleep,' she said.

'Drunk?'

'Same as ever.'

'Why didn't you tell me yesterday who was Lulu's steady lover?'

'Because you didn't ask me. I remember very well, you asked me if I'd ever seen a man in her flat.'

'And you've never seen him?'

'No.'

'But you knew that it was the Professor?'

By her expression, it was plain that she knew a great deal more than that. Only she was determined to say nothing, unless obliged and coerced. Not because, on her part, she had anything to hide. Nor even, probably, in order to shield someone else. It was simply a matter of principle with her not to help the police; and this was, on the whole, natural enough, considering that they had harried her all her life. She just did not like policemen. They were her natural enemies.

'Did your employer ever discuss him?'

'That happened.'

'What did she tell you about him?'

'She told me so many things!'

'Did she want to leave him?'

'I don't know whether she wanted to leave him, but she was not happy in that house.'

Without being invited, he had sat down in a chair with a straw bottom that creaked.

'What prevented her leaving?'

'I never asked her.'

'Was she in love with Pierrot?'

'It certainly looked like it.'

'Did she get much money from Gouin?'

'He gave her some whenever she asked.'

'Did she ask him often?'

'Whenever there was none in the house. Sometimes when I was about to go shopping I'd find only a few small notes in her bag and in the drawer. I'd tell her about it and she would reply:

' "I'll ask for some." '

'Did she give any to Pierrot?'

'That's no business of mine. If she had been cleverer . . .'

She fell silent.

'What would she have done?'

'First she should never have moved into that house, where she lived like a prisoner.'

'He didn't let her go out?'

'For the most part, it was she who didn't dare go out, in case the gentleman should take it into his head to bid her a good morning as he passed by. She wasn't her own mistress, but a sort of servant, with the difference that she was not expected to work but to go to bed. If she had kept up a flat somewhere else, and if he had been the one who had to go out of his way . . . But what's the use of all this? What exactly do you want from me?'

'A piece of information.'

'Today you want information, and you take your hat off. To-morrow if I had the bad luck to stop beside a show case, you'd run me into gaol. What information?'

She was hanging the washing up to dry on a cord across the kitchen.

'Did you know that Lulu was pregnant?'

She turned round quickly.

'Who told you that?'

'The autopsy.'

'So she hadn't made a mistake.'

'When did she tell you?'

'About three days before she was shot.'

'She wasn't sure?'

'No. She hadn't yet gone to a doctor. She was afraid of going.'

'Why?'

'For fear, I suppose, of being disappointed.'

'She wanted a child?'

'I think she was glad to be pregnant. But it was still too early to celebrate. I told her that doctors today have a dodge by which they can tell for certain even at two or three weeks.'

'Did she go to consult one?'

'She asked me if I knew one and I gave her the address of someone I know, near here, in the Rue des Dames.'

'Do you know if she saw him?'

'If she did, she didn't tell me.'

'Did Pierrot know?'

'Don't you know anything about women? Have you ever met a woman who told a man about things like that before she was sure?'

'You think she didn't speak to the Professor, either?'

'Use your own gumption.'

'What would have happened, do you think, if she hadn't been murdered?'

'I don't read tea leaves.'

'Would she have kept the child?'

'Of course.'

'Would she have stayed with the Professor?'

'Unless she had gone off with Pierrot.'

'Who did she think was the father?'

Once again she looked at him as if he couldn't tell chalk from cheese.

'You don't imagine it was the old man?'

'It could be.'

'You read about that sort of thing in the papers. But as women are not kept locked up in a stable like cows, and led to the bull once a year, it's hard to swear to whatever it might be.'

Her husband in the next room shifted in bed and groaned. She opened the door.

'In a minute, Jules. I've got someone here. I'll bring your coffee in a minute.'

Turning to Maigret, she added:

'Any more questions?'

'Not exactly. Do you hate Professor Gouin?'

'I've never seen him, I said.'

'But, all the same, you do hate him?'

'I hate all people like that.'

'Supposing that when you arrived that morning you had found in Lulu's hand or on the carpet, within her reach, a revolver. Wouldn't you have been tempted to get rid of it, in order to remove the possibility of suicide and put the Professor under suspicion?'

'You make me tired. Do you think I'm fool enough not to know that when the police have a choice between a big shot and a poor bastard of a musician like Pierrot, it's the poor bastard they'll go for?'

She poured some coffee into a bowl, added sugar, and shouted to her husband:

'Coming.'

Maigret did not persist. Only in the doorway did he turn round to ask the name and address of the doctor in the Rue des Dames.

He was a certain Duclos. He had not been long settled in the practice, and had probably just completed his studies, for his consulting-room was nearly bare, with merely the indispensable instruments bought second-hand. When Maigret told him who he was, the doctor at once showed his awareness.

'I suspected somebody would come one day or another.'

'She gave you her name?'

'Yes. I filled in a form for her.'

'How long had she known she was pregnant?'

The doctor looked more like a student, and to give himself importance he consulted his almost empty filing cabinet.

'She came on Saturday, recommended by a woman I looked after.'

'Madame Brault, I know.'

'She told me that she thought she was pregnant and wanted to be sure.'

'One moment. Did she seem worried?'

'I can assure you that she wasn't. When a girl of her sort puts that question to me, I always expect her to ask me if I'll do what's necessary to induce an abortion. That happens twenty times a week. I don't know whether it is the same in other districts. In short, I examined her. I asked for the usual sample of urine. She wanted to know what happened next, and I told her about the rabbit test.'

'What was her reaction?'

'She was anxious to know whether we had to kill the rabbit. I told her to come back on Monday afternoon.'

'And she came?'

'At half past five. I informed her that she was well and truly pregnant, and she thanked me.'

'She didn't say anything else?'

'She was insistent, and I assured her it was an absolute certainty.'

'Did she seem happy about it?'

'I'd swear she was.'

On Monday, therefore, about six o'clock, Lulu had left the Rue des Dames and returned to the Avenue Carnot. Towards eight, after dinner, the Professor, according to Madame Gouin, had spent a few minutes in the third-floor flat, and then proceeded to the hospital.

Until around ten, Louise Filon had been at home alone. She had eaten tinned lobster and drunk a little wine. Then, apparently, she went to bed, which had been found unmade—not in disorder, as if she had been sleeping with a man, but simply unmade.

During that period Pierrot was already at the Grelot and she could have telephoned him immediately. Instead, she had not called until about nine-fifteen.

Was it to tell him her news that she had fetched him out to the Etoile during his working hours? If so, why had she delayed so long?

Had Pierrot jumped into a taxi? According to the concierge he had stayed about twenty minutes in the flat.

Gouin, according to the concierge and also according to his wife, had returned from the hospital a little after eleven and had not visited his mistress.

Next morning, at eight, Madame Brault, starting her job, had found Louise dead on the sitting-room sofa, and she maintained that there was no weapon near the body.

Doctor Paul, always cautious in his conclusions, placed the time of death between nine and eleven. Because of the telephone call to the Grelot, nine-thirty could be substituted for nine.

As for the finger-prints taken in the flat, they belonged to four people only: Lulu herself, the charwoman, the Professor and Pierre Eyraud. Moers had sent someone to Cochin to photograph Gouin's prints on a hospital form he had just signed. The other three sets had caused no trouble, for they were all on record in the P.J.

Lulu had evidently not been expecting an attack, since someone had been able to shoot her point-blank.

The flat had not been ransacked, which meant that the murderer had not killed for money, nor to lay his hands on papers of any sort.

'Thank you, Doctor. I suppose that after her appointment no one called to question you about her? Nobody telephoned to discuss her affairs with you?'

'No. When I saw in the paper that she'd been murdered, I expected a visit from the police, given that her charwoman had sent her to me and that she must be in the know. To tell you the truth, if you hadn't come this morning, I was intending to put through a call to you this afternoon.'

A few minutes later, from a *bistrot* in the Rue des Dames, Maigret was telephoning Madame Gouin. She recognized his voice and did not sound surprised.

'Yes, Inspector.'

'You told me yesterday that your sister works in a library. May I ask which one?'

'The municipal library in the Place Saint-Sulpice.'

'Thank you.'

'Have you found out anything?'

'Only that Louise Filon was pregnant.'

'Oh!'

He was sorry he had said this over the wire, for he could not judge her reaction.

'Does that surprise you?'

'Well . . . yes. . . . It's probably silly, but one never expects that to happen to certain kinds of women. One forgets that they are built the same as others.'

'Do you know if your husband was aware of it?'

'He would have spoken to me.'

'Has he ever had a child?'

'Never.'

'He didn't want one?'

'I don't think he cares one way or the other. The fact is that we haven't had one. Very likely because of me.'

The little black car drove him to the Place Saint-Sulpice, which for some reason was the Paris square he disliked most. There he always felt as if he were in some place in the provinces. To his eyes, even the shops appeared different from elsewhere, and the passers-by seemed more sluggish and depressed.

The library was gloomier still, badly lit, and quiet as an empty church; at that time of day only three or four people, regulars probably, were consulting the dusty volumes.

Antoinette Ollivier, Madame Gouin's sister, watched him approach; she looked more than her fifty years, and she had the rather disdainful assurance of women who think they have penetrated all the great truths of life.

'I am Inspector Maigret of the *Police Judiciaire*.'

'I recognized you from your pictures.'

As in a church, she was speaking in low tones. But it reminded him more of school than of a church, when she made him sit down in front of a table covered in green baize which served as her desk. She was fleshier than her sister Germaine, but it was a scarcely living flesh, and her complexion was of a neutral tint such as nuns sometimes have.

'I suppose you are here to put some questions to me?'

'Quite right. Your sister informed me that you paid her a visit yesterday evening.'

'So I did. I arrived about half past eight, and left at half past eleven, as soon as the individual you know had come in.'

For her, it must have represented the height of contempt to avoid mentioning even the name of her brother-in-law, and she seemed very pleased by the word 'individual', in which she carefully drew out all the syllables.

'Do you often happen to spend an evening with your sister?'

For some reason or another, Maigret suspected that she was on her guard and that she would be even more reticent than the concierge or Madame Brault.

The other two had replied with caution, because they were afraid of incriminating the Professor.

This woman, on the contrary, was probably afraid of exonerating him.

'Not very often,' she said regretfully.

'Does that mean once every six months, once a year, or once every two years?'

'Perhaps once a year.'

'You had made an appointment with her?'

'One doesn't make appointments with one's sister.'

'You went out there without knowing whether she would be at home? Haven't you a telephone in your flat?'

'Yes.'

'Didn't you call your sister?'

'She called me.'

'To ask you to go and see her?'

'Not exactly. She talked about one thing and another.'

'What things?'

'Mostly about the family. She doesn't write often. And I am in touch with our brothers and sisters.'

'She said she would like to see you?'

'More or less. She asked me if I was free.'

'What time was that?'

'About half past six. I had just got home and had started cooking.'

'You weren't surprised?'

'No. I merely made certain that HE was not going to be in. What has HE told you?'

'You are referring to Professor Gouin?'

'Yes.'

'I haven't interviewed him yet.'

'Because you think he is innocent? Because he's a famous surgeon, a member of the Academy of Medicine and because . . .'

Without raising her voice, her tone had become more resonant.

'What happened,' he interrupted, 'when you reached the Avenue Carnot?'

'I went up, kissed my sister and took off my coat and hat.'

'Where were you?'

'In the little room, next to Germaine's bedroom, which she calls her *boudoir*. The big sitting-room is gloomy and hardly ever used.'

'What did you do?'

'What sisters of our age usually do when they meet again after an interval of some months. We chatted. I gave her the news about everyone. I talked especially about François, a nephew of ours who was ordained a year ago and is about to go to the north of Canada as a missionary.'

'Did you drink anything?'

The question surprised her, startling her to such a degree that she coloured a little.

'First, we had coffee.'

'And then?'

'I sneezed several times. I told my sister I was afraid I had caught cold coming out of the Metro, where it was stifling hot. It was too hot at my sister's, also.'

'Were the servants in the flat?'

'They both went to bed about nine, after saying good night. My sister has had the same cook for eleven years. The maids come and go more frequently, for obvious reasons.'

He did not ask her for the reasons, he understood.

'So, you sneezed. . . .'

'Germaine suggested a hot toddy, and went to the kitchen to make it.'

'What did you do while she was out of the room?'

'I read a magazine article about our own village.'

'Was your sister long away?'

'As long as it takes to boil a couple of glasses of water.'

'On previous occasions, did you wait for your brother-in-law to come back before you left?'

'I always tried to avoid meeting him.'

'Were you surprised when you saw him come in?'

'My sister had assured me he would not be back before midnight.'

'How did he look?'

'As he always does, like a man who thinks himself above the ordinary laws of decency and morality.'

'You noticed nothing special about him?'

'I didn't take the trouble to observe him. I put on my hat and coat and went off, banging the door.'

'In the course of the evening, you didn't hear a noise that might have been a shot?'

'No. Until eleven o'clock or so someone in the house on the floor above was playing the piano. I recognized it as Chopin.'

'Did you know that your brother-in-law's mistress was pregnant?'

'It doesn't surprise me.'

'Did your sister mention it?'

'She didn't speak to me about that girl.'

'Did she never discuss her?'

'No.'

'However, you know all about her?'

She blushed.

'She must have referred to her in the beginning, when that individual installed her in the house.'

'Did it weigh on her mind?'

'Everyone has his own ideas. One can't live for years with such a person without something rubbing off.'

'In other words, your sister didn't take her husband to task for this liaison and didn't resent his bringing Louise Filon into the house?'

'What are you driving at?'

He would have had some difficulty in replying to that question. He had a feeling of burrowing forward little by little, without knowing where he would end up, anxious to form a more or less precise conception of the persons connected with Lulu, and of Lulu herself.

They were disturbed by a young man wanting some books, and Antoinette left the inspector for a few minutes. When she returned, she had worked up a fresh store of hatred for her brother-in-law and she gave Maigret no time to open his mouth.

'When are you going to arrest him?'

'You think it was he who killed Louise Filon?'

'Who else could it be?'

'It could be her lover, Pierrot, for instance.'

'What reason would he have?'

'Jealousy, or because she intended to break with him.'

'But do you imagine that the other man wasn't jealous, too? Don't you think that someone of his age would be furious when he saw a girl preferring a younger man to himself? And supposing it was him she'd decided to leave?'

She seemed anxious to hypnotize him, the more surely to plant in his head the idea of the Professor's guilt.

'If you knew him better, you would realize that he is not a man to think twice about eliminating a human being.'

'I thought, on the contrary, that he devoted himself to saving human life.'

'Absolute vanity! To prove to the world that he is the greatest surgeon of the age. The proof is that he only undertakes difficult operations.'

'Perhaps because other doctors can deal with the easy cases.'

'You are defending him, without knowing him.'

'I am trying to understand.'

'It isn't so complicated as all that.'

'You are forgetting that according to the medical examiner, who is seldom wrong, the murder was committed before eleven o'clock.

Now, it was after eleven when the concierge saw the Professor come in, and he went up at once to the fourth floor.'

'What is there to prove that he didn't come back for a first time, earlier?'

'I imagine it is simple to check at the hospital on how he spent his time.'

'Have you done so?'

It was Maigret's turn to be on the point of blushing.

'Not yet.'

'Well, you'd better do so! It is probably more worth while than tracking down a young fellow who's done nothing at all.'

'You hate the Professor?'

'Him and all his kind.'

She spoke these words with so much conviction that the three or four readers doing research work simultaneously looked up.

'You have forgotten your hat!'

'I thought I had left it at the entrance.'

With a finger of scorn she pointed to it on the green baize of the table, where the presence of a man's hat probably was for her the height of incongruity.


# VI

In a sense, and from the technical point of view, Antoinette had not been far wrong.

When Maigret reached the Cochin hospital in the Faubourg Saint-Jacques, Etienne Gouin had already left with his assistant for the Saint-Joseph Clinic at Passy. As it was after eleven o'clock the inspector was not surprised. It was not to meet the Professor that he had come. Actually, and without quite knowing why, perhaps he did not yet want to confront him?

Gouin's department was on the second floor, and Maigret had to negotiate with the secretariat before he was allowed to go up. He found the long corridor busier than he expected, the nurses working at full pressure. The one he spoke to, as she came out of a ward, looked less anxious than the rest; she was a middle-aged woman with hair already turned white.

'Are you the matron?'

'The day-matron.'

He told who he was and explained that he wanted to put some questions to her.

'What about?'

He was reluctant to admit that it was about the Professor. She had led him to the door of a small office, but did not invite him in.

'Is that the operating theatre at the end of the corridor?'

'One of them, yes.'

'What happens when a surgeon spends part of the night in the hospital?'

'I don't follow. You mean when a surgeon is here to perform an operation?'

'No. Unless I'm mistaken, it sometimes happens that they are here for other reasons; for instance, if they are afraid of complications setting in, or waiting for the results of an operation.'

'Yes, that happens. But what about it?'

'Where do they spend the night?'

'That depends.'

'On what?'

'On how long they are staying. If it is not for long, they use my office or walk about in the corridor. On the other hand, if it is a matter of waiting several hours, in order to be available in case of emergency they go upstairs to the house-doctors' quarters where there are two or three rooms at their disposal.'

'They go up by the stairs?'

'Or they take the lift. The rooms are on the fourth floor. For the most part, they rest until they are called.'

She was obviously wondering what was the point of these questions. The newspapers had not mentioned Gouin's name in connexion with Lulu's death. It was likely that no one here knew about his relations with Pierrot's girl.

'I suppose I couldn't have a talk with someone who was on duty the night before last?'

'After eight o'clock?'

'Yes. I should have said during the night of Monday to Tuesday.'

'The nurses on duty now are in the same position as myself. They belong to the day staff. But possibly one of the house-doctors was on duty. Wait a moment.'

She looked into two or three rooms, and eventually returned with a tall, bony, red-haired young fellow, wearing thick glasses.

'Someone from the police,' she offered before going to sit down in her office, into which she did not invite them.

'Inspector Maigret,' he explained.

'I thought I recognized you. You want some information?'

'Were you here on the night of Monday to Tuesday?'

'A large part of the night. The Professor operated on a child on Monday afternoon. It was a difficult case, and he asked me to keep a close watch on the patient.'

'Didn't he come himself?'

'He spent most of the night in the hospital.'

'Was he on this floor with you?'

'He arrived a little after eight, together with his assistant. We all went in to see the patient, and stayed there, waiting for a development that did not materialize. I suppose you don't want the technical details?'

'I probably shouldn't understand a word of them. You stayed an hour or two with the patient?'

'Less than an hour. Mademoiselle Decaux insisted that the Professor should go and get some rest, for he had operated on an urgent case the night before. Eventually he went to lie down.'

'How was he dressed?'

'He wasn't expecting to operate. Nor did he have to. He was wearing his day-time clothes.'

'Did Mademoiselle Decaux stay with you?'

'Yes. We chatted. A little after eleven the Professor came down. I had been looking in on the patient every fifteen minutes. We went in together once more, and as the crisis seemed to have passed, the Professor decided to go home.'

'With Mademoiselle Decaux?'

'They nearly always come and go together.'

'So that from eight-forty-five until eleven, the Professor was alone on the fourth floor?'

'Alone in a room, at any rate. I can't make out why you are asking these questions.'

'Could he have left without your noticing?'

'By the stairs, yes.'

'Could he have walked past the entrance-desk without attracting attention?'

'It's possible. People don't pay attention to the comings and goings of the doctors, especially at night.'

'Thank you very much. May I have your name?'

'Mansuy. Raoul Mansuy.'

This was the point on which Madame Gouin's sister had not been so far out. Materially speaking, Etienne Gouin could have left the hospital, been driven to the Avenue Carnot and returned, without anyone having noticed his absence.

'I suppose I may not ask why . . . ?' the house-doctor began just as Maigret was walking away.

The inspector shook his head and went downstairs, crossed the courtyard and found the little black car and P.J. driver waiting by the kerb. When he reached the Quai des Orfèvres, he omitted to cast his usual glance through the windows of the waiting-room. Before entering his office, he walked into the inspectors' room, where Lucas rose to speak to him.

'I have news from Béziers.'

Maigret had almost forgotten Louise Filon's father.

'The man died three years ago of cirrhosis of the liver. Before that he did occasional work in the town slaughterhouses.'

*

No one had so far appeared to claim Louise's estate—if there was one.

*

'A man named Louis has been waiting half an hour to see you.'

'A musician?'

'I think so.'

'Bring him into my office.'

Maigret went in, took off his hat and overcoat, sat down at his desk and picked up one of the pipes stacked beside his blotting-pad. A few moments later, the accordionist was introduced, looking far from easy, and glancing round before he took a seat, as if he expected a trap.

'You may leave us, Lucas.'

And to Louis:

'If it's going to take some time, you had better take off your coat.'

'It's not worth it. He's telephoned.'

'When?'

'This morning, a little after nine.'

He considered the inspector, paused, and asked:

'Does it still hold?'

'What I said yesterday? Certainly. If Pierrot is innocent, he has nothing to fear.'

'He didn't kill her. He would have told me. I passed on your message, explaining that you were prepared to meet him wherever he wanted and that afterwards he would be set at liberty again.'

'Let's make certain we understand one another. I don't want any mistakes. If I think him innocent, he will go entirely free. If I think him guilty, or have any doubts, I promise not to take advantage of our meeting—that is to say, to let him go, but the search for him will be resumed at once.'

'That's more or less what I told him.'

'What did he say?'

'That he's ready to see you. He has nothing to hide.'

'Would he come here?'

'So long as he's not set upon by reporters and photographers. And on condition that he can reach the building without being jumped on by the police.'

Louis was speaking slowly, weighing his words, without taking his eyes off Maigret.

'Can it be arranged quickly?' the inspector asked.

He looked at the time. It was not yet twelve. Between twelve and two o'clock the offices of the Quai des Orfèvres are quiet and almost deserted. It was the time of day that Maigret liked to choose, whenever he could, to conduct a delicate interview.

'He can be here in half an hour.'

'In that case, listen. I suppose he has some money on him. Tell him to take a taxi to the opposite side of the *Dépôt* on the Quai d'Horloge. There are very few people about on the quay. Nobody will pay any attention to him. One of my inspectors will be waiting for him at the gate, and will bring him here through the *Palais de Justice.*'

Louis rose, and looked steadily into Maigret's eyes, conscious of the responsibility he was undertaking in regard to his friend.

'I believe you,' he muttered finally. 'In half an hour, or an hour at the outside.'

When he had left, Maigret telephoned the Brasserie Dauphine to order something to eat.

'Send it up for two. And four half-pints.'

Next he called his wife to warn her that he would not be back for lunch.

Then, in a fit of conscientiousness, he went into the Chief's office, to inform him about the experiment he was about to make.

'You think he's innocent?'

'Until proved otherwise. If he were guilty, there would be no sense in his wanting to see me. Or else, he's devilish tough.'

'The Professor?'

'I don't know. I don't know anything yet.'

'Have you interviewed him?'

'No. Janvier has had a short talk with him.'

The Chief knew it was useless to ask questions. Maigret had the brooding, obstinate look that was well known at the Quai, and at such times he was even less talkative than usual.

'The girl was pregnant,' was all he chose to say, as if this fact particularly bothered him.

Returning to the inspectors' room, he found that Lucas had not yet gone out to lunch.

'I suppose they haven't found the taxi-driver?'

'There's no hope of finding him till this evening. Drivers on night-shift are all in bed now.'

'It wouldn't be a bad idea to look for two taxis.'

'I don't follow.'

'It's conceivable, for instance, that earlier in the evening, a little before ten, the Professor may have been driven to the Avenue Carnot and then returned to hospital.'

'I'll check.'

He was looking round for the detective whom he was to post in front of the *Dépôt* to bring in Pierrot, and he picked young Lapointe.

'Go and station yourself on the pavement opposite the *Dépôt*. At a given moment someone will get out of a taxi. It will be the saxophonist.'

'Is he giving himself up?'

'He's coming to have a talk. Treat him gently. Bring him to me by way of the little courtyard and the corridors of the *Palais*. I have promised that he won't be spotted by the Press.'

Reporters were nearly always prowling about in the corridors, but temporarily it was not hard to dodge them.

When Maigret stepped back into his office, the sandwiches and the beers were waiting for him on a tray. He drank one of the half-pints, but did not eat, whiling away a quarter of an hour on his feet at the window, watching the barges gliding on the grey water.

At last he heard the footsteps of two men, opened the door, and signalled to Lapointe that he could go.

'Come in, Pierrot.'

Pale and with shadows under his eyes, Pierrot was obviously upset. As his friend had done, he began by looking all round like a man who suspects a trap.

'You and I are the only people in the room,' Maigret reassured him. 'You may take off your coat. Give it to me.'

He put it over the back of a chair.

'Have a drink?'

He held out a glass of beer, and took one himself.

'Sit down, I rather thought you would come.'

'Why?'

His voice was hoarse, as of someone who has not slept all night and who has smoked one cigarette after another. Two fingers of his right hand were stained with nicotine. He had not shaved. No doubt, wherever he had gone to earth, he had no opportunity to do so.

'Have you had anything to eat?'

'I am not hungry.'

He looked younger than his years, and he was so nervous that it was exhausting to watch him. Even now that he was sitting down, he still trembled from top to toe.

'You promised . . .' he began.

'I shall keep my word.'

'I've come of my own free will.'

'You were right to do so.'

'I did not kill Lulu.'

Suddenly, when Maigret was least expecting it, he burst into sobs. Very likely it was the first time he had let himself go since he had heard of the death of his girl-friend. He was sobbing like a child, hiding his face with both hands, and the inspector took care not to intervene. In fact, since in the little restaurant on the Boulevard Barbès he had read in the paper that Lulu was dead, he had not had a moment to think about her—only about the threat hanging over his own head.

Within a single moment he had become a hunted man, who at every minute was risking his liberty, if not his life.

Now that he was present in the Quai des Orfèvres, face to face with the police who had been his nightmare, he had abruptly broken down.

'I swear that I didn't kill her. . . .' he repeated.

Maigret believed him. These were not the tones nor the behaviour of a murderer. Louis had been right, the night before, when he had spoken of his friend as a weakling who acted tough.

With his fair hair, blue eyes and almost babyish features, here was no butcher's apprentice; he reminded one rather of an office clerk who could easily be imagined taking a Sunday afternoon stroll in the Champs-Elysées with his wife.

'You really thought it was me?'

'No.'

'Then why did you say so to the papers?'

'I said nothing to the reporters. They write what they like. And in the circumstances . . .'

'I didn't kill her.'

'Take it easy. You may smoke.'

Pierrot's hand was still trembling as he lit his cigarette.

'There is one question I must put to you first of all. When you went to the Avenue Carnot on Monday evening, was Louise still alive?'

Pierrot gaped at him and cried:

'Of course she was!'

It was probably true; otherwise he would not have had to wait for the paper at lunch-time next day to give him a fright and send him into hiding.

'When she telephoned you at the Grelot, did you have any suspicion of what she was going to tell you?'

'I had no idea. She sounded beside herself, and wanted to see me at once.'

'What did you think?'

'That she'd made up her mind.'

'To do what?'

'To ditch it all.'

'Ditch what?'

'The old man.'

'You'd asked her to do so?'

'For two years I'd been begging her to come and live with me.'

With an air of defying the inspector, and the whole world, too, he added:

'I loved her.'

There was no emphasis in his tones. On the contrary, he was clipping his words.

'You're sure you won't have a bite?'

This time Pierrot automatically took a sandwich, and so did Maigret. It was better like this. They both started eating, and the atmosphere relaxed. No noise was to be heard in the offices except for the distant clacking of a typewriter.

'Had it ever happened before that Lulu summoned you to the Avenue Carnot in your working hours?'

'No. Not the Avenue Carnot. Once, when she was still living in the Rue La Fayette and suddenly felt ill. . . . It was only an attack of indigestion, but she was frightened. . . . She was always afraid of death. . . .'

Because of that word, and the images it conjured up, his eyes once more filled with tears, and there was a pause before he next took a bite of the sandwich.

'What did she say on Monday evening? One moment. Before you answer, tell me if you have a key to the flat?'

'No.'

'Why not?'

'I don't know. No reason, really. I seldom went to see her there, and when I did she was always at home to let me in.'

'So you rang the bell, and she opened the door.'

'I didn't have to ring. She was looking out for me, and opened the door as soon as I came out of the lift.'

'I thought she had gone to bed.'

'She had done, earlier. She must have telephoned from her bed. But she got up a little before I arrived, and was wearing a dressing-gown.'

'Did she seem in a normal state of mind?'

'No.'

'What was she like?'

'It's hard to say. She looked as if she had been thinking hard and was on the point of making a serious decision. I was frightened when I saw her.'

'What of?'

The musician paused.

'All right,' he muttered eventually, 'I was frightened because of the old man.'

'You mean the Professor when you say that?'

'Yes. I was always afraid he'd decide to get a divorce and marry Lulu.'

'Did the question ever come up?'

'If it did, she didn't mention it to me.'

'Did she want him to marry her?'

'I don't know. I think not.'

'She was in love with you?'

'I think so.'

'You aren't sure?'

'I suppose women are different from men.'

'What do you mean?'

He did not elaborate—possibly because he was incapable of it—and merely shrugged his shoulders.

'She was a poor little thing,' he finally murmured as though to himself.

The food stuck in his throat, but he mechanically kept on eating.

'Where did she sit when you came in?'

'She didn't sit. She was much too excited to sit down. She started pacing up and down and, without looking at me, said:

' "I've some very important news for you."

'Then as if to get it off her chest:

' "I am pregnant." '

'Did she seem glad?'

'Neither glad nor sorry.'

'You thought it was your child?'

He did not venture a reply, but by his attitude it was clear that he thought the answer obvious.

'What did you say?'

'Nothing. It made me feel funny. I wanted to take her in my arms.'

'But she didn't let you?'

'No. She went on pacing the room. She was talking to herself, saying more or less:

' "I wonder what I ought to do. This alters everything. It could be very important. If I speak to him about it. . . ." '

'She was alluding to the Professor?'

'Yes. She didn't know whether or not she should tell him the truth. She wasn't sure what his reaction would be.'

And Pierrot, who had finished his sandwich, sighed dejectedly:

'I don't know how to explain it. I remember the smallest details, and yet it's all confused. I hadn't thought it would happen like that.'

'What had you hoped for?'

'That she'd fall into my arms, swearing that at last she'd made up her mind to come to me.'

'But the idea didn't occur to her?'

'Perhaps it did. I'm almost certain it did. She'd always wanted to. In the beginning, when she came out of hospital, she claimed she was obliged to act as she did out of gratitude.'

'She felt she owed a debt to Gouin?'

'He had saved her life. I think he spent more time over her case than over any of his other patients.'

'You believed that?'

'Believed what?'

'In Lulu's sense of gratitude?'

'I told her she wasn't compelled to remain his mistress. He had plenty of others.'

'Do you think he was in love with her?'

'He wanted her, for sure. I suppose she'd got under his skin.'

'And you?'

'I loved her.'

'To sum up, why did she ask you round?'

'I wondered, too.'

'It was about half past five at the doctor's in the Rue des Dames that she definitely learnt she was pregnant. Couldn't she have seen you then?'

'Oh yes. She knew where I generally had dinner before turning up at the Grelot.'

'She went home. Later, between seven-thirty and eight the Professor looked in.'

'She spoke to me about that.'

'Did she say whether she'd told him her news?'

'She didn't tell him anything.'

'She had dinner and went to bed. Probably she didn't fall asleep. And around nine she telephoned you.'

'I know. I've been thinking about it all, trying to understand. But so far, I can't make it out. All I know for certain is that I didn't kill her.'

'Tell me frankly, Pierrot: if on Monday evening she had declared that she didn't want to see you any more, would you have killed her?'

The young man looked at him, with the hint of a smile rising to his lips.

'You want me to put the noose round my neck?'

'You don't have to answer.'

'I might perhaps have killed her. But, firstly, she didn't say that, and secondly I had no revolver.'

'You had one last time you were arrested.'

'That was years ago and the police never gave it me back. I haven't had one since. In any case, I wouldn't have killed her that way.'

'How would you have done it?'

'I don't know. Perhaps I might have struck her without knowing what I was doing, or would I have strangled her?'

He gazed at the parquet floor at his feet and took some time before he added in a more hesitant tone of voice:

'I might have done nothing at all. There are things you think about when you're half asleep, but never carry out.'

'Killing Lulu had occurred to you when you were half asleep?'

'Yes.'

'Because you were jealous of Gouin?'

He shrugged his shoulders again, probably meaning that words were inadequate, and that the truth was much more complicated.

'Before Gouin, you were already Louise Filon's lover, and I think I am right in saying that you did not stop her from walking the streets?'

'That's different.'

Maigret was doing his utmost to come as close to the truth as possible, but he well knew that the absolute truth was beyond reach.

'You've never taken a whack of the Professor's money?'

'Never!' he retorted sharply, with a fierce shake of the head that suggested he was about to explode with rage.

'Did Louise give you presents?'

'Nothing but trifles, a ring, ties, socks . . .'

'But you accepted them?'

'I didn't want to hurt her feelings.'

'What would you have done if she had left Gouin?'

'We should have lived together.'

'As before?'

'No.'

'Why not?'

'I never liked that sort of life.'

'What would you have lived on?'

'I earn my own living.'

'Not much of a living, so Louis tells me.'

'Not much of one, no. But I didn't expect to stay in Paris.'

'Where were you thinking of going?'

'Anywhere. South America or Canada.'

He was even less mature in mind than Maigret had thought.

'Was Lulu enthusiastic about this idea?'

'Sometimes it appealed to her, and now and again she'd promise that we should set off together in a month or so.'

'I imagine it was in the evening that she talked like that?'

'How do you know?'

'And in the morning she saw things in a different light?'

'She was frightened.'

'What of?'

'Of starving to death.'

In the end, one really came down to it. And an inevitable feeling of resentment was obviously welling up in Pierrot.

'Wouldn't you agree that it was because of this fear of hers that she stayed with the Professor?'

'Possibly.'

'Isn't it true that she'd often gone hungry in the course of her life?'

The young man replied challengingly:

'So have I !'

'But her fear was of starting to starve all over again.'

'What are you trying to prove?'

'Nothing. I am simply trying to understand. One thing is certain: on Monday evening someone shot Lulu at point-blank range. You maintain it was not you, and I believe you.'

'You really do believe me?' Pierrot murmured doubtfully.

'Until I have proof to the contrary.'

'And you'll let me go?'

'As soon as we have finished this interview.'

'You'll call off the search, and tell your men to leave me alone?'

'I shall even allow you to go back to your job at the Grelot.'

'But the papers?'

'I shall issue a communiqué straight away, announcing that you presented yourself to the P.J. of your own free will, and that after the explanations you gave you were set at liberty.'

'That doesn't mean that I'm not still a suspect.'

'I shall add that there is no evidence against you.'

'That's a little better.'

'Did Lulu own a revolver?'

'No.'

'You said just now that she was afraid.'

'Afraid of poverty and life, but not of people. She wouldn't have had any use for a revolver.'

'You stayed a bare quarter of an hour with her on Monday evening?'

'I had to get back to the Grelot. Besides, I did not like being there at a time when the old man might come in at any minute. He has a key.'

'Had that ever occurred?'

'Once.'

'What happened?'

'Nothing. It was in the afternoon when he never usually called at Lulu's. We had made an appointment in town, but something had happened to stop me keeping it. As I was in the neighbourhood, I went up to see her. We were both in the sitting-room, chatting, when we heard the key turn in the lock. He came in. I didn't try to hide. He didn't even look at me. He walked into the middle of the room, with his hat on his head, and stood there without saying a word. It was rather as if I hadn't been a human being.'

'In short you still don't know exactly why Lulu asked you round on Monday night?'

'I suppose she needed to talk to someone.'

'How did your meeting end?'

'She said: "I wanted you to know. I've no idea what I'm going to do. At any rate, it doesn't show yet. You think about it, too."'

'Had Lulu ever spoken to you of marrying the Professor?'

He looked as if he were racking his memory.

'Once, when we were in a restaurant in the Boulevard Roche-chouart and we were talking about a girl we know who had just married. She said: "It all depends on me whether he gets a divorce in order to marry me."'

'Did you believe her?'

'He might have done so. At that age, men are capable of anything.'

Maigret could not repress a smile.

'I am not asking you where you've been hiding since yesterday lunch-time.'

'I wouldn't tell you. Am I free to go?'

'Entirely.'

'If I go out, your men won't arrest me?'

'It might be wise to spend an hour or two in this neighbourhood without making yourself too conspicuous, so that I shall have time to give my orders. There is a Brasserie in the Place Dauphine where you'll be safe.'

'Pass me my coat.'

He seemed much more tired than when he had come in, because he was no longer living on his nerves.

'You would do better still to take a room in the first hotel you come across and go to bed.'

'I shouldn't sleep.'

In the doorway, he turned back.

'What's going to be done?'

Maigret understood.

'If no one comes forward . . .' he began.

'I can claim her?'

'In the absence of family . . .'

'Will you let me know how I ought to go about it?'

He wanted to give Lulu a decent funeral, and no doubt their friends in the dance-hall and in the Barbès district would follow behind the hearse.

Maigret watched his weary figure disappearing down the long corridor, and slowly shut the door; he stood motionless for a while in the middle of his office, and then made for the inspectors' room.

# VII

IT was about six o'clock when the P.J. car stopped in the Avenue Carnot in front of the block where the Gouins lived, but on the oppo-site of the road, and headed towards the Ternes district. Night had fallen early, for as on the past three days, the sun had never shone.

The light was on in the concierge's lodge. It was on, too, in the left-hand part of the Gouins' flat on the fourth floor. A few other windows, here and there, were also lit up.

Some of the flats were temporarily unoccupied. The Ottrebons, for instance, who were Belgians and in high finance, were wintering in Egypt. On the second floor, the Comte de Tavera and his family had gone shooting for the season to their château somewhere south of the Loire.

Wedged in the back of the car and hunched up in his overcoat, with only his pipe protruding through its raised collar, Maigret made no move, and seemed in such an evil temper that after a few moments the driver pulled a newspaper from his pocket, muttering:

'May I?'

It was a wonder how he could read with no more light than the beam of a street-lamp.

All afternoon Maigret had worn the same expression. It was not really bad temper, as his colleagues knew, but the effect was the same, and word had been passed round at the Quai des Orfèvres not to disturb him.

He had hardly left his office, except once or twice to loom up in the inspectors' room where he'd look round heavily, as if he had forgotten what he meant to do.

He had dealt with files that had been pending for weeks with as much zeal as if they had suddenly become extremely urgent. About four-thirty he had called the American Hospital at Neuilly for the first time.

'Is Professor Gouin engaged on an operation?'

'Yes. He won't finish for another hour. Who is wanting him?'

He had hung up, and re-read the report drawn up by Janvier on the tenants in the house and the replies they had made to him. Nobody had heard the shot. On the same floor as Louise, a certain Madame Mattetal occupied the flat on the right; she was a young widow who had spent the evening at the theatre. On the floor below the Crémieux had given a dinner party for ten, which had ended noisily.

Maigret had worked on another case, and made a few unimportant telephone calls.

At half past five, when he had called Neuilly for the second time, he was told that the operation was over and that the Professor was dressing. It was then that he had taken the car.

Not many people were passing along the pavements of the Avenue Carnot, and motors were few. Over the driver's shoulder he could read the newspaper's front-page headline:

'*Pierrot-the-Musician Released.*'

As he had promised, Maigret had given the news to the reporters.

The dashboard clock was dimly luminous, and showed six-twenty. Had there been a *bistrot* nearby he would have got out for a drink and he was sorry he had not stopped on the way.

Not until ten to seven did a taxi stop in front of the block. Etienne Gouin alighted first, and stood still for a moment on the pavement while his assistant followed him out of the cab.

They were near a street-lamp, and his figure was outlined in its light. He must have been half a head taller than Maigret and almost as broad in the shoulders. It was hard to guess his weight, because of his flowing overcoat, which looked too big for him and was cut much longer than was fashionable that year. Obviously he did not bother overmuch about his appearance, and his hat had been put on anyhow.

As he was, he gave the impression of a stout man who had grown thin, and in whose body only the big-boned structure remained.

He waited without showing impatience, gazing absent-mindedly into space, while the young woman drew some money from her bag to pay the driver. Then, as the taxi went off, he stood listening to what she had to say. Probably she reminded him of next day's appointments.

She walked with him as far as the entrance-hall, where she handed him the black leather brief-case she was holding, and watched him enter the lift before she set off towards the Ternes.

'Follow her.'

'Yes, sir.'

The car had only to coast down the slope of the avenue. Lucile Decaux was walking fast, without looking back. She was a small brunette, and so far as could be made out, slightly plump. She turned the corner of the Rue des Acacias, entered a *delicatessen*, then a baker's shop next door, and finally, a hundred yards farther on, a dilapidated-looking block of flats.

Maigret waited ten minutes in his car before he approached the block and addressed the concierge; her lodge was very different from the one in the Avenue Carnot, being cluttered up with a grown-up's bed and a child's cot.

'Mademoiselle Decaux?'

'The fourth floor, on the right. She has just come in.'

There was no lift. On the fourth floor he rang the doorbell and heard footsteps within. A voice asked from behind the door:

'Who is it?'

'Inspector Maigret.'

'One moment, please.'

The voice betrayed neither surprise nor alarm. Before she let him in, she went into another room, and a few seconds passed before she returned; Maigret saw why when the door was drawn open: she was wearing a dressing-gown and slippers.

'Come in,' she said, eyeing him with interest.

The flat consisted of three rooms and a kitchen; it was extremely clean, and the floor was so highly waxed that it was as easy to slip as on a skating rink. He was shown into a sitting-room which was rather like a studio, with a divan covered in striped material, plenty of books on shelves, a gramophone and shelves loaded with records. Over the fireplace, in which the young woman had just lit a log-fire, was a framed photograph of Etienne Gouin.

'May I take off my coat?'

'Please do. I was just making myself comfortable when you rang the bell.'

She was not pretty. Her features were irregular and her lips too thick, but she seemed to have an attractive figure.

'Am I holding up your dinner?'

'It doesn't matter. Sit down.'

She pointed to an armchair, and herself sat down on the edge of the divan, drawing the skirt of her dressing-gown around her bare legs.

She asked no questions, but studied him as some people study a celebrated person whom they are seeing for the first time in flesh and blood.

'I preferred not to trouble you at the hospital.'

'You would have found it difficult, for I was in the operating theatre.'

'Are you generally present at the Professor's operations?'

'Always.'

'Since when?'

'Ten years ago. Before then I was his pupil.'

'You are a doctor?'

'Yes.'

'May I ask your age?'

'Thirty-six.'

She replied without hesitation, in an almost expressionless voice, but he could sense in it none the less a certain distrust, and perhaps even hostility.

'I have come to clear up a few points of detail. I expect you know that in an investigation such as I am conducting, everything has to be verified.'

She waited for his questions.

'On Monday evening, unless I am mistaken, you went to pick up your chief at the Avenue Carnot, a little before eight?'

'That is true. I kept the taxi waiting and telephoned the Professor from the concierge's lodge to tell him I was waiting.'

'That's your normal procedure?'

'Yes. I only go up to the flat when there is work to do in the office or papers to collect.'

'Where did you stand while the Professor was coming down?'

'In front of the lift-gate.'

'So you know that he stopped on his way down?'

'He stopped a few moments at the third floor. I suppose you know all about it?'

'I do.'

'Why haven't you asked the Professor himself?'

He preferred not to answer.

'Did he behave the same as on any other evening? Was he at all preoccupied?'

'Only over the condition of his patient.'

'Did he say anything on the way?'

'He never says much.'

'You must have reached Cochin a few minutes after eight. What happened then?'

'We at once went into the patient's room together with the house-doctor on duty.'

'You spent the rest of the evening there?'

'No. The Professor stayed in the room about half an hour, watching for certain symptoms that did not develop. I told him he would do better to get some rest.'

'What time did he go up to the fourth floor?'

'I know that you have already asked these questions at the hospital.'

'The matron in charge told you?'

'It doesn't matter.' .

'What time was it?'

'Not yet nine.'

'You didn't go up with him?'

'I stayed with the patient. It's a child.'

'I know. What time did the Professor come down again?'

'I went to warn him about eleven o'clock that what he'd been expecting had happened.'

'You went into the room where he was lying down?'

'Yes.'

'Was he dressed?'

'At the hospital he usually lies down fully dressed. He had merely taken off his jacket and undone his tie.'

'So you spent the whole of the time between eight-thirty and eleven at the patient's bedside. This being so, your chief could have walked down the stairs and left the hospital without your knowing?'

She must have been expecting it, for he had asked the same question at Cochin and someone would have warned her. In spite of that, he noticed her breasts rise and fall more rapidly. Had she prepared her reply in advance?

'That would have been impossible. For I went up at ten-fifteen to make sure there was nothing he wanted.'

Looking into her eyes, and putting much gentleness into his voice, Maigret remarked, without raising his tones:

'You're lying, aren't you?'

'Why do you say that?'

'Because I can feel that you are lying. Listen, Mademoiselle Decaux, it is easy for me to reconstruct, this very evening, your actions and movements at the hospital. Even if you have told the staff what to say, somebody can be found who will get flustered and reveal the truth. You did not go up before eleven o'clock.'

'The Professor did not leave the hospital.'

'How do you know?'

'Because I know him better than anyone does.'

She pointed to the evening paper lying on an occasional table.

'I picked it up from a table at Neuilly, and I've read it. Why did you let the young man go?'

She was referring to Pierrot, whose name he could see, upside-down, where he was sitting.

'You're so sure that he's not guilty?'

'I'm not sure about anything.'

'But you suspect the Professor of having murdered that girl?'

Instead of replying, he asked:

'You knew her?'

'You're forgetting that I am Monsieur Gouin's assistant. I was present when he operated on her.'

'You didn't like her?'

'Why should I have disliked her?'

As he had his pipe in his hand, she said:

'You may smoke. I don't mind.'

'Is it not true that you and the Professor had a more intimate relationship than the purely professional connexion?'

'They've told you that, too?'

She smiled, with a certain air of condescension.

'Are you very middle-class, Monsieur Maigret?'

'It depends on what you mean by that.'

'I am trying to find out whether you have preconceived ideas about conventional morality.'

'My dear, I've been in the police for nearly thirty-five years.'

'In that case, don't talk about intimate relations. There were intimate relations, but they were our working relations. The rest is of no importance.'

'You mean that there is no love between the two of you?'

'Certainly not in the sense that you give to the word. I admire Professor Gouin more than any other human being on earth. I do my best to help him. For ten or twelve hours on end, sometimes for longer, I am at his side and often he does not even notice it—so natural has our association become. It often happens that we spend the night waiting for symptoms to develop in a patient. When he operates in the provinces or abroad, I go with him. In the street I pay his taxis; I remind him of his appointments, and I telephone his wife to warn her that he won't be back.

'Long ago, in the beginning, there happened between us what usually occurs between a man and a woman constantly in close touch. He did not attach any importance to it. He has done the same with the nurses and with many other women.'

'You didn't attach any importance to it, either?'

'None.'

And she looked him straight in the eye as if challenging him to contradict her.

'You've never been in love?'

'With whom?'

'With any man. With the Professor.'

'Not in the sense that you give the word.'

'But you have devoted your life to him?'

'Yes.'

'Was it he who chose you as his assistant when you'd taken your degrees?'

'I am the one who applied. I'd had the idea in mind ever since I began to attend his lectures.'

'You said that in the beginning certain things happened between you. Am I to understand that they occur no longer?'

'You are a first-rate confessor, Monsieur Maigret. It still happens occasionally.'

'In your flat?'

'He's never set foot in here. I can't see him climbing four flights of stairs and entering these quarters.'

'At the hospital?'

'Sometimes. Sometimes also in his flat. You're overlooking that I also act as his secretary and that we often spend part of the day in the Avenue Carnot.'

'You know his wife well?'

'We are in touch practically every day.'

'What are your relations with her?'

He thought that Lucile's expression hardened a little.

'Indifferent,' she let fall.

'Mutually?'

'What are you trying to make me say?'

'The truth.'

'Let's say that Madame Gouin looks upon me in the same way as on her servants. Probably she does it to persuade herself that she is the Professor's wife. You've seen her?'

Once more Maigret forbore to reply.

'Why did your chief marry her?'

'Because he didn't want to be alone, I suppose.'

'It was before you became his assistant, wasn't it?'

'Several years before.'

'Does he get on well with her?'

'He is not the sort of man to quarrel with anyone, and he possesses an extraordinary capacity for failing to notice people.'

'Does he fail to notice his wife?'

'He eats a certain number of meals with her.'

'Is that all?'

'So far as I know.'

'Why do you think she married him?'

'She was only an insignificant nurse, remember. The Professor is reported to be a wealthy man.'

'Is he?'

'He makes a lot of money. He doesn't care about that.'

'But he's made a considerable fortune?'

She nodded in agreement and uncrossed her legs, taking care to draw the skirt of her dressing-gown round them.

'In short, in your view, he isn't happy in his marriage?'

'That's not quite right. His wife couldn't make him unhappy.'

'Nor Lulu?'

'Lulu, neither, that's my opinion.'

'If he wasn't in love with her, how do you explain that for more than two years . . .'

'I can't explain it to you. You must work it out for yourself.'

'Someone told me that he "had her under his skin".'

'Who?'

'Isn't it true?'

'It's true, and it's also false. She had become something that belonged to him.'

'But he wouldn't have sought a divorce in order to marry her?'

She looked at him, dumbfounded, and exclaimed:

'Never in the world! Besides, he would never have complicated his life with a divorce.'

'Not even to marry you?'

'He's never thought of it.'

'Have you?'

She blushed.

'Nor have I. What more would it have brought me? On the contrary, I should have lost in the bargain. You see, it is I who have had the better part, really. He does hardly anything without me. I share in his work. I know all about his books while he's actually writing them, and often I do his research for him. He never crosses Paris in a taxi unless I am at his side.'

'He is afraid of a sudden death?'

'Why do you ask that?'

She seemed surprised by the inspector's insight.

'For some years past it's true, more or less since he found out that his heart is not all it should be. At that time he consulted several of his colleagues. Perhaps you don't know, but most doctors are more terrified of illness than their patients.'

'I know.'

'He hasn't said anything to me on the subject, but he's gradually acquired the habit of never remaining alone.'

'If he had an attack in a taxi, for instance, what could you do?'

'Hardly anything. But I understand him.'

'In short, it is the idea of dying alone that terrifies him.'

'For what reason exactly did you come to see me, Inspector?'

'Perhaps in order not to bother your chief unnecessarily. His mistress was murdered on Monday night.'

'I don't like that word. It's inaccurate.'

'I use it in the sense it customarily has. Gouin had the material opportunity of committing the crime. As you admitted just now, he was alone on the fourth floor of the hospital from eight-forty-five until eleven. Nothing prevented him from walking out and driving to the Avenue Carnot.'

'If only you knew him, the notion that he could kill anyone would never occur to you.'

'Oh yes, it could have.'

His reply was so categorical that she looked at him in astonishment, without thinking of arguing.

'What do you mean?'

'You admit that his work, his career, his scientific research, his surgical and professional activity—put it how you will—is the only thing of value in his eyes?'

'To some extent.'

'To an extent much greater than in anyone else I have ever come across. Someone has applied to him the phrase "a force of nature".'

This time she did not ask who.

'Forces of nature are not concerned with the damage they may do. If, for one reason or another, Lulu had become a menace to his activities?'

'In what way could Lulu be a menace to the Professor?'

'You know that she was pregnant?'

'Did that alter the situation?'

She had not looked surprised.

'You knew?'

'The Professor spoke to me about it.'

'When?'

'Last Saturday.'

'You're sure it was last Saturday?'

'Absolutely. We were returning by taxi from the hospital. He told me, just as he tells me many things, without attaching any importance to it and rather as if he were talking to himself: "I think Louise is pregnant."'

'What was his expression?'

'None at all. A little ironical, as usual. You see, there are many things to which most people attach importance, but which have none for him.'

'What surprises me is that he should have told you on Saturday, whereas it was only on Monday evening, about six o'clock, that Lulu learnt the truth.'

'You forget he is a doctor, and was sleeping with her.'

'Do you think he also spoke to his wife about it?'

'It's unlikely.'

'Suppose Louise Filon had got it into her head that she wanted to marry him?'

'I don't think the idea ever occurred to her. Even in that case, he wouldn't have killed her. You're on the wrong track, Inspector. I don't maintain that you've let the guilty man go. For I don't see either, why Pierrot should have killed the girl.'

'In a passion, if she'd threatened not to see him any more.'

She shrugged her shoulders.

'You're very wide of the mark.'

'You have your own view?'

'I don't care to have one.'

He rose to empty his pipe into the grate, and automatically, as if he had been at home, he picked up the tongs to rearrange the logs.

'You're thinking of his wife?' he asked in a blank tone of voice, his back turned to her.

'I'm not thinking of anyone.'

'You don't like her?'

How could she have liked her? Germaine Gouin was a mere nurse, a fisherman's daughter, who had become overnight the Professor's legitimate wife, whereas Lucile Decaux, who had devoted her life to him and was trained to help him in his work, was only his assistant. Every evening when they came back from the hospital, she accompanied him out of the taxi, but it was to say good night on the threshold and to return to her own lodging in the Rue des Acacias, while he rode up in the lift to his wife.

'You suspect her, Mademoiselle Decaux?'

'I have never said that.'

'But it's in your thoughts.'

'I think that you don't hesitate to investigate the actions and movements of my chief on Monday evening, but that you aren't bothering about hers.'

'What do you know about that?'

'You've spoken to her?'

'I have at least found out, and it doesn't matter how, that she spent the evening with her sister. Do you know Antoinette?'

'Not personally. The Professor has mentioned her to me.'

'He doesn't like her?'

'It's she who hates him. He told me once that he always expects, whenever they accidentally meet, that she'll spit in his face.'

'You know nothing more about Madame Gouin?'

'Nothing,' she remarked curtly.

'Has she a lover?'

'Not to my knowledge. Besides, it's not my business.'

'Is she the kind of woman, supposing she were guilty, to let her husband be condemned in her place?'

As she was silent, Maigret could not help smiling.

'You must confess you wouldn't be annoyed if she had killed Lulu and we were able to prove it.'

'What I am sure about, is that the Professor didn't kill her.'

'Did he speak to you about the murder?'

'Not on Tuesday morning. He didn't know about it then. In the afternoon he told me incidentally that the police would probably be telephoning to ask for an appointment.'

'And since then?'

'He hasn't mentioned it.'

'Has he seemed upset by Lulu's death?'

'If it has affected him, he hasn't shown it. He's the same as he always is.'

'I suppose there's nothing else you have to tell me? Has he ever spoken of Pierre Eyraud, the musician?'

'Never.'

'Have you ever considered that he might have been jealous of him?'

'He's not a man to feel jealous of anybody.'

'Thank you very much, my dear, and forgive me for delaying your dinner. If you happen to remember any detail of interest, just give me a ring.'

'You won't be seeing my chief?'

'I don't know yet. Is he at home tonight?'

'It's the only free night in his week.'

'What will he be doing?'

'Working as usual. He has the proofs of his new book to read.'

Maigret sighed as he put on his overcoat.

'You're a funny sort of girl,' he murmured, almost to himself.

'There's nothing extraordinary about me.'

'Good night.'

'Good night, Monsieur Maigret.'

She accompanied him on to the landing and watched him walk downstairs. Outside, he found his black car, and the driver opened the door.

He almost gave him the Avenue Carnot address. Sooner or later he would have to decide on a *tête-à-tête* with Gouin. Why was he perpetually putting it off? He seemed to be circling round him, without daring to approach him, as if the personality of the Professor awed him.

'To the Quai!'

By this time, Etienne Gouin would be in the middle of dinner with his wife. Passing by, Maigret noticed that there were no lights in the right-hand side of the flat.

There was at least one point on which Lucile Decaux was wrong. Contrary to her statements, Gouin's conjugal relations were not so negative as she thought. The assistant maintained that her chief never talked about his business to his wife. On the other hand, Madame Gouin had provided the inspector with details of which only her husband could be the source.

Had he also told her that Lulu was pregnant?

He stopped the car a little higher up the Avenue in front of the *bistrot* where he had once before broken his journey to drink hot toddy. The wind was not so chill this evening, and he ordered a *marc*, although it was not the time for neat spirits, simply because it was the drink he had had the night before. At the Quai des Orfèvres they used to tease him about this peculiarity. If, for instance, he began an investigation on *calvados*, it was *calvados* throughout; the result was that there had been cases on beer, cases on red wine, and even a few on whisky.

He was on the point of telephoning his office to ask if there was anything new, and then of driving straight home. It was only because the telephone booth was occupied that he changed his mind.

On the way he did not utter a word.

'Will you still need me?' the driver asked when they had reached the courtyard of the P.J.

'You can take me to the Boulevard Lenoir in a few minutes. Unless you're due to go off duty.'

'I don't finish till eight.'

He went up and turned on the light in his office; immediately the second door opened, disclosing Lucas.

'Inspector Janin telephoned. He is annoyed because no one told him that Pierrot had been found.'

Everybody had forgotten Janin, who had continued searching the La Chapelle district, until he had learnt from the newspapers that Maigret had interviewed the musician and let him go.

'He asks if he ought to keep his eye on him.'

'It's no longer worth it. Anything else?'

Lucas was opening his mouth to speak when the telephone rang. Maigret lifted the receiver.

'Inspector Maigret,' he announced frowning.

Suddenly Lucas realized that it was something important.

'Etienne Gouin here,' said the voice from the other end.

'Yes?'

'I understand you have just been questioning my assistant.'

Lucile Decaux had telephoned her chief to tell him all about it.

'So I have,' Maigret admitted.

'I should have thought it more correct, if you wanted information on my account, to apply direct to me.'

It seemed to Lucas that Maigret was a little dismayed and had to make an effort to regain his composure.

'It's a matter of opinion,' he replied rather shortly.

'You know where I live.'

'Very well. I shall come and see you.'

At the other end of the line there was a silence. The inspector heard indistinctly a woman's voice. Probably it was Madame Gouin saying something to her husband, who asked:

'When?'

'In an hour or an hour-and-a-half's time. I haven't eaten yet.'

'I shall expect you.'

Maigret was cut off.

'The Professor?' Lucas asked.

Maigret nodded.

'What does he want?'

'He wants to be interviewed. Are you free?'

'To go down there with you?'

'Yes. But first we'll go and have a bite.'

They did so in the Place Dauphine, at the table where the inspector had lunched and dined so often that it was known as Maigret's table.

Throughout the meal, he never uttered a word.


# VIII

IN the course of his career Maigret had interviewed thousands of people—perhaps tens of thousands—some of them men of considerable position, others who were more famous for their wealth, and others still who were reckoned among the cleverest of international crooks.

Nevertheless he attached an importance to this coming interview that he had never ascribed to any that had gone before, and it was not Gouin's social position that impressed him, nor the renown he enjoyed throughout the world.

He was well aware that ever since the beginning of the case, Lucas had been wondering why he had not fairly and squarely put a few searching questions to the Professor, and even now poor Lucas was nonplussed by his chief's bad temper.

Maigret could not admit the truth to him, nor to anyone else—even to his wife. In fact, he hardly dared to formulate it precisely in his own mind.

He was impressed, it is true, by what he knew of Gouin and what he had found out. But for a reason that no one, very likely, could have guessed.

Like the Professor, Maigret had been born in a little village in central France, and, like him, from his earliest years he had been thrown on his own resources.

Had not Maigret started to study medicine? If he had been in a position to continue his studies, he would probably not have become a surgeon, for lack of the necessary manual dexterity, but he had an idea, none the less, that he and Lulu's lover had some characteristics in common.

It was vain of him, and that is why he preferred not to think of it. But they both possessed, so it seemed to him, a comparable knowledge of life and of mankind.

By no means the same, and above all not the same reactions. They were, as it might be, opposites, but opposites of equal value.

What he knew of Gouin he had learnt through the words and attitudes of five different women. All he had seen of him had been his outline on the pavement of the Avenue Carnot and a photograph over a chimney-piece; and certainly the most revealing incident had been Janvier's short telephone account of the Professor's appearance in Louise Filon's flat.

He was now going to find out whether he was wrong. He had prepared himself for the interview to the best of his ability, and if he was taking Lucas with him it was not for the sake of his help, but to give the occasion a more official air, and perhaps to remind himself that he was going to the Avenue Carnot in his capacity as an Inspector of the P.J. and not simply as a man interested in another human being.

He had drunk wine with his dinner. When the waiter had asked him if he wanted brandy or a liqueur, he had ordered an old *marc de Bourgogne*, with the result that he was feeling a certain warmth within him as he drove along in the car.

The Avenue Carnot was quiet and deserted, with subdued lights showing through the curtains of the flats. When he passed by the lodge, he thought the concierge looked at him with a reproachful expression.

The two men took the lift, and the house around seemed hushed and turned in upon itself and its secrets.

It was eight-forty when Maigret pulled the shining brass handle that worked the electric bell; steps were heard inside and a young, rather pretty, maid, wearing a smart apron over her black uniform, opened the door and said:

'If the gentlemen would like to take off their coats . . .'

He had wondered whether Gouin would receive them in the sitting-room, in the more or less family part of the flat. He did not at once get an answer. The maid hung up their coats in a cupboard, left the visitors in the hall, and disappeared.

She did not return, but Gouin wasted no time in presenting himself; here he seemed taller and thinner than in the street. He scarcely glanced at them and did no more than to murmur:

'Would you kindly come this way . . .'

He preceded them down a corridor leading to his library. The walls were almost entirely lined with bound volumes. The room was suffused with a soft light, and logs were burning in a fireplace much grander than Lucile Decaux's.

'Please sit down.'

He indicated some chairs, and took one himself. All this was of no account. So far the two men had not looked at each other. Lucas, who felt himself one too many, was made even more uncomfortable by the fact that the chair was too deep for his short legs, and he was sitting too near the fire.

'I had expected that you would come alone.'

Maigret introduced his colleague.

'I brought Sergeant Lucas who will take shorthand notes.'

It was at this moment that their eyes for the first time crossed, and Maigret thought he read in the Professor's something like a reproach. Perhaps there was also, though he could not be sure of this, a certain disappointment. It was difficult to say because, outwardly, Gouin seemed ordinary enough. Actors at the theatre, and specially operatic basses, are often of his kind of large-boned build, with strongly chiselled features and pouches under the eyes.

His eyes were small and pale, and without any particular brilliance, but in his glance there was an uncommon power of penetration.

While this glance rested upon him, Maigret could have sworn that Gouin was as curious about him as he was about the Professor.

Did he, too, find him more ordinary than he had imagined?

Lucas had taken a notebook and pencil out of his pocket, and this kept him in countenance.

It was impossible to forecast what tone the conversation would take, and Maigret was careful to hold his peace and wait.

'Do you not think, Monsieur Maigret, that it would have been more rational to apply to me in the first instance instead of bothering that poor girl?'

He was speaking naturally, in unemphatic tones, as if he were talking of quite ordinary things.

'You are referring to Mademoiselle Decaux? She didn't seem to me to be in the least upset. I suppose that as soon as I left her she telephoned to tell you all about it?'

'She reported your questions and her replies. She thought it was important. Women are everlastingly anxious to convince themselves of their importance.'

'Lucile Decaux is your closest colleague, isn't she?'

'She is my assistant.'

'Doesn't she also act as your secretary?'

'She does. And as she must have told you, she follows me about wherever I go. That gives her the impression that she plays a major part in my life.'

'She is in love with you?'

'As she would be with whatever chief she had, provided he were famous.'

'She seemed to me devoted to you, up to the point of committing perjury, if need be, in order to get you out of a difficulty.'

'She would do so without a moment's hesitation. My wife has also been in touch with you.'

'She told you?'

'Just like Lucile, she has given me the fullest details of your conversation.'

He spoke of his wife in the same detached way in which he had referred to his assistant. There was no warmth in his voice. He was stating facts, without attaching any sentimental importance to them.

People of no account who came into contact with him probably went into rhapsodies over his directness of manner, and he had in fact no pose about him; he was not in the least concerned with the effect he produced on others.

It is very rarely one meets human beings who are not playing a part, even when they are alone with themselves. Most men experience a need to observe themselves living and hear themselves speaking.

Not so with Gouin. He was completely himself and he took no trouble to conceal his feelings.

When he had spoken of Lucile Decaux, he had meant by his words and his attitude:

'What she takes for devotion is really only a kind of vanity, a need to consider herself exceptional. Any one of my women students would do the same as she does. Thus, she makes her life seem interesting to herself, and probably imagines that I owe her a debt of gratitude.'

If he was not explicit, it was because he judged Maigret capable of understanding, and spoke to him as to an equal.

'I have not yet told you why I telephoned you this evening and asked you to call. But in any case, please note that I wanted to meet you.'

He was a man, and he was sincere. Since they had met face to face, he had been incessantly watching the inspector and had not concealed it, observing him as if he were a specimen of humanity whom he wished to know better.

'While my wife and I were at dinner, I had a telephone call. It was from someone you know already, from the Madame Brault who was Louise's charwoman.'

He did not say Lulu, but Louise, referring to her as simply as he had to the others, well understanding that it was superfluous to offer explanations.

'Madame Brault has got it into her head that she has grounds for blackmailing me. She did not beat about the bush, although I did not at once understand her first remark. She said :

' "I have the revolver, Monsieur Gouin."

'To begin with, I wondered what revolver she meant.'

'May I ask a question?'

'Please do.'

'Have you ever met Madame Brault?'

'I don't think so. Louise has spoken to me about her. She knew her before she moved in here. Apparently she is a strange creature who has many times been to prison. As she only worked in the flat in the mornings, and I hardly ever had occasion to call there at that time, I do not remember having met her. Though I may have passed her on the stairs.'

'Please go on.'

'She told me that when she went into the sitting-room on Monday morning, she found the revolver on the table and . . .'

'Did she say specifically : on the table?'

'Yes. She added that she had hidden it on the landing, in a flower-pot that contains an evergreen plant. Your men must have searched the flat without thinking of looking outside it.'

'It was ingenious on her part.'

'In short, she claims now to be in possession of the revolver and for a considerable sum would be willing to let me have it back.'

'Have it *back*?'

'It belongs to me.'

'How do you know?'

'She gave me a description, including the serial number.'

'Have you had this weapon for long?'

'Eight or nine years. I had gone to Belgium to operate. At that time I travelled more than I do now. It has even happened that I have been called to go as far afield as the United States and India. My wife often told me that she was afraid to be alone in the house for days on end, and sometimes for several weeks. At the hotel where I was staying, in Liège, some locally manufactured guns were on exhibition in a glass-case. It occurred to me to buy a small automatic. I ought to add that I did not declare it to the Customs.'

Maigret smiled.

'What room was it kept in?'

'In a drawer in my desk. That's where I saw it last, some months ago. I have never made use of it. I had completely forgotten it when I received this telephone call.'

'What did you say to Madame Brault?'

'That I would give her an answer later.'

'When?'

'Probably this evening. It was then that I telephoned you.'

'Will you go down there, Lucas? You have the address?'

'Yes, Chief.'

Lucas was obviously delighted to escape from the heavy atmosphere of the room, for though the two men were talking in low tones and apparently saying quite ordinary things, a veiled tension could be distinctly felt.

'Can you find your overcoat? Would you like me to ring for the maid?'

'I can find it, thank you.'

After the door had shut, they were silent for a moment. It was Maigret who spoke first.

'Is your wife aware of this?'

'Of Madame Brault's blackmail?'

'Yes.'

'She heard what I said on the telephone, for I took the call in the dining-room. I told her the rest.'

'What was her reaction?'

'She advised me to come to terms.'

'Have you wondered why?'

'Well now, Monsieur Maigret, whether it is my wife, Lucile Decaux, or any of the others—they all derive a deep satisfaction from persuading themselves that they are devoted to me. In short, it is a question of which of them can help and protect me best.'

There was no irony in his words. Wholly without acrimony, he was dissecting their states of mind with the same detachment as he would have brought to the dissection of a body.

'Why do you suppose my wife felt the need to go down to talk to you? In order to cast herself in the role of a wife protecting the work and peace of mind of her husband.'

'Isn't that really the case?'

He looked at Maigret without replying.

'Your wife seemed to me, Professor, to be exhibiting for you a sort of understanding that is pretty rare.'

'True enough, she maintains that she is not jealous.'

'But it is only a pretence?'

'That depends on the meaning you give to the word. It probably is a matter of indifference to her whether I sleep with other people.'

'Even with Louise Filon?'

'Yes, at the start. Don't forget that Germaine, who was only an insignificant nurse, became Madame Gouin overnight.'

'Were you in love with her?'

'No.'

'Why did you marry her?'

'To have someone in the house. The old woman who looked after me had not much longer to live. I do not like being alone, Monsieur Maigret. I do not know if you have experienced that feeling?'

'Perhaps you also like the people around yourself to owe everything to you?'

He did not object. On the contrary the remark seemed to have pleased him.

'In a sense, yes.'

'Was it for that reason that you chose a girl of modest family?'

'The others exasperate me.'

'She knew what to expect when she married you?'

'Very precisely.'

'At what moment did she begin to make herself unpleasant?'

'She has never made herself unpleasant. You have seen her. She is admirable, takes excellent care of the house and never insists on my taking her out for an evening or inviting friends to dinner.'

'If I understand it rightly, she spends her days waiting for you.'

'More or less. It is enough for her to be Madame Gouin and to know that one day she will be Etienne Gouin's widow.'

'You think she's self-seeking?'

'Let us put it that she will not be sorry to have at her disposal the fortune I shall leave her. At this minute I am prepared to bet that she is listening behind the door. She was worried when I telephoned you. She would have preferred me to receive you in the sitting-room with her present.'

He had not lowered his voice when he declared that Germaine was listening behind the door, and Maigret could have sworn that he heard a slight noise in the adjoining room.

'According to her, it was she who suggested installing Louise Filon in this house.'

'So she did. I had not thought of it. I did not even know that a flat was vacant.'

'Didn't this arrangement seem strange to you?'

'Why should it?'

The question had surprised him.

'Were you in love with Louise?'

'Now, listen, Monsieur Maigret, that is the second time you have used that word. In medicine we do not recognize it.'

'You needed her?'

'Physically, yes. Do I have to explain? I am sixty-two years old.'

'I know.'

'That's all there is to it.'

'You weren't jealous of Pierrot?'

'I would rather he had not existed.'

As he had done at Lucile Decaux's, Maigret rose to rearrange a log that had slipped. He was thirsty. The Professor had not thought of offering him a drink. The *marc* he had drunk after dinner furred his mouth, and he had been smoking continuously.

'Have you met him?' he asked.

'Who?'

'Pierrot.'

'Once. Usually they both contrived that it should not happen.'

'What were Lulu's feelings towards you?'

'What feelings do you suppose she would have? I imagine you know her story. Naturally, she spoke to me of gratitude and affection. The truth is simpler. She had no desire to be poor again. You ought to know that. People who have really gone hungry, and suffered poverty in the darkest sense of the word, and who have managed in one way or another to climb out of it, are willing to do anything in the world to avoid falling back into their former life.'

It was true, as Maigret was in a good position to know.

'Was she in love with Pierrot?'

'If you insist on the words!' the Professor sighed resignedly. 'She needed some sentimental interest in her life. She also needed to create problems for herself. I said just now that women like to feel themselves important. Because of that, I suppose, they have to complicate their lives, perplex themselves and constantly imagine that a choice lies before them.'

'A choice between what?' Maigret asked, with the shadow of a smile, to oblige the speaker to be more precise.

'Louise thought that she had a choice between her musician and myself.'

'And she hadn't?'

'Not in reality. I have told you why.'

'Did she ever threaten to leave you?'

'She sometimes claimed to be thinking it over.'

'But you weren't afraid that it would happen?'

'No.'

'She didn't try, either, to persuade you to marry her?'

'Her ambition didn't rise so high as that. I am convinced that she would have been a little alarmed of becoming Madame Gouin. What she needed was security. A flat with heating, three meals a day, and decent clothes.'

'What would have happened if you had disappeared?'

'I had taken out a life-assurance in her favour.'

'Have you also taken one out in favour of Lucile Decaux?'

'No. There is no point. When I die, she will attach herself to my successor as she has done to me, and nothing will change in her life.'

They were interrupted by the telephone bell. Gouin was about to get up to reply when he stopped:

'That will be your detective.'

It was indeed Lucas, speaking from the Batignolles police station, the nearest to Madame Brault's home.

'I have the weapon, sir. She pretended at first that she didn't know what I was talking about.'

'What have you done with her?'

'She's with me, here.'

'Have her sent to the Quai. Where did she find the revolver?'

'She maintains it was on the table.'

'Why did she decide that it belonged to the Professor?'

'According to her, it was obvious. She won't give any details. She is furiously angry, and tried to scratch my face. What does he have to say?'

'Nothing definite. We are having a talk.'

'Shall I join you?'

'Go to the laboratory first to make sure there are no finger-prints on the automatic. That will enable you to take your prisoner along with you to the Quai.'

'Very good, sir,' Lucas sighed, without enthusiasm.

Only now did Gouin think of offering him a drink.

'Will you have a brandy?'

'Gladly.'

He rang. The maid who had let Maigret and Lucas in appeared at once.

'The *fine*!'

They did not speak while they were waiting. When the maid came back, there was only one glass on the tray.

'Forgive me, but I never drink,' the Professor said, leaving Maigret to help himself.

It was probably not on principle, nor for reasons of diet, but simply because he did not need it.

# IX

MAIGRET took his time. Glass in hand, he gazed at the Professor, who calmly returned his gaze.

'The concierge, too, owes you a debt of gratitude, doesn't she? Unless I'm wrong, you saved her son?'

'I don't expect gratitude from anybody.'

'She is none the less devoted to you, and like Lucile Decaux is ready to tell lies to get you out of trouble.'

'Quite so. It is always pleasant to think of oneself as heroic.'

'Don't you sometimes feel alone in the world as you conceive it?'

'Human beings are always alone, whatever they may think. It is enough to admit it once and for all, and to adapt oneself accordingly.'

'I thought you had a horror of being alone?'

'That is not the kind of solitude I had in mind. Let us say, if you like, that I find it distressing to have emptiness around me. I do not like to be alone in a flat, in the street, or in a car. But that is a matter of physical loneliness, not solitude of mind.'

'You are afraid of death?'

'The thought of being dead does not disturb me. But I hate the act of dying and all that goes with it. In your profession, Inspector, you have witnessed death almost as often as I have.'

He understood very well that this was his weak point, and that his fear of dying alone was the little touch of human cowardice that made him a man like any other. Nor was he ashamed of it.

'Since my last heart attack, someone has nearly always been with me. Medically, there is no point in it. However, though it may seem odd, anybody's presence is reassuring. Once when I was about in town, and suddenly felt slightly faint, I went into the first bar I came to.'

It was at this moment that Maigret sprang the question he had long been holding in reserve.

'What was your reaction when you observed that Louise was pregnant?'

He seemed surprised, not that this fact was mentioned, but that it might be considered as a possible complication.

'None,' was all he said.

'Didn't she speak to you about it?'

'No. I suppose she didn't know.'

'She found out about six on Monday. You saw her later. She didn't mention it?'

'All she said was that she didn't feel well, and was going to lie down.'

'Did you think that the child was yours?'

'I never gave it a thought.'

'You've never had children?'

'Not to my knowledge.'

'Have you never wanted one?'

His reply shocked Maigret, who for thirty years had very much wanted to be a father.

'*For what reason?*' the Professor demanded.

'Surely!'

'What do you mean?'

'Nothing.'

'Some people, with no serious interests in life, imagine that a child will give them importance and a sort of value; that they will thus have something to leave behind them. It is not so in my case.'

'Don't you think that, given your age and her lover's, Lulu would have decided that the child was his?'

'Scientifically, there is nothing in it.'

'I am speaking of what she may have thought.'

'It is possible.'

'Wouldn't that be enough for her to make up her mind to leave you for Pierrot?'

He did not hesitate.

'No,' he replied, like a man certain of possessing the truth. 'She would certainly have sworn to me that the child was mine.'

'Would you have recognized it?'

'Why not?'

'Even though you doubted whether you were the father?'

'What difference does that make? One child is as good as another.'

'Would you have married the mother?'

'I see no reason for it.'

'In your opinion, she would not have tried to make you marry her?'

'If she had tried, she would not have succeeded.'

'Because you do not wish to give up your wife?'

'Simply because I find these complications ridiculous. I am answering frankly, because I think you are capable of understanding me.'

'Have you spoken to your wife about it?'

'On Sunday afternoon, if I remember rightly. Yes, it was Sunday. I spent part of the afternoon at home.'

'Why did you tell your wife about it?'

'I also told my assistant.'

'I know.'

'Well, then?'

He was right in thinking that Maigret understood. There was something terribly disdainful and at the same time tragic, in the way in which the Professor spoke of people around him, or rather of the women around him. He took them at their own value, without any illusions, and asked from each only what she could give him. In his eyes it was as if they were little more than inanimate objects.

He did not even take the trouble to hold his tongue in their presence. For what difference did it make? He could think aloud, without bothering about their reactions, still less about what their thoughts or sentiments might be.

'What did your wife say?'

'She asked me what I intended to do.'

'And you replied that you would recognize the child?'

He nodded.

'It did not occur to you that this avowal of yours might cause her some anxiety?'

'Perhaps.'

This time Maigret thought he noticed in the speaker something he had not perceived up to then, or that he had not been able to fathom. There had seemed to be a note of private satisfaction in the Professor's voice as he said '*Perhaps.*'

'You did it on purpose?' he attacked.

'Telling her about it?'

Maigret was sure that Gouin would have preferred not to smile and to have remained impassive, but his feelings were stronger than he was, and for the first time his lips parted curiously.

'In short, you were not sorry to upset your wife, nor your assistant?'

Gouin's silence amounted to an assent.

'Might not one of them have conceived the idea of putting Louise Filon out of the way?'

'The idea must long since have occurred to them. They both hated Louise. I know of no one who has not at some time wished for the death of another person. But people capable of putting these ideas into execution are rare. Luckily for you!'

All this was true. And that indeed was the preposterous thing about this conversation. Everything the Professor had said from the start, Maigret himself believed deep within him. Their ideas about men and their motives were not very far apart.

The difference lay in the attitudes with which they faced the problem.

Gouin only made use of what Maigret would have called pure reason. Whereas the inspector was trying . . .

He would have been hard put to it to define what he was trying to do. Perhaps from understanding people he derived not merely a feeling of pity, but also a kind of affection.

Gouin observed them from on high.

Maigret placed himself on the same level as they.

'Louise Filon has been murdered,' he said slowly.

'That is the fact. Someone has gone to the very limit.'

'Have you wondered who it might be?'

'That is your job, not mine.'

'Have you considered that it might be yourself?'

'Of course. Before I knew that my wife had spoken to you, I was surprised that you did not come and interview me. The concierge had warned me that people had been talking to you about me.'

She, too! And Gouin accepted it as his natural due.

'You went to Cochin on Monday evening, but you only stayed half an hour at your patient's bedside.'

'I went upstairs to lie down in a room on the fourth floor that is kept at my disposal.'

'You were alone, and there was nothing to stop you from leaving the hospital without being seen, coming here by taxi and then returning to your room.'

'At what time, do you think, these comings and goings could have taken place?'

'It has to be between nine o'clock and eleven.'

'What time was Pierre Eyraud in Louise's flat?'

'At a quarter to ten.'

'So that I should have had to kill Louise some time after that?'

Maigret assented.

'Given the time necessary for the journey, I could not have been back at the hospital between ten and ten-thirty.'

Maigret worked it out in his mind. The Professor's reasoning was sound. Of a sudden, Maigret felt disillusioned. Something was not happening as he had foreseen. He knew what was to follow, and hardly paid attention to the speaker's words.

'The fact is, Monsieur Maigret, that at five past ten one of my colleagues, Dr. Lanvin, who had been seeing a patient on the third floor, came up to see me. He did not quite trust his own diagnosis. He asked me to accompany him. I went down to the third floor. Neither my assistant, nor my staff, could have told you about this, for they knew nothing about it.

'This is not the testimony of an anxious woman, but of five or six people, among whom was the patient, who had never previously seen me and probably does not know my name.'

'I never thought that you had killed Lulu.'

He made a point of calling her by this name, which seemed to annoy the Professor. He, too, was experiencing the need to be cruel.

'I merely expected that you would try to cover up for the person who did kill her.'

Gouin showed that the shot had gone home. A slight flush rose to his cheeks, and for an instant his eyes turned away from the inspector's.

Someone rang the doorbell. It was Lucas, carrying a small parcel, whom the maid showed into the room.

'No finger-prints,' he said, unwrapping the weapon and handing it to his chief.

He glanced from one to the other, surprised by the prevailing calm, and by the fact that they were still in the same places and in the same attitudes, as if while he had been running about Paris, time had stood still in the library.

'Is this your revolver, Monsieur Gouin?'

It was a toy-like weapon, with a nickel-plated barrel and a butt in mother-of-pearl; if the shot had not been fired point-blank, it would probably not have done much harm.

'One bullet is missing from the magazine,' Lucas explained. 'I telephoned Gastine-Renette, who will supply the usual tests tomorrow. But he is already convinced that this is the weapon from which the shot was fired on Monday.'

'I suppose, Monsieur Gouin, that your wife, like your assistant, had access to your desk-drawer? It wasn't kept locked?'

'I never lock up anything.'

This, too, came from a kind of contempt for people. He had nothing to hide. It mattered little to him, if others read his private papers.

'Weren't you surprised on Monday evening when you came in to find your sister-in-law in the flat?'

'She generally tries to avoid me.'

'I think she, at least, detests you, doesn't she?'

'That is merely another way of making her life seem interesting.'

'Your wife told me that her sister had called by chance, because she happened to be in the neighbourhood.'

'It could be.'

'When I questioned Antoinette, she told me that her sister had telephoned her to ask her to come round.'

Gouin was listening attentively, without displaying any perceptible emotions. Lying back in his chair, with his legs crossed, he had interlaced his fingers, and Maigret was struck by their length, as slender as a pianist's.

'Sit down, Lucas.'

'Shall I get a drink for your detective?'

Lucas shook his head.

'There is another statement of your wife's which I should like to have confirmed, and only you can do so.'

The Professor motioned that he was waiting.

'Some time ago you had a heart attack when you were in Lulu's flat.'

'That's right. A little exaggerated, but true.'

'Is it also true that your distracted mistress called in your wife?'

Gouin seemed surprised.

'Who told you that?'

'It doesn't matter. But is it true?'

'Not entirely.'

'You realize that your reply is of enormous importance.'

'I realize it from the manner in which you are putting the question, but I do not know why. I did not feel well on that particular night. I asked Louise to go upstairs and fetch a medicine bottle that is kept in my bathroom. She did so. My wife opened the door for her, for the servants had gone to bed, and their bedrooms are on the sixth floor. My wife, who was in bed, too, when Louise came, went to find the bottle.'

'Did they come down together?'

'Yes. But, in the meantime, the attack had passed and I had already left the third-floor flat. I had just walked through the door when Louise and my wife appeared, both in nightgowns.'

'Allow me, a moment.'

Maigret said a few words in a low voice to Lucas, who left the room. Gouin asked no questions and did not seem surprised.

'Was the door wide open, behind you?'

'No. It was pulled to.'

Maigret would have preferred him to tell a lie. For the last hour he would have liked to see Gouin attempting to tell an untruth, but he was a man of relentless sincerity.

'You are sure?'

He was giving him a last chance.

'Absolutely.'

'To your knowledge your wife has never been to see Lulu in her third-floor flat?'

'You little know her.'

Had not Germaine Gouin stated that this was the sole occasion on which she had previously been in the flat?

Now, in fact, she had not entered it on that night. Yet, when she had come down to see the inspector, she had not cast a single curious glance around her, and had behaved as if the place were well known to her.

That was her second lie, to which ought to be added that she had not mentioned the fact that Lulu was pregnant.

'Do you think she is still eavesdropping at the door?'

Sending Lucas to post himself in the vestibule of the flat had been a needless precaution.

'I am convinced she is . . .' the Professor began.

And the communicating door immediately opened. Madame Gouin took a few steps forward into the room, just enough to be able to look her husband in the face, and never had Maigret seen in human eyes so much hatred and contempt. The Professor did not turn away, but received the impact without flinching.

The inspector rose to his feet.

'I am compelled to place you under arrest, Madame Gouin.'

Almost absent-mindedly, and still turned towards her husband, she said :

'I know.'

'I suppose you have heard everything?'

'Yes.'

'You admit that you killed Louise Filon?'

She nodded, looking as if she were about to throw herself like a fury upon the man who was still meeting her gaze.

'He knew that this would happen,' she announced at length, in a jerky voice, while her breast rapidly rose and fell. 'I wonder now whether it is not what he really wanted, if it was not consciously and in order to egg me on, that he told me certain things.'

'You called your sister in order to provide yourself with an alibi?'

Again she nodded assent. Maigret continued:

'I suppose you went downstairs when you left the dressing-room on the pretext of preparing hot toddy?'

He saw her begin to frown, and she turned her glance away from Gouin to level it at the inspector. She seemed to hesitate. One could feel she was waging a battle with herself. At length she uttered :

'That is not true.'

'What is not true?'

'That my sister stayed here alone.'

In Gouin's eyes there flashed an ironic expression. Maigret coloured, for this expression clearly meant :

'What did I tell you?'

And it was true that Germaine was not willing to bear the whole weight of the crime. She had only to remain silent. But she was talking.

'Antoinette knew what I was going to do. As at the last moment I did not have enough courage, she came downstairs with me.'

'Did she go in?'

'She remained on the stairs.'

And after a pause, with an air of defying the world, she added :

'So much the worse. It is the truth.'

Her lips were trembling with stifled anger.

'Now he can set about renewing his harem!'

*

Madame Gouin was wrong. Little change took place in the Professor's life. A few months later Lucile Decaux came to live with him, while continuing to serve as his secretary and assistant.

If she tried to get him to marry her, Maigret never knew.

In any event, the Professor did not remarry.

And when his name turns up in conversation, Maigret pretends not to hear it, or quickly changes the subject.

*Shadow Rock Farm,*
*Lakeville, Conn.*
*31 August, 1953*

# MAIGRET HAS SCRUPLES

# MAIGRET HAS SCRUPLES

## I

THIS scarcely happens more than once or twice a year at the Quai des Orfèvres, and sometimes it is over so soon that no one has time to notice it: suddenly, after a period of feverish activity, during which cases follow one after another without a breathing-space, when they are not cropping up three or four at a time, working the whole staff so hard that the inspectors, for want of sleep, end up haggard and red-eyed, suddenly there is a dead calm, a blank, one might say, barely punctuated by a few telephone calls of no importance.

This had been the case the day before, a Monday, it is true, a day which is always slacker than the rest, and at eleven o'clock in the morning this was still the atmosphere on Tuesday. In the vast corridor, there were at most two or three seedy-looking informers, who had come to make their reports and were hanging about uneasily, while in the inspectors' office everyone, except for those who were suffering from influenza, was at his post.

Whereas in an emergency Maigret was generally short-handed and had the utmost difficulty in finding enough men to put on to a case, he could have drawn, today, on almost his entire squad.

It is true that it was the same nearly everywhere in Paris. It was January 10th. People, after the holidays, were living at a slower pace, with a vague hang-over, and the prospect of rent to pay and income-tax returns to make close at hand.

The sky, in keeping with their consciences and their spirits, was a dull grey, more or less the same grey as the pavements. There was a chill in the air, but not enough to be interesting and to be mentioned in the papers, an unpleasant chill, nothing more, which you only noticed after you had been walking in the streets for some time.

The radiators, in the offices, were burning hot, making the atmosphere closer than ever, and from time to time there were gurgling sounds in the pipes, mysterious noises which came from the boiler-room.

Like schoolboys in their classrooms after the examinations, all and sundry were attending to those little jobs which are usually put off until later, finding in their drawers forgotten reports, statistics to be worked out, dreary administrative tasks.

The people who are talked about in the papers were nearly all on the Côte d'Azur or at winter sports.

If Maigret had still been in possession of his stove, which had been left long after the central heating had been installed but which had finally been removed, he would have broken off from time to time to stoke it up, poking the fire so as to produce a rain of red ashes.

He was not feeling out of sorts, but he was not in good form either, and he had wondered for a moment, in the bus bringing him from the Boulevard Richard-Lenoir, whether he might not be sickening for the influenza.

Perhaps it was his wife who was worrying him? The day before, his friend Pardon, the doctor in the Rue Picpus, had telephoned him unexpectedly.

'Hullo, Maigret. . . . Now don't tell Madame Maigret that I've told you about this . . .'

'Told me about what?'

'She has just been to see me and she insisted that I wasn't to speak to you about it. . . .'

It was less than a year since the chief-inspector himself had been to see Pardon and had asked him to say nothing to his wife about his visit.

'Above all, don't go and start worrying. I've examined her carefully. There's nothing seriously wrong. . . .'

Maigret had been as dull-witted, the day before, when he had had this telephone call, as he was this morning, with the same administrative report in front of him, waiting to be put into shape.

'What does she say is the matter with her?'

'For some time now, she has been getting out of breath going upstairs, and her legs feel heavy too, especially in the morning. Nothing to worry about, as I said before. Only, her circulation isn't quite what it ought to be. I've prescribed some tablets for her to take with every meal. I ought to tell you too, so that you won't be taken by surprise, that I've put her on a diet. I should like her to lose ten or twelve pounds, because that would ease the strain on her heart.'

'You are sure that . . .'

'I swear to you there's absolutely no danger at all, but I thought it best to let you know about it. If I were you, I should pretend I hadn't noticed anything. What frightens her most of all is the thought of your worrying about her. . . .'

Knowing his wife, he felt sure that she had gone and bought the prescribed medicine at the first chemist's she had come to. The telephone call had come in the morning. At midday, he had watched Madame Maigret, who had taken no tablets while he was there. In the evening it was the same. He had hunted for a bottle or a pillbox in the sideboard drawers, and then, in a casual way, in the kitchen.

Where could she have hidden her tablets? She had eaten less, and had not taken any dessert, though she usually enjoyed it.

'I think I must start slimming a bit,' she had said jokingly. 'I'm beginning to burst out of my dresses. . . .'

He had every confidence in Pardon. He was not alarmed. All the same it worried him, or rather, to be more precise, it made him sad.

He had been the first, the year before, with three weeks of complete rest. Now it was his wife's turn. This meant that they had arrived almost imperceptibly at the age of petty tribulations, when minor repairs are necessary, rather like cars which, all of a sudden, need to be sent to the garage nearly every week.

Only, for cars, you can buy spare parts. You can even put in a new engine.

When the porter knocked at his door, which he opened as usual without waiting for an answer, Maigret was not conscious of these thoughts. He raised his head from his file, and looked at old Joseph with big eyes that you might have thought were asleep.

'What is it?'

'Somebody who insists on seeing you personally.'

And Joseph, who made no noise as he walked, put a form on the corner of the desk.

Maigret read a name written in pencil but, as this name meant nothing to him, took no notice of it. Later he would only remember that it was a two-syllabled name, which probably began with an M. Only the Christian name, Xavier, stuck in his memory, because it was that of his first chief at the Quai des Orfèvres, old Xavier Guichard.

Under the printed words: 'Purpose of Call', there was something like: 'Urgently needs to talk to Chief-Inspector Maigret.'

Joseph waited, impassively. It was gloomy enough in the office for the lamps to be lit, but the chief-inspector had not thought of it.

'Will you see him?'

He said yes with a nod of the head, shrugging his shoulders slightly. Why not? The next moment, a visitor of about forty was shown in, whose appearance had nothing special about it and who could have been any one of the thousands of men you see, at six o'clock in the evening, walking hurriedly towards the nearest Metro station.

'I must apologize for troubling you, Chief-Inspector . . .'

'Sit down.'

His visitor was a little nervous, though not inordinately so, over-awed rather, like so many others who entered this same office. He was wearing a dark overcoat, which he unbuttoned before sitting down, keeping his hat on his knees at first, then, a little later, putting it by his feet on the carpet.

He smiled then, a mechanical smile, no doubt a sign of timidity. After giving a little cough, he said:

'The hardest thing is getting started, isn't it? Of course, like every-body else, I've repeated to myself I don't know how many times what I was going to say to you, but, now the time has come, it's all getting muddled up. . . .'

Another smile, angling for some sign of approval or encouragement from the chief-inspector. But the latter's interest had not been awakened. The man had come at the wrong time, when his mind was asleep.

'You must have lots of calls of this sort, from people who come to talk to you about their little troubles, convinced that they are interesting.'

He was dark, and not bad-looking, although his nose was a little crooked and his lower lip too fleshy.

'I can assure you that that isn't the case with me and that I hesitated a long time before bothering a man as busy as you are.'

He must have expected to find a desk littered with files, with two or three telephones ringing at once, inspectors coming and going, and witnesses or suspects slumped on chairs. That was indeed more or less what he would have found on any other day, but his disappointment failed to amuse the chief-inspector, who looked as if he were thinking of nothing in particular.

In fact, he was looking at his visitor's suit, and thinking that it was made of a good cloth and that it must have been cut by a local tailor. A suit of a grey colour that was almost black. Black shoes. A quiet tie.

'Let me assure you, Chief-Inspector, that I'm not mad. I don't know if you know Dr. Steiner, in the Place Denfert-Rochereau. He's a neurologist, which, I believe, is more or less the same as a psychiatrist, and he has appeared several times as an expert witness in the assize courts.'

Maigret's thick eyebrows rose a little way, but not unduly far.

'You've been to see Steiner?'

'Yes, I went and asked him to examine me, and incidentally I might say that his examinations last a full hour and that he leaves nothing to chance. He found nothing wrong. He regards me as completely normal. As for my wife, whom he hasn't seen . . .'

He stopped, because his monologue was not exactly the one he had prepared, and he tried to remember the precise wording. With a mechanical gesture, he had taken a packet of cigarettes out of his pocket and did not dare to ask permission to smoke.

'You may,' said Maigret.

'Thank you.'

His fingers were somewhat clumsy. He was nervous.

'I beg your pardon. I ought to control myself better than this. I can't help being agitated. This is the first time I've seen you in the flesh, all of a sudden, in your office, with your pipes . . .'

'May I ask what your occupation is?'

'I ought to have begun with that. It isn't a very common occupation and, like so many people, you are probably going to smile. I work at the Grands Magasins du Louvre, in the Rue de Rivoli. My official title is head salesman in the toy department. So you can imagine that in the holiday season I was worked to death. Actually, I have a special job which takes most of my time: you see, I'm in charge of the electric trains.'

It was as if he had forgotten where he was, and why he was there, and was letting himself go on his favourite topic.

'Did you go past the Magasins du Louvre in December?'

Maigret said neither yes nor no. He could not remember. He vaguely recalled a gigantic luminous design, on the façade, but he could not have said what the multicoloured moving figures represented.

'If you did, you must have seen, in the third window on the Rue de Rivoli, an exact reconstruction of Saint-Lazare Station, with all its tracks, its suburban trains and its expresses, its signals, its signal-boxes. It took me three months' work and I had to go to Switzerland and Germany to buy some of the material. It may seem childish to you, but if I told you the amount of money we make on electric trains alone . . . Above all, don't imagine that our customers are just children. There are grown-ups, including men with important positions, who are passionately interested in electric trains, and I'm often called to private residences to . . .'

He broke off again.

'Am I boring you?'

'No.'

'You're listening?'

Maigret nodded. His caller must have been between forty and forty-five years old and wore a broad, flat wedding-ring in red gold, almost the same as the chief-inspector's. He also had a tie-pin representing a railway signal.

'Now I've forgotten what I was saying. Of course, it wasn't to talk to you about electric trains that I came to see you, and I realize that I'm wasting your time. However, it is essential that you should be able to place me, isn't it? That I should tell you too that I live in the Avenue de Châtillon, near the church of Saint-Pierre de Montrouge, in the XIVth *arrondissement*, and that I've been in the same place for eighteen years. No: nineteen . . . Anyhow, it will be nineteen years in March . . . I'm married . . .'

He was upset at not being any clearer, at having too many details to give. One felt that as ideas came to him he considered them carefully, asking himself whether they were important or not, then expressed them or rejected them.

He looked at his watch.

'It's precisely because I'm married . . .'

He smiled apologetically.

'It would be easier if you asked the questions, but you can't do that, because you don't know what it's all about . . .'

Maigret came close to reproaching himself for being so static. It was not his fault. It was something physical. He found it difficult to take an interest in what he was being told and felt sorry that he had allowed Joseph to introduce the caller.

'I'm listening . . .'

He filled a pipe, for something to do, and threw a glance at the window, behind which there was nothing but a pale grey colour. It was like a worn-out back-cloth in some provincial theatre.

'Above all I must stress that I'm not making any accusations, Chief-Inspector. I love my wife. We've been married now for fifteen years, Gisèle and I, and we've never really had a quarrel. I talked about her to Dr. Steiner, after he'd examined me, and he looked anxious and said :

' "I'd rather like you to bring your wife along to see me."

'Only, on what pretext can I ask Gisèle to accompany me on a visit to a neurologist? I can't even say for certain that she's mad, because she goes on with her work without anybody complaining about her.

'You see, I'm not very well educated. I'm a ward of the Board of Guardians, and I've had to teach myself. Anything I know, I've learnt out of books, in my spare time.

'I'm interested in everything, not just in electric trains, as you might imagine, and I consider that knowledge is man's most precious possession.

'I must apologize for going on like this. What I wanted to explain was that, when Gisèle began behaving differently towards me, I went to various libraries, among them the Bibliothèque Nationale, to consult works which I couldn't afford to buy. Apart from that, my wife would have been worried if she'd found them at home . . .'

The proof that Maigret was following this speech more or less closely was that he asked :

'Works on psychiatry?'

'Yes. I don't claim to have understood everything. Most of them are written in a language which is too learned for me. All the same I found some books on neuroses and psychoses which made me think. I suppose you know the difference between neuroses and psychoses? I've also made a study of schizophrenia, but I believe, in all conscience, that it doesn't go as far as that . . .'

Maigret thought of his wife, of Pardon, and noticed a little brown mole at the corner of his visitor's mouth.

'If I've not misunderstood you, you suspect your wife of not being in her normal condition?'

The moment had come and the man went rather pale, swallowed his

saliva two or three times, and then, looking as if he were choosing his
words carefully and weighing their meaning, declared:

'I am convinced that for several months, five or six at least, my wife
has been meaning to kill me. That, Chief-Inspector, is why I came to
see you personally. I haven't got any positive proof, otherwise I would
have begun with that. But I'm ready to give you what evidence I have,
which is of two sorts. First of all the moral evidence, the most difficult
to set out, as you will understand, because it consists above all of trifles
which are not important in themselves, but which taken all together
end up by meaning something.

'As for the material clues, there is one piece of evidence, which I've
brought here to show you, and which is the most worrying of all . . .'

He opened his overcoat, then his jacket, took his wallet out of his
hip-pocket, and extracted from it a fold of paper such as some chemists
still use for headache powders.

It was in fact powder that the paper contained, a powder of a dirty
white colour.

'I'm leaving this sample with you, so that you can have it analysed.
Before coming to see you, I asked for an analysis from a salesman at the
Louvre, who is keen on chemistry and has set up a real laboratory at his
home. He was quite definite. It is white phosphide. Not phosphorus,
as you might imagine, but phosphide, I've checked it in the dictionary.
And I didn't just trust to Larousse. I've also looked up some books on
chemistry. White phosphide is a practically colourless powder, which is
extremely poisonous. They used it in the old days, in infinitesimal
doses, as a cure for certain illnesses, and it's precisely because it's so
poisonous that they had to give it up.'

He paused for a moment, a little puzzled at having before him a
Maigret who remained impassive and apparently distrait.

'My wife doesn't go in for chemistry. She isn't following any course
of treatment. She isn't suffering from any of the illnesses for which a
doctor might, just possibly, prescribe zinc phosphide. Now, it wasn't
just a few grammes that I found at home, but a bottle containing at
least fifty grammes. As it happens, I came across it by accident. On
the ground floor, I've got a sort of workshop where I work on the models
of my displays and where I do a little research into mechanics. It's only
a matter of toys, I know, but, as I explained to you, toys represent . . .'

'I know.'

'One day when my wife was out, I knocked a pot of glue over on my
workbench. I opened the cupboard where the brooms and cleaning
materials are kept. Looking for a detergent, I found, quite by accident,
a bottle without a label which struck me as being a curious shape.

'Now, if you link this find with the fact that, in the course of these
last few months, I've felt, for the first time in my life, certain pains
which I've described to Dr. Steiner . . .'

The telephone started ringing on the desk. Maigret picked up the receiver, and recognized the voice of the Chief of Police Headquarters.

'Is that you, Maigret? Have you a few minutes to spare? I should like you to meet an American criminologist who is in my office and who very much wants to make your acquaintance . . .'

Putting down the receiver, Maigret looked around. There was nothing of a confidential nature lying on the desk. His visitor did not look like a dangerous man.

'Will you excuse me? It's only for a few minutes . . .'

'Of course . . .'

At the door, however, he stopped automatically, came back across the office, and opened, as he usually did, the door of the inspectors' office. But he gave them no special instructions. He did not think of it.

A few moments later he pushed open the baize door of the chief's office. A big, red-haired fellow got up from an armchair and shook him vigorously by the hand, saying in French, with only the slightest trace of a foreign accent:

'It's a great pleasure for me to see you in the flesh, Monsieur Maigret. When you came to my country, I missed you, because I was in San Francisco and you didn't come as far as that. My friend Fred Ward, who met you in New York and accompanied you to Washington, has told me some fascinating things about you.'

The chief motioned to Maigret to sit down.

'I hope that I'm not disturbing you right in the middle of one of those interrogations that seem so quaint to us Americans?'

The chief-inspector reassured him. The chief's guest offered him a cigarette, then changed his mind.

'I was forgetting that you're a devotee of the pipe . . .'

This happened periodically and there were always the same remarks, the same questions, the same exaggerated and embarrassing admiration. Maigret, who loathed being examined as if he were a freak, used to put a brave face on things and, at these times, he had a special smile which greatly amused his chief.

One question led to another. After talking of technical matters, they recalled some famous cases, on which he was obliged to give his own opinion.

Inevitably, mention was made of his methods, something which always annoyed him because, as he kept repeating without succeeding in destroying the legends, he had never had any methods.

To release him, the chief got up, saying:

'And now, if you would like to come upstairs and see our museum . . .'

This formed part of every visit of this sort and Maigret, after having his hand crushed once more in a clasp stronger than his own, was able to go back to his office.

He stopped short, surprised, on the threshold, for there was no longer anybody in the armchair he had offered his electric-train sales-man. The office was empty, with just some cigarette smoke floating about half-way up to the ceiling.

He made for the inspectors' office.

'Has he gone?'

'Who?'

Janvier and Lucas were playing cards, something they did not do as often as three times a year, except when they were on duty all night.

'Never mind . . . It doesn't matter. . . .'

He went into the corridor, where old Joseph was reading the paper.

'So my customer's gone, has he?'

'Not long since. He came out of your office and told me he couldn't wait any longer, and he just had to get back to the shop, where they were waiting for him. Should I have . . . ?'

'No. It doesn't matter.'

The man was free to go, since nobody had asked him to come. It was just then that Maigret realized that he had forgotten his name.

'I suppose, Joseph, that you don't know what he was called either?'

'I must admit, Chief-Inspector, that I didn't look at his form.'

Maigret went back to his room, sat down again, and immersed himself once more in his report, which was anything but exciting. Anyone would have thought that the boiler-room had got out of control, for the radiators had never been so hot and alarming noises could be heard. He nearly got up to turn the control lever, did not feel equal to it, and stretched his hand out towards the telephone.

He meant to ring up the Magasins du Louvre and inquire about the head of the toy department. But, if he did so, wouldn't they wonder why the police were suddenly taking an interest in one of the staff? Wasn't Maigret running the risk of doing his caller a disservice?

He did a little more work, then picked up the receiver almost automatically.

'Will you try to get me a certain Dr. Steiner, who lives in the Place Denfert-Rochereau?'

Less than two minutes later, the telephone rang.

'You are through to Dr. Steiner.'

'Forgive me for troubling you, Doctor . . . This is Maigret speaking . . . The chief-inspector at Police Headquarters, yes . . . I believe you have had a patient recently whose Christian name is Xavier and whose surname escapes me . . .'

The doctor, at the other end of the line, did not appear to remember.

'His job is selling toys . . . Particularly electric trains . . . He apparently went to see you to make sure that he wasn't mad and, after that, he spoke to you about his wife . . .'

'Just a moment, please. I shall have to consult my records.'

Maigret could hear him saying to somebody:

'Mademoiselle Berthe, will you be so kind as to . . .'

He must have moved away from the telephone, for there was nothing more to be heard and the silence lasted for quite a time, so long in fact that Maigret thought that he had been cut off.

Judging by his voice, Steiner was a cold man, probably conceited, conscious, in any case, of his own importance.

'May I ask, Chief-Inspector, why you have rung me up?'

'Because this man was in my office just now and went off before our conversation had finished. Now it so happens that, while I was listening to him, I tore the form on which he'd written his name into little pieces.'

'Had you asked him to come and see you?'

'No.'

'What is he suspected of?'

'Nothing. He came of his own accord to tell me his story.'

'Has something happened?'

'I don't think so. He spoke to me about certain fears which, I believe, he has mentioned to you . . .'

There is scarcely one doctor in a hundred who is as unco-operative as this, and Maigret had happened on that one.

'You know, I suppose,' said Steiner, 'that my professional oath prevents me from . . .'

'I'm not asking you, Doctor, to break your oath. I'm asking you, first of all, for the surname of this Xavier. I can find it out straight away by telephoning the Grands Magasins du Louvre, where he works, but I thought that if I did that I should risk harming him in the eyes of his superiors.'

'Yes, that seems quite likely.'

'I know too that he lives in the Avenue de Châtillon, and my men, by questioning the concierges, would get the same result. In that way, too, we might harm your patient by stirring up gossip.'

'I understand.'

'Well?'

'He's called Marton, Xavier Marton,' said the neurologist, reluctantly.

'When did he go and see you?'

'I think that I can answer that question too. It was about three weeks ago, the twenty-first of December to be precise . . .'

'In other words, just when he was at his busiest with the Christmas rush. I suppose that he was in an excited condition?'

'I beg your pardon?'

'Listen, Doctor, let me tell you once again, I'm not asking you to betray any secrets. We have, as you know, expeditious ways of getting information.'

Silence at the other end of the line, and Maigret could have sworn that it was a disapproving silence. Dr. Steiner clearly had no liking for the police.

'Xavier Marton, since Marton is his name,' Maigret went on, 'behaved like a normal man in my office. However . . .'

The doctor repeated:

'However?'

'I'm not a psychiatrist and, after listening to him, I should like to know whether I've been dealing with an unbalanced character or whether . . .'

'What do you mean by unbalanced?'

Maigret was red in the face and was holding the receiver in a clenched and threatening hand.

'If you have certain responsibilities, Doctor, and if you are pledged to maintain a professional secrecy which I am not trying in any way to make you infringe, we have certain responsibilities too. I don't like to think that I let a man go who, tomorrow, might . . .'

'I let him walk out of my office too.'

'So you don't think that he's mad?'

Another silence.

'What do you think of what he told you about his wife? Here, he didn't have time to get to the end of his story . . .'

'I haven't examined his wife.'

'And from what he told you, you've no idea of . . .'

'No idea.'

'You've nothing to add?'

'Nothing, I'm afraid. Will you excuse me? I have someone here who's getting impatient.'

Maigret hung up as if he would have liked to break the receiver over the doctor's head.

Then, almost immediately, his anger subsided and he shrugged his shoulders, even smiling after a while.

'Janvier!' he shouted, so as to be heard in the next room.

'Yes, Chief.'

'You're to go to the Grands Magasins du Louvre and go up to the toy department. Try to look like a customer. And look for a man who should be the head of the department, between forty and forty-five years old, dark-haired, with a hairy mole to the left of his mouth.'

'What do I ask him?'

'Nothing. If the head of the department answers to that description, then his name is Xavier Marton and that's all that I want to know. Though, while you're there, you might show an interest in electric trains so as to get him to talk. Have a good look at him. That's all.'

'Was it about him you were talking on the phone just now?'

'Yes. You heard all that, did you?'

'You want to know whether he's mad?'

Maigret just shrugged his shoulders. Any other day, he would probably not have given more than a few minutes' attention to Marton's call. At Police Headquarters, they are used to visits from lunatics and semi-lunatics, cranks, inventors, males and females who consider themselves marked out to save the world from perdition and others who are convinced that mysterious enemies have designs on their lives or their secrets.

The Special Squad, or the Criminal Squad as it is usually called, is not a mental hospital and, if it deals with these people, it is generally only when they end up by breaking the law, something which, luckily, does not happen straight away.

It was getting on for midday. He thought of telephoning Pardon, but told himself that it was not worth the trouble, that there was nothing in this morning's call more worrying than in a hundred other calls of the same sort that he had had.

Why did he think of the pills his wife had to take with every meal? Because of the zinc phosphide which Xavier Marton claimed to have found in the broom cupboard. Where did Madame Maigret, for her part, hide her pills, so as not to worry her husband?

Intrigued, he resolved to hunt everywhere. She must have thought about it for a long time, and found an artful hiding-place where he would never think of looking.

Well, they would see. In the meantime, he closed his file, and turned the radiator half-off at last, preferring not to leave the window open during the lunch hour.

Just as he was going out, he noticed the packet of white powder on his desk and took it to Lucas.

'Send that to the laboratory. Tell them to let me know what it is this afternoon.'

On the embankment, the cold took him by surprise and he turned up the collar of his overcoat, plunged his hands into his pockets and made for the bus stop.

He did not like Dr. Steiner at all, and it was about him that he thought much more than about the specialist in electric trains.

II

As on every day for years past, he had no need to knock at the door, which opened just as he was stepping on the mat, and he could not remember ever having used the electric bell.

'You're back early,' remarked his wife.

And, straight away, she frowned imperceptibly, as she did when she saw that he was preoccupied. She never failed in this either. She noticed the slightest change in his mood and, if she did not ask him any outright questions, she none the less tried to guess what was worrying him.

Now, for the moment, it was not the visit of the electric-train man. He might have thought about that on the bus, but what had just given him a serious expression, indeed a rather melancholy look, was a memory which had come to the surface while he was pausing on the second-floor landing. The previous winter, the old woman who lived in the flat above theirs had said to him, when he passed her in front of the concierge's lodge and touched his hat to her:

'You ought to see a doctor, Monsieur Maigret.'

'You think I look ill?'

'No. I hadn't even looked. It's the way you come upstairs. For some time, you've been treading more heavily and, every four or five steps, I can hear you hesitating.'

It was not because of her that he had gone to see Pardon some weeks later, but she was right for all that. How could he explain to his wife that it was because of that memory that his thoughts appeared to be a long way off?

She had not yet laid the table. As usual, he roamed round the dining-room and the sitting-room and, almost unconsciously, began opening drawers, lifting the lid of the sewing-box, and of a red lacquer casket in which they kept odds and ends.

'Are you looking for something?'

'No.'

He was looking for the pills. It intrigued him. He wondered if he would end up by finding the hiding-place.

And then, after all, it was true that he had none of his usual go. Hadn't he the right, like other people, to be grumpy on a cold, grey winter's day? He had been like that since morning and it was not particularly unpleasant. One can quite easily be a crosspatch without being unhappy.

He did not like his wife watching him, darting furtive little glances at him. It gave him a guilty feeling, when he was not guilty of anything. What could he have said to her to reassure her? That Pardon had told him about her visit?

The fact of the matter, as he was only just beginning to realize, was that he was annoyed, even a little sad. All because of his customer that morning. This was the sort of intimate little secret which you tell nobody and which you do not like to confess to yourself.

This fellow, for all that he was a specialist in electric trains, was not a crank, like so many of the people who turn up at the Quai des

Orfèvres. He had a problem. He had chosen to explain it frankly to Maigret. Not to any police officer. To Maigret.

And then, when the latter had come back to his office, after going to the chief's room to meet the American, Xavier Marton was no longer there.

He had gone without getting to the end of his confidences. Why? Was he in such a hurry? Wasn't it rather because he had been disappointed?

Before coming, he had formed a definite idea of the chief-inspector. He must have expected understanding, an immediate human contact. He had found a rather dull-witted fellow, stupefied by the warmth from the over-heated radiators, who looked at him without a word of encouragement, and with a wearied or bored expression.

All right, it was nothing. Just a passing shadow. Soon, Maigret would have forgotten all about it. And at table, he took care to talk about anything but that.

'Don't you think it's time we had a maid? We've got a room on the sixth floor which we've never used for anything . . .'

'And what would she do?'

'The housework, dammit! Or at least the heavy work.'

He would have been wiser not to have broached that particular subject.

'Don't you like your lunch?'

'Yes, I do. The thing is, you're tiring yourself out.'

'I've got a woman who comes two mornings a week to do the cleaning. Will you tell me what I should do with myself all day if I had a maid?'

'You could go out for walks.'

'By myself?'

'There's no reason why you shouldn't have some women friends.'

Good! Now it was his wife's turn to be upset. As she saw things, it was rather as if he wanted to rob her of one of her prerogatives, the one she had most at heart.

'You think I'm growing old?'

'We are all growing old. That isn't what I meant to say. It seemed to me . . .'

There are days like that, when one does everything wrong, with the best will in the world. Once lunch was over, he dialled a number on the telephone. A familiar voice answered. He said:

'Is that you, Pardon?'

And he realized that he had just done another needlessly cruel thing. His wife was looking at him in alarm, telling herself that he had discovered her secret.

'Maigret here.'

'Is there something wrong?'

'No. I'm quite all right . . .'

He hastily added:

'My wife too . . . Look, are you terribly busy?'

Pardon's answer brought a smile to his lips. It was funny, because he could have said exactly the same thing himself.

'Dead calm! In November and December, everybody arranged to fall ill at the same time and I didn't have three whole nights in bed. On some days the waiting-room was too small and the telephone never stopped ringing. During the holidays, a few hang-overs and a few liver complaints. And now that people have spent their money, keeping just enough back to pay the rent, they are all well again . . .'

'Could I come round and see you? I'd like to have a chat with you about a case that cropped up this morning at Headquarters.'

'I'll be expecting you.'

'Now?'

'If you like.'

Madame Maigret asked him:

'You're sure it isn't you? You aren't feeling ill?'

'No, I swear I'm not.'

He kissed her, and came back to pat her cheeks and murmur:

'Don't you worry. I think I must have got out of bed on the wrong side.'

He made his way leisurely to the Rue Picpus where Pardon lived in an old block of flats without a lift. The maid, who knew him, did not take him through the waiting-room, but along the corridor and in at the back door.

'He won't be a minute. As soon as his patient has gone, I'll show you in.'

He found Pardon in a white coat, in his consulting-room with the frosted-glass windows.

'I hope you haven't told your wife that I let you know about her? She would hold it against me for the rest of her life.'

'I'm delighted that she has decided to take care of herself. You're sure there's nothing seriously wrong?'

'Nothing at all. In a few weeks' time, perhaps three months, when she has lost a few pounds, she'll feel ten years younger.'

Maigret pointed to the waiting-room.

'I'm not taking your patients' time?'

'There are only two of them, and they've got nothing else to do.'

'Do you know a certain Dr. Steiner?'

'The neurologist?'

'Yes. He lives in the Place Denfert-Rochereau.'

'I knew him vaguely at the Medical School, because he's roughly the same age as I am, and after that I lost sight of him. But I've heard about him from my colleagues. He's one of the most brilliant men of his generation. After passing his examinations with every possible distinction, he was first a houseman, then a registrar at Sainte-Anne. Next, he passed his *agrégation* and he might have been expected to become one of the youngest professors.'

'What happened?'

'Nothing. His character. It may be that he's too conscious of his merit. He makes it felt, and likes behaving in a dry, almost arrogant way. At the same time, he's an over-anxious type, for whom every case poses moral problems. During the war, he refused to wear the yellow star, claiming that he hadn't a drop of Jewish blood in him. The Germans finally proved him wrong and sent him off to a concentration camp. He came back from it thoroughly embittered and he imagines that it's on account of his origins that obstructions are put in his way—which is absurd because the Faculty contains a certain number of Jewish professors. You are having some dealings with him?'

'I telephoned him this morning. I wanted some information from him, but I see now that there's no point in pressing for it.'

Rather like his visitor that morning, Maigret did not know where to begin.

'Although this isn't your speciality, I'd like to ask your opinion on a story I've been told lately. I've had in my office a fellow of forty or so, who seems normal and who talked to me without any hysteria, without any exaggeration, weighing his words. He has been married about twelve years, if I remember rightly, and he has been living longer than that in the Avenue de Châtillon.'

Pardon, who had lit a cigarette, was listening attentively.

'His line is electric trains.'

'You mean he's an engineer on the railways?'

'No. I'm talking about toys.'

Pardon frowned.

'I know,' said Maigret. 'That struck me too. But trains aren't just a hobby with him. He's the head salesman in the toy department of a big store and it was he who, among other things, rigged up the electric train in the window display for Christmas. As far as I can judge, he's perfectly fit.'

'What offence has he committed?'

'None. At least, I suppose not. He told me that his wife, for some time past, has been meaning to kill him.'

'How did he find that out?'

'He went off before he could give me any details. All I know is that he found, hidden in a cupboard for brooms and cleaning materials, a bottle containing quite a large quantity of zinc phosphide.'

Pardon became more attentive.

'It was he who had the stuff analysed and he seems to have read up everything there is to read about zinc phosphide. He also brought me a sample of it.'

'You want to know whether it's a poison?'

'I imagine it's a poisonous chemical?'

'Very poisonous and, in certain country districts, they use it to destroy meadow mice. Has he been ill?'

'He has felt unwell several times.'

'Has he laid a complaint?'

'No. He disappeared from my office without telling me what he was getting at. That's precisely what's worrying me.'

'I think I understand. It was he who went to see Steiner? . . . With his wife? . . .'

'No. Alone. He had himself examined, about a month ago, to make sure . . .'

'. . . that he wasn't mad?'

Maigret nodded, lighting his pipe before going on:

'I could summon him to my office, and even have him examined myself, since Steiner is taking refuge behind his professional oath of secrecy. When I say that I could, I'm exaggerating a little because, in point of fact, there's nothing against him. He came to see me of his own free will. He told me a story which sounds reasonable. Neither he nor anyone else has laid a complaint, and there's no law against possessing a certain amount of any poisonous chemical. You see the problem?'

'I see.'

'It may be that his story's true. If I go and see his superiors to ask about his behaviour, I run the risk of doing him harm because, in the big stores, as in the Civil Service, they mistrust people who attract the attention of the police. If I arrange to have his concierge and his neighbours questioned, rumours will spread round his district . . .'

'You realize what you're asking me for, Maigret. An opinion about a man whom I've never seen, whom you don't know, so to speak, yourself. And I'm only a family doctor, with just a vague smattering of neurology and psychiatry.'

'I remember seeing, in your library, a certain number of works on . . .'

'Between being interested in these things and making a diagnosis, there's an enormous gulf. In short, what you'd like to know is why he came and told you his story?'

'That's the first question. He goes on living with his wife and he doesn't appear to be thinking of parting from her. He didn't ask me to arrest her, nor to start an inquiry into her conduct. And, when I had to leave my office for a few minutes, because the chief wanted to see me, he disappeared, as if he didn't want to go any further with his confidences. Does that mean anything to you?'

'It can mean any number of things. You see, Maigret, in the days when I was a student, these questions were much simpler than they are today. Like the whole of medicine, indeed, and like nearly all the sciences. When, in a court of law, they asked an expert whether a man was mad or of sound mind, the expert more often than not replied with a yes or a no. Do you read the criminological journals?'

'Some of them.'

'In that case, you know as well as I do that it isn't so easy nowadays to make a clear distinction between psychoses, neuroses, psycho-neuroses and even, sometimes, schizophrenia. The barrier between a man of sound mind and a psychopath or a neuropath is more and more fragile and, if one followed certain foreign specialists . . . But I'm not going to embark on a scientific or pseudo-scientific lecture . . .'

'At first sight . . .'

'At first sight, the answer to your question depends on the specialist to whom you put it. For instance, this business of electric trains, even if that's his occupation—*because he chose that occupation*—can be inter-preted as a sign that he's incapable of adapting himself to reality, and that would point to a psycho-neurosis. The fact of his coming to see you at the Quai des Orfèvres and complacently exposing his private life would make any psychiatrist prick up his ears, as would that of his going of his own accord to a neurologist to make sure that he was of sound mind.'

Maigret was not much better off, for he had thought of all this himself.

'You tell me that he was calm, that he spoke deliberately, without obvious emotion, in any case without excessive emotion, and that can just as easily count against him as it can be considered in his favour, like the fact that he had the zinc phosphide analysed and read everything he could about that chemical. He hasn't suggested that his wife was going mad?'

'Not exactly. I can't remember every detail. To tell the truth, at the beginning I was only listening to him with half an ear. It was very warm in my office. I was feeling sleepy . . .'

'If he suspects his wife of being mad, that would be another indica-tion. But it's also quite possible that it's his wife who . . .'

Maigret got up from his armchair and began walking up and down.

'I'd do better not to bother about it,' he grumbled, as much to him-self as to his friend Pardon.

He added straight away:

'And yet, I know that I am going to bother about it.'

'It isn't absolutely impossible that the whole thing only exists in his imagination and that he bought the phosphide himself.'

'You can buy it freely?' asked Maigret.

'No. But the shop where he works may have got some to destroy rats, for instance.'

'Let us suppose that that's the case, that Marton belongs to the category you've thought of: is he a dangerous man?'

'He can become one at any moment.'

'And supposing that his wife is really trying to . . .'

Maigret suddenly turned to face the doctor and growled:

'Hell and damnation!'

Then he smiled.

'Forgive me. That wasn't meant for you. We were so peaceful at the Quai. Like you here! The off season, in fact. And then along comes this braggart who sends in a form, sits down in my office and, in the twinkling of an eye, saddles me with responsibilities which . . .'

'You aren't responsible.'

'From the official, professional point of view, no. All the same, if, tomorrow or next week, one of the two, the man or the woman, happens to die, I shall be convinced that it's my fault . . .'

'Sorry, Maigret, that I can't help you any more. Would you like me to try to get in touch with Steiner to ask his opinion?'

Maigret nodded, without conviction. Pardon rang the Place Denfert-Rochereau, then the clinic where Steiner was to be found at that time. Though Pardon spoke humbly and respectfully, as befitted an obscure family doctor addressing a famous specialist, Maigret understood, from his face and from the cutting voice which he heard vibrating in the receiver, that this approach was having no more success than his own.

'He put me in my place.'

'Forgive me.'

'But no! We had to try. Don't worry about it too much. If everybody who behaved in a peculiar way was to become a murderer or a victim, there would be more vacant flats available than there are today.'

Maigret walked as far as the Place de la République, where he caught his bus. At the Quai des Orfèvres, Janvier, who was in the inspectors' office, came over straight away to make his report, wearing a sheepish expression.

'He can't have seen me here, can he?' he said. 'And my photo has never as you might say appeared in the papers. Do I look so very much like a copper?'

Of the whole staff, Janvier was the man who looked least like one.

'I went up to the toy department and I recognized him straight away, from the description you gave me. Over there, he wears a long grey overall, with the firm's initials embroidered in red. An electric train was running, and I watched it working. Then I beckoned to our man and I started asking him a few innocent questions, like a father who's thinking of buying a train for his kid. I know what it's like, because I bought one for my son the Christmas before last. Well, he scarcely let me say three or four sentences. Then he interrupted me and muttered:

' "Tell Chief-Inspector Maigret that it's pretty shabby of him sending you here and that he's running the risk of getting me the sack."

'He spoke almost without moving his lips, and looking anxiously at a shop-walker who was watching us from a distance.'

On the chief-inspector's desk there was a slip of paper from the laboratory with, written on it in red: *zinc phosphide.*

For two pins, Maigret would have let the matter drop. As he had said to Pardon, or as Pardon had said to him, he could not remember exactly which, it did not concern him from the strictly professional point of view and, if he annoyed Xavier Marton, the latter might very well complain about it and stir up trouble for him.

'I'd like to send you to the Avenue de Châtillon to question the concierge and the neighbours. Only, they mustn't suspect in the district that the police are taking an interest in our man. You might do a bit of door-to-door salesmanship, with a vacuum cleaner, for instance . . .'

Janvier could not help pulling a face at the idea of lugging a vacuum cleaner from house to house.

'If you prefer, you can say you're an insurance agent . . .'

Janvier preferred, obviously.

'Try to find out how they live, what the wife looks like, what people think of them in the district. If the wife is at home, you can always ring and offer her a life-assurance policy. . . .'

'I'll do my best, Chief.'

The weather was still just as grey, just as cold, and the office, in which the chief-inspector had forgotten to switch the radiator on again, was almost freezing. He went and turned the handle, wondering for a moment whether to go and ask the chief's advice. If he did not do so, it was for fear of looking ridiculous. He had realized, while he was telling the story to Pardon, how little he had to go on.

Slowly filling a pipe, he immersed himself once more in the file which he had abandoned that morning and in which he could not succeed in summoning up any interest. An hour went by. The air became more opaque, because of the smoke and the falling dusk. He lit the lamp with the green shade, and got up to regulate the radiator, which was once more getting out of control. There was a knock at the door. Old Joseph put a form on the corner of the desk, murmuring:

'A lady.'

She must have impressed the old porter, for him to use that particular word.

Joseph added:

'I think it's the wife of the chap who came this morning.'

The name written on the form had reminded him of something: 'Madame Marton.' And, underneath, the word 'personal' had been entered below the words 'Purpose of Call'.

'Where is she?'

'In the waiting-room. Shall I show her in?'

He nearly said yes, then thought better of it.

'No. I'll see to her myself.'

He took his time, going through the inspectors' office, then two other offices, so as not to come out into the vast corridor until he was on the other side of the glazed waiting-room. As it was not yet completely dark, the lamps seemed to be shedding less light than usual, and the atmosphere was as yellowish and dismal as in a little provincial railway station.

From a doorway, he inspected the aquarium-like room, in which there were only three people, two of whom were obviously there to see the Vice Squad, for one of them was a little pimp who had Place Pigalle written all over him, and the other was a buxom young woman who had all the self-assurance of a regular customer.

Both of them kept glancing at another woman who was waiting there and who looked out of place on account of her simple yet faultless elegance.

Maigret, taking his time, finally got to the glass door and opened it.

'Madame Marton?'

He had noticed the crocodile handbag matching the shoes, the severe costume under a beaver fur coat.

She got up with just the right degree of confusion one would expect in somebody who had never had anything to do with the police and suddenly found herself faced with one of their most important representatives.

'It's Chief-Inspector Maigret, isn't it?'

The other two, old customers that they were, exchanged meaning looks. Maigret showed her into his office, and gave her the armchair which her husband had occupied that morning.

'I must apologize for bothering you like this . . .'

She took off her right glove, which was made of soft suède, and crossed her legs.

'I suppose you can guess why I'm here?'

It was she who was attacking and Maigret did not like that. Accordingly he refrained from answering.

'Doubtless you too are going to talk to me about professional secrecy . . .'

He noticed particularly the *you too*. Did that mean that she had been to see Dr. Steiner?

It was not only by her attitude that Madame Marton surprised him.

The husband, it was true, was not at all bad-looking, and he presumably made a decent living. Madame Marton belonged none the less to a different class. Her elegance had nothing forced, nothing vulgar about it. Nor had her self-assurance.

Already, in the waiting-room, he had noticed the perfect cut of her shoes and the richness of her hand-bag. Her gloves were not of inferior quality, nor was the rest of what she was wearing. Nothing aggressive, nothing obvious. No showiness. Everything she was wearing had come from excellent shops.

She too looked about forty, that special forty peculiar to Parisian women who take care of their appearance and, in her voice as in her behaviour, she gave the impression of someone who is at ease everywhere and under all circumstances.

Was there really a flaw? He thought he could sense one, a very small discordant note, but he was incapable of putting his finger on it. It was an impression rather than something he had observed.

'I think, Chief-Inspector, that it would save time if I spoke frankly to you. In any case it would be presumptuous to try any artful tricks with a man like you.'

He remained impassive, but this impassivity did not worry her, or else she had marvellous self-control.

'I know that my husband came to see you this morning.'

He finally opened his mouth, hoping to startle her.

'Did he tell you so?' he asked.

'No. I saw him entering this building and I realized that it was you he had come to see. He takes a passionate interest in all your cases. For years he has spoken enthusiastically about you on every possible occasion.'

'You mean to say that you followed your husband?'

'Yes,' she admitted simply.

There was a short and rather embarrassed silence.

'Does that surprise you, after seeing and hearing him?'

'Do you also know what he said to me?'

'I can easily guess. We've been married now for twelve years and I know Xavier well. He's the most honest, the most courageous, the most likeable person imaginable. You probably know that he never knew his parents and that he was brought up by the Board of Guardians?'

He gave a slight nod of the head.

'He was brought up on a farm in Sologne, where they snatched out of his hands and burnt any books that he managed to get hold of. He has none the less arrived where he is now and, in my opinion, he's a long way from having the job he deserves. For my part, I'm constantly surprised by the extent of his knowledge. He has read everything. He knows about everything. And, of course, people take advantage of him. He kills himself over his work. Six months before Christmas he's already getting ready for the festive season, and the season, for him, is exhausting.'

She had opened her handbag, and was hesitating whether to take out a silver cigarette-case.

'You may smoke,' he said.

'Thank you. It's a bad habit of mine. I smoke far too much. I hope my presence isn't preventing you from lighting your pipe?'

He could make out some fine crow's-feet at the corners of her eyelids, but, instead of making her look older, this lent her an added charm. Her grey-blue eyes had the gentle sparkle that comes from short sight.

'We must seem ridiculous to you, the two of us, I mean my husband and I, coming here in turn as if we were coming to confession. It's rather like that when you come to think of it. For months, I've been concerned about my husband. He's over-worked and worried, with periods of utter despondency during which he doesn't say a word to me.'

Maigret would have liked Pardon to be present, for perhaps the doctor would have been able to make something out of this.

'Already in October . . . yes, at the beginning of October . . . I told him that he was getting neurotic and that he ought to go and see a doctor . . .'

'It was you who mentioned neurosis to him?'

'Yes. Shouldn't I have done so?'

'Go on.'

'I watched him a great deal. He began by complaining about one of his superiors whom he has never liked. But, for the first time, he spoke of a sort of conspiracy. Then he started going for a young salesman . . .'

'What about?'

'This sounds ridiculous, but to a certain extent I understand Xavier's reactions. I'm not exaggerating when I say that he is, in France, the greatest specialist in electric trains. I hope that doesn't make you smile? People don't make fun of someone who, for instance, spends his life designing brassières or corsets.'

Why did he ask:

'Do you have something to do with brassières and corsets?'

She laughed.

'I sell them. But I wasn't talking about myself. As I was saying, the new salesman started watching my husband, worming his little tricks out of him, designing circuits. . . . In short, he gave him the impression that he was out to take his place. . . . I only really began worrying when I saw that Xavier's suspicions were extending to me . . .'

'What did he suspect you of?'

'I imagine he has told you. It all began one evening when, looking at me closely, he murmured:

' "You'd make a beautiful widow, wouldn't you?"

'That word often came up again in conversations. For example:

' "All women are made to be widows. Besides, statistics prove . . ."

'You see the theme. From there to telling me that, without him, I should have a more brilliant career, that he was the only obstacle to my success . . .'

She did not falter, despite the expressionless gaze which Maigret deliberately brought to bear on her.

'You know the rest. He's convinced that I've decided to get rid of him. At table, he's apt to exchange his glass for mine, without concealing what he's doing, gazing at me on the contrary with a mocking expression. Before eating, he waits until I've swallowed the first mouthful. Sometimes, when I come home after him, I find him hunting about all over the kitchen.

'I don't know what Dr. Steiner said to him . . .'

'Did you go there with him?'

'No. Xavier told me that he was going to go and see him. Again, it was a sort of challenge on his part. He said to me:

' "I know that you're trying to convince me that I'm going mad. Oh, you're going about it very cleverly, drop by drop, so to speak. But we shall see what a specialist has to say about it." '

'Did he tell you the result of the consultation?'

'He told me nothing, but, since then—it was about a month ago—he has been looking at me with an air of ironical superiority. I don't know if you can understand what I mean. Like a man who has a secret and who's gloating over it. He follows me with his eyes. All the time I have the impression that he's thinking:

' "Go on, my girl! Do what you like. You won't succeed, because I know what you're up to . . ." '

Maigret sucked his pipe and said:

'So this morning you followed him. Are you in the habit of following him?'

'Not every day, no, because I have my own work too. Usually, we set off together, at half past eight, from the Avenue de Châtillon, and we take the same bus as far as the Rue des Pyramides. Then I go to the shop, in the Rue Saint-Honoré, while he carries on along the Rue de Rivoli as far as the Magasins du Louvre. Well, for some time, as I've already mentioned, I think, your name has been cropping up fairly frequently in conversation. Two days ago, he said to me, in a voice that was sardonic and threatening at the same time:

' "Whatever you do, however cunning you are, there will be somebody who will know all about it." '

She added:

'I realized that it was you he meant. Yesterday, already, I followed him as far as the Louvre and stayed for some time watching the staff entrance, to make sure that he didn't come out again. This morning, I did the same . . .'

'And you followed him here?'

She said yes, openly, and bent forward to stub out her cigarette in the glass ash-tray.

'I've tried to give you some idea of the situation. Now, I am ready to answer your questions.'

Only her hands, folded on top of the crocodile handbag, betrayed a certain nervousness.

# III

IF, that morning, he had been dull-witted and absent-minded when faced with the electric-train salesman, it had been an involuntary dullness, something more akin to torpor, to a sort of somnolence. Contact, in fact, had not been established; or to be more precise, it had been established too late.

At present, with Madame Marton, it was his professional dullness that he had recovered, the dullness which he had assumed long ago, when he was still shy, in order to mislead the people he had to talk to, and which had become an almost unconscious reflex.

She did not seem to be impressed by it and went on looking at him in the way a child looks at a big bear which does not frighten him, but which he watches none the less out of the corner of his eye.

Wasn't it she who, so far, had conducted the conversation, ending up with a remark which Maigret had rarely heard in this office of his:

'Now, I await your questions . . .'

He made her wait for some time, deliberately letting the silence deepen, pulling at his pipe, and finally saying with the air of someone who does not quite know what he is doing:

'Exactly why have you come to tell me all this?'

And that did indeed throw her off her balance. She began:

'But . . .'

She fluttered her eyelashes like a short-sighted person, failed to think of anything else to say, and gave a little smile to suggest that the answer was obvious.

He went on, as if he attached no importance to the matter, as if he were a civil servant doing a routine duty:

'Are you asking us to have your husband certified?'

This time, her face immediately flushed scarlet, her eyes glazed and her lips quivered with anger.

'I don't remember saying anything which would entitle you to . . .'

The thrust had gone so deep that she made as if to get up and bring the conversation to an end.

'Sit down, please. Compose yourself. I don't see why such a perfectly natural question should upset you like that. In point of fact, what did you come here to tell me? Don't forget that here we are at Police Headquarters, where our business is with crimes and misdemeanours, either trying to arrest the culprits, or, more rarely, trying to prevent the crimes themselves. First of all, you told me that, for several months, your husband has seemed to be getting neurotic . . .'

'I said . . .'

'You said neurotic. And his behaviour worried you so much that you sent him to see a neurologist . . .'

'I advised him . . .'

'Let us say you advised him to consult a neurologist. Did you expect the neurologist to say that he ought to be certified?'

Her features drawn, her voice changed, she retorted:

'I expected him to look after my husband.'

'Good. I suppose he did?'

'I have no idea.'

'You rang up Dr. Steiner, or you went to see him, and he took refuge behind his oath of professional secrecy.'

She was looking at him with unremitting attention, her nerves keyed up, as if to guess what the next attack was going to be.

'Since his visit to the doctor, has your husband been taking any medicine?'

'Not as far as I know.'

'Has his behaviour altered?'

'He still seems to me to be just as depressed as before.'

'Depressed, but not excited?'

'I don't know. I don't see what you're driving at.'

'What are you afraid of?'

This time, it was she who took her time, asking herself what the question referred to.

'Are you asking me whether I'm afraid of my husband?'

'Yes.'

'I'm afraid *for* him. I'm not afraid *of* him.'

'Why not?'

'Because, whatever happens, I'm capable of defending myself.'

'In that case, I come back to what I asked you at the beginning. Why did you come to see me this afternoon?'

'Because he came to see you this morning.'

They did not reason the same way, the two of them. Or was it that she did not want to reason the same way as the chief-inspector?

'Did you know what he was going to tell me?'

'If I'd known that, I . . .'

She bit her lip. Wasn't she going on to say:

'. . . I wouldn't have had to bother.'

Maigret did not have time to think about it, for the telephone on his desk started ringing. He picked up the receiver.

'Hullo, Chief . . . Janvier here . . . I'm in the office next door . . . They told me who you were with and I thought it best not to show my face . . . I'd like to talk to you for a moment . . .'

'I'm coming.'

He got up and apologized.

'Will you excuse me? Someone needs to see me about another business. I shan't be long.'

In the inspectors' office he said to Lucas:

'Go into the corridor and, if she tries to get away like her husband, stop her.'

He had shut the communicating door. Torrence had had a glass of beer sent up and, automatically, Maigret drank it with relish.

'You've got some news?'

'I've been over there. You know the Avenue de Châtillon. You might think yourself in the provinces, for all that the Avenue d'Orléans is so close. No. 17, where they live, is a new block of flats, with seven stories, in yellow brick, and the tenants are mostly office workers and commercial travellers.

'You must be able to hear everything that's going on in the next flat, and there are kids on every floor.

'The Martons don't live in the apartment-house proper. Where it stands there used to be a sort of big private house which has been demolished. The courtyard is still there, with a tree in the middle and, at the far end, a two-floored cottage.

'An outside staircase goes up to the first floor, where there are only two bedrooms and a bathroom.

'Eighteen years ago, when Xavier Marton, who was still a bachelor, rented this place, the ground floor, which has a glass front, was a carpenter's workshop.

'Later, the carpenter disappeared, Marton rented the ground floor and turned it into an attractive room, half studio, half living-room.

'The over-all effect is unusual, stylish, amusing. It isn't an ordinary house. I started by offering a life-assurance policy to the concierge, who listened to my patter without interrupting me, only to tell me at the end that she didn't need one because she would have her old-age pension one day. I asked if there were any tenants who might be interested. She mentioned a few names.

' "They're all in social insurance schemes," she added. "You haven't got much hope . . ."

' "Haven't you got a Monsieur Marton?"

' "At the far end of the courtyard, yes . . . Perhaps they might . . . They make a decent living . . . Last year, they bought a car . . . Yes, try them . . ."

' "Will there be anybody at home?" '

' "I think so." '

'As you can see, Chief, it wasn't too difficult. I rang at the studio door. A youngish woman answered the bell.

' "Madame Marton?" I asked.

' "No. My sister won't be back till about seven." '

Maigret had started frowning.

'What's the sister like?'

'A woman men are bound to turn round and look at in the street. Speaking for myself . . .'

'You were impressed?'

'She's difficult to describe. I should say she was about thirty-five at the outside. It isn't that she's pretty, or striking. I wasn't impressed by her elegance, either, because she was wearing a little black woollen dress and her hair was untidy—like any woman doing the housework. Only . . .'

'Only?'

'Well, there's something very feminine about her, something touching. You feel that she's very sweet, a little frightened by life, and that's the kind of woman a man wants to protect. You know what I mean? Her figure too is very feminine, very . . .'

He blushed at Maigret's smile of amusement.

'Did you stay with her for long?'

'Ten minutes or so. I talked about insurance to begin with. She replied that her brother-in-law and her sister had both taken out heavy insurance policies about a year ago . . .'

'She didn't specify the amount?'

'No. All I know is that it was with the Mutual. She added that, for her part, she doesn't need any insurance, because she has a pension. Alongside one of the walls there's a table, with a complicated electric train on it, close to a work-bench. I said that I'd just bought my son an electric train. That enabled me to stay there longer. She asked if I'd bought the train at the Magasins du Louvre and I said yes.

' "In that case, it must have been my brother-in-law who served you . . ." '

'That's all?' asked Maigret.

'Just about. I saw two or three shopkeepers, but I didn't dare to be too precise. The Martons seem to be well thought of in the district and to pay their bills promptly.'

Only now did Maigret notice that it was Torrence's glass he had emptied.

'I beg your pardon, old man. Have another one sent up at my expense. . . .'

He added:

'And one for me. I'll come and drink it when I've finished with this customer of mine.'

The latter, during his absence, had not stirred from her armchair, but had lit a cigarette.

He sat down again, his hands flat on the desk.

'I can't remember where we were. Oh, yes! You'd invited me to question you. But I don't really see what I can ask you. Have you got a maid, Madame Marton? Because, if I've understood you rightly, you work all day?'

'All day, yes.'

'On your own account?'

'Not exactly. All the same, my employer, Monsieur Harris, who started the lingerie shop in the Rue Saint-Honoré, gives me quite a high percentage of the profits, because I'm the one who really runs the business.'

'So you have a very good position?'

'Quite good, yes.'

'I seem to have heard of the Maison Harris.'

'It's one of the three best in Paris for fine lingerie. We have a high-class clientèle, including several crowned heads.'

He began to understand certain details which had struck him at the beginning, the discreet yet rather unusual elegance of his visitor. As often happens in fashion houses and certain branches of business, she had gradually acquired the tastes and the attitudes of her clientèle, while at the same time retaining a certain indispensable modesty.

'Your parents were in the lingerie business?'

She relaxed, now that they were on more ordinary ground and the questions appeared to be innocent.

'Far from it. My father was a history master at the Rouen *lycée*, and my mother did nothing all her life apart from being a general's daughter.'

'Have you any brothers and sisters?'

'A sister, who lived for some time in the United States, at Green Village, in New Jersey, not far from New York, with her husband. Her husband was an engineer in a petrol-refining company.'

'You say: was?'

'He was killed two years ago in an explosion in the laboratories. My sister came back to France, so unsettled, so depressed, that we took her in.'

'I asked you just now whether you had a maid.'

'No. My sister doesn't go out to work. She has never done any work in her life. She's younger than I am and married at twenty, while she was still living with my parents. She has always been a spoilt child.'

'It's your sister who keeps house for you?'

'It's her way, if you like, of paying her share. It wasn't we who asked her to do it, but she who insisted.'

'You were living with your parents too when you met your husband?'

'No. Unlike Jenny—that's my sister—I didn't feel that I was made to live in Rouen and I didn't get on very well with my mother. As soon as I'd got my baccalaureate I came to Paris.'

'By yourself?'

'What do you mean?'

'You hadn't got a friend here?'

'I see what you're driving at. Since I asked you to question me, I haven't any excuse for not answering you. I came here, it is true, to join someone I knew, a young lawyer, and we lived together for a few months. That didn't work and I started looking for a job. I then discovered that the baccalaureate, which my father was so keen on that he martyred me for years on end, was no use whatever. All that I could find, after weeks of coming and going in Paris, was a post as a saleswoman at the Magasins du Louvre.'

'And then you met Marton.'

'Not straight away. We weren't in the same department. It was in the Metro that we finally made each other's acquaintance.'

'He was already a head salesman?'

'No, of course not.'

'You got married?'

'He was the one who wanted to. As for myself, I should have been content to have lived with him . . .'

'You love him?'

'Why should I be here if I didn't?'

'When did you leave the shop?'

'Wait a minute. . . . It will be five years ago next month.'

'That's to say, after seven years of marriage.'

'About that.'

'And, by that time, your husband had become the head of a department?'

'Yes.'

'But you were still just an ordinary saleswoman.'

'I don't see what you're driving at.'

He murmured, absent-mindedly:

'Nor do I. So then you entered Monsieur Harris's service.'

'It didn't happen quite like that. In the first place, Harris is the name of the firm. My employer's real name is Maurice Schwob. He used to work at the Magasins du Louvre, where he was the buyer in lingerie.'

'What age?'

'Now?'

'Yes.'

'Forty-nine. But it isn't what you think. Our relations are on a purely business footing. He'd always intended to set up on his own account. He needed a young woman in the shop who knew the business. When it comes to lingerie and corsets, women don't like being served by a man. He'd noticed me at the Louvre. That's all there is to it.'

'You are practically partners?'

'In a sense, yes, although my stake in the business is much smaller than his, which is natural enough, seeing that he supplied the capital and it's he who designs the models.'

'In short, until about five years ago, your husband's position was much better than yours. His pay too. But for the past five years, the reverse has been the case. Is that correct?'

'That is correct, yes, but please believe me when I say that I don't so much as give it a thought.'

'Your husband doesn't give it a thought, either?'

She hesitated.

'To begin with, a man doesn't like it. He has got used to it. We continue to live a quiet life.'

'You have a car?'

'That's true, but we scarcely ever use it except at week-ends and in the holidays.'

'You go on holiday with your sister?'

'Why not?'

'Why not, indeed?'

There was quite a long silence. Maigret looked embarrassed.

'Now that I can't think of any other questions to ask you, tell me, Madame Marton, what you want me to do.'

This was enough to put her on the defensive once more.

'I still don't understand,' she murmured.

'You don't want us to watch your husband?'

'Why watch him?'

'You aren't prepared to sign a formal application which would enable us to have him examined by a mental specialist?'

'Certainly not.'

'Then that's all?'

'That's all . . . I suppose.'

'In that case, I don't see, either, why I should detain you any longer. . . .'

He got up. She copied him, a little stiffly. Just as he was about to show her to the door, he appeared to change his mind.

'Do you use zinc phosphide?'

She did not start. She must have been expecting that question all the time, and who knows if she hadn't come in order to answer it?

'I use some, yes.'

'What for?'

'The Rue Saint-Honoré is one of the oldest streets in Paris and, behind the luxury shops, the houses are mostly in poor condition; there's a whole network of courtyards, alleys and passages which you'd never dream existed. The nearness of the market too attracts an incredible number of rats and these have caused damage to our stock. We've tried several products without success. Someone advised Monsieur Schwob to use zinc phosphide, which has produced excellent results.

'In the Avenue de Châtillon too we had some rats, and my husband used to complain about them. I took a certain amount of phosphide from the shop . . .'

'Without telling your husband?'

'I can't remember now whether I told him or not.'

She opened her eyes wide, as if an idea had struck her.

'I suppose he can't have imagined . . . ?'

He did not finish the sentence for her and she went on:

'If he spoke to you about it, it means that . . . Heavens above! And there was I racking my brains to guess what was worrying him . . . I must have it out with him tonight . . . Or rather . . . If I bring that subject up, he'll know that I've been to see you. . . .'

'You expected to be able to keep it from him?'

'I don't know, I don't know any more, Monsieur Maigret. I came here . . . how shall I put it? . . . I came here in all simplicity, with the idea—a naïve idea, I know—of confiding in you. I told you the truth about Xavier and about my worries. Instead of helping me, you have asked me questions which, I can see, show that you don't believe me, that you suspect me of heaven knows what intentions . . .'

She was not crying, but she was none the less showing signs of a certain distress.

'Well, it can't be helped! . . . I had hoped . . . All that I can do now is try my best . . .'

She opened the door with her gloved hand. Standing in the corridor, she said again:

'Good-bye, Chief-Inspector. . . . Thank you all the same for being good enough to see me . . .'

Maigret watched her walking away with neat steps, perched on very high heels, and he shrugged his shoulders as he went back into his office. A good quarter of an hour had passed before he came out again and made for the chief's office, asking Joseph on the way:

'Is the Director in?'

'No. He's in conference with the Prefect and told me that he probably wouldn't come back this afternoon.'

All the same Maigret went into the office of the Director of Police Headquarters, turned on the light, and began reading the titles of the works which filled the two mahogany book-cases. There were statistical works which nobody had ever opened, and technical books in several languages which the authors or publishers had sent as a matter of course. There were numerous treatises on criminology, as also on scientific detection and forensic medicine.

Maigret finally found on one shelf several works on psychiatry and skimmed through three or four before picking one which seemed to him to be written in simpler and more comprehensible language than the others.

That evening, he took the book home with him. After dinner, sitting in his slippers in front of the log fire, with the radio playing quietly in the background, he started reading, while Madame Maigret mended shirt cuffs.

He had no intention of reading the bulky volume from cover to cover and there were whole pages which, in spite of his brief medical studies, he was incapable of understanding.

He looked for certain chapter headings, certain words which had been used that morning in the course of his conversation with Pardon, words whose meaning everybody thinks he knows but which, for professionals, have a very different resonance.

*. . . Neuroses . . . In Adler's opinion, the starting-point of neurosis is an alarming feeling of inferiority and insecurity . . . A defensive reaction against this feeling leads the patient to identify himself with an imaginary ideal. . . .*

He repeated under his breath, thus causing his wife to raise her head:

'. . . imaginary ideal . . .'

*. . . Physical syndrome . . . Neurasthenics are well known to specialists of every sort . . . Without any appreciable organic lesion, they feel ill and above all worry about possible complications; they undergo innumerable consultations and examinations. . . .*

*. . . Mental syndrome . . . The feeling of incapacity is dominant . . . Physically, the patient feels dull-witted, full of aches and pains, exhausted by the slightest effort. . . .*

Like Maigret that very morning. Even now, he felt dull-witted, not full of aches and pains perhaps, but . . .

He turned the pages, in a grumpy mood.

*. . . So-called paranoiac constitution . . . Hypertrophy of the Ego. . . .*

*. . . Unlike the sensitive type, these patients project into family and above all social life a personality, an Ego, which is clumsy and domineering. . . .*

*. . . Never do they consider themselves blameworthy or at fault . . . Their pride is characteristic . . . Even when they are not very intelligent, they often dominate their family by means of the authoritarianism and their arrogant dogmatism. . . .*

Did that apply best to Xavier Marton, or to his wife? And couldn't it serve to describe a quarter of the population of Paris?

*Revenge psychosis . . . Persecuted persecutors . . .*

*. . . This is a typical emotional psychosis of which the nosological setting has aroused interminable discussions . . . Like Kraepelin and Capgras, I consider that it does not belong to the class of true delusions . . . The patient considers himself to be the victim of an injustice which he wishes to redress, and attempts to obtain satisfaction at any price. . . .*

Xavier Marton? Madame Marton?

He went from neuroses to psychoses, from psychoses to psychoneuroses, from hysteria to paranoia, and, like those good folk who when they immerse themselves in a medical dictionary discover that they are suffering from each illness in turn, he found, under every heading symptoms which would apply just as well to the one as to the other of his two characters.

From time to time he grunted, or repeated a word or a phrase, and Madame Maigret darted anxious little glances at him.

In the end he got up, like someone who has had enough, threw the book on to the table and, opening the sideboard in the diningroom, took the bottle of *prunelle* and filled one of the little gilt-edged glasses.

It was a sort of protest on behalf of common sense against all this learned rubbish, a way of getting back to earth with both feet firmly on the ground.

Pardon was right: the result of too much studying of the anomalies of human behaviour, classifying them and subdividing them, was that you ended up not knowing what a man of sound mind was like any more.

Was he one himself? After what he had just been reading, he was not so sure.

'Have you got a difficult case on?' ventured Madame Maigret, who rarely bothered about her husband's work at the Quai des Orfèvres.

He contented himself with shrugging his shoulders and growling:

'A mad business!'

A little later, after emptying his glass, he added:

'Let's go to bed.'

\*

The next morning, however, he asked to see the Director a few minutes before the daily report, and the chief saw straight away that he was worried.

'What's the matter, Maigret?'

He tried to tell him the story of the two calls as succinctly as possible. The chief's first reaction was to look at him in some surprise.

'I don't see what's bothering you. Seeing that no formal complaint has been made to us . . .'

'Quite. Each came to tell me his or her little story. And neither story, in itself, is really alarming. But, as soon as you try to superimpose them, you realize that they don't fit . . . Incidentally, I'm returning your book.'

He put it on the desk and the Director glanced at the title, then looked at the chief-inspector in even greater surprise.

'Let me make myself clear, Chief. And don't imagine that I've allowed this book to carry me away. I don't say that one of the two is absolutely mad. All the same, there's something wrong somewhere. It's not for nothing that two people, husband and wife, come to see me the same day as if they were coming to confession. And if, tomorrow or in a week, or in a month from now, we found we had a corpse on our hands, I wouldn't feel I had a clear conscience . . .'

'You think that will happen?'

'I don't know. I do and I don't. It's like working on a case the wrong way round. Usually, we have a crime to begin with, and it's only after it's been committed that we have to hunt for the motives. This time, we've got the motives, but so far no crime.'

'Don't you think there are thousands of cases where the motives aren't followed by a crime?'

'I'm sure there are. Only, in those cases, people don't come and tell me their motives *beforehand*.'

The chief thought for a moment.

'I'm beginning to understand.'

'As things are at the moment, there's nothing I can do. Especially after the recent campaign in the Press about the liberties the police have been taking with suspects.'

'Well then?'

'I came to ask you for permission to mention it on the off-chance to the Public Prosecutor.'

'To get him to order an investigation?'

'Something like that. In any case, to set my conscience at rest.'

'I doubt if it will come off.'

'So do I.'

'Go ahead if it will make you happier.'

'Thank you, Chief.'

He had not said exactly what he had promised himself he would say. This was doubtless because it was too complicated, still obscure. Whereas the day before, at this time, he had never heard of the Martons, the specialist in electric trains was beginning to haunt his thoughts, and also the elegant young wife who, he admitted to himself, had stood up to him bravely although he had done everything he could to shake her.

Even the widowed sister-in-law, a touching figure according to Janvier, was engrossing him as if he had always known her.

'Hullo! Maigret here. Will you ask the Public Prosecutor for me if he can spare me a minute or two? . . . This morning, if possible, yes . . . Hullo! I'll hold the line.'

The Public Prosecutor's office was in the *Palais de Justice* too, in the same buildings, but in a different world, where the walls were covered with carved panelling and where people talked in velvet voices.

'Straight away? . . . Yes . . . I'm coming. . . .'

He went through the glass door separating the two worlds, passed some barristers in black robes, and noticed, waiting between a couple of gendarmes beside nameless doors, people who had gone through his hands a few weeks or a few months before. Some of them looked pleased to see him again and said good morning to him in an almost familiar way.

'If you will wait a moment, the Public Prosecutor will see you straight away. . . .'

It was almost as awe-inspiring as going into the headmaster's study at school.

'Come in, Maigret . . . You wanted to see me? . . . But there's nothing new, is there?'

'I wanted to consult you on a matter which is almost a matter of conscience . . .'

He told the story very badly, much worse even than to the Director of Police Headquarters.

'If I understand you correctly, you're under the impression that there may be an incident, or perhaps a crime?'

'That's roughly it.'

'But this impression is based on nothing specific, apart from a man's vague confidences and the explanation his wife came and gave you afterwards of her own accord? Tell me, Maigret, how many lunatics, semi-lunatics, maniacs and common-or-garden cranks do you see every year in your office?'

'Hundreds . . .'

'And here, I get thousands of letters from the very same people.'

The Public Prosecutor looked at him in silence, as if he had said everything there was to say.

'All the same, I'd like to have carried out an investigation,' the chief-inspector murmured timidly.

'What sort of investigation? Let's be precise. Questioning the neighbours, the employers, the sister-in-law, the tradesmen, and heaven knows who else? In the first place, I don't see what good that will do you. And secondly, if the Martons are trouble-makers, they'll have a perfect right to complain . . .'

'I know . . .'

'As for forcing them, either of them, to be examined by a psychiatrist, we can't do that as long as we haven't received a formal request to that effect from the husband or the wife. And even then . . . !'

'And if a crime is committed . . .'

A short silence. A slight shrug of the shoulders.

'That would be regrettable, of course, but there's nothing we could do about it. And at least, in that event, we shouldn't have far to go to find the culprit.'

'Will you allow me all the same to have them kept under observation?'

'On condition, first of all, that it is done discreetly enough not to get us into trouble. And on a second condition, and that is that it doesn't force you to use inspectors who would be more usefully employed somewhere else . . .'

'We are in a period of dead calm . . .'

'That sort of period never lasts long. If you really want to know my opinion, you're letting your scruples run away with you. In your place, Maigret, I would let the matter drop. Once again, as things are at the moment, we have no right to intervene, and no means of doing so either. These cases of a husband and wife suspecting each other—I'm convinced there are thousands of them all around us . . .'

'But neither the husband nor the wife has ever appealed to me before.'

'Have these two really appealed to you?'

He had to admit that they had not. Marton had not asked him for anything, when it came to the point. Nor had Madame Marton. Sister Jenny even less.

'Forgive me if I don't keep you any longer. There are five or six people waiting to see me and I have an appointment at the Ministry at eleven.'

'I am sorry to have disturbed you.'

Maigret was not pleased with himself. He had the impression that he had stated his case badly. Perhaps he ought not to have immersed hin\self, the night before, in that treatise on psychiatry.

He walked towards the door. The Public Prosecutor called him back at the last moment, and his tone was no longer the same, his voice was suddenly as cold as when he pronounced one of his famous indictments.

'It is clearly understood that I don't give you any cover at all and that I've forbidden you, until some fresh development occurs, to do anything about this affair?'

'Very good, sir.'

And, in the corridor, head down, he growled:

'. . . fresh development . . . fresh development . . .'

Who was to be the *fresh development*, in other words the victim? He or she?

He shut the glass door so hard that he nearly broke the panes.

# IV

IT was not the first time, nor in all probability would it be the last, that Maigret had flown into a temper on leaving the Public Prosecutor's office, and his differences with certain judges, particularly Judge Coméliau, who for over twenty years had been as it were his private enemy, were a legend at the Quai des Orfèvres.

In his more collected moments, he did not take too seriously the antagonism which existed between the two worlds. On their different sides of the glass door, each did its job more or less conscientiously. The same people—delinquents, criminals, suspects and witnesses—passed in turn through their hands.

What distinguished them most of all from each other, what created hidden conflicts between them, was the point of view each adopted—a point of view which was probably determined by their different methods of recruitment. The people in the Parquet—attorneys, deputies and examining magistrates—nearly all belonged to the middle, if not the upper, strata of the *bourgeoisie*. Their way of life, after a period of purely theoretical study, scarcely ever brought them into contact, except in their chambers, with those whom they had to prosecute in the name of society.

Hence their well-nigh congenital incomprehension of certain problems, their irritating attitude towards certain cases which the men of Police Headquarters, living in permanent and almost physical intimacy with the criminal world, appraised instinctively.

There was also a certain tendency, in the *Palais de Justice*, to hypocrisy. In spite of their apparent independence, which they talked about a great deal, they were more afraid than anyone else of the Minister's frown and, if a case which aroused public interest was hanging fire, they would spur on the police, who never went fast enough for their liking. It was for the police to make their plans and use what methods they thought fit.

But if the newspapers came to criticize those methods, then the magistrates of the Parquet were quick to share their indignation.

It was not for nothing that the chief-inspector had gone to see the Public Prosecutor. As happens periodically, they were in a tight corner. There had been an incident, for which not Police Headquarters, fortunately, but the Sûreté Générale, of the Rue des Saussaies, was to blame, and which had assumed serious proportions, giving rise to questions in the Chamber.

In a night-club, the son of a Deputy had made a violent attack on an inspector who, he alleged, had been following him for several days. A general free-for-all had followed. It had proved impossible to hush up the affair and the Sûreté had been forced to admit that it had been making inquiries about the young man, who was suspected not only of being a heroin addict, but also of acting as a tout for drug traffickers.

The result had been a sickening show-down. According to the Deputy whose son had been convicted, one of the traffickers was a police spy, and the father alleged that it was with premeditation, on instructions from the Place Beauvau, in order to compromise him, the Deputy, in his political career, that the young man had been turned into a drug addict.

As if by chance—these things never come singly—there had been a case, the following week, of someone being beaten up in a police station.

For some time, therefore, the police had been having a bad Press, and, Maigret, that morning, had preferred to take precautions.

Back in his office, he was none the less determined to get round the instructions he had been given, especially as instructions of that sort are never intended to be taken literally. The Public Prosecutor had been covering himself, that was all, and if, the next day, a corpse was found in the Avenue de Châtillon, he would be the first to blame the chief-inspector for his inactivity.

Since he had to cheat, he cheated, but half-heartedly. He would no longer use Janvier whom, curiously enough, Marton had spotted straight away in the Magasins du Louvre, and who had already shown his face in the Martons' house.

Of all the others, it was Lucas who would have shown the greatest flair and judgment, but Lucas had one great fault: it was easy to guess his profession.

He picked young Lapointe, who had less training and less experience, but who often passed for a student or a young clerk.

'Listen, my lad . . .'

He gave him his instructions at length and at leisure, with all the more details in that these instructions, at bottom, were vague. First of all he was to buy a toy of some sort, without hanging about, without making a fuss, at the Magasins du Louvre, in order to register Marton's appearance so that he would know him again.

Then, at lunch-time, he was to stand close to the staff entrance and shadow the specialist in electric trains.

At night, he was to do it again, if need be. Meanwhile, in the afternoon, he was to go and have a look at the lingerie shop in the Rue Saint-Honoré.

'For all they know, you might be engaged . . .'

Lapointe blushed, for this was almost the case. Almost, but not quite, for the engagement was not yet official.

'You could buy, say, a nightdress for your fiancée. Preferably not too dear . . .'

To which Lapointe shyly retorted:

'You think it's done to give a nightdress to one's fiancée? Isn't it rather intimate?'

Afterwards they would see how they could find out more about the Martons and the young sister-in-law, without giving themselves away.

When Lapointe had gone, Maigret set to work, signing documents and letters, listening to his inspectors' reports on minor matters. Marton and his wife remained none the less, like a backcloth, behind his preoccupations of the moment.

He had one faint hope, on which he was not counting too heavily, and that was that he would be told that Xavier Marton was asking to see him.

Why not? If he had gone off, the day before, while Maigret was with the chief, wasn't that because the time he had allowed himself had run out, because he had to be back at the shop before a certain time? In that sort of establishment, the discipline is strict. Maigret knew this all the better in that in his early days he had spent nearly two years policing the big stores. He knew the atmosphere in them, the machinery, the rules and the intrigues.

At midday, he went back to the Boulevard Richard-Lenoir for lunch, and eventually noticed that it was the third day they were having grilled meat. He remembered in time about his wife's visit to Pardon. She must have been expecting him to express surprise at the new menus and no doubt she had got ready a more or less plausible explanation.

He avoided putting her in this predicament, and showed a certain tenderness towards her, perhaps a little too much, for she looked at him with a hint of anxiety in her eyes.

Of course, he was not thinking all the time about the trio in the Avenue de Châtillon. This affair only came back to him from time to time, in brief snatches, almost without his knowing it.

It was rather like a jigsaw puzzle and it irritated him in the way a puzzle does which you come back to in spite of yourself to try and fit a piece into place. The difference was that the pieces, in this case, were so to speak pieces of human beings.

Had he been unkind to Gisèle Marton, whose lip, when she had left him, had been trembling as if she had been going to cry?

It was possible. He had not done it on purpose. It was his job to try to find things out. In fact, he had taken rather a liking to her, as he had to the husband, too.

The two of them must have been in love when they were both working at the Magasins du Louvre, at the time when they had only two uncomfortable rooms over the workshop at their disposal.

Little by little, they had made improvements in their home. When the carpenter had left, they had extended their living-quarters by renting the ground floor, which, according to Janvier, had become an attractive room, and they had had an interior staircase put in so that they would not have to go outside to get from one floor to the next.

At present, they both had what is known as a good position, and they had bought a car.

There was a flaw somewhere, that was obvious. But where?

An idea came into his head and it was to come back to him several times. Marton's visit to Dr. Steiner worried him because, in the whole of his career, he could not remember coming across a man who had been to a neurologist or a psychiatrist to ask him:

'Do you think I am mad?'

His idea was that perhaps Marton had read, accidentally or otherwise, a treatise on psychiatry such as the one the chief-inspector had dipped into the night before.

At the same time as he was conjuring up the Avenue de Châtillon household in this way, Maigret took several telephone calls, saw a tradeswoman who had come to complain about a case of shop-lifting and sent her to see her local inspector, and went for a prowl round the inspectors' room where a dead calm still reigned.

Lapointe gave no sign of life and about five o'clock Maigret found himself back at his desk, lining up words in columns on the yellow jacket of a file.

First of all he had written; *frustration.*

Then, underneath: *inferiority complex.*

These were terms which he was not in the habit of using, and which he distrusted. Some years before, there had been an inspector who had come from university and who had only stayed a few months at the Quai. He was probably working in a legal bureau at present. He had read Freud, Adler and a few others and had been so deeply impressed by them that he claimed to be able to explain every case by psycho-analysis.

During his brief stay at Police Headquarters, he had been wrong every time and his colleagues had nicknamed him Inspector Complex.

The case of Xavier Marton was none the less an odd one in that it might have come straight out of the book which Maigret had read the day before and which he had finally closed in exasperation.

There were whole pages of the book dealing with frustration and its effects on the behaviour of the individual. Examples were given which might have been portraits of Marton.

A ward of the Board of Guardians, he had spent his childhood in a poverty-stricken farm in Sologne, with rough, brutish peasants who snatched his books out of his hands whenever they caught him reading.

He had none the less devoured every printed page he could get hold of, going from a popular novel to a scientific treatise, from mechanics to poetry, swallowing good and bad indiscriminately.

He had taken his first step forward by getting into a big store where, to begin with, only the humblest jobs had been entrusted to him.

One fact was characteristic. As soon as Marton could, he stopped living in more or less shabby furnished rooms, like most people starting their careers in Paris, and had his own flat instead. It only consisted of two rooms at the far end of a courtyard; the furniture was scanty, the comfort non-existent, but it was his home.

He went up in the world. Soon he could imagine that he was leading an orderly, middle-class life, and his first thought was, with his meagre means, to improve his living-quarters.

This was what Maigret put under the heading: inferiority complex. To be more precise, it was Marton's reaction against that complex.

The man needed to reassure himself. He also needed to show other people that he was not an inferior being, and he worked desperately hard to become an undisputed master in his field.

In his mind, didn't he consider himself rather as *King of the Electric Train?*

He was becoming somebody. He had become somebody. And, when he got married, it was to a girl of middle-class origins, a schoolmaster's daughter, who had her baccalaureate, and whose manners were different from those of the little salesgirls all around her.

Maigret, after some hesitation, wrote down a third word: *humiliation.*

His wife had outstripped him. She was now practically in business on her own account, in a luxury trade where every day she met famous women, high society, the rank and fashion of Paris. She was earning more than he was.

Certain phrases remained with Maigret from what he had read the day before. He could not remember them word for word but, in spite of himself, he tried to apply them to his problem.

One, for example, which said in substance that 'psychopaths shut themselves up in a world of their own, a dream-world which is more important to them than reality'. It was not quite that, but he was not going to make a fool of himself by going back to the chief's office for the book and consulting it all over again.

Besides, he did not really believe in it. All that stuff was just idle speculation.

But didn't electric trains, which were to be found not only in the Rue de Rivoli, but also in the studio in the Avenue de Châtillon, correspond fairly closely to this 'dream-world', to this 'shut-in world'?

Another passage reminded him of Xavier Marton's sang-froid, the conversation at the Quai des Orfèvres, the apparent logic of the way he had presented his case.

Maigret could no longer remember whether it was under the heading of neuroses, psychoses or paranoia, for the frontiers between these different domains did not seem to him to be very clearly defined.

'. . . *starting from false premises* . . .'

No. The text was different.

'. . . *on false or imaginary premises, the patient builds a closely reasoned argument, which is sometimes subtle and brilliant* . . .'

There was something similar about persecution mania, but here '*the patient starts from real facts, and draws conclusions from them which have an appearance of logic.* . . .'

The zinc phosphide was real. And in the Harris–Gisèle Marton, or rather Maurice Schwob–Gisèle Marton relationship, wasn't there something equivocal which was liable to affect the husband?

The most disturbing thing about this case was that, on closer examination, the young wife's behaviour, studied in the light of the same texts, produced an almost identical diagnosis.

She too was intelligent. She too discussed their case with apparent logic. She too . . .

'Oh, to blazes with it!'

Maigret looked for an india-rubber to erase the words he had written on the yellow file, filled his pipe, and went and planked himself down in front of the window, through which, in the darkness, he could see nothing but the dots of light that were the street-lamps.

When young Lapointe knocked at his door, half an hour later, he was dutifully filling in the blanks in an administrative questionnaire.

Lapointe had the advantage of coming from outside, from real life, and there remained a little fresh air in the folds of his overcoat, his nose was pink with cold and he was rubbing his hands together to warm them.

'I've done what you told me to, Chief.'

'He didn't smell a rat?'

'I don't think he noticed me.'

'Fire away.'

'First of all, I went up to the toy department and I bought the cheapest thing I could find, a little car that doesn't even go by clockwork. . . .'

He took it out of his pocket, and put it on the desk. It was canary yellow.

'A hundred and ten francs. I recognized Marton straight away from your description, but it was a woman who served me. Next, while I was waiting for the lunch-hour, I went and had a look at the Rue Saint-Honoré, without going in. The shop isn't far from the Place Vendôme. A narrow window, with practically nothing on display: a dressing-gown, a black silk slip and a pair of mules in gold-embroidered satin. On the glass, two words: 'Harris, lingerie'. Inside, it looks more like a drawing-room than a shop and you can tell it's a high-class firm.'

'Did you see her?'

'Yes. I'll come to that in a minute. It was time for me to go back to the Louvre, where I waited near the staff entrance. At midday, there's a regular stampede, like kids coming out of school, and everybody rushes off to the restaurants round about. Marton came out, in even more of a hurry than the others, and started walking very fast along the Rue du Louvre. He kept glancing all around him and he looked back two or three times, without paying any attention to me. At that time of day there's a lot of traffic and the pavements are crowded. . . .

'He turned left into the Rue Coquillière, where he hadn't gone more than a hundred yards before he went into a little restaurant called the "Trou Normand". The front is painted brown, with yellow letters, and the cyclostyled menu is stuck up on the left of the door.

'I hesitated and then decided to go in a few moments after him. It was full up. You could see that the people there were regulars and besides that, on one wall, there's a set of pigeon-holes where they keep the customers' napkins. I stopped at the bar and bought an *apéritif*.

' "Can I have lunch?"

'The manager, in a blue apron, looked into the dining-room, where there are only ten or so tables.

' "In a few minutes, there'll be a place for you. No. 3 has got to his cheese course."

'Marton was at the far end, by the kitchen door, sitting by himself in front of a paper table-cloth and a single cover. There was an empty place facing him. He said something to one of the two waitresses who seemed to know him and she laid a second cover.

'A few minutes went by. Marton, who had unfolded a newspaper, kept looking over it in the direction of the door.

'And soon, sure enough, a woman came in, spotted the table at the back straight away and went and sat down on the empty chair as if she was in the habit of doing this. They didn't kiss, they didn't shake hands. They just smiled at each other, and it seemed to me that their smiles were a little sad, or at least a little melancholy.'

'It wasn't his wife?' interrupted Maigret.

'No. I'd just seen his wife in the Rue Saint-Honoré and I'll come back to her later. From what you've told me, I should say it was the sister-in-law. The age and appearance tally. I don't know how to put it. . . .'

Well, well! Janvier, speaking about the same woman, had used almost exactly the same words.

'You get the impression of a real woman—I don't know if you understand what I mean—a woman who was born to love a man. Not to love in an ordinary way, but as men dream of being loved. . . .'

Maigret could not repress a smile on seeing Lapointe blush.

'I thought you were practically engaged?'

'I'm trying to explain to you the effect she must produce on most people. Sometimes, just like that, you meet a woman who starts you thinking straight away about . . .'

He could not find the right words any more.

'About what?'

'In spite of yourself you see her curling up in her companion's arms, you can almost feel her warmth. . . . At the same time you know that she's meant for one man alone, that she's a true mistress, an authentic lover. . . . After a while I got a place, two tables away from them, and that impression remained with me all through the meal . . . They didn't make the slightest suspicious gesture . . . They didn't hold hands . . . I don't think they even looked into each other's eyes . . . And yet . . .'

'You think they're in love?'

'I don't think they are. I'm certain of it. Even the waitress in her black dress and white apron, a great slatternly gawk of a girl, didn't serve them the way she served the other people and seemed to be making herself their accomplice. . . .'

'But you said at the beginning that they looked sad.'

'Let us say serious . . . I don't know, Chief . . . I'm sure they aren't unhappy, because you can't be really unhappy when you . . .'

Maigret smiled again as he wondered what would have been the report of a Lucas, for example, who would certainly not have had the same reactions as young Lapointe.

'Not unhappy, then, but sad, like lovers who aren't free to show their love . . .'

'If you like. At one point, he got up to help her off with her coat, because she'd glanced at the stove. It's a black woollen coat, with a bit of fur at the collar and the wrists. She was wearing a black dress too, in jersey, and I was surprised to see that she's rather on the plump side. . . .

'He looked at his watch several times. Then he asked the waitress to bring him his sweet and his coffee, while his companion had only got to roast veal.

'He got up while she was still eating, and, by way of leave-taking, he put his hand on her shoulder, in a gesture that was simple and tender at the same time.

'At the door he turned round. She smiled at him and he blinked his eyes. . . .

'I don't know if I did right to remain. I decided that he would be going back to the shop. I finished my dinner almost at the same time as the woman. Marton had paid the bill before going. I paid mine. I went out behind her and, without hurrying, she went and caught the Porte d'Orléans bus. I imagined she was going home to the Avenue de Châtillon and I didn't follow her. Did I do wrong?'

'You did right. And then?'

'I walked about a bit before going to the Rue Saint-Honoré, because the luxury shops scarcely ever open before two o'clock, and some of them not until half past two. I didn't want to arrive too early. I must admit too that I was a bit windy. Apart from that, I wanted to see the boss and I said to myself that he's probably the sort who lunches in the big restaurants and isn't in any hurry.'

Maigret was looking at Lapointe with almost fatherly benevolence, for he had taken him under his wing when, two years earlier, the young man had come to the Quai des Orfèvres, where he had made remarkable progress.

'I'll tell you something, Chief. I was so scared at the idea of going into a shop like that that first of all I treated myself to a *calvados*.'

'Go on.'

'The first time I had almost pushed open the glass door when I saw two old ladies in mink coats sitting in the armchairs, facing the saleswoman, and I didn't dare. I waited till they came out. A Rolls with a chauffeur was waiting for them a little way off.

'Then, for fear another customer might arrive, I rushed in.

'At first, I didn't look at anything around me, I was so nervous.

' "I want a nightdress for a young lady," I said.

'I supposed it was Madame Marton who stood before me. Besides, when, a little later, I looked at her, I noticed that she had certain features in common with the young woman at the "Trou Normand". Madame Marton is a little taller, with a good figure too, but her body looks harder, what they call a statuesque figure. You see what I mean?

' "What sort of nightdress?" she asked me. "Please sit down. . . ."

'Because it isn't the kind of shop where you stay on your feet. I told you it looks like a drawing-room. At the back, there are curtains hiding some cubicles which must be used for trying on, and I noticed, in one of them, a big mirror and a cane stool.

' "What is the young lady's size?"

' "She's a bit shorter than you, and not so broad across the shoulders. . . ."

'I don't think she smelt a rat. She looked at me all the time in a patronizing sort of way and I felt that she was thinking I must have come to the wrong shop.

' "We have this one, in real silk, with hand-made lace. I suppose it's for a present?"

'I stammered that it was.

' "This is the model we created for the trousseau of Princess Helen of Greece."

'I was determined to stay as long as possible. I said hesitantly:

' "I suppose it's very dear?"

' "Forty-five thousand . . . It's a 40 . . . If the young lady's size is different, we shall have to make it to measure, for this is the only one we have in stock . . ."

' "You haven't something less exotic? In nylon, for instance? . . ." '
Maigret remarked:

'I say, Lapointe, you seem to know all about it. I thought it wasn't done to buy lingerie for a fiancée.'

'I had to play the game properly. At the word "nylon", she took on a scornful, supercilious expression.

' "We don't stock nylon here. Only pure silk and batiste . . ."

'The door opened. It was in the mirror, to begin with, that I saw a man in a camel-hair coat to whom, straight away, the saleswoman gave a wink. I imagine, Chief, that that meant she had a queer customer on her hands.

'The man took his hat and coat off, and went behind the counter into a narrow office where he hung his things on a coat-stand. He left a whiff of perfume behind him. I could see him bending over some papers which he was glancing at casually.

'Then he came back into the shop where, looking at his fingernails, then at us in turn, like someone who is completely at home, he seemed to be patiently waiting for me to make up my mind.

'I asked at a venture:

' "What have you got in white? I'd like something very simple, without any lace. . . ."

'They exchanged another glance and the woman bent down to take a box out of a drawer.

'Monsieur Harris, or Schwob, is the sort of man you meet around the Place Vendôme and the Champs-Elysées, and he might just as easily be in the cinema trade as in exports, pictures or antiques. You know what I mean, don't you? He must go to his barber's every morning and have a facial massage. His suit is beautifully cut, without a single crease, and he certainly doesn't buy his shoes ready-made.

'He has dark hair, with a touch of silver at the temples, a clean-shaven face, a matt complexion, a distant and sardonic gaze.

' "This is the least expensive thing we have . . ."

'A nightdress that looked nothing at all, with just a few stitches of embroidery.

' "How much?"

' "Eighteen thousand."

'Another glance between them.

' "I suppose it isn't what you're looking for?"

'And already she was opening the box to put the nightdress back.

' "I'll have to think about it . . . I'll come back. . . ."

' "Yes, do."

'I nearly forgot my hat on the counter and had to go back for it.

Once I was outside, and the door shut, I turned round and saw the two of them laughing.

'I walked about a hundred yards, then I came past on the opposite pavement. There was nobody left in the shop. The curtain of the little office was open, the woman sitting there, and Harris busy, in front of a mirror, running a comb through his hair. . . .

'That's all, Chief. I can't swear that they sleep together. What is certain is that they make a good pair and they don't need to speak to understand each other. You can tell that straight away.

'Madame Marton doesn't lunch with her husband although they work a quarter of a mile from each other, and it was the sister-in-law who went to meet Xavier Marton.

'Finally, I imagine that these two have to keep their meetings secret. Marton, in fact, has very little time at his disposal for his midday meal. Close to the Magasins du Louvre, there are lots of cheap restaurants which I saw the salesmen and saleswomen dashing into.

'But he takes the trouble to go quite a distance, to a restaurant with a different clientele where no one would think of looking for him.

'Is Madame Marton in the habit of lunching with Monsieur Harris? I just don't know. The fact that he arrived at the shop after her doesn't prove anything.'

Maigret got up to regulate the radiator which, as on the day before, was showing a tendency to get out of hand. All day long, they had been expecting snow, which was forecast and was already covering the North and Normandy.

Hadn't the chief-inspector been right to send the treatises on psychiatry and all those stories of psychoses and complexes to the devil?

He had, at last, the impression of finding himself face to face with people of flesh and blood, men and women with their passions and their interests.

Yesterday, it had just been a question of a couple of people.

Today there seemed to be two couples and that made a tremendous difference.

'Where are you sending me now?' asked Lapointe, who in his turn was becoming passionately interested in the case and was afraid of being taken off it.

'You can't go to the Rue Saint-Honoré any more, or to the Avenue de Châtillon, now that the two women have seen you. . . .'

Besides, what could he have gone and done there? It was the Public Prosecutor who appeared to be in the right. Nothing had happened. Probably nothing would. Unless one of the two couples, growing impatient. . . .

Just at that moment the telephone rang, Maigret looked at the black marble clock which was always ten minutes fast. It said twenty to six.

'Inspector Maigret, yes . . .'

Why did he feel a slight shock on recognizing the voice? Was it because, ever since the morning before, his only thoughts had been about the man at the other end of the line?

There were noises and voices in the background. Maigret could have sworn that his caller, full of anxiety, was holding his hand cupped in front of his mouth. He was speaking in a low voice.

'I must apologize about yesterday, but I was forced to go. All I want to know is whether you will still be at your office about a quarter to seven, or perhaps ten to seven. We close at half past six . . .'

'Today?'

'If you don't mind . . .'

'I'll be expecting you.'

Marton rang off straight away, after stammering a thank-you, and Maigret looked at Lapointe rather as Madame Marton and Monsieur Harris looked at one another in the lingerie shop.

'It's him?'

'Yes.'

'He's coming here?'

'In an hour and a quarter.'

Maigret felt tempted to laugh at himself, and at all the ideas he had thought up about a case which, in an hour and a quarter, would no doubt appear perfectly simple to him.

'We've time to go and have a pint at the Brasserie Dauphine,' he growled, opening his cupboard to take his hat and coat.


# V

IT was just as he was going downstairs with Lapointe that the idea struck Maigret.

'I'll be with you in a minute. Wait for me.'

And, still hesitating, he made for the inspectors' office. His idea was for one of his men to start shadowing Xavier Marton at the entrance to the Magasins du Louvre. He did not know precisely why, in fact. Or rather, he felt that several things might happen. To begin with, Marton was capable of changing his mind at the last moment, as had happened a first time when he had left Maigret's office during the latter's absence. Or else his wife, who admitted having followed him the previous day, might well shadow him again.

If she accosted him in the street, wouldn't he accompany her to the Avenue de Châtillon? There were other possibilities too. And, even if nothing happened, Maigret would not be sorry to find out how the electric-train salesman behaved while taking this important step, whether he hesitated, whether he stopped on the way, for example, to steel himself by drinking a glass or two.

Janvier risked being recognized. Another inspector working on his own, Lucas, for instance, who was free, but who had never seen Marton, might not be able to recognize him, from his description, among all the staff coming out.

'Lucas and Janvier! Cut along, both of you, to the Magasins du Louvre. When the staff come out, don't show your face, Janvier, but just point out Marton as he goes by and you, Lucas, will do the shadowing alone.'

Lucas, who did not know much about the case, asked:

'Do you think it will be a long job, that he'll go very far?'

'Here, probably.'

He nearly added:

'Above all, no taxis, no expenses!'

For there are certain administrative rules of which the public knows nothing but which, for the men of Police Headquarters, are sometimes of great importance. When a crime, or an offence, is committed, and when the police, in consequence, make investigations on the basis of powers delegated by the judiciary, the professional expenses of the chief-inspectors, inspectors and technicians are as a rule chargeable to the culprit. If he is not arrested, or if the courts later find him not guilty, the Ministry of Justice foots the bill.

If on the other hand it is a case which Police Headquarters are investigating on their own initiative and if, in the end, there is neither crime nor culprit, then the bill for expenses is charged to the Prefecture, that is to say to the Ministry of the Interior.

Now, for the police, this makes an enormous difference. The Ministry of Justice, which always thinks that the criminal will pay, is not too close-fisted and does not make a fuss about a taxi more or less. The Prefecture, on the contrary, scrutinizes every bill, demanding an account of the most trifling comings and goings which cost the treasury anything.

In the present affair, wasn't Maigret working to ensure that there was neither a crime nor a culprit?

This meant therefore no bill for expenses, or a bill which was as modest as possible, and he knew that, if nothing happened, he would have to justify the use of his men.

'Let's go!'

There was no snow, as the radio had forecast, but a cold, yellowish fog. The two men, in the heat and light of the Brasserie Dauphine, did not order beers, which seemed unseasonable, but *apéritifs*. Elbows on the bar, they said nothing about Marton, chatted a little with the *patron*, and when, with their coat-collars turned up, went back to the Quai.

Maigret had decided to leave the door of the inspectors' office slightly ajar and behind that door to install Lapointe who was a fairly good shorthand writer. It was a precaution, just in case.

At ten to seven, he was sitting at his desk, waiting for old Joseph to knock at the door. At five to seven, he was still waiting and Lapointe, with a well-sharpened pencil in his hand, was also waiting behind the door.

The chief-inspector was beginning to lose patience when, at one minute to seven, he finally heard footsteps, a familiar little knock, and saw the white porcelain handle turning.

It was Joseph. Notified beforehand, he contented himself with murmuring:

'It's the gentleman you're expecting.'

'Show him in.'

'Forgive me for being a little late,' said Marton. 'It was useless for me to take the Metro at this time of day. Two buses were full and so I came on foot, thinking it would be quicker. . . .'

He was panting slightly, and looked hot from running.

'If you want to take your coat off . . .'

'Perhaps it would be a good idea. I think I'm starting a cold. . . .'

Settling down took some time. He did not know where to put his overcoat. First he put it on a chair, noticed that it was the one where he ought to sit to face the chief-inspector, and carried it to the other end of the room.

At last, they were sitting together in conversation, Maigret smoking his pipe and studying his caller more closely than on the day before. He was almost disappointed. For twenty-four hours, his thoughts had been revolving round Marton, who had ended up by becoming an extraordinary figure, and now all he had before him was an ordinary little man, such as you rub shoulders with by the hundred in the Metro or in the street.

He was a little vexed with him for being so commonplace, for behaving in such a normal way.

'I must apologize again for leaving your office without telling you. At the shop, discipline is strict. I had obtained permission to be away for an hour to go and see my dentist, who lives in the Rue Saint-Roch, a stone's throw from the Louvre. Here I suddenly noticed that time was passing and I had to be at my post at eleven to take delivery of some goods. I meant to leave a message with your porter, the old man who showed me in, but he wasn't in the corridor. I ought to have rung you up, but we are forbidden to make private calls and most of the telephones are connected to the switchboard.'

'How did you manage this afternoon?'

'To ring you up, I took advantage of the fact that there wasn't anybody in the floor manager's office, where there's an outside telephone.

You'll have noticed that I was quick about saying what I had to say to you and that I rang off in a hurry. . . .'

There was nothing extraordinary in all that. But the chief-inspector insisted :

'At midday, when you went to lunch . . .'

'In the first place, I said to myself that you'd be out at lunch too. And then, it seemed to me that you didn't regard my business as very serious . . .'

'And is it serious?'

'Certainly. It was you who sent somebody to prowl round my department, wasn't it?'

Maigret did not answer. The other continued :

'You won't admit it, but I'm sure that it was a detective.'

He must have prepared this conversation as he had prepared the first. There were however some moments of hesitation, like gaps. He hesitated for quite a while before asking :

'My wife has been to see you, hasn't she?'

'What makes you think that?'

'I don't know. I've known her a long time. I'm sure she suspects something. Women have antennae. And, with her character, if she senses the slightest danger, she'll attack. You understand what I'm getting at?'

A silence, during which he looked at Maigret reproachfully, as if he were vexed with him for not playing fair with him.

'Has she been?'

The chief-inspector hesitated in his turn, realizing that it was a heavy responsibility to take on. If Marton was, to any extent, mentally ill, the answer could have a capital influence on his future behaviour.

A little earlier, alone in his office, Maigret had nearly telephoned his friend Pardon to ask him to be present at the interview. But hadn't the doctor already told him that he knew next to nothing about psychiatry?

Xavier Marton was there, in his chair, three feet away from the chief-inspector, talking and gesticulating like any other caller. Perhaps he was a normal man, who felt that his life was in danger and had honestly come to tell the police all about it.

Perhaps too he was a neurotic, suffering from persecution mania, who needed reassurance.

Perhaps he was a lunatic.

And finally, perhaps he was a man tormented by diabolical ideas, a madman too, in a certain sense, but a lucid, intelligent madman, who had drawn up a detailed plan which he intended to carry out at all costs.

His face was very ordinary. He had a nose, a mouth, eyes and ears like everybody else. The blood had gone to his head, as a result of the contrast between the cold outside and the heat of the office, and perhaps that was what was making his eyes shine, or else it was the cold in the head of which he had spoken.

Was he really starting a cold in the head or had he just mentioned it because he knew that his eyes were going to shine?

Maigret felt ill at ease. He began to suspect that the man had only come back in order to ask the question about his wife.

Had he in his turn spied on her? Did he know that she had been to the Quai des Orfèvres and did he hope to find out what she had said?

'She has been here,' the chief-inspector finally admitted.

'What did she tell you?'

'Here, as a rule, people answer questions, they don't ask them.'

'I beg your pardon.'

'Your wife is very elegant, Monsieur Marton.'

He gave a mechanical twitch of the lips which did duty for a smile and which was not without irony, or bitterness.

'I know. She has always dreamt of being elegant. She decided to be elegant.'

He had stressed the word *decided* as, in a letter, he would have underlined it, and Maigret remembered that it had happened before that his caller had emphasized a word.

Hadn't he read, in the treatise on psychiatry, that insistently underlining words was a sign of . . . ?

But he refused to put the interview on that particular plane.

'Yesterday morning, you came and told me that you were afraid for your life. You spoke to me about the attitude your wife had adopted for some time, and of a poisonous chemical which you had found in a cupboard. You also told me that several times, after a meal, you had felt ill. At that point, I was called to see the Director and our conversation did not continue later, for you had gone. I suppose you had some other details to give me?'

Marton gave the rather melancholy smile of a man who is being treated unjustly.

'There's a way of asking questions which makes it difficult to answer them,' he observed.

Maigret nearly lost his temper, for it seemed that he was being taught a lesson and he was aware that he deserved it.

'But, dammit all, you aren't going to tell me that you came here without any definite object? Are you lodging a complaint against your wife?'

Marton shook his head.

'You aren't accusing her?'

'What of?' he asked.

'If what you've told me is true, you can accuse her of attempted murder.'

'Do you really think that that would result in anything? What proof have I got? You yourself don't believe me. I've given you a sample of zinc phosphide, but I might just as well have put it in the broom-cupboard myself. From the fact that I went, of my own accord, to see a neurologist, it will be assumed that I'm not entirely sane, or else—and this would be just as plausible—that I'm trying to create that impression.'

It was the first time that Maigret had had a customer like this before him and he could not help staring at him in amazement.

Every reply, every new attitude baffled him. He kept hunting in vain for a flaw, a weak point, and, without fail, it was he himself who was put in his place.

'My wife is sure to have spoken to you about my neurasthenia. She will have told you too that, in the evening, when I'm pottering about, I'll often stamp my feet and actually burst into tears because I can't do something I have in mind . . .'

'You've mentioned this to Dr. Steiner?'

'I told him everything. For a whole hour, he asked me questions that you would never dream of asking.'

'Well?'

He looked Maigret in the eyes.

'Well, I'm not mad.'

'And you're still convinced that your wife intends to kill you?'

'Yes.'

'But you don't want us to start inquiries?'

'That wouldn't do any good.'

'Or to protect you?'

'How?'

'Then, once again, why did you come here?'

'So that you would know. So that, if anything happened to me, you wouldn't think it was death from natural causes, as would be the case if you hadn't been told. I've read a lot about poisonings. According to your own experts, you have to reckon nine cases of criminal poisoning that are unknown, and therefore unpunished, to one case where the culprit is discovered.'

'Where did you read that?'

'In a scientific detection review.'

'You take it regularly?'

'No. I read it in a public library. Now, I can tell you one last thing: I don't intend to go quietly.'

Maigret gave a slight start, feeling that at last they were coming to the heart of the matter.

'What exactly do you mean?'

'First of all, that I'm taking precautions, as I told you yesterday. And then that, precisely because of the statistics I've just quoted, I'm not going to rely on the law and, if I have enough time, I'll mete out justice myself.'

'Am I to understand that you are going to kill your wife *in advance*?'

'Before dying, of course, but not before she has succeeded in poisoning me. There are very few poisons which can cause instantaneous death and they are nearly all extremely difficult to get hold of. Therefore there will be a certain lapse of time between the moment I shall know she has succeeded and the moment I shall be incapable of action. I have a loaded revolver at home. I should add that it is properly licensed, as you can find out from the town hall. My wife knows about it, because I've had it for years. Only, for some time now, it has been hidden somewhere where she won't find it. She has been looking for it. She's still looking . . .'

There were moments when Maigret asked himself whether he wouldn't be well advised to take the man, straight away, to the special infirmary at the *Dépôt*.

'Suppose that tonight, half an hour after dinner, you feel a pain in the stomach?'

'Don't worry, Monsieur Maigret. I'm capable of telling the difference between poisoning and ordinary indigestion. Apart from that, I've always had an excellent stomach.'

'But if you think that you've been poisoned, you'll act?'

'If I *feel* that I've been poisoned, I shan't hesitate.'

'You'll shoot?'

'Yes.'

The telephone started ringing and it seemed to the chief-inspector that it was making an unusual din in the room, where the atmosphere had finally become oppressive, tense, almost unhealthy . . .

'It's Lucas, Chief.'

'Yes . . .'

'I couldn't let you know any sooner, because I didn't want to leave her alone on the embankment . . .'

'Who?'

'The woman . . . I'll explain in a minute . . . I had to wait until an inspector passed near me before I could hand over to him and come up here to phone you . . . It's Torrence who's taken my place . . .'

'Be quick about it. Don't talk too loud, because you're making the receiver vibrate . . .'

Had Marton realized that all this concerned him indirectly?

'I understand, Chief . . . Here goes! . . . Janvier showed me your man as he was coming out of the shop . . . I started following him, by myself, while Janvier waited for a bus . . .'

'And then?'

'As long as we were walking through the crowds, which are dense at this time of day, I didn't notice anything. But, crossing the courtyard

of the Louvre, and then getting on to the embankment, I realized that
I wasn't the only one who was following him . . .'

'Go on.'

'There was a woman close on his heels . . . I don't think she noticed
me, but I can't be sure . . . She followed him as far as the Quai des
Orfèvres and she's still there, about a hundred yards from the entrance . . .'

'Describe . . .'

'It isn't worth it. When Torrence came near me and I'd handed over
to him, I came up here and asked Janvier to go and have a look down
below, seeing that he's been on the case . . . He's just come back and
he's beside me now . . . Would you like to have a word with him?'

'Yes.'

'Hullo, Chief . . . It's the sister-in-law, Jenny . . .'

'You're sure?'

'Certain.'

'She didn't recognize you?'

'No. I took precautions.'

'Thanks.'

'No instructions?'

'Torrence is to go on watching her.'

'And what about the man? Has Lucas to keep on following him when
he comes out?'

'Yes.'

He rang off, and found Marton's inquiring gaze fixed on him.

'Is it my wife?' asked the electric-train enthusiast.

'What do you mean?'

'Nothing. I should have known that you wouldn't tell me the truth
anyway.'

'You heard?'

'No. Only, it isn't difficult to understand, from the little you said
yourself. If it is my wife . . .'

'Well? What then?'

'Nothing. I was wrong to come and see you yesterday, and even
more so to come back today. Seeing that you don't believe me . . .'

'I ask nothing better than to believe you. Why, look here! Since
you're so sure of yourself, I'll make you a proposal. Dr. Steiner, re-
strained by his professional oath of secrecy, won't tell me anything.'

'You want me to submit to an examination by another doctor?'

'By the specialist at the special infirmary at the *Dépôt*. He's a trust-
worthy man, a professor known all over the world.'

'When? Straight away?'

Was Maigret wrong? Was there, in his caller, a moment of panic?

'No. At this hour, I can't possibly bother him. He'll be in his
department tomorrow morning.'

Calmly, Marton replied:

'If it isn't too early, I'll have time to tell the shop.'

'You agree to it?'

'Why shouldn't I agree to it?'

'You also agree to sign a paper for me stating that it's of your own free will that you're having this examination?'

'If you insist.'

'You're a curious fellow, Monsieur Marton.'

'You think so?'

'You are here of your own free will too, I'm not forgetting that. You aren't obliged to answer my questions. However, there are a few I should like to ask you.'

'Will you believe me?'

'I shall try, and I can assure you that I'm not prejudiced against you in any way.'

This declaration only called forth a disabused smile.

'Do you love your wife?'

'Now?'

'Now, of course.'

'In that case, no.'

'Does she love you?'

'She hates me.'

'That isn't the impression I'd got of the couple you form when you left here yesterday morning.'

'We didn't have time to go to the root of the matter, and you didn't want to anyway.'

'Just as you like. Shall I go on?'

'Do, please.'

'Did you ever love her?'

'I thought I did.'

'Explain to me what you mean by that.'

'Till then, I'd lived on my own, without allowing myself the slightest distraction. I've worked hard, you know. Starting as low as I did, I had to make a tremendous effort to become what I have become.'

'You'd never had anything to do with women before you met your wife?'

'Rarely. The sort of adventure you can imagine. It left me with more shame than pleasure. So that, when I met Gisèle, I saw her as the ideal woman and it was that ideal woman that I loved. At that time the word *couple* was a marvellous word to me. I dreamt about it. We were going to be a couple. I was going to become one of the halves of a couple. I wouldn't be alone any more at home, in life. And, one day, we would have children . . .'

'You haven't any?'

'Gisèle doesn't want any.'

'Had she told you beforehand?'

'No. If she had told me, I'd have married her all the same and I'd have been satisfied with just the couple . . .'

'Did she love you?'

'I thought so.'

'You realized one day that you'd been mistaken?'

'Yes.'

'When?'

He did not reply straight away. He seemed to have found himself faced with a serious matter of conscience and he was thinking. Maigret, for his part, did not hustle him.

'I suppose,' Marton murmured at last, 'that you've made inquiries. If you sent somebody to spy on me at the shop, you must have sent one of your men too to the Avenue de Châtillon.'

'That's correct.'

'In that case, I'd better speak frankly. To the question you've just asked me, I answer: Two years ago.'

'In other words, it was about the time your sister-in-law came to live with you both that you realized that your wife didn't love you and that she had never loved you?'

'Yes.'

'Can you explain to me why?'

'That's easy. Before knowing my sister-in-law, who was living in America with her husband, I wasn't always happy at home, but I used to tell myself that I was as happy as anyone could be. You understand? In other words, I considered my disappointments to be unavoidable, imagining that other men were all in the same boat. In short, Gisèle was a woman and I'd come to believe that her faults were the faults inherent in every woman.'

He was still searching for his words, pronouncing some with greater emphasis than others.

'Like everybody else, I suppose, I'd dreamt of a certain form of love, of union, of fusion, call it what you will, and, after a few years or a few months, I'd come to the conclusion that it doesn't exist.'

'You mean, that love doesn't exist.'

'That sort of love, at least.'

'What is it that you hold against your wife?'

'What you're making me do probably isn't in very good taste, but if I don't answer you truthfully, you'll go and draw the wrong conclusions again. I know now, for instance, that, if Gisèle left Rouen and her family, it was just out of ambition. Not out of love for the man she followed at that time and who dropped her after a few months, as she would like people to think. That man, he was the first rung of the ladder, he was Paris. Even if he hadn't left her, she wouldn't have stayed with him for long.'

It was strange to hear him talking like this, coolly, dispassionately, as if he were studying an impersonal case, and trying to be clear and precise.

'Only, she imagined that things would move faster than they did. She was young, pretty, desirable. She didn't expect to go running from one waiting-room to the next and copying out advertisements of situations vacant from the windows of newspaper offices just to finish up in the lingerie department of a big store.'

'You aren't ambitious yourself, I suppose?'

'It isn't the same. Let me finish with her. She went out in the evenings with colleagues, mostly heads of departments, but either they were married, or else they didn't propose to her. It was at that moment, just as she felt that she was growing old, that I came on the scene. Three or four years earlier, she would have laughed at me. Experience had shown her that I was an acceptable last resource and she did what was necessary.'

'That is to say?'

'She allowed me to believe that she loved me. For years, I thought of nothing but the couple we formed, of what I called our nest, of what I also called our future. I found her cold, but I consoled myself with the thought that women who aren't are putting on an act. I found her selfish, even avaricious, and promptly persuaded myself that women are all like that.'

'You were unhappy?'

'I had my work. She poked fun at it, called me a maniac, was ashamed, I know that now, to be married to a man whose job was children's toys and electric trains. She had found something better.'

Maigret could tell what was coming.

'What do you mean?'

'She made the acquaintance of a man who worked for some time at the shop, a certain Maurice Schwob. I don't know whether she loves him. It's possible. At least, he has helped her to take another step forward, and a big step at that. He's married to a former actress who was kept for a long time and who has a lot of money . . .'

'Is that why your wife hasn't asked for a divorce in order to marry Schwob?'

'I suppose so. The fact remains that they've opened a shop together with the old woman's money.'

'You think they are lovers?'

'I know they are.'

'You've followed them?'

'I'm as inquisitive as the next man.'

'But you haven't asked for a divorce yourself?'

He did not reply. They seemed to have come to a dead end.

'This situation already existed before your sister-in-law's arrival?'

'That is probably so, but my eyes weren't open yet.'

'You told me just now that it's since your sister-in-law has been living with you in the Avenue de Châtillon that you've understood. What have you understood?'

'That there are other sorts of women, of women such as those I'd always dreamt of.'

'You love her?'

'Yes.'

'She's your mistress?'

'No.'

'Yet you sometimes meet each other unknown to your wife?'

'You know that too?'

'I know the little restaurant called the "Trou Normand".'

'That's correct. Jenny often comes and joins me at lunch-time. My wife, for her part, nearly always goes with Schwob to more expensive places. She no longer belongs to our world, you understand?'

This last word kept cropping up, as if Marton were afraid that Maigret was incapable of following him.

'You understand?'

'Does your sister-in-law love you too?'

'I think she's beginning to.'

'She's just beginning?'

'She was really in love with her husband. They formed a real couple, those two. They lived in New Jersey, not far from New York, in a pretty country house. Edgar was killed in an accident and Jenny tried to commit suicide. She turned on the gas, one evening, and was saved only just in time. Then, not knowing what to do any more, she came back to Europe and we took her in. She was still in deep mourning. Gisèle pokes fun at her, and advises her to go out and enjoy herself, to change her ideas. I, on the other hand, am gently trying to give her back a taste for life. . . .'

'Have you succeeded?'

He blushed like an adolescent.

'I think so. You understand now why she isn't my mistress? I love her and I respect her. I wouldn't want, for the sake of selfish satisfaction . . .'

Was Lapointe taking all this down in shorthand? If this interrogation went through the ordinary administrative channels, it was probably Maigret who would look silly.

'Does Jenny know that her sister wants you out of the way?'

'I haven't spoken to her about it.'

'She knows that you don't get on together?'

'She's living with us. I ought to point out that we never quarrel, my wife and I. On the surface, we lead the same life as any other couple. Gisèle is too intelligent to provoke any quarrels. And then there are ten million francs to be picked up, which would allow her to have an equal share in the Rue Saint-Honoré business, with this Schwob who calls himself Harris.'

'What ten million francs?'

'The insurance money.'

'When did you take out an insurance policy? Before or after your sister-in-law's arrival?'

'Before. It was about four years ago. Gisèle was already working with Schwob. An insurance agent came to see us, apparently by chance, but I realized later that it was my wife who'd asked him to call. You know how it goes. "You don't know who's going to live or who's going to die," he said. "It's a comfort to the one who's going to know that the one who remains . . ." '

He laughed, for the first time, a short unpleasant laugh.

'I was still very ignorant. To cut a long story short, we ended up by signing a policy for ten million.'

'You say *we*?'

'Yes, because it's a joint life policy, as they call it.'

'In other words, if your wife happens to die you collect ten million too?'

'Certainly.'

'So that you have as much interest in her death as she has in yours?'

'I make no secret of the fact.'

'And you hate each other?'

'She hates me, yes.'

'And you?'

'I don't hate her. I'm just taking precautions.'

'But you love your sister-in-law.'

'I make no secret of that, either.'

'And your wife is Schwob-Harris's mistress.'

'That's a fact.'

'Have you anything else to tell me?'

'I can't think of anything. I've answered all your questions. I think I've even anticipated some of them. I'm ready to submit, tomorrow morning, to the examination you've told me about. What time do I have to be here?'

'Between ten o'clock and midday. What time would suit you best?'

'Will it take long?'

'About as long as at Dr. Steiner's.'

'That means an hour. Let's say eleven o'clock, if that's all right with you, because that way I won't need to go back to the shop.'

He got up, hesitantly, perhaps expecting some more questions. While he was putting on his overcoat, Maigret murmured:

'Your sister-in-law is waiting for you on the embankment.'

He stayed for a moment with one arm in the air, the sleeve half on.

'Oh!'

'Does that surprise you? Didn't she know you were coming here?'

There was a second's hesitation, but it did not escape Maigret's notice.

'Of course she didn't.'

This time, he was lying, that was obvious. He was suddenly in a hurry to get away. He was not so sure of himself any more.

'Good-bye till tomorrow,' he stammered.

And, as he had automatically begun to put out his hand, he had to go through with it. Maigret shook hands with him, watched him making for the stairs, and shut the door, standing stock-still behind it for a good few moments and breathing hard.

'Whew!' he sighed as Lapointe, his wrist aching, appeared in the other doorway.

He could not remember an interrogation as astonishing as this had been.

# VI

'LUCAS?' asked Maigret, with a jerk of the head towards the communicating door between the two offices.

Not only did Lapointe grasp the meaning of the question, but he also understood that just then the chief-inspector had no desire to talk a lot.

'He's gone back to take Torrence's place on the embankment. As Torrence wasn't in the picture . . .'

Suddenly, Maigret went straight from one idea to another and, once again, the inspector followed him without difficulty.

'What do you think about it?'

Except with Janvier, to whom he had always spoken familiarly, Maigret only used the *tu* form of address—and then only with a few people—in the heat of action, or else when he was very worried. It always gave pleasure to Lapointe, for, when it happened, it was rather as if the two men had suddenly confided secrets to each other.

'I don't know, Chief. I heard him without seeing him, which is rather different. . . .'

That was precisely why the chief-inspector was asking for his opinion. They had heard the same words. But the young man, behind the door, had not been distracted by a face, eyes and hands on which his attention was dispersed. He was rather in the position of the attendants, at the theatre, who hear the play from the corridors and for whom the tirades being declaimed have a different resonance.

'He gave me the impression of being an honest man.'

'Not rather mad?'

'It must be difficult to explain oneself, faced with somebody like you . . .'

Lapointe had hesitated about saying that, for fear of being misunderstood, when in his eyes it was a compliment.

'You'll see what I mean better when you read your side of the interview. It was only at the end . . .'

'What, at the end?'

'That he was probably lying. At least in my opinion. The sister-in-law must have known that he was coming here. He knew that she knew. What he didn't know was that she'd followed him and that she was waiting for him on the embankment. I think that made him angry. You want me to type the text out straight away?'

Maigret shook his head, adding:

'I hope that you won't need to type it out.'

He was beginning to grow impatient, wondering why Lucas had not come back. There was no point in following the couple to the Avenue de Châtillon. The chief-inspector was eager to know how the reunion had gone and Lapointe shared his curiosity.

'I wonder,' murmured the inspector, 'why he said that his sister-in-law wasn't in the know.'

'He could have had a reason.'

'What reason?'

'A desire to avoid compromising her, to make sure that she couldn't be accused one day of complicity.'

'She couldn't be unless . . .'

Lapointe broke off, and threw a look of surprise at his chief. Maigret's words implied that something was going to happen, something which would put Xavier Marton in a difficult position. He had no time to say any more on the subject, for some quick, rather short footsteps were heard which could only be Lucas's. The latter came through the inspectors' office, and appeared framed in the half-open doorway.

'Can I come in, Chief?'

He was still wearing his overcoat, a black overcoat, in a shaggy material on which there could still be seen a few small white specks.

'It's snowing?'

'It's beginning. Fine snow, but heavy.'

'Fire away.'

'The poor kid, on the embankment, couldn't have been any warmer than I was, especially as she's wearing light shoes, and I could hear her heels tapping on the pavement. First of all, she stood still by the stone parapet, avoiding the lamps. From the way she was standing, I could guess, although I only saw her silhouette, that she was looking at the lighted windows. There aren't many left in the building. I saw them too, going out one after the other. From time to time, you could hear voices under the archway. I'd never realized before that our voices, when we go out, carry so far. Inspectors, in groups of two or three, came out, wished each other good night, and separated . . .

'She gradually drew nearer, as if the lights in your office fascinated her, and she became more and more nervous. I'm sure that several times she was on the point of crossing the road and coming in . . .'

'She must have thought I'd arrested him?'

'I don't know. Finally he came out, all alone, and walked past the policeman on duty. Straight away, he peered around him, as if he were looking for somebody. . . .'

'He was looking for her. I'd just told him that she was there.'

'Now I understand. It was difficult for him to see her where she was. First of all he looked for her towards the Pont-Neuf, but she was standing in the opposite direction. He came back. I thought she was going to take advantage of the moment he had his back turned to slip away, or to go down on to the loading quay, but he found her before she could move. I couldn't hear what they said. From their attitudes, I got the impression that he began by reproving her. He wasn't gesticulating but his attitude was that of an angry man.

'It was she who slipped her hand under his arm, pointing out the duty policeman to him, and pulled him away towards the Pont Saint-Michel . . .'

'One moment,' Maigret broke in. 'How did she put her hand under his arm?'

If Lucas did not appear to see the purport of this question, Lapointe, who was in love, did.

'In a normal way, like any woman you see in the street with her lover or her husband. He must have reproached her some more, not so energetically. Then I suppose he noticed she was cold and he put his arm round her waist. Their bodies came a little closer together. They began walking in step, at the same pace . . .'

Lapointe and Maigret looked at each other, thinking the same thing.

'When they got to the Pont Saint-Michel, they hesitated and then, crossing the line of cars, still holding each other round the waist, they went into the bar on the corner. There were a lot of people round the counter. It's *apéritif* time. I could see them through the steamy window-panes. I didn't go in. They were both standing near the cash-desk. The barman prepared a hot toddy and put it on the counter in front of the young woman, who seemed to be protesting. Marton insisted. Finally she drank the toddy, blowing on it, while he just had a coffee.'

'Now I come to think of it,' Maigret said to Lapointe, 'what did he drink at midday in the restaurant?'

'Mineral water.'

It was curious. If anybody had asked him, Maigret would in fact have sworn that the electric-train enthusiast drank neither wine nor spirits.

'When they came out,' concluded Lucas, 'they made for the bus stop and waited there. I saw them get on the bus. They were going in the direction of the Porte d'Orléans and I thought it best to come and report to you. Did I do right?'

Maigret nodded. The snow had disappeared from Lucas's overcoat. During this conversation, he had been warming his hands on the radiator.

The chief-inspector used the familiar *tu* with him as well.

'Have you anything fixed for this evening?'

'Nothing special.'

'Nor have I,' said Lapointe quickly.

'I don't know which of the two of you I'm going to ask to spend the night outside. In this weather, it won't be very pleasant . . .'

'Me!' said the young inspector, raising his hand like a schoolboy.

And Lucas said:

'Why don't we share the job? I can phone my wife to say that I won't be home for dinner. I'll have a sandwich in the bar opposite Montrouge Church. Later, Lapointe can come and relieve me. . . .'

'I'll be there about ten o'clock,' decided Lapointe.

'Later if you like. Why not divide the night in two and say midnight?'

'I'll be there earlier than that. If I'm not going to bed, I'd rather be doing something.'

'What orders, Chief?'

'None, boys. And, tomorrow, if they call me to account, I shall be hard put to it to explain this particular job. They've both been here, husband and wife. They've insisted, both of them, on telling me all about their little troubles. Logically speaking, nothing ought to happen. But it's precisely because . . .'

He did not finish what he had in mind, which was not clear enough to be put into words.

'Perhaps I did wrong in letting him know his wife had been here. I hesitated about it. Then I said to myself . . .'

He shrugged his shoulders, feeling sick of the whole business, and opened the cupboard where his hat and coat were hanging, growling:

'Anyway, we'll see what happens . . . Good night all the same, boys. . . .'

'Good night, Chief.'

And Lucas added:

'I'll be over there in an hour.'

Outside, the cold had become sharper and the snowflakes, hard and tiny, scarcely visible in the haloes of the street-lamps, pricked the skin, which they seemed to want to penetrate, settling on eyelashes, eyebrows and lips.

Maigret did not feel up to waiting for a bus and took a taxi, huddling in the back, well wrapped up in his heavy coat.

All the other cases he had investigated struck him as having been almost childishly simple compared with this one, and this annoyed him. Never had he felt so unsure of himself, to the extent of telephoning Pardon, going to see the chief and the Public Prosecutor, and, only a moment ago, angling for Lapointe's approval.

He had the impression of being all at sea. Then, while the taxi was going round the Place de la République, a thought came to him which comforted him a little.

If this case was unlike the others and if he did not know how to set about it, wasn't that because, this time, it was not a question of a crime which had already been committed, which only needed to be reconstructed, but of a crime which might be committed at any moment?

Just as it might quite well not be committed at all! How many potential crimes, crimes *in posse*, some of them meticulously prepared in the criminal's mind, are never perpetrated? How many people intend to do away with somebody, consider all the means of attaining this end and, at the last moment, lose their nerve?

Some cases which he had dealt with came back to mind. Some of them would never have come to anything but for a favourable opportunity, or sometimes an accident. In certain cases, if, at a given moment, the victim had not pronounced some particular phrase, or assumed some particular attitude, nothing would have happened.

What he had to do, this time, was not to reconstruct the acts and gestures of a human being, but to forecast his behaviour, which was much more difficult.

None of the treatises on psychology, psycho-analysis or psychiatry were of any use to him.

He had known other couples of which one of the parties, for some reason, wanted the death of the other.

Precedents did not help him either. It is only with professionals that precedents can be turned to account, or else with certain maniacs. And then only with maniacs who have already killed one or more times and are repeating themselves.

He did not realize that the taxi had stopped at the kerb. The driver said to him:

'Here we are, Chief.'

The door of the flat opened as usual and Maigret rediscovered the light, the familiar smells, the furniture and the other objects which had been in their places for so many years.

He also rediscovered Madame Maigret's gaze which, as always, especially when she knew that he was worried, contained a mute inquiry.

'What do you say to going to the cinema?' he suggested.

'It's snowing!'

'You're afraid of catching cold?'

'No. I'd like to go to the cinema.'

She suspected that he did not want to stay in his armchair turning the same question over and over in his mind as he had done the evening before. An hour later, they were walking in the direction of the Place de la République and the Boulevard Bonne-Nouvelle, and Madame Maigret had hooked her hand on to her husband's arm.

Xavier Marton's sister-in-law, Jenny, had done the same thing when he had surprised her on the embankment. Maigret asked himself how long it had been, after their first meeting, before his wife had made that particular gesture.

A hundred yards from the cinema, where he did not even know what film they were showing, he put the question to her.

'Oh, I know that,' she said with a smile. 'I can remember it exactly. We'd known each other for three months. The week before, you'd kissed me, on the landing, and after that, you'd kissed me every night at the same place. One Tuesday, you took me to the Opéra-Comique, where they were doing *Carmen*, and I wore a blue taffeta dress. I could even tell you which perfume I'd used. On our way to the taxi, you didn't hold me, and you just gave me your hand to help me to get into the car.

'After the theatre, you asked me if I was hungry. We went towards the Grands Boulevards, where the Taverne Pousset was still in existence.

'I pretended to stumble because of my high heels and I put my hand in your arm. My boldness impressed me so much that I started trembling, and you had the good sense to pretend you hadn't noticed anything.

'Coming out of the restaurant, I made the same gesture, and I've been doing the same ever since.'

In other words, Jenny, too, had got into the habit. It followed that she and her brother-in-law often went walking together in the streets.

Didn't that suggest that they made no secret of their love and that, contrary to what Marton had implied, Gisèle Marton knew all about it?

He went down to the box-office window, then made for the entrance, holding two pink tickets in his hand.

They were showing a thriller, with shots, fights, and a hard-boiled hero who jumped out of a window to land in an open car and who, in the middle of the town, knocking the driver out, took his place at the wheel, drove at a reckless speed, and got away from the police cars with their screaming sirens.

He smiled in spite of himself. As a matter of fact, he was enjoying himself. He managed to forget the Martons and the sister-in-law, the Harris whose name was Schwob, and the more or less complicated affairs of the two couples.

At the interval, he bought some sweets for his wife, for this was a tradition going back almost as far as Madame Maigret's gesture in taking his arm. Another tradition, while she was eating her sweets, was for him to smoke half a pipe in the entrance-hall, where he had a vague look at the posters advertising the films that were coming.

The snow was still falling when they came out and the flakes were thicker, so that you could see them trembling for a moment on the ground before dissolving.

People were walking with their heads down, to avoid getting flakes in their eyes. The next day, no doubt, the snow would be whitening the roofs and the parked cars.

'Taxi!'

He was afraid that his wife would catch cold. He thought she already looked thinner and even though he knew that it was on Pardon's orders, it worried him all the same. It seemed to him that she was going to become more fragile, that she might lose her optimism, her good humour.

As the car was drawing up in front of their home, in the Boulevard Richard-Lenoir, he murmured:

'Would you mind terribly if I didn't come in for another hour?'

In any other case, he would not have asked: he would just have told her that he had some work to do. This evening, it was a question of doing something which was not necessary, which had not even any justification, and he felt the need to apologize about it.

'Shall I wait up for you?'

'No. Go to bed. I might be delayed.'

He saw her cross the pavement looking for the key of the flat in her handbag.

'The church of Saint-Pierre de Montrouge,' he said to the driver.

The streets were almost empty, the roadway slippery, with serpentine tracks where cars had skidded.

'Not too fast . . .'

He was thinking:

'If anything is really going to happen . . .'

Why had he got the impression that it would be very soon? Xavier Marton had come to see him the day before. Not a week before, when the situation was the same, but only the day before. Didn't that indicate that the drama was coming to some sort of maturity?

Gisèle, too, had come to the Quai the day before.

And her husband had come again this very day.

He tried to remember what was said about this subject in the book on psychiatry he had dipped into. Perhaps, after all, he had been wrong not to take a greater interest in it? There were several pages about the development of crises, but he had skipped them.

Now, there was one thing which might bring the drama to a head, if there was a drama. Xavier Marton had agreed to undergo an examination the next day, at eleven o'clock in the morning, in the special infirmary at the *Dépôt*.

Would he mention it to his sister-in-law? To his wife? And would the latter pass on the news to her lover in the Rue Saint-Honoré?

Once the examination was over, and whatever the result might be, it seemed certain that it would be too late for fresh developments.

The taxi stopped in front of the church. Maigret paid the fare. Opposite, a café-bar was still open, where there were only two or three customers. Maigret pushed open the door and ordered a toddy, not so much to warm himself up as because somebody had mentioned a toddy to him not long before. As he was making for the call-box the barman shouted to him:

'You want a *jeton*?'

'I'm just going to have a look at the directory.'

For no particular reason, as it happened. Thinking about Monsieur Harris, he had wondered whether the Martons were on the telephone and he wanted to make sure.

They were not. Plenty of Mortons and Martins, but not a single Marton.

'What do I owe you?'

He turned into the Avenue de Châtillon, which was deserted and where there were only two or three windows still lighted. He could see neither Lucas nor Lapointe, and he was beginning to feel anxious when, about the middle of the Avenue, not far past the Rue Antoine-Chantin, he heard a voice near him say:

'Here, Chief . . .'

It was young Lapointe, huddled in a corner, a muffler covering half his face, his hands as deep as they would go in his coat pockets.

'I recognized your step as soon as you turned the corner of the avenue.'

'It's over there?' asked the chief-inspector, pointing to an apartment-house in yellow brick where all the windows were in darkness.

'Yes. You see that dark gap, to the right of the door?'

It was a kind of blind alley, or passage, such as you often still see in Paris, even in the heart of the city. In a passage of this sort, off the Boulevard Saint-Martin, they had once found a murdered man, at five o'clock in the afternoon, a few yards from the crowds going by on the pavement.

'That leads into the courtyard?'

'Yes. They can go in and out without calling the concierge.'

'You've been to have a look?'

'I go every ten minutes. If you're going over there, mind how you walk. A huge ginger cat will come and quietly rub against your legs. The first time, it miaowed and I was afraid it would give the show away.'

'Have they gone to bed?'

'They hadn't a few minutes ago.'

'What are they doing?'

'I don't know. Somebody must still be up on the first floor, as there's a light on, but you can't see anything because of the blinds. I've waited in vain for a silhouette to appear; it looks as though the person or persons in the room aren't moving about or are staying at the back. There's a light on the ground floor as well. You don't realize it's there for some time, because the steel shutters only allow thin strips of light to shine through.'

Maigret crossed the road and Lapointe followed him. Both of them took care not to make any noise. The passage, which was vaulted over for three or four yards, was as cold and damp as a cellar. In the court-yard they found complete darkness and, as they stood still, a cat came sure enough and rubbed against, not the chief-inspector, but Lapointe, whom it already seemed to have adopted.

'They've gone to bed,' whispered the inspector. 'The lighted window was just in front of you.'

He tip-toed up to the shutters on the ground floor, bent down, then came back to the chief-inspector. Just as the two men were about to turn away, a light went on, not in the cottage, but on the second floor of the block of flats.

They both stood stock-still in the shadows, afraid that they had been heard by one of the tenants, and expecting to see a face pressed against the window-pane.

Nothing of the kind happened. A shadow passed behind the curtain. They heard a cistern flush.

'Somebody piddling,' sighed Lapointe in relief.

A moment later, they were back on the opposite pavement. Curiously enough, they were almost disappointed, the two of them. It was Lapointe who murmured:

'They've gone to bed.'

Didn't that mean that nothing was going to happen, that the chief-inspector had been worrying needlessly?

'I wonder . . .' began Maigret.

Two policemen on bicycles appeared, heading straight towards them. They had spotted them from a distance and, from the kerb, one of the two challenged them in a loud voice:

'What are you two up to?'

Maigret stepped forward. The beam of an electric torch picked out his face. The policeman frowned.

'You aren't . . . ? Oh! I beg your pardon, sir . . . I didn't recognize you at first . . .'

He added, after a glance at the house opposite:

'Do you want us to lend a hand?'

'Not at the moment.'

'Anyway, we come by every hour.'

The two men in their capes moved off, sprinkled with snow, and Maigret rejoined Lapointe, who had not stirred.

'What was I saying?'

'That you were wondering . . .'

'Ah, yes . . . I was wondering whether husband and wife still slept in the same bed. . . .'

'I don't know. From what Janvier told me this afternoon, there's a divan on the ground floor, though that doesn't necessarily mean somebody sleeps on it. Logically speaking, if anybody uses it, it ought to be the sister-in-law, don't you think?'

'Good night, old chap. Perhaps you can . . .'

He wondered if he should send Lapointe home to bed. What was the use of mounting guard in front of a house where nothing was happening?

'If it's on my account you're hesitating . . .'

In point of fact, Lapointe would be annoyed not to see the job through to the end.

'Stay if you like. Good night. You don't want to go and have a drink?'

'I must admit I went and had one a few minutes before you arrived. From the bar on the corner, I could see the whole street.'

When Maigret arrived at Saint-Pierre de Montrouge, the gates of the Metro were shut and there was not a single taxi in sight. He hesitated between heading towards the Lion de Belfort and going down the Avenue du Maine in the direction of the Gare Montparnasse. He decided on the Avenue du Maine because of the station, and in fact he soon hailed a taxi coming away from the station empty.

'Boulevard Richard-Lenoir.'

He had not got the key of the flat, but he knew he would find it under the door-mat. For all that he was head of the Criminal Squad, he had never thought of telling his wife that this hiding-place was, to say the least, illusory.

She was asleep and he started undressing in the half-light, only leaving the corridor lamp on. A few moments later, a voice from the bed asked:

'Is it late?'

'I don't know. Half past one perhaps . . .'

'You haven't caught cold?'

'No.'

'You don't want me to make you a hot drink?'

'No, thanks, I had a toddy a little while ago.'

'And you went out again afterwards?'

These were ordinary little phrases which he had heard hundreds of times, but they struck him tonight because he wondered whether Gisèle Marton had ever pronounced them.

Wasn't it precisely for want of hearing them that her husband . . . ?

'You can put the light on.'

He just switched on the bedside lamp, on his side of the bed, and went and turned out the light in the corridor.

'You're sure you've shut the hall door?'

He would not have been surprised to hear his wife get up, in a few minutes, to go and make certain.

That too formed part of a whole, a whole which Xavier Marton had no doubt looked for, which he had not found, which . . .

He slipped between the warm sheets, turned out the light, and in the dark, without fumbling, found his wife's lips.

He thought he would find it difficult to get off to sleep and yet, a few moments later, he was asleep. It is true that, if the light had been turned on suddenly, it would have been seen that he was wearing a frown, an expression of concentration, as if he were still in pursuit of a truth which was slipping away.

As a rule, Madame Maigret got up quietly at half past six and went to the kitchen without his noticing. He only began to become aware of the new day when the smell of coffee reached him.

It was the time when other windows lit up on the Boulevard Richard-Lenoir and in every part of Paris, the time when the footsteps of early risers could be heard on the pavements.

That day he was not roused from sleep by the familiar smell of coffee, nor by his wife's noiseless tread. It was the telephone bell, suddenly ringing, that snatched him out of the world of darkness and, when he opened his eyes, Madame Maigret, already sitting up in bed, was shaking him by the shoulder.

'What time is it?' he stammered.

She groped about for the button on the bedside lamp, then the light shone on the alarm-clock and the hands were pointing to ten to six.

'Hullo!' said Maigret in a thick voice. 'Is that you, Lapointe?'

'Chief-Inspector Maigret?'

He could not recognize the voice, and frowned.

'Who's that speaking?'

'This is the emergency service. Inspector Joffre.'

It sometimes happened, in certain specific cases, that he left instructions with the emergency service to get in touch with him direct if something in particular occurred. He had not done anything of the sort the day before. His ideas were not connecting yet. However, he was only slightly surprised.

'What is it, Joffre? Is it Lapointe?'

'What about Lapointe?'

'Is it Lapointe who's asked you to ring me up?'

'I haven't had any news from Lapointe. Just a phone call, a moment ago, asking us to pass a message on to you.'

'What message?'

'To go straight away to the Avenue de Châtillon . . . Hang on! I made a note of the number . . .'

'I know it. Who was it speaking?'

'I don't know. They didn't give a name.'

'A man? A woman?'

'A woman. She says you know all about it and that you'll know what it means. It seems that she looked for your number in the directory but that . . .'

Maigret was not listed in the directory.

'There's nothing I can do for you?'

The chief-inspector hesitated. He nearly asked Joffre to telephone on his behalf to the police station in the XIVth *arrondissement* to ask them to send someone to the Avenue de Châtillon. Then, on reflection, he decided not to. Sitting on the edge of his bed, he felt around with his feet for his slippers. As for his wife, she was already in the kitchen and he heard the pop of the gas on which she was putting some water to heat.

'Nothing, thanks . . .'

What surprised him was that it was not Lapointe who had rung him up, although he was on the spot.

Which woman had it been? Gisèle Marton? The sister-in-law?

If it was one of those two, she could not have left the apartment-house, for Lapointe would have seen her and telephoned Maigret himself.

Now, the Martons were not on the telephone.

He called his wife.

'While I'm getting dressed, will you look in the telephone directory, the one with the classification by streets, and see who's on the telephone at No. 17, Avenue de Châtillon?'

He hesitated about shaving, and decided not to, despite his reluctance to go out like that, in order to save time.

'No. 17 . . . Here we are . . . Apartment-house . . .'

'Good. That means there's a telephone in the lodge.'

'I can see a Madame Boussard too, a midwife. That's all. There'll be some coffee for you in two minutes.'

He ought to have told Joffre to send him one of the cars from the Quai des Orfèvres, but now it would take longer than calling a taxi.

Madame Maigret said she would see to this. Five minutes later, after scalding his mouth swallowing coffee that was too hot, the chief-inspector was going downstairs.

'Will you ring me up?' asked his wife, leaning over the banisters.

This was something she rarely asked him. She must have sensed that he was more worried than usual.

He promised:

'I'll try.'

The taxi arrived. He plunged into it, scarcely noticing that it was not snowing any more, that there were no white patches in the street or on the roofs, but that an icy rain was blackening the roadway.

'Avenue de Châtillon.'

He gave a sniff, for the taxi still smelt of scent. No doubt it had just taken home a couple who had spent the night dancing in a fashionable restaurant. A little later, he bent down and picked up a little ball of pink cotton-wool such as grown-ups throw at one another, after midnight, while they are drinking champagne.

## VII

MAIGRET had asked to be set down at the corner of the Avenue de Châtillon and, as in his own district, the pavements were deserted in the rain; as in the Boulevard Richard-Lenoir too, there were a few lighted windows, three or four in each block; in the time it took him to walk a hundred yards, he saw two light up, and heard, on a ground floor that was still dark, an alarm-clock ringing.

He looked to see if Lapointe was in his corner, could not find him, and growled a few syllables under his breath, disgruntled, anxious, only half-awake.

In the passage-way into the yellow-brick apartment-house, he finally saw a very short woman, with hips as broad as her shoulders, who was obviously the concierge, a Metro employee holding in his hand the tin box containing his dinner, and another woman, an old one this time, her white hair in curling-pins, dressed in a sky-blue woollen dressing-gown and a shawl of a violent purple colour.

All three looked at him in silence and it was only later that he discovered what had happened, and found out why Lapointe was not outside on the pavement. For some moments, at the very least, he had felt an emptiness in his chest, for he had thought that as the result of circumstances which he did not try to imagine, his inspector was perhaps the victim.

As usual, it was simpler than that. When Gisèle Marton had come to telephone from the lodge, the concierge was up and busy making coffee, but she had not yet put out the dustbins. She had heard a call being made to the emergency service, then the message from her tenant, who had left the lodge without giving her the least information.

The concierge had gone and opened one half of the door, as she did every morning, before dragging the dustbins out on to the pavement. Just at that moment Lapointe had been crossing the road, with the intention of having a look inside the courtyard as he had done several times during the night. Because of the telephone call which she had just heard, the woman had looked at him suspiciously.

'What do you want?'

'I suppose nothing out of the ordinary has happened in the house?' He showed her his badge.

'You're from the police, are you? Well now, there's somebody at the back of the courtyard who's just sent for the police. What's happening, with all these goings-on?'

That was how Lapointe had come to cross the courtyard, without any attempt at concealment, this time, and knock at the door, under which he could see a strip of light. The three windows on the first floor were lighted too.

Maigret, for his part, had no need to knock. His footsteps had been heard and it was Lapointe who, from the inside, opened the door to him, a Lapointe pale from fatigue, and also from what he had just found. He did not say a word, the sight which met his chief's eyes speaking for itself.

The divan in the studio-cum-sitting-room did in fact turn into a bed at night and it was Xavier Marton who used it. The sheets were in disorder, the pillow askew, and on the floor, on the beige-coloured jute carpet, half-way between the bed and the spiral staircase leading to the first floor, was the body of the electric-train enthusiast, dressed in pyjamas, and lying face down.

The red stripes of the pyjamas gave added emphasis to the contortion of the body. One had the impression that he had collapsed while crawling on all fours and he was all twisted, his right arm stretched out in front, his hands clenched, as if, in a final effort, he had tried to reach the revolver which was also lying on the floor, about eight inches away from his fingers.

Maigret did not ask whether he was dead. That was obvious. Three people were looking at him in silence, for the two women were there, almost as motionless as the corpse, in their nightwear too, with dressing-gowns over their nightdresses, and their bare feet in slippers. Jenny's hair, which was darker than her sister's, was partly falling over her face and hiding one of her eyes.

Automatically, without thinking of what he was saying, Maigret murmured to Lapointe:

'You haven't touched anything?'

Lapointe shook his head. There were shadows under his eyes, and his beard, like the dead man's and Maigret's, had grown during the night.

'Notify the local police station. Telephone the Criminal Records Office and ask them to send us photographers and experts straight away. Ring up Dr. Paul as well. . . .'

'And the Parquet?'

'There'll be time for that later.'

In that part of the *Palais de Justice* life did not begin as early as at the Quai des Orfèvres and Maigret did not want to have those gentlemen getting in his way sooner than he could help.

He looked at the two women. Neither of them had thought of sitting down. With her back to the wall, by the table for the electric train, the sister-in-law, holding a handkerchief rolled into a ball in one hand, kept dabbing her red eyes, and sniffing as if she had a cold in the head. She had big dark eyes, which were soft and timorous, rather like the eyes of forest animals, of squirrels for example, and she gave off a warm smell of bed.

Colder or more composed, Gisèle Marton was watching the chief-inspector and from time to time her hands contracted in an involuntary movement.

Lapointe had gone out and crossed the courtyard. He would be busy telephoning from the concierge's lodge. The two women were doubtless expecting Maigret to question them. Perhaps for a moment he had thought of doing so, but, in the end, he just said in a low voice:

'Go and get dressed.'

This baffled them, Jenny even more than Gisèle. She opened her mouth to speak, said nothing, and decided, after a hard look of bitter hatred at her sister, to go upstairs first; while she was going up, the chief-inspector could see her bare white thighs.

'You too . . .'

In a rather hoarse voice, Gisèle said:

'I know.'

She seemed to be waiting until her sister had shut herself in her room before going up herself.

Maigret only remained alone with Marton's body for a few moments, and he scarcely had time to make an inventory of the room with his eyes. The room was none the less photographed in his mind, down to its smallest details, and he knew that he would be able to find them again in his memory when he needed them.

He heard a car stopping, brakes squealing, a door slamming shut. Then there were footsteps in the courtyard and, just as Lapointe had done for him, he opened the door.

He knew Boisset, the inspector of the XIVth *arrondissement*, who was accompanied by a policeman in uniform and a tubby little man carrying a doctor's bag.

'Come in, all three of you . . . I think, Doctor, that all you've got to do is to certify the death . . . Dr. Paul will be here before long . . .'

Boisset looked inquiringly at him.

'A case I've been dealing with for the last two days,' murmured Maigret. 'I'll explain later . . . At the moment, there's nothing to be done . . .'

They heard footsteps overhead, the noise of a tap, a cistern flushing. As Boisset raised his eyes in surprise towards the ceiling, Maigret added:

'The wife and the sister-in-law . . .'

He felt as weary as if it had been he, and not Lapointe, who had spent the night outside, in the cold and the rain. The inspector was soon back. The doctor, after kneeling for a moment, stood up again. He had shone an electric torch into the dead man's staring eyes; then he had put his face close to the man's lips and sniffed.

'At first sight, it looks like a case of poisoning.'

'It *is* a case of poisoning.'

Lapointe motioned to Maigret that he had completed his mission. Voices could be heard whispering in the courtyard. Several people had come up to the shutters, which were still closed.

Maigret said to the policeman in uniform:

'You might go out and stop them gathering together.'

The doctor asked:

'Do you need me any more?'

'No. You'll be given the identification details later for the death certificate.'

'Good-bye, gentlemen! Boisset knows where to find me.'

Gisèle Marton came down first and Maigret noticed straight away that she was wearing her costume and carrying her fur coat on her arm. She was also holding a handbag, which suggested that she expected to be taken away. She had seized the opportunity to make up, in a discreet way. The expression on her face was serious and thoughtful, with a few traces of shock still apparent.

When Jenny in her turn appeared, she was wearing a black dress. Noticing her sister's outfit, she asked, after wetting her lips:

'Shall I fetch my coat?'

Maigret blinked his eyes. The one who was watching him most closely was Lapointe, who had rarely been so impressed by his chief's behaviour . . . He sensed that this was not an ordinary investigation, and that the chief-inspector did not intend to use ordinary methods, but he had not the faintest idea what he meant to do.

Everyone's nerves were so on edge that it was a relief to see Boisset light a cigarette. He offered his packet to Lapointe, who refused, then, noticing Gisèle who stood waiting as if she were on a station platform, he said:

'Do you smoke?'

She took one. He held the flame of his lighter up to her cigarette, and she began breathing in nervously.

'Have you got a police car at the door?' Maigret asked the local inspector.

'I kept it in case.'

'Can I use it?'

He was still looking all round as if to make sure that he was not forgetting a single detail. He was about to give the two women the signal to go when he changed his mind.

'One moment . . .'

And he went upstairs himself, alone, to the first floor, where the lights had been left on. There were only two bedrooms, a bathroom, and a lumber-room where suitcases, old trunks and a dressmaker's dummy were piled together, with two old oil-lamps and some dusty books lying on the floor.

He went into the first bedroom, the bigger of the two. It contained a small double bed and the smell told him that he was in Madame Marton's room. The wardrobe confirmed him in this opinion, for in it he found clothes of the sort he knew she wore, simple, elegant, even rich. On a shelf a little way above the floor, a dozen pairs of shoes were arranged in a row.

The bed was unmade, like the one downstairs. The nightdress and the salmon-pink dressing-gown had been carelessly thrown on to it. On the dressing-table, pots of cream, bottles, a silver manicure-set, and some pins in a Chinese bowl.

In another wardrobe, some men's clothes, just two suits, a sports jacket, two pairs of shoes, and some sandals. There was obviously no wardrobe downstairs and Marton had gone on leaving his things in the double bedroom.

He opened the chest of drawers, pushed a door, and found himself in the bathroom. On the glass shelf, he saw three toothmugs, with a toothbrush in each one, which suggested that each person came here in turn. Lipstick on some crumpled towels, one of which had been thrown on the floor. And, on the porcelain bowl of the lavatory, and on the tiled floor round it, some little dried-up stains, as if someone, in the course of the night, had been sick.

The other bedroom did not connect with the bathroom. You had to go through the corridor. It was smaller, with a blue floral wallpaper, and the bed was a single bed.

There was greater disorder here than in the first bedroom. The wardrobe door had been left open. There was a tweed coat bearing the label of a New York firm. Far fewer shoes, only four pairs in fact, two of which also came from America. Finally, on the table covered with an embroidered cloth which served as a dressing-table, a jumble of incongruous objects: a pencil with the lead broken, a fountain-pen, some small change, combs, hairpins, and a brush which had lost some of its bristles.

Maigret went on registering. When he went downstairs again, he looked as slow-witted as before, with eyes which scarcely moved.

He discovered that the kitchen was on the ground floor, behind a partition which had been built in one corner of what had been the carpenter's workshop. He pushed the door open, while Gisèle Marton continued to follow him with her eyes. The kitchen was minute. It comprised a gas-cooker, a white cupboard, a sink, and a table covered with oilcloth.

There was no crockery lying around. The porcelain of the sink was dry.

He went back to the others, who were still as motionless as if they were in a waxworks.

'You'll receive the gentlemen of the Parquet,' he said to Lapointe. 'Tender my apologies to Dr. Paul for not waiting for him. Ask him to telephone me as soon as he's done the necessary. I'll send you somebody, I don't know yet whom . . .'

He turned to the two women.

'If you will follow me . . .'

Of the two, the sister-in-law was the more frightened and it seemed as if she were reluctant to leave the house. Gisèle, on the other hand, had opened the door and, standing very upright, was waiting in the rain.

The policeman had shepherded the inquisitive spectators out of the courtyard, but he could not prevent them forming a circle opposite the passage, on the pavement. The old woman was still there, with her purple shawl over her head in lieu of an umbrella. The Metro employee must have had to go off, regretfully, to his work.

They looked at them as the public always looks at these comings and goings which strike it as at once mysterious and dramatic. The policeman pushed back the crowd to clear a way to the car and the chief-inspector let the two women go in front of him.

A voice said:

'He's arresting them . . .'

He shut the door after them, and went round the car to take his place beside the uniformed driver.

'Headquarters.'

One could feel, albeit vaguely, the beginning of a new day. The rain was turning grey, the sky a dirty colour. They drove past some buses, and half-awake people were diving down the Metro staircases.

When they got to the embankments, the street-lamps had lost nearly all their brilliance and the towers of Notre-Dame were standing out against the sky.

The car entered the courtyard. During the journey, the two women had not said a word, but one of them, Jenny, had sniffed several times. Once, she had given her nose a long blow. When she got out of the car, her nose was red, like Marton's on his first visit.

'This way, ladies.'

He went in front of them up the big staircase which was in process of being swept, pushed open the glass door, and looked for Joseph whom he could not see. He ended up by showing them into his office, where he turned on the lights, and glanced inside the inspectors' office, where there were only three men, three who knew nothing about the case.

He picked Janin out at random.

'Will you stay for a minute in my office with these ladies?'

And, turning towards them:

'Sit down, please. I suppose you haven't had any coffee?'

Jenny did not reply. Madame Marton shook her head.

Ostentatiously, Maigret went to the door, locked it from the inside, and put the key in his pocket.

'You'd be well advised to sit down,' he repeated, 'because you'll be here for some time.'

He went into the other office.

'Baron! Telephone the Brasserie Dauphine, will you. Tell them to send up a big pot of coffee. Black coffee . . . Three cups and some *croissants* . . .'

After which, he dropped into a chair near the window, picked up another telephone, and asked to be put through to the Public Prosecutor. The latter could only just have got up and was doubtless busy dressing or having his breakfast. However, it was not a servant who answered, but he himself.

'Maigret here, sir. Marton is dead . . . The man I spoke to you about yesterday morning . . . No, I'm at the Quai des Orfèvres . . . I've left an inspector at the Avenue de Châtillon—Lapointe . . . Dr. Paul has been notified . . . Criminal Records too, yes . . . I don't know . . . I've got the two women in my office . . .'

He spoke in a low voice, although the communicating door between the two rooms was shut.

'I don't think I can go over there this morning . . . I'm going to send another inspector to relieve Lapointe . . .'

He wore a rather guilty expression. When the conversation was over, he looked at his watch, and decided to wait for Janvier, who would not be long now and who was familiar with the case, to send him to the scene of the crime.

After passing his hand over his cheeks, he asked the third inspector, Bonfils, who was busy writing his report on the night's minor incidents:

'Will you go to my cupboard and get my razor, shaving-brush and towel?'

He preferred not to do this himself in front of the two women. With his shaving-kit in his hand, he went down the corridor and into the cloakroom, where he took his jacket off and shaved. He took his time over it, as if to put off the moment when he would have to do what remained to be done. After washing his face in cold water, he rejoined his colleagues and, in addition, the waiter from the Brasserie Dauphine, who did not know where to put his tray.

'In my office . . . This way . . .'

He picked up the telephone again and this time it was to his wife that he spoke.

'I'm going to have a busy morning. I don't know yet whether I'll be able to come home for lunch.'

Because of his tired voice, she anxiously asked:

'There's nothing wrong, is there?'

What could he say in reply?

'Don't worry. I'm going to have my breakfast.'

Finally he gave instructions to Bonfils:

'When Janvier arrives, tell him to come and see me.'

He went into his office, which the waiter was just leaving, and released Janin. Then, still as if he were acting in slow motion, or as if he were in a dream, he poured coffee into the three cups.

'Sugar?' he asked, addressing Gisèle Marton first.

'Two lumps.'

He handed her her cup, and the plate of *croissants*, but she gave a sign that she did not want anything to eat.

'Sugar?'

The sister-in-law shook her head. She did not eat anything either, and he was the only one to nibble, without any appetite, at a *croissant* that was still warm.

The day had dawned, but it was not bright enough yet to turn out the lights. Twice, Jenny had opened her mouth to ask a question and both times a look from the chief-inspector had robbed her of any desire to speak.

The moment had come. Maigret, who had poured himself out a second cup of coffee, was slowly filling a pipe chosen from among the pipes scattered about on his desk.

Standing up, he looked at each of the women in turn.

'I think I'll begin with you,' he murmured, stopping at Madame Marton.

Jenny gave a slight start and, once again, tried to say something.

'As for you, I'd like you to wait in another room with one of my inspectors.'

He called Janin back.

'You'll take this lady into the green office and you'll stay with her until I call you.'

This was not the first time this had happened. They were used to it.

'Right, Chief.'

'Janvier still isn't there?'

'I think I heard his voice in the corridor.'

'Tell him to come here straight away.'

Janin went off with the sister-in-law. A moment later, Janvier came in, and stopped short in surprise at the sight of Madame Marton sitting in a chair, a cup of coffee in her hand.

'Marton is dead,' said Maigret. 'Lapointe is on the spot. He's spent the night outside and you'd do well to go and relieve him.'

'No instructions, Chief?'

'Lapointe will pass them on to you. If you take a car, you'll still get there before the Parquet.'

'You won't be coming?'

'I don't think so.'

Both doors were finally shut and there was nobody left in the office but Maigret and Madame Marton. It seemed as if she had been waiting for this particular moment and, while he remained silent in front of her, drawing on his pipe, she slowly came back to life, emerging little by little from her torpor, or rather from her rigidity.

It was strange to see her face becoming human once more, her complexion colouring slightly, her eyes expressing something other than expectation.

'You think I've poisoned him, don't you?'

He took his time. It was not the first time that he had refrained, as he had done that morning, from asking questions as soon as a crime was discovered. It is often preferable not to have people speaking too soon, whether they are suspects or witnesses, for if, right at the beginning, they have made a statement, they often stick to it later for fear of being accused of lying.

He had deliberately given them, both of them, time to think, time to decide on their attitude and the statements they would make.

'I don't think anything,' he murmured at last. 'You will have noticed that I haven't called in the stenographer. I shan't take any notes of what you say to me. Just tell me what happened.'

He knew that his composure, the simple way in which he spoke to her, puzzled her.

'Begin, for example, with yesterday evening.'

'What do you want to know?'

'Everything.'

It was embarrassing. She wondered where to begin her story and in spite of everything he gave her a little help.

'You came home . . .'

'As I do every night of course.'

'At what time?'

'Eight o'clock. After closing the shop, I had an *apéritif* in a bar in the Rue Castiglione.'

'With Monsieur Harris?'

'Yes.'

'And then?'

'My husband had come home before me. My sister was in too. We sat down at table.'

'It was your sister who'd cooked the dinner?'

'As usual.'

'You eat downstairs, in the living-room which serves your husband as a workshop and a bedroom at the same time?'

'Several months ago, he decided to sleep there.'

'How many months ago?'

She did some mental arithmetic. Her lips moved.

'Eight months,' she said in the end.

'What did you eat?'

'First of all, soup . . . The same as the day before . . . Jenny always makes enough soup for two days. . . . Then ham and salad, cheese and pears. . . .'

'Coffee?'

'We never drink coffee in the evening.'

'You didn't notice anything unusual?'

She hesitated, looking him straight in the eye.

'That depends on what you call unusual. I don't quite know what to tell you, because I suspect that there are certain things you know better than I do. The proof of that is that there was an inspector at the door. Before sitting down to dinner, I went upstairs to take my coat off and get into slippers. That was how I found out that my sister had been out and that she'd only just got back.'

'How did you find out?'

'Because I opened the door of her room and saw some shoes of hers that were still wet. Her coat was damp too.'

'Why did you go into her room?'

'Just to make sure that she'd been out.'

'Why?'

Still not averting her eyes, she replied:

'So as to know.'

'Jenny cleared the table?'

'Yes.'

'It's always she who clears away?'

'She insists on paying her share by doing the housework.'

'She does the washing-up too?'

'Sometimes my husband gives her a hand.'

'Not you?'

'No.'

'Go on.'

'She made some herbal tea, as she did every evening. It was she who got us into the habit of drinking herbal tea, at night.'

'Lime-blossom? Camomile?'

'No. Chinese anise. My sister has a sluggish liver. Since she came back from the States, she's had a cup of Chinese anise every night, and my husband wanted to try it, and then I copied him. You know how it is . . .'

'She brought in the cups on a tray?'

'Yes.'

'With the teapot?'

'No. She filled the cups in the kitchen and then came and put the tray on the table.'

'What was your husband doing just then?'

'He was trying to get a station on the radio.'

'So that, if I remember the room correctly, he had his back to you?'

'Yes.'

'What were you doing?'

'I'd just opened a magazine.'

'Near the table?'

'Yes.'

'And your sister?'

'She went back to the kitchen to start the washing-up. I know what you're getting at, but I'll tell you the truth all the same. I didn't put anything in the cups, either in my husband's or in the others. I just took a precaution which I've been taking for some time whenever possible.'

'What's that?'

'Unobtrusively turning the tray so that the cup which is meant for me becomes my husband's or my sister's.'

'And, last night, your cup became . . . ?'

'My husband's.'

'He drank it?'

'Yes. He picked it up and then put it on the radio. . . .'

'You didn't at any moment leave the room? There couldn't have been another substitution?'

'I've been thinking about that for nearly two hours.'

'And what conclusion have you reached?'

'Before my sister brought the tray in, my husband went to the kitchen. Jenny will probably deny it, but it's the truth.'

'What did he go there for?'

'Ostensibly to see whether his spectacles were there. He wears spectacles for reading. He needs them too to see the control panel of the radio. From the studio, you can hear everything that is said in the kitchen. He didn't speak to my sister, came back almost immediately, and found his spectacles by the electric train.'

'It was because of this visit to the kitchen that you changed the cups round?'

'Possibly. Not necessarily. As I've just told you, I often did it.'

'Because you were afraid of his poisoning you?'

She looked at him without answering.

'What happened next?'

'Nothing different from any other evening. My sister came and drank her tea and went back to the kitchen. Xavier listened to a programme on the radio while he repaired a little electric motor he meant to use for something or other.'

'And you went on reading?'

'For an hour or two. It was about ten o'clock when I went upstairs.'

'You went first?'

'Yes.'

'What was your sister doing then?'

'She was making my husband's bed.'

'You were in the habit of leaving them alone together?'

'Why not? What difference could it make?'

'You think they took the opportunity to kiss each other?'

'If they did, it's all the same to me.'

'Have you any reason to believe that your husband was your sister's lover?'

'I don't know if they were lovers. I doubt it. He behaved like a boy of seventeen with her.'

'Why did you say "I doubt it" just now?'

She did not reply immediately. Maigret's gaze was insistent. Finally she answered his question with another question.

'Why do you think we haven't any children?'

'Because you didn't want any.'

'That's what he told you, isn't it? And it's probably what he told his colleagues. A man doesn't like to admit that he's impotent.'

'That was the case, was it?'

She nodded, not without a certain weariness.

'Look here, Chief-Inspector, there are still a lot of things you don't know. Xavier gave you his version of our life. When I came to see you, I didn't bother to go into details. Things happened last night which I don't understand and I know that, when I tell you about them, you won't believe me.'

He did not hurry her. He wanted, on the contrary, to give her plenty of time to speak, and even to weigh her words.

'I heard the doctor, this morning, saying that Xavier had been poisoned. That may be true. But so had I.'

He could not help giving a start, and looking at her more closely.

'You had been poisoned?'

He remembered something which made him feel inclined to believe her: the stains, already dry, on the porcelain of the lavatory and on the tiling.

'I woke up about the middle of the night with horrible burning pains in the stomach. When I got up, I was surprised to feel light-headed and weak in the legs. I made a dash for the bathroom, and I stuck two fingers into my mouth to make myself sick. I'm sorry if this isn't very pleasant. It was like fire, with an after-taste that I would recognize among a thousand others.'

'Did you call your sister, or your husband?'

'No. They may have heard me, because I pulled the chain several times. Twice, I washed my stomach out, and both times I brought up a liquid which left the same after-taste.'

'You didn't think of calling a doctor?'

'What for? Seeing that I'd tackled it in time. . . .'

'You went back to bed?'

'Yes.'

'You weren't tempted to go downstairs?'

'I just listened. I heard Xavier tossing about in his bed as if he were sleeping badly.'

'You realize that it was his cup you drank?'

'I suppose so.'

'You still maintain that you changed the cups round on the tray?'

'Yes.'

'And, afterwards, you didn't let the tray out of your sight? Your husband, or your sister, couldn't have effected another substitution?'

'My sister was in the kitchen.'

'So your husband must have taken the cup that was meant for you?'

'It looks like it.'

'Which amounts to saying that it was your sister who tried to poison your husband?'

'I don't know.'

'Or else, seeing that your husband was poisoned as well, that she tried to poison both of you?'

She said again:

'I don't know.'

They looked at each other for a long time. In the end, it was Maigret who broke contact and went and planted himself in front of the window where, looking at the Seine flowing by in the rain, he filled another pipe.

# VIII

PRESSING his forehead against the cold window-pane, as he used to do when he was a child and kept it there until the skin turned white and he felt pins and needles in his head, Maigret, without realizing it, followed the movements of two workmen who, on the other side of the Seine, were working on some scaffolding.

When he turned round, his face wore an expression of resignation and, making for his desk and sitting down at it again, he said, taking care not to look at Gisèle Marton:

'Have you anything else to tell me?'

She did not hesitate for long and, when she spoke, he could not help looking up, for in calm, measured tones, without either defiance or despondency, she said:

'I saw Xavier die.'

Did she know what sort of impression she made on the chief-inspector? Did she realize that she inspired in him an involuntary, almost professional admiration? He could not remember seeing, in this office where so many people had appeared in turn, a being possessed of such lucidity and sang-froid. He could not remember either anybody so *detached*.

It was impossible to detect in her the slightest human vibration. There was not a single flaw in her make-up.

With his elbows on his blotting-pad, he sighed:

'Fire away.'

'I had gone back to bed and I was finding it hard to get to sleep again. I was trying to understand, without any success, what had happened. I no longer had any clear idea of the passage of time. You know how it is. You get the impression of following a continuous line of thought, but, in reality, there are gaps. I must have dozed off several times. Once or twice, I seemed to hear a noise downstairs, the noise my husband made turning over suddenly in his bed. At least that's what I thought.

'Once, I'm sure, I caught the sound of a groan and I said to myself that he was having nightmares. It wasn't the first time he'd talked and struggled in his sleep. He'd told me that, as a boy, he used to walk in his sleep, and he did that several times with me.'

She continued to choose her words carefully, without any more emotion than if she had been telling a story.

'At one point, I heard a louder noise, as if something heavy had fallen on the floor. I hesitated about getting up, because I felt frightened. Straining my ears, I thought I could make out a rattling groan. I got up then, slipped my dressing-gown on, and quietly made for the stairs.'

'You didn't see your sister?'

'No.'

'And you didn't hear any sound from her bedroom? There wasn't a light under her door?'

'No. To see into the downstairs room, I had to go down several steps and I hesitated, conscious of some danger. I went down, all the same, reluctantly. I bent forward.'

'How many steps did you go down?'

'Six or seven. I didn't count them. There was a light in the studio, just the bedside lamp. Xavier was lying on the floor, roughly half-way between his bed and the spiral staircase. It looked as if he had been crawling along, as if he were still crawling along. He had raised himself on one elbow, the left elbow, and his right arm was stretched out in front to try to grasp the revolver lying about a foot away from his hand.'

'Did he see you?'

'Yes. Raising his head, he gave me a look of bitter hatred, his face all distorted, and froth or saliva on his lips. I realized that, as he was walking towards the stairs, already weakened, holding his gun in his hand, in order to kill me, his strength had failed him, he had fallen down and the revolver had rolled out of his reach.'

His eyes half-shut, Maigret recalled the studio, the staircase going up towards the ceiling, and Marton's body as it had been found.

'You continued to go downstairs?'

'No. I stayed there, incapable of taking my eyes off him. I couldn't be sure exactly how much energy he had left. I was hypnotized.'

'How long did he take to die?'

'I don't know. He kept trying both to reach the gun and to speak, to shout insults or threats at me. At the same time, he was afraid that I should come down, get hold of the revolver before him and shoot. That was doubtless partly why I didn't go down. I don't know for certain. I wasn't thinking. He was breathing hard. Some spasms shook him. I thought that he was going to be sick too. Then he gave a howl, his body shook several times, his hands contracted and finally, all of a sudden, he was still.'

Without averting her eyes, she added:

'I realized that it was all over.'

'It was then that you went down to make sure that he was dead?'

'No. I knew that he was. I don't know why I felt so certain. I went back to my room and sat on the edge of my bed. I felt cold. I put the blanket round my shoulders.'

'Your sister still hadn't left her room?'

'No.'

'Yet you said just now that he gave a howl.'

'That is correct. She must have heard it. She couldn't help hearing it, but she stayed in bed.'

'You didn't think of calling a doctor? Or of telephoning the police?'

'If there had been a telephone in the house, I might have done so. I can't be sure.'

'What time was it?'

'I don't know. I didn't think of looking at the alarm-clock. I was still trying to understand.'

'If you'd been on the telephone, wouldn't you have rung up your friend Harris?'

'Certainly not. He's married.'

'So you don't know, even approximately, how long it was from the time you saw your husband die to the time, about six o'clock in the morning, when you went to telephone from the concierge's lodge? Was it an hour? Two hours? Three hours?'

'Over an hour, I could swear to that. Less than three.'

'You expected to be arrested?'

'I hadn't any illusions.'

'And you wondered what you'd say to the questions you were going to be asked?'

'Possibly. Without realizing. I thought a great deal. Then I heard the familiar sound of dustbins being dragged across a nearby court-yard and I went downstairs.'

'Still without meeting your sister?'

'Yes. On the way, I touched my husband's hand. It was already cold. I looked for your telephone number in the directory and, as I couldn't find it, I rang the emergency service and asked them to notify you.'

'After which you went back to the house?'

'From the courtyard, I saw a light in my sister's room. When I opened the door, Jenny was coming downstairs.'

'She'd already seen the body?'

'Yes.'

'She didn't say anything?'

'She might have said something if there hadn't been a knock at the door almost immediately. It was your inspector.'

She added after a pause:

'If there's a little coffee left . . .'

'It's cold.'

'That doesn't matter.'

He gave her some, and poured out a cup for himself too.

Beyond the door, beyond the window, life was going on, everyday life, life as men had organized it to reassure themselves.

Here, between these four walls, there was another world, which could be felt palpitating behind every word, every phrase, a dark and fearful world, in which the young woman none the less seemed to move about easily.

'Did you love Marton?' asked Maigret in a low voice, almost despite himself.

'No. I don't think so.'

'Yet you married him.'

'I was twenty-eight. I was sickened by all the attempts I'd made.'

'You wanted respectability?'

She did not look offended.

'Tranquillity, at any rate.'

'Did you choose Marton in preference to other men because he was more malleable?'

'Unconsciously perhaps.'

'You already knew that he was practically impotent?'

'Yes. That wasn't what I was looking for.'

'In the early days you were happy with him?'

'That's a big word. We got on quite well together.'

'Because he did what you wanted?'

She pretended not to notice either the aggressive note vibrating in the chief-inspector's voice, or the way in which he was looking at her.

'I didn't ask myself that question.'

Nothing put her off her stride, and yet she was beginning to show a certain weariness.

'When you met Harris, or, if you prefer, Maurice Schwob, did you love him?'

She pondered, with a kind of honesty, as if she were determined to be precise.

'You keep on using that word. To begin with, Maurice was able to change my position, and I never considered that I belonged behind a counter in a big store.'

'Did he become your lover straight away?'

'That depends on what you mean by straight away. A few days, if I remember correctly. We neither of us attached any importance to it.'

'Your relations were established rather on a business footing?'

'If you like. I know that of two hypotheses you'll choose the dirtier. I'd prefer to say that Maurice and I felt that we were the same sort of people . . .'

'Because you had the same ambitions. You never thought of getting a divorce to marry him?'

'What good would that have done? He's married, to a woman older than himself, who has a private fortune and thanks to whom he's been able to start the Rue Saint-Honoré business. As for the rest . . .'

She implied that the rest was so very unimportant!

'When did you begin to suspect that your husband's mind was unbalanced? Because that was the impression you had, wasn't it?'

'It wasn't an impression. It was a conviction. From the start, I knew that he wasn't quite like other people. He had periods of exaltation, during which he spoke of his work as a man of genius would, and others in which he complained that he was just a failure everybody laughed at.'

'Including yourself.'

'Of course. I understand that it's always like that. During these latter periods, he was gloomy and nervous, watching me suspiciously and then, suddenly, just when I least expected it, launching out into recriminations. At other times, on the contrary, he indulged in insinuations.'

'This didn't make you want to leave him?'

'I think I felt sorry for him. He was unhappy. When my sister arrived from the States, in deep mourning, playing the inconsolable widow, he began by sulking in her company. She upset his routine and he couldn't forgive her for that. He'd go whole days without saying a word to her.

'I still wonder how she managed it. What did it, no doubt, was her putting on a helpless act.

'That way, he finally had somebody available who was weaker than himself. At least, that was what he thought. You understand? With my sister, he had the impression of being a man, a stalwart, superior creature. . . .'

'You still didn't think of getting a divorce so as to leave him a clear field?'

'They'd have been unhappy together anyway, because my sister, in actual fact, isn't made of putty. On the contrary.'

'You hate her?'

'We've never liked each other.'

'Why, in that case, did you take her under your roof?'

'Because she forced herself on us.'

If Maigret felt a weight on his shoulders, and something like a bad taste in his mouth, it was because he felt that this was all true.

Life, in the cottage in the Avenue de Châtillon, had indeed been lived in the atmosphere which Madame Marton described in a few phrases, and he could imagine the virtually silent evenings in the course of which each person remained wrapped in his hatred.

'What were you hoping for? That it wouldn't last much longer?'

'I went to see a doctor.'

'Steiner?'

'No. Another one. I told him everything.'

'He didn't advise you to try to have your husband certified?'

'He advised me to wait, telling me that the symptoms weren't clear enough yet, that a more violent crisis would occur before long . . .'

'So that you expected this crisis and you were on your guard?'

She gave an imperceptible shrug of the shoulders.

'Have I answered all your questions?' she asked after a silence.

Maigret hunted in his mind, but could not think of anything else he could ask her, for there were scarcely any obscure points left.

'When you stopped on the stairs and saw your husband on the floor, you weren't tempted to go to his help?'

'I couldn't be sure that he hadn't enough strength left to grab the revolver . . .'

'You are convinced that your sister knew about everything you've just told me?'

She looked at him without answering.

What was the good of going on? He would have liked to make her contradict herself. He would have liked to charge her. She gave him no hold over her. She did not shy away either.

'I suppose,' he murmured, throwing a final shaft, 'you never had any intention of getting rid of your husband?'

'By killing him?'

She made a clear distinction between killing and putting away. When he said yes, she stated simply:

'If I'd found it necessary to kill him, I wouldn't have left anything to chance and I wouldn't be here now.'

This too was true. If anyone was capable of committing a perfect crime, it was this woman.

Unfortunately, she had not killed Marton, and, after relighting his pipe and giving her a malevolent look, Maigret slowly got up, his body and mind both feeling numb, and made for the door to the inspectors' office.

'Get me No. 17, Avenue de Châtillon . . . The concierge's lodge . . . Janvier is in the cottage, at the back of the courtyard . . . I'd like to speak to him on the telephone . . .'

He came back to his place and, while he waited, she put a little powder on her face, as she would have done at the theatre during the interval. Finally the telephone rang.

'Janvier? . . . I'd like you to go to the cottage, without hanging up, and have a good look at a tray, which ought to be in the kitchen . . .'

He turned towards Gisèle Marton.

'A round tray or a square tray?'

'An oblong tray, in wood.'

'An oblong wooden tray, big enough to take three cups and saucers . . . What I want to know is whether there's a mark, a scratch, any sort of sign which makes it possible to tell if the tray has been put one way or another . . . You see what I mean? . . . Just a moment . . . Are the experts still there? . . . Good! Ask them to have a look at a bottle in the broom-cupboard which contains some white powder . . . and test it for finger-prints . . .'

Janvier was able to answer the second question straight away.

'There aren't any prints. They've already examined it. The bottle has been wiped with a wet, rather greasy rag, probably a dishcloth.'

'Has the Parquet arrived?'

'Yes. The examining magistrate isn't pleased.'

'Because I didn't wait for him?'

'More particularly because you took the two women away.'

'Tell him that, by the time he gets to his chambers, it will probably be all over. Which magistrate is it?'

'Coméliau.'

The two men could not stand each other.

'Go and have a quick look at the tray. I'll hold the line.'

He heard the voice of Gisèle Marton, to whom he was no longer paying any attention.

'If you had asked me, I would have told you what you want to know. There is a mark. It wasn't made on purpose. It's the varnish which has formed a blister, on one of the short sides of the oblong.'

Sure enough, a few moments later, Janvier, a little out of breath, told him:

'There's a blister in the varnish.'

'Thank you. Nothing else?'

'In Marton's pocket, they've found a bit of crumpled paper which had contained some zinc phosphide.'

'I know.'

Not that the paper would be in the dead man's pocket, but that they would find it somewhere in the room.

He hung up.

'When you saw your husband go into the kitchen, you suspected what he was going to do, didn't you? That was why you changed the cups round?'

'I changed them round whenever I had the chance.'

'He sometimes changed them round too?'

'That's correct. Only, last night, he wasn't able to, because I didn't let the tray out of my sight.'

At the Boulevard Richard-Lenoir too, there was a tray, not in wood, but in electroplate, which was a wedding present. Maigret's cup and his wife's were the same, except that the chief-inspector's had a scarcely visible crack in it.

Now, they never made a mistake. When Madame Maigret put the tray on the pedestal table, by her husband's armchair, he knew for certain that his cup was on his side, within his reach.

He had got up once more. Madame Marton followed him with her eyes, curious but not afraid.

'Will you come here a minute, Lucas? Find an empty office, never mind which, and go there with her. Stay there until I call you. On your way, tell them to bring me the sister-in-law.'

Madame Marton followed Lucas without putting a single question
to the chief-inspector. The latter, once he was on his own, opened his
cupboard, took the bottle of cognac that he kept there, not so much for
himself as for certain of his customers who sometimes needed it, and
poured a spot into the water-tumbler.

When somebody knocked, he shut the cupboard door and just had
time to wipe his lips.

'Come in!'

Jenny was shown in, wearing the wan, swollen face, streaked with
red, of someone who has been crying.

'Sit down.'

The chair her sister had been sitting in was still warm. Jenny looked
around her, puzzled to find herself alone with the chief-inspector.

He remained on his feet, walking round in a circle, not knowing how
to tackle her, and finally, planting himself in front of her, said:

'Which lawyer do you want?'

She raised her head sharply, her eyes wide open and moist. Her lips
moved, but she did not manage to say anything.

'I would prefer to question you in the presence of your lawyer, so
that you don't get the impression that I'm catching you off your
guard.'

With tears running down her cheeks, she ended up by stammering:

'I don't know any lawyers.'

He took a Bar year-book from the shelves of the book-case and held
it out to her.

'Choose from this list.'

She shook her head.

'What's the use?'

He would so much have preferred it to be the other one!

'You confess?'

She nodded, looked for her handkerchief in her handbag, and un-
affectedly blew her nose, so that it became redder than ever.

'You admit that you intended to poison your sister?'

At that, she burst out sobbing.

'I don't know any more . . . Don't torture me . . . I want to get
it over quickly. . . .'

Great sobs shook her. She did not think of hiding her wet face.

'You were in love with your brother-in-law?'

'I don't know. I don't know any more. I suppose so . . .'

Her eyes looked at him beseechingly.

'Make it quick, Inspector! . . . I can't stand it any longer. . . .'

And, now that he knew, he took the shortest cuts. Sometimes, as he
went past her, he even touched the young woman's shoulders with
his hand, as if he understood that she needed some human contact.

'You realized that Xavier wasn't like other people?'

She nodded. She shook her head. She was wrestling with problems that were too complicated for her, and finally she cried:

'It was she who didn't understand him and was driving him mad . . .'

'On purpose?'

'I don't know. He needed . . .'

The words were having trouble in coming.

'I tried . . .'

'To reassure him?'

'You can't imagine the sort of atmosphere we were living in . . . It was only when we were alone, he and I . . . Because, with me, he felt well and confident . . .'

'When he joined you on the embankment, yesterday evening, did he tell you that he was to come here for an examination this morning?'

Surprised that Maigret knew all about it, she gaped at him for a moment.

'Answer me . . . I'm trying, for my part, to set you free as soon as possible . . .'

This she understood. She did not think that the chief-inspector was talking of letting her go, but rather of setting her free from herself, as it were.

'He told me,' she admitted reluctantly.

'Did that frighten him?'

She said yes, with a sniff, and added, once more on the brink of tears:

'He fancied she had won . . .'

Her choice of words revealed the disorder of her thoughts.

'Because it was she who drove him to all that . . . She'd foreseen that he would find the poison, that he would get ideas into his head . . .'

'He hated her?'

She stared at him apprehensively, without daring to reply.

'And you too, you began to hate your sister, didn't you?'

She shook her head. That meant neither yes nor no. She was trying rather to chase away the nightmare.

'Yesterday evening, leaving here,' continued Maigret, 'Marton fancied that after the medical examination he wouldn't be allowed to go free again . . . So he had only one evening left . . . It was his last chance . . .'

The behaviour of the toy salesman might appear incoherent, but none the less it followed a certain logical pattern, and Maigret began to understand certain passages in the treatise on psychiatry. Only, what the author of the book set out in difficult terms and complicated phrases was, in fact, nothing but human nature.

'When he came into the kitchen while you were there . . .'

She shivered, wishing she could stop him talking.

'The tea was already in the cups?'

He was sure of it, and did not need an answer.

'You didn't see him put the powder in?'

'I'd got my back to him. He opened the cutlery drawer and took out a knife. I heard the noise the knives made . . .'

'And you thought he hadn't the courage to put the poison in?'

Maigret recalled the knife, with its dark wooden handle, lying beside the radio which had a catalogue on top of it.

Under the chief-inspector's stern gaze, Jenny struggled a little longer before groaning:

'I felt sorry . . .'

He could have retorted:

'Not for your sister, at any rate!'

And she went on:

'I was sure that he was going to be put away, that Gisèle had won the game . . . So . . .'

'So you took the bottle of phosphide and you poured a good dose into your sister's cup. You had the presence of mind to wipe the bottle.'

'I'd got a wet towel in my hand.'

'You made sure that the cup meant for your sister was on the right side of the tray.'

'Please, Inspector! . . . If you knew what a night I'd had . . .'

'You heard everything?'

How could she have failed to hear?

'And you didn't go downstairs?'

'I was too frightened.'

She trembled at the memory and it was for her sake that he went and opened the cupboard again.

'Drink this.'

She obeyed, choked, and nearly brought up the cognac which was burning her throat.

It was obvious that she had reached the point where she wanted to lie down on the floor and stay still and not hear anything more.

'If only your brother-in-law had told you everything . . .'

Huddled up small, she wondered what she was going to hear now.

And Maigret, remembering things that Marton had said in this very office, explained:

'It wasn't poison that he meant to use to get rid of his wife or to take his revenge on her, but his revolver.'

Hadn't he very nearly brought it off? Don't psychiatrists speak of the strict logic of certain lunatics?

It was in his own cup that he had poured some phosphide while rattling the knives, so quickly that his sister-in-law, who had her back to him, had imagined that he had lost his nerve at the last moment.

He had calculated the dose so as to be ill enough to justify the action he was going to take later, but not enough to die. It was not for nothing that, for months past, he had been haunting public libraries, immersing himself in medical and chemical treatises.

It was Gisèle Marton, by changing the cups round on the tray, who had had this dose, and it had done no more than upset her.

Hadn't Jenny understood all this, during the interminable night she had spent in her room, listening to the noises in the house?

The proof that she understood it now was that she slumped further down in her chair, hanging her head, and that she stammered as if she no longer had the strength to form her words properly:

'It was I who killed him . . .'

He left her to her grief, trying not to make any noise, only afraid of seeing her fall to the floor, then finally, on tip-toe, he went into the inspectors' office.

'Take her downstairs . . . Gently . . . To the infirmary first,' he said.

He preferred to have nothing to do with it. Standing in front of the window, he did not even bother to see which inspectors were making for his office.

It was not his fault. He could not, straight after Marton's first visit, have taken him to the psychiatrist. And the latter, no doubt, would not have taken on the responsibility of certifying him.

There exists, between responsibility and irresponsibility, an indefinite zone, a realm of shadows into which it is dangerous to venture.

Two people, at least, had struggled about in it, while a third . . .

'What shall we do with the other one, Chief?'

He gave a start, turned round, and looked at the vast inspectors' office like a man who has come back from afar.

'Let her go.'

He had nearly said:

'Chuck her out.'

He waited till his own office was free. Then he went back there and, finding traces of foreign smells lingering in the air, opened the window.

He was taking deep breaths of the damp air when Lucas said behind him:

'I don't know if I've done right. Before going, Madame Marton asked me for permission to make a phone call. I said yes, thinking that it might tell us something.'

'What did she say to him?'

'You know who she spoke to?'

'Harris.'

'She calls him Maurice. She apologized for not being there to open the shop. She didn't give any details. She just said:

' "I'll explain everything to you directly . . ." '

Maigret shut the window, turning his back to it, and Lucas, looking at him, asked uneasily:

'What's the matter, Chief?'

'Nothing. What should be the matter? She said it and she isn't the sort of woman who's wrong. Just now, she's in a taxi, holding a little mirror in front of her nose and repairing her make-up. . . .'

He knocked his pipe out in the ash-tray.

'Ring up the Parquet and, if Coméliau is back, tell him I'm coming over to see him straight away.'

For him, it was all over. The rest was the judges' concern, and he had no desire to be in their place.

*Noland, 16 December, 1957*

# MAIGRET AND THE RELUCTANT WITNESSES

# MAIGRET AND THE RELUCTANT
# WITNESSES

---

## I

'You haven't forgotten your umbrella?'

'No.'

In a moment the door would close behind Maigret; he had already turned towards the stairs.

'You'd better wear your muffler.'

Madame Maigret bustled away to fetch it, with no inkling that those simple words would stick in her husband's mind for quite a time, with depressing effect.

It was only November—November 3rd—and the weather wasn't particularly cold. But rain was falling from a sky of low, unbroken grey, one of those steady showers that seem wetter and somehow more perfidious, especially first thing in the morning, than ordinary rain.

A while ago, getting out of bed, he had winced because his neck hurt when he turned his head. You couldn't call it a proper stiff neck, but he couldn't move it quite as usual, something felt wrong.

The evening before, after the cinema, they had walked for a good distance along the Boulevards, and it had been raining already.

All this was of no importance. And yet, because of the muffler, perhaps also because it was a thick muffler that his wife had knitted for him, he felt old.

Going downstairs, where there were damp footmarks on the steps, and then outside, walking under his umbrella, he remembered what she had said to him last evening. In two years' time he'd be retiring.

He had shared her pleasure at the idea. For a long time they had chatted lazily about the part of the country where they were going to live, near Meung-sur-Loire, a district they were both fond of.

A bare-headed little boy ran into him and didn't apologize. A young married couple went past, arm-in-arm, sharing an umbrella; they doubtless worked in offices near each other.

It had been an emptier Sunday than usual, possibly because this year it happened to be All Souls' Day. He would have sworn that he could still smell the chrysanthemums this morning. From their window they had watched the family groups setting off for the cemeteries; but neither of them had any relations buried in Paris.

He waited for his bus at the corner of the Boulevard Voltaire, and felt glummer than ever when he saw the large vehicle drive up; it was one of the new kind without a platform, so that he was not only obliged to sit down, but had to knock out his pipe as well.

We all have days like that, don't we?

He longed for the next two years to be over; then he wouldn't have to wind a muffler round his neck and set out across Paris on beastly wet mornings like this, with the place looking the same black and white as in an old silent film.

The bus was full of young people; some recognized him, others took no notice.

On the quays the rain slanted down more sharply and felt colder. He hurried into the arched, draughty entrance of Police Headquarters, strode towards the stairs; and then, all of a sudden, recognizing the characteristic smell of the building, the greenish glimmer of the lamps, which were still alight, he felt sad to think that in such a short time he would stop coming here each morning.

Old Joseph, who for some mysterious reason had escaped the retired-list, greeted him with a conspiratorial air and murmured:

'Inspector Lapointe is waiting for you, Chief-Inspector.'

As usual on Mondays, there were a lot of people in the waiting-room and in the long corridor. Some new faces; two or three young women who were hardly the type one would expect to see there, but mostly old acquaintances who turned up every now and then at one door or another.

He went into his office, hung his overcoat in the cupboard together with his hat and that muffler, hesitated whether to open the umbrella and leave it out to dry, according to Madame Maigret's instructions, finally stood it in a corner of the cupboard.

It was barely half past eight. There were letters waiting on his blotter. He went across and opened the door into the inspectors' office, greeted Lucas, Torrence and two or three others with a gesture of the hand.

'Somebody tell Lapointe I'm here.'

That would touch off a rumour that the Chief was in a bad mood today, which was not true. Sometimes, looking back on days when one has been grumpy, glum, touchy, one sees them in memory as among the happiest.

'Good morning, Chief.'

Lapointe was pale, his eyes a little bloodshot from lack of sleep, but sparkling with satisfaction. He was quivering with impatience.

'Done it! I've got him!'

'Where is he?'

'In the little room at the end of the corridor; Torrence has gone to keep an eye on him.'

'What time?'

'Four o'clock this morning.'

'Has he talked?'

'I had coffee sent up, and then, about six o'clock, breakfast for both of us, and we chatted like old friends.'

'Go and fetch him.'

This was nice work. Grégoire Brau, known as Patience, also as the Canon, had been at his game for years without ever being caught in the act.

Only once, twelve years ago, he had been nabbed because he had overslept, but when he came out of prison he had gone right back to his old ways.

He came into the office now, preceded by Lapointe looking as proud as though he'd caught the biggest trout or pike of the year, and stood, sheepishly, in front of Maigret, who was deep in his papers.

'Sit down.'

The chief-inspector added, as he finished scanning a letter:

'Have you got any cigarettes?'

'Yes, Monsieur Maigret.'

'You can smoke.'

Brau was a fat fellow of forty-three, who must have been plump and flabby even in his schooldays. He had a fresh complexion, a pink face that reddened easily, a blunt nose, a double chin, a guileless mouth.

'So they got you after all?'

'They got me.'

It was Maigret who had arrested him the first time, and they had often met again since then, greeting each other without ill-feeling.

'You've been at it again!' continued the chief-inspector, alluding to the burglary of a flat.

Instead of denying the statement, the Canon smiled modestly. There was no proof. But though he never left a single finger-print his jobs were signed, as it were.

He worked alone, planning each job with incredible patience. He was the very image of a quiet man, with no vices, no passions, no nerves.

He spent most of his time sitting in a corner of some bar, café or restaurant, apparently deep in a newspaper, or dozing; but his keen ears lost nothing of what was being said around him.

Moreover he was a great reader of weekly magazines; he studied their society and gossip columns with care and had an unparalleled knowledge of the comings and goings of celebrities.

Sooner or later Police Headquarters would be rung up by some famous person, sometimes an actor or film star, who had just got back from Hollywood, London, Rome or Cannes to find that their flat had been broken into.

Without needing to hear the whole story, Maigret would ask:
'What about the refrigerator?'

'Empty!'

All the liqueurs would have vanished from the cellar too. One could be sure, too, that the bed would have been slept in, and the pyjamas, dressing-gown and slippers of the owner would have been used.

That was the Canon's signature, an obsession that had come over him right at the start, when he was only twenty-two, perhaps because in those days he was really hungry and longed for a comfortable bed. When he was sure that a flat was empty for several weeks, that no servants were left there, that the concierge had not been told to go up and air it, he would move in, without the aid of a jemmy, for no lock could keep its secrets from him.

Once inside, instead of hastily making off with any valuables such as jewellery, pictures, ornaments, he would settle down for a time, usually until the supply of provisions was exhausted.

As many as thirty empty tins had been found after one of his visits; and a number of bottles too, of course. He read. He slept. He made use of the bathroom with a kind of voluptuous satisfaction, unsuspected by the other occupants of the house.

Then he would go home and resume his regular habits, going out only in the evenings, for a game of *belote*, to a rather ill-famed bar in the Avenue des Ternes, where, because he worked alone and never talked about his exploits, he was regarded with a mixture of respect and distrust.

'Did she write to you, or ring up?'

He put this question in a kind of melancholy that resembled the feeling with which Maigret had left home a while earlier.

'What are you talking about?'

'You know very well, Monsieur Maigret. Otherwise you wouldn't have picked me up. Your inspector'—he looked at Lapointe—'was in the house, on the stairs, before I got there, and I suppose he'd left one of his pals in the street outside? Correct?'

'Correct.'

Lapointe had spent not one night, but two, on the stairs of the house at Passy where a certain Monsieur Ailevard owned a flat. That gentleman had gone to London for a fortnight. The newspapers had announced his trip, for it was connected with a film and with a very well-known star.

The Canon didn't always rush into a house the moment people had left it. He took his time and his precautions.

'Can't think how I missed seeing your inspector. Well, that'll teach me . . . Did she ring you up?'

Maigret shook his head.

'She wrote to you?'

He nodded.

'I suppose you couldn't show me the letter? She must have disguised her writing, of course?'

Not even that. No point in telling him, though.

'I rather thought, without letting myself believe it, that this would happen one day. She's a bitch, if you'll excuse my language, and yet I can't hold it against her . . . After all, I've had two pretty good years, when you come to think of it.'

He had gone on for years without any woman in his life, and because of his appearance some people used to tease him for this, declaring that there were good reasons for his virtuous behaviour.

Suddenly, at the age of forty-one, he had set up house with a certain Germaine, twenty years his junior, who had had her pitch on the Avenue de Wagram for a short time past.

'Did you marry her in the registry office?'

'And in church. She's from Brittany. I suppose she's already moved in on Henri?'

He was referring to a young pimp known as Henri-My-Eye.

'No, he's moved into your place.'

The Canon displayed no indignation, did not rail against fate, blamed only himself.

'What'll I get?'

'From two to five years. Did Inspector Lapointe take down your statement?'

'He made notes of what I told him.'

The telephone rang.

'Hello? Chief-Inspector Maigret here.'

He listened, frowned.

'The name again, please.'

He pulled a pad towards him, scribbled : 'Lachaume.'

'Quai de la Gare? . . . At Ivry? . . . Very well. . . . Is there a doctor there? . . . Fellow's definitely dead, is he? . . .'

The Canon's importance had instantly dwindled, as he himself seemed to realize. He got up without being told.

'I suppose you've other things to see to . . .'

Maigret turned to Lapointe.

'Take him to the *Dépôt*, then go and get some sleep.'

He opened the cupboard to take out his hat and coat, then, on second thoughts, held out his hand to the fat man with pink cheeks.

'It isn't our fault, old man.'

'I know.'

He didn't put on the muffler. Going to the inspectors' room he chose Janvier, who had only just arrived and was not yet at work.

'You're coming with me.'

'Yes, Chief.'

'Lucas, you ring up the Public Prosecutor's office. A man has been killed by a bullet in the heart, on the Quai de la Gare at Ivry. Name of Lachaume . . . Lachaume's Biscuits. . . .'

This called up memories that took him right back to his country childhood. In those days, in every dimly lit village grocery, where dried vegetables were offered for sale alongside clogs and sewing-cotton, you were sure to find cellophane-wrapped packets labelled *'Biscuiterie Lachaume'*.

Lachaume's made *petits-beurre* and wafer-biscuits, both of which had the same rather cardboardy taste.

He had not heard of them since those days. Neither had he seen any more of those calendars showing a little boy with exaggeratedly rosy cheeks and an inane grin, eating a Lachaume wafer, and it was even rare nowadays to see the name in faded letters on a wall in some isolated village.

'Tell the Identity people too, of course.'

'Yes, Chief.'

Lucas was reaching for the telephone already. Maigret and Janvier went downstairs.

'Are we taking the car?'

Maigret's depression had evaporated in the everyday atmosphere of Police Headquarters. Caught up in the routine, he had forgotten to be introspective or to put questions to himself.

Sundays have a pernicious influence. Sitting in the car and lighting a pipe that tasted delicious again, he asked:

'D'you know Lachaume's Biscuits?'

'No, Chief.'

'You're too young, of course.'

Besides, perhaps they had never been on sale in Paris? A whole lot of things are manufactured just for country districts. Then there are the makes that go out of fashion, but still have a limited following. He could remember some *apéritifs* that were celebrated in his young days, but you never came across them now except in some lost inn, far from any main road.

After crossing the bridge they could not follow the river, because of the one-way system along the quays, and Janvier had to go a long way round before getting back to the Seine, opposite Charenton. On the other side they could see the Halle aux Vins, and to the left a train was going over an iron bridge across the river.

In the old days there had been nothing here except small detached houses and brick and timber yards; now there were blocks of flats, six or seven storeys high, with shops and *bistrots* on the ground floor; but every so often came a gap, a patch of waste ground, some studios, or two or three low houses.

'What number?'

Maigret told him, and they pulled up in front of what must once have been a handsome house, a three-storey affair in brick and stone, with behind it a tall chimney, like a factory chimney. There was a car at the door. A policeman was walking to and fro along the pavement. It was difficult to tell whether this was still Paris or already Ivry, and the turning they had just passed was probably the dividing street.

'Good morning, Chief-Inspector. The door isn't locked. They're waiting for you upstairs.'

The house had a carriage entrance, with a gate painted green and a smaller door let in on one side. Going in, the two men found themselves in an arched passage, not unlike that of the Quai des Orfèvres, except that the far end was closed by a door with frosted glass panes. One of the panes was missing and the gap had been filled with a piece of cardboard.

It was cold and damp. A door opened off on either side of the passage, and Maigret, wondering which to choose, opened the one on the right; evidently the right choice, for it revealed a kind of hall and the foot of a wide staircase.

The walls, once white, had taken on a yellow tinge with browner patches here and there, and the cracking plaster had fallen off in places. The three lowest steps were of marble; the others were wooden, looked as though they had not been swept for a long time, and creaked when trodden on.

It was rather like one of those municipal offices where you always feel, on entering, that you have come to the wrong place. Each man felt that if he spoke his voice might echo back at him.

Footsteps were heard on the first floor and a man leant over the banisters, a youngish, tired-looking man, who introduced himself as soon as Maigret reached the top of the stairs.

'My name's Legrand, I'm the secretary of the Ivry Police Station. . . . The superintendent is waiting for you. . . .'

Another hall upstairs, with a marble floor, an uncurtained window looking out at the Seine and the falling rain.

It was an enormous house, with doors on all sides, corridors like some government building, and everywhere the same drab aspect and the same smell of long-settled dust.

At the end of a narrower passage, on the left, the secretary knocked at a door and opened it, revealing a bedroom so dark that the local superintendent had kept the light on.

This room looked into the courtyard, and through the dusty muslin curtains could be seen the chimney that Maigret had already noticed from outside.

He was vaguely acquainted with the Ivry superintendent, who was of a younger generation and shook his hand with exaggerated respect.

'I came as soon as I had the telephone call. . . .'

'Has the doctor left?'

'He had an urgent case. I didn't think I need keep him, because in any case the official pathologist will be here soon. . . .'

The body was lying on the bed, and except for the superintendent there was no one in the room.

'What about the family?'

'I told them to go to their own rooms or to the drawing-room. I thought you'd rather . . .'

Maigret took his watch out of his pocket. It was a quarter to ten.

'When did you hear about it?'

'An hour or so ago. I'd just got to the office. Someone rang up my secretary to ask me to come round here.'

'Did he say who he was?'

'Yes. The brother, Armand Lachaume.'

'D'you know him?'

'Only by name. He must have come to the station sometimes, to have a signature witnessed for some formality or other. They're not people one takes much notice of. . . .'

Maigret was struck by the phrase. *Not people one takes much notice of.* He could understand it, for like Lachaume's Biscuits, the house seemed to be at one remove from time, from present-day life.

It was years since Maigret had seen such a bedroom, which must have remained for a century without the slightest change. There was even a washstand with drawers, topped with a slab of grey marble on which stood a flowered china jug and basin, and dishes of the same china to hold soap and combs.

The furniture and other objects were not in themselves particularly ugly. Some of them would perhaps have fetched good prices at an auction, or in an antique shop, but there was something dreary and oppressive about the way they were arranged.

It seemed as though suddenly, long ago, life in this place had stopped, not the life of the man on the bed, but the life of the house, the life surrounding it, and even the factory chimney, seen through the curtains, looked absurd and old-fashioned, with its 'L' inlaid in black bricks.

'Theft?'

Two or three drawers were open. Ties and linen were scattered on the floor in front of the wardrobe.

'It seems that a pocket-book with a biggish sum in it has disappeared.'

'Who is he?'

Maigret pointed to the dead man on the bed. The sheets and blankets were in disorder. The pillow had fallen on the ground. One arm was dangling. There was blood on the pyjama jacket where it had been torn or burnt by the powder.

Just as Maigret had been thinking earlier that morning of the sharply-contrasted black and white of silent films, now, in this room, he was suddenly reminded of those illustrations in the old-time Sunday papers, before photographs began to be reproduced and the week's sensations were depicted in engravings.

'Léonard Lachaume, the eldest son.'

'Married?'

'A widower.'

'When did it happen?'

'In the night. According to Dr. Voisin, death took place at about two in the morning.'

'Who was in the house?'

'Let me see. . . . The old couple, his father and mother, on the floor above, in the left wing. . . . That's two. . . . The little boy. . . .'

'What little boy?'

'The dead man's son. . . . A boy of twelve. . . . At the moment, he's at school. . . .'

'In spite of the tragedy?'

'Apparently no one knew about that at eight o'clock, when he went off to school.'

'So no one heard anything? . . . Who else lives here?'

'The maid. . . . I think her name is Catherine. . . . She sleeps up above, near the old couple and the boy. . . . She looks as old as the house and just as rickety. . . . Then there's Armand, the younger brother. . . .'

'Whose brother?'

'The dead man's. . . . He sleeps on the other side of the corridor, and so does his wife.'

'They were all here last night, and the shot didn't wake one of them?'

'So they say. I only asked them a few questions. It's difficult. You'll see!'

'What's difficult?'

'To know. When I got here, I had no idea what it was about. Armand Lachaume, the one who rang me up, opened the downstairs door the moment my car stopped. He seemed as though he were still half-asleep, and said, without looking at me:

' "My brother has been killed, Superintendent."

'He brought me here and pointed to the bed. I asked him when it had happened and he said he hadn't the remotest idea.

'I insisted:

' "But you were in the house?"

' "I suppose so. I slept in my room." '

The police superintendent seemed to be annoyed with himself.

'I don't know how to explain. Usually, when there's a tragedy like this in a family, you find everyone gathered round the corpse, some in tears, others explaining, a bit too talkative if anything. . . .

'Whereas in this case it took me quite a time to discover that the men weren't alone in the house. . . .'

'Have you seen the others?'

'The wife.'

'You mean the wife of Armand, the one who telephoned you?'

'Yes. At some stage I heard a rustling sound in the corridor. I opened the door and found her outside. She had the same air of weariness as her husband. She didn't seem embarrassed. I asked her who she was, and Armand answered for her:

' "She's my wife. . . ."'

'I asked whether she hadn't heard anything in the night and she said no, she always took some tablets—I forget what—so as to sleep. . . .'

'Who found the body? And when?'

'The old servant, at a quarter to nine.'

'Have you seen her?'

'Yes. She must have gone back to her kitchen. I suspect she's a bit deaf. She got worried when the eldest son didn't appear at breakfast, which they all have together in the dining-room. In the end she came and knocked on his door. Then she went in, and it was she who told the others.'

'What about the old people?'

'They don't say a word. The wife is half-paralysed and stares straight ahead of her as though she hadn't got all her wits. Her husband seems so distressed that he can hardly follow what one says to him.'

Once more the superintendent added:

'You'll see!'

Maigret turned to Janvier.

'Will you go and have a look round?'

Janvier departed and the chief-inspector at last went over to the body, which was lying on its left side, facing the window. Someone had already closed the man's eyes. His mouth was half-open, beneath a drooping brown moustache with some grey hairs in it. His thin hair clung to his temples and forehead.

It was difficult to gauge the expression on his face. He did not seem to have felt pain, and looked more astonished than anything else. But perhaps that came from the open mouth, and he hadn't looked like that till he was dead?

Maigret heard steps in the upstairs hall, then along the corridor. Opening the door, he encountered one of the public prosecutor's deputies, whom he had known for a long time and who shook his hand silently, looking across at the bed. He knew the clerk too, and nodded to him, but he had never set eyes on the tall young man who came in behind them, hatless and coatless.

'This is Monsieur Angelot, the examining magistrate. . . .'

The young man, thus named, extended a firm, well-manicured

hand, the hand of a tennis-player, and Maigret reflected once again that a new generation was already taking over.

However, old Dr. Paul came in shortly afterwards, out of breath, but alert, with a well-fed look about his eyes and mouth.

'Where's the stiff?'

Maigret noticed that the grey-blue eyes of the examining magistrate remained cold and that he frowned slightly, doubtless in disapproval.

'Have the photographers finished?' went on Dr. Paul.

'They haven't arrived yet. I think I can hear them now.'

That meant waiting till the photographers were through, and then the Judicial Identity experts invaded the room and set to work.

In a corner, the public prosecutor's deputy asked Maigret:

'A family quarrel?'

'Apparently there's been theft.'

'No one heard anything?'

'They say not.'

'How many people in the house?'

'Wait till I count. . . . The old couple and the servant, that's three. . . . The little boy. . . .'

'What little boy?'

'The dead man's son. . . . That's four. . . . Then the brother and his wife. . . . Six! Six people beside the fellow who got killed, and none of them heard a thing. . . .'

The public prosecutor's deputy went over to the doorway and ran his hand over the wallpaper.

'The walls are thick, but all the same! . . . No weapon been found?'

'I don't know. . . . The Ivry police superintendent said nothing about that. I'm waiting till the formalities are over, before beginning my investigation. . . .'

The photographers were looking for electric points where they could plug in their lamps, and finding none, they had to take the bulb out of the centre light. They strode about, grumbling, getting in one another's way, calling out hasty instructions, while the examining magistrate, who looked like an athletic student, stood waiting, grey-suited and motionless, without a word.

'Do you think I could go now?' asked the local superintendent. 'There must be a mob in my waiting-room. I could send you two or three men in case the rubber-neckers start collecting outside the house a bit later on. . . .'

'That would be very kind. Thank you.'

'Would you like to have one of my inspectors as well, one who knows the neighbourhood?'

'I expect I shall need one later. I'll ring you up. Thank you again.'

As he went out, the superintendent said once again:

'You'll see!'

The public prosecutor's deputy asked in an undertone:
'See what?'

'The family. . . . The whole set-up. . . . There was no one in the room when the police superintendent arrived. . . . They're all in their own rooms, or in the dining-room. . . . Nobody stirs. . . . There isn't a sound. . . .'

The deputy glanced at the furniture, the damp-marked wallpaper, the mirror above the fireplace, where generations of flies had left traces of their passage.

'It doesn't surprise me. . . .'

The photographers were the first to leave, which cleared the room a bit. Dr. Paul was able to make a preliminary examination, while the Identity experts looked for finger-prints and went through drawers and cupboards.

'What time, Doctor?'

'I shall be able to say more definitely after the post-mortem, but he's been dead a good six hours, if not more.'

'Killed instantaneously?'

'The shot was fired at very close range. . . . The external wound is as big as a saucer, the flesh scorched. . . .'

'What about the bullet?'

'I shall find it inside him presently, for it didn't go right through, which suggests that it was of small calibre.'

His hands were covered with blood. He went across to the wash-stand, but the jug was empty.

'There must be a tap somewhere. . . .'

One of the others opened the door for him. Armand Lachaume, the younger brother, was in the corridor, and it was he who, without a word, led him to an old-fashioned bathroom where stood an antique, claw-footed bath-tub, whose tap must have been dribbling for years past, for it had left rusty streaks on the enamel.

'I'll leave you to it, Maigret,' sighed the public prosecutor's deputy, turning towards the examining magistrate. 'I'm going back to the *Palais de Justice*.'

Whereupon the magistrate murmured:

'I hope you don't mind if I don't come with you. I'm staying here.'

Maigret started, and almost blushed to see that the young judge had noticed it. The latter went on at once:

'I hope you have no objection, Chief-Inspector. I'm only a beginner, you know, and this will be valuable experience for me.'

Wasn't there the faintest trace of irony in his voice? He was polite, too polite even. And completely cold beneath his surface friendliness.

He was one of the new school, the school that regards an investigation as the affair of the examining magistrate from start to finish, with the role of the police reduced to obeying his instructions.

Janvier, who appeared in the doorway at that moment and had heard what was said, exchanged a highly expressive glance with Maigret.


# II


MAIGRET could not hide his annoyance and almost lost his temper altogether at the thought that the examining magistrate was not only noticing it, but must inevitably be putting it down to his own presence, which in fact was only part of the reason. For hadn't that muffler business, even as he left the Boulevard Richard-Lenoir, started a procession of gloomy reflections?

This fellow Angelot, so fresh and brisk, had only just left college. Either he was an exceptional chap, one of the few in each generation, whom you can count on your fingers, or else he was being backed by people in high places; otherwise, instead of getting a job in Paris, he'd have been sent to kick his heels for years in some sub-prefecture magistrate's court.

Just now, when the deputy had introduced them, the examining magistrate had simply shaken Maigret's hand with an energy that might be taken for warmth, but hadn't said any of the things people usually said to the chief-inspector. Naturally he couldn't say, as the older men did:

'Nice to run into you again.'

But there were some who always murmured:

'So glad to be working with you.'

It was hard to believe that Angelot had never heard of him. Yet he had shown neither satisfaction nor curiosity.

Was it a deliberate pose, intended to show Maigret that he wasn't impressed by his reputation? Or simply lack of curiosity, the genuine indifference of the young generation?

Catching certain glances, the chief-inspector wondered whether it might be more in the nature of shyness, a kind of modesty.

That embarrassed him even more than smartness would have done. Feeling himself under observation he struggled for composure.

He said to Lapointe in an undertone:

'You go through the routine stuff. . . .'

They both knew what that meant.

Then he turned to Armand Lachaume, who was unshaven and wearing no tie.

'I suppose there's some room where we could talk more comfortably?' And, noticing the raw cold, he added:

'One that's heated, for choice.'

He had just touched the radiator, an old-fashioned type, and discovered that the central heating was not working.

Lachaume did not go out of his way to be polite either. He seemed to think for a moment, then, his shoulders slumped in resignation, he said:

'This way. . . .'

There was something ambiguous, not only in the atmosphere of the house, but in the attitude of its occupants. As the Ivry superintendent had remarked, one expected weeping, confused hurrying to and fro, people talking all at once; whereas here were only stealthy footsteps, doors opening slightly, faces peering through the crack.

For instance, going along the dimly lit corridor, Maigret glimpsed, through the narrow chink of a doorway, an eye, dark hair, a silhouette which seemed to be that of a woman.

They reached the upstairs hall, and Armand Lachaume opened a door in the left wing, to reveal a strange drawing-room where two old people were sitting in front of an iron stove.

The son said nothing, made no introductions. The father was a man of at least seventy-five, perhaps eighty. Unlike Armand, he was freshly shaved and had on a clean shirt, a black tie.

He stood up, as placid and dignified as though this were a directors' meeting, bowed slightly, then stepped forward to bend over his wife, who seemed to be the same age as himself; one side of her face was motionless, with a staring eye like a glass eye.

He helped her out of her arm-chair, and both of them, without a word, vanished through another door.

This was the room where the family usually assembled; that was evident from the arrangement of the furniture and from the oddments lying about. Maigret sat down on a chair and turned to Angelot, the examining magistrate.

'Do you wish to ask any questions?'

'I would rather leave it to you.'

The magistrate stood leaning against the side of the door.

'Would you mind sitting down, Monsieur Lachaume?' pursued Maigret.

It was like groping his way through cotton-wool. There was nothing to get hold of, nothing seemed real, except the rain still falling outside.

'Please tell me what you know.'

'I know nothing.'

Even the man's voice was expressionless, impersonal, and he was avoiding Maigret's eye.

'The dead man is your elder brother, is he not?'

'My brother Léonard, as I already told your colleague.'

'Is the biscuit factory still going?'

'Certainly.'

'Was it he who ran it?'

'Our father is still chairman of the board of directors.'

'But who was the actual manager?'

'My brother.'

'And you?'

'I look after stocks and distribution.'

'Is it long since your brother lost his wife?'

'Eight years.'

'Are you acquainted with his private life?'

'He has always lived here, with us.'

'All the same, outside this house he presumably had a life of his own, men and women friends, connexions of various kinds?'

'I don't know.'

'You told the police superintendent that a wallet had disappeared.'

He nodded.

'About how much money might be in the wallet?'

'I can't say.'

'A large sum?'

'I don't know.'

'Was your brother in the habit, for instance, of keeping several hundred thousand francs in his room?'

'I don't think so.'

'Was it he who handled the firm's money?'

'He and the book-keeper.'

'Where is the book-keeper?'

'I presume he is downstairs.'

'And where was the money put when it came in?'

'In the bank.'

'Every day?'

'Money doesn't come in every day.'

Maigret was forcing himself to remain calm and courteous, beneath the dispassionate gaze of the young magistrate.

'But surely there was some money somewhere . . .'

'In the safe.'

'Where is the safe?'

'On the ground floor, in my brother's office.'

'Was it tampered with during the night?'

'No.'

'You have made sure of that?'

'Yes.'

'You think your brother's murderer came from outside, with theft as his intention?'

'Yes.'

'Someone he didn't know from Adam?'

'I suppose so.'

'How many people work in the factory?'

'At present, about twenty. At one time we employed over a hundred men and women.'

'You know them all?'

'Yes.'

'You don't suspect one of them?'

'No.'

'You heard nothing last night, although your room is only a few yards away from your brother Léonard's?'

'I heard nothing.'

'You are a heavy sleeper?'

'Perhaps.'

'You sleep heavily enough not to be disturbed by a shot fired less than ten paces away?'

'I don't know.'

Just then there was a rumbling sound, and the house, despite its thick walls, seemed to shake a little. Maigret's eye caught that of the examining magistrate.

'Is that a train?'

'Yes. The line runs close by here.'

'Do many trains go past at night?'

'I've never counted them. About forty, most of them long goods trains.'

There was a knock on the door. It was Janvier, who signed to Maigret that he had something to tell him.

'Come in. Tell us.'

'There's a ladder in the courtyard, lying on the ground a few yards from the wall. I found the marks of the uprights on the window-sill.'

'Which window?'

'A window of the landing, next to this room. It looks into the court-yard. The ladder must have been leant up there recently, and a pane of the window has been broken, after having been coated with soap.'

'You knew this, Monsieur Lachaume?'

'I had noted the fact.'

'Why did you say nothing to me about it?'

'I have had no opportunity of doing so.'

'Where was this ladder, in the usual way?'

'Against the warehouse, on the left of the courtyard.'

'Was it there yesterday evening?'

'Normally it should be there.'

'Excuse me for a moment.'

Maigret left the room, partly to see for himself and partly to let off steam, and he seized the chance to fill a pipe. The upstairs hall was lit by two windows, one overlooking the quay, the other, opposite it, over the courtyard. This latter had a broken pane, and some fragments of glass lay on the floor.

Opening the window, he saw that the grey stone bore two lighter marks, as far apart as the uprights of a ladder.

As Janvier had told him, a ladder was lying on the flagstones of the courtyard. Faint smoke was rising from the tall chimney. In a building on the left, women were bending over a long table.

He was just going back to the others, when he heard a sound and saw a woman in a blue dressing-gown, who had just opened her door.

'Might I ask you, Madame, to come to the drawing-room for a moment?'

She seemed to hesitate, then tied the belt of her dressing-gown and at last came forward.

She was young. She had not yet made up her face and it was a little shiny.

'Please come in.' And to Armand Lachaume:

'I take it this is your wife?'

'Yes.'

Husband and wife did not look at each other.

'Please sit down, Madame.'

'Thank you.'

'You, too, heard nothing in the night?'

'I always take a sleeping-tablet before going to bed.'

'When did you hear that your brother-in-law was dead?'

She stared into space for a moment, as though pondering this.

'I didn't look at the time.'

'Where were you?'

'In my room.'

'That is your husband's room as well?'

Again she hesitated.

'No.'

'But your room is in the corridor, nearly opposite your brother-in-law's room?'

'Yes. There are two rooms on the right of the corridor, my husband's and mine.'

'How long have you had separate rooms?'

Armand Lachaume coughed, turned towards the examining magistrate, who was still standing up, and said in an ill-assured voice, the voice of a timid man who feels obliged to make an effort.

'I wonder whether the chief-inspector is entitled to ask us these questions concerning our private lives. My brother was killed last night by a burglar, and so far it is only our movements that seem to be the subject of inquiry.'

The ghost of a smile twitched Angelot's lips.

'I imagine that when Chief-Inspector Maigret puts these questions to you he is regarding you as witnesses.'

'I don't want my wife to be pestered, and I'd like her to be left outside all this.'

It was the anger of a shy man, of one who seldom expressed his feelings, and it had brought a flush to his cheeks.

Maigret went on again gently:

'Who had been regarded as the head of the family until now, Monsieur Lachaume?'

'Which family?'

'Let us say, of the group of people living in this house.'

'That is our business. Don't answer him, Paulette.'

Maigret noticed that he spoke to his wife with the formal *vous*, but that is customary in a certain class, is often a kind of snobbish affectation.

'If this kind of thing goes on, you will be annoying my father and mother presently. Then the employees, the staff . . .'

'That is my intention.'

'I do not know your precise rights . . .

The magistrate volunteered:

'I can tell you what they are.'

'No. I prefer our lawyer to be present. I suppose I am allowed to send for him?'

The examining magistrate hesitated before replying:

'There is nothing in the regulations to prevent the presence of your lawyer. But I would anyway like to point out once again that you and the members of your family are being questioned as witnesses, and that it is not usual, in such circumstances, to call upon . . .'

'We shall say nothing further until he is here.'

'Just as you like.'

'I will go and telephone him.'

'Where is the telephone?'

'In the dining-room.'

This was the room next door, and they had a glimpse of the two old people who had settled in front of the fireplace where two meagre logs were burning. Thinking this was a fresh invasion, they made as if to get up in order to take refuge somewhere else, but Armand Lachaume closed the door behind him.

'Your husband seems to have been considerably shaken, Madame.'

She looked stonily at the chief-inspector.

'It's natural, don't you think?'

'Were they twins, he and his brother?'

'There is seven years' difference between them.'

Yet their features were the same, even to the identical thin, drooping moustaches. A murmur of voices came from the next room. The magistrate showed no sign of impatience, no desire to sit down.

'You have no suspicion, no idea of your own, about . . .'

'My husband told you we would not answer questions except in the presence of our lawyer.'

'Who is he?'

'Ask my husband.'

'Are there any other brothers or sisters?'

She looked at him in silence. And yet she seemed to be of a different race from the rest of the family. One could feel that in other circumstances she would be pretty, desirable, and she had a muted vitality which she was obliged to hold in check.

She was an unexpected figure in this house where everything was so far removed from time and real life.

Armand Lachaume reappeared. There was another glimpse of the two old people, sitting in front of the fireplace like waxen images.

'He will be here in a few minutes.'

He gave a start, as the footsteps of several men were heard on the stairs. Maigret reassured him.

'They've come for the body,' he explained. 'I'm sorry, but as the examining magistrate will tell you, this is a regulation : the body must be taken to the medico-legal institute for a post-mortem to be performed.'

The curious thing was that there seemed to be no grief here, only a strange dejection, a kind of uneasy stupor.

Many a time in his career Maigret had been in much the same position, forced to intrude into the life of a family in which a crime had just been committed.

Never had he received such an impression of unreality.

And into the bargain, an examining magistrate, belonging to a younger generation, had to complicate things by dogging his heels.

'I'll have a word with those fellows,' he muttered. 'I must give some instructions . . .'

They needed neither instruction nor advice. The men with the stretcher knew their job. Maigret simply watched them at it, lifted the sheet that covered the dead man's face for a moment, to have a final brief glance at him.

Then, looking round the room, he saw a door at one side, opened it, and found himself in a dusty, untidy room which must have been Léonard Lachaume's private office.

Janvier was there, bending over a piece of furniture, and gave a start :

'Oh! it's you, Chief . . .'

He was opening the drawers of an old desk, one by one.

'Have you found anything?'

'No. I don't like this ladder business.'

Neither did Maigret. He had not yet had a chance to prowl round the house, or outside it, but all the same that ladder struck him as somehow incongruous.

'You see,' went on Janvier, 'there's a glass-panelled door just below the window with the broken pane. It opens into the entry, and anyone can come up here from there with nothing to stop them. Coming in that way it wouldn't even have been necessary to break a pane in the door, for there was already that broken one that's filled in with cardboard. So why carry a very heavy ladder across the courtyard and . . .'

'I know.'

'Is *he* going to hang around till the bitter end?'

*He*, of course, was the examining magistrate.

'I don't know. He may.'

This time both of them jumped, for there was someone standing in the doorway, a little old woman, almost a hunchback, who was glaring at them with dark, indignant eyes.

It was the servant to whom the police superintendent had referred. Her glance travelled from the two men to the open drawers, the scattered papers, and at last she muttered, with a visible effort to keep from reviling them:

'Would Chief-Inspector Maigret come to the drawing-room, please.'

Janvier inquired in a low voice:

'Shall I go on, Chief?'

'At the present stage I really don't know. Do as you like.'

He followed the waiting hunchback, who opened the door for him into the drawing-room, where there was a newcomer. He introduced himself:

'Maître Radel . . .'

Was he going to refer to himself in the third person?

'Pleased to meet you, Maître.'

Another young fellow, though not so young as the magistrate. In this house, this survival from another age, Maigret would have expected some old, dirty, pettifogging lawyer.

Radel could hardly be over thirty-five and he was almost as well turned-out as the examining magistrate.

'Gentlemen, I only know what Monsieur Armand Lachaume thought fit to tell me on the telephone, and I would like first of all to apologize for my client's reactions. Try to put yourselves in his place, and you will perhaps understand him. I have come here as a friend rather than as a lawyer, and in order to clear up any misunderstanding. Armand Lachaume is a sick man. The death of his brother, who was the life and soul of this house, has been a great shock to him, and it is not surprising that, in his ignorance of police methods, he should have been riled by certain questions.'

Maigret sighed in resignation to the inevitable, and relit his pipe which had gone out.

'Since he has asked me to be present at any interrogations you may

decide to hold, I will do so, but I must emphasize that my presence is
not to be regarded as implying any defensive attitude on the part of the
family . . .'

He turned to the examining magistrate, then to the chief-inspector.
'Whom do you wish to question?'

'Madame Lachaume,' said Maigret, indicating the young woman.

'I will only ask you to bear in mind that Madame Lachaume is just
as distressed as her husband.'

'I would like,' went on Maigret, 'to question each person separately.'

The husband scowled. Maître Radel spoke to him quietly and
persuaded him to leave the room.

'To your knowledge, Madame, had your brother-in-law received
any threatening letters recently?'

'Certainly not.'

'He would have told you?'

'I imagine so.'

'Told you, or the rest of the family?'

'He would have told us all.'

'Including his parents?'

'Perhaps not, in view of their age.'

'So he would have told your husband and yourself.'

'That would have been natural, I think.'

'The brothers were on close, confident terms?'

'Very close and very confident.'

'And with you?'

'I don't know what you mean.'

'On what terms were you, exactly, with your brother-in-law?'

'I apologize for interrupting,' put in Maître Radel, 'but expressed
in those words, that might seem to be a leading question. I take it,
Monsieur Maigret, that it is not your intention to insinuate . . .'

'I am not insinuating anything at all. I am merely asking whether
Madame Lachaume and her brother-in-law were on friendly terms.'

'Certainly we were,' she replied.

'On affectionate terms?'

'The same as in any other family, I suppose.'

'When did you see him for the last time?'

'Well . . . this morning . . .'

'You mean that this morning you saw him dead in his room?'

She nodded.

'When did you last see him alive?'

'Last night.'

'At what time?'

She could not restrain a quick glance at the lawyer.

'It must have been about half past eleven.'

'Where were you?'

'In the corridor.'

'The one that goes past your room and his?'

'Yes.'

'You were coming from this drawing-room?'

'No.'

'You were with your husband?'

'No. I had been out by myself.'

'Your husband had remained at home?'

'Yes. He seldom goes out. Especially since he nearly died of pleurisy. He has always been delicate and . . .'

'What time did you go out?'

She asked the lawyer:

'Do I have to answer that?'

'I advise you to, although these questions relate only to your private life and obviously have no connexion whatever with the tragedy.'

'I went out about six o'clock.'

'In the evening?'

'Certainly not at six in the morning.'

'Your lawyer will perhaps allow you to tell us what you did up to half past eleven?'

'I had dinner out.'

'Alone?'

'That's my affair.'

'And then?'

'I went to the cinema.'

'A local one?'

'No, in the Champs-Elysées. When I got back the house was in darkness, at least on the side that overlooks the quay. I went upstairs, into the corridor, and I saw my brother-in-law's door opening.'

'He was waiting for you?'

'I see no reason why he should have been. He usually sat up very late, reading, in the little study next to his room.'

'He came out of the study?'

'Out of his bedroom.'

'How was he dressed?'

'In a dressing-gown. Pyjamas and a dressing-gown. He said:

' "Ah, it's you, Paulette . . ."

'And I replied:

' "Good night, Léonard.'

' "Good night . . ."

'That was all.'

'You both went to your rooms?'

'Yes.'

'Did you speak to your husband?'

'I had nothing to say to him.'

'You have communicating rooms?'

'Yes. But the door between them is nearly always shut.'

'And locked?'

The lawyer intervened:

'I think you're going too far, Chief-Inspector.'

The young woman shrugged her shoulders wearily.

'No, not locked,' she said in an off-hand, scornful tone.

'So you didn't see your husband?'

'No. I undressed and got into bed at once.'

'You have your own bathroom?'

'This is an old house. There is only one bathroom on this floor, at the end of the corridor.'

'You went there?'

'I did. Do I have to give you fuller details?'

'Did you notice whether the light in your brother-in-law's room was still on?'

'I saw light under the door.'

'You heard nothing?'

'Nothing.'

'Did your brother-in-law sometimes confide in you?'

'That depends on what you mean by confiding.'

'There are sometimes things that a man would rather talk about to a woman than to his brother or his parents, for instance. A sister-in-law is a member of the family, without being a relative . . .'

She was waiting patiently.

'Léonard Lachaume had been a widower for years; did he talk to you about his affairs with women?'

'I don't even know whether he had any.'

'Did he go out a great deal?'

'Very little.'

'Do you know where he used to go?'

'That was no business of mine.'

'His son is twelve years old, I understand?'

'He was twelve last month.'

'Did Léonard pay much attention to him?'

'The same as any parents who work. Léonard worked hard, and sometimes went down to the office again after dinner.'

'Your mother-in-law is practically helpless, isn't she?'

'She can only walk with a stick, and someone has to help her up and down stairs.'

'Your father-in-law is not very active either?'

'He is seventy-eight years old.'

'So far as I can see, the servant is hardly more sprightly. Yet, unless I am mistaken, the boy's room is on the second floor, in the left wing, with those three old people.'

She began to answer:

'Jean-Paul . . .'

Then, changing her mind, she broke off.

'You were about to say that Jean-Paul, your nephew . . .'

'I've forgotten what I was going to say.'

'How long has he been sleeping on the second floor?'

'Not long.'

'For years? . . . Months? . . . Weeks?'

'About a week.'

Maigret felt certain she had given this information unwillingly, and the lawyer realized it too, for he immediately interrupted.

'Chief-Inspector, I wonder whether you couldn't ask other members of the household for these particulars? Madame Lachaume has had a distressing morning and has not had time to get dressed. I think her husband would be in a better position to . . .'

'In any case, Maître Radel, I have finished with her, at least for the moment. Unless the examining magistrate has any questions to put to her.'

The magistrate made a slight negative gesture.

'I must apologize for keeping you so long, Madame . . .'

'Do you want me to send my husband in?'

'Not at present. I would rather ask a few questions of that old servant, whose name is . . ?'

'Catherine. She has been with my parents-in-law for more than forty years, and she's almost as old as they are. I'll go and see if she's in the kitchen.'

She went out, and the lawyer was on the point of saying something, but thought better of it and lit a cigarette, after tapping it on his silver case.

He had offered one to the magistrate, who had refused, replying:

'No thank you. I don't smoke.'

Maigret, who was thirsty, didn't dare to ask for a drink, and was in a hurry to get out of the house.

A long time went by before they heard a patter of footsteps, followed by a kind of scratching on the door.

'Come in!'

It was old Catherine, who glared at each of them in turn with an even more sombre expression than shortly before, in the study, and then demanded fiercely:

'What do you want with me? And for one thing, if you go on smoking like that in this house, Monsieur Félix will have another attack of asthma.'

What else could one do? Under the sardonic gaze of the magistrate, Maigret, heaving a sigh, laid his pipe down on the little marble-topped table.

# III

MORE embarrassed than ever by the magistrate's attitude and by the presence of the lawyer, Maigret began, in the diffident tone of one who is feeling his way:

'I'm told you have been in this house for forty years?'

He thought this would appease her, give her pleasure. Instead of which, she croaked:

'Who told you that?'

And while he was wondering whether their roles were being reversed, so that he would be answering questions from the old woman, she went on:

'It's not forty years I've been here, it's fifty. I took service when my poor lady was scarcely more than twenty and was expecting Monsieur Léonard.'

A rapid calculation. So old Madame Lachaume, who looked the same age as her husband, could hardly be more than seventy. What had the house been like when Catherine, as a little maid doubtless straight up from the country, had arrived in it, to find her young mistress expecting a first baby?

Absurd questions came thronging into Maigret's mind. There must have been an elder Lachaume couple in those days too, another pair of old people, for on the brass plate he had read 'Established in 1817'. Not long after Waterloo.

Perhaps some of the drawing-room furniture had been just where it stood today; the Empire sofa, for instance, that would have been a very handsome piece if they hadn't covered it in garish blue velvet?

Logs must have blazed in all the marble fireplaces. A later generation had put in central heating, which was now no longer used, either to save money or because the boiler was in bad condition.

The stove fascinated him, a little round stove of rusty iron, such as one used to see in small country railway stations and in some government buildings.

Everything had grown seedy, things and people alike. Family and house had withdrawn into themselves and taken on an unfriendly aspect.

Old Catherine let fall a phrase which placed the period more clearly than anything else. Speaking of Léonard as a baby, she announced proudly:

'I nursed him myself!'

So it was not as a servant but as a wet-nurse that she had come to Paris, and Maigret stared, in spite of himself, at her flat chest, her draggling, dirty black skirts.

For she was dirty. Everything here was dirty or grubby, broken, worn, or patched up by the first means to hand.

Because his mind was on these images, Maigret asked a silly question, which Angelot, the young magistrate, doubtless repeated to his colleagues afterwards.

'Did you nurse Monsieur Armand too?'

The retort came pat:

'Where would I have got the milk?'

'The Lachaumes have no other children?'

'Mademoiselle Véronique.'

'She isn't here?'

'Not since a long time.'

'I suppose you heard nothing during the night?'

'No.'

'What time does Monsieur Léonard usually get up?'

'He gets up when he feels like it.'

'Do you know his friends, the people he's in touch with?'

'I've never poked my nose into my masters' private lives, and you'd do well to follow my example. You're here to find the criminal who killed Monsieur Léonard, and not to interfere in the family's concerns.'

Turning her back on him, she made for the dining-room door.

He was on the point of calling her back. But what was the good? If he needed to ask her anything, he would do it when the examining magistrate and the lawyer were not there looking at him in silent jubilation.

He was floundering, true. But he'd be bound to have the last word.

Should he send for old Félix Lachaume, and his semi-paralysed wife? It would have been logical to give them their turn of questioning, but he was afraid of again showing himself, Maigret, not on top of the situation.

The servant had no sooner left the room than he lit his pipe, went out to the landing, where he looked through the window at the long ladder lying across the courtyard. As he had expected, the magistrate and the lawyer followed him.

At least once during his career he had been obliged to work like this, in front of a witness who studied his every move attentively, but on an infinitely less unpleasant case. A certain Inspector Pyke, of Scotland Yard, had obtained permission to follow one of Maigret's cases in order to study his methods, and seldom in his life had Maigret felt so awkward.

People were far too apt to imagine that those celebrated methods were something in the nature of a cookery recipe, laid down once and for all, needing only to be followed to the letter.

'I suppose you intend to question Armand Lachaume?'

It was the lawyer who put this question. Maigret looked at him, undecided, then shook his head.

'No. I'm going to have a look round downstairs.'

'You won't object if I come too? Seeing that my clients . . .'

He shrugged and set off down the stairs of what had once been a handsome, elegant patrician house.

Downstairs, he opened at random a double door, came upon an immense ballroom, plunged in darkness because the shutters were closed. It was stuffy, smelling of mildew. He felt for the electric switch, and two bulbs out of twelve lit up in a chandelier, several of whose festoons of crystal drops were dangling down, broken.

There was a piano in one corner, an ancient harpsichord in another, and carpets rolled up along the walls. In the middle of the floor were piles of magazines, green cardboard files and biscuit-tins.

Though there had once been music and dancing here, no one had set foot in the room for a long time, and the crimson silk that covered the walls had come unstuck in places.

A door stood ajar, opening into a library whose shelves were almost empty, except for red-bound school prizes and a few battered volumes like those in certain of the booksellers' boxes along the quays.

Had the rest been sold? It was more than likely. The furniture as well, no doubt, for there was none left here, except, in a third and even damper room, a billiard table whose green felt top was mouldering.

Maigret's voice sounded strange, as though it came from some vault, when he remarked, speaking more to himself than to the others who were still following him:

'I suppose the offices are on the other side of the entry.'

They went across, heard voices outside on the pavement, where the police were holding back a score or so of inquisitive idlers.

Opposite the ballroom, they at last found a room that was more or less alive, an office that really looked like an office, though still an old-fashioned one. Its walls were panelled, hung with two oil paintings dating from the previous century, and some photographs, the most recent of which presumably represented Félix Lachaume at the age of fifty or sixty. The Lachaume dynasty, in which Léonard's effigy had not yet taken its place.

The furniture was a mixture of Gothic and Renaissance in style, like that which still survives in the head offices of some very old-established businesses in Paris. Tins of various biscuits made by the firm were displayed on shelves.

Maigret knocked on a door, to the right.

'Come in!' called a voice.

They went into a second office, equally old-fashioned but more untidy, where a man of about fifty, with a bald, shiny head, was bent over a ledger.

'I suppose you are the book-keeper?'

'Justin Brême, the book-keeper, yes.'

'Chief-Inspector Maigret.'

'I know.'

'Monsieur Angelot, the examining magistrate, and Maître Radel, the family's lawyer.'

'Pleased to meet you.'

'I imagine, Monsieur Brême, that you have heard what happened last night?'

'Sit down, gentlemen. . . .'

There was an unoccupied desk facing his own.

'Is this Monsieur Armand Lachaume's desk?'

'Yes, gentlemen. The firm of Lachaume has been a family business for several generations, and not long ago, Monsieur Félix was still working in the next-door office, which his father and grandfather had worked in before him.'

He was stout, rather sallow. Through an open door they could see into a third office, where a man in a grey overall and an elderly typist were at work.

'I'd like to ask you a few questions.'

Maigret pointed to a safe, one of an old type which, despite its size and weight, would not have held out against even a novice among burglars.

'Is it in that safe that you keep the ready cash?'

Monsieur Brême first went and closed the door of the next office, came back, looking embarrassed, glanced at the lawyer as though seeking his advice.

'What ready cash?' he finally inquired, with a sort of wily ingenuousness.

'You employ staff. So you have pay-days. . . .'

'Unfortunately! They come only too often.'

'You must have a cash reserve. . . .'

'I *should* have one, Chief-Inspector! Unhappily we have been living from hand to mouth for a long time now, and this morning there isn't more than ten thousand francs in that safe. Even that will be needed presently, for I have to pay something on account of a bill.'

'Do the employees know about this?'

'They often have to wait several days for their wages, and sometimes they are not paid in full.'

'So it wouldn't occur to any of them to burgle the place?'

Monsieur Brême laughed soundlessly at this idea.

'Certainly not.'

'The local people know how things are?'

'The grocer, the butcher and the dairy woman sometimes call round three or four times for their money . . .'

It was unpleasant to have to see it through. It was like stripping the clothes off someone, and yet it had to be done.

'The Lachaumes have no private fortune?'

'None.'

'How much, in your opinion, might there have been in Monsieur Léonard's pocket-book?'

The book-keeper made a vague gesture.

'Not a lot.'

'Yet the firm keeps going,' objected Maigret.

Monsieur Brême again looked at the young lawyer.

'It seems to me,' the latter intervened, 'that this inquiry is tending more and more to concentrate on my clients instead of on the criminal.'

And Maigret growled:

'You talk like old Catherine, Maître. How do you expect me to trace a murderer unless I discover his motives? We're told he was a burglar . . .'

'The ladder proves it. . . .'

The chief-inspector grunted sceptically:

'Yes! And the disappearance of the pocket-book! And the fact that no weapon has been found yet . . .'

He had not sat down. Neither had the others, despite the suggestion made by the book-keeper, who stood there casting covert glances towards his cushioned chair.

'Tell me, Monsieur Brême, you do pay your employees sooner or later all the same; otherwise they wouldn't go on working. . . .'

'It's a miracle each time.'

'And where does this miraculous money come from?'

The man began to show signs of nervousness.

'Monsieur Léonard used to give it to me.'

'In cash?'

Maître Radel put in:

'You are not obliged to answer, Monsieur Brême.'

'They will find out anyhow, by going through the books or asking the bank. . . . The money is generally given to me in the form of a cheque. . . .'

'You mean Monsieur Léonard had a personal bank account, separate from the firm's account, and that he drew cheques on it when the need became too urgent?'

'No. It was Madame Lachaume.'

'The mother?'

'Madame Paulette.'

At last they were getting somewhere, and Maigret sat down, in satisfaction.

'Sit down at your desk, Monsieur Brême. Take your time to answer me. For how long has Madame Paulette, as you call her, in other words Armand Lachaume's wife, been acting as the good angel of this house?'

'Practically ever since she came into it.'

'When did the marriage take place?'

'Six years ago. Two years after the death of Madame Marcelle.'

'Excuse me, but who was Madame Marcelle?'

'Monsieur Léonard's wife.'

'So it is six years since Armand Lachaume married Paulette . . . Paulette who?'

'Paulette Zuber.'

'She had money?'

'A great deal.'

'Are any of her family still alive?'

'Her father died five months ago and she was his only daughter. As for her mother, she never knew her.'

'Who was Zuber?'

The name was familiar, and he seemed to remember hearing it in some professional connexion.

'Frédéric Zuberski, known as Zuber, the leather-merchant.'

'He had some trouble, didn't he?'

'The income-tax authorities were hot on his heels for a time. And after the war it was said that he . . .'

'Now I've got it!'

Zuberski, who preferred to be called Zuber, had had his hour of fame. He had started his career by driving round the countryside in a little cart, collecting skins and raw-hide from peasants, then he had set up a warehouse, at Ivry, as it happened, probably not far from Lachaume's.

Even before the war his business was already doing well and Zuber owned a number of lorries, besides several warehouses in the provinces.

Later on, two or three years after the Liberation, there had been a rumour that he had piled up a considerable fortune and that his arrest was imminent.

He had awakened the attention of the Press, largely because he was such a quaint character: misshapen, shabbily dressed, speaking French with a strong foreign accent, and scarcely able to read or write.

Millions, some people said thousands of millions, of francs passed through his hands, and he was believed to have a virtual monopoly of the trade in raw-hides, either by direct ownership or through middle-men.

It was not Maigret who had had to deal with him, but the financial branch. In the end the matter had been forgotten, and the chief-inspector did not know how it had ended.

'What did Zuber die of?'

'Cancer; he was operated on at the Saint-Joseph Clinic.'

'If I understand rightly, it's thanks to his money that the firm of Lachaume keeps more or less afloat?'

'Not exactly. When she married, Madame Paulette brought a considerable dowry. . . .'

'Which she invested in Lachaume's Biscuits?'

'More or less. Let's say it was drawn upon whenever the need arose.'

'And afterwards, when the dowry was all used up? For it was soon used up?'

'Yes.'

'How did they manage after that?'

'Madame Paulette used to go and see her father.'

'Didn't he come here?'

'I don't remember ever seeing him. If he ever came it must have been upstairs, in the evening, but I'm not sure about that.'

'I really do not see what you are trying to get at, Chief-Inspector,' the lawyer protested again.

The magistrate, for his part, seemed keenly interested, and there was even a glint of amusement in his pale eyes.

'Neither do I,' admitted Maigret. 'You see, Maître, at the beginning of an investigation one is in the dark and one can only grope about. So Frédéric Zuber, who had one daughter, gave her in marriage to the younger of the Lachaume sons, Armand, providing her with a comfortable sum by way of dowry. You don't happen to know the exact figure?'

'I protest. . . .'

Radel again, of course; he was on thorns.

'Very well. I'll let that go. The biscuits ate up the dowry. Then, every so often, Paulette was dispatched to see her father, who was not received here. . . .'

'He didn't say that.'

'I will correct myself: who was not received here or who was not a frequent visitor. . . . Old man Zuber used to spit . . .'

It was largely as a protest against the presence of the magistrate and the young lawyer that Maigret took this vulgar tone.

'Then Zuber died. Did the Lachaumes go to his funeral?'

Monsieur Brême smiled wanly.

'That is not my affair. . . .'

'Did you go yourself?'

'No.'

'I suppose there was a marriage settlement? An old fox like Zuber can hardly have . . .'

'They were married under the system of separate property.'

'And a few months ago, Paulette Lachaume inherited her father's fortune. Is that correct?'

'That is correct.'

'So it is she, now, who holds the purse-strings? It is she who must be appealed to when there is no money in the till to settle bills or pay the employees?'

Radel again, as bothersome as a great bluebottle:

'I don't see where this is getting you.'

'Nor do I, Maître. But neither do I see where I should get to by hunting through Paris for a burglar stupid enough to break into a house where there is no money, using a heavy ladder and smashing a window-pane when there is a glass-panelled door on the ground floor, all this in order to get into the bedroom where a man is asleep, kill him with a noisy revolver, and make off with an almost empty pocket-book.'

'You don't know about that.'

'True enough! Léonard Lachaume may have asked his sister-in-law for money last night. But the fact remains that in this office there is a safe, monumental in size but childishly simple to open, which has not been touched. The further fact remains that when the crime was committed there were at least six people in the house.'

'More puzzling burglaries have been known.'

'Granted. To get into the courtyard where the ladder was standing, somebody had to climb a wall which, if my eyes tell me correctly, is about twelve feet high. Lastly, two people were sleeping within a few yards of the room where the shot was fired, and they heard nothing.'

'We are near a railway line where trains follow one another almost without pause.'

'I am not denying that, Monsieur Radel. My job is to search for the truth, and I am doing so. The mere fact of your presence here would disincline me from searching very far off, for it is unusual, when someone has been murdered, for the relatives to send for a lawyer even before the police have had time to interrogate them.

'I am going to ask you a question you will probably refuse to answer. Armand Lachaume telephoned to you, in my presence, to ask you to come here. Where do you live, Maître?'

'Place de l'Odéon. Very near here.'

'It's true you arrived within ten minutes. You showed no great surprise. You asked very few questions. Are you sure you didn't know before we did what happened last night?'

'I protest vigorously against . . .'

'Against what? I am not, of course, accusing you of entering the house by night, through a window. I am only wondering if you may not have received, early this morning, a previous telephone call, informing you of what had happened and asking your advice. . . .'

'I reserve the full right, in the presence of the examining magistrate, to take any action I may think fit in the light of such an accusation.'

'I'm not accusing you, Maître. I'm only asking. And, if you prefer, I'm asking myself.'

Maigret's hackles were up.

'As for you, Monsieur Brême, I am obliged to you. I shall probably have to come back and ask you some more questions. It is for the examining magistrate to decide whether these offices should be placed under seal. . . .'

'What do you think?'

He was leaving the decision to Maigret.

'I don't think there would be any point in it, and the books would most likely add nothing to what Monsieur Brême has told us already.'

He looked round for his hat, realized that he had left it upstairs.

'I'll go and fetch it,' the book-keeper proposed.

'Oh, don't trouble.'

Maigret started upstairs, had the feeling of a presence, looked up, and saw Catherine peering down over the banisters. She must have been watching for him.

'Is it your hat you want?'

'Yes. Isn't my inspector up there?'

'He left a long time ago. Catch!'

Without letting him reach the top, she threw his felt hat down at him, and just as he bent to pick it up, she spat.

\*

The lawyer had not followed them into the street. Because of the rain that was still falling, as cold and gloomy as it had been all morning, only a few idlers had stayed on, and one uniformed policeman was enough to keep them at a distance. The newspapers, for a wonder, had not yet got wind of the case.

The two black cars, the magistrate's and the one from Police Headquarters, were still parked at the side of the road.

'Are you going back to the Quai des Orfèvres?' asked the magistrate, as he opened his car-door.

'I don't know yet. I'll wait for Janvier, he must be somewhere about.'

'Why do you have to wait for him?'

'Because I can't drive a car,' replied Maigret frankly, pointing to the little police Renault.

'Would you like me to drop you?'

'No thank you. I'd rather wait and sniff the local air.'

He foresaw a risk of searching questions, perhaps even of protests, exhortations to caution and restraint.

'I'd be glad if you would telephone me before midday, Chief-Inspector, to keep me informed. I intend to follow this case very closely.'

'I know. Good-bye for the present.'

The small group of idlers watched them, and a woman hugging a black shawl around her murmured to her neighbour:

'That's the famous Maigret.'
'And who's the young one?'
'I don't know.'

Maigret turned up his coat collar and set out along the pavement.
He had scarcely gone fifty yards when someone signed to him from the
entrance of a little bar: *Aux Copains du Quai*. It was Janvier.

There was nobody there except the proprietress behind the bar, a
fat, tousle-headed woman, watching from a distance, through the
kitchen door, over a pot which was steaming on the stove and giving
off a strong smell of onions.

'What will you have, Chief?'

Janvier added:

'I had a hot toddy. This is just the weather for catching 'flu.'

Maigret had a toddy too.

'Did you come across anything?'

'I don't know. I thought it might be as well to put seals on the bedroom door before I left.'

'Have you rung up Dr. Paul?'

'He's still on the job. One of his assistants told me they'd found a
certain quantity of alcohol in the stomach. They'll ascertain what
percentage was in the blood.'

'Nothing else?'

'They've discovered the bullet and are sending it to the expert. The
doctor said it was a small calibre, probably a 6.35. What do you think
about it yourself, Chief?'

The bar-keeper had gone off to stir her stew with a wooden spoon.

'I preferred this morning's case.'

'The Canon?'

'Chaps like that don't kill people, at any rate.'

'You don't believe their yarn about the burglary?'

'No.'

'Neither do I. The specialists looked for finger-prints on the ladder
and the window-pane, but they didn't find any. Except some old prints
left on the ladder by the foreman.'

'The fellow might have had gloves on. That doesn't prove anything.'

'I took a look at the outer wall.'

'Well?'

'It's all stuck with broken glass. At one place, not far from the
house, some of the glass has been smashed. I had some photos taken.'

'Why?'

'Well, Chief, you know that a cat-burglar makes his plans beforehand. If he knows there's broken glass along a wall, he brings an old
sack, or a bit of board. Then you find the glass smashed in a particular
way. Whereas here, it had been crushed as though with a hammer.'

'You questioned the neighbours?'

'They didn't hear anything. They all tell me that the trains make an infernal row and that it takes years to get used to them. I noticed there were no shutters on the first- and second-floor windows, so I went to question the crew of the barge you can see unloading over there. I wanted to know if any of them had seen lights in the house after midnight.

'They'd been asleep, as I expected. Those people go to bed early and get up early. But the wife told me one thing that might turn out to be interesting. Last night there was a Belgian barge tied up alongside them, and it left early this morning. It was the *Notre-Dame*, making for the flour-mills at Corbeil.

'Yesterday was the skipper's birthday. Some people from another barge, also a Belgian one, that was moored up-stream, spent part of the night on board the *Notre-Dame*, and one of the chaps had an accordion ...'

'Have you got the name of the other barge?'

'No. The woman said that must have left, too.'

Maigret called the proprietress, paid for the two drinks.

'Where are we going?' inquired Janvier.

'Drive round the district for a bit. There's something I want to find.'

The little black car had only a few hundred yards to travel along the neighbouring streets.

'Stop. It's here.'

They saw a long wall, full of cracks, an unpaved yard, with buildings, some wooden, some brick-built, which had open-work walls, like those of the store-houses where tobacco is put to dry. Above the entrance was a notice:

### F. ZUBER
*Leathers and Hides*

Below, in more recent paint of a glaring yellow:

*David Hirschfeld, Successor*

Janvier, who didn't know what this had to do with the case, kept his foot on the clutch.

'The goose that's been laying golden eggs for the Lachaumes for the last six years,' muttered Maigret. 'I'll explain later.'

'Do I wait for you?'

'Yes. I shan't be more than a few minutes.'

He found the office without difficulty, for the word was written above the smallest of the buildings, more like a hut, where a typist was at work beside a stove resembling the one he had just seen in the house on the quay.

'Is Monsieur Hirschfeld here?'

'No. He's at the slaughterhouse. What have you come about?'

He showed his Police Headquarters badge.

'Were you here already in Monsieur Zuber's time?'

'No. I've always worked for Monsieur Hirschfeld.'

'When did Monsieur Zuber sell the business?'

'Just over a year ago, when he had to go into hospital.'

'Did you know him?'

'I typed the deed of sale.'

'Was he an old man?'

'One couldn't put an age to him, because he was already ill, and very thin. His clothes hung on him like sacks and his skin was as white as that wall over there. I know he was only fifty-eight.'

'Did you ever meet his daughter?'

'No. I heard about her.'

'In what connexion?'

'When the two men were discussing the sale. Monsieur Zuber had no illusions about his health. He knew he couldn't last more than a few months, a year at the outside. The doctor had told him so straight out. That's why he preferred to make a deed of gift, keeping in his own name only what he needed to pay the hospital and the doctors, which saved a lot in death-duties.'

'Can you tell me the figure?'

'You mean the price Monsieur Hirschfeld paid him?'

Maigret nodded.

'There was so much talk about it in the trade that I don't think I'm being indiscreet. Three hundred.'

'Three hundred what?'

'Millions, of course!'

Maigret couldn't prevent himself from looking round at the scruffy office, the muddy yard, the dilapidated buildings that gave off a disgusting stench.

'And Monsieur Hirschfeld paid that amount cash down?'

She smiled with a touch of pity.

'A sum like that is never paid cash down. He paid part of it. I won't tell you exactly how much, but you can ask him. The rest is to be spread over a period of ten years. . . .'

'The whole lot goes to Zuber's daughter?'

'Yes, in the name of Madame Armand Lachaume. If you'd like to talk to Monsieur Hirschfeld, he's usually back from the slaughterhouse about half past eleven, except on days when he has lunch at La Villette. . . .'

Janvier looked inquisitively at the dreamy, slightly stunned Maigret who returned towards the car, with head bent, and paused on the kerb to fill a pipe.

'Notice a smell here?'

'It stinks, Chief.'

'You see that yard, those huts?'

Janvier waited expectantly.

'Well, my boy, that little lot is worth three hundred million francs. And you know who's getting that three hundred million?'

He slid into his seat, closed the door.

'Paulette Lachaume! Now back to the Quai!'

Until he walked into his office, with Janvier still close behind, he didn't utter another word.


# IV

MAIGRET opened the cupboard to hang up his wet coat and hat, caught sight of himself in the mirror above the wash-basin, and nearly put out his tongue, from sheer disgust, at himself. Of course that glass did distort things a bit. But all the same the chief-inspector felt as though he had come back from the Quai de la Gare with a face not unlike those of the people who lived in that weird house.

After so many years in the police force one doesn't, it's true, believe any longer in Father Christmas, in the world as described in improving books and twopence-coloured prints, with the rich on one side, the poor on the other, with the honest people and the scoundrels, the exemplary families gathered, as though at the photographer's, around a smiling patriarch.

But now and then, without realizing it, he went harking back to childhood memories, and was as much shocked by some things as though he were still a lad.

He had seldom been so shocked as in the Lachaume household. For once, he had really felt he was losing his grip, and even now he still had a kind of bitter aftertaste in his mouth, needed to settle back into his office again, drop heavily into his chair, stroke his pipes, as though to remind himself of the reality of everyday things.

It was one of those days when the lights would be left on all the time, and trickles of rain were zigzagging down the windows. Janvier, who had followed him into the room, was waiting for his instructions.

'Wasn't that Loureau I caught sight of in the corridor?'

Loureau was a journalist who had already been haunting Police Headquarters in the days when Maigret was a mere inspector.

'You might tip him off. . . .'

In the ordinary way he avoided putting the Press on the track at the beginning of a case, for in their eagerness to find everything out at top speed, they are apt to confuse the issue, even to give the alarm to suspects.

It was not a spirit of vengeance against the Lachaumes or against the examining magistrate that prompted him this time to send the journalists to the Quai de la Gare; but in that sealed house where no one said a word and he was forced to go to work with kid gloves on, he felt defenceless, and would not be sorry to see the reporters stirring things up a bit. They didn't have to be as cautious as he did. They weren't saddled with a young magistrate, or with a man like Radel, who would make the hell of a row over the slightest abuse of authority or breach of the regulations.

'Don't give him any details. He'll find those out for himself. After that, come back here.'

He picked up his telephone, asking for the superintendent of police at Ivry.

'Hello? Maigret here. You were kind enough this morning to offer me the help of your inspectors. I shall be very glad of it. I'd like them to look into everything that may have happened around that house during the night. You understand? Particularly between midnight and, say, three in the morning. Perhaps you could find me, in your registers, the present address of Véronique Lachaume, the dead man's sister, who seems to have left the Quai de la Gare home some years ago. Will you give me a ring as soon as you have it? Thank you. Good-bye for the moment.'

He might have summoned Lucas by telephone too, but when he wanted one of the inspectors, he preferred to get up from his armchair and go and open the door into their office. It was not to keep an eye on them, but to take the temperature of the place, so to speak.

'Will you come in here for a second, Lucas?'

There were at least six of them in the big room that morning, which was a lot for a Monday.

'How's the Canon?' was his first question after sitting down again at his desk.

'I had him committed.'

'How did it go?'

'Very well. We chatted a bit. You know what I discovered, Chief? In a way he's rather glad someone blew the gaff on him, even if it was his wife. He didn't admit it in so many words, but I could see he'd have been more upset if we'd caught him by our own methods, or because he'd slipped up somehow.'

This was almost refreshing, after the Lachaume household. Maigret wasn't surprised. This was not the first time he had noticed a kind of professional pride among men like the Canon.

'Not that he's exactly pleased to be going to prison, or to discover that it was his wife who gave him away so as to go off for good with another man. But he doesn't grumble, or talk about taking his revenge when he comes out of clink. While he was being weighed and measured, without a stitch on, he gave me a funny look and muttered:

' "Only a silly b—— would get married when he's as ugly as I am!" '

Maigret had called Lucas to give him instructions.

'Ring through to Corbeil. Ask their flying squad to send down to the flour-mills and see if the barge *Notre-Dame* has arrived. If she's not there yet, they'll find her somewhere near the last lock. She tied up last night at the Ivry dock, just opposite the Lachaumes' house. There was a little party on board, and it lasted till very late. Somebody may have noticed lights in the house, or movements around it. There were some other bargemen at the celebration and I want to know their names, the name of their boat, the place where they might be got hold of. You understand?'

'Yes, Chief.'

'That's all, old man.'

Janvier had come back.

'And what am I to do?'

This was the disagreeable period that occurs during every investigation, the moment of uncertainty as to where to turn next.

'Telephone Paul, he must have finished the post-mortem. He may have some extra particulars to give you before he sends in his report. After that, go up to the laboratory. See whether they've found out anything.'

Left alone with his pipes, Maigret selected one of them, the oldest, and filled it slowly, watching the rain trickling down the window-panes.

'Three hundred million! . . .' the words escaped him in a growl, as he saw in his mind's eye the shabby house on the Quai de la Gare, the little stove in the drawing-room, the old furniture which had once been handsome, but had been re-covered in ill-assorted materials, the icy radiators, the great ballroom on the ground floor, the library and the billiard-room, where one expected to see a ghost at any moment.

He called to mind, too, the rather contorted features of Armand Lachaume, who was obviously a weakling, possibly a coward, and seemed to have lived completely overshadowed by his brother.

'Which of you is free?' he asked, standing in the doorway of the inspectors' office.

Torrence was the first to stand up, as if at school.

'Come into my office, Torrence. Sit down. You're to go to the Quai de la Gare, at Ivry. I'd rather you didn't go into the house, or into the factory or offices. I imagine that at midday the employees, some of them at any rate, go out to lunch.

'Get what you can out of them, and try to make a point of finding the answers to these questions:

'*Firstly*: have the Lachaumes a car, and if so, what make is it?

'*Secondly :* who usually drives it, and was it out last night?

'*Thirdly :* does Paulette Lachaume often go out to dinner? Does nayone know with whom she goes? and have they any idea what she does afterwards?

'*Fourthly :* how do things stand between her and her husband? I can tell you, for what it may be worth, that they have separate rooms.

'*Fifthly :* how did she get along with her brother-in-law? . . .

You've made a note of all that? Lastly, I wouldn't mind knowing who Léonard Lachaume's wife was. She died about eight years ago. Her maiden name. Her family. Was she well off? What did she die of? . . .'

The hefty Torrence was placidly jotting this down in his note-book.

'I think that's all. Naturally it's urgent.'

'I'll go right away, Chief.'

Had he forgotten anything? If the examining magistrate and the lawyer hadn't been there, he would have stayed on at the Quai de la Gare himself and put certain questions direct. He would have liked, too, if only out of curiosity, to take a look at Armand Lachaume's room and still more at his wife's.

Did that heiress, with her three hundred million francs, live as shabbily as the rest of the family?

It was almost noon, and he had promised to telephone to Angelot, the magistrate. He called him up.

'Maigret speaking. I've rung up to report, as you asked me to. There's nothing important to tell you, except that Paulette Lachaume is the daughter of a leather-merchant named Zuber, who left her at least three hundred million francs.'

There was a silence at the other end, then the calm voice of the young magistrate :

'You're certain of that?'

'Practically certain. I shall have the confirmation presently.'

'Has she been long in control of that money?'

'About a year, if my information is correct. When he knew the doctors gave him no hope, Zuber made a deed of gift to his daughter, so as to avoid death-duties as far as possible.'

'Paulette Lachaume is married under the system of separate property, is she not?'

'That's what we were told this morning. I haven't checked it.'

'Thank you. Please continue to keep me informed. You have nothing else to tell me?'

'My men are busy on routine work.'

He had no sooner rung off than he picked up the telephone again.

'Get me Maître Radel, please.'

This brought the reply that the lawyer was not at his home, where they were waiting for him to return to lunch.

'Ring up the Lachaumes' house on the Quai de la Gare. He may still be there.'

So indeed he was, a fact which set Maigret speculating.

'I have two or three small points to clear up, Maître Radel. As I know you prefer your clients to be disturbed as little as possible, I would rather apply to you. In the first place, what is the name of the Lachaume family's notary . . . ?'

'Just a moment. . . .'

There was a fairly long pause, during which the lawyer must have kept his hand carefully over the telephone.

'Hello? Chief-Inspector Maigret? Are you still there? I don't see what you're getting at, but my clients have no objection to my telling you that their notary is Maître Barbarin, Quai Voltaire.'

'I imagine that if Léonard Lachaume left a will, it was with Maître Barbarin that he deposited it?'

'I imagine so too, though I doubt whether a will exists, for the family has said nothing about it.'

'Has Léonard Lachaume's son . . . his name is Jean-Paul, I believe? . . . got back from school yet?'

'One moment, please.'

Another silence. The lawyer's hand was not so squarely over the mouthpiece, and Maigret could hear a hum of voices.

'He will not be coming home. His uncle has arranged, by telephone, for him to remain at school.'

'As a boarder?'

'For the time being, yes. His things will be taken to him presently. Is that all you wish to know?'

'Will you ask Madame Lachaume—junior, of course—the name of her own notary, the one who wound up her father's estate, and probably drew up her marriage settlement?'

This time the silence lasted so long that Maigret wondered whether the man at the other end had not hung up. Only once he heard the voice of the lawyer, who seemed to be angry and was declaring forcibly:

'But I tell you that . . .'

Silence again. Were the Lachaumes putting up a fight? Was Radel trying to convince them that the police would anyhow get to know what they wanted? Who was arguing with the lawyer? Armand Lachaume? His wife? And were the two old people listening to the argument, they who already looked like family portraits?

'Hello? . . . Excuse me, Chief-Inspector. . . . We were interrupted and I couldn't attend to your question at once. . . . Zuber's estate was wound up by his notary, Maître Léon Wurmster, Rue de Rivoli. . . . You got the name? . . . Wurmster . . . Léon. . . . I want to emphasize that, because there's a Georges Wurmster who is a notary at Passy. . . . As for the marriage settlement, Maître Barbarin saw to that. . . .'

'Thank you.'

'Hello? . . . Don't ring off. . . . I am ready to give you any further information you may consider necessary. . . . Contrary to what you may have supposed, my clients have no intention of withholding anything from the police. . . . What would you like to know?'

'First of all, the marriage settlement. . . .'

'Separate properties.'

'Was that all?'

'Madame Lachaume's money to go to her children, if any.'

'And if there were no children?'

'To the survivor of the couple.'

'If I am not mistaken, the sum involved is over three hundred million francs?'

'One moment.'

The silence did not last long.

'There is some exaggeration, but the figure is approximately correct, nevertheless.'

'Thank you.'

'I had the impression there were other points you wished to clear up?'

'Not for the moment.'

He rang up Maître Barbarin, and it took some time to get him, for the notary was at a meeting.

'Chief-Inspector Maigret here. I suppose you already know that one of your clients, Léonard Lachaume, died last night?'

Caught unprepared, the notary answered:

'I have just heard about it.'

'By telephone?'

'Yes.'

'I am not asking you to commit a breach of professional etiquette, but I need to know whether Léonard Lachaume left a will.'

'Not to my knowledge.'

'So he never drew it up in your presence, or left any such document in your office?'

'No. He certainly didn't concern himself with the matter.'

'Why not?'

'Because he owned nothing, except a parcel of shares in Lachaume's Biscuits, and those are valueless.'

'Don't ring off yet, Maître Barbarin. I haven't quite finished. Léonard Lachaume was a widower. Could you tell me the name of his wife?'

'Marcelle Donat.'

He had not needed to look up his files.

'What sort of family did she come from?'

'You've heard of the firm of Donat & Moutier?'

Maigret had often seen these two names on hoardings and outside building sites. They belonged to a big firm of government contractors.

'Did she have a dowry?'

'Of course.'

'Can you tell me the amount?'

'Not without an order from the examining magistrate.'

'I'll let that go. Considering how wealthy her family is, I presume it was a large sum?'

Silence.

'Did the marriage take place under the system of separate property?'

'My answer is the same as before.'

'And you can't tell me what Madame Léonard Lachaume died of?'

'The family will be able to give you more accurate information than I can as to that.'

'Thank you, Maître.'

Only the background of the picture was beginning to be filled in as yet. Most of the people in it were still hazy, indeterminate, with, here and there, a few features standing out more sharply.

At several years' interval, each of the Lachaume sons, first Léonard, then Armand, had married a rich girl.

Their brides had brought with them dowries, probably large ones, of which nothing apparently remained.

Might it not be these successive contributions that had enabled the once prosperous business, founded in 1817, to survive to the present day?

True, it was tottering on the verge of collapse. Maigret wondered whether, even in the depths of the country, those packets of wafer-biscuits, with their after-taste of cardboard, could be found nowadays as they were in his childhood.

The two old people, in their drawing-room heated by an iron stove, had practically no individual existence any more; like the billiard-table on the ground floor, like the crystal chandelier, they were merely survivals from the past.

Was not even Armand Lachaume an insubstantial figure, a kind of shadow or partly-faded replica of his brother?

Yet a miracle had happened, had been going on for years; however decayed, the place was still there and smoke still rose from the tall chimney.

The biscuit factory served no purpose, met no standards of business. It had been a thriving, even celebrated concern in the days of small enterprise, but now the market had been won by more up-to-date organizations, two or three of which vied for supremacy in it.

Logically, the biscuit factory on the Quai de la Gare should have closed down long ago.

Whose determination had kept it going in spite of everything?

It was hard to believe that Félix Lachaume was responsible, that dignified, silent old man who no longer seemed fully aware of what was going on around him.

For how long had he been reduced to being merely a kind of ornament?

There remained Léonard. The fact that it was Léonard who was dead to some extent accounted for the family's bewilderment, its reticences, or rather silence, its panic-stricken summoning of a lawyer.

Could one not imagine how, up to last night, it had been Léonard who thought, who *willed* for everybody?

Even for Paulette Lachaume?

That last question was a more perplexing one, and Maigret tried hard to envisage the young woman as he had seen her that morning, tousle-headed, wearing a rather commonplace blue dressing-gown.

His one surprise had been to discover, in that house, amid that family, a young woman who had a certain vitality, even a degree of animal magnetism. He couldn't have said whether she was pretty; but he would have sworn she was desirable.

He would decidedly have liked to see her room, and he wondered whether it was different from the rest of the house.

He wondered, too, how Paulette had come into the place, why she had married such a ludicrous creature as Armand, whose bedroom she did not share.

There were other questions, so many questions, in fact, that he preferred to put off worrying about them.

The telephone rang and he picked up the receiver.

'Maigret here . . .'

It was Lucas.

'I've got Corbeil on the line. They've already questioned the barge people. Shall I put them through to you?'

He assented and heard the voice of an inspector belonging to the Corbeil flying squad.

'I found the *Notre-Dame* in the lock, Chief-Inspector. The skipper and his son have a frightful hangover and don't remember anything much. They were playing, singing, eating and drinking nearly all night.

'Each of them went up on deck at one time or another, to discharge his overflow into the Seine. They paid no attention to what might have been happening on the quay.

'They did notice lights in some of the windows of a big house, but don't know whether it was the one just opposite the barge, or another.

'Their friends' name is Van Cauwelaert and their barge is called the *Twee Gebroeders*; apparently that means the Two Brothers. They're Flemish. They must be unloading somewhere along the Canal Saint-Martin by now. I doubt if they'll be able to tell you much, for at least one of the brothers was so tight that he had to be carried to his own boat.'

'About what time was that?'

'Around four in the morning.'

Once again Maigret opened the door into the next office. Only three inspectors were left in there now.

'Are you very busy, Bonfils?'

'I'm finishing a report, but it's not urgent.'

'Cut along to the Canal Saint-Martin and look for a Belgian barge called the *Twee Gebroeders . . .*'

He completed his instructions and was just back in his office, with his mind bent on lunch, when the telephone rang yet again.

'Torrence here, Chief. I've not got many details yet, but I thought I'd better keep you informed. The Lachaumes have got a car, as well as two old delivery vans and a lorry that's been out of commission for several years. The car is a blue Pontiac, registered under the name of Paulette Lachaume. Her husband doesn't drive. I don't know whether it's true, but people in the district say he's had epileptic fits.'

'Did Léonard ever drive the Pontiac?'

'Yes. He used it as much as his sister-in-law did.'

'Yesterday evening?'

'Paulette didn't take the car. But about six o'clock, when she went out, it was at the door.'

'You don't know whether she left by taxi?'

'I don't know for certain. Most likely she did. From what I'm told she isn't the kind of woman who'd travel by Metro or bus.'

'Did Léonard go out?'

'The Ivry inspectors are dealing with that and questioning the people who live along the quay. According to the men on duty at the time, the blue car was no longer outside the door at eight o'clock. One of them thinks he saw it coming back about ten that evening, but he was some way from the house and didn't see it driven in.'

'Who was at the wheel?'

'He didn't notice. He only remembers a blue Pontiac coming from the direction of Paris and driving towards the quay.'

'That all?'

'No. I have the sister's address. It wasn't easy to get hold of, because she's moved five or six times in the last few years.'

'Did she keep in touch with her family?'

'Apparently not. At the moment she's living in the Rue François I*er*, at No. 17, *bis.*'

'Married?'

'I don't think so. Do you want me to go to the Rue François I*er*?'

Maigret hesitated, thinking of lunch, of his wife waiting for him at home, then shrugged his shoulders:

'No. I'll attend to that. You keep on poking about down there and ring me every now and then.'

He was curious to meet the third Lachaume, who he anticipated would be unlike the others, since she had been the only one to break away from home.

He put on his still damp overcoat, hesitated whether to take an official car. Like Armand Lachaume, he didn't drive, and he'd have to take someone along with him.

He didn't feel inclined to talk. He went out, and made for the Place Dauphine, knowing that at the last moment he would look in at the *brasserie* for a drink. Some inspectors from other branches were standing at the bar, but none from his own, because they were all out on jobs.

'What will you have, Monsieur Maigret?'

'A toddy.'

Since he'd begun with a toddy he might as well go on, even though this wasn't the time of day for it. The men from the Quai didn't need to watch him for long in order to realize that this was not the moment to speak to him. Some of them even dropped their voices suddenly.

Unconsciously he was trying to fit the occupants of the Ivry house into their places, to imagine them in their daily life, which was not easy.

For instance, they apparently took their meals together. How would a woman like Paulette behave in the presence of the old couple? What was her attitude towards that subdued, withdrawn husband of hers, and towards her brother-in-law, who seemed to be the life and soul of the family?

And in the evenings? . . . Where did they all sit? . . . What did they do? . . . He hadn't seen a wireless or a television set . . .

To run that huge house, though part of it, of course, was left to rack and ruin, there was only one servant, nearly eighty years old.

He mustn't forget the boy, Jean-Paul, whom they'd suddenly pushed into boarding-school but who had so far been coming home every afternoon.

How would a kid of twelve react to that atmosphere?

'Taxi!'

He gave the address in the Rue François I<sup>er</sup> and sat back in a corner, still imagining the house at various times of day.

If he had not been dogged by the examining magistrate, he would probably have known more by now. In particular, he had the impression that by questioning Armand Lachaume for long enough, in the right way, he could have made him talk.

'Here we are, sir!'

He paid, looked at the six-storey building in front of which they had stopped. On the ground floor there was a hat shop, and several brass plates bore the names of well-known firms. He went through the main

entrance, opened the glass door of a well-kept, almost luxurious lodge
There was not a cat in sight. The place didn't smell of stew, and the
concierge was young and prepossessing.

He showed his badge, muttering:

'Chief-Inspector Maigret.'

She at once pointed to a chair upholstered in red velvet.

'My husband has driven you several times and often talked to me
about you. He's a taxi-driver. He works at night . . .'

She gestured towards a curtain dividing the lodge from the bedroom.

'He's there. He's asleep . . .'

'You have a tenant called Mademoiselle Lachaume?'

Why did she give that mysterious, amused smile?

'Véronique Lachaume, yes. You're interested in her?'

'Has she lived here for long?'

'Wait a minute . . . It's easy, because she renewed her lease last
month . . . So it must be just over three years . . .'

'Which floor?'

'The fifth, one of the two flats that have big balconies.'

'Is she up there now?'

She shook her head and smiled again.

'Does she work?'

'Yes. Not at this time of day.'

Maigret misunderstood her.

'You mean she . . .'

'No. It's not what you're thinking. You know the *Amazone*, just
round the corner in the Rue Marbeuf?'

Though Maigret knew there was a night-club of that name, he had
never set foot in it. All he could recollect was a glass-panelled door
between two shop-fronts, a neon sign, and some photographs of
scantily clad women.

'Does that place belong to her?' he queried.

'Not exactly. She's the barmaid and hostess.'

'The clientele is a bit unusual, isn't it?'

This seemed to amuse the concierge considerably.

'I don't think many men go there. But there are women in dinner-
jackets . . .'

'I understand. That being so, Mademoiselle Lachaume presumably
isn't home much before four in the morning?'

'Five o'clock, half past five . . . She used to be very regular. For some
months now, there've been times when she hasn't come home at all . . .'

'Is she having an affair?'

'A proper one, with a man.'

'Do you know who he is?'

'I can tell you what he looks like: a fellow of about forty, smartly
dressed, who drives a Panhard convertible.'

'Does he sometimes spend part of the night up there?'

'He has done two or three times. More often it's she who goes to his place.'

'You don't know where he lives?'

'I'm pretty certain it can't be far. Mademoiselle Véronique, as I call her, goes everywhere by taxi. She doesn't like the Metros or buses. But when she's spent the night out I see her coming home on foot, so I take it she hasn't far to come.'

'You don't remember the number of the Panhard?'

'It begins with seven-seven . . . I'd almost bet it ends with a three, but I'm not positive . . . Why? . . . Is it urgent?'

At the beginning of an investigation everything is urgent, for one never knows what unexpected developments there may be.

'She has the telephone?'

'Of course.'

'What's the flat like?'

'Three fine rooms and a bathroom. She's furnished it in very good taste. I'm pretty certain she earns a very good living.'

'Is she a pleasant woman?'

'You mean, is she pretty?'

The concierge's eyes twinkled again.

'She's thirty-four and makes no bones about it. She's fat, with about twice as much bosom as me. Her hair's cut short, like a man's, and when she goes out she always wears a suit. Her features are rather heavy, and yet she's attractive, perhaps because she's always in a good temper and doesn't seem to have a care in the world.'

Maigret was beginning to understand better why the youngest of the Lachaumes had been in a hurry to leave her ancestral home.

'Before this latest affair you told me about, did she have any others?'

'Fairly often, but they never lasted. She would sometimes bring a man back with her at five in the morning, as I told you. Regularly, about three o'clock in the afternoon, I'd see a man leaving, keeping his face turned away and slinking close along the wall . . .'

'In other words this is her first real liaison since she came to live here?'

'That's what I think.'

'Does she seem to be in love?'

'She's gayer than ever. Draw your own conclusions.'

'You don't know at what time I'd be likely to find her at home?'

'Anything's possible. She may come back late in the afternoon, or she may equally well go straight to the night-club without looking in here. That's happened two or three times. Don't you think I ought to wake my husband? If he finds out that you've been here and that he missed you . . .'

Maigret pulled out his watch.

'I'm in a hurry, but I'm sure to be round again

A few minutes later he was standing in front of the women's photographs displayed at the entrance of the *Amazone*. The iron-barred door was shut and there was no bell.

An errand-boy cast an ironic glance over his shoulder at the elderly gentleman who seemed to be rapt in the contemplation of suggestive photographs, and Maigret, noticing this, moved away with a growl.

## V

IN actual fact—as his wife must have suspected long ago—if Maigret seldom went home for meals when he was in the thick of an investigation, it wasn't so much to save time as to remain withdrawn into himself, so to speak, like a sleeper who curls up when morning comes, swathed in his bedclothes, to get his own smell into his nostrils.

It was the private lives of other people, in reality, that Maigret was sniffing up, and at this moment, for instance, in the street, with his hands in the pockets of his overcoat, the rain on his face, he was still lost in the bewildering atmosphere of the Quai de la Gare.

Was it surprising that he should be reluctant to go home, back to his flat, his wife, his furniture, to a kind of unchanging order that had no connexion with the more or less degenerate Lachaumes?

This withdrawal into his shell, and certain other tricks, such as his legendary grumpiness at such times, his hunched shoulders, his gruff manner, were all part of a technique that he had unconsciously built up as the years went by.

For example, it was not merely by chance that he finally went into an Alsatian *brasserie*, where he took a table near the window. He needed to feel solid ground under his feet, that afternoon. He wanted to be weighty, impervious.

He was glad to find that the waitress, in her regional costume, was sturdy and healthy-looking, with a laughing, dimpled face and curly fair hair, unburdened with any psychological complexities. Following the same train of thought, he found it natural to order a *choucroute*, which in this place was lavish and plentifully garnished, accompanied by shiny sausages and fresh pink pickled pork.

After giving his order—including the traditional beer—he went to telephone to his wife, who betrayed her curiosity only by three short questions.

'A murder?'

'Something of the kind.'

'Where?'

'Ivry.'

'Difficult?'

'I think so.'

She did not ask whether he would be home for dinner, for she knew beforehand that it might be a day or two before she set eyes on him again.

He ate abstractedly, tossed off two big mugs of beer, drank his coffee while watching the rain that was still slanting down, almost horizontally, and the passers-by who bent forward as they walked and held their umbrellas like shields in front of them.

He had forgotten his stiff neck. It must have worn off as he moved about. When he got back to his office, a little after two o'clock, there were several messages waiting for him.

He took time to make himself comfortable, to fill a fresh pipe, and remembering the little iron stove at the Quai de la Gare he regretted the almost identical stove he had kept in his office long after central heating had been put in at the Quai des Orfèvres, which the powers that be had finally taken away from him.

For years people had laughed about the way he was always poking that stove; it was because he liked to see the shower of falling sparks, just as he liked the booming sound the thing made at every gust of wind.

The first message he looked at was from one of the Ivry inspectors.

A certain Mélanie Cacheux, housewife, who lived next door to the Lachaumes, had been to visit her sister in the Rue Saint-Antoine the evening before. She had dined there and come home by Metro at about nine o'clock.

As she drew near her home, she had seen the blue Pontiac outside the biscuit factory. Léonard Lachaume was opening the double doors, and while she hunted in her bag for her key, he had got back into the car and driven it through to the courtyard.

She had not spoken to him, for though she had been living on the quay for fifteen years she was not acquainted with the Lachaumes and knew them only by sight.

The inspector had asked her if she was sure of this. Mélanie Cacheux had been quite positive it was Léonard, the elder of the sons. She had added what Maigret already knew:

'Besides, his brother never drives the car.'

Had Léonard Lachaume gone out again later?

Not for the time being, at any rate. The woman lived on the first floor. Her flat overlooked the quay. She had taken the opportunity of her outing to air it. When she got in she had gone straight to the window and had heard the neighbours' heavy double doors being closed, with a familiar squeak of bolts. She had automatically glanced down at the pavement and there had been nobody in sight.

The second note was from Inspector Bonfils, whom Maigret had sent to the Canal Saint-Martin. He had found the boat, the *Twee Gebroeders*, which was unloading bricks. Bonfils had had to visit several *bistrots* before finding one of the two brothers, Jef Van Cauwelaert, who seemed disposed to continue the previous night's festivities.

Jef had gone up on deck several times during the evening and night. It was his brother, not he, who was playing the accordion. On one occasion he had heard a noise on the quay. A peculiar sound, which had caused him to look up while he was relieving his bladder:

'*As though someone was smashing glass, see what I mean?*'

It came from the wall of the biscuit factory. There was no one on the pavement, or beside the wall.

Yes, he was sure he had caught sight of a head projecting above it, the head of someone in the yard, who must have been standing on a ladder.

How far from the house? About ten yards. And at that time Jef Van Cauwelaert had not had more than five or six glasses of gin.

Maigret turned to the plan drawn up by the Judicial Identity people. The spot where the broken glass had been crushed, on the top of the wall, was marked by a cross, twelve yards or so from the house. Now there was a street-lamp less than three yards away, which added plausibility to the bargeman's statement.

Bonfils had emphasized the question of the time, wanting to make sure that it had not been during one of the man's other visits to the deck that he had witnessed the incident.

'It's easy to find out, because they hadn't cut the cake yet.'

Bonfils had gone back on board the barge to ask Jef's wife. The cake had been cut about half past ten.

Maigret registered this in his mind, without attempting to fit the particulars into place and draw conclusions from them.

He glanced over a third message, again from Ivry, later by a few minutes than the first. These scraps of paper, none of them bearing more than a few lines, each represented hours of going round in the rain, and an impressive number of people who had been asked what appeared to them to be ridiculous questions.

At six o'clock on the previous evening—working backwards—a certain Madame Gaudois, who kept a little grocery just opposite the Pont National, had seen a red sports car parked a few yards away from her shop. She had noticed that the windscreen-wipers were working and that a man was seated at the wheel. The man had switched on the inside lamp and was reading a newspaper. He seemed to be waiting for someone.

The car had stood there for a long time. Counting how many customers she had served while it was there, Madame Gaudois estimated that it must have waited for about twenty minutes.

No. The man was not very young. About forty. He was wearing a
yellow raincoat. She had seen him more clearly when, growing impatient, he had got out of the car and begun to walk up and down the
pavement. At one time he had even come and looked in the window of
the grocery.

He wore a brown hat. He had a little moustache.

It wasn't one of the Lachaumes; neither Monsieur Léonard nor
Monsieur Armand. She knew them both by sight. Not to mention that
old Catherine sometimes bought things from her, and owed her money.
Those people had a trail of bills in every shop in the district.

The keeper of the grocery had heard the footsteps of a woman
walking in high-heeled shoes. The lamp in a shop window lit up part
of the pavement, and she was sure it had been Paulette Lachaume who
had joined the man, even to the point of describing her as wearing a fur
coat and a beige hat.

The man in the driving-seat had opened the door. Paulette Lachaume
had stooped to get in, because it was a very low car.

'You don't know what make it was?'

She knew nothing about makes. She had never owned a car. She
was a widow and . . .

The inspector's professional conscience had impelled him to bring
her a sheaf of prospectuses with pictures of different cars.

'It was like that one!' the grocer had said, pointing to a Panhard.

That was all, except an afternoon paper in which Lucas had ringed
a short snipped with a blue line:

### BURGLAR'S CRIME

*Last night, a burglar broke into a house on the Quai de la Gare at Ivry,
occupied by the Lachaume family. Léonard Lachaume, the elder son of the family,
caught him in the act, but was shot in doing so.*

*It was not until this morning that the family found the body and . . .*

Details would come later. By this time there must be at least a dozen
journalists prowling round Ivry.

Maigret sat placidly in his office, where the smoke from his pipe was
beginning to form a blue cloud on a level with his forehead, and sorted
out this information.

At six o'clock, which corroborated what they already knew, Paulette
Lachaume left the house on the quay, wearing a fur coat and a beige
hat. She did not take her own car, but hurried off on foot to the Pont
National, some two hundred yards away, where a man was waiting for
her in a red sports car which seemed to have been a Panhard.

At about the same hour, her own car, the blue Pontiac, was parked
outside the biscuit factory.

There was no precise information as to the time at which that car
had been used.

All that was known was that towards seven o'clock it was no longer there, and that around nine o'clock Léonard Lachaume brought it back and ran it into the garage at the far end of the courtyard.

What time did the Lachaumes have dinner? In the ordinary way there should be six of them at table, because young Jean-Paul was not yet a boarder at his school.

Paulette was definitely out that evening. Léonard too, almost certainly.

So in the dining-room there were only the two old people, Armand, and the boy.

At about ten o'clock the bargeman belonging to the *Twee Gebroeders* heard the sound of glass being smashed on the top of the wall, and caught sight of a face.

At half past eleven Paulette came home, by some unknown means Had she taken a taxi? Or had the red car brought her back?

While she was going down the first-floor corridor, her brother-in-law, in pyjamas and dressing-gown, half-opened his door and wished her good-night.

Was Armand already asleep then? Had he heard his wife come in?

Once undressed, Paulette had gone to the general bathroom, at the far end of the corridor, and had noticed a streak of light under Léonard's door.

Then, as was her custom, she would have taken a sleeping-drug, and apparently slept until morning without hearing anything.

The rest was more in the nature of conjecture, except the time of Léonard's death, which Dr. Paul put between two and three in the morning.

When and where had he drunk the fairly considerable quantity of alcohol revealed by the examination of the stomach and by the blood-analysis?

Maigret turned to the experts' first report. It included a meticulous inventory of everything in the dead man's room, with a description of the furniture, hangings and miscellaneous objects. There was no mention of a bottle or a glass.

'Get me Dr. Paul, please. He's pretty sure to be at home at this time of day.'

So he was, just returned from a lunch out, which had put him into an excellent temper.

'Maigret here. I wonder if you could clear up one point for me. It's about the alcohol found in Léonard Lachaume's body.'

'In the stomach, at any rate, it was brandy,' replied Paul.

'What I would like is to get some idea of the time at which he drank it. Do you know at all?'

'I could even fix it to within half an hour by scientific methods, for the organism eliminates alcohol at a regular rate, though the rate does vary slightly from one individual to another. Some of the alcohol found in the blood was drunk early in the evening, perhaps before that, but only a comparatively small proportion. The brandy that was still in his stomach when he was killed had been drunk quite a long time after his last meal; to leave a safe margin, I would say between eleven in the evening and one o'clock at night. If you want me to tell you how much he'd drunk, I'd rather not commit myself quite so positively, but I should put it not far short of half a pint.'

Maigret remained silent for a moment, digesting this information.

'Is that all you wanted to know?'

'Just a moment, Doctor. Would you say from the post-mortem that Léonard was a heavy drinker, or even a habitual drunkard?'

'Neither one nor the other. His liver and arteries were in perfect condition. The only thing I discovered was that he'd had a touch of TB in his childhood, perhaps without knowing it, a thing that happens more often than people imagine.'

'Thank you, Doctor.'

Léonard Lachaume had left the house on the quay at some undetermined hour, in any case later than his sister-in-law, since the Pontiac was still drawn up by the kerb when she had gone off to join an unknown man.

He might have gone out immediately after her, or not until later. At all events he had come home at nine o'clock.

The household would not all have gone to bed by that hour. What about young Jean-Paul, for instance? It wasn't certain. And it was unlikely that Léonard would have gone to his room without looking into the drawing-room first.

So there had been an encounter between him, his brother and the old couple, at any rate some sort of meeting of uncertain duration, while Catherine was busy in the kitchen, washing up.

Had Léonard begun to drink at that stage already? What had they talked about? When had his parents gone up to bed on the floor above?

If it hadn't been for the zeal and doggedness of Angelot, the examining magistrate, who had prevented him from questioning the family as he would have liked to do, Maigret would doubtless have known all this by now.

Had the two brothers been left to each other's company? What did they do at such times? Did each of them sit reading in opposite corners of the room? Or did they chat?

It wasn't in his own room that Léonard had drunk the brandy, for neither glass nor bottle had been found there.

Either Armand had gone to bed first, leaving his elder brother in the drawing-room, or the latter had come back there later on.

Léonard was not a drunkard. Paul, who had cut up thousands of corpses in the course of his career, was positive, and Maigret had learnt to rely on him.

Yet between eleven at night and two in the morning, the elder Lachaume had drunk roughly half a pint of brandy.

Where was drink kept, in the house? In some drawing-room or dining-room cupboard? Had Léonard been obliged to go down to the cellar?

At eleven-thirty or midnight he was in his room, when his sister-in-law had returned home.

Had he been drinking already? Or hadn't he begun until after that?

Various inspectors, at least ten of them, were still going around in the rain, ringing doorbells, questioning people, trying to jog their memories.

Other particulars would gradually be added to those Maigret already possessed, confirming or conflicting with previous ones.

He was just feeling inclined to get up and stroll into the inspectors' room to change his train of thought, when the telephone rang.

'There's a Madame Boinet on the line, who says she must speak to you personally.'

The name meant nothing to him.

'Ask her what it's about.'

Because his name appeared with undue frequency in the papers, complete strangers were always insisting that they must speak to him personally, even on subjects that had nothing to do with him, such as a lost dog or the renewal of the passport.

'Hello? She says she's the concierge from the Rue François I$^{er}$.'

'Put her through to me.... Hello?... Good afternoon, Madame.... Maigret here.'

'It isn't easy to get hold of you, Chief-Inspector, and I was afraid they wouldn't give you a message. I wanted to tell you she's just come in.'

'By herself?'

'Yes, loaded with provisions, which means she'll be having dinner at home.'

'I'll be right round.'

Again he decided to take a taxi, rather than one of the black Police Headquarters cars, which were too well known. It was beginning to get dark. He was delayed by two traffic blocks in the Rue de Rivoli, and it took ten minutes to cross the Place de la Concorde, where the wet roofs of the cars seemed to be practically touching one another.

As soon as he entered No. 17 *bis*, the concierge peeped out of her door.

'Fifth floor, on the left. I can tell you already that among the things she brought back there were some leeks.'

He gave her a conspiratorial wink, but did not go into the lodge, for he had caught sight of the husband and did not want to waste time chatting.

The house was prosperous-looking, the lift slow but silent. On the fifth floor there was no name on the left-hand door, and Maigret pushed the bell, heard footsteps coming from some distance, muffled by a carpet.

The door was opened eagerly. It was not he who was expected. The woman who received him frowned slightly, as though trying to remember his face.

'Aren't you . . . ?'

'Chief-Inspector Maigret.'

'I was sure I'd seen your face somewhere. I thought at first it was at the cinema, but it was in the papers. Come in.'

Maigret was surprised, for Véronique Lachaume bore only a distant resemblance to the concierge's description of her. True, she was buxom, even fat, to be frank, but she was wearing a dainty housecoat, not a mannish suit, and the room into which she led him was more like a boudoir than a living-room.

Everything was white, the walls, the satin-covered furniture, except for a touch of blue provided by some pieces of china and the old rose colour of the thick-piled carpet, a colour scheme that was reminiscent of a picture by Marie Laurencin.

'What are you surprised about?' she inquired, indicating an arm-chair.

He was afraid to sit down, because of his damp overcoat.

'Take off your coat and give it to me.'

She went to hang it up in the hall. The concierge had been right about one thing, at least: an appetizing smell of leeks was already coming from the kitchen.

'I hadn't expected the police to be here so quickly,' she remarked, sitting down opposite Maigret.

Instead of making her plain, her plumpness rendered her attractive and very likeable, and Maigret suspected that a lot of men must find her desirable. She didn't simper, didn't even bother to fold her house-coat over a considerable stretch of bare leg.

Her feet, with their painted toenails, played in and out of a pair of white mules trimmed with swansdown.

'You may smoke your pipe, Chief-Inspector.'

She took a cigarette from a case, got up to fetch matches, sat down again.

'What rather surprises me is that the family should have told you about me. You must have bombarded them with questions to induce them to do so, because they look upon me as the black sheep, and I imagine my name is taboo in the household.'

'You know what happened last night?'

She pointed to an open newspaper lying on a chair.

'I only know what I've just read.'

'You looked through the paper when you got back here?'

She hesitated only for a second.

'No. At my friend's flat.'

She added good-humouredly:

'I'm thirty-four, you know; I'm a big girl now.'

Her full bosom, scantily covered by the white frills, seemed almost to have a life of its own and to quiver in sympathy with her mood. Maigret would have been inclined to call it a gay, good-natured bosom rather than a voluptuous one.

Her eyes were prominent, bright blue in colour, shrewd and innocent at the same time.

'You're not too surprised that I didn't rush off to the Quai de la Gare? I must admit I probably shan't go to the funeral. I wasn't invited to my brothers' weddings, nor to the funeral of my first sister-in-law. I wasn't told when my nephew was born. It's a complete break, as you see!'

'Didn't you want it to be like that?'

'It was I who left home, yes.'

'For some definite reason? If I'm not mistaken, you were eighteen at the time.'

'And the family wanted to marry me to a dealer in non-ferrous metals. Mark you, even without that, I should have left, though a bit later, perhaps. Have you been down there?'

He nodded.

'I don't suppose it's changed for the better? As sinister as ever? What surprises me most is that the burglar wasn't scared. Either he was drunk, or he hadn't seen the house by daylight.'

'You believe in the burglar?'

'The newspaper . . .' she began.

Her brow wrinkled.

'Isn't that true?'

'I'm not sure. Your family isn't talkative.'

'I can remember times, when I was a girl, when they'd spend a whole evening without opening their mouths a dozen times. What's my sister-in-law like?'

'Rather pretty, so far as I could judge.'

'Is it true she's very rich?'

'Very.'

'Do you understand why that is?'

'I hope I shall end by understanding everything.'

'I read what the papers said about her at the time of the marriage. I saw some photos. I felt sorry for the poor girl, then I began to wonder.'

'What conclusion did you come to?'

'If she'd been ugly it would have been easier. Perhaps it was her father who put me on the track, in the end. He'd had difficulties, hadn't he? He started at the bottom. They say that in the beginning he drove his own trap from one farm to another, and that he couldn't read or write. I don't know whether his daughter went to a convent. Whatever school she went to, convent or not, the girls must have given her a hard time of it.

'To some people, especially at Ivry, the name of Lachaume still sounds impressive. That house on the quay remains a kind of fortress. You see what I mean?

'Those Zubers, father and daughter, jumped into the upper middle class at one go. . . .'

Maigret had thought of this.

'I suspect she's paying a high price for it,' she went on. 'Won't you have a drink?'

'No, thank you. You haven't seen any member of your family again recently?'

'Not one.'

'You've never been back there?'

'I'd rather go out of my way not to set eyes on the house; it's left me too many unpleasant memories. Though my father is probably a good sort. It isn't his fault that he was born a Lachaume and it's turned him into what he is now.'

'What about Léonard?'

'Léonard was much more of a Lachaume than Father. It was Léonard who was determined to make me marry the metal-dealer, a frightful creature, and he used to talk to me about the marriage in the tone of a king explaining to his children that it was their duty to carry on the dynasty.'

'Did you know your first sister-in-law?'

'No. In my time, my brother, in spite of his efforts, hadn't yet found an heiress for himself. I was to be the first to be asked to sacrifice myself. As for Armand, he was an invalid in those days. He's never been strong. But even when he was still only a boy he was a bad copy of Léonard. He'd go to great trouble imitating his movements, his bearing, his voice. I used to make fun of him. He's rather pathetic, really. . . .'

'You have no idea what can have happened last night?'

'None at all. Remember, I know less about it than you do. Was it really not a burglar?'

'I'm beginning to doubt it more and more.'

'You mean you think the crime was committed by someone inside the house?'

She pondered for a moment, and her conclusion was unexpected, to say the least of it:

'That's priceless!'

'Why?'

'I don't know. It takes a bit of courage to kill someone and I don't see who, in my family . . .'

'Where were you last night?'

She was not offended.

'It's surprising, now I come to think of it, that you didn't ask me that before. I was behind the bar of the *Amazone*. I take it you know about that? That's probably why you seemed astonished to find me in the kind of get-up the magazines call 'frothy'. The *Amazone* is my work. Black velvet dinner-jacket and monocle. Here, I'm me. See what I mean?'

'Yes.'

'When I'm at home I tend to exaggerate in the opposite direction, a kind of revenge for having to spend part of my time pretending to be a masterful woman.'

'You even have a lover.'

'I've had lots. I'll tell you something that caused a bit of a stir in the family at the time, and helped me to make up my mind: at the age of sixteen I was the mistress of my drawing-master. I had no choice, he was the only man who taught at my school.'

'It's never happened for one of your brothers, or your sister-in-law, to turn up at the *Amazone*?'

'To begin with, I don't suppose they know I work there, since I never gave them my address, and I'm not well known except in a small and rather specialized circle. Secondly, I doubt whether they'd be keen on seeing a member of the Lachaume family behind the bar of a night-club. But . . .'

She hesitated, not sure of herself.

'I don't actually know my sister-in-law Paulette. And her photo hasn't been in the papers for years, not since the wedding. One evening I had the impression I recognized her at one of the tables, but it was only a vague impression, that's why I hesitated to mention it. What struck me was the way that woman stared at me, with a curiosity that's difficult to account for. There was also the fact that she was alone.'

'When did this happen?'

'Six weeks ago, two months perhaps.'

'You haven't seen her again?'

'No. Do you mind if I go and take a look at my soup?'

She stayed for some little time in the kitchen, whence he could hear the sound of pans, plates and forks being moved.

'I took the chance of putting the joint into the oven. You mustn't tell this to the proprietress of the *Amazone*, or the clients, because they'd stop taking me seriously and I might lose my job, but I adore cooking.'

'Just for yourself?'

'For myself and sometimes for two.'

'This evening it's for two?'

'How did you guess?'

'You just mentioned a joint.'

'So I did. My friend will be here presently.'

'It's a serious affair this time, isn't it?'

'Who's been telling you that? One of the girls at the *Amazone*? Not that it matters, for I don't hide it. Well, Chief-Inspector, just imagine, at the age of thirty-four I've fallen in love and I've half a mind to throw up everything and get married. I enjoy housekeeping, marketing, going to the butcher's and the dairy. I like staying at home and cooking tasty things. All that becomes far and away more delightful if one's expecting somebody and laying the table for two. So . . .'

'Who is it?'

'A man, of course. Not young. Forty-four. Just the right difference in age. Not specially handsome either, but not ugly. On his side, he's tired of furnished rooms and restaurants. He's an advertising agent. He chiefly handles film advertising, so he's obliged to go every day to *Fouquet's, Maxim's*, the *Elysée Club*. . . .

'He's had all the starlets he wanted, but they too live mostly in hotels and eat at restaurants.

'So he's beginning to think that a woman like me . . .'

Beneath the surface irony it was clear that she was in love, perhaps passionately.

'I've just come back from his place, and we shall be having dinner alone here presently. It's time I laid the table. If you have any more questions to ask, come along with me. I can work while I'm listening and answering. . . .'

'I'd just like you to give me his name and address.'

'You need him?'

'It's unlikely.'

'Jacques Sainval, 23 Rue de Ponthieu. Jacques Sainval isn't his real name. He's actually Arthur Baquet, but that's too ordinary-sounding for an advertising man. So he adopted a pseudonym.'

'Thank you very much.'

'What for?'

'For receiving me so nicely.'

'Why shouldn't I? You wouldn't even have a drink! As a matter of fact I haven't got much here in the flat. I'm obliged to drink champagne all night, and that's quite enough. Most of the time I just take a sip or two and empty the rest down the sink.'

Here was a woman still getting fun out of life.

'You mustn't be shocked that I've not been weeping. I should have, perhaps, but I can't manage it. I'm longing to know who killed Léonard.'

'So am I.'

'You'll tell me?'

'I promise.'

It was rather as though the two of them had become fellow-conspi-
rators, for Maigret, as he left, was smiling almost as light-heartedly
as the plump young woman in her rustling housecoat.

He stood alone on the landing, waiting for the lift, and when it came
up there was someone in it, a man with brown hair, starting to thin at
the temples.

He was wearing a light-coloured raincoat, with a brown felt hat in
his hand.

'Excuse me . . .' he murmured, as he went past the chief-inspector.

Then he turned back for a better look, as though he, too, found the
face familiar.

The lift went down. The concierge was on the watch, behind her
glass-panelled door.

'Did you see him? He's just gone up.'

'Yes.'

'What do you think of her?'

'She's charming.'

He thanked her and smiled. He might need her again and he mustn't
discourage her. He also shook hands with the taxi-driver husband, who
had driven him several times.

When at last he emerged on the pavement, he saw a red Panhard
convertible outside the door.


# IV

I T was a little time before Maigret could thread his way across between
the cars, for this was the after-office rush-hour. On reaching the opposite
pavement, he looked up at the flat he had just left. The balcony ran the
whole width of the house, divided half-way along by a wrought-iron
fence. It was quite dark now, and light was shining through at least
half of the curtained windows.

The french windows on the fifth floor stood half-open, and a man
with a cigarette in his mouth, who was leaning on the balcony rail to
look down into the street, drew back hastily when he saw the chief-
inspector.

It was the one who had just gone up and who had frowned when he
passed Maigret at the door of the lift, the man who called himself
Jacques Sainval and whose business was cinema advertising.

He had gone back into the flat. The french window was closing now. What would he be saying to Véronique Lachaume, as she laid the table?

There was a bar opposite the block, not a *bistrot*, but one of those American bars with high stools and soft lighting that are becoming more and more numerous in the Champs-Elysées district.

Maigret went in; the place was crowded, but he found a stool by the wall. It was hot. There was a lot of noise, women's laughter, cigarette-smoke. A pretty girl in a black dress and white apron waited, smiling, to take his coat and hat.

When the barman turned his way, also looking as if he were wondering where he'd seen him before, Maigret hesitated briefly before ordering:

'A hot toddy!'

Then he inquired:

'The telephone?'

'In the basement.'

'Can you give me a *jeton*?'

'See the girl at the switchboard.'

It wasn't the sort of spot he went to for choice, and he felt, as usual, a bit out of place there, for in his young days such bars hadn't existed. The wooden panelling on the walls was painted with hunting scenes full of pink-coated riders, and a real hunting-horn was hanging just above the bar.

As he made for the stairs at the far end of the room, he could feel himself being stared at. The barman had finally recognized him. So, probably, had others. Most of the women were young. The men, though rather older, didn't belong to his generation.

He too had noticed several familiar faces, and he remembered that there were some television studios just up the street.

He went down the oak staircase, found another pretty woman sitting in front of a telephone switchboard near the cloakroom door.

'A *jeton*, please.'

There were three glass-fronted cabins, but the telephones inside were without dials.

'What number do you want?'

He was obliged to give the number of Police Headquarters, and the young woman recognized it herself, and looked more closely at Maigret.

'Cabin 2.'

'Police Headquarters.'

'Maigret speaking. Would you put me on to Lucas?'

'One minute, Chief-Inspector. . . .'

He had to wait, Lucas was already speaking to someone. At last his voice came over the line.

'I'm sorry, Chief. As it happens, that was the examining magistrate.

He called up for the third time since you left, and he's surprised at getting no news from you.'

'Go on.'

'He asked me a whole lot of questions. . . .'

'What about?'

'He began by asking whether you'd been back to the Quai de la Gare. . . . I said I thought not. . . . He wanted to know whether you'd interrogated any other witnesses. . . . Finally, a few minutes ago, he left a message for you. . . . He has to go home to change, because he's dining out. . . . He'll be all the evening at Balzac 23.74. . . .'

This was in the Champs-Elysées district, where Maigret was now.

'He insisted that if you planned to question anybody, he particularly wanted it to be done in his office. . . .'

Lucas was clearly embarrassed.

'Is that all?'

'No. He asked me where the inspectors were, what they were doing, what they'd found out. . . .'

'Did you tell him?'

'No. I made out I didn't know anything. He wasn't pleased.'

'Is there any news?'

Through the glass door he could see the switchboard operator watching him while she put on lipstick, and a woman customer adjusting her suspenders in front of a mirror.

'No. Lapointe has just come on duty. He's getting impatient. He'd love to have something to do.'

'Let me speak to him.'

This was a stroke of luck.

'Lapointe? Take one of the cars and go to Ivry. At the corner of a street just opposite the Pont National, you'll see a badly-lit grocery. I've forgotten the woman's name. Something like Chaudais, Chaudon, or Chaudois . . . She wears her hair in a bun and has one eye a bit askew. Be very nice to her, very polite.

'Tell her we need her for a short time. She'll want to dress up in her best. Try not to let her take too long about it. Then bring her to the Rue François I$^{er}$, opposite No. 17 bis. You'll most likely see a red car parked outside. Pull up as close to it as you can. Stay in the car, both of you, till I get in touch with you. . . .'

'Right, Chief.'

He went out of the cabin, paid for the call.

'Thank you, Monsieur Maigret.'

That had long ago ceased to thrill him. There were more people in the bar upstairs by this time, and a red-headed young woman had to draw aside so that he could get back on his stool. He could feel her warm thigh against his, and she was using very strong scent.

At one table a man of his own age, with grizzled hair and a balding head, had his arm round the waist of a dimpled girl hardly twenty years old, and Maigret, for the first time, found this shocking. Perhaps because of that examining magistrate, fresh from college, he was suddenly feeling an old man, a survival from the past.

All these girls smoking, and drinking whisky and cocktails, were not for the men of his generation any more. A few of them, talking loudly, turned to stare at him curiously and rather brazenly.

He only had to bend forward and he could see the lighted fifth-floor windows up there, with a shadow passing across them now and then.

He had weighed the pros and cons. His first idea had been to wait for Jacques Sainval when he came out again. Fat, kindly Véronique Lachaume was in love, no doubt about that. Mightn't he cause her unhappiness? Wasn't there a danger of his causing a lovers' quarrel?

It was not the first time he'd been held back by scruples of that kind. But if his intuition was correct, wouldn't it be better for her to know how things stood?

He sipped his drink slowly, trying to imagine what was happening in the flat. Dinner must be ready. The two of them would be sitting down to it. He was giving them time to eat, and similarly time for Lapointe and the grocery woman to get under way.

'The same again . . .' he ordered.

Everything changes. It's like children growing up, you don't notice it while it's happening, only when it's happened.

His intimate enemy, as he liked to call him, the examining magistrate Coméliau, had retired now and become just an old gentleman taking his dog for its morning walk, arm-in-arm with a lady whose hair was dyed mauve.

Maigret had begun by finding around him, and later under his orders, inspectors who had never been on traffic duty, or taken their turn at the railway stations, but came from colleges. Nowadays he had some colleagues, with the same grade and salary as himself, who were scarcely forty years old. True, they all had law degrees, and many of them had two or three other university qualifications as well. Those chaps seldom left their offices, simply sending their subordinates out on investigations, and then sifting the results thus obtained.

In the course of his career he had seen police prerogatives being gradually whittled away, and now a new generation of examining magistrates was taking over. A team of young athletes was replacing the Coméliaus; like Angelot, they claimed the right to conduct an investigation from start to finish.

'How much is that?'

'Six hundred francs. . . .'

Prices were different too. He sighed, looked round for his coat, had to wait by the door till the cloakroom girl came.

'Thank you, Monsieur Maigret.'

Would the examining magistrate have been so punctilious in dealing with the Canon, for example, or some other professional thief, or with a navvy from the Quai de Javel?

Even though they were reduced to the almost disgusting poverty revealed on the Quai de la Gare, the Lachaumes were still patricians, a great *bourgeois* family whose name had been respected for over a century.

Would the younger generation still take that into account?

He was not actually asking himself questions, but he couldn't prevent his thoughts from revolving round various bothersome points. There are days when one is more than usually sensitive to certain aspects of the world. Yesterday had been All Souls' Day, the Feast of the Dead.

He shrugged his shoulders and crossed the street. Through their muslin curtains he saw the concierge and her husband sitting at a round table, gave them a slight wave as he went by, without being sure whether they had noticed him.

He took the lift to the fifth floor, rang the door bell, heard voices, followed by footsteps. It was fat Véronique who opened the door to him; her face was pinker than before, because she had just finished her hot soup, as he was soon to discover.

She was surprised to see him again, but did not seem worried.

'Did you forget something? Had you an umbrella?'

She glanced automatically towards the hat-stand in the passage.

'No. I'd just like a few words with your friend.'

'Ah!'

She closed the front door.

'Come in! This way. . . .'

She did not take him to the sitting-room, but to the kitchen. This was white-painted too, with chromium-plated electrical gadgets like those shown at Ideal Homes exhibitions. It was divided by a sort of balustrade, on one side of which a miniature dining-room had been fitted up. The steaming tureen was still on the table. Jacques Sainval had his spoon in his hand.

'It's Chief-Inspector Maigret, who'd like to talk to you. . . .'

The man got up, obviously ill at ease, hesitated whether to hold out his hand, finally did so.

'Delighted to meet you.'

'Please sit down. Go ahead with your dinner. . . .'

'I was just going to take away the soup.'

'Pay no attention to me.'

'You'd better give me your coat. It's very hot in here.'

She took his overcoat out to the hall. Maigret sat down, holding his unlighted pipe, with the feeling that Angelot, the magistrate, would have strongly disapproved of his behaviour.

'I only want to ask you one or two questions, Monsieur Sainval. I noticed your car down below. The red Panhard is yours, isn't it?'

'Yes.'

'Wasn't that car standing opposite the Pont National, yesterday evening, about six o'clock?'

Had Sainval been expecting this question? He showed no sign of alarm, appeared to be searching his memory.

'The Pont National?' he echoed.

'It's the last bridge before Ivry, a railway bridge. . . .'

Véronique, who had come back, was watching them both in surprise.

'I don't see. . . . No. . . . Wait a minute. . . . Yesterday afternoon. . . .'

'About six o'clock.'

'No. . . . Definitely not. . . .'

'You hadn't lent your car to anyone?'

It was not without reason that the chief-inspector offered him this loophole.

'I didn't exactly lend it, but one of my colleagues may possibly have used it. . . .'

'Do you generally park it in front of your office?'

'Yes.'

'With the key in it?'

'One has to take the risk, doesn't one? A bright-coloured car like that isn't very liable to be stolen, it would be too easy to trace.'

'Do you and your colleagues go to the office on Sundays?'

'We often do. . . .'

'Are you sure you're not lying, Jacquot?'

This was Véronique interrupting, as she put the joint on the table.

'Why should I be lying? You know perfectly well that the firm pays for the garage and the petrol. . . . If one of us has something urgent on hand and can't get hold of a car . . .'

'You don't know Paulette, of course?'

'Paulette who?'

Véronique Lachaume was not laughing now. In fact she had become extremely serious.

'My sister-in-law,' she explained.

'Ah, yes. . . . I vaguely remember your speaking about her. . . .'

'Do you know her?'

'By name.'

'And you know she lives on the Quai de la Gare?'

'Now you mention it. . . . Her address had slipped my memory. . . .'

Maigret had noticed a telephone in the concierge's lodge. There was one in Véronique's drawing-room as well.

'Might I make a telephone call?'

'You know where it is?'

He went to it by himself, rang down to the lodge.

'Maigret here. I'm on the fifth floor. . . . Yes. . . . Would you have a look out in the street to see whether a small black car has arrived? There should be a youngish man and an elderly woman sitting in it. . . . Ask them from me to be kind enough to come up here. . . .'

He had not lowered his voice. The pair in the kitchen had heard. It wasn't pleasant work, and he was trying to be as above-board as he could.

'I'm sorry, but I have to check up on something. . . .'

It looked to him as though Véronique's prominent eyes, so merry a little while ago, were moist. Her bosom had changed the rhythm of its rise and fall. She was forcing herself to eat, but her appetite had gone.

'You swear you're not hiding anything from me, Jacquot?'

Even the pet name 'Jacquot' was becoming embarrassing.

'I assure you, Nique . . .'

As Véronique had admitted, this was her first regular liaison, and despite her apparent cynicism it must mean a lot to her, this love. Did she already feel it threatened? Had she always had some doubt about the publicity agent's sincerity? Had she shut her eyes deliberately, because at the age of thirty-four she was tired of fooling around in a dinner-jacket and was yearning to get married like other women?

He was listening for the bell. When it rang he hurried into the passage and went to open the door.

As he had expected, the grocery woman had put on her Sunday best, with a black-fur-collared coat and an elaborate hat. Lapointe merely winked at his chief and said:

'I was as quick as I could manage.'

'Come in, Madame. It was you, I believe, who noticed a red car, yesterday evening, standing outside your premises?'

He was careful not to say 'shop'.

'Yes, Monsieur.'

'Come this way, please. . . .'

She stopped at the kitchen door in silence, turned to the chief-inspector and asked:

'What am I supposed to do?'

'Do you recognize anyone here?'

'Indeed I do.'

'Who?'

'The gentleman who's eating.'

Maigret went to the hat-stand for Sainval's hat and raincoat.

'I recognize those, too. Anyway, I'd already recognized the car out in the street. There's a dent in the right wing.'

Dry-eyed, with clenched teeth, Véronique Lachaume got up and put her plate into the sink. Her friend, too, stopped eating, sat hesitantly for a moment, then stood up, murmuring:

'All right!'

'What's all right?'

'I was there.'

'Thank you, Madame. You can drive her home now, Lapointe. Get her to sign a statement, just in case.'

When the three of them were alone again, Véronique said in a slightly hoarse voice:

'I wonder if you two would mind discussing your little affairs somewhere else than in my kitchen? . . . In the drawing-room, if you like. . . .'

Maigret realized that she wanted to be alone, perhaps to have a cry. He had spoilt her evening, and more than that, very likely. The little dinner for two had turned out badly.

'Come along. . . .'

He left the door open on purpose, for he felt that as the daughter of the Lachaume family she had a right to hear what was said.

'Sit down, Monsieur Sainval.'

'May I smoke?'

'By all means.'

'Do you realize what you've just done?'

'What about you?'

Véronique's lover looked like a schoolboy caught in some prank; he had a sulky, shifty expression.

'I can tell you right away that you're mistaken.'

Maigret sat down facing him, filled his pipe. He said nothing, not wanting to make things easier for the other man. This, he realized, was a little unfair. Angelot, the magistrate, was not there. And Sainval wasn't insisting on his lawyer being present.

Some women doubtless found him handsome, but seen at close quarters, especially just now, he looked rather the worse for wear. Without the air of assurance that he usually assumed, one could feel he was weak, hesitant.

He would have been more at ease and at home in the American bar across the street.

'I've read the paper, like everyone else, and I can guess what you're thinking.'

'I'm not thinking anything, as yet.'

'Then why did you bring up that woman whom I don't know?'

'To make you admit that you were on the Quai de la Gare yesterday.'

'What does that prove?'

'Nothing, except that you know Paulette Lachaume.'

'And so what?'

He was regaining confidence; or rather, he was trying to put a bold face on things.

'I know hundreds of women, and I've never heard that that's a crime.'

'I am not accusing you of any crime, Monsieur Sainval.'

'Yet you come here, to my friend's flat, knowing quite well that . . . that . . .'

'That I'm putting you in an awkward position. For I imagine you've never told her about your goings-on with Paulette Lachaume?'

The man hung his head in silence. They could hear the rattle of plates and cutlery. To all appearances, Véronique was not listening.

'How long have you known her?'

Sainval was searching for an answer, still wondering whether or not to tell a lie. Whereupon Véronique broke in, showing that she had followed the conversation after all.

'It's my fault, Monsieur Maigret. Now I know. I've been nothing but an idiot, and I ought to have known where it would land me. . . .'

She had been crying in the kitchen, not much, but enough to make her eyes red. She was clutching a handkerchief, and her nostrils were still damp.

'Just now, when you came the first time, I gave you the answer to your question, without realizing it. You remember that about six weeks or two months ago I thought I recognized my sister-in-law in the night-club? Jacques came to call for me that night, as he often does. I don't know why I mentioned it to him, because I'd never told him anything about my family.

'I don't remember exactly how it came up. I think I said:

' "My brother would have a nice surprise if he knew the kind of place his wife goes to ! . . ."'

'Something like that. . . . Jacques asked what my brother did, and it struck me as amusing to say:

' "Wafer biscuits!"'

'We were very gay. We were walking arm-in-arm through the night.

' "Is he a pastrycook?"'

' "Not exactly. Have you never heard of Lachaume's wafer-biscuits?"'

'And as this meant nothing to him, I added:

' "His wife's worth at least two hundred million, perhaps more."'

'Now do you understand?'

Though Maigret understood, he needed to know more.

'Did he question you about your sister-in-law?'

'Not then and there. That came later, one question at a time, casually, as it were. . . .'

'Were the two of you already thinking of getting married?'

'We'd been considering it, more or less seriously, for several weeks.'

'And you went on considering it?'

'I assumed it was settled, once and for all.'

Sainval muttered, in a voice he tried to make convincing:

'I've never changed my mind.'

'Then why did you get yourself acquainted with my sister-in-law?'

'Out of curiosity. . . . With no special purpose. . . . To begin with, she's married. . . . So . . .'

'So what?'

'It wasn't in my interest to . . .'

'Will you excuse me?' interrupted Maigret. 'I'd like to put a few more precise questions on my own. Tell me, Monsieur Sainval, where and when did you first meet Paulette Lachaume?'

'You want the exact date?'

'As near as you can manage.'

'It was on a Thursday, about four weeks ago, in a tea-room in the Rue Royale. . . .'

'So you go in for tea-rooms nowadays?' exclaimed Véronique with a burst of laughter.

She had no illusions left. She wasn't going to hang on. She knew it was all over and bore no grudge against her companion. It was only herself she was angry with.

'I don't suppose,' persisted Maigret, 'that you were there by pure chance. You had followed her. Probably since she left home. For how many days had you been watching her?'

'That was the second day.'

'In other words, hoping to make her acquaintance, you'd been on the watch in the afternoon, with your car, on the Quai de la Gare.'

He did not deny it.

'Paulette came out, probably in her blue Pontiac, and you followed her.'

'She left the car in the Place Vendôme and went shopping in the Rue Saint-Honoré.'

'In the tea-room you spoke to her?'

'Yes.'

'Did she seem surprised?'

'Very.'

'From which you inferred that she wasn't used to having men make up to her?'

It all hung together.

'When did you take her to your rooms?'

'I didn't take her home,' he protested.

'To an hotel?'

'No. A friend lent me his flat.'

Véronique interrupted again, sarcastically:

'You understand, Monsieur Maigret? The Rue de Ponthieu was quite good enough for me. But for a woman worth several hundred million francs he had to find somewhere more glamorous. Where was it, Jacques?'

'It belongs to an Englishman you don't know, on the Île Saint-Louis.'

'Did she often come to see you there?'

'Fairly often.'

'Every day?'

'Only just lately.'

'In the afternoon?'

'Sometimes in the evening too.'

'Yesterday?'

'Yes.'

'What happened yesterday evening?'

'Nothing in particular.'

'What did you talk about?'

Véronique again:

'Do you suppose they spent much time talking?'

'Answer me, Sainval.'

'Have you interrogated her?'

'Not yet.'

'You're going to?'

'Tomorrow morning, in the examining magistrate's office.'

'I didn't kill her brother-in-law. Anyhow, I had no reason to kill him.'

He fell silent for a moment, looking more thoughtful, added in a low voice:

'Neither had she.'

'Have you ever seen Léonard Lachaume?'

'Once when I was waiting on the quay, I saw him come out of the house.'

'Did he see you too?'

'No.'

'Where did you and Paulette have dinner yesterday?'

'In a restaurant in the Palais-Royal. You can verify that. We had a table on the *entresol*.'

'I know it!' broke in Véronique. 'It's called *Chez Marcel*. He's taken me there on the *entresol* too, the same table, I expect, in the left-hand corner. Am I right, Jacques?'

He made no reply.

'When you left the Quai de la Gare you didn't notice whether another car was following you?'

'No. It was raining. I didn't even look into the driving-mirror.'

'Afterwards you went to the flat on the Île Saint-Louis?'

'Yes.'

'You drove Paulette home?'

'No. She insisted on taking a taxi.'

'Why?'

'Because a red car is more noticeable at night, when the quay is deserted.'

'She was very much afraid of being seen with you?'

It was evident that Sainval didn't know what Maigret was getting at, or rather, that he was wondering what kind of a trap his questions concealed.

'I suppose so. It's fairly natural.'

'I take it, however, that she was on rather chilly terms with her husband?'

'There had been no intimate relations between them for years, and they had separate rooms. Armand's health is not good.'

'You were already calling him Armand?'

'There had to be some way of referring to him.'

'In fact, without ever having set foot in the Lachaumes' house, you regarded yourself in some sort as one of the family?'

Once again Véronique intervened, and this time she went straight to the point.

'Listen, both of you, there's no point in this cat-and-mouse game. You both know how things stand. So do I, I'm sorry to say, and I'm just a big fool.

'Although he's often at *Fouquet's*, *Maxim's*, and other smart places, Jacques has always been hard up, and his only possession is his car, assuming that's been paid for.

'I'd noticed already that he had bills chalked up in bars and restaurants. When he met me, he said to himself that a woman of my age, who's worked all her life, must have some money tucked away, and I was misguided enough to bring him here and tell him I'd just bought the flat.'

'It's true. This place is my own. I'm even about to build myself a little house on the banks of the Marne.

'That sounded magnificent to him, and though I wasn't asking for anything of the kind, he began talking marriage.

'Only then I had the idiotic idea of telling him all about my sister-in-law and her millions. . . .'

'I have never taken money from women,' declared Sainval in a colourless voice.

'That's just what I'm saying. It wasn't worth while to get a small sum out of her now and then. Whereas by marrying her . . .'

'She's married. . . .'

'What's divorce for, then? Admit you've discussed it together.'

He hesitated, not knowing which way to turn. Hadn't Maigret told him he would be interrogating Paulette next day?

'I didn't take her seriously. I had put out a feeler, just from curiosity. . . .'

'So she was thinking of divorce. . . . And it was so that the decree shouldn't go against her, that she was anxious not to be caught. . . . You see the idea, Monsieur Maigret? . . . I don't bear you any malice for bringing all this out. . . . It's not your fault. . . . You were looking for something else. . . . Sometimes when one's after big game one puts up a rabbit. . . .

'As for you, Jacquot, I'd be glad if you'd take away your dressing-gown and slippers and send me back my things. . . .

'It's almost time for me to go to work, and I must get into uniform. . . . The ladies are expecting me!'

A burst of slightly hysterical laughter shook her plump bosom.

'That'll teach me! . . . But you'd be making a mistake, Inspector, if you suspected Jacques of killing Léonard. . . . For one thing I don't see why he should have done it. . . . For another, between you and me, he's a phoney tough. . . . He'd have lost his nerve before he was over the wall. . . .

'Excuse me for not offering you a drink. . . .'

Her tears suddenly began to fall, without her being aware of it, and she didn't think to turn away her face. In a muffled voice, she commanded:

'Clear out, both of you. . . . It's high time I got dressed. . . .'

She pushed them into the passage, towards the hat-stand. Out on the landing, Sainval turned back:

'My dressing-gown and slippers . . . ?'

Instead of going to fetch them, she flung back at him:

'I'll send them to you all right. . . . Don't worry! No one else will use them. . . .'

The door closed behind them, and Maigret could have sworn he heard a sob, just one, followed by hurried footsteps.

Sainval and he waited in silence for the lift. As they stepped into it, the advertising agent murmured:

'Do you realize what you've done?'

'What about you?' retorted Maigret, lighting his pipe at last.

And that fool of a magistrate would have liked to be present right through the investigation! For the fun of it, no doubt?

# VII

HE dreamt about it, like a schoolboy worrying over tomorrow's exam. And though Angelot, the magistrate, never put in an appearance, though Maigret never saw his face, his presence permeated the background all the same. It wasn't just one dream. It was a kind of string of dreams, separated by periods when the chief-inspector was half-awake, sometimes even wide awake, during which he went on making the same effort.

It had begun rather pompously. He was informing the invisible magistrate:

'Very well, I'll show you my method. . . .'

To his mind this was a kind of rehearsal. He used the word 'method' ironically, of course, because for thirty years he'd been denying that he had any method. But never mind! He was not sorry to have things out with this insolently youthful magistrate.

Maigret was at the Quai de la Gare, all by himself in the dilapidated buildings, which had become so insubstantial that he could pass through the walls. But the interior was true to life, down to the least detail, including some the chief-inspector had forgotten in his waking moments.

'There you are! . . . Every evening, for years, they'd be sitting here . . .'

It was the drawing-room, and Maigret was stoking the little stove, whose iron front showed a crack of brighter red, like a scar. He was arranging the characters in their places: the old couple, carved in wood; Léonard, whom he had to try to imagine alive and to whom he gave a thin, bitter smile; an impatient Paulette who kept jumping to her feet, thumbing through magazines, and was the first to announce that she was going to bed; and last of all Armand, who was tired and was taking some medicine.

'You understand, Monsieur Angelot, that is the capital point. . . .'

He didn't know what point.

'Every evening, for years. . . . Jean-Paul is already in bed. . . . The others, except Paulette, are all thinking the same thing. Léonard and his brother exchange glances from time to time. . . . Léonard will have to do the talking, because he's the eldest and because Armand doesn't dare. . . .'

Talking, in the dream, meant asking Zuber's daughter for money.

The firm of Lachaume was on the verge of collapse; it was the oldest biscuit factory in Paris, an important institution, as valuable as one of those pictures of family groups that are put in museums, which have taken generations to create.

Somebody had a whole heap of money, dirty money, so dirty that old Zuber had been only too glad to give his daughter to a Lachaume so that she should have a respectable position in the world.

'You understand?'

For it was still in front of an invisible Angelot that he was working like this; an acrobat without a net. Difficult work. As when, in other dreams, he was raising himself through space by the strength of his hands.

He mustn't let the characters escape, melt into thin air.

'The old couple go away, followed by Armand, so as to leave the other two alone. It would be simpler if she would hand over a big sum at one go, but she stubbornly refuses to do that; perhaps her father, who was no fool, gave her that advice before he died. Only small amounts, for the end of the month. So that it has to be done over and over again. . . .'

The Lachaumes must have lied at the start, making out that given a few million francs the business would become prosperous once more, the house comfortable and cheerful, a setting for dinner-parties and receptions like any other big middle-class household. Paulette believed them, then ceased to do so.

The little talks with Léonard were repeated every month.

'How much?'

After which they would shut themselves up separately, each in one of those rooms. Each in one of those cells, to go on calculating. . . .

The corridor . . . the doors . . . The bathroom, at the far end, an ancient bathroom with a brown stain on the enamel, where the tap drips . . .

The Lachaumes are used to it . . . Perhaps in Zuber's household, in spite of the millions, they didn't use the bathroom? . . .

'All that, Monsieur Angelot, you have to assimilate . . .'

He repeated the word, stressing each syllable:

'As-si-mi-late!'

. . . Léonard in his office downstairs, Armand in his, opposite the book-keeper, the biscuits being packed in the dispatch room, and an absurd trickle of smoke rising from the tall chimney, that imitation of a factory chimney . . .

Paulette in her car . . .

The day, the evening before. The grocery woman in her shop. It was Sunday, but the day before that was a public holiday, and the small local shopkeepers don't like to close for two days in succession. The red Panhard, towards six o'clock, with the so-called Sainval in his raincoat. Léonard following. In the blue Pontiac. The Palais-Royal. The restaurant . . .

It would have been interesting to superimpose the different images, as in certain photographs, showing the Ivry police, the inspectors, Janvier, Lucas, all those who were questioning people, a barge at Corbeil, another on the Canal Saint-Martin, and Paul cutting up muscles and viscera, putting samples in test-tubes, the laboratory people measuring, analysing, looking through magnifying-glasses and microscopes . . .

Maigret smiled ironically.

'But what really matters . . .'

He refrained, out of modesty, from saying what really mattered, continuing to move from room to room, through the walls . . .

When Madame Maigret shook him awake, he was worn out, as if after a night in a train, and his neck was painful again.

'You talked several times during the night.'

'What did I say?'

'I couldn't understand. You mixed up the syllables . . .'

She didn't continue the subject. He had eaten without speaking to her, as though forgetting that he was at home and she was sitting opposite him.

Jacques Sainval had seemed surprised, the evening before, at being left free on the one condition that he didn't go out of Paris.

On reaching home, the chief-inspector had telephoned to Lapointe, who was on night-duty for the whole of this week, and had asked him to make certain investigations, to get a file together.

It was no longer raining, but the sky was no lighter, nor more cheerful-looking, and the people in the bus were crotchety.

Maigret had had himself roused earlier than usual, and when he arrived at the Quai des Orfèvres there was hardly anyone in the offices.

The first thing he saw, placed in full view, was the series of messages from the examining magistrate, who demanded that the chief-inspector should ring him up first thing in the morning, which, for a member of the Public Prosecutor's staff, presumably meant nine o'clock.

This left him some time in hand, and he began by studying the statistics that Lapointe had left on his desk before going home to bed. He made no notes, merely memorizing some of the figures, not without a smile of satisfaction, for he had been pretty well right.

Next, he turned to the plan of the house at Ivry, prepared by the Judicial Identity branch.

With the plan went a bulky, meticulous report, for those fellows were not in the habit of overlooking the smallest detail. For instance, they had listed an old wheel off a child's bicycle, rusty and twisted, found in a corner of the courtyard.

Had it belonged to Jean-Paul's bicycle, or, very likely, to a bicycle once used by Armand, if not by Léonard? Or had some local resident got rid of it by throwing it over the wall instead of into the Seine?

The detail was suggestive, and there were a lot of others equally so, too many for them all to be kept in mind.

What he studied at greatest length was the inventory of the contents of Léonard's bedroom.

Eight white shirts, six of them very much worn, with darned collars and cuffs. . . . Six pairs of pants, patched. . . . Ten pairs of cotton socks and four pairs of woollen ones. . . . Five pairs of striped pyjamas. . . .

Everything was mentioned, the number of handkerchiefs, the condition of the comb, of the hairbrush and clothes-brush, with sketches showing the position of each item. As he had done in his dream during the night, Maigret strove to visualize the room and to place the various objects mentioned in the list.

... A black marble and bronze clock, no longer in working order. ... Two three-branched marble and bronze candlesticks. ... A wicker wastepaper basket containing a crumpled newspaper. ... A 14-inch adjustable spanner, of the type used by plumbers. ...

The bed was described with equal precision. One of the sheets, of fine linen and in excellent condition, was embroidered with the letter 'P', 1½ inches in height. ...

Maigret held up two parted fingers, pictured the embroidered letter, sighed and, still reading, picked up the telephone.

'Get me Maître Radel. . . . The lawyer. . . . I don't know his number. . . .'

A few seconds later he was through to him.

'Hello? Maigret here. . . . I'd like you to ask your clients two questions, which will save my going to the Quai de la Gare and taking you along there. . . . Hello? Are you there?'

'Yes. I'm listening.'

The lawyer must be surprised at such punctilio from Maigret.

'The first question is about a spanner. . . . A fourteen-inch spanner. . . . It's in Léonard Lachaume's room, which is sealed up. . . . I'd like to know why it was there. . . . What? . . . Yes. . . . . There may be some perfectly simple reason and I'd be glad to know it. . . .

'Another thing. . . . How many sheets are there in the house? . . . Yes, I'm sorry, I know it's a very down-to-earth subject. . . . Just a moment! . . . Ask whether all the sheets are embroidered with the letter "P", and if not, who were the embroidered ones used for. . . . How many sheets marked like that, and how many without a mark, or with a different one. . . . What? . . . Yes, that's all. . . . At least. . . . I expect you'll take refuge in professional secrecy. . . . How long have you been the Lachaumes' lawyer? . . .'

There was no answer from the other end. Maître Radel was hesitating. Maigret had been surprised, the day before, to find such a young, practically unknown lawyer in a house where he would have expected to meet a crafty old pettifogger.

'What did you say? . . . A week? . . . And lastly, might I ask for whom, precisely, you are acting? . . . Somebody sent for you a week ago, or called on you. . . .'

He listened, shrugged his shoulders, and finally, when the voice stopped speaking, rang off. As he had expected, Radel refused to answer that last question.

He was reaching out for one of his pipes when the telephone rang.

It was Angelot, the magistrate, already in his office well before nine o'clock.

'Chief-Inspector Maigret?'

'Yes, Monsieur Angelot.'

'You had my messages?'

'Certainly. I have read them carefully.'

'I should like to see you as soon as possible.'

'I know. I'm just waiting for one telephone call, in a few minutes, I hope, before coming round to your office.'

Whereupon he did wait, without doing anything else, except smoke and stand looking out of the window. It took six minutes. Radel had been quick.

'I asked first about the spanner. . . . Old Catherine remembers that very well. . . . About a fortnight ago, Léonard Lachaume was indisposed by a smell of gas in his room. . . . They don't use gas any more except in the kitchen, but in the old days the bedrooms were lit by gas and the system is still there. All that was done was to block the pipes with bolts. So Léonard fetched a spanner from the ground-floor workshop. . . . He forgot to take it back, and it's been in a corner of his room ever since. . . .'

'What about the sheets?'

'I couldn't get an exact list, because there are some at the laundry. . . . There are several different marks. . . . The oldest, which are very worn, bear the initials "N.F." and date from the time when the old couple were married. . . . In those days a bride brought with her enough sheets to last a lifetime. . . . They're made of thick cambric and there are several pairs left. . . . Then there are sheets marked "M.L.", that belonged to Léonard's late wife. . . . Twelve pairs, I'm told. . . . Including one scorched by an over-heated iron. . . . Six pairs of almost new sheets, cotton, without initials. . . . Lastly, two dozen better-quality sheets coming from Paulette Lachaume. . . .'

'Are they marked with a "P"?'

'Yes.'

'I suppose the idea was that only she used those?'

'I didn't venture to press that point. I was just told those were her own sheets.'

'Thank you.'

'Might I ask you . . .'

'Nothing, Maître. . . . I know nothing as yet. . . . Excuse me. . . .'

Taking no file with him, he opened the door of the inspectors' office, where Lucas had just arrived.

'If anyone asks for me, I'm with the examining magistrate.'

He had a key to the glass-panelled door leading from Police Headquarters into the *Palais de Justice*, which has been kept carefully locked ever since a prisoner made a getaway through it.

As usual, he recognized several old acquaintances sitting on the benches, some of them between two policemen. He also saw the Canon, who was waiting by the door of one of the examining magistrates and who, without a word, indicated the handcuffs that had been clamped on him, shrugging his shoulders as though to say:

'That's what they're like on this side of the door!'

It was indeed a different world, with a dull smell of bureaucracy and red tape.

He knocked on Angelot's door, found him seated at his desk, smooth-shaven, surrounded by a faint smell of lavender. His secretary, at the end of the table, was hardly older than he.

'Sit down, Chief-Inspector. I was rather surprised, yesterday, to have no news from you right through the afternoon and evening. Am I to conclude that you have discovered nothing, that you have taken no steps likely to interest me?'

The secretary was still there, holding a pencil as though ready to make notes, but fortunately he was not making any.

'Have you been back to the Quai de la Gare?'

'I myself, no.'

'So you have not seen any members of the family or staff again?'

'No.'

'I take it that you and your subordinates have been attending to the case, all the same? I've been thinking about it a great deal myself, and I must admit that although the sum stolen was so trifling, I keep coming back to the idea of a burglary. . . .'

Maigret said nothing, reflecting on the difference between his dream and reality. Was it truly worth while explaining, trying to get the magistrate to understand what . . .

He waited for definite questions.

'What do you think about it?' he was asked at last.

'About a burglary?'

'Yes.'

'I had some figures looked up for you. Do you know how many burglaries there have been in Paris in the last ten years, at night, in private houses or flats, while the occupants were at home?'

The magistrate looked at him, surprised, intrigued.

'Thirty-two,' went on Maigret off-handedly. 'Just over three per year. Apart from the fact that more than a dozen of them must be credited to a kind of artist or lunatic whom we arrested three years ago and who's still in prison, a young chap of twenty-five, who lived with his sister, had no mistress and no men friends, and whose one passion was to bring off the most difficult feats, such as going into a bedroom where a married couple lay asleep and taking the jewellery without giving the alarm. He was never armed, of course.'

'Why do you say "of course"?'

'Because the professional burglar never is armed. He knows the law, from experience, and keeps his risks down to the minimum.'

'But nearly every week . . .'

'Yes, nearly every week you see in the papers that an old trades-woman, a haberdasher, or the keepers of some back-street or suburban shop have been done in. . . . But those aren't really burglaries. . . . Crimes like that are committed by young thugs who are simple-minded, often even half-witted. . . . I also wanted to find out how many real burglaries, in the last ten years, were accompanied or followed by murder. . . . Three, Monsieur. . . . One burglar used a monkey-wrench he had in his pocket. . . . The second picked up a poker on the spot, which he used when he was taken by surprise and threatened. . . . The third did have a firearm, a Luger he'd brought back from the war. . . .'

He repeated:

'Only one! . . . And that was not a 6·35 automatic. . . . I don't think you'd find in the whole of Paris a single professional burglar or criminal using one of those weapons; they are what honest citizens keep in the drawer of the bedside table, and jealous women carry in their hand-bags. . . .'

'If I understand correctly, you rule out the hypothesis of a burglary?'

'I do.'

'Even by an employee, or former employee, for instance?'

'During the evening a Belgian bargeman, whom my men managed to trace, saw somebody propped on a ladder inside the yard, smashing the broken glass on top of the wall.'

'During the evening, or after two o'clock in the morning?'

'During the evening, about ten o'clock.'

'In other words, four hours before the crime?'

'Four hours before the crime.'

'If that is correct, what do you infer from it?'

'Nothing so far. You asked me to keep you informed.'

'Have you made any other discoveries?'

'Paulette Lachaume has a lover.'

'She told you so? I thought you . . .'

'I haven't seen her. She has told me nothing. It was her sister-in-law who unintentionally put me on the track. . . .'

'What sister-in-law?'

'Véronique Lachaume.'

'Where did you find her?'

'In her flat, in the Rue François I$^{er}$. She works as hostess in a night-club of a rather specialized type, the *Amazone*, in the Rue Marbeuf. Her lover, whom she was expecting to marry in the near future, is also Paulette's lover. . . .'

'Did he admit it?'

'Yes.'

'What sort of man is he?'

'The kind you see a great many of round about the Champs-Elysées. . . . His job is advertising. . . . Owes money in all the bars. . . . To begin with, he thought he'd marry Véronique, who owns her flat and has some savings. . . . When he heard about the sister-in-law and her millions, he arranged things so as to meet her, became her lover, and the day before yesterday he had dinner with her and then took her to a flat on the Île Saint-Louis which is lent to him on occasion by an English friend. . . .'

Purposely, not without a mischievous satisfaction, he was pouring out this mixture of information which the magistrate was struggling to classify in his mind.

'You kept him at the Quai des Orfèvres?'

'I didn't take him there.'

'Where does that get us?'

'I don't know. If we dismiss the hypothesis of a burglar or a lunatic and if we credit what the bargeman said, we are driven to the conclusion that the crime was committed by a member of the household. Now, the Judicial Identity men have found a fourteen-inch spanner in Léonard Lachaume's room.'

'The murderer used a revolver. . . .'

'I know. That spanner weighs over two pounds. According to Catherine, the servant, it had been in Léonard's room for the last fortnight, since he had used it to tighten a bolt stopping up the gas pipe. . . .'

'What other information have you?'

The magistrate was becoming irritated by Maigret's ironical placidity. It was obvious, even to the secretary, who was gazing down at the table in embarrassment, that the chief-inspector had deliberately adopted an attitude which, though not hostile nor definitely truculent, was hardly friendly.

'One can't really call it information. . . . For instance, I've just obtained a list of the sheets used in the house. . . .'

'The sheets?'

'Only one sheet, in Léonard's room, is bloodstained. . . . But it is embroidered with a "P" and belongs to Paulette. . . .'

'Is that all?'

'The day before yesterday she left the house on foot, in the rain, at about six o'clock, to meet her lover, who was waiting for her, in a red car, a little way along the quay in front of a grocery. At about the same time, Léonard Lachaume went out, driving his sister-in-law's car, a blue Pontiac. . . . The couple went to a quiet restaurant in the Palais-Royal. *Chez Marcel.* . . Léonard is said to have arrived home at nine o'clock. . . . An hour later, someone, from inside the yard, was crushing the broken glass along the top of the wall with some heavy object, probably a hammer. . . .

'Paulette, after a visit to the Englishman's flat, on the Quai de Bourbon, went home by taxi. . . .'

'Why not in her lover's car?'

'Because at night she was afraid of being noticed.'

'She told you that?'

'Her lover told me. In the corridor she exchanged greetings with Léonard, who was in his dressing-gown. . . .'

Maigret's features suddenly froze, and for a moment he seemed abstracted.

'What are you thinking about?'

'I don't know yet. I shall have to check up. . . .'

All this was very different from his dream, when he had given such a brilliant demonstration of his methods to the invisible examining magistrate. And they were not at the Quai de la Gare. The atmosphere of the house was lacking, the things in it, the past and the present, the visible and the invisible.

All the same he was playing a part, consciously. With poor Coméliau, who had for so long been his personal enemy, there had been open hostility, the old, unacknowledged but always latent rivalry between the Public Prosecutor's Office and the Quai des Orfèvres.

Other magistrates preferred to let him have his own way and wait patiently for him to bring them a complete file, preferably including a signed confession.

In dealing with the new magistrate, Angelot, he was swaggering, in spite of himself, playing, so to speak, the character of Maigret as some people imagined him.

He was a bit ashamed of himself, but he couldn't help it. This was a meeting of two generations, and he wasn't sorry to show this green-horn . . .

'In conclusion . . . ?'

'I have come to no conclusion, *Monsieur le Juge*.'

'If, as you seem to say, it was a member of the family . . .'

'Of the family or the household.'

'Meaning you include the old hunchbacked servant among the suspects?'

'I don't rule out anyone. I'm not going to quote you any more statistics. Three months ago a man killed his neighbour, with a 6·35 automatic, by the way, because the neighbour persisted in playing his wireless at full volume.'

'I don't see the connexion.'

'At first sight it was an idiotic, inexplicable crime. But the murderer is a completely disabled ex-serviceman, who's been trepanned twice and spends his days in pain in an arm-chair. He has nothing but his pension to live on. The neighbour was a tailor, of foreign extraction, who worked at home; he'd been in trouble after the Liberation, and had got out of it. . . .'

'I still don't see . . .'

'What I'm getting at is this. . . . What at first sight appears to be a ridiculous motive—a little music more or less—becomes for the disabled man, when you come to think it over, a vital question. . . . In other words, in the circumstances, the crime was explicable, almost inevitable.'

'I can't see any similar situation at the Quai de la Gare.'

'Yet there must be something, *at least in the mind of the person who killed Léonard Lachaume*. Except for certain rather rare pathological cases, people don't kill except for definite, imperative motives.'

'Have you found that motive in the case we are considering?'

'I've found several.'

But the chief-inspector was suddenly tired of the role he had been drawn into playing.

'I must apologize . . .' he murmured.

He was sincere about it.

'What for?'

'For everything. Never mind. Just now, while talking to you, I had an idea. If you will allow me to make a telephone call, we shall perhaps find things growing clearer.'

The magistrate pushed the telephone towards him.

'Get me the Judicial Identity branch, please. . . . Hello? . . . Yes. . . . Hello? . . . Who's speaking? . . . That you, Moers? Maigret here. . . . I had the report. . . . Yes. . . . It isn't about that I want to talk to you, it's about the inventory. . . . It's quite complete, I suppose? . . . What? . . . I know. . . . I'm quite sure it was done very thoroughly. . . . I just want to be certain that nothing can have been left out. . . .

'. . . The man who typed it may have skipped a line? . . . You have the original list by you? . . . If you'll take it. . . . Good. . . . Now, see if there's no mention of a dressing-gown. . . . I ran over the list rather hurriedly in my office, and it might have escaped me. . . . A dressing-gown, yes. . . . A man's, that's it. . . . I'll hold on. . . .'

He listened while Moers read the list in an undertone.

'No. There's no mention of a dressing-gown. Anyhow, I was there and I didn't see one. . . .'

'Thanks, old man.'

The magistrate and he looked at each other in silence. At last Maigret murmured, as though he were unsure of himself:

'Perhaps, at the stage we've reached, an interrogation might produce some results!'

'An interrogation of whom?'

'That's what I'm wondering.'

And not merely because he was seeking what he sometimes called the point of least resistance. Today there was a personal question as well.

He felt sure Judge Angelot would insist on the interrogation taking place in his office. Perhaps he might even want to conduct it himself?

Maigret felt uncomfortable at the thought of summoning old Lachaume, who already resembled one of the ancestral portraits hanging in the ground-floor office. He would have to be separated from his wife, who could hardly be brought along too. It wasn't even certain that old Lachaume still had all his wits. His eyes seemed to be gazing inwards, and Maigret suspected that he was living entirely among his memories.

As for Catherine, she'd be aggressive, for she was a woman of one idea and would not depart from it. She would deny everything in the teeth of the evidence, not giving a fig for logic. He'd have to look at her hunchbacked figure, listen to her shrill voice.

He didn't know Jean-Paul, had never had a chance to set eyes on him, since the boy had been hurriedly whisked away to boarding-school.

The kid might accidentally have provided some valuable information, but the chief-inspector could imagine how much the examining magistrate would shrink from the idea of bothering a child whose father had died two nights before.

There remained Armand and Paulette.

Armand's epileptic fits were an argument against choosing him. With his back to the wall, might he not be tempted to indulge in one, whether real or sham?

'I think Paulette Lachaume would be the best person to interrogate,' he finally decided, heaving a sigh.

'Have you any specific questions to ask her?'

'Some. Others will develop out of her replies.'

'Do you want me to inform her lawyer?'

Radel would be there, of course. With Angelot, everything would be done according to the rules. It was not without regret that Maigret relinquished his own office, his habits, his little ways, such as choosing the moment to have sandwiches and beer or coffee sent up, or having himself relieved by one of his inspectors, who would innocently begin the interrogation all over again.

The day would come before long when all that would be over and done with, and Maigret's work would be carried out by fellows like Angelot, gentlemanly chaps with a sheaf of degrees.

'I rang him up this morning,' the chief-inspector confessed.

The magistrate frowned.

'About this interrogation?'

He was already prompt to insist on his rights.

'No. To ask him for two of the pieces of information I've just given you. To avoid disturbing the Lachaume family, I decided to apply for it through him.'

'Hello? . . . Get me Maître Radel's office, please. André Radel, that's it. . . . Hello? . . . André? . . .'

The day before, at the Quai de la Gare, Maigret had not heard the two men calling one another by their Christian names.

'Listen. . . . I have Chief-Inspector Maigret in my office. . . . The investigation has reached a point at which certain interrogations seem to be necessary. . . . Yes, of course, in my office. . . . No! I don't intend to disturb the old parents. . . . Nor him . . . for the moment, at any rate. . . . What? . . . What does the doctor say? Oh! . . . Paulette Lachaume, yes. . . . This morning, for choice. . . . Very well. . . . I'll wait for you to call me. . . .'

He rang off, thought fit to explain:

'We went through law school together. . . . He tells me Armand Lachaume is in bed. . . . He had a rather serious attack yesterday evening. . . . The doctor was sent for and is at his bedside again this morning. . . .'

'And Paulette?'

'Radel's going to ring me back. He hopes to bring her along here later in the morning.'

The magistrate seemed embarrassed, cleared his throat, fidgeted with his paper-knife.

'It would be more in order, at the present stage, for me to put the questions, while you intervene only if it becomes necessary. . . . I take it you see no objection to that?'

Maigret saw a great many objections, but what would be the use of saying so?

'Just as you wish.'

'On the other hand it is only natural, I think, for you to give me in writing, before she arrives, the points on which you think I should lay emphasis.'

Maigret nodded.

'Just a few words on a piece of paper. Quite unofficially.'

'Of course.'

'Have you any information about Léonard Lachaume's late wife?'

'She served the same function as Zuber's daughter.'

'That being?'

'To keep the house on the quay and the biscuit factory alive, if one can call it alive, for a time. A similar background, too. Her father began as a foreman and made a fortune as a government contractor. Her dowry was used to stop the leaks.'

'And the money she left?'

'She didn't leave anything, because her father is still alive and may last a long time.'

First Léonard. Then Armand.

Wasn't there something rather touching about this determination to keep the firm afloat, when by all the laws of the business world it should have foundered long ago?

Was it not something like the behaviour of the disabled ex-serviceman who had shot his neighbour because he tortured him from morning to night by turning his radio full on?

It was no accident that Maigret had referred to that case. True, he had been acting a part before the examining magistrate, but in essentials he had been honest with himself.

'Hello, yes. . . . What did she say? . . . How long do you think that will take? . . . About half past eleven? . . . Right. . . . Oh no! It'll be in my office. . . .'

Was Radel so afraid of the interrogation taking place in Maigret's office? Angelot had reassured him, as though saying:

'In my office it will all be done in the proper way. . . .'

The chief-inspector sighed and stood up:

'I'll be here a little before half past eleven.'

'Don't forget to note down the questions that . . .'

'I'll think about them.'

The poor Canon was still waiting resignedly on his bench, between two policemen, for 'his' magistrate to deign to receive him. Maigret winked at him as he went by, and when he got back to his own office, banged the door savagely behind him.


# VIII

WITH his elbows resting heavily on his desk, his forehead supported on his left hand, he wrote a few words, between short puffs of his pipe, then sat for quite a time staring at the watery-looking rectangle of the window.

As though on the eve of an examination, in the days when he had been for two years a medical student, he had re-read all the reports, including, three times over, the famous inventory, of which he was becoming heartily sick.

But he felt less like a student than like a boxer who, within an hour, perhaps within a few minutes, would be staking his reputation, his very career, calling forth jeers or an ovation.

The comparison was not accurate, of course. The magistrate,

Angelot, could not influence a career which in any case would soon end in retirement. And the journalists would know nothing of what was about to take place within the four walls of an office in the *Palais de Justice*.

So there was no question of an ovation. The worst that could happen to Maigret was a reprimand, and, in future, ironical or pitying glances from certain young magistrates to whom Angelot would undoubtedly relate the story.

'As for Maigret and his hunches, have you ever heard . . .'

As soon as he got back to his office, he had called Lucas to give him instructions, and all the inspectors available were now on footwork, as it is called, in the neighbourhood of the Palais-Royal this time, questioning shopkeepers, newsvendors, visiting in their homes or offices any customers of *Chez Marcel* who had been dining on the ground floor on Sunday evening and might have seen something through the windows.

There was only a tiny detail involved, but at the last moment it might become important, even prove conclusive.

Maigret had written out his questions once, then, thinking his writing was not legible enough, had re-copied them.

At ten minutes past eleven, after some hesitation, he had put the sheet of paper into an envelope and sent it by hand to the *Palais de Justice*.

This was a sporting gesture on his part. He was giving Judge Angelot time to get ready, and, in so doing, revealing his own cards.

He did this not so much out of generosity, however, as by the wish to arrive at the last moment and thus avoid another conversation with the magistrate before the interrogation began.

'If anyone rings me up, I'm not in, unless it's one of our chaps.'

He would not speak to Angelot before Paulette appeared, not even on the telephone. Now he was roaming round his office, pausing a moment to look out at the cruel grey Seine, at the black ants going to and fro across the Pont Saint-Michel and weaving their way among the buses.

From time to time he shut his eyes, the better to envisage the house on the Quai de la Gare, and occasionally he uttered a few words under his breath.

Eleven-twenty . . . twenty-three . . . twenty-five. . . .

'I'll be off now, Lucas. If anything fresh comes in, tell them to let me know, and to insist on speaking to me personally.'

As the chief-inspector's bulky figure moved away along the corridor, Lucas's lips outlined, as it were, an inaudible word which began with an 's'.

Maigret caught sight of Maître Radel in the distance, steering Paulette Lachaume towards the magistrate's office; she was wearing a beaver coat, and a hat of the same fur, and the three of them went in almost together, which made the magistrate raise his eyebrows. Did he imagine Maigret had stolen a march on him by waylaying the young woman and her lawyer?

Radel unconsciously reassured him:

'Hullo! Were you just behind us?'

'I came by the side door.'

The magistrate had risen, though he did not actually advance to meet his visitor.

'I must apologize, Madame, for bringing you here. . . .'

She was tired, that could be seen in her face, which looked blurred, almost ravaged. Glancing round mechanically for a chair, she murmured:

'I understand. . . .'

'Please sit down. You too, Maître Radel. . . .'

The two men were not using each other's Christian names now, and to all appearances their relations had never been on anything but a strictly professional footing.

'I believe, Madame, that you already know Chief-Inspector Maigret. . . .'

'Yes, we met at the Quai de la Gare. . . .'

He waited for Maigret to sit down in his turn, near the door, a little behind the others. The seating arrangements took some time. At last the magistrate sat down, looked to see that his secretary was ready to take down the conversation in shorthand, then cleared his throat.

It was his turn to feel awkward, for this time the roles were reversed: he was in the centre of the stage, while Maigret had become the spectator, the onlooker.

'Maître Radel, some of my questions may seem curious to you, as well as to your client. . . . But I think she owes it to herself to answer them frankly, even those that concern her private life. . . .'

She had been expecting this; Maigret felt sure of it, just by looking at her. So she wouldn't be taken by surprise. Radel must have warned her that the police had certainly got wind of her liaison with Sainval.

'The first question concerns you, too, Maître, but I particularly wish the reply to come from Madame Lachaume. . . . On what date, Madame, did you feel the need to consult a barrister? . . .'

Radel was about to protest. A glance from his fellow-lawyer gave him pause, and he turned to his client, who had herself turned towards him, murmuring timidly:

'Must I answer?'

'It will be better if you do.'

'Three weeks ago.'

Looking at the desk, where the judge, on purpose, had laid out various documents, including copies of the reports and the inventory,

Maigret noticed that Angelot was not using his little sheet of paper, but that the questions had been copied on another sheet.

From now on, Angelot regularly glanced at his secretary whenever he was about to speak, to make sure that he was allowing time for everything to be taken down.

The atmosphere was still impersonal, official, and there was no sense of emotion in the air as yet.

'When your father died, it was his usual notary, Maître Wurmster, who dealt with the estate, was it not? And he had the assistance of a barrister who had also acted for your father, Maître Tobias?'

She nodded, but he insisted on an audible reply.

'Yes.'

'Had you a particular reason, three weeks ago, not to turn to your father's lawyer, that is, to Maître Tobias, but to another member of the Bar?'

Radel intervened.

'I do not see the connexion between that question and the events at the Quai de la Gare.'

'You will see it presently, Maître. I would ask your client to be good enough to reply.'

And Paulette Lachaume, almost inaudibly:

'Yes, I think so.'

'You mean you had a reason for changing your lawyer?'

'Yes.'

'Wasn't it that you wished for the help of a specialist?'

Radel was about to protest again, when the magistrate forestalled him.

'By specialist, I mean a lawyer well known for his success in a particular field. . . .'

'Perhaps.'

'And was it not, in fact, about the prospect of a divorce that you went to consult Maître Radel?'

'Yes.'

'Did your husband know of this at the time?'

'I had said nothing to him about it.'

'Might he have suspected your intentions?'

'I don't think so.'

'And your brother-in-law?'

'I don't think so either. Not at that time.'

'Did you pay out money to meet the expenses at the end of last month?'

'Yes.'

'You signed the cheque without arguing about the amount?'

'Yes. I hoped it would be the last. I didn't want a scene.'

'The plans for the divorce were ready?'

Yes.'

'When was it that someone in the house on the Quai de la Gare got wind of your intentions?'

'I don't know.'

'But the suspicion did exist, during these last few days at any rate?'

'I believe so.'

'What makes you believe so?'

'A letter from Maître Radel never reached me.'

'How long ago should that letter have reached you?'

'A week ago.'

'Who used to open the mail?'

'My brother-in-law.'

'So that in all probability Léonard Lachaume intercepted the letter from Maître Radel. Did you have the impression that from then onwards there was something different about the Lachaumes' attitude towards you?'

She visibly hesitated.

'I'm not sure.'

'You did have that impression?'

'My husband seemed to be avoiding me. One evening, when I got home . . .'

'When was that?'

'Last Friday.'

'Go on. You were saying that last Friday, when you got home . . . What time was it?'

'Seven o'clock. . . . I'd been shopping in town. . . . I found everybody in the drawing-room. . . .'

'Old Catherine too?'

'No.'

'So there were your father- and mother-in-law, Léonard and your husband. Was Jean-Paul there?'

'I didn't see him. I suppose he was in his own room.'

'What happened when you arrived?'

'Nothing. Usually I got back later. They weren't expecting me and they all stopped talking. It seemed to me that they were all embarrassed. That evening my mother-in-law didn't dine with us, but went straight up to her room. . . .'

'Until recently, if I'm not mistaken, Jean-Paul slept on the first floor, in the room next to his father's, the room that had formerly been his mother's. . . . When did he move up to the second floor, where he is now alone with the three old people?'

'A week ago.'

'Was it the boy himself who proposed the change?'

'No. He didn't like it.'

'It was your brother-in-law's idea?'

'He wanted to turn Jean-Paul's room into a private study, where he could go after dinner.'

'Was he in the habit of working in the evening?'

'No.'

'What was your reaction?'

'I felt worried.'

'Why?'

She looked at her lawyer. The latter uneasily lit a cigarette. Maigret, motionless in his corner, would have liked to light his pipe, which lay, ready filled, in his pocket, but he didn't dare.

'I don't know. I was frightened. . . .'

'Frightened of what?'

'Of nothing definite. . . . I'd have preferred to get things over without a row, without arguments, tears, pleading. . . .'

'You mean your divorce?'

'Yes. For them, I knew it was a catastrophe. . . .'

'Because since your marriage it is you who have kept the place going. Is that not so?'

'Yes. In any case I meant to leave a certain sum for my husband. I'd spoken to Maître Radel about it. But I wanted to be out of the house the day Armand was served with the papers. . . .'

'Jacques Sainval knew about all this?'

On hearing the name she blinked, and then murmured, with no further sign of surprise:

'Of course. . . .'

The magistrate sat in silence for a little while, looking down at his notes. Before resuming, not without a touch of solemnity, he could not resist a glance at Maigret.

'In fact, Madame Lachaume, your departure meant final collapse for the biscuit factory and for the family as well.'

'I've already told you I would have left money for them.'

'Enough to manage for a long time?'

'For a year at any rate.'

Maigret remembered the words engraved on the brass plate: *Established in 1817.*

Nearly a century and a half. What was one year in comparison? For a century and a half the Lachaumes had held out, and all of a sudden, because a chit like Paulette had made the acquaintance of a greedy advertising agent . . .

'Have you made a will?'

'No.'

'Why not?'

'In the first place, because I have no children. In the second place, because I intended to marry again as soon as it was legally possible.'

'According to your marriage settlement, the fortune goes to the surviving partner of the marriage?'

'Yes.'

'How long have you been frightened?'

Radel tried to put her on her guard, but too late, for she was already answering, without realizing the danger:

'I don't know. . . . A few days. . . .'

'Frightened of what?'

This time she did react, and they saw her fingers clench, her face take on an expression of terror.

'I don't see what you're getting at. Why are you questioning me and not *them*?'

Maigret thought fit to glance encouragingly at the hesitant magistrate.

'Your decision to divorce was final?'

'Yes.'

'Nothing the Lachaumes might have said would have induced you to stay?'

'No. I'd sacrificed myself for long enough. . . .'

For once the words, so often pronounced by women, were not exaggerated. For how long, once she was married, could she have preserved any illusion as to the part she played in the patrician house on the Quai de la Gare?

She had not rebelled. She had done her best to refloat the firm, at least to stop up the holes, and prevent it from foundering once and for all.

'Did you love your husband?'

'I thought so, right at the beginning.'

'You never had any sexual relations with your brother-in-law?'

The magistrate brought out this question with visible distaste, and resented Maigret's having obliged him to ask it.

As she hesitated, he added:

'Did he never try?'

'Once, a long time ago. . . .'

'A year, two years, three years after your marriage?'

'About a year after, when Armand and I moved into separate rooms.'

'You rejected Léonard's advances?'

'Yes.'

The silence that followed was graver, more oppressive than on previous occasions. The atmosphere had imperceptibly changed, and there was a feeling that from now on every word would carry weight, that they were moving towards some redoubtable truth not yet mentioned by anyone.

'Who used to use the sheets embroidered with your initial?'

She answered too quickly. Radel hadn't time to warn her of the trap·
'I did, of course.'
'And no one else?'
'I don't think so. Possibly my husband, occasionally.'
'Not your brother-in-law?'
As she remained silent, he repeated:
'Not your brother-in-law?'
'Not in the ordinary way.'
'There were enough other sheets in the house for all the family's beds?'
'I suppose so.'
'Did you tell Jacques Sainval you were afraid?'
She was beginning to give ground, not knowing which way to look, her hands so tightly clenched that the knuckles were turning white.
'He wanted me to leave the Quai de la Gare at once. . . .'
'Why did you not do so?'
'I was waiting for the divorce papers to be ready. It was only a matter of two or three days longer. . . .'
'In other words, if it were not for your brother-in-law's death, you would have left the house today or tomorrow?'
She sighed.
'Did it occur to you, last week, that someone might try to stop you from going?'
She turned to her lawyer.
'Give me a cigarette. . . .'
And Angelot continued:
'. . . to stop you by no matter what means?'
'I don't know now. You're confusing me.'
She lit the cigarette, put the lighter back into her bag.
'Didn't Sainval warn you to be careful, especially after noticing that your brother-in-law was following you?'
She raised her head sharply.
'How do you know that?'
'When did he follow you?'
'The day before yesterday.'
'Not before that?'
'I'm not sure. . . . Last Thursday, I thought I caught sight of him on the Quai de Bourbon. . . .'
'You were in Sainval's friend's flat?'
She looked at Maigret reproachfully, as though she knew it was he who was responsible for these discoveries.
'Léonard had taken your car?'
'I allowed him to. . . .'
'And you saw him out of the window as he went past?'
'He was driving slowly and looking up at the house. . . .'

'It was then that Sainval gave you a revolver?'

'*Monsieur le Juge* . . .'

Radel raised his hand, stood up.

'At the point we have now reached, I ask your permission to have a short talk with my client.'

The judge and Maigret exchanged glances. Maigret batted his eyelids.

'On condition that it is really short. You may use this room.'

He signed to his secretary. The three men went out into the corridor where Maigret, without loss of time, lit his pipe. He and the magistrate walked up and down among the general concourse, while the secretary sat on the bench beside the door.

'Do you still consider, Monsieur Maigret, that it is not possible to obtain the same results, quietly, without shouting, without theatrical effects, in an examining magistrate's office as at the Quai des Orfèvres?'

What would be the use of replying that all he had done was to reel off the questions prepared by the chief-inspector?

'If things happened as I am beginning to believe they did, Radel will advise her to speak up. . . . It's in her own interest. . . . He should have insisted on it from the first. . . . Unless she hadn't even told the truth to him. . . . Suppose she hadn't replied to my questions, or had been a good liar. Where should we be now?'

Maigret nudged his arm, for he had just caught sight of a faltering figure, a good way off along the endless corridor.

It was Armand Lachaume, obviously lost in the maze of the *Palais de Justice*, reading the notices outside the doors.

'You saw him? We'd better go in again before . . .'

Lachaume had not caught sight of them as yet, and the magistrate knocked at the door of his own office and went in, followed by the chief-inspector and the secretary.

'I apologize. Unforeseen circumstances oblige me to . . .'

Paulette Lachaume, whom they had caught standing up, sat down again, paler than before but more composed, as though relieved. Radel seemed about to make a speech. Just as he opened his mouth the telephone rang, the magistrate picked up the receiver, listened, held it out to the chief-inspector.

'It's for you.'

'Maigret here, yes . . . Two people saw the car? . . . Good! . . . The description fits? . . . Thank you. No . . . See you later. . . .'

He rang off and announced in an expressionless voice:

'Léonard Lachaume was outside the restaurant in the Palais-Royal the night before last.'

Maître Radel gave a shrug, as though all that business was over and done with now. But if the interrogation had taken a different turn, the information would have been valuable, nevertheless.

'My client, *Monsieur le Juge*, is prepared to tell the whole truth, and as you will see, it puts others in a worse light than herself. You must understand, too, and I would like this to be put on record, that her reason for keeping silence so far was not to evade her responsibilities, but out of pity for a family of which she has been a member for several years. . . .

'A jury will ultimately have to express its opinion. We are not putting the Lachaumes in the dock here, but she, who knew them better than we do, has succeeded, for a few days at least, in finding extenuating circumstances for them. . . .'

He sat down, in satisfaction, and straightened his tie.

Paulette Lachaume, not knowing where to start from, began by murmuring:

'For a week, since that letter was intercepted, and specially since I'd caught sight of Léonard on the Quai de Bourbon, I'd been afraid . . .'

If this had been the Quai des Orfèvres, Maigret would have spared her a difficult confession, for he would have told the story himself and she would only have had to agree or, where necessary, to correct him.

'Go on, Madame. . . .'

She was not accustomed to talking in front of a stenographer who took down all she said. It intimidated her. She was groping for words, and several times Maigret had a job to keep from interfering. He had forgotten to put out his pipe, and was still smoking it, in his corner, without realizing the fact.

'It was Léonard who frightened me most, for it was he who kept the firm going, at all costs. . . . Once, a long time ago, when I didn't want to give him a sum that was bigger than usual, he made a speech to me, comparing big business firms to old aristocratic families. . . .

' "We have no right," he said, looking very stern, "to let a firm like ours go out of business. . . . I'd do anything on earth rather than let that happen. . . ."

'I remembered that just lately. . . . I almost walked out of the house at once, without a word, to stay at an hotel until the divorce had gone through. . . .'

'What prevented you?'

'I don't know. I wanted to play the game to the end, everything to be done fairly. . . . It's difficult to explain. . . . You'd need to have lived in that house for years, in order to understand. . . . Armand is a weakling, a sick man, the mere shadow of his brother. . . . And I'd grown fond of Jean-Paul. . . . At the beginning I hoped I'd have children. . . . They hoped so too, were always watching for signs of pregnancy. . . . They were terribly disappointed when nothing happened. . . .

'I wonder if that wasn't why Léonard . . .'

She changed the subject.

'It's true Jacques gave me a revolver. . . . I didn't want to take it. . . .

I was afraid it would be found. . . . At night I used to put it on my bedside table, and in the daytime I kept it in my handbag. . . .'

'Where is it now?'

'I don't know what *they* did with it. Everything was so confused and so crazy, *after* . . .'

'Tell us what happened *before*.'

'I got in about midnight. . . . Half past eleven, perhaps. . . . I didn't notice the time. . . . I'd decided that in any case this was to be the last night but one. . . . I jumped when I saw Léonard's door opening. . . . He watched me go into my room without a word, without saying good night, and that scared me. . . . On my way to the bathroom, after I'd undressed, I saw light under his door. . . . I was even more frightened. . . . It may have been a presentiment. . . . I felt inclined not to get into bed, to sit in an arm-chair and wait in the dark till daybreak. . . .'

'Did you take your sleeping drug?'

'No. I didn't dare. . . . In the end I lay down, with the gun within reach, determined not to fall asleep. I kept my eyes open, listening to the sounds in the house. . . .'

'You heard him coming?'

'More than an hour went by. . . . I think I dozed off for a moment. . . . Then I heard the boards creak in the corridor. . . . I sat up in bed. . . .'

'Your door was not locked?'

'There's no key; hardly any doors in the house have keys, and the lock had been out of order for ages. . . . I had the impression that someone was turning the handle, and then I crept carefully out of bed and flattened myself against the wall, a yard away.'

'Was there a light in the passage?'

'No. Someone came in. I couldn't see anything. I was afraid to shoot too soon, because I was certain that if I missed . . .'

She could not remain seated any longer. She jumped up and went on, looking now not at the magistrate, but at Maigret:

'I could hear someone's breath coming closer. A body nearly touched me. I'm positive an arm was raised to strike at the place on the bed where my head ought to have been. Then, without realizing it, I pressed the trigger. . . .'

Maigret had suddenly frowned. Suddenly careless of his status, he burst out:

'Will you allow me, *Monsieur le Juge?*'

He continued, without waiting for a reply:

'Who turned on the light?'

'I didn't. . . . At least I don't remember doing so. . . . I rushed out into the corridor, without knowing where I was going. . . . I'd probably have run into the street in my nightdress . . .'

'Who did you run into?'

'My husband . . . I suppose it was he who put the light on. . . .'

'He was fully dressed?'

She looked at him with round eyes. After an effort, as though trying to form a definite picture, she murmured:

'Yes. . . . That hadn't occurred to me. . . .'

'What happened?'

'I must have screamed. . . . Anyhow, I remember opening my mouth to do so. . . . Then I fainted. . . . It wasn't till later that the nightmare began. . . . My father-in-law had come down. . . . So had Catherine. . . . It was her voice one heard most. . . . I could hear her in the distance, ordering Jean-Paul back to his room. . . . I saw Armand coming out of my room with a big spanner. . . .'

'The spanner Léonard had tried to hit you with.'

'I suppose so. . . . They ordered me to be quiet, to stop moaning. . . .'

'Who were *they*?'

'My father-in-law. . . . That old witch Catherine. . . . She most of all! . . . It was she who washed the floor and helped Armand to carry the body. . . . And it was she who noticed that there was blood on my sheet, because Léonard had fallen across the turned-down bed. . . .'

'Did they seem astonished at what had happened?' the examining magistrate now asked.

'I wouldn't say that. . . . Distressed, but not astonished. . . . It seemed to be me they were angry with . . .'

The magistrate resumed:

'It was then that they got busy with the ladder and the window-pane?'

'No.'

Maigret took over again.

'Remember, *Monsieur le Juge*, that about ten o'clock that evening, someone, most probably Léonard, had been seen smashing the broken glass on the wall. . . . At about the same time, no doubt, somebody attended to the ladder, the marks on the window-sill, the window-pane smeared with soap. . . .'

She sighed:

'I suppose so. . . .'

Radel began:

'As you see, gentlemen, my client . . .'

'Just a moment!'

The magistrate took a dry, severe tone.

'Who asked you to say nothing and allow the idea of a burglary to be put forward?'

'No one in particular.'

'I'm afraid I don't understand.'

Of course he didn't! He'd been stuffed with theories, and expected the truth to adapt itself to them, to fit into one category or another.

Paulette replied, regardless of putting the magistrate's back up:

'It's easy to see you didn't live through that night! . . . I ended by not knowing what was true and what wasn't. . . . For instance I seem to remember, without being sure it really happened, Catherine's voice croaking:

' "The windows!"

'Because at first they'd turned on all the lights. There are no shutters to the windows, only curtains that don't quite meet in the middle. . . . She had all the lights put out. . . .

'It was she, too, who found an electric torch, in the kitchen, I imagine. . . .

'Then she came back with a bucket. . . .

' "You'd do better to get to bed, Monsieur Armand. . . . You too, Monsieur Félix. . . ."

'But they both stayed there. Another time I asked for some brandy and they wouldn't give it me, saying I mustn't have a drunkard's breath in the morning. . . .'

'What happened in the morning? Did they tell Jean-Paul?'

'No! They told him his uncle had had an attack. . . . When he maintained that he'd heard a shot, everyone assured him it must have been the noise of a train, or a car on the quay, that he'd heard in his sleep. . . .

'As soon as he'd gone off to school, there was a kind of rehearsal. . . .'

She glanced at her lawyer. Was she about to add that she had rung him up to ask his advice? Did he motion to her to keep quiet?

For the last few seconds Maigret had stopped listening, straining his ears to catch a faint sound, as of something brushing against the door.

Just as Paulette was about to resume her story, there was a sharp report, followed by hurried steps, the murmuring of voices.

In the space of a second, the five people in the magistrate's office had stiffened like wax effigies.

There was a knock on the door. Maigret was the first to get up, slowly, and before he opened the door he said quietly, in Paulette's direction:

'I think your husband is dead.'

Armand was sprawled on the dusty floor. He had shot himself in the mouth, and within a few inches of his clenched hand lay a 6·35 automatic.

Then Maigret looked back at the motionless young woman, at the lawyer, who had turned slightly pale, at the magistrate, who had not yet had time to strike an attitude.

All he said was:

'I take it you don't need me any more, *Monsieur le Juge?*'

He made no further remark before walking away along the corridor, towards the small door that led into Police Headquarters.

If all this had taken place through there, perhaps it would have gone differently?

Paulette Lachaume had made a regulation confession.

Her husband had died a regulation death.

Who could say whether that might not be the best thing for both of them?

Now only the three old people were left in the house on the Quai de la Gare, and the descendant of the Lachaumes of 1817 was a boarder at school.

The moment Maigret set foot in his office, Lucas sprang out of the next room, with a question on the tip of his tongue. The chief-inspector had already picked up the telephone to ask for Véronique's number, in the Rue François I$^{er}$.

It would take her some time to get over things; meanwhile she was certainly entitled to know what had happened.

*Noland, 23 October, 1958.*

MAIGRET GOES TO SCHOOL

# MAIGRET GOES TO SCHOOL

---

## I

THERE are certain images which one registers unconsciously, with the precision of a camera, and later, recalling them to memory, racks one's brain to discover where this took place.

Maigret had ceased to realize, after so many years, that each time he arrived, always slightly out of breath, at the top of the steep, dusty staircase at Police Headquarters, he would make a brief pause and glance automatically towards the glass cage which served as a waiting-room and was known to some of his colleagues as 'the aquarium', to others as 'Purgatory'. Perhaps they all did this and it had become a kind of professional reflex.

Even on mornings like this, when bright, pale sunlight, gay as lilies-of-the-valley, was shimmering down on Paris and casting a glow on the pink chimney-pots above the roofs, a lamp was kept burning all day in 'Purgatory', which had no window and whose only light came from the immense corridor.

Sometimes one saw, seated in the arm-chairs or on the green velvet chairs, various seedy-looking characters, old-timers picked up by some inspector during the night and now waiting to be questioned, or else stool-pigeons, or witnesses who had received their summons the day before and now raised melancholy heads whenever anyone went by.

For some mysterious reason, this had been chosen as the place to hang the two black frames, with their gold fillets, which held the photographs of policemen killed while on duty.

There were other people who passed through Purgatory, men and women belonging to what is called 'good society'; and they would remain standing at first, as though about to be sent for at any moment—as though they were just here for an unimportant visit. After a longish time they would be seen to move over to a chair on which they would finally sit down, and it was not unusual to find them still there three hours later, shrunk into themselves, mournful-eyed, having lost all sense of their social precedence.

On this particular morning there was only one man in Purgatory, and Maigret noticed that he belonged to the type commonly known as 'rat-faced'. He was on the thin side. His bare, receding forehead was crowned by a fluff of reddish hair. His eyes were doubtless blue or violet, and the forward thrust of his nose was all the more apparent in contrast to his receding chin.

Everywhere, from schooldays onward, we meet people of this kind, and there is, heaven knows why, a tendency not to take them seriously.

Maigret felt he paid so little attention to the man that if, as he opened the door of his own office, he had been asked who was in the waiting-room, he might have been unable to reply. It was five minutes to nine. The window was wide open and a light, goldish-blue haze was drifting up from the Seine. For the first time this year he had put on his thinner overcoat, but the air was still cool; you wanted to drink it in like some light, white wine, and it made the skin on your face feel taut.

Taking off his hat, he glanced at the visiting-card which lay in full view on his blotter. It bore, in pale ink, the words '*Joseph Gastin, schoolmaster*'. And in the right-hand corner, in small letters which he had to bend forward to read, '*Saint-André-sur-Mer*'.

He did not connect this card with the rat-faced man, only wondered where he had heard of Saint-André-sur-Mer. The bell rang in the corridor as a summons to the daily report. He removed his overcoat, picked up the file he had prepared the day before, and set off, as he had done for so many years, to the Chief's office. On the way he met other chief-inspectors, and their eyes all reflected the mood he had noticed in the passers-by in the street.

'This time it's really spring!'

'Seems like it.'

'Going to be a wonderful day.'

Sunshine was pouring in through the big windows of the Chief's office, as though through the windows of a country church, and pigeons were cooing on the stone ledge outside.

Each man, as he came in, rubbed his hands and made the same remark:

'This is spring.'

They were all over forty-five years old; the matters they were about to discuss were serious, in some cases ghastly, but all the same they were as happy as children because of the sudden mildness of the air, and above all because of the light that was flooding down on the city and transforming every street-corner, the house-fronts, the roofs, the cars crossing the Pont Saint-Michel, into pictures that one would have liked to hang on the wall.

'Have you seen the assistant manager of the bank in the Rue de Rivoli, Maigret?'

'I have an appointment with him in half an hour.'

An unimportant affair. This was an almost empty week. The assistant manager of the branch office of a bank in the Rue de Rivoli, just near the central markets, suspected one of his clerks of dishonesty.

He filled his pipe and looked out of a window while his colleague from General Information was discussing another matter—some business about a Senator's daughter who had got herself into an awkward situation.

Back in his own office, he found Lucas waiting, with his hat already on, to go to the Rue de Rivoli with him.

'Shall we walk?'

It was quite near. Maigret didn't give another thought to the visiting-card. Going past Purgatory, he saw the rat-faced man again, and two or three other 'clients', one of whom was a night-club proprietor whom he recognized and who was there because of the Senator's daughter.

They walked to the Pont Neuf, the pair of them, Maigret with long strides, and the short-legged Lucas obliged to take many more steps in order to keep up with him. They couldn't have said, afterwards, what they had talked about. Perhaps they had merely been looking around them. In the Rue de Rivoli there was a strong smell of vegetables and fruit, and lorries were removing loads of crates and baskets.

They went into the bank, listened to the assistant manager's explanations, walked round the premises, casting sidelong glances at the suspected clerk.

For lack of proofs, they decided to set a trap for him. They discussed the details, then said good-bye. Maigret and Lucas left and found it so warm outside that they carried their overcoats instead of putting them on again, which gave them a kind of holiday feeling.

In the Place Dauphine, they stopped with one accord.

'Shall we have a quick one?'

It was too early for an *apéritif*, but they both felt that the taste of *pernod* would make a wonderful accompaniment to the spring atmosphere, and in they went to the Brasserie Dauphine.

'Two *pernods*, quickly!'

'D'you happen to know Saint-André-sur-Mer?'

'Isn't it somewhere in the Charentes?'

This reminded Maigret of the beach at Fourras, in the sunshine, the oysters he had eaten at about this time, half past ten in the morning, on the terrace of a little *bistrot*, washing them down with a bottle of the local white wine, at the bottom of which lay a few grains of sand.

'Think that clerk is a swindler?'

'His boss seems positive about it.'

'He looked a poor devil to me.'

'We shall know in a couple of days.'

They strolled along the Quai des Orfèvres, went up the big staircase, and once again Maigret paused. Rat-face was still there, leaning forward, his long, bony hands clasped on his knees. He looked up at Maigret with what the chief-inspector felt to be a reproachful expression.

In his office he found the visiting-card lying where he had left it, and rang for the office-boy.

'Is he still here?'

'Ever since eight o'clock. He was here before me. He insists on speaking to you personally.'

Any number of people, most of them mad or half-crazy, used to ask to speak personally to the Chief or to Maigret, whose names they had come to know from the newspapers. They would refuse to be fobbed off with an inspector, and some would wait all day and come back next morning, standing up hopefully whenever the chief-inspector went by, only to sit down and wait again.

'Bring him in.'

He sat down, filled two or three pipes, signed to the man, when he was shown in, to sit down opposite him. Picking up the visiting-card, he asked:

'Is this yours?'

Looking more closely, he realized that the man had probably had no sleep, for he was grey-faced, with red eyelids and unnaturally bright eyes. His hands were folded, as they had been in the waiting-room, with the fingers clenched so tightly that the joints cracked.

Instead of answering the question, he muttered, with an anxious yet resigned glance at the chief-inspector:

'You know about it?'

'About what?'

The man looked surprised, confused, disappointed perhaps.

'I thought it was already known. I left Saint-André yesterday evening and a journalist had arrived by then. I took the night train. I've come straight here.'

'Why?'

He seemed to be intelligent, but was obviously very upset and didn't know where to begin his story. Maigret awed him. He had doubtless known him by repute for a long time and, like a lot of people, looked upon him as someone endowed with almost divine powers.

At a distance he had thought it would be easy. But now he was confronted by a man in flesh and blood, smoking his pipe with short puffs and watching him with wide-open, almost expressionless eyes.

Was that how he had imagined him? Wasn't he beginning to be sorry he had come?

'They must be thinking I've run away,' he said nervously, with a bitter smile. 'If I were guilty, as they feel sure I am, and if I'd meant to run away, I shouldn't be here now, should I?'

'I can't very well answer that question till I know more about it,' murmured Maigret. 'What are you accused of?'

'Of killing Léonie Birard.'

'Who's accusing you?'

'The whole village, more or less openly. The local police chief didn't dare to arrest me. He admitted frankly that he hadn't sufficient evidence, but he asked me not to go away.'

'All the same, you went?'

'Yes.'

'Why?'

The visitor, too tense to remain seated for long, sprang to his feet, stuttering:

'Do you mind?'

He didn't know where to stand or what to do with himself.

'I sometimes even forget what's going on.'

He pulled a grubby handkerchief from his pocket, mopped his forehead. The handkerchief probably still smelt of the train, and of his sweat.

'Have you had breakfast?'

'No. I was in a hurry to get here. Above all, I didn't want to be arrested before that, you understand.'

How could Maigret have understood?

'Why, exactly, have you come to see me?'

'Because I have confidence in you. I know that if you will, you can find out the truth.'

'When did this lady . . . what did you say her name was?'

'Léonie Birard. She used to be our postmistress.'

'When did she die?'

'She was killed on Tuesday morning. The day before yesterday. Soon after ten o'clock in the morning.'

'And you are being accused of the crime?'

'You were born in the country, I saw that in a magazine. You spent most of your childhood there. So you must know the sort of thing that happens in a small village. The population of Saint-André is only three hundred and twenty.'

'Just a minute. This crime was committed in the Charentes?'

'Yes. About nine miles north-west of La Rochelle, not far from the Aiguillon headland. You know it?'

'A little. But it so happens that I belong to Police Headquarters in Paris and have no authority in the Charentes.'

'I thought of that.'

'Well, then . . .'

The man was wearing his best suit, which was threadbare; his shirt had a frayed collar. Standing in the middle of the room he had his head lowered, and was staring at the carpet.

'Of course . . .' he sighed.

'What do you mean?'

'I was wrong. I don't know, now. It seemed quite natural at the time.'

'What did?'

'Coming to put myself under your protection.'

'Under my protection?' repeated Maigret in surprise.

Gastin ventured to glance at him, with the air of a man wondering how he stands.

'Down there, even if they don't arrest me, something unpleasant may happen to me.'

'They don't like you?'

'No.'

'Why not?'

'In the first place, because I'm the schoolmaster and the secretary of the *mairie*.'

'I don't understand.'

'It's a long time since you lived in the country. They've all got money. They're farmers or else *bouchoteurs*. You know the *bouchots*?'

'The mussel-beds, along the coast?'

'Yes. We're right in the *bouchot* and oyster district. Everybody owns at least part of one. It's very profitable. They're rich. Nearly everyone has a car or a small van. But do you know how many of them pay income-tax?'

'Very few, I dare say.'

'Not one! In our village, the doctor and I are the only tax-payers. Naturally, they call me an idler. They imagine it's they who pay my salary. When I complain because the children don't come to school, they tell me to mind my own business. And when I told my pupils to touch their caps to me in the street, they asked me who I thought I was.'

'Tell me about the Léonie Birard business.'

'You mean it?'

With the return of hope, his expression had become firmer. He made himself sit down, tried to speak calmly, though he could not prevent his voice from trembling with ill-controlled emotion.

'You'd need to know the lay-out of the village. It's difficult to explain at this distance. As in almost all villages, the school is just behind the *mairie*. I live there too, on the other side of the courtyard, and I have a scrap of kitchen-garden. On Tuesday, the day before yesterday, the weather was just about what it is today, a real spring day, and it was a neap-tide.'

'Is that important?'

'At the neap-tide, that is to say during the period when the ebb and flow of the tides is slight, nobody goes out for mussels or oysters. You understand?'

'Yes.'

'Beyond the school playground there are gardens and the backs of several houses, including Léonie Birard's.'

'What sort of age was she?'

'Sixty-six. Being the secretary of the *mairie*, I know everyone's exact age.'

'Of course.'

'She retired eight years ago and became practically crippled. She never goes out any more, and hobbles round the house with a stick. She's a nasty woman.'

'In what way nasty?'

'She hates everybody.'

'Why?'

'I don't know. She's never married. She had a niece who lived with her a long time and who's married to Julien, the ironmonger, who is also the village policeman.'

On another day Maigret might have found these stories boring. That morning, what with the sun shining in through his window and bringing a spring-like warmth with it, and his pipe which had an unaccustomed taste, he was listening with a vague smile to words that reminded him of another village, which had also had its dramatic incidents between the postmistress, the schoolmaster and the village policeman.

'The two women aren't on speaking terms any longer, because Léonie didn't want her niece to get married. She's not on speaking terms with Dr. Bresselles, either; she said he'd tried to poison her with his drugs.'

'Did he try to poison her?'

'Of course not! That's just to show you the kind of woman she is, or rather was. When she was postmistress she used to listen in on telephone calls, read postcards, so that she knew everyone's secrets. She found no difficulty in working up bad feeling between people. Most quarrels in families or between neighbours were started by her.'

'So she wasn't popular?'

'She certainly wasn't.'

'Well, then . . .'

Maigret's manner suggested that this simplified everything, that the death of a woman who was universally hated could bring nothing but delight to everyone.

'But I'm not popular either.'

'Because of what you told me?'

'Because of that and all the rest. I'm not a local man. I was born in Paris, in the Rue Caulaincourt in the XVIIIth *arrondissement*, and my wife comes from the Rue Lamarck.'

'Does your wife live at Saint-André with you?'

'We live together, with our son, who's thirteen years old.'

'Does he go to your school?'

'There's no other for him to go to.'

'Do the other boys hold it against him, that he's the teacher's son?'

Maigret remembered about that, too. He remembered it from his own boyhood. The tenant-farmers' sons had held it against him that his father was the estate manager, to whom their fathers had to submit accounts.

'I don't favour him, I assure you. In fact I rather suspect he purposely works less well than he could.'

He had gradually calmed down. His eyes had lost their frightened expression. This was no lunatic, inventing a story to make himself interesting.

'Léonie Birard had developed a special dislike of me.'

'For no reason?'

'She used to say I stirred up the children against her. But that was quite untrue, Inspector. On the contrary, I always tried to make them behave politely. She was very fat, huge in fact. It seems she wore a wig. And she had a hairy face, a definite moustache and black bristles on her chin. That's enough to set the children off, don't you see? Added to which, she would get into a rage at the slightest thing, for instance, if she saw some child peering in at her window and putting its tongue out. She'd get up from her arm-chair and shake her stick threateningly. That amused them. One of their favourite games was to go and make old mother Birard angry.'

Hadn't there been an old woman like that in his own village? In his day it was old mother Tatin, who kept the draper's shop, and the children used to tease her cat.

'I'm afraid I'm boring you with these details, but they have a certain importance. There were some more serious incidents, such as when some of the boys broke glass panes at her house, and when they threw filth in at the windows. She complained to the police any number of times. The constable called on me, asked me who'd done it.'

'Did you tell him?'

'I said they were all more or less mixed up in it, and that if only she'd stop trying to play at scarecrow by brandishing her stick, they'd probably calm down.'

'What happened on Tuesday?'

'Early in the afternoon, about half past one, Maria, a Polish woman with five children, who works as a char, went to Mère Birard's house, as she did every day. The windows were open, and from the school I heard her shrieks, the words she started to rattle off in her own language, as she does whenever she's upset. Her full name is Maria Smelker, and she came to the village when she was sixteen, as a farm servant; she's never been married. Her children have various fathers. It's said that at least two of them belong to the deputy-mayor. He hates me too, but that's another story. I'll tell you later about that.'

'So on Tuesday, about half past one, Maria cried for help?'

'Yes. I didn't leave the classroom, because I heard other people hurrying towards the old woman's house. After a short time I saw the doctor's little car go by.'

'You didn't go to have a look?'

'No. Some people are blaming me for that now, saying that the reason why I didn't move was because I knew what they'd found.'

'You couldn't leave the class, I suppose?'

'I could have done. I sometimes do, for a moment, to sign documents in the office at the *mairie*. Besides, I could have called my wife.'

'Is she a teacher?'

'She used to be.'

'In the country?'

'No. We were both teaching at Courbevoie, where we stayed for seven years. When I asked to be moved to the country, she handed in her resignation.'

'Why did you leave Courbevoie?'

'Because of my wife's health.'

The subject embarrassed him. He was answering less frankly.

'So, you didn't call your wife, as you sometimes do, and you stayed with your pupils.'

'Yes.'

'What happened next?'

'For more than an hour there was a great to-do. The village is usually very quiet. Noises can be heard a long way off. The hammering at Marchandon's smithy stopped. People were calling out to one another across the garden hedges. You know how it is when anything like that happens. So that the pupils shouldn't get excited, I went and closed the windows.'

'From the school windows you can see into Léonie Birard's house?'

'From one of the windows, yes.'

'What did you see?'

'To begin with, the village policeman; that surprised me, as he wasn't on speaking terms with his wife's aunt. And then Théo, the deputy-mayor, who must have been half drunk, as he usually is after ten o'clock in the morning. I saw the doctor, too, other neighbours, the whole lot bustling about in one room and looking down at the floor. Later on, the police lieutenant arrived from La Rochelle with two of his men. But I didn't know that until he knocked on the classroom door, and by that time he'd already put questions to a number of people.'

'He accused you of killing Léonie Birard?'

Gastin threw the chief-inspector a reproachful glance, as if to say:

'You know quite well it doesn't happen like that.'

And in rather flat tones, he explained:

'I noticed at once that he was looking strangely at me. The first thing he asked was:

'"Do you own a rifle, Gastin?"'

'I said I didn't, but that Jean-Paul, my son, had one. That's another complicated story. You know what it's like with children, I expect. One morning one of them arrives at school with some marbles, and by next day all the boys are playing marbles, their pockets are bulging with them. Another day someone produces a kite, and kites are in fashion for weeks.

'Well, last autumn, someone or other brought a .22 rifle, and began shooting at sparrows with it. Within a month we had half a dozen guns of the same type. My boy wanted one for Christmas. I saw no reason to refuse. . . .'

Even the gun stirred memories in Maigret; the only difference was that his, in the old days, had been an air-gun and fired pellets that did no more than ruffle the birds' feathers.

'I told the police lieutenant that so far as I knew, the gun was in Jean-Paul's room. He sent one of his men to find out. I ought to have asked the boy. It didn't occur to me. As it happened, the gun wasn't there, he'd left it in the hut in the kitchen garden, where I keep the wheelbarrow and the tools.'

'Léonie Birard was killed with a .22 rifle?'

'That's the most extraordinary thing. And it isn't all. The police lieutenant then asked me whether I'd left the classroom during that morning, and unfortunately I said no.'

'You had left?'

'For about ten minutes, soon after the morning break. When you're asked a question like that, you answer without thinking. Break finishes at ten o'clock. A little later—five minutes, perhaps—Piedbœuf, from Gros-Chêne farm, came to ask me to sign a paper he needed in order to draw his pension—he was disabled in the war. I usually have the *mairie* stamp in the classroom. That morning I hadn't got it, and I took the farmer along to the office. The children seemed quiet. As my wife isn't well, I went across the yard afterwards, to see if she needed anything.'

'Your wife has bad health?'

'It's chiefly nerves. In all, I may have been away for ten or fifteen minutes, more like ten than fifteen.'

'You didn't hear anything?'

'I remember Marchandon was shoeing a horse, because I heard the hammer clanging on the anvil and there was a smell of singed horn in the air. The forge is next to the church, nearly opposite the school.'

'That's the time when Léonie Birard's supposed to have been killed?'

'Yes. They think someone must have shot her from one of the gardens, or from a window, when she was in her kitchen, at the back of the house.'

'She was killed by a .22 bullet?'

'That's the strangest thing of all. A bullet like that, fired from some way off, ought not to have done her much harm. But the fact is that it went into her head through the left eye and flattened against the skull.'

'Are you a good shot?'

'People think so, because they saw me at target-practice with my son during the winter. It happened three or four times, perhaps. Apart from that I've never touched a rifle, except on a fairground.'

'Didn't the lieutenant believe you?'

'He didn't definitely accuse me, but he seemed surprised that I hadn't admitted leaving the classroom. Afterwards, when I wasn't there, he questioned the children. He didn't tell me what the interrogation led to. He went back to La Rochelle. Next day—yesterday, that is—he came and settled down in my office, at the *mairie*, with Théo, the deputy-mayor, beside him.'

'Where were you then?'

'I was taking school. Out of thirty-two pupils, only eight had turned up. They sent for me twice to ask me the same questions, and the second time they made me sign my statement. They questioned my wife too. They asked her how long I'd stayed with her. They interrogated my son about the rifle.'

'But you weren't arrested.'

'I wasn't arrested yesterday. I feel sure I would have been today if I'd stayed at Saint-André. Just after dark, stones were thrown at our house. It upset my wife a lot.'

'You went off by yourself, leaving her there alone with your son?'

'Yes. I don't think they'll dare do anything to them. Whereas if they arrest me, they'll give me no chance to defend myself. Once I'm shut up I shan't be able to communicate with the outside world. No one will believe me. They'll do whatever they like with me.'

Again his forehead was damp with sweat and his linked fingers so tightly clenched that the blood could not circulate.

'Perhaps I was wrong? I thought that if I told you all about it, you would perhaps come and find out the truth. I'm not offering you money. I know that isn't what interests you. I swear to you, Inspector, that I didn't kill Léonie Birard.'

Maigret extended a hesitant hand towards the telephone, finally lifted the receiver.

'What's the name of your constabulary lieutenant?'

'Daniélou.'

'Hello! Get me the constabulary at La Rochelle. If Lieutenant Daniélou isn't there, see if you can find him at the *mairie* at Saint-André-sur-Mer. Put him through to me in Lucas's office.'

He rang off, lit a pipe, and went over to stand facing the window.

He was pretending to take no further notice of the schoolmaster, who had opened his mouth two or three times to thank him, but had not found the words.

The brilliant yellow glow in the air was gradually gaining over the blue, and the house-fronts across the Seine were changing to a creamy hue; the sun was reflected in an attic window somewhere at a distance.

'Was it you who asked for Saint André-sur-Mer, Chief?'

'Yes, Lucas. Stay here a minute.'

He went into the next-door office.

'Lieutenant Daniélou? This is Maigret, of Police Headquarters in Paris. I hear you're looking for someone?'

At the other end of the line, the constabulary officer was astounded.

'How did you know that already?'

'It's the schoolmaster?'

'Yes. I was a fool not to keep an eye on him. It never occurred to me that he'd try to give me the slip. He took the train to Paris last night, and . . .'

'You're bringing a charge against him?'

'A very serious one. And I have at least one damaging piece of evidence, acquired this morning.'

'Who from?'

'One of his pupils.'

'He saw something?'

'Yes.'

'What?'

'He saw the schoolmaster coming out of his tool-shed on Tuesday morning, about twenty past ten. And it was at a quarter past ten that the deputy-mayor heard a shot.'

'Have you asked the examining magistrate for an arrest warrant?'

'I was just off to La Rochelle to do it when you rang up. How did you know about it? Have the newspapers . . . ?'

'I haven't seen the newspapers. Joseph Gastin is in my office.'

There was a silence, then the lieutenant let out an:

'Ah!'

Whereupon he would doubtless have liked to ask a question. But he didn't do so. Maigret, for his part, was rather at a loss what to say. He had not made up his mind. If the sun had not been shining so brightly that morning, if the chief inspector hadn't, a little time ago, suddenly remembered Fourras, the oysters and the white wine, if he hadn't been over ten months without a chance of a holiday, even for three days, if . . .

'Hello? Are you still there?'

'Yes. What do you intend to do with him?'

'Bring him back to you.'

'Yourself?'

The tone was not enthusiastic, and the chief-inspector smiled.

'You may be sure I shall not dream of interfering in any way in your investigation.'

'You don't think he's . . .'

'I don't know. Perhaps he's guilty. Perhaps he isn't. Anyhow, I'm bringing him back to you.'

'Thank you. I'll be at the station.'

Back in his own office, he found Lucas gazing curiously at the schoolmaster.

'Wait another minute. I must have a word with the Chief.'

His work would allow him to take a few days off. When he came back, he asked Gastin:

'Is there an inn at Saint-André?'

'Yes, the *Bon Coin*, run by Louis Paumelle. The food's good, but the rooms don't have running water.'

'Are you going away, Chief?'

'Get my wife on the phone for me.'

All this was so unexpected that poor Gastin was dumbfounded, not yet daring to feel delighted.

'What did he say to you?'

'He'll probably arrest you the moment we get out of the train.'

'But . . . you're coming with me . . . ?'

Maigret nodded and took the telephone receiver which Lucas was holding out to him.

'That you, dear? Would you pack me a small suitcase, just underclothes and toilet things? . . . Yes. . . . Yes. . . . I don't know. . . . Three or four days, perhaps. . . .'

He added gleefully:

'I'm going to the seaside, in the Charentes. Right among the oysters and mussels. Meantime, I'll be lunching at a restaurant. See you presently. . . .'

He felt as though he were playing a joke on someone, like the small boys who had teased old Léonie Birard so much and for so long.

'Come along and have a bite with me,' he said finally to the schoolmaster, who got up and followed him as though in a dream.


II


AT Poitiers, while the train was in the station, the lights went up all at once along the platforms, but it wasn't dark yet. It was not until later, when they were crossing the open fields, that they noticed that night was falling, the windows of the scattered farm-houses starting to gleam like stars.

Then suddenly, a few miles outside La Rochelle, a light mist, which came not from the country but from the sea, began to mingle with the darkness, and the spark of a distant lighthouse shone for a moment.

There were two other people in the carriage, a man and a woman, who had been reading throughout the journey, looking up occasionally to exchange a few words. Most of the time, especially towards the end, Joseph Gastin had kept his weary eyes fixed on the chief-inspector.

The train crossed some points. Small houses slid past. The lines became more numerous, and at last they reached the platforms, the doors with their familiar notices, the people waiting, looking just like the people in previous stations. The moment the carriage door opened one felt a strong, cool breath from the empty blackness into which the rails seemed to vanish; and looking more attentively, one saw ships' masts and gently-rocking funnels, heard gulls screaming, recognized the smell of salt water and tar.

The three uniformed men standing near the entrance did not move. Lieutenant Daniélou was still young, with a little black moustache and thick eyebrows. Not until Maigret and his companion were within a few paces did he step forward, holding out his hand with a military gesture.

'Delighted, Chief-Inspector,' he said.

Maigret, noticing that one of the policemen was producing a pair of handcuffs from his pocket, murmured to the lieutenant:

'I don't think that's necessary.'

The lieutenant made a sign to his subordinate. A few heads had turned in their direction, not many. The passengers were trooping out, weighed down by their suitcases, now walking diagonally across the entrance hall.

'I have no intention of interfering in your inquiry in any way, Lieutenant. I hope you understand that. I'm not here in any official capacity.'

'I know. I discussed it with the examining magistrate.'

'I hope he isn't annoyed?'

'On the contrary, he's delighted that we'll be able to have your help. As things stand at present we can't do otherwise than put him under arrest.'

Joseph Gastin, three feet away, was pretending not to listen, could not help overhearing.

'Anyway, it's in his own interest. He'll be safer in prison than anywhere else. You know how people react in small towns and villages.'

All this was rather stilted. Maigret himself didn't feel too comfortable.

'Have you had dinner?'

'Yes, on the train.'

'Do you mean to spend the night at La Rochelle?'

'I'm told there's an inn at Saint-André.'

'May I offer you a drink?'

As Maigret neither accepted nor refused, the lieutenant turned to give orders to his men, who moved towards the schoolmaster. There was nothing the chief-inspector could say to Gastin, so he merely gave him a serious look.

'You heard. You'll have to go through with it,' he seemed to be saying apologetically. 'I'll do my best.'

Gastin gazed back at him, turned his head shortly afterwards for another glance, finally went out of the door, walking between the two constables.

'We'll do best to go to the buffet,' murmured Daniélou. 'Unless you'd like to come to my place?'

'Not tonight.'

A few travellers were eating in the ill-lit refreshment-room.

'What will you have?'

'I don't know. A brandy.'

They sat down in a corner, at a table which was still laid for dinner.

'You're not having anything to eat?' asked the waitress.

They shook their heads. Not until the drinks came did the lieutenant inquire, with an air of embarrassment:

'You think he's innocent?'

'I don't know.'

'Until the boy gave his evidence we were able to leave him at liberty. Unfortunately for him that evidence is conclusive, and the boy seems sincere, he has no reason to be lying.'

'When did he tell his story?'

'This morning, when I questioned the whole class for the second time.'

'He hadn't said anything yesterday?'

'He was scared. You'll see him. If you like I'll give you the file tomorrow morning, when I'm down there. I spend most of my time at the *mairie*.'

There was still a certain awkwardness. The lieutenant seemed over-awed by the chief-inspector's massive bulk and by his reputation.

'You're accustomed to the things and people of Paris. I don't know if you're used to the atmosphere of our small villages.'

'I was born in a village. What about you?'

'At Toulouse.'

He managed to smile.

'Would you like me to drive you out there?'

'I think I'll find a taxi.'

'If you'd rather. There's a rank outside the station.'

They parted at the door of the taxi, which drove off along the sea-front, and Maigret leant forward to make out the fishing-boats in the darkness of the harbour.

He was disappointed to have arrived at night. When they turned away from the sea and left the town, they drove through a stretch of country that looked like any other stretch, and soon, at the third village, the car stopped outside a lighted window.

'Is this it?'

'You said the *Bon Coin*, didn't you?'

A very stout man came to look out through the glass-panelled door, and, without opening it, watched while Maigret went to and fro, took out his suitcase, put it on the ground, paid the driver, finally walked towards the inn.

Men were playing cards in a corner. The inn smelt of wine and stew, and smoke hovered round the two lamps.

'Have you a room?'

Everyone was staring at him. A woman came to the kitchen door to look at him.

'For the night?'

'For two or three days, perhaps.'

They looked him up and down.

'Have you your identity card? The constables come here every morning and we have to keep the register up to date.'

The four men had stopped playing, were listening. Maigret, now standing at the counter, which was loaded with bottles, held out his card and the landlord put on his glasses to read it. When he looked up again, he gave a sly wink.

'So you're the famous inspector? My name's Paumelle, Louis Paumelle.'

He turned towards the kitchen and called:

'Thérèse! Take the inspector's suitcase up to the front room.'

Without paying special attention to the woman, who looked about thirty years old, Maigret had the impression that he'd seen her before somewhere. It only struck him later on, as with the people he used to see when he went past 'Purgatory'. He thought she had given a slight start, too.

'What will you take?'

'Whatever you have. A brandy, if you like.'

The others, for the sake of appearances, had returned to their game of *belote*.

'You've come because of Léonie?'

'Not officially.'

'Is it true the schoolmaster has been found in Paris?'

'He's in the prison at La Rochelle by now.'

It was hard to guess what Paumelle thought of the business. Although he was an innkeeper, he looked more like a peasant in his own farm.

'You don't think he did it?'

'I don't know.'

'I imagine that if you reckoned he was guilty you wouldn't have come all this way. Am I right?'

'Maybe.'

'Your very good health! There's a man here who heard the shot. Théo! It's true you heard the shot, isn't it?'

One of the card-players, sixty-five years old or perhaps more, his reddish hair going white here and there, cheeks unshaven, and his eyes shifty and spiteful, turned towards them.

'Why shouldn't I have heard it?'

'This is Inspector Maigret, who's come from Paris to . . .'

'The lieutenant told me about it.'

He did not get up nor give any greeting; he was holding his grimy cards between black-nailed fingers. Paumelle explained in an undertone:

'That's the deputy-mayor.'

And Maigret, in his turn, answered just as laconically:

'I know.'

'You mustn't take any notice. By this time of night . . .'

He made the gesture of emptying a glass.

'What about you, Ferdinand, what did you see?'

The man he called Ferdinand had only one arm. His complexion was ruddy-brown, that of a man who spent all his time out of doors.

'The postman,' explained Louis. 'Ferdinand Cornu. What did you see, Ferdinand?'

'Nothing at all.'

'You saw Théo in his garden.'

'I even brought him a letter.'

'What was he doing?'

'Planting out onions.'

'What time was it?'

'Just ten by the church clock. I could see the clock-face, above the houses. *Belote! Rebelote!* My nine beats it . . . Ace of spades, King of diamonds, takes all . . .'

He flung down his cards on the table where the glasses had left a wet circle, and glared defiantly at the other players.

'And to hell with people who come here to make trouble for us!' he added, getting to his feet. 'Pay up, Théo.'

His movements were clumsy, his gait unsteady. He took down his postman's cap from a peg and made for the door, growling out something indistinguishable.

'Is he like that every evening?'

'Pretty much.'

Louis Paumelle was about to fill the two glasses, and Maigret put out a hand to stop him.

'Not for the moment. . . . You won't be closing just yet, I suppose, and I've time for a stroll before going to bed?'

'I'll wait for you.'

He went out, amid dead silence. He found himself in a small open space, neither round nor square, with the dark mass of the church to his right, opposite him an unlighted shop, above whose window he could just decipher the words: '*Coopérative Charentaise*'.

There was a light in the house at the corner, a grey stone-built place. The light came from the first floor. Going up to the door, with its three steps, Maigret noticed a brass plate, lit a match, and read:

### *Xavier Bresselles: M.D.*

For lack of something to do, and puzzled as to how to make a beginning, he was on the point of ringing the bell; then he shrugged his shoulders and reflected that the doctor was probably getting ready for bed.

Most of the houses were in darkness. He recognized the *mairie*, a one-storey building, by its flagstaff. It was a very small *mairie*, and above its courtyard a lamp was burning in a first-floor room of a building, probably the Gastins' house.

He went down the road, turned to the right, strolled past some houses and gardens, not long afterwards met the deputy-mayor, who was coming up from the opposite direction and gave a grunt by way of good night.

He could neither hear the sea nor get any glimpse of it. The slumbering village looked like any small country place and did not fit in with his expectation of oysters with white wine on a café terrace overlooking the ocean.

He was disappointed, for no definite reason. The lieutenant's greeting at the station had chilled him, to begin with. He could not blame the man. Daniélou knew the district, where he had most likely been stationed for some years. A crime had been committed, he had done his best to clear it up, and now Maigret had arrived from Paris, without warning, and appeared to think he was mistaken.

The examining magistrate must be annoyed too. Neither of them would dare to show their irritation, they would be polite, would put their files at his disposal. Maigret would still be a nuisance, interfering in what wasn't his business, and he began to wonder what had suddenly decided him to come on this trip.

He heard footsteps and voices, probably the other two *belote* players on their way home. Then, further on, a yellowish dog brushed against his leg and he gave a startled jump.

When he opened the door of the *Bon Coin* only one of the lamps was still burning, and the landlord, behind the counter, was putting away the glasses and bottles. He was wearing neither waistcoat nor jacket. His dark-coloured trousers were hanging very low on his bulging stomach, and his sleeves were rolled up, revealing fat, hairy arms.

'Made any discoveries?'

He was trying to be clever, doubtless thought himself the most important person in the village.

'A nightcap?'

'If you'll let this be my round.'

Ever since morning Maigret had been thirsting for some local white wine, but he asked for brandy again, feeling that this was not an hour to drink wine.

'Here's how!'

'I thought,' remarked the chief-inspector quietly, wiping his mouth, 'that Léonie Birard wasn't very popular.'

'She was the nastiest shrew on earth. She's dead. May the Lord have her soul, or more likely the devil, but she was undoubtedly the most unpleasant woman I've ever known. And I knew her when she still had pigtails down her back, and we went to school together. She was . . . wait a minute . . . three years older than me. That's right. I'm sixty-four. So she must have been sixty-seven. Even at twelve she was poisonous.'

'What I don't understand . . .' began Maigret.

'There are lots of things you won't understand, although you're such a smart chap, let me warn you.'

'I don't understand,' he began again, as though talking to himself, 'that although she was so much hated, everybody is so down on the schoolmaster. Because after all, even if he did kill her, one would rather expect . . .'

'That people would say, *Good riddance!* That's what you're thinking, isn't it?'

'More or less.'

'Yes, but you're forgetting that Léonie was a local woman.'

He refilled the glasses without being asked.

'It's like in a family, don't you see. Relations have the right to hate one another, and they certainly do. But if an outsider gets mixed up in it, things change. People loathed Léonie. They loathe Gastin and his wife still more.'

'His wife as well?'

'His wife particularly.'

'Why? What has she done?'

'Nothing—here.'

'Why: "here"?'

'Everything gets known in the end, even in a godforsaken village like ours. And we don't like to be landed with people who aren't wanted anywhere else. This isn't the first time the Gastins have been mixed up in some funny business.'

He was interesting to watch, as he stood leaning on his bar. He obviously wanted to talk, but after each sentence he was peering at Maigret to see what effect he was producing, ready to retreat, or even to contradict himself, like a peasant bargaining for a yoke of oxen in the market.

'Looks as though you'd come here without knowing anything?'

'Except that Léonie Birard was killed by a bullet through her left eye.'

'And you came all this way!'

He was laughing at Maigret, after his own fashion.

'You hadn't the curiosity to break the journey at Courbevoie?'

'Ought I to have?'

'You'd have heard a fine tale. It took a long time to get here. It's only about two years since we heard it, at Saint-André.'

'What tale?'

'Madame Gastin was a schoolteacher, together with her husband. They taught in the same school, she on the girls' side, he on the boys'.'

'I know.'

'Have you heard about Chevassou?'

'Who's Chevassou?'

'One of the municipal councillors there, a handsome fellow, tall and strong, with black hair and a southern accent. There was a Madame Chevassou too. One fine day when the children were going home from school, Madame Chevassou turned up in the street and shot at the schoolmistress, hitting her in the shoulder. Guess why? Because she'd discovered that her husband and Gastin's wife were having fun and games together. It seems she was acquitted. After which, the best thing the Gastins could do was to leave Courbevoie, and they suddenly developed a hankering for country air.'

'I don't see the connexion with the murder of Léonie Birard.'

'There may be no connexion.'

'From what you tell me, Joseph Gastin did nothing wrong.'

'He's a cuckold.'

Louis was grinning, thoroughly pleased with himself.

'He's not the only one, of course. This village is full of them. I wish you joy. One more drop?'

'No, thank you.'

'Thérèse will show you to your room. Tell her what time you'd like your hot water brought up.'

'Thank you. Good night.'

'Thérèse!'

She went ahead of him up a staircase with uneven steps, turned into a corridor with flower-patterned wallpaper, opened a door.

'Call me about eight,' he said.

She didn't move, but stood watching him as though she wanted to tell him something. He looked more closely at her.

'Haven't I met you before?'

'You remember?'

He didn't admit that it was a rather vague recollection.

'You won't talk about it here, will you?'

'Aren't you from the village?'

'Yes. But I went away when I was fifteen, to work in Paris.'

'Did you really work there?'

'For four years.'

'And then?'

'You saw me, so you know. Inspector Priollet will tell you I didn't take the pocket-book. It was my friend Lucille, and I didn't even know about it.'

A picture came back to his mind and he remembered where he had seen her. One morning he had called in, as he often did, at the office of his colleague Priollet, head of the '*mondaine*' section, the Vice Squad. On a chair sat a dark, tousled-haired girl, dabbing at her eyes and snivelling. There was something about her pale, sickly face which had appealed to him.

'What's she done?' he had asked Priollet.

'The old story. A skivvy who's started picking up men along the Boulevard Sébastopol. Two days ago a shopkeeper from Béziers came to complain that his pocket had been picked, and was able, for once, to give us a fairly accurate description. Last night we caught her in a dance-hall in the Rue de Lappe.'

'It wasn't me!' stammered the girl between sobs. 'I swear to you on my mother's head that it wasn't me that took the pocket-book.'

The two men had exchanged winks.

'What do you think, Maigret?'

'Has she never been arrested before?'

'Not so far.'

'Where does she come from?'

'Somewhere in the Charentes.'

They often put on a little act of this kind.

'Have you found her girl friend?'

'Not yet.'

'Why not send this one home to her village?'

Priollet had turned solemnly to the girl.

'Would you like to go back to your village?'

'As long as they don't know about it there.'

It was strange to find her here now, five or six years older, still pale-faced, with big dark eyes that looked pleadingly at the chief-inspector.

'Is Louis Paumelle married?' he asked in a low voice.

'A widower.'

'Do you sleep with him?'

She nodded.

'Does he know what you were doing in Paris?'

'No. He mustn't find out. He's always promising to marry me. He's been promising for years, and sooner or later he's sure to make up his mind.'

'Thérèse!' called the landlord from the foot of the stairs.

'Just coming!'

And, to Maigret:

'You won't tell him?'

He shook his head, with an encouraging smile.

'Don't forget my hot water at eight o'clock.'

He was glad to have come across her again, because really with her he felt he was on familiar ground, and it was rather like meeting an old acquaintance.

He felt as though he knew the rest of them too, although he had only had a glimpse of them, because in his own village there had been a deputy-mayor who drank, there had been card-players—it wasn't *belote* in those days, it was piquet—a postman who thought himself somebody, and an innkeeper who knew everyone's secrets.

Their faces were still graven in his memory. But he had seen them with a child's eyes, and he realized, now, that he hadn't really known them.

While he was undressing he heard Paumelle coming upstairs, and then some thuds in the next room. Thérèse joined the innkeeper a little later and began undressing in her turn. Both were talking in low voices, like a married couple getting to bed, and the last sound was the creaking springs.

He had some difficulty in hollowing out a place for himself in the two huge feather mattresses. He recognized the country smell of hay and damp and, either because of the feathers or because of the brandies in tumblers which he had drunk with the landlord, he began to sweat profusely.

Before daylight, sounds began to reach him through his sleep, including those of a herd of cows which went past the inn, with an occasional moo. The forge began work soon afterwards. Downstairs, someone was taking down the shutters. He opened his eyes, found the sun shining even more brilliantly than the day before in Paris, sat up and pulled on his trousers.

With slippers on his bare feet he went downstairs, found Thérèse in the kitchen, busy making coffee. She had put on a kind of dressing-gown with a sprigged pattern over her nightdress, and her legs were bare; she smelt of bed.

'It isn't eight yet. Only half past six. Would you like a cup of coffee? It'll be ready in five minutes.'

Paumelle came down in his turn, unwashed and unshaven, wearing bedroom slippers like the chief-inspector.

'I thought you didn't want to get up before eight o'clock.'

They drank their first cup of coffee in thick china bowls, standing up near the stove.

Outside the house there was a group of women dressed in black, carrying baskets and shopping-bags.

'What are they waiting for?' inquired Maigret.

'The bus. It's market day at La Rochelle.'

Hens could be heard cackling in crates.

'Who's taking school now?'

'Yesterday there was nobody. This morning they're expecting a substitute from La Rochelle. He's to come on the bus. He'll sleep here, in the back room, as you've got the front one.'

He was up in his room again when the bus stopped in the square and he saw a timid-looking young man get out, carrying a big gladstone-bag; this must be the schoolmaster.

The crates were piled on the roof of the bus. The women packed themselves into it. Thérèse knocked on his door.

'Your hot water!'

Casually, without looking at her, he asked:

'Are you another who thinks Gastin killed Léonie?'

Before replying she glanced towards the half-open door.

'I don't know,' she said in a very low tone.

'You don't think so?'

'It doesn't seem like him. But they all want it to be him, you understand?'

The chief thing he was beginning to understand was that, for no reason, he had taken a difficult, if not impossible, job.

'Who stood to benefit by the old woman's death?'

'I don't know. They say she disinherited her niece for getting married.'

'Who'll get her money?'

'Some charity, perhaps. She changed her mind so often! . . . Or it might be Maria, the Polish woman. . . .'

'Is it true she's had one or two children by the deputy-mayor?'

'Maria? So they say. He often goes to see her, and sometimes stays for the night.'

'In spite of the children?'

'That doesn't worry Maria. Everybody goes there.'

'Paumelle too?'

'I expect he did when she was younger. She's not very tempting nowadays.'

'How old is she?'

'About thirty. She takes no trouble about herself, and her house is worse than a pigsty.'

'Thérèse!' came the landlord's voice, as on the previous evening.

Better not detain her, Paumelle didn't seem to like it. Was he perhaps jealous? Or merely anxious that she shouldn't tell too much?

When Maigret went downstairs, the young schoolmaster was having breakfast and looked inquisitively at him.

'What will you have, Inspector?'

'Have you any oysters?'

'Not at neap-tide.'

'Will that last much longer?'

'Another five or six days.'

Ever since Paris he'd been wanting to eat oysters washed down with white wine, and it looked as though he wouldn't get any all the time he was here.

'There's soup. Or we can do you some ham and eggs.'

He ate nothing at all, drank another cup of coffee, standing at the open door and looking at the sunlit square and at two dark figures moving about in the '*Coopérative Charentaise*'.

He was wondering whether to ask for a glass of white wine all the same, to take away the taste of the abominable coffee, when a cheerful voice exclaimed, close beside him:

'Inspector Maigret?'

It was a small, thin, lively man, whose expression was youthful although he must be over forty. He held out his hand with a cordial gesture.

'Dr. Bresselles!' he introduced himself. 'The lieutenant told me yesterday that you were expected. I came along before surgery, to know if I could help you. An hour from now my waiting-room will be packed.'

'Will you have something to drink?'

'In my house, if you'll come, it's next door.'

'I know.'

Maigret followed him to the grey stone house. All the other houses in the village were colour-washed, some in harsh white, others in a creamier shade, and the pink roofs gave the whole place a very gay appearance.

'Come in! What would you like to drink?'

'Ever since I left Paris I've been longing for oysters and local white wine,' confessed Maigret. 'But I've already discovered that I shall have to do without the oysters.'

'Armande!' he called, crossing to the door. 'Bring up a bottle of white wine. From the red bin.'

He explained:

'That's my sister. She's been keeping house for me since my wife died. I have two boys, one at Niort, at the *Lycée*, the other's doing his military service. What do you think of Saint-André?'

Everything seemed to amuse him.

'I'm forgetting you've not seen much of it yet. Just wait! By way of a sample, you have that scoundrel Paumelle, who was a farm-hand and married the owner of the *Bon Coin* when her husband died. She was twenty years older than Louis. She liked her little drop to drink. So as she was fiendishly jealous and the money was hers, he killed her by encouraging her weakness. See what I mean? He did his best to fill her up with drink, and by the time lunch was over she often had to go upstairs to bed. She held out for seven years, with a liver as hard as stone, and in the end he was able to give her a handsome funeral. Since then, he's been going to bed with his servants. One after another they left, till it came to Thérèse, who seems to be sticking it out.'

The sister came in, timid and colourless, carrying a tray with a bottle and two glasses, and Maigret thought she looked like a priest's house-keeper.

'My sister. Inspector Maigret.'

She went out backwards, and this, too, seemed to amuse the doctor.

'Armande has never married. I'm inclined to think she's been wait-ing all her life for me to be a widower. Now she has her own house at last, and can spoil me as she would have spoilt a husband.'

'What do you think of Gastin?'

'He's pathetic.'

'Why?'

'Because he does his best, despairingly, and people who do their best are pathetic. He gets no thanks from anyone. He struggles away to teach something to a bunch of snotty little boys whom their parents would rather keep at home on the farm. He even tried to get them to wash. I remember the day he sent one of them home because his head was lousy. A quarter of an hour later the father turned up, furious, and they nearly came to blows.'

'His wife is an invalid?'

'Your very good health! She isn't really an invalid, but she isn't very well either. I've learnt not to put too much confidence in medicine, you know. Madame Gastin pines. She's ashamed. She blames herself, day in and day out, for ruining her husband's career.'

'Because of Chevassou?'

'You know about that? Yes, because of Chevassou. She must have been really in love with him. What's called a devouring passion. You'd never think it to look at her, for she's an insignificant little woman; she and her husband are as like as two peas. Maybe that's the real trouble. They're too much alike. Chevassou, who's a big brute full of vitality, a kind of satisfied bull, did what he liked with her. Her right arm still hurts her now and then, it's remained a bit stiff.'

'How did she get on with Léonie Birard?'

'They never saw each other except through their windows, across the courtyard and the gardens, and Léonie put out her tongue at her now and then, as she did at everyone. What strikes me as most extraordinary in this business is that Léonie, whom one would have imagined to be indestructible, was killed by a little bullet fired from a child's rifle. And that isn't all. There are some incredible coincidences. The left eye, the one that was hit, was her bad eye; she'd always been slightly wall-eyed, and she hadn't been able to see with it for years. What do you say to that?'

The doctor raised his glass. The wine had greenish lights in it, it was dry and light, with a strong local flavour.

'Your good health! They'll all try to put spokes in your wheel. Don't believe a word they say, whether it's the parents or the children. Come and see me whenever you like, and I'll do my utmost to help.'

'You don't like them?'

The doctor's eyes began to sparkle with laughter, and he retorted emphatically:

'I adore them! They're quite crazy!'

## III

THE door of the *mairie* stood open into a corridor on whose recently whitewashed walls various official notices were fixed with drawing-pins. Some of the smaller ones, such as the announcement of a special meeting of the Council, were written in pen and ink, with the headings in round-hand, probably by the schoolmaster. The floor was grey-tiled, the woodwork painted in grey also. The door on the left presumably led into the council-room, with its bust of Marianne and its flag, while the right-hand door, which stood ajar, gave into the secretary's office.

The room was empty; it smelt of stale cigar-smoke; Lieutenant Daniélou, who had made the office his headquarters for the past two days, had not yet arrived.

Opposite the street entrance, at the far end of the passage, a double door stood open on to the courtyard, in the middle of which grew a lime-tree. To the right of this yard, the low building, of which three windows were visible, was the school, with rows of boys' and girls' heads and, standing up, the outline of the substitute teacher whom Maigret had seen at the inn.

There was a monastic hush over all this, and only the clang of the blacksmith's hammer could be heard. Beyond, there were hedges and gardens, with the tender green of budding leaves on lilac bushes, white and yellow houses, an open window here and there.

Maigret turned left, towards the Gastins' two-storey house. As he was about to knock on the door it opened, and he found himself on the threshold of a kitchen where a small, spectacled boy was seated at the oilcloth-covered table, bending over an exercise-book.

It was Madame Gastin who had opened the door to him. Looking out of the window, she had seen him in the yard, glance around, come slowly forward.

'I heard yesterday that you were coming,' she said, standing aside to let him pass. 'Come in, Inspector. If you only knew how relieved I feel!'

She wiped her wet hands on her apron, turned towards her son, who had not looked up and seemed to be ignoring the visitor.

'Aren't you going to say how do you do to Inspector Maigret, Jean-Paul?'

'How do you do.'

'Run along up to your room now.'

The kitchen was small but, even at this early hour, meticulously clean, without a trace of untidiness. Young Gastin picked up his book without protest, went out into the corridor and up the stairs to the floor above.

'Come this way, Inspector.'

They crossed the passage in their turn, went into a room which served as a parlour and was doubtless never used. There was an upright piano against one wall, a round, massive oak table, arm-chairs with lace antimacassars, photographs on the walls, ornaments all over the place.

'Please sit down.'

The house had four rooms, all tiny, and it made Maigret feel too tall and too broad, in addition to which he had had, ever since he came in, the impression of having suddenly entered an unreal world.

He had been warned that Madame Gastin was the same type as her husband, but he had never imagined that she was so much like him that they might practically have been taken for brother and sister. Her hair was of the same indeterminate colour, already thinning too, the middle of her face was, as it were, thrust forward, and she had pale, short-sighted eyes. And the child, too, was like a caricature of both his parents combined.

Was he trying, from upstairs, to overhear the conversation, or had he gone back to his exercise-book? He was only about twelve and already he looked like a little old man, or, to be more exact, like a being with no definite age.

'I kept him away from school,' explained Madame Gastin as she closed the door. 'I thought it was better. You know how cruel children are.'

If Maigret had remained standing he would almost have filled the room, and he now sat motionless in an arm-chair, signed to his hostess to sit down too, because it made him feel tired to see her standing.

She was as ageless as her son. He knew she was only thirty-four, but he had seldom seen a woman who had so completely discarded every feminine touch. Under her dress, whose colour was undefinable, her body was thin, tired; there was a hint of breasts that hung down like empty pockets, and her shoulders were already slightly rounded, her face, instead of being tanned by the country sunshine, had turned grey. Even her voice sounded washed-out!

But she was doing her best to smile, put forward a timid hand to touch Maigret's arm as she said:

'I'm so grateful to you for having confidence in him!'

He couldn't reply that he didn't know yet, couldn't confess to her that it was because of the first spring sunshine in Paris, of a memory of oysters and white wine, that he had suddenly decided to come.

'If you knew how much I blame myself, Inspector! Because what is happening is all my fault. I've ruined his life and the boy's. I'm doing my best to make up for it. I try so hard, you know. . . .'

He felt as uncomfortable as if he had come unawares into a house where someone he didn't know had died, and was at a loss for words. All of a sudden he was in a world apart, which didn't belong to the village in the centre of which he was now ensconced.

These three, Gastin, his wife and their son, belonged to a race so different that the chief-inspector could understand the peasants' mistrust.

'I don't know how it will all end,' she was continuing after a sigh, 'but I can't believe that the law will condemn an innocent man. He's such an exceptional character! You've met him, but you don't know him. Tell me, how was he, last night?'

'Very well. Very calm.'

'Is it true they handcuffed him, on the station platform?'

'No. He went freely between the two constables.'

'Were there any people there to see him?'

'It was all done discreetly.'

'Do you think there's anything he needs? His health isn't good. He's never been very strong.'

She was not crying. She must have wept so much in her life that there were no more tears left in her. Just above her head, to the right of the window, hung the photograph of a young woman who was almost plump, and Maigret could not tear his eyes away from this, wondering if she had really looked like that, with laughing eyes and dimpled cheeks even.

'You're looking at my picture when I was young?'

There was another, of Gastin, to match it. He had scarcely changed at all, except that in those days he had longish hair, like an artist, as people used to say, and no doubt he used to write poems.

'Have you been told?' she asked softly, after glancing at the door.

And he could feel that that was what she chiefly wanted to talk about, it had been in her mind ever since she had been told he was coming, it was the only thing that mattered to her.

'You mean about what happened at Courbevoie?'

'Yes, about Charles . . .'

She stopped short and blushed, as though the name were taboo.

'Chevassou?'

She nodded.

'I'm still wondering how it could ever have happened. I've been so miserable, Inspector! And I do wish someone would explain to me! I'm not a bad woman, you know. I met Joseph when I was only fifteen, and I knew at once that he was the man I should marry. We planned our lives together. We both decided to take up teaching.'

'Was it he who gave you the idea?'

'I think so. He's cleverer than I am. He's a very exceptional man. People don't always realize that, because he's too modest. We took our degrees the same year and got married; thanks to a cousin who had influence, we managed to get appointments at Courbevoie together.'

'Do you think that has any connexion with what happened here on Tuesday?'

She looked at him in surprise. He would have done better not to interrupt her, for she lost the thread of what she was saying.

'It's all my fault.'

She frowned, anxious to explain.

'If it hadn't been for what happened at Courbevoie, we shouldn't have come here. People thought well of Joseph there. Their ideas are more modern, you know. He was getting on. He had good prospects.'

'And you?'

'I had, too. He used to help me, give me advice. And then, from one day to the next, it was as though I'd gone mad. I still can't understand what took possession of me. I didn't want it. I fought against it. I told myself I'd never do such a thing. And then, when Charles was there . . .'

She blushed again, stammered, as though it were an offence to Maigret himself to refer to the man:

'I beg your pardon. . . . When he was there I couldn't resist. I don't think it was love, because I love Joseph, I always have loved him. It was like a sort of fever, and I lost all thought of anything else, even of our boy, who was quite a baby. I was ready to leave him, Inspector. I really thought of leaving them both, going off somewhere, anywhere. . . . Can you understand it?'

He hadn't the courage to tell her that she had doubtless never had any sexual enjoyment with her husband and that her story was a commonplace one. She needed to believe that her adventure had been exceptional, she needed to lament, to be filled with remorse, to regard herself as the lowest of women.

'You are a Catholic, Madame Gastin?'

He was touching on another sensitive point.

'I was, like my parents, until I met Joseph. He only believes in science and progress. He loathes priests.'

'You stopped being a practising Catholic?'

'Yes.'

'Since those things happened, you haven't been back to church?'

'I couldn't. I feel as though I should be betraying him again. Besides, what would be the good! During our first few years here I did hope we were beginning a new life. The people looked at us suspiciously, as country people always do. But I felt sure that one day they would learn to appreciate my husband's qualities. Then, I don't know how, they found out about Courbevoie, and after that even the children didn't respect him any more. I told you it is all my fault . . .'

'Did your husband have arguments with Léonie Birard?'

'Now and then. As secretary of the *mairie*. She was a woman who always made difficulties. There were questions of pensions to be settled. Joseph is strict. He refuses to go beyond his duty, he'll never sign a false certificate to please anybody.'

'Did she know your story?'

'Yes, everyone did.'

'She used to put out her tongue at you too?'

'And make filthy remarks when I went past her house. I used to avoid going that way. Not only did she put her tongue out, but sometimes, when she saw me at the window, she'd turn round and pull up her skirts. I beg your pardon. One would hardly believe it, of such an old woman. She was like that. But it would never have occurred to Joseph to kill her, all the same. He'd never kill anyone. You've seen him. He's a gentle creature, who'd like everyone to be happy.'

'Tell me about your son.'

'What is there to tell you? He takes after his father. He's a quiet, studious boy, very advanced for his age. The only reason he isn't head of the class is that then my husband would be accused of favouritism. Joseph gives him lower marks than he deserves, on purpose.'

'Doesn't the boy object to that?'

'He understands. We've explained to him why it has to be that way.'

'Does he know about the Courbevoie business?'

'We've never mentioned it to him. But the other boys do. He pretends to know nothing about it.'

'Does he ever go to play with the others?'

'He used to at first. The last two years, since the village became openly hostile to us, he's preferred to stay at home. He reads a great deal. I'm teaching him the piano. He already plays very well for his age.'

The window was shut, and Maigret was beginning to feel stifled, to wonder whether he hadn't suddenly been caught fast, in an old photograph-album.

'Your husband came into the house on Tuesday morning, soon after ten o'clock?'

'Yes. I think so. I've been asked that so often, in all kinds of ways, as though they were determined to make me contradict myself, that I'm no longer positive about anything. He usually comes to the kitchen for a moment during the break, and helps himself to a cup of coffee. I'm generally upstairs at that time.'

'He doesn't drink wine?'

'Never. He doesn't smoke either.'

'On Tuesday, didn't he come in during the break?'

'He says he didn't. So I said the same, because he always tells the truth. Then they maintained he'd come in later.'

'You denied that?'

'I was speaking in good faith, Monsieur Maigret. Some time afterwards, I remembered finding his empty coffee-bowl on the kitchen table. I don't know whether it was during break or later, that he came.'

'He could have gone to the tool-shed without your seeing him?'

'The room I was in upstairs doesn't overlook the kitchen-garden.'

'You could see Léonie Birard's house?'

'If I'd looked that way, yes.'

'You didn't hear the shot?'

'I didn't hear anything. The window was shut. I feel the cold a great deal. I always have. And even in summer I shut the windows during the break, because of the noise.'

'You tell me the local people don't like your husband. I'd like to get that clearer. Is there anyone in the village who particularly dislikes him?'

'Indeed there is. The deputy-mayor.'

'Théo?'

'Théo Coumart, yes, who lives just behind us. Our gardens are end to end. First thing in the morning he begins to drink white wine in his cellar, where there's always a barrel on tap. By ten or eleven o'clock he's at Louis's, and he goes on drinking till evening.'

'Hasn't he any work?'

'His parents owned a big farm. He's never done a stroke of work in his life. One afternoon last winter, when Joseph had gone to La Rochelle with Jean-Paul, he came into the house, at about half past four. I was upstairs, changing. I heard heavy footsteps on the stairs. It was he. He was drunk. He pushed the door open and began to laugh. Then, all of a sudden, as though this were a brothel, he tried to push me over on to the bed. I grabbed at his face, giving him a long scratch down his nose. It bled. He began to swear, shouting that a woman like me had no business to put on airs. I opened the window and threatened to call for help. I was in my underclothes. At last he went away, chiefly because of his bleeding face, I think. He's never spoken to me since.

'He's the village leader. The mayor, Monsieur Rateau, owns a mussel-bed; he's occupied all the time with his business, and only comes to the *mairie* for Council meetings.

'Théo arranges the elections just as he likes, does good turns to people, is always ready to sign any paper they want . . .'

'You don't know whether he was in his garden on Tuesday morning, as he makes out?'

'If he says so it's probably true, because other people must have seen him. Though of course if he asked them to oblige him by telling a lie, they wouldn't hesitate to do it.'

'Would you mind if I had a little chat with your son?'

She stood up resignedly, and opened the door.

'Jean-Paul, come down, will you?'

'Why?' asked the voice from upstairs.

'Inspector Maigret wants a word with you.'

Hesitant steps were heard. The little boy appeared, carrying a book, and stood waiting in the doorway, with a suspicious expression on his face.

'Come in, my boy. You're not afraid of me, I take it?'

'I'm not afraid of anyone.'

He spoke in almost the same toneless voice as his mother.

'You were at school on Tuesday morning?'

He glanced from the chief-inspector to his mother, as though uncertain whether he should answer even such a harmless question.

'Go on, Jean-Paul. The inspector's on our side.'

She looked at Maigret as though silently apologizing for this statement. But she could elicit no more than a nod from the boy.

'What happened after break?'

The same silence. Maigret was becoming a monument of patience.

'You want your father to come out of prison, don't you, and the real murderer to be arrested?'

It was hard to read the expression in his eyes, through the thick lenses of his spectacles. He did not look aside, but stared his questioner straight in the face, without the slightest flicker of his pinched features.

'Just now,' the chief-inspector went on, 'I don't know what people are saying. Some little thing, that seems quite unimportant, may give me a clue  How many of you are there in the school?'

'Answer, Jean-Paul.'

Reluctantly, he said:

'Thirty-two altogether.'

'What do you mean by "altogether"?'

'Seniors and juniors. The whole lot whose names are on the list.'

His mother explained:

'There are always some who are away. At times, especially in the summer, only about fifteen come, and we can't always be sending constables to their homes.'

'Have you any school-friends?'

He replied shortly: 'No.'

'Not one friend, among the village children?'

The answer came with an air of defiance:

'I'm the schoolmaster's son.'

'Is that why they don't like you?'

He didn't reply.

'What do you do in the breaks?'

'Nothing.'

'You don't come to see your mother?'

'No.'

'Why not?'

'Father doesn't let me.'

Madame Gastin explained again:

'He doesn't want to make any difference between his boy and the others. If Jean-Paul came here during break there would be no reason why the forester's boy, or the butcher's, for instance, shouldn't cross the road to their own homes.'

'I see. Do you remember what your father was doing on Tuesday during the break?'

'No.'

'Doesn't he keep an eye on the boys?'

'Yes.'

'Standing in the middle of the playground?'

'Sometimes.'

'He didn't come in here?'

'I don't know.'

He had seldom questioned anyone so recalcitrant. If he had been dealing with a grown-up person he would probably have lost his temper, and Madame Gastin, feeling this, stood protectively beside her son, laid a conciliatory hand on his shoulder.

'Answer the inspector politely, Jean-Paul.'

'I'm not being rude.'

'At ten o'clock you all went back into the classroom. Did your father go to the blackboard?'

Through the window-curtains he could see a section of the board, with words written on it in chalk, in the opposite building.

'Perhaps.'

'What lesson was it?'

'Grammar.'

'Did someone knock at the door?'

'Perhaps.'

'Aren't you sure? Didn't you see your father go out?'

'I don't know.'

'Now listen. When the teacher leaves the class, the boys generally begin jumping up, chattering, playing the fool.'

Jean-Paul said nothing.

'Is that what happened on Tuesday?'

'I don't remember.'

'You didn't leave the room?'

'What for?'

'You might have gone to the lavatory, for instance. I see it's in the yard.'

'I didn't go there.'

'Who went to look out of the window?'

'I don't know.'

By this time Maigret was standing up, and his fists, in his pockets, were tightly clenched.

'Now listen . . .'

'I don't know anything. I didn't see anything. I've nothing to tell you.'

And the boy suddenly rushed out of the room and up the stairs; they heard him, up above, shutting his door.

'You mustn't be cross with him, Inspector. Put yourself in his place. Yesterday the lieutenant questioned him for over an hour, and when he got home he didn't say a word to me, went and lay down on his bed and stayed there till it was dark, with his eyes wide open.'

'Is he fond of his father?'

She didn't quite understand the question.

'I mean, has he a particular affection or admiration for his father? Or does he prefer you, for instance? Is it in you that he confides, or in his father?'

'He doesn't confide in anyone. He's undoubtedly fonder of me than of his father.'

'How did he behave when your husband was accused?'

'Just as you've seen him now.'

'He didn't cry?'

'I've never seen him cry since he was a baby.'

'How long has he had that gun?'

'We gave it to him for Christmas.'

'Does he often use it?'

'He goes off alone now and then, with his gun on his arm, like a sportsman, but I don't think he often fires it. Two or three times he pinned a paper target to the lime-tree in the yard, but my husband explained that he was wounding the tree.'

'If he'd left the classroom on Tuesday while your husband was away, I suppose the other boys would have noticed it?'

'Certainly.'

'And they would have said so.'

'You can't have thought that Jean-Paul . . . ?'

'I have to think of every possibility. Who is the boy who claims to have seen your husband come out of the tool-shed?'

'Marcel Sellier.'

'Whose son is he?'

'His father is the village policeman, who's also the ironmonger, the electrician and the plumber. He mends roofs too, when it's needed.'

'How old is Marcel Sellier?'

'The same age as Jean-Paul, to within two or three months.'

'Does he work well?'

'The best of them all, with my son. So as not to seem to favour Jean-Paul, my husband always puts Marcel at the head of the class. His father is intelligent too, and hard-working. They're a good kind of people, I think. Are you very cross with him?'

'With whom?'

'Jean-Paul. He was almost rude to you. And here am I, not even offering you anything to drink. Won't you have something?'

'Thank you, but the lieutenant must have arrived by now, and I promised to go and see him.'

'You'll keep on helping us?'

'Why do you ask me that?'

'Because if I were you, I think I should have lost heart. You've come so far, and what you find here is so uninspiring. . . .'

'I'll do my best.'

He went towards the door, to prevent her from seizing his hands in a gesture he could feel she was on the point of making, and kissing them, perhaps. He was eager to get out, to feel the fresh air on his face, to hear sounds other than the tired voice of the schoolmaster's wife.

'I shall be coming to see you again, I expect.'

'You don't think there's anything he needs?'

'If there is, I'll let you know.'

'Oughtn't he to choose a lawyer?'

'There's no need to do that yet.'

While he was crossing the yard without looking back, the double, glass-paned doors of the school were thrown open and a pack of children rushed out, yelling. Some of them stopped dead on seeing him, knowing doubtless from their parents who he was, and stared.

They were of all ages, from shrimps of six to big lads of fourteen or fifteen, who looked almost grown-up already. There were girls, too, who collected in one corner of the yard, as though taking refuge from the boys.

At the far end of the corridor, where both doors were open, Maigret saw the car from the constabulary. He stopped at the secretary's office and knocked. Daniélou's voice said:

'Come in!'

The lieutenant, who had taken off his belt and unbuttoned his tunic, stood up to shake hands. He was sitting in Gastin's chair, papers spread in front of him, *mairie* stamps lying all round. Because she was seated in a dark corner, Maigret did not immediately notice a stout girl with a baby in her arms.

'Sit down, Chief-Inspector. I'll be with you in a moment. I thought it would be a good thing to send for all the witnesses again and go right through the interrogations a second time.'

Doubtless because the chief-inspector had come to Saint-André.

'A cigar?'

'No, thank you. I only smoke a pipe.'

'I was forgetting.'

The lieutenant himself smoked very black cigars, which he chewed as he talked.

'Excuse me.'

And, turning to the girl:

'You say she promised to leave you all she had, including the house?'

'Yes. She promised.'

'Before witnesses?'

She didn't seem to understand what this meant. In fact she didn't seem to understand anything much; she looked as though she might be the village idiot.

She was a big, stolid, manly girl, wearing a black dress that someone must have given her, and there were wisps of hay in her untidy hair. She stank. The baby, too, smelt dirty and unkempt.

'When did she give this promise?'

'A long time ago.'

Her large eyes were of an almost transparent blue and she was frowning with the effort to understand what was wanted of her.

'What do you call a long time? A year?'

'Maybe a year.'

'Two years?'

'Maybe.'

'How long have you been working for Léonie Birard?'

'Wait a minute. . . . After I had my second baby. . . . No, the third. . . .'

'How old is he now?'

Her lips moved, as though in church, while she made a mental calculation.

'Five.'

'Where is he now?'

'At home.'

'How many of them are there at home?'

'Three. I've got one here, and the eldest is at school.'

'Who's looking after them?'

'Nobody.'

The two men exchanged glances.

'So you've been working for Léonie Birard for about five years. Did she promise at once that she'd leave you her money?'

'No.'

'After two years, or three?'

'Yes.'

'Was it two, or three?'

'I don't know.'

'Didn't she sign a paper?'

'I don't know.'

'You don't know either why she made you that promise?'

'To annoy her niece. She told me so.'

'Used her niece to come and visit her?'

'Never.'

'She's Madame Sellier, the village policeman's wife, isn't she?'

'That's right.'

'Didn't the policeman ever come to see her either?'

'Yes.'

'They had quarrelled?'

'Yes.'

'Why did he come to see her?'

'To threaten to summons her for throwing her rubbish out of the window.'

'Did they get angry?'

'They shouted insults at each other.'

'Were you fond of your employer?'

She gazed at him with her round eyes, as though the notion of being fond of anyone, or the contrary, had never occurred to her.

'I don't know.'

'Was she kind to you?'

'She used to give me left-overs.'

'Left-overs from what?'

'Food. And her old dresses too.'

'Did she pay you regularly?'

'Not much.'

'What do you mean by not much?'

'Half what other women give me to work for them. But she took me every afternoon. So that . . .'

'Have you heard her quarrelling with other people?'

'With nearly everyone.'

'In her own home?'

'She never left home lately; she used to shout things at people through the window.'

'What things?'

'Things they'd done and didn't want known about.'

'So everyone hated her?'

'I think so.'

'Did anyone hate her especially, enough to want to kill her?'

'Must have, seeing she was killed.'

'But you haven't the faintest idea who can have done it?'

'I thought you knew.'

'What do you mean?'

'Well, you've arrested the schoolmaster.'

'You think he did it?'

'I don't know.'

'Do you mind if I ask a question?' intervened Maigret, turning to the lieutenant.

'By all means.'

'Is Théo, the deputy-mayor, the father of one or more of your children?'

She was not offended, seemed to be pondering.

'He may be. I'm not sure.'

'Did he get along well with Léonie Birard?'

She thought again.

'Same as the rest.'

'He knew she'd promised to remember you in her will?'

'I told him.'

'What was his reaction?'

She didn't understand the word. He tried again:

'What did he say to that?'

'He told me to ask her for a paper.'

'You did so?'

'Yes.'

'When?'

'A long time ago.'

'Did she refuse?'

'She said everything was arranged.'

'When you found her dead, what did you do?'

'I called out.'

'Straight away?'

'As soon as I saw there was blood. At first I thought she'd fainted.'

'You didn't hunt through her drawers?'

'What drawers?'

Maigret signed to the lieutenant that he had finished. The latter stood up.

'Thank you, Maria. If I need you again, I'll send for you.'

'Didn't she sign any paper?' inquired the woman, pausing near the door, with her baby in her arms.

'We've found nothing so far.'

Turning her back on them, she grumbled:

'I might have known she'd cheat me.'

They saw her going past the window, talking to herself with a discontented air.

# IV

THE lieutenant sighed, as though apologizing:

'You see? I do my best.'

And that was undoubtedly true. He was all the more conscientious now that there was a witness to his investigation, someone from the famous Police Headquarters, who must seem very impressive to him.

His was a curious story. He came of a well-known family at Toulouse, and on the insistence of his parents he had gone to the Polytechnique, where he acquitted himself more than creditably. And then, instead of choosing between the army and a business career, he had opted for the constabulary and decided to read law for two years.

He had a pretty wife, who also came of a good family, and they were one of the most popular couples at La Rochelle.

He was doing his best to appear at ease in the greyish room in the *mairie*, into which the sun was not yet shining, so that, in contrast with the brightness outside, it was almost dark.

'It's not easy to discover what they think!' he remarked, lighting another cigar.

Six .22 rifles were leaning against the wall in a corner of the room; four of them were exactly alike and one was of an older type, with a carved butt.

'I think I've got them all. If there are any more around, my men will find them this morning.'

From the mantelpiece he picked up what looked like a cardboard pill-box, and took out a flattened scrap of lead.

'I've inspected this carefully. I studied ballistics at one time, and we've no expert at La Rochelle. It's a lead bullet, of the type sometimes called "soft", which squashes flat as soon as it hits anything, even a pinewood plank. So it's no use looking it over for the kind of marks one finds on other bullets, which often help to identify the actual weapon used.'

Maigret nodded his understanding.

'You're familiar with the .22 rifle, Chief-Inspector?'

'More or less.'

Less rather than more, for he could not recall any crime committed in Paris with such a weapon.

'Two types of cartridge can be used in it, short or long. The short ones have a small range, but the long .22 can hit its target at over a hundred and fifty yards.'

On the veined marble mantelpiece other scraps of lead, some twenty in all, lay in a little heap.

'Yesterday we made some tests with these different rifles. The bullet which hit Léonie Birard is a long .22, of the same weight as those we fired.'

'The cartridge-case hasn't been found?'

'My men have been over the gardens, behind the house, with a fine-tooth comb. They'll make another search this afternoon. It's not impossible that whoever fired the shot picked up the case. What I'm trying to explain is that we have very few definite clues.'

'Have all these guns been used recently?'

'Fairly recently. It's difficult to be quite sure, because the boys don't bother to clean and oil them after use. The medical report, which I've got here, doesn't help much, either, because the doctor couldn't say, even approximately, from what distance the shot was fired. It might be fifty yards or it might be over a hundred.'

Maigret, standing near the window, was filling his pipe and listening with only half an ear. In the opposite building, next to the church, he could see a man with tangled black hair, shoeing a horse whose hoof was being held by a younger lad.

'I've been over all the different possibilities with the examining magistrate. The first thing we thought of, strange as it may seem, was that it might have been an accident. There's something so incredible about the crime, there was so little chance of killing the old woman with a .22 bullet, that we wondered whether she hadn't been shot by pure chance. Somebody in one of the gardens might have been taking pot-shots at sparrows, as the kids often do. One hears of stranger coincidences. You see what I mean?'

Maigret nodded. The lieutenant had an almost childish desire for his approval, and his good intentions were touching.

'That's what we called the pure and simple accident theory. If Léonie Birard had been killed at any other time of day, or on a holiday, or in another part of the village, we should probably have been satisfied with that, for it's the most plausible. But when she was killed the children were at school.'

'All of them?'

'Practically all. The three or four absentees, one of them a girl, live a good way off, on farms, and weren't seen in the village that morning. Another, the butcher's son, has been in bed for nearly a month.

'Then we turned to a second possibility, that of mischief-making.

'Someone, any one of the neighbours, who'd quarrelled with old Léonie as nearly all of them had, someone she'd made fun of once too often, might, in a fit of anger, have fired from a distance, meaning to frighten her or break one of her windows, without even dreaming that she might be killed.

'I haven't quite rejected that theory yet, because the third possibility, that of deliberate murder, implies a crack shot, to begin with. If she'd been hit anywhere except in the eye, she'd have been only slightly wounded. And to shoot her deliberately in the eye from some distance, an exceptionally fine shot would be needed.

'Don't forget that this happened in broad daylight, in this group of buildings, at a time of day when most women are at home doing their housework. There's a maze of yards and gardens all around. It was a fine day, and most windows were open.'

'Have you tried to discover where everybody was at about a quarter past ten?'

'You heard Maria Smelker. The other statements aren't much clearer than hers. People are reluctant to answer questions. When they go into details they get so confused that it only complicates things.'

'The deputy-mayor was in his garden?'

'Apparently. It depends whether we're to go by wireless time or by the church clock, because the clock is fifteen or twenty minutes fast. Someone who was listening to the wireless claims to have seen Théo on his way to the *Bon Coin*, at about a quarter past ten. The people at the *Bon Coin* declare that he didn't arrive there till after half past ten. The butcher's wife, who was hanging out her washing, says she saw him go into his cellar for a drink, as he usually does.'

'Has he a rifle?'

'No. Only a double-barrelled sporting gun. That shows you how difficult it is to get hold of reliable evidence. The boy's the only one whose statement holds together.'

'That's the policeman's boy?'

'Yes.'

'Why didn't he say anything the first day?'

'I asked him that. His reply is plausible. I expect you know that his father, Julien Sellier, is married to the old woman's niece?'

'Yes, and Léonie Birard had said she was disinheriting her.'

'Marcel Sellier felt it would look as though he were trying to shelter his father. He didn't mention it at home till the following evening. And Julien Sellier brought him along to us on Thursday morning. You'll be seeing them. They're pleasant people and seem to be sincere.'

'Marcel saw the schoolmaster coming out of his tool-shed?'

'So he says. The children were left to themselves in the classroom. Most of them were fooling around; Marcel Sellier, who's rather a serious, quiet boy, went across to the window and saw Joseph Gastin coming out of the shed.'

'He didn't see him go in?'

'Only coming out. The shot must have been fired then. The schoolmaster, however, stubbornly denies setting foot in the tool-shed that morning. Either he's lying, or the boy made up the story. But why?'

'Yes, why?' muttered Maigret in a detached tone.

He felt like a glass of wine. It was, he felt, the right time of day. The break was over, in the playground. Two old women went past with shopping-bags, on their way to the Co-operative.

'Might I have a look at Léonie Birard's house?' he asked.

'I'll take you there. I've got the key.'

That, too, was on the mantelpiece. He put it into his pocket, buttoned up his tunic and put his cap on. The air outside had a smell of the sea, but not enough to satisfy Maigret. They walked along to the corner of the street, and as they reached Louis Paumelle's inn, the chief-inspector asked casually:

'What about a drink?'

'Do you think so?' said the lieutenant, awkwardly.

He wasn't the type of man to go for drinks to a *bistrot* or an inn. The invitation embarrassed him, and he didn't know how to refuse.

'I wonder whether . . .'

'Just a quick glass of white wine.'

Théo was there, seated in a corner, his long legs outstretched, a jug of wine and a glass at his elbow. The postman, who had an iron hook where his left arm should have been, was standing in front of him. They both stopped talking as the other men came in.

'What will you take, gentlemen?' inquired Louis, who stood behind his bar, shirt-sleeves rolled up high.

'A *chopine*.'

Daniélou was uncomfortable, but trying to carry it off. Perhaps that was why the deputy-mayor stared mockingly at the two of them. He was tall and must once have been stout. Now that he had lost weight, his skin seemed to hang in folds, like a garment that was too loose.

The expression on his face combined the cunning self-assurance of the peasant with that of the politician, skilled in juggling with the village elections.

'Well, what's become of that scoundrel Gastin?' he inquired, as though speaking to nobody in particular.

And Maigret, without quite knowing why, retorted in the same tone: 'He's waiting for someone to go and take his place.'

The lieutenant was shocked at this. The postman turned his head sharply.

'You've discovered something?' he demanded.

'You must know the district better than anyone, you make the round of it every day.'

'And what a round! At one time, not so long ago, there were still people who practically never had any letters. I remember some farms where I only used to set foot once a year, to take the almanac. Nowadays they not only all get newspapers, which have to be delivered to them, but there isn't one who doesn't claim some allowance or pension. If you knew what a lot of papers that means! . . .'

He repeated, with an air of profound dejection: 'Papers! Papers!'

To hear him, one might have supposed that he had to fill them in himself.

'To begin with, there are the ex-servicemen. That I can understand. Then there are the widows' pensions. Then the health insurance, the large family allowances, and the allowances for . . .'

He turned to the deputy-mayor.

'Can you sort them all out? I sometimes wonder whether there's a soul in the village who doesn't draw something or other from the government. And I'm certain some of them have kids just for the sake of the children's allowance.'

His glass misted over in his hand, Maigret inquired jokingly:

'Do you think the allowances have something to do with Léonie Birard's death?'

'One never knows.'

It seemed to be an obsession. He must draw a pension himself, for his arm. He was paid by the government. And it infuriated him that other people benefited as well. In fact, he was jealous.

'Give me a *chopine*, Louis.'

Théo's eyes were still twinkling. Maigret drank his wine in sips, and this was almost like what he had expected of his trip to the seaside. The air was the same colour as the white wine, tasted the same. Out in the square, two hens were pecking at the hard ground; they could hardly be finding worms there. Thérèse was in the kitchen, peeling onions, wiping her eyes from time to time with the corner of her apron.

'Shall we be going?'

Daniélou, who had scarcely touched his wine, followed him with relief.

'Don't you think those peasants seemed to be laughing at us?' he murmured, when they were outside.

'And how!'

'You seem to find it funny!'

Maigret made no reply. He was beginning to find his feet in the village, and no longer regretted the Quai des Orfèvres. He hadn't telephoned to his wife that morning, as he had promised to do. He hadn't even noticed the post office. He'd have to take a look at that, presently.

They went past a haberdashery, and the chief-inspector saw, through the window, a woman so old and so emaciated that he felt she might snap in two at any moment.

'Who's that?'

'There are a couple of them, about the same age, the Demoiselles Thévenard.'

Two old maids had kept a shop in his native village, too. One would really think French villagers were interchangeable. Years had gone by. The roads had become crowded with fast cars. Buses and vans had replaced the former carts. Cinemas had sprung up all over the place. Wireless and numbers of other things had been invented. And yet Maigret was finding, in this village, the characters of his childhood, unchanged as figures in a holy picture.

'Here is the house.'

It was an old one, and the only one in the street which had not been whitewashed for years. The lieutenant put the big key into the lock of the green-painted door, pushed it open, and they were met by a sickly smell, doubtless also to be found next door, where the two old maids lived, a smell that clings to places where very old people live with the windows shut.

The first room was not unlike the one where Madame Gastin had received him, except that the oak furniture was not so well polished, the upholstery was shabbier, and there was a set of huge copper fire-irons. There was also, in one corner, a bed which must have been brought in from another room, and which was still unmade.

'The bedrooms are upstairs,' explained the lieutenant. 'For the last few years Léonie Birard had refused to go up. She lived on the ground floor, slept in this room. Nothing has been touched.'

A half-open door led into a fair-sized kitchen, with a stone fireplace beside which a coal-burning kitchen range had been installed. Every-thing was dirty. Saucepans had left rusty circles on the stove. Splashes starred the walls. The leather arm-chair near the window must be the one in which the old woman had spent the greater part of her time.

Maigret understood why she preferred this room to the front one. There were hardly any passers-by on the road, which led to the sea, whereas from the back, just as from the schoolmaster's house, one could see the liveliest part of the houses, the yards and gardens, in-cluding the school playground.

It was almost homely. From her arm-chair, Léonie Birard could share the daily life of nine or ten families, and if she had sharp eyes she could see what they all had for their meals.

'The chalk line shows where she was found, of course. That stain you can see . . .'

'I understand.'

'She hadn't bled much.'

'Where is she now?'

'They took her to the morgue at La Rochelle, for the post-mortem. The funeral's tomorrow morning.'

'You still don't know who gets her property?'

'I've looked everywhere for a will. I telephoned to a solicitor at La Rochelle. She'd often talked to him about making a will, but she'd never done it with him. He has some securities she deposited with him, some bonds, the title-deeds of this house and of another one she owns, a mile from here.'

'So that if nothing is found, her niece will get the lot?'

'I imagine so.'

'What does she say about it?'

'She doesn't seem to count on it. The Selliers aren't hard up. They're not rich, but they have a flourishing little business. You'll be seeing them. I haven't your experience with people. These seemed frank, honest, hard-working.'

Maigret was opening and closing drawers, discovering half-rusted kitchen utensils, odds and ends of all kinds, old buttons, nails, bills, jumbled up with threadless cotton-reels, stockings, hairpins.

He went back to the front room, where there stood an old chest of drawers which was not without value, and there too he opened the drawers.

'You've been through these papers?'

The lieutenant blushed slightly, as though he had been caught out or brought face to face with some disagreeable fact.

He had had the same expression at Louis's bar, when he had been obliged to take the glass of white wine held out to him by Maigret.

'They're letters.'

'So I see.'

'They go back more than ten years, to the time when she was still postmistress.'

'So far as I can see, they aren't addressed to her.'

'That's true. I shall put the whole lot in the file, of course. I've already mentioned them to the examining magistrate. I can't do everything at once.'

The letters were still in their envelopes, each of which bore a different name: Évariste Cornu, Augustin Cornu, Jules Marchandon, Célestin Marchandon, Théodore Coumar, and so on; women's names too, including those of the Thévenard sisters, who kept the haber-dashery.

'It looks to me as though Léonie Birard, in the days when she was postmistress, didn't give *all* the letters to the people they were addressed to.'

He glanced over a few of them:

'*Dear Mamma,*
 '*This comes to tell you that I am well, as I hope you are. I like my new place, except that the grandfather, who lives with the family, coughs all day and spits on the floor. . . .*'

Another said:

 '*I met cousin Jules in the street and he looked ashamed when he saw me. He was dead drunk and for a moment I thought he didn't recognize me.*'

Léonie Birard had evidently not opened all the letters. She seemed to be more interested in some families than in others—especially the Cornus and Rateaus, who were numerous in the district.

Several envelopes bore the Senate postmark. They were signed by a well-known politician who had now been dead for two years.

'*My dear Sir,*
 '*I have received your letter about the storm that wrecked your mussel-beds and washed away more than two hundred posts. I am prepared to arrange for the funds earmarked for victims of national calamities . . .*'

'I asked about that,' explained the lieutenant. 'The mussel-beds consist of pinewood piles driven into the sea-bed, with bundles of twigs hung between them. The bunches of young mussels are slung there and left to grow. Whenever the tide comes in a bit violently, some of the piles are washed out to sea. They're expensive, because they have to be brought from a distance.'

'So the clever chaps get them paid for by the Government under the heading of "national calamity"!'

'That Senator was very popular,' said Daniélou with a wry smile. 'He never had any difficulty in getting re-elected.'

'You've read all these letters?'

'I've glanced through them.'

'They don't provide any clues?'

'They explain why the Birard woman was detested by everyone in the village. She knew too much about them all. She was probably pretty outspoken with them. But I found nothing really serious, any-how nothing serious enough to induce anyone, especially after ten years had gone by, to finish her off with a bullet through the head. Most of the people those letters were meant for are dead now, and their children don't bother much about what went on in the old days.'

'Are you taking these letters away with you?'

'I needn't take them this evening. I can leave you the key of the house. You don't want to go upstairs?'

Maigret went up, to satisfy his conscience. He learnt nothing from the two upper rooms, which were full of odds and ends and pieces of dilapidated furniture.

Outside, he accepted the key the lieutenant proffered.

'What are you going to do now?'

'When is school over?'

'Morning class ends at half past eleven. Some of the children, those who live fairly near, go home for lunch. The rest, those who come from the farms and the seaside, bring sandwiches and eat them at school. Lessons begin again at half past one and finish at four o'clock.'

Maigret pulled out his watch. It was ten past eleven.

'Are you staying in the village?'

'I must go and see the examining magistrate, who's been questioning the schoolmaster this morning, but I'll be back sometime in the afternoon.'

'See you later, then.'

Maigret shook his hand. He felt inclined for another glass of white wine before the end of morning school. He stood for a moment in the sunshine, watching the lieutenant move away with a light step, as though a weight had fallen from his shoulders.

Théo was still at Louis's. In the opposite corner there now sat an old man dressed almost in rags, looking like a tramp, with a bushy white beard. Filling his glass with an unsteady hand, he had only an indifferent glance to spare for Maigret.

'A *chopine*?' inquired Louis.

'The same as before.'

'It's the only one I've got. I suppose you'll be eating here? Thérèse is cooking a rabbit that'll make your mouth water.'

The maid appeared.

'You like rabbit with white wine sauce, Monsieur Maigret?'

It was only to get a glimpse of him, to shoot him a conspiratorial, grateful glance. He hadn't given her away. In her relief she looked almost pretty.

'You get along back to your kitchen.'

A van drew up, and a man in butcher's overalls came into the tap-room. Unlike most butchers he was thin and sickly-looking, with a crooked nose and bad teeth.

'A *pernod*, Louis.'

He turned towards Théo, who was smiling seraphically.

'Hello, you old scoundrel!'

The deputy-mayor's sole response was a vague movement of the hand.

'Not too tired? I can't think how lazy hounds like you get by!'

He switched his attention to Maigret.

'So it's you who're going to dig out the secret, is it?'

'I'm trying to!'

'Try hard. If you find anything you'll deserve a medal.'

He dipped his drooping moustache in his glass.

'How's your boy getting on?' asked Théo, still lazily sprawling in his corner.

'Doctor says it's time he began to walk. Easier said than done. As soon as he's put on his feet, he falls down. Doctors don't know their job. No more than deputy-mayors!'

He spoke jokingly, but with a bitter undercurrent in his voice.

'Have you finished your round?'

'I've still to go to Bourrages.'

He asked for a second glass, swallowed it at one gulp, wiped his moustache, and called to Louis:

'Chalk that up with the rest.'

Then, turning to the chief-inspector:

'Enjoy yourself!'

Finally, on his way out, he deliberately knocked against Théo's legs.

'So long, you dirty dog!'

They watched him start up the van and turn it in the square.

'His father and mother died of TB,' explained Louis. 'His sister is in a sanatorium. He's got a brother shut up in a lunatic asylum.'

'And he himself?'

'He does his best, sells his meat in the villages round here. He opened a butcher's shop at La Rochelle once, and it swallowed up every penny he'd got.'

'Has he several children?'

'A boy and a girl. The two others died at birth. The boy was knocked down by a motor-bike a month ago, and he's still in plaster. The girl, who's seven, is at school, I suppose. By the time he's finished his round he'll have swallowed at least half a bottle of *pernod*.'

'Amuses you, does it?' Théo asked in his mocking voice.

'What amuses me?'

'Telling all that.'

'I'm not saying any harm of anyone.'

'Would you like me to tell about your little affairs?'

This seemed to frighten Louis, who seized a *chopine* of wine from under the counter and went across to put it on the table.

'You know there's nothing to tell. One has to make conversation, doesn't one?'

Théo seemed somehow jubilant. His mouth was unsmiling, but there was a strange glint in his eyes. Maigret couldn't help thinking the man

was like an old faun who'd retired from active life. There he was, in the
midst of the village, like a mischievous god who knew everything that
went on behind people's walls, inside people's heads, and who was
watching with solitary relish the spectacle the world presented.

He regarded Maigret as an equal rather than an enemy.

'You're a very smart chap,' he seemed to be saying.'You're supposed
to be the star performer in your game. In Paris, you unearth everything
people try to hide from you.

'But I'm a smart chap too. And down here, I'm the one who knows.

'Go ahead! Play your game. Ask people questions. Drag out their
secret thoughts.

'We'll see whether you tumble to it in the end!'

He slept with Maria, an unlovely slattern. He had tried to sleep with
Madame Gastin, who had nothing feminine left about her. He drank
from morning to night, never entirely fuddled, floating in a private
world which must be comic, since it brought a grin to his face.

The old woman Birard, too, had known the little village secrets,
but they had infuriated her, acting on her like a poison that she had
to work out of her system in one way or another.

His way was to watch the people, mock them, and when any of
them wanted a fake certificate in order to draw one of those allowances
that made the postman so angry, he supplied it, endorsing the paper
with one of the *mairie* stamps which he always carried in the pockets of
his shapeless trousers.

He didn't take them seriously.

'Another glass, Inspector?'

'Not just now.'

Maigret could hear children's voices from the direction of the
school. Those who went home for lunch were coming out. He saw two
or three going across the square.

'I'll be back in half an hour.'

'The rabbit will be ready.'

'Still no oysters?'

'No oysters.'

Hands in pockets, he strolled over to the Selliers' shop. A little boy
had gone in just ahead of him, making his way among the buckets,
hose-pipes, spraying apparatus that cluttered the floor and hung from
the ceiling. There were other tools to be seen everywhere, in the dusty
light.

A woman's voice asked:

'What can I do for you?'

He had to peer through the dimness to make out a youngish face, the
light patch of a blue-and-white checked apron.

'Is your husband here?'

'At the back, in the workshop.'

The little boy had gone into the kitchen and was washing his hands at the pump.

'If you'll come this way, I'll call him.'

She knew who he was, and did not seem to be alarmed. In the kitchen, which was the centre of life in the house, she pushed forward a rush-bottomed chair for him, then opened a door into the yard.

'Julien! . . . Someone to see you. . . .'

The little boy was drying his hands and gazing inquisitively at Maigret. And he, too, brought childhood memories back to the chief-inspector. In his form at school, in every form he had been in, there had always been one boy who was fatter than the others and had this same innocent, intent expression, this same clear skin, this same air of having been well brought-up.

His mother was not a big woman, but his father, who came in a moment later, must have weighed well over fourteen stone; he was very tall, very broad, with an almost babyish face and guileless eyes.

He wiped his feet on the doormat before coming in. Three places were laid on the round table.

'Excuse me,' he murmured, going in his turn to the pump.

One could feel that in this house there was a ritual, each person doing certain things at certain times of day.

'Were you just going to have your meal?'

It was the woman who answered:

'Not at once. Dinner's not ready yet.'

'As a matter of fact, what I really wanted was to have a word with your little boy.'

Both parents looked at the child, with no sign of surprise or uneasiness.

'You hear that, Marcel?' asked his father.

'Yes, Papa.'

'Answer the inspector's questions.'

'Yes, Papa.'

Turning squarely to face Maigret, the boy settled into the attitude of a pupil preparing to answer his schoolmaster.

V

WHILE Maigret was lighting his pipe there took place a kind of silent ceremony which reminded him, more vividly than anything else he had seen at Saint-André since the previous evening, of the village of his childhood. For a moment, in fact, Madame Sellier seemed to have been transformed into one of his own aunts, in a blue-and-white checked apron, her hair screwed into a knot on top of her head.

The woman had merely looked at her husband, with the very slightest widening of her eyes, and Julien had understood the message, gone over to the back door, through which his tall figure had vanished for a moment. His wife, without waiting for him to come back, had opened the cupboard and taken out two glasses belonging to the best service, those that were kept for when visitors came, and she was now wiping them with a clean cloth.

When the ironmonger reappeared, he was carrying a corked-up bottle of wine. He said nothing. Nobody needed to say anything. Anyone who had come from a great distance, or from some other planet, might have imagined that these actions formed part of a rite. They heard the sound of the cork being drawn from the bottle, the splash of the golden wine into the two glasses.

Obviously a little shy, Julien Sellier picked up one glass, looked through it sideways, and finally said:

'Your very good health.'

'Your very good health,' responded Maigret.

After which the man withdrew to a shadowy corner of the room, while his wife went across to the stove.

'Tell me, Marcel,' began the chief-inspector, turning back to the boy, who had not moved, 'I suppose you've never told a lie?'

The hesitation, if any, was brief, accompanied by a quick sidelong glance towards his mother.

'Yes, sir, I have.'

He added hastily:

'But I've always confessed.'

'You mean you've gone to confession afterwards?'

'Yes, sir.'

'At once?'

'As soon as I could, because I didn't want to die in sin.'

'But they can't have been very important lies?'

'Pretty important.'

'Would you very much mind telling me one of them, as an example?'

'There was the time I tore my trousers, climbing a tree. When I got home I said I'd caught them on a nail in Joseph's yard.'

'And you went to confession that same day?'

'The next day.'

'And when did you own up to your father and mother?'

'Not till a week later. Another time I fell into the pond when I was catching frogs. Papa and Mamma don't let me play round the pond, because I catch cold easily. My clothes were all wet. I said another boy had pushed me when I was crossing the little bridge over the stream.'

'And did you wait a week that time, before telling them the truth?'

'Only two days.'

'Do you often tell lies like that?'

'No, sir.'

'About every how often?'

Marcel paused for reflection, just as though this were an oral examination.

'Less than once a month.'

'Do your friends do it more often?'

'Not all of them. Some do.'

'Do they go to confession afterwards, like you?'

'I don't know. I expect so.'

'Is the schoolmaster's son a friend of yours?'

'No, sir.'

'Don't you play with him?'

'He doesn't play with anybody.'

'Why not?'

'Perhaps because he doesn't like playing. Or perhaps because his father's the teacher. I did try to be friends with him.'

'You don't like Monsieur Gastin?'

'He's unfair.'

'In what way unfair?'

'He always gives me top marks, even when it's his son who ought to have them. I like to be top of the class when I've deserved it, but not when I haven't.'

'Why do you suppose he does that?'

'I don't know. Perhaps he's afraid.'

'Afraid of what?'

The boy struggled to find a reply. He undoubtedly knew what he wanted to say, but realized that it was too complicated, that he wouldn't find the words. He merely repeated:

'I don't know.'

'You remember Tuesday morning?'

'Yes, sir.'

'What did you do during break?'

'I played with the others.'

'What happened a little time after you'd gone back to the classroom?'

'Old Piedbœuf, from Gros-Chêne, knocked on the door, and Monsieur Gastin went over to the *mairie* with him, after telling us to keep quiet.'

'Does that often happen?'

'Yes, sir. Fairly often.'

'Do you keep quiet?'

'Not all of us.'

'You yourself keep quiet?'

'Most of the time.'

'When had this happened last?'

'The day before, on Monday, when there was a funeral. Someone came to have a paper signed.'

'What did you do on Tuesday?'

'At first I stayed in my place.'

'Had the other boys begun to fool about?'

'Yes, sir. Most of them.'

'What exactly were they doing?'

'They were fighting for fun, throwing things at each other, india-rubbers and pencils.'

'And then?'

The boy occasionally hesitated before replying, but not from embarrassment, merely like someone searching for the exact answer.

'I went to the window.'

'Which window?'

'The one overlooking the yards and kitchen gardens. That's the one I always go to.'

'Why?'

'I don't know. It's the one nearest to my desk.'

'It wasn't the sound of a shot that made you go to the window?'

'No, sir.'

'If a shot had been fired outside, would you have heard it?'

'I mightn't have. The others were making a lot of noise. And a horse was being shod at the forge.'

'Have you a .22 gun?'

'Yes, sir. I took it to the *mairie* yesterday, like the others. Everybody who had a gun was asked to take it to the *mairie*.'

'You didn't leave the classroom while the master was away?'

'No, sir.'

Maigret was speaking in a quiet, encouraging tone. Madame Sellier had tactfully departed to tidy the shop, while her husband, glass in hand, was watching Marcel with an air of pride.

'You saw the schoolmaster crossing the yard?'

'Yes, sir.'

'You saw him when he was on his way to the tool-shed?'

'No, sir. He was coming back from it.'

'You saw him come out of the shed?'

'I saw him shutting the door behind him. Then he came across the yard and I said to the others:

' "Look out!"

'Then they all went back to their places. Me too.'

'Do you play a great deal with the other boys?'

'Not much, no.'

'Don't you like playing?'

'I'm too fat.'

He blushed as he said this, glanced at his father, as though apologizing.

'Haven't you any friends?'

'Joseph's my best friend.'

'Who's Joseph?'

'Monsieur Rateau's son.'

'The mayor's son?'

Julien Sellier broke in to explain.

'There are a lot of Rateaus at Saint-André and in the neighbourhood,' he said, 'nearly all cousins. Joseph's father is Marcellin Rateau, the butcher.'

Maigret took a sip of wine and relit his pipe, which he had allowed to go out.

'Was Joseph with you at the window?'

'He wasn't at school. He's been at home for a month, because of his accident.'

'Is he the boy who was knocked down by a motor-bicycle?'

'Yes, sir.'

'Were you with him when it happened?'

'Yes, sir.'

'Do you often go to see him?'

'Nearly every day.'

'Did you go yesterday?'

'No.'

'The day before yesterday?'

'Not then either.'

'Why not?'

'Because of what had happened. Nobody was thinking of anything except the crime.'

'You wouldn't have dared to tell a lie to the constabulary lieutenant, I suppose?'

'No, sir.'

'Are you glad the schoolmaster's in prison?'

'No, sir.'

'Do you realize it's your evidence that sent him there?'

'I don't understand what you mean.'

'If you hadn't said you'd seen him coming out of the tool-shed, they probably wouldn't have arrested him.'

He made no reply to this, embarrassed, shifting from one foot to the other, glancing again at his father.

'If you really did see him, you were quite right to tell the truth.'

'I did tell the truth.'

'You didn't like Léonie Birard?'

'No, sir.'

'Why not?'

'Because she used to shout rude things at me when I went past.'

'More at you than at the others?'

'Yes, sir.'

'Do you know why?'

'Because she was cross with Mamma for marrying my father.'

Maigret half closed his eyes, trying to think of another question, failed to find one and emptied his glass instead. He rose to his feet, rather heavily, for he had already that morning drunk quite a few glasses of white wine.

'Thank you, Marcel. If you had anything to say to me—for instance, if you remembered any little thing you'd forgotten, I'd like you to come and see me at once. You're not scared of me?'

'No, sir.'

'Another glass?' asked the boy's father, reaching out for the bottle.

'No, thank you. I don't want to delay your lunch any longer. Your son's an intelligent boy, Monsieur Sellier.'

The ironmonger flushed with pleasure.

'We're doing our best to bring him up properly. I don't think he often tells lies.'

'That reminds me: when did he tell you about the schoolmaster going to the tool-shed?'

'On Wednesday evening.'

'He hadn't said anything about it on Tuesday, when the whole village was talking about Léonie Birard's death?'

'No. I think he was a bit overcome. On Wednesday, while we were at dinner, he looked rather strange, and suddenly he said to me:

' "Papa, I think I saw something." '

'He told me the story, and I went and reported it to the police lieutenant.'

'Thank you.'

Something was bothering him, he didn't know exactly what. Once outside, he made first for the *Bon Coin*, where he saw the substitute schoolmaster seated near the window, eating his lunch and reading a book. He remembered he had meant to telephone to his wife, walked to the post office, which was one of another group of houses, and was received there by a girl of about twenty-five, who wore a black overall.

'Would it take very long to get Paris?'

'Not at this time of day, Monsieur Maigret.'

While he waited for his call he watched her doing her accounts, wondered whether she was married, whether she would get married one day, or if she would turn out like the old Birard woman.

He stayed in the telephone booth for about five minutes, and the only words the girl at the switchboard could hear through the door were:

'No, no oysters. . . . Because there aren't any. . . . No. . . . The weather's lovely. . . . Not in the least cold. . . .'

He decided to go to lunch. The schoolmaster was still there, and Maigret was shown to a seat at the opposite table. The whole village knew who he was by this time. They didn't speak to him, but they watched him go along the street, and no sooner had he gone by, than they began to talk about him. The schoolmaster looked up from his book three or four times. Just as he went away he seemed to hesitate for a moment. Perhaps he had something he wanted to say? One couldn't be sure. In any case, as he went past he gave him a nod which might have been interpreted as an unintentional jerk of the head.

Thérèse had a spotless white apron over her black dress. Louis was eating in the kitchen, where he could be heard calling to the girl from time to time. When he had finished he came over to Maigret, his mouth still greasy.

'Well, what did you think of the rabbit?'

'It was first-class!'

'A drop of *marc* to wash it down? This is on me.'

His manner towards the chief-inspector was protective, as though without him he would have been lost in the jungle of Saint-André.

'Queer chap, that!' he growled as he sat down, legs wide apart because of his fat stomach.

'Who?'

'Théo. Cleverest fellow I know. All his life he's managed to take things easy, without doing a stroke of work.'

'Do you really think nobody else heard that shot?'

'Well, in the country, people don't pay much attention to a rifle-shot. If it had been a sporting gun, everybody would have noticed. But those little things don't make much noise, and we've got so used to them since all the kids began to have them. . . .'

'Théo was in his garden and is supposed not to have seen anything?'

'In his garden or in his wine-cellar, since what he calls gardening usually means going to tap the barrel. But if he did see anything he probably wouldn't say so.'

'Even if he saw someone fire the shot?'

'All the more reason to keep quiet.'

Louis was pleased with himself, refilled the little glasses.

'I warned you you wouldn't understand a thing.'

'Do you believe the schoolmaster wanted to kill the old woman?'

'Do you?'

Maigret replied positively:

'No.'

Louis looked at him, smiling as though to say:

'Neither do I.'

But he did not say it. The two of them were probably in the same torpid condition, because of what they had had to eat and drink. They sat in silence for a moment, looking out at the square which was cut in two by the sun, at the greenish glass windows of the co-operative stores, the stone porch of the church.

'What's the priest like?' asked Maigret, for the sake of something to say.

'He's a priest.'

'Is he on the schoolmaster's side?'

'No.'

At last Maigret got up, stood hesitating for a moment in the middle of the room, then decided on laziness and moved towards the staircase.

'You can call me in an hour,' he said to Thérèse.

He had been wrong to use the familiar 'tu'. Officials at Police Head-quarters usually speak like that to women of her type, and it had not been lost on Louis, who frowned. In the bedroom the green shutters were closed, with only thin shafts of sunlight stealing through. He did not undress, only took off his jacket and shoes, lay on the bed without turning it down.

A little later, while he was still only dozing, he seemed to hear the regular sound of the sea—could it be that? Then he went right off to sleep and did not wake until there was a knock on the door.

'It's more than an hour, Monsieur Maigret. Would you like a cup of coffee?'

He still felt heavy, sluggish, uncertain as to what he really wanted to do. Downstairs, going through the front room, he saw four men playing cards; one was Théo and another Marcellin, the butcher, still in his working clothes.

He still felt there was a detail jarring somewhere, though he couldn't think what it was. He had had that impression during his talk with little Sellier. At what moment exactly?

He began walking, first to Léonie Birard's house, the key of which was in his pocket. He went in, sat down in the front room, where he read all the letters he had glanced over that morning. They did not tell him anything important, merely familiarized him with certain names, the Dubards, the Cornus, the Gillets, Rateaus and Boncœurs.

On leaving the house he meant to go down the path to the sea, but a little way along he found the cemetery and went in, spelt out the names on the tombs, much the same as those he had found in the letters.

He could have pieced together the family histories, telling how the Rateaus had been related by marriage to the Dubards for two genera-tions back, and that a Cornu daughter had married a Piedbœuf who had died at the age of twenty-six.

He went on for another two or three hundred yards, and the sea was still not in sight, the meadows were sloping gently upwards on either side; all he could see, far ahead, was a shimmering mist that he gave up hope of reaching.

The villagers kept meeting him in their streets and alleys, hands in pockets, stopping now and then, aimlessly, to stare at a house-front or a passer-by.

He couldn't resist another glass of white wine before going to the *mairie*. The four men were still playing cards and Louis sat astride a chair, watching the game.

The sun was shining full on the *mairie* steps, and looking down the corridor he could see the caps of the two *gendarmes*, in the kitchen-garden at the back. They must be still hunting for the cartridge-case.

The windows of the schoolmaster's house were shut. Rows of children's heads could be seen through the schoolroom window.

He found the lieutenant making notes, in red pencil, on a witness's statement.

'Come in, Chief-Inspector. I've seen the examining magistrate. He questioned Gastin this morning.'

'How is he?'

'Like a man who's just spent his first night in prison. He was anxious to know whether you were still here.'

'He sticks to his denial, I suppose?'

'Closer than ever.'

'Has he any theory of his own?'

'He doesn't believe anyone meant to kill the old woman. He thinks it was more likely a practical joke that proved fatal. People often played tricks of that kind.'

'On Léonie Birard?'

'Yes. Not only the children, but grown-ups as well. You know what it is when a whole village takes a dislike to someone. Whenever a cat died it would be tossed into her garden, if it wasn't thrown through the window into the house. A couple of weeks ago she found her door all plastered with dung. The schoolmaster thinks someone fired a shot to frighten her or make her angry.'

'What about the tool-shed?'

'He still makes out that he never set foot in it on Tuesday.'

'He didn't do any gardening on Tuesday morning, before school?'

'Not on Tuesday, but on Monday he did. He gets up at six o'clock every morning, it's only then that he has a little time to himself. Did you see the Sellier boy? What do you think about him?'

'He answered my questions without hesitation.'

'Mine, too, without once contradicting himself. I questioned the other boys, who all declare he didn't leave the classroom after break. If that had been a lie, I imagine one of them would certainly have slipped up on it.'

'I imagine so. Do they know who inherits?'

'They still haven't found a will. Madame Sellier's chances look good.'

'Did you check on how her husband spent his time on Tuesday morning?'

'He was busy in his workshop.'

'Any witnesses to that?'

'His wife, for one. And for another, Marchandon, the blacksmith, who went across to speak to him.'

'What time was that?'

'He doesn't know exactly. Before eleven o'clock, he says. According to him, they chatted for at least a quarter of an hour. Not that that proves anything, of course.'

He leafed through his papers.

'Especially as young Sellier says the forge was working when the schoolmaster left the classroom.'

'So his father could have gone away?'

'Yes, but don't forget that everybody knows him. He'd have had to go across the square and into the gardens. If he'd been carrying a rifle they'd have noticed him all the more.'

'But they mightn't say so.'

In fact there was nothing reliable, no firm foundation, except two contradictory statements: one from Marcel Sellier, who said that from the schoolroom window he had seen Gastin coming out of the tool-shed; and the other from Gastin himself, who would swear that he had never set foot in the shed that day.

All these happenings were recent. The villagers had been questioned on the evening of the very day, Tuesday, and the questioning had gone on during Wednesday. They had had no time to forget things.

If the schoolmaster had not fired the shot, why should he tell a lie? And, above all, what motive had he for killing Léonie Birard?

Neither had Marcel Sellier any motive for making up the tool-shed story.

As for Théo, he maintained, in his bantering style, that he had heard a shot, but seen nothing at all.

Had he been in his kitchen-garden? Had he been in his wine-cellar? Impossible to rely on the times given by any of them, for time doesn't count much in the country, except when it comes to meals. Neither was Maigret very convinced by assurances that such and such a person had or had not gone past along the street at a particular moment. When you're accustomed to seeing people a dozen times a day in the same familiar places, you don't pay attention any longer, and you may quite sincerely mix up one meeting with another, say that a particular incident took place on Tuesday whereas really it happened on Monday.

The wine was making him feel hot.

'What time is the funeral?'

'Nine o'clock. Everybody will be there. It isn't every day that they have the pleasure of burying the local bugbear. Have you got an idea?'

Maigret shook his head, went on pottering about the office, fingered the rifles, the lead pellets.

'I believe you told me the doctor wasn't certain what time she was killed?'

'He puts it at between ten and eleven in the morning.'

'So that if it weren't for young Sellier's evidence . . .'

They always came up against that. And each time, Maigret had the same impression that the truth had given him the slip again, that he had been on the verge, at one moment, of discovering it.

He wasn't interested in Léonie Birard. What did it matter to him whether someone had meant to kill her or only to frighten her, or whether it was by accident that the bullet had gone through her left eye?

It was the Gastin business that excited him, and consequently, little Sellier's evidence.

He walked into the courtyard, and was half-way across it when the children began emerging from the schoolhouse, less hurriedly than at break, and making their way in small groups to the gate. Brothers and sisters could be distinguished among them. The big girls were leading smaller children by the hand, and some of them would have nearly two miles to walk home.

Only one boy greeted him, except Marcel Sellier, who raised his cap politely. The others went past, staring inquisitively. The schoolmaster was standing in the doorway. Maigret went up to him and the young man stepped aside to let him in, stammering:

'Did you want to speak to me?'

'Not particularly. Had you been to Saint-André before this?'

'No. This is the first time. I've taught in schools at La Rochelle and at Fourras.'

'Did you know Joseph Gastin?'

'No.'

The desks and forms were black, cut about with penknives and splashed with patches of purple ink, which had a bronze sheen here and there against the varnish. Maigret went to the first window on the left, through which he saw part of the courtyard, the gardens, the tool-shed. Then, from the right-hand window, he could see the back of Léonie Birard's house.

'Did you notice anything special about the children's behaviour today?'

'They're quieter than town children. Perhaps they're shy.'

'They've not been holding discussions in groups, or passing notes in class?'

The deputy teacher was less than twenty-two years old. He was obviously in awe of Maigret, rather because he was a celebrity than because he belonged to the police. He would no doubt have behaved in the same way if confronted with a famous politician or a film star.

'I'm afraid I didn't pay attention to that. Should I have done?'

'What do you think of young Sellier?'

'Just a moment . . . which one is that? . . . I don't know their names yet. . . .'

'A taller, fatter boy than the others, who's very good at his lessons. . . .'

The young man's eyes turned towards the seat at the end of the front row, which was evidently Marcel's place, and Maigret went and sat down there, though the desk was too low for him to get his knees under it. Sitting here and looking out of the second window, it was not the kitchen-gardens he saw, but the lime-tree in the courtyard and the Gastins' house.

'He didn't strike you as uneasy or worried?'

'No. I remember asking him some questions in arithmetic and noticing that he was very intelligent.'

To the right of the schoolmaster's house, further off, one could see the first-floor windows of two other houses.

'Tomorrow I may perhaps ask you to let me come and see them for a moment during school.'

'Whenever you like. We're both staying at the inn, I believe. It'll be easier for me to prepare my lessons over here.'

Maigret left him, and was about to go to the schoolmaster's house. It was not Madame Gastin he wanted to see, but Jean-Paul. He walked more than half the distance, saw a curtain move at one of the windows, stopped, depressed at the thought of finding himself once again in a stuffy little room, confronted with the tragic faces of the woman and her little boy.

He felt cowardly. Overcome by laziness which must be due to the leisurely village life, the white wine, the sun which was now beginning to sink behind the roofs.

What, in fact, was he doing here? Scores of times before, during an investigation, he had had this same feeling of helplessness, or rather of futility. He was suddenly pitchforked into the life of a group of people he had never set eyes on before, and his job was to worm out their deepest secrets. This time it wasn't even his job. He had come of his own accord, because a schoolmaster had waited for him for hours in the Purgatory at Police Headquarters.

The air was taking on a bluish tint, becoming cooler, damper. Windows were lighting up here and there, and Marchandon's forge stood out, red; one could see the flames dancing every time the bellows blew them.

In the shop opposite were two women, as motionless as the picture on an advertisement calendar, with only their lips moving slightly. They seemed to be speaking in turns, and at the end of every sentence the shopwoman shook her head disconsolately. Were they talking about Léonie Birard? Very likely. And about tomorrow's funeral, which would be a memorable event in the history of Saint-André.

The men were still playing cards. They must spend hours this way, every afternoon, exchanging the same phrases, now and again putting out a hand to pick up a glass, then wipe their lips.

He was about to go in, order a *chopine* for himself, sit down in a corner to wait for dinner-time, when a car pulled up close beside him, making him jump.

'Did I frighten you?' called the cheery voice of the doctor. 'You haven't fathomed the mystery yet?'

He got out of the car, lit a cigarette.

'Makes a change from the Grands Boulevards,' he remarked, with a wave of the hand at the village around them, the dimly-lit shop-windows, the forge, the church door, which was half open, letting out a faint glow of light. 'You should just see it in the middle of the winter. Have you begun to get used to our local life?'

'Léonie Birard used to keep letters addressed to different people.'

'She was an old scoundrel. Some people called her the louse. You can't imagine how scared she was of dying!'

'Was she ill?'

'Ill enough to have died long ago. But she didn't die. Like Théo, who ought to have been in his grave these ten years or more, and yet goes on drinking his two quarts of white wine a day, not to mention *apéritifs.*'

'What do you think of the Selliers?'

'They're doing their best to join the middle class. Julien came here as an apprentice from the Waifs and Strays, and worked hard to establish himself. They've only one child, a boy.'

'I know. He's intelligent.'

'Yes.'

It seemed to Maigret that there was a certain reserve in the doctor's tone.

'What do you mean?'

'Nothing. He's a well-brought-up lad. He's one of the choirboys. The priest's pet.'

It looked as though the doctor didn't like priests, either.

'You believe he's been lying?'

'I didn't say that. I don't believe anything. If you'd been a country doctor for twenty-two years, you'd be like me. The only thing that interests them is making money, turning it into gold, putting the gold into bottles and burying the bottles in their gardens. Even when they're ill or injured, they have to make something out of it.'

'I don't understand.'

'There's always the insurance, or the allowances, one way or another of turning everything into money.'

He was talking almost like the postman.

'A bunch of scoundrels!' he concluded, in a tone which seemed to contradict his words. 'They're a scream. I'm quite fond of them.'

'Léonie Birard too?'

'She was phenomenal!'

'And Germaine Gastin?'

'She'll spend the rest of her life tormenting herself and everybody else because she went to bed with Chevassou. I'll bet it didn't happen often, perhaps only once. And just because she enjoyed herself once in her life . . . If you're still here tomorrow, come and have lunch with me. This evening I have to go to La Rochelle.'

It was dark already. Maigret hung about a little longer in the square, emptied his pipe, knocking the bowl against his heel, and, with a sigh, went into Louis's inn, walked over to a table which was already his table, and Thérèse, without being asked, put a *chopine* of white wine and a glass in front of him.

Théo, sitting opposite with his pack of cards, glanced at him from time to time with eyes that sparkled with malice, as though to say:

'You're coming on: You're coming on: A few years of that, and you'll be like the rest of them.'

# VI

I T was not because of the postmistress's funeral, which was to take place that day, that Maigret woke up with a weight on his mind. The death of Léonie Birard, in the sunshine, had not upset anyone, there had been nothing tragic about it, and the people of Saint-André, in the houses and farms, were doubtless dressing for her burial as cheerfully as for a wedding. So much so that Louis Paumelle, out in the yard very early, already wearing his starched white shirt and black cloth trousers, but with no collar or tie, was pouring wine into an impressive number of *chopines*, which he was lining up not only behind the bar, but on the kitchen table as well, as though this were a fair-day.

The men were shaving themselves. Everybody would be wearing black, as though the whole village were in mourning. Maigret remembered how once, when he was little, his father had asked one of his aunts why she had bought yet another black dress.

'Well you know, my sister-in-law has cancer of the breast and may be dead in a few months or even in a few weeks. It is so bad for clothes, to dye them!'

In any village people have so many relations who may die any moment, that they spend all their time dressed in black.

Maigret shaved himself, too.

He saw the La Rochelle bus go off almost empty, although this was a Saturday. Thérèse had brought him up a cup of coffee and his hot water, because she had seen him sitting for hours in his corner, the previous evening, drinking wine and then, after dinner, glass upon glass of brandy.

But it wasn't, either, because of the amount he had drunk, that he now had a feeling of tragedy. Perhaps, after all, it was simply because he had slept badly. All night he had been seeing children's faces, in close-up, as though at the cinema, faces which all resembled little Gastin and little Sellier, but were not exactly either of theirs.

He tried, without success, to recall those dreams. Someone had a grudge against him, one of the boys; he couldn't say which, they were indistinguishable. He kept telling himself that it was easy to recognize them apart, because the schoolmaster's son wore glasses. But immediately afterwards he saw Marcel Sellier wearing glasses too and saying, when he expressed surprise:

'I only put them on when I go to confession.'

Gastin's being in prison was not so very tragic, for the police lieutenant did not really believe he was guilty; neither, in all probability, did the examining magistrate. He was better off there for a few days than going about the village or shut up in his own house. And he couldn't be found guilty on the evidence of a single witness, especially when that witness was a child.

It seemed to Maigret to be more complicated than that. This often happened to him. One could even say that during each case that came along, his mood followed more or less the same curve.

At the beginning you see people from the outside. Their little traits are what show most clearly, and that's amusing. Then, gradually, you begin to put yourself in their shoes, to wonder why they behave in this or that fashion; you catch yourself thinking like them, and that's much less amusing.

Later on, perhaps, when you've seen so much of them that nothing surprises you any longer, you may be able to laugh at them, like Dr. Bresselles.

Maigret had not reached that stage. He was worried about the little boys. At least one of them, somewhere, he felt must be living in a kind of nightmare, in spite of the bright sunlight that was still shining over the village.

By the time he went downstairs to his corner for breakfast, farmers from the outlying districts were already arriving in the square in carts. They did not come straight into the café, but stood in dark-clad groups in the street and outside the church, and their tanned skin made their shirts look dazzling white by contrast.

He did not know who had made the arrangements for the funeral, it had not occurred to him to ask. In any case the coffin had been brought from La Rochelle and taken straight to the church.

The black figures were rapidly increasing in number. Maigret noticed faces he had not seen before. The police lieutenant came up and shook hands.

'Anything fresh?'

'Not a thing. I saw him last night in his cell. He sticks to his denial, can't understand why Marcel Sellier persists in accusing him.'

Maigret went into the school playground; there were to be no lessons today, and the windows of the schoolmaster's house were closed, no one to be seen: the boy and his mother would certainly not go to the funeral, they would stay at home, silent, terrified, waiting for something to happen.

But the crowd did not seem to be angry. The men were calling to one another, some were going into Louis's for a quick glass, and coming out again, wiping their lips. As the chief-inspector went past they all fell silent, then began to talk in low voices, following him with their eyes.

A young man who, despite the cloudless sky, was wearing a tightly-belted raincoat, came up to him, an outsized pipe in his mouth.

'Albert Raymond, reporter on *La Charente*,' he announced cockily. He was not more than twenty-two. He was thin, long-haired, kept his mouth twisted into a sardonic smile.

Maigret merely nodded.

'I tried to get along to see you yesterday, but I hadn't the time.'

His way of speaking and general manner implied that he felt himself to be on equal terms with the chief-inspector. Or rather, that they were both outside this crowd. They could both look down on it with con-descension, as men who knew, who had penetrated to the most hidden springs of human nature.

'Is it true,' he asked, grasping his pencil and notebook, 'that the schoolmaster came and offered you all his savings if you'd get him out of the mess?'

Maigret turned towards him, looked him up and down, was about to say something, then, with a shrug of the shoulders, turned his back on him.

The idiot would probably think he'd guessed right. It didn't matter. The bells were ringing. The women were pouring into the church, with a few men as well. Then came the soft notes of the organ, the tinkle of a choirboy's bell.

'Is it to be a mass, or only an intercession?' the chief-inspector inquired of a man he did not know.

'A mass and an intercession. We've got plenty of time.'

Time to go to Louis's for a drink. Most of the men had gradually gathered in front of the inn or went inside in groups to drink a *chopine* or two of wine without sitting down, and then emerge again. There was a perpetual coming and going: there were people in the kitchen and even in the yard. Louis Paumelle, who had already been into the church for a moment, was now in his shirt-sleeves again and bustling about, helped by Thérèse and by a young man who seemed to be accustomed to lending him a hand.

Sellier was in church, with his wife. Maigret had not seen Marcel go past, but a little later, when he too went to the church, he understood why. Marcel was there, in his choirboy's surplice, serving mass. He could apparently get straight into the vestry by going through his parents' backyard.

'*Dies irae, dies illa . . .*'

The women really seemed to be praying, their lips were moving. Were they praying for Léonie Birard's soul, or for themselves? A few old men were standing, hat in hand, at the back of the nave, and others peeped in from time to time, half opening the door, to see how the service was getting along.

Maigret went out again, caught sight of Théo, who acknowledged his presence with his usual juicy, sarcastic grin.

Somebody obviously must know. There might even be several who knew and were keeping quiet. The voices in Louis's bar-parlour were growing louder now, and one thin farmer, with a drooping moustache, was already more than half drunk.

The butcher, too, seemed to Maigret to have brighter eyes and a more unsteady gait than usual, and the chief-inspector saw him drain three large glasses within a few minutes, invited by one man or another.

The lieutenant, either less inquisitive than he or more sensitive to the curiosity of the crowd, had taken refuge in the office at the *mairie*, where the courtyard was empty around its lime-tree.

A cart went by, which was to serve as a hearse, drawn by a chestnut horse with a black rug draped over its back. It pulled up outside the porch and the driver came across for a drink.

A light breeze was stirring the air. Far up in the sky, a few clouds were gleaming like mother-of-pearl.

At length the church doors opened. The drinkers rushed outside. The coffin appeared, carried by four men among whom Maigret recognized Julien Sellier and the deputy-mayor.

It was hoisted, not without difficulty, on to the cart. It was then covered with a black, silver-fringed pall. Young Sellier appeared next, bearing a silver cross on a black wooden shaft, and his surplice blew out round him two or three times, like a balloon.

The priest followed, repeating prayers, finding the time to glance at each person in turn; his eyes lingered for a moment on Maigret's face.

Julien Sellier and his wife led the procession; both were in black and she had a veil over her face. Next came the mayor, a tall, powerful man with a placid face and grey hair, surrounded by the members of the local council, then the general public, men in front and women behind; some of the latter, especially those at the tail end of the procession, were dragging children by the hand.

The young journalist was hurrying to and fro, making notes, talking to people whom Maigret did not know. Slowly the procession moved on, passing Louis's inn where Thérèse stood alone in the doorway, for Paumelle was with the local councillors' group.

For the second time that morning, Maigret was tempted to go and knock on the Gastins' front door and talk to Jean-Paul. Now that all the inhabitants were off to the cemetery, the mother and son must surely be feeling lonelier than ever in the deserted village.

He followed the others, however, for no definite reason. They went past Léonie Birard's house, then past a farm; a calf in the farmyard began to bellow.

As they turned into the cemetery there was a certain amount of trampling and confusion. The priest and the choirboy were already at the grave-side before the rest had all come through the gate.

It was then that Maigret noticed someone looking over the wall. He recognized Jean-Paul. One of his glasses was reflecting the sun like a mirror.

Instead of following the crowd, the chief-inspector remained outside and began to walk round the cemetery, meaning to join the boy. The latter was, he thought, probably too concentrated on what was happening beside the grave to notice this manoeuvre.

He was walking along a strip of waste ground. He had got to within about thirty yards of the boy, when he trod on a dead branch.

Jean-Paul looked round quickly, jumped down from the stone he had been standing on, and bolted for the road.

Maigret was about to call to him, refrained because the others would have heard him, merely walked on more quickly, hoping to catch up with the boy on the road.

The situation was, he realized, ridiculous. He could not venture to run. Neither could Jean-Paul. The child was afraid even to glance behind him. He was probably the only one in the village who was wearing his school clothes, not dressed in his best.

To make his way home, as he probably wanted to do, he would have had to pass the cemetery gate, outside which stood a group of farmers.

He turned left, towards the sea, hoping, perhaps, that the chief-inspector would not follow him.

Maigret followed. There were no more farms or houses to be seen, only fields and meadows where a few cows were grazing. The sea was still invisible, behind a low hill. The road sloped gently upwards.

The boy was walking as fast as he could do without breaking into a run, and Maigret, too, had lengthened his stride. He did not even know exactly why he was pursuing him like this, began to realize it was cruel.

To Jean-Paul it must seem as though a terrifying power were on his tracks. But the chief-inspector could not very well begin to shout:

'Jean-Paul! . . . Stop! . . . I only want to talk to you. . . .'

The cemetery had vanished behind them, and the village. Little Gastin had now reached the top of the hill and began to go down the other side; and Maigret could only see his head and shoulders, then only his head. There came a moment when he saw nothing at all, until he, in his turn, reached the top of the hill; and then, at last, the sparkling expanse of sea lay before him, with what he took to be an island in the distance, or perhaps the Pointe de l'Aiguillon, and a few brown-sailed fishing-boats, looking as though they were floating in space.

Jean-Paul was still walking. There was no path, either to right or left. Down beside the sea stood five or six red-roofed huts, where the mussel-breeders kept their tackle.

'Jean-Paul!' he made up his mind and called.

His voice sounded so strange that he hardly recognized it, and he turned his head to make sure nobody was watching. He noticed a momentary change in the rhythm of the boy's step. Surprise at hearing his name called had made him hesitate, almost pause, but now the surprise was over he was walking as fast as ever, practically running, panic-stricken.

The chief-inspector was ashamed of his persistence, he felt like a hulking brute bearing down on a defenceless creature.

'Wait for me, boy. . . .'

What made the position even sillier was that he was out of breath and his voice didn't carry. The distance between them remained about the same. To reduce it, he would have had to run.

What was Jean-Paul hoping? That Maigret would be disheartened and turn back?

It was more likely that he wasn't thinking at all, that he was just plunging on as though it were the only hope of escaping a danger. All that lay ahead of him was the sea, its shining fringe of foam washing over the pebbles.

'Jean-Paul . . .'

At the point he had reached, it would be as silly to give up as to go on.

The boy came to the beach, halted as though uncertain whether to take the path which no doubt led to the next village, finally stopped, still with his back turned, and only when he heard the chief-inspector's footsteps quite close by, did he swing round to face him.

He was not red but pale, his nostrils pinched. His chest was visibly heaving fast, his lips were parted, it seemed as though his heart-beats must be audible, like those of a bird held in the hand.

Maigret said nothing. For the moment he could think of nothing to say, and he, too, was out of breath.

Jean-Paul had turned away from him and was looking at the sea. They both stared in that direction, and the silence lasted a long time, as long as was needed for their hearts to return to a calm, regular rhythm.

Then Maigret walked a few steps and sat down on a stack of posts which smelt of fresh pinewood. He took off his hat, unashamedly mopped his forehead, and began, very slowly, to fill his pipe.

'You're a fast walker,' he muttered at last.

The boy, who was standing with his legs braced like a young cock, made no reply.

'Won't you come and sit by me?'

'I don't want to sit down.'

'Are you angry?'

Jean-Paul threw him a quick glance and asked:

'Why?'

'I wanted to talk to you without your mother being present. At your home it can't be done. When I saw you over the cemetery wall, I thought that was my chance.'

So as not to startle the child, he paused for a long time between sentences.

'What were you looking at?'

'The people.'

'You couldn't have been watching them all at the same time. I'm sure you were watching one particular person. Am I right?'

Jean-Paul neither admitted this nor denied it.

'Do you usually go to church?'

'No.'

'Why not?'

'Because my father and mother don't go.'

Conversation would have been easier with a grown-up. It was so long since Maigret's childhood. He had no son or daughter of his own. But he had to try to see things from this boy's standpoint.

'Did you tell your mother you were going out this morning?'

'No.'

'You didn't want her to know?'

'She'd have stopped me.'

'So you waited till she was upstairs, so as to slip out quietly? And you went round by the back lanes?'

'I wanted to see.'

'What?'

It wasn't the crowd, nor the coffin being lowered into the grave. Maigret felt certain of that.

He remembered the surplice puffed out by the wind, and the cross

Marcel had been carrying; he recalled the time when, hardly seven years old, he himself had yearned to be a choirboy. He had had to wait two years. Then it had been his turn to carry the silver cross and trot towards the cemetery, with a rustic hearse following behind.

'You wanted to see Marcel?'

He saw the boy give a start, the astonishment of the child on suddenly realizing that a grown-up is capable of guessing his thoughts.

'Why aren't you friends with Marcel?'

'I'm not friends with anyone.'

'Is there no one you like?'

'I'm the schoolmaster's son, I told you that already.'

'You'd rather be the ironmonger's son, or the mayor's, or the son of one of the local farmers?'

'I didn't say that.'

It was important not to frighten him, for he would have been capable of taking to his heels again. Yet it was not only fear of being caught up by Maigret that kept him where he was. He could move faster than the chief-inspector. Could it be that now they were face to face he felt a kind of relief? Could it be that at the bottom of his heart he had a secret longing to talk to somebody?

'Won't you sit down now?'

'I'd rather stand.'

'Are you very sorry your father's in prison?'

Instead of replying at once in the negative, he said nothing.

'You aren't sorry?'

Maigret was feeling like a stalker, creeping forward only with infinite caution. He must not go too quickly. The slightest word would be enough to startle the child, and then there would be nothing to be got out of him.

'Does it make you unhappy to be different from the others?'

'Why am I different from the others? Who said I was?'

'Suppose I had a little boy and he went to school, and played in the street near our home. The other boys would say,

' "His father's the chief-inspector!"'

'And because of that, they wouldn't treat him quite like one of themselves. You understand?

'Well, your father is the schoolmaster.'

The little boy looked at him again, longer and more intently than before.

'Would you have liked to be in the choir?'

He could feel he was on the wrong track. It was hard to say how he knew it. Some of the things he had said caused an almost imperceptible reaction. Others seemed to make Jean-Paul close up in himself.

'Marcel has friends?'

'Yes.'

'When they're together, they talk in whispers? They tell one another secrets, begin to laugh when they look at the rest of you?'

This was all coming back to him from so long ago that it astonished him. Never before, he thought, had he recalled such vivid memories of his own childhood; he could even smell the scent of the lilacs that flowered in the school playground in spring-time.

'Have you tried to be friends with them?'

'No.'

'Why not?'

'No reason.'

'You thought they wouldn't want you?'

'Why are you asking me all these questions?'

'Because your father's in prison. He didn't shoot Léonie Birard.'

He was staring hard at the boy, who did not blink.

'You know quite well he didn't. So someone else must have done it. Would you like your father to be found guilty?'

'No.'

There had been an almost imperceptible hesitation, and Maigret decided to let this point drop. It had occurred to him already, sitting in his corner the evening before, that Jean-Paul might feel some concealed resentment against his father and mother for being different from other people.

Not only because his father was the schoolmaster. They didn't go to church. They didn't dress him the same way as the other boys. Their house wasn't like the other houses either, nor was their way of life. His mother never laughed, she glided about like a shadow, humble and contrite. She had done something very wrong, and a woman had shot at her, to punish her.

The woman hadn't been sent to prison, which proved that she must have been right.

But perhaps Jean-Paul was fond of them all the same. Whether he liked it or not, he belonged to their clan, their race.

It was difficult to express all this. There were shades of meaning that vanished when one tried to put them into words.

'Suppose you knew something that would get your father out of prison . . .'

He himself didn't know what he was making for, and was surprised when Jean-Paul suddenly raised his head, stared at him with a mixture of terror and admiration. The boy opened his mouth, was about to say something, but bit it back, clenching his fists in the effort to restrain himself.

'Look, I'm only trying to understand. I don't know your father very well, but I feel sure he's not a man to tell lies. He says he didn't set foot in the tool-shed on Tuesday morning, and I believe him.'

The boy, still on the defensive, continued to watch him closely.

'On the other hand, Marcel Sellier seems like a good boy. When he does tell a lie, he goes to confession at once, so as not to remain in a state of sin. He has no reason to make trouble for your father. He's never unfair to him, in fact always puts him at the top of the class when you're the one who should be there.

'But Marcel says he saw your father coming out of the shed.'

It was like a bubble bursting suddenly at the surface of a pool. Jean-Paul, hanging his head, without looking at Maigret, declared:

'He's telling a lie.'

'You're quite sure of that, aren't you? It isn't just your own impression. You aren't saying it out of jealousy.'

'I'm not jealous of Marcel.'

'Why didn't you say so before?'

'What?'

'That Marcel was telling a lie.'

'Because!'

'You're quite certain he didn't see your father?'

'Yes.'

'What makes you so certain?'

Maigret had expected tears, perhaps even screams, but Jean-Paul's eyes, behind his spectacles, were dry. Only, his body had relaxed. There was nothing aggressive in his attitude now. He was not even on the defensive any longer.

The only visible sign of his surrender was that, feeling unsteady on his feet, he now sat down, at a little distance from the chief-inspector.

'I saw him.'

'Who did you see?'

'Marcel.'

'Where? When?'

'In class, standing by the window.'

'Tell me exactly what happened.'

'Nothing happened. Monsieur Piedbœuf came to fetch Father. They went together to the *mairie* office.'

'You saw them go?'

'Yes. I could see them from where I sat. They went in at the front door, and all the other boys began to fool about, as usual.'

'You stayed at your desk?'

'Yes.'

'Don't you ever fool about?'

'No.'

'Where was Marcel?'

'Standing by the first window on the left, the one that looks on to the playground and the gardens.'

'What was he doing?'

'Nothing. He was just looking out.'

'Doesn't he fool around either?'

'Not often.'

'Sometimes?'

'When Joseph's there.'

'The butcher's son?'

'Yes.'

'You were sitting at your desk. Marcel was standing at the left-hand window. Your father and Monsieur Piedbœuf were in the office. That's right, is it?'

'Yes.'

'Were the windows open?'

'They were shut.'

'You could hear the noise of the forge all the same?'

'I think so. I'm almost certain.'

'What happened?'

'Marcel left the window and walked across the room.'

'Where was he going?'

'To one of the two windows on the right.'

'The one that overlooks the back of Madame Birard's house?'

'Yes.'

'Your father was still at the *mairie* then?'

'Yes.'

'Marcel didn't say anything?'

'No. He looked out of the window.'

'You don't know what he was looking at?'

'From where I was sitting I couldn't see.'

'Do you often watch Marcel?'

He admitted awkwardly:

'Yes.'

This time, Maigret did not ask him why. The two boys were both good at their lessons, but because Jean-Paul was the schoolmaster's son, Marcel was put at the head of the class. Marcel was a choirboy and wore a surplice on Sundays. Marcel had friends, he had Joseph, the butcher's son, with whom he talked in whispers at break and to whose house he went to play when school was over.

'You saw your father come out of the *mairie* after that?'

'He walked over to our house, and went in for a cup of coffee.'

'Was the kitchen window open?'

'No. I know he had a cup of coffee. He always does.'

'Was your mother downstairs?'

'Upstairs in my room. I could see her through the open window.'

'After that your father didn't go into the tool-shed?'

'No. He came across the playground, back to the classroom.'

'Marcel was still standing at the window, the one on the right?'

'Yes.'

'Why didn't you say so at once?'

'When?'

Maigret paused for a moment to sort out his recollections.

'Wait a minute. Léonie Birard's body was found at the beginning of the afternoon. They didn't question you children at once?'

'They didn't question us at all that day. We didn't know exactly what had happened. We just noticed people coming and going. Then we saw the *gendarmes*.'

In fact, on Tuesday no one had openly accused the schoolmaster. Marcel Sellier had said nothing, either to his parents or to anyone else. So Jean-Paul had had no reason to contradict him and no chance of doing so.

'Were you there next day, when they questioned Marcel?'

'No. They sent for us one by one, in the office.'

'And when he came back on Thursday morning? When did you first hear that he was maintaining he had seen your father?'

'I can't remember now.'

'Did your parents talk about Léonie Birard on Tuesday evening?'

'Not till I was in bed. I heard part of what they were saying. Mother said it was her fault. Father said no, it was only rumours, people would soon realize he'd had nothing to do with it.'

'Why didn't you protest when you discovered that Marcel was accusing him?'

'Nobody would have believed me.'

Again Maigret seemed to catch a flicker, a mere nothing, something too subtle to be put into words. The little boy had not been pleased when his father was accused. He had probably been rather ashamed to think that he was in prison. But hadn't he been rather cowardly? Hadn't he been tempted, however slightly, without admitting it even to himself, to desert his parents' cause?

He already bore them a grudge for not being like other people. Now they were even less like other people, and the village, instead of simply cold-shouldering them, had turned against them.

Jean-Paul envied Marcel.

Was he to accuse him in his turn?

When one came to think of it, he had not been carried away by bad feelings. It hadn't been a question of cowardice, at any rate not only of cowardice.

Couldn't it even be said to be a kind of loyalty to the others?

He had had a chance of contradicting Marcel, showing him up as a liar. It would have been easy. Had it seemed to him to be too easy, too cheap a triumph?

Besides, it was a fact that people wouldn't have believed him. Who indeed in the village would have believed him, if he had gone to them and said:

'Sellier is a liar. My father didn't come out of the tool-shed. I saw
him go into our house, come out again, cross the playground. And at
that time Marcel was standing at the opposite window, where he
couldn't see him.'

'You haven't told this to your mother?'

'No.'

'Is she crying a lot?'

'She doesn't cry.'

That was even worse. Maigret could imagine the atmosphere in their
house during the last few days.

'Why did you come out this morning?'

'To see.'

'To see Marcel?'

'Perhaps.'

Perhaps also, without realizing it, from an urge to share, even at a
distance, in the village life? He must surely feel smothered in that little
house at the far end of the yard, where his mother was afraid to open
the windows.

'Are you going to tell the lieutenant?'

'I must have a word with Marcel first.'

'Will you tell him you heard about it from me?'

'Would you rather he didn't know that?'

'Yes.'

It looked as though he hadn't entirely given up hope of one day being
admitted to the alluring company of Marcel, Joseph and the rest.

'I think he'll tell me the truth without my needing to bring you into
it. Some of the others must have seen which window he was standing by.'

'They were fooling about.'

'All of them?'

'All except one of the girls, Louise Boncœur.'

'How old is she?'

'Fifteen.'

'Doesn't she fool about with the rest of them?'

'No.'

'You think she was watching Marcel?'

For the first time the boy's face was red, especially his ears.

'She watches him all the time,' he mumbled.

Was it because she was in love with Marcel that she hadn't contra-
dicted him, or simply because she hadn't distinguished between one
window and another? Marcel had said he was standing by the window. The other children probably hadn't thought twice about which
one it had been.

'It's time we went back to the village.'

'I'd rather not go back with you.'

'Would you like to go ahead?'

'Yes. You're sure you won't say anything to Marcel?'

Maigret nodded, and the boy hesitated, touched his cap, set out in the direction of the fields, soon breaking from a walk into a run.

The chief-inspector, who was at last by the sea, forgot to look at it, was gazing after the small figure departing along the lane.

Then he set out in his turn, stopped to fill his pipe, blew his nose, muttered something unintelligible, and anyone seeing him advancing slowly along the road would doubtless have wondered why he shook his head every now and then.

When he went past the cemetery the grave-diggers had finished heaping yellowish earth on Léonie Birard's coffin; her tomb could be recognized from a long way off, because of the bunches of flowers and fresh wreaths.


# VII

The women had gone home and, except for a few who came from distant farms, had probably taken off their black dresses and best shoes by this time. The men were still there, as though this were fair-day, and were overflowing from Louis's inn on to the pavement and into the yard, where they stood, putting down their bottles on the windowsills or on an old iron table that had been left outside all winter.

The pitch of their voices, their laughter, their slow, fuddled gestures made it clear that they had drunk a lot, and one, whose face Maigret did not see, was relieving himself behind the hedge.

Thérèse, busy as she was, had found time to pass him a *chopine* and a glass. He had gone only a few paces into the room, and could hear snatches of several conversations at once; he had had a glimpse of the doctor in the kitchen, but there were so many people in the way that he could not join him for the moment.

'I'd never have thought we'd have had the burying of her,' one old man was saying, shaking his head.

There were three of them, all much of an age. All three were certainly over seventy-five, and behind them, as they stood in a corner, against the white wall, was a copy of the law on establishments for the sale of alcoholic beverages and on public intoxication. They held themselves more stiffly than usual, because of their black Sunday suits and starched shirts, and this lent them a certain solemnity.

It was strange to see that though their faces were wrinkled with deep furrows, their eyes, when they looked at one another, had an innocent, childish expression. Each of them had a glass in his hand. The tallest of the three, who had a magnificent crop of white hair and a silky moustache, was swaying slightly, and whenever he was disposed to speak he laid a finger on the shoulder of one of his companions.

Why did Maigret suddenly imagine them in the school playground? They were just like schoolboys in their laughter and in the glances they exchanged. They had been to school together. Later in life they had pulled the same girls into ditches and had seen one another married, attended the funerals of their respective parents, their children's weddings and the christenings of their grandchildren.

'She might almost have been my sister; my father used to tell me he didn't know how often he'd pushed her mother down under the hay-stack. It seems she was a hot bitch and her husband was a cuckold from start to finish.'

Didn't that go far to explain the village? Behind Maigret, in another group, someone was saying:

'When he sold me that cow, I said to him:

' "Look here, Victor, I know you're a thief. But don't forget we did our military service together at Montpellier, and there was that evening . . ." '

Louis hadn't had time to change, he had only taken off his jacket. Maigret was edging slowly forward, remembering that the doctor had invited him to lunch at his house that day. Could Bresselles have forgotten about it?

He had a glass in his hand, like everyone else, but he had not lost his head, and was trying to quieten Marcellin, the butcher, who was the most drunk of them all and seemed very excited. It was difficult, from a distance, to make out exactly what was going on. Marcellin appeared to be angry with somebody, was trying to thrust the little doctor aside and push his way into the front room.

'I tell you I'm going to tell him!' the chief-inspector heard him say.

'Be quiet, Marcellin. You're drunk.'

'I've a right to be drunk, haven't I?'

'What did I tell you the last time you came to me for a check-up?'

'Be damned to what you told me!'

'If you go on like this, the next funeral will be yours.'

'I won't be spied on. I'm a free man.'

Wine did not suit him. He was white-faced, with an unhealthy flush on his cheekbones and eyelids. He was losing control of his movements. His voice was becoming thick.

'You hear that, Doc? I never could stand spies. And what's he doing here, except . . .'

It was Maigret he was looking at, from a distance, struggling to rush at him and vent his feelings. Two or three of the others were watching him and laughing. Someone held out a glass, which the doctor intercepted, emptying its contents on the ground.

'Don't you see he's had a skinful, Firmin?'

So far there had been no quarrelling, no scuffle. Indeed, they all knew one another too well to start fighting, and everyone knew exactly who was strongest among them.

Maigret went no closer; to avoid irritating the butcher he pretended not to notice what was going on. But he kept an eye on the group, and witnessed a little scene which distinctly surprised him.

The tall figure of Théo, the deputy-mayor, came lounging up, with the usual glint of mockery in his eyes, and joined the others; he was brandishing a glass which contained not wine but *pernod*, a strong dose, to judge by the colour.

He made some remark to the doctor in an undertone and passed the glass to the butcher, laying a hand on his shoulder. He said something to him too, and Marcellin at first seemed inclined to struggle, to push him away.

Finally, he grabbed the glass, swallowed its contents at one gulp, and almost at once his eyes glazed over, losing all expression. He made one more attempt to point a threatening finger at the chief-inspector, but his arm had grown too heavy to lift.

Whereupon, as though he had just felled him with a blow, Théo pushed him towards and up the stairs; after the first few steps he had to hoist him on to his shoulder.

'You haven't forgotten my invitation?'

The doctor, who had walked across to Maigret, gave a sigh of relief as he remarked, in almost the same words as the old man in the corner:

'*They've put her underground!* Shall we go now?'

They both slipped through the crowd and out on to the pavement, where they strolled a few steps.

'Before three months are up it'll be Marcellin's turn. I'm telling him regularly:

' "Marcellin, if you don't stop drinking you won't last long!"

'He's reached a stage where he eats practically nothing.'

'He's a sick man?'

'They're all sick, in his family. He's a pathetic case.'

'Théo's putting him to bed upstairs?'

'He had to be got rid of somehow.'

He opened the door. There was a good smell of cooking in the house.

'Will you have an *apéritif*?'

'Thank you, I'd rather not.'

The smell of wine had been so strong at Louis's inn that one could have got drunk just by breathing it in.

'Did you see the funeral?'

'From a distance.'

'I looked for you as I left the cemetery, but I didn't see you. Is lunch ready, Armande?'

'In five minutes.'

Only two places were laid. The doctor's sister, just like a priest's housekeeper, preferred not to sit down at table. She no doubt took her meals standing up in the kitchen, between two courses.

'Sit down. What do you think about it?'

'About what?'

'About nothing. About everything. She had a terrific funeral!'

Maigret grunted: 'The schoolmaster's still in prison.'

'Somebody had to go there.'

'I'd like to ask you a question, Doctor. Do you think that among all that crowd at the funeral there were many people who believed that Gastin killed Léonie Birard?'

'There must have been a few. Some people will believe anything.'

'And what about the rest?'

At first the doctor did not see the point of the question. Maigret explained:

'Let's suppose that one person in ten believes that Gastin fired that shot.'

'That's about the proportion.'

'Then the other nine-tenths have their own idea.'

'Undoubtedly.'

'Who do they suspect?'

'That depends. In my opinion each of them suspects, more or less sincerely, the person he himself would prefer to be found guilty.'

'And nobody says anything about it?'

'Among themselves, I expect they do.'

'Have you heard any such suspicions expressed?'

The doctor looked at him with something of Théo's irony.

'They don't say that kind of thing to me.'

'But although they know or believe that the schoolmaster is innocent, it doesn't worry them that he's in prison.'

'It assuredly doesn't worry them. Gastin isn't a local man. They consider that if the constabulary lieutenant and the examining magistrate have thought fit to arrest him, that's their affair. That's what those two are paid for.'

'Would they let him be condemned?'

'Without batting an eyelid. Of course, if it had been one of their own folk, it'd be a different story. Are you beginning to understand? If there has to be a guilty party, they'd rather it was an outsider.'

'Do they think the Sellier boy is telling the truth?'

'Marcel's a good boy.'

'He's told a lie.'

'Perhaps so.'

'I wonder why.'

'He may have thought his father would be accused. Don't forget that his mother is old Léonie's niece and will get all she's left.'

'I thought the old post-woman had always said her niece wouldn't get a penny.'

The doctor looked slightly embarrassed. His sister brought in the *hors-d'œuvre*.

'Did you go to the funeral?' Maigret asked her.

'Armande never goes to funerals.'

They began to eat in silence. Maigret was the first to break it, by saying, as though to himself:

'It wasn't on Tuesday that Marcel Sellier saw Gastin coming out of the tool-shed, it was on Monday.'

'He's admitted that?'

'I haven't asked him yet, but I'm practically certain of it. On Monday, before school, Gastin worked in his garden. Going across the playground during the morning, he noticed a hoe lying around and went to put it away. On Tuesday evening, after the body had been found, Marcel said nothing, and it didn't occur to him to accuse his teacher then.

'The idea came to him later, or some conversation he overheard made him decide to do it.

'He didn't tell an outright lie. Women and children specialize in such half-lies. He didn't make anything up, he simply changed a real event to another day.'

'That's rather comic!'

'I'll bet he's trying now to convince himself that it really was on Tuesday that he saw the schoolteacher coming out of the shed. He can't manage it, of course, and he must have been to confession.'

'Why don't you ask the priest?'

'Because if he told me, he'd be indirectly betraying the secrets of the confessional. The priest won't do that. I was thinking of asking the neighbours, the people at the co-operative stores, for instance, whether they'd seen Marcel going into the church at a time when there was no service, but now I know he goes in from the courtyard.'

The mutton was done to a turn and the beans melted in the mouth. The doctor had produced a bottle of old wine. A dull humming sound could be heard from outside, the noise of people talking in the inn yard and on the square.

Did the doctor realize that Maigret was simply talking in order to try out his ideas on a listener? He was going round and round the same subject, lazily, never coming right to the point.

'Actually, I don't think it was to save his father from suspicion that Marcel told that lie.'

At that moment he had the impression that Bresselles knew more about the matter than he would admit.

'Really?'

'You see, I'm trying to look at things from a child's point of view.

From the very beginning I've had the impression that this is some children's business in which grown-ups have become mixed up just by accident.'

Looking the doctor straight in the face he added placidly, weightily:

'And I'm more and more convinced that other people know it too.'

'In that case perhaps you'll be able to persuade them to talk?'

'Perhaps. It's difficult, isn't it?'

'Very difficult.'

Bresselles was laughing at him, just as the deputy-mayor did, again.

'I had a long talk with the little Gastin boy this morning.'

'You went to their house?'

'No. I saw him watching the funeral, over the cemetery wall, and I followed him down to the sea-shore.'

'Why did he go down to the sea?'

'He was running away from me. At the same time he wanted me to catch up with him.'

'What did he tell you?'

'That Marcel Sellier was standing at the right-hand window, not the left. Marcel might, at a pinch, have seen Léonie Birard fall when the bullet hit her in the eye, but he couldn't possibly have seen the schoolmaster coming out of the shed.'

'What conclusion do you draw from that?'

'That it was in order to protect somebody that little Sellier decided to tell his lie. Not at once. He took his time. The idea probably didn't enter his head straight away.'

'Why did he choose the schoolmaster?'

'For one thing because he was the most likely person. And for another because it just so happened that he'd seen him the day before, almost at the same time, coming out of the shed. And perhaps because of Jean-Paul, too.'

'You think he hates him?'

'I'm not saying anything positive, Doctor. I'm simply groping in the dark. I've questioned both boys. This morning I was watching some old men who were children themselves once, in this very village. If the village people are so liable to be hostile to strangers, isn't it because, without realizing it, they're envious of them? They themselves spend the whole of their lives at Saint-André, except for a trip to La Rochelle now and then, with only an occasional wedding or funeral by way of distraction.'

'I see what you're getting at.'

'The schoolmaster comes from Paris. In their eyes, he's an educated man who pokes into their little affairs and takes upon himself to give them advice. Among the children, the schoolmaster's boy has much the same status.'

'So Marcel told his lie because he hates Jean-Paul?'

'Partly because he envies him. The funny thing is that Jean-Paul, on his side, envies Marcel and his friends. He feels lonely, different from the others, rejected by them.'

'All the same, somebody shot the old Birard woman, and it can't have been either of the boys.'

'That's true.'

A home-made apple-tart was brought in, and the smell of coffee came in from the kitchen.

'I feel more and more convinced that Théo knows the truth.'

'Because he was in his garden?'

'Because of that and for other reasons. Last night, Doctor, you informed me cheerfully that they were all scoundrels.'

'I was joking.'

'Only half-joking, isn't that it? They all cheat, to some extent, they all go in for what you would call little mean tricks. You're an outspoken man. You haul them over the coals now and then. But you'd never actually give them away. Or am I wrong?'

'You say the *curé* would refuse to answer any questions you might put to him about Marcel, and I think you're right. Well, I'm their doctor. It's the same thing, in a way. Doesn't it strike you, Inspector, that this lunch is beginning to be rather like an interrogation? What will you have with your coffee? Brandy or *calvados*?'

'*Calvados*.'

Bresselles got up to fetch the bottle from an antique sideboard, and filled the glasses, still gay and playful, but his eyes rather more serious now.

'Your good health.'

'I'd like to talk to you about the accident,' said Maigret, almost timidly.

'What accident?'

It was only to gain time for thought that the doctor asked this question, for accidents in the village were few and far between.

'The motor-bicycle accident.'

'You've heard about that?'

'All I've heard is that Marcellin's son was knocked down by a motorbike. When did it happen?'

'One Saturday, just over a month ago.'

'Near old mother Birard's house?'

'Not far away. A hundred yards, perhaps.'

'In the evening?'

'Not long before dinner-time. It was dark. The two boys . . .'

'What boys?'

'Joseph, Marcellin's lad, and Marcel.'

'Were they by themselves?'

'Yes. They were going home. A motor-bike came up from the direction of the beach. Nobody knows exactly how it happened.'

'Who was on the bike?'

'Hervé Jusseau, a man of about thirty, who owns some mussel-beds, and got married last year.'

'Was he drunk?'

'He doesn't drink. He was brought up by his aunts, who are very strict and who still live in his house.'

'Was his headlamp lit?'

'Yes, that was established by the inquiry. The boys must have been playing about. Joseph tried to cross the road, and got knocked down.'

'Was his leg broken?'

'In two places.'

'Will he be lame?'

'No. In a week or two he'll be as good as new.'

'He can't walk yet?'

'No.'

'Will Marcellin get anything out of the accident?'

'The insurance will pay a fair amount, because Jusseau admitted that it was probably his fault.'

'Do you think it was?'

The doctor was obviously ill at ease, and took refuge in a burst of laughter.

'I'm beginning to understand what you chaps at Police Head-quarters mean by "third degree" questioning. I'd rather come clean. That's what you call it, isn't it?'

He refilled the glasses.

'Marcellin's a pathetic chap. Everyone knows he won't last much longer. He can't be blamed for drinking, because he's been unlucky all his life. There's always been illness somewhere in his family, and every-thing he's undertaken has gone wrong. Three years ago he rented some pasture-land to fatten bullocks, and there was such a drought that he lost every penny. He can hardly make both ends meet. His van is more often broken down by the roadside than on its way delivering meat.'

'So Jusseau, who, being insured, has nothing to lose, took the blame on himself?'

'That's about it.'

'Everyone knows this?'

'Pretty well everyone. An insurance company is a vague, far-away set-up, like the government, and people feel quite justified in taking money off it.'

'You made out the certificates?'

'Of course.'

'And worded them in such a way that Marcellin would get the highest possible sum?'

'Let's say I stressed the possibility of complications.'

'Were there any complications?'

'There might have been. As often as not, when a cow dies of some sudden illness, the vet certifies that it was an accident.'

It was Maigret's turn to laugh.

'Unless I'm mistaken, Marcellin's boy might have been up and about for the last week or two.'

'For the last week.'

'By keeping the plaster on his leg, you're enabling his father to demand more money from the insurance?'

'Even the doctor has to be a bit of a scoundrel, you see. If I refused that kind of thing, I'd have been gone from here long ago. And it's because the schoolmaster won't oblige with certificates, that he's in prison today. If he'd been more adaptable, if he hadn't been constantly scolding Théo for being too generous with Government money, they might have ended by adopting him.'

'In spite of what happened to his wife?'

'All the men here are cuckolds themselves.'

'So Marcel Sellier was the only witness of the accident?'

'I told you it was after dark. There was nobody else on the road.'

'Somebody might have seen them from a window.'

'You're thinking of old Léonie?'

'Well, I suppose she wasn't *always* in her kitchen; she must have gone into the front room now and then.'

'There was no mention of her during the inquiry. She didn't come forward.'

The doctor scratched his head, perfectly serious now.

'I have the impression you're beginning to see your way. Not that I can follow you yet.'

'Are you sure of that?'

'Of what?'

'Why did Marcellin try to throw himself on me this morning?'

'He was drunk.'

'Why pick on me particularly?'

'You were the only stranger in the inn. When he's tight he gets persecution mania. So he began to imagine you'd come here simply to spy on him. . . .'

'You were trying hard to calm him down.'

'Would you have preferred a fight?'

'Théo finished him off by making him drink a double or triple *pernod*, and carted him upstairs. It's the first time I've seen the deputy-mayor do a good turn.'

'Marcellin's his cousin.'

'I'd rather he'd been allowed to come out with what he wanted to say to me.'

The others had obviously wanted to stop him talking, they'd whisked him away, so to speak, and at present he must be sleeping off his drink in one of the first-floor bedrooms.

'I must be getting back to my surgery,' said Bresselles. 'There'll be at least a dozen people in the waiting-room by now.'

The consulting surgery was a low-roofed, two-roomed building in the yard. People could be seen sitting in a row against the wall; among them a child with a bandaged head and an old man with crutches.

'I think you'll end by getting somewhere!' sighed the little doctor, referring, of course, not to Maigret's career, but to the present investigation.

His attitude now betokened some respect, but a certain embarrassment as well.

'You'd rather I didn't find out anything at all?'

'I'm wondering. It might have been better if you hadn't come.'

'That depends on how it's all going to end. Have you no idea about that?'

'I know about as much as you do on the subject.'

'And you'd have left Gastin in prison?'

'They can't keep him there for long, in any case.'

Bresselles wasn't a local man. He was a townsman like the schoolmaster. But he had been living with the village for over twenty years, and couldn't help feeling himself a part of it.

'Come and see me whenever you like. Please believe I do what I can. It's just that I'd rather live here and spend most of my day on the road, than be shut up in a surgery in a town or in some suburb or other.'

'Thank you for the lunch.'

'Are you going to question young Marcel again?'

'I haven't decided yet.'

'If you want him to talk, you'd better see him when his father isn't there.'

'Is he afraid of his father?'

'I don't think it's that. It's more that he admires him. If he's told a lie he must be in a state of terror.'

When Maigret emerged from the house, there were only a few people clustered at Louis's and on the square. Théo was sitting in a corner, playing cards, as on any other day, with the postman, the blacksmith and a farmer. His eyes met Maigret's, and though they were still mocking they held a dawning respect as well.

'Is Marcellin still upstairs?' the chief-inspector asked Thérèse.

'Snoring! He's messed up the whole room. He can't carry drink any longer. The same thing happens every time.'

'Nobody been asking for me?'

'The lieutenant came past just now. He didn't come in, he only gave a glance round as though looking for somebody, it may have been you. Will you have something to drink?'

'No, thank you.'

The very smell of wine was making him feel sick. He strolled over to the *mairie*. One of the gendarmes was talking to Lieutenant Daniélou.

'Were you wanting to see me?'

'Not specially. I went across the square a little time ago and took a look in case you were at the inn.'

'Nothing fresh?'

'It may be of no importance. Nouli, here, has found a seventh rifle.'

'A .22?'

'Yes. Here it is. It's the same type as the others.'

'Where was it?'

'In the stable behind the butcher's house.'

'Hidden?'

It was the gendarme himself who replied:

'I was still hunting for the cartridge-case, with one of the other men. We were going through the gardens. I noticed that one of the stable doors was open, and there were bloodstains all over the place. Then I saw the rifle in a corner.'

'Did you question the butcher's wife?'

'Yes. She said that when Sellier went round with his drum to announce that all rifles must be taken to the *mairie*, she forgot all about her little boy's gun, because he was in bed. He had an accident about a month ago, and . . .'

'I know.'

Maigret stood holding the weapon, puffing at his pipe. Finally he put down the rifle, propping it in a different corner from the others.

'Will you come with me for a moment, Lieutenant?'

They went across the courtyard and opened the door of the schoolroom, which smelt of ink and chalk.

'Now I don't know yet where this is going to lead us. On Tuesday morning, when the schoolmaster left this room with Piedbœuf, the farmer, Marcel Sellier came over to this window.'

'That's what he told us.'

'To the right of that lime-tree, one can see the tool-shed. One can also see certain windows, including those on the first floor of the butcher's house.'

The lieutenant was listening, with a slight frown.

'The boy didn't remain here long. Before the schoolmaster left the office, he went to the other side of the classroom.'

Maigret was doing the same, walking past the blackboard and the teacher's desk to the window right opposite the first one.

'From here, as you can see for yourself, there's a view of Léonie Birard's house. If, as the investigation seems to have established, she

was standing at her window when she was shot, Marcel may have seen
her fall.'

'You think he had some reason for crossing from one window to the
other? He might have seen something, and . . .'

'Not necessarily.'

'Why did he tell a lie?'

Maigret preferred not to answer this.

'You have suspicions?'

'I think so.'

'What are you going to do?'

'What has to be done,' replied Maigret without enthusiasm.

He sighed, emptied his pipe on the greyish floorboards, looked down
at the ashes with an air of embarrassment and added, as though
regretfully:

'It isn't going to be pleasant.'

From a first-floor window in the opposite house, Jean-Paul was
watching them across the courtyard.


# VIII

BEFORE he left the classroom, Maigret noticed another figure, at a
window, an open one this time, in a more distant house, beyond the
gardens. Someone was sitting on the windowsill, with his back turned,
but from the shape of the head and the plump body, he recognized
Marcel Sellier.

'That's the butcher's house, I suppose?'

The lieutenant followed the direction of his glance.

'Yes . . . Joseph, the son, and Marcel are great friends.'

The boy at the window turned round and looked down at a woman
who was hanging out washing in a garden. Automatically, his eyes
swept round in a half-circle just as Maigret and the lieutenant were
coming out of the school and facing his way.

In spite of the distance it was clear, from his movements, that he was
saying something to somebody in the room; then he slid off the windowsill and disappeared.

Daniélou turned to the chief-inspector and said quietly, pensively:
'Good luck!'

'Are you going back to La Rochelle?'

'Would you rather I waited for you?'

'If you did I might perhaps be able to take the evening train.'

He had not more than a hundred and fifty yards to go. He covered the distance at a swinging stride. The butcher's was a low, squat house. There was no proper shop. The left-hand ground-floor room had been fitted up for the purpose with a quaint-looking counter, a pair of scales, an old-fashioned refrigerator and a table on which the meat was cut up.

The front door opened into a passage at the far end of which, to the left of the stairs, one saw through to the backyard.

Before knocking, Maigret had gone past the right-hand window, the kitchen window, which was open; inside, at a round table, sat three women, one of whom was old and wore a white cap; they were eating slices of tart. One of them must be Marcellin's wife and the others her mother and sister, who lived in the neighbouring village and had come over for the funeral.

They had seen him go by. The windows were so small that for a moment his bulk had blocked this one. They listened while he paused at the open door, looked for a bell and, not finding one, took two steps forward, purposely making a noise.

The butcher's wife got up, half-opened the kitchen door, began by asking:

'What is it?'

Then, recognizing him, probably from having seen him about the village, she went on:

'You're the policeman from Paris, aren't you?'

If she had been to the funeral, she had already changed her clothes. She could not be very old, but she was round-shouldered, hollow-cheeked, with feverish eyes. Avoiding his eye, she added:

'My husband's out. I don't know when he'll be back. Did you want to see him?'

She did not ask him into the kitchen, where the other two women sat silent.

'I'd like a word with your little boy.'

She was frightened, but that didn't mean anything; she was the kind of woman who would always be frightened, always expecting some disaster.

'He's in bed.'

'I know.'

'He's been up there for over a month.'

'You don't mind if I go up?'

What could she do? She let him pass without daring to protest, as she crumpled a corner of her apron with tense fingers. He had only gone up four or five steps when he saw Marcel coming down towards him, and it was he, Maigret, who stood back against the wall.

'Excuse me . . .' stammered the boy, avoiding Maigret's eye in his turn.

He was in a hurry to get outside, must have expected Maigret to stop him or call him back, but the chief-inspector did neither and continued on his way upstairs.

'The door on the right,' said the mother when he reached the landing.

He knocked. A child's voice said:

'Come in.'

The mother was still standing below, looking up at him while he opened the door and closed it behind him.

'Don't trouble to move.'

Joseph had made as if to get up from the bed where he was sitting with several pillows at his back and one leg in plaster to well above the knee.

'I passed your friend on the stairs.'

'I know.'

'Why didn't he wait for me?'

The room was low-ceilinged, and Maigret's head nearly came up to the central rafter. It was a small room. The bed took up the greater part of it. It was untidy, scattered with illustrated magazines and pieces of wood hacked with a penknife.

'Are you bored?'

There was in fact a chair, but it was heaped with a variety of objects, a jacket, a catapult, two or three books, and some more bits of wood.

'You can take off all that stuff,' said the boy.

Jean-Paul Gastin took after his father and mother. Marcel took after his father.

Joseph resembled neither the butcher nor his wife. He was undoubtedly the handsomest of the three boys, and seemed to be the healthiest and most well-balanced.

Maigret sat down on the windowsill, with his back to the view of yards and gardens, in the place where Marcel had been sitting a few minutes ago, and he seemed to be in no hurry to talk. This was not because he wanted to puzzle the other person present, as sometimes happened at the Quai des Orfèvres, but because he didn't know where to begin.

Joseph opened the conversation by inquiring:

'Where's my father?'

'At Louis's.'

The boy hesitated, then asked:

'How is he?'

Why try to conceal what he must know perfectly well?

'Théo's put him to bed.'

He seemed to be relieved rather than worried by this.

'Mother's downstairs with my grandmother?'

'Yes.'

The sun, now low although the sky was still bright, was gently warming Maigret's back, and the song of birds came up from the gardens; some unseen child was blowing a tin trumpet.

'Wouldn't you like me to take off that plaster?'

It seemed almost as though Joseph was expecting this, he understood the hint. He was not uneasy, like his mother. He didn't seem scared. He was gazing at the heavy figure of his visitor and at his apparently inscrutable face, and considering what line to take.

'You know about that?'

'Yes.'

'Did the doctor tell you?'

'I'd already guessed. What were you up to, you and Marcel, when the motor-bike knocked you down?'

Joseph showed genuine relief.

'You haven't found the horse-shoe?' he asked.

And these words brought a picture into Maigret's mind. He had seen a horse-shoe somewhere. It was while he'd been going round Léonie Birard's house. There had been a rusty horse-shoe lying on the floor, in the corner to the right of the window, not far from the chalk marks which showed where the body had been found.

He had noticed it at the time. He had been on the point of asking about it. Then, as he straightened up, he had caught sight of a nail and reflected that the horse-shoe had probably been hung on that. Many country people will pick up a horse-shoe on the road and keep it, for luck.

Daniélou and his men, who had searched the house before him, must have thought the same.

'Yes, there was a horse-shoe in Léonie Birard's house,' he replied.

'It was me that found it, the evening I had the accident. I was coming along the sea lane with Marcel when I stumbled over it. It was in the dark. I picked it up. We got to the old woman's house and I was carrying the horse-shoe. The window that looks on to the road was open. We crept close up to it without making a noise.'

'Was the postmistress in the front room?'

'In the kitchen. The door was half-open.'

He couldn't prevent himself from grinning.

'First of all I thought of throwing the horse-shoe into the house, to frighten her.'

'Just as you used to throw in dead cats and other filth?'

'I wasn't the only one who did that.'

'You changed your mind?'

'Yes. I thought it would be more fun to put it in her bed. I climbed over the windowsill, without any noise, and went two or three steps inside: then, by bad luck, I knocked into something, I don't know what. She heard. I dropped the horse-shoe and jumped out of the window.'

'Where was Marcel?'

'He was waiting for me, a bit further on. I began to run. I heard the old woman yelling threats out of her window, and that's when the motor-bike ran over me.'

'Why didn't you say so?'

'To begin with, they took me to the doctor, and it hurt a lot. They gave me some medicine to put me to sleep. When I woke up, Father was there, and he began at once to talk to me about the insurance. I understood that if I told the truth, they'd say it had been my own fault and the insurance wouldn't pay up. Father needs money.'

'Did Marcel come to see you?'

'Yes. I made him promise not to say anything either.'

'And since then he's been to see you every day?'

'Nearly every day. We're friends.'

'Isn't Jean-Paul friends with you?'

'He isn't friends with anybody.'

'Why not?'

'I don't know. He doesn't want to be, I suppose. He's like his mother. His mother never talks to the other women in the village.'

'Aren't you bored, staying up in this room all alone for a month?'

'Yes.'

'What do you do all day?'

'Nothing. I read. I carve little boats and people out of bits of wood.'

There were dozens scattered around him, some of them quite skilfully made.

'Don't you ever go to the window?'

'I oughtn't to.'

'For fear people may find out you can walk?'

He answered frankly:

'Yes.'

Then he asked:

'Are you going to tell the insurance people?'

'It's no business of mine.'

There was a silence, during which Maigret turned to look out at the backs of the houses opposite, and the school playground.

'I suppose it's mostly during playtime that you look out of the window?'

'Often.'

Just opposite, on the far side of the little gardens, he could see Léonie Birard's windows.

'Did the postwoman ever notice you?'

'Yes.'

The boy's face clouded at this; he hesitated for a moment, but already knew he would have to tell.

'Even before, whenever she saw me, she used to pull faces.'

'Used she to put out her tongue at you?'

'Yes. After the accident she used to tease me by holding up the horse-shoe.'

'Why?'

'It must have been to make me understand that she might go and tell the whole story.'

'She didn't do so.'

'No.'

The ex-postmistress had behaved rather as though she were the same age as the little boys she used to curse, who made a set against her. She would shout, threaten, put out her tongue at them. She had been reminding Joseph, from a distance, that she could make trouble for him if she chose.

'Did she frighten you?'

'Yes. Father and Mother needed the money.'

'Do they know about the horse-shoe business?'

'Father does.'

'Did you tell him?'

'He guessed I'd done something I hadn't told him about, and he made me own up.'

'Was he cross with you?'

'He said I'd better keep quiet about it.'

'How many times did Léonie Birard show you the horse-shoe through the window?'

'Twenty times, perhaps. She did it every time she saw me.'

Just as he had done in the morning with Jean-Paul, Maigret slowly lit his pipe; his manner was as reassuring as possible. He seemed to be listening absent-mindedly to some trivial story, and his relaxed attitude and innocent face might have led the boy to forget that he was not talking to one of his own school-friends.

'What did Marcel come to tell you just now?'

'That if he was questioned again he'd have to own up.'

'Why? Is he scared?'

'He's been to confession. Besides, I think the funeral made him feel a bit funny.'

'He'll say he saw you at this window before he went across to the opposite window of the schoolroom?'

'How did you know that? You see! Everything goes wrong, in this house. Other people do worse things and nothing happens to them. In our family it's the other way round.'

'What were you doing at the window?'

'I was looking out.'

'The old woman was showing you the horse-shoe?'

'Yes.'

'Tell me exactly what happened.'

'There's nothing else I can do, is there?'

'Not at the point we've reached.'

'I took my rifle.'

'Where was your rifle?'

'In that corner, by the cupboard.'

'Was it loaded?'

An almost imperceptible hesitation.

'Yes.'

'With long or short .22 cartridges?'

'Long ones.'

'Do you generally keep the rifle in your bedroom?'

'Often.'

'Have you ever shot at sparrows through the window, lately?'

He hesitated again, thinking as rapidly as possible, as though he could not afford to make the slightest slip.

'No. I don't think so.'

'You wanted to scare the old woman?'

'I suppose so. I'm not quite sure what I wanted. She was teasing me. I thought she'd end by telling everything to the insurance people, and then Father wouldn't be able to buy a new van.'

'That's what he's decided to do with the money?'

'Yes. He feels sure that if he had a good van and could make a longer round, he'd earn money.'

'Doesn't he earn any as it is?'

'Some months he makes a loss, and it's Grandma who . . .'

'She helps you?'

'When there's no other way. She makes a scene every time.'

'Did you fire the gun?'

He nodded, with a kind of apologetic smile.

'Did you aim it?'

'I was aiming at the window.'

'In other words, you meant to break a pane of glass?'

He nodded again, eagerly.

'Will they send me to prison?'

'Boys of your age aren't sent to prison.'

He seemed disappointed at this.

'Then what will they do?'

'The judge will lecture you.'

'And then?'

'He'll talk severely to your father. The final responsibility is his.'

'Why, when he didn't do anything?'

'Where was he when you fired?'

'I don't know.'

'Was he on his round?'

'I don't suppose so. He never goes off as early as that.'

'Was he in the shop?'

'Perhaps.'

'He didn't hear anything? Nor your mother?'

'No. They didn't say anything to me.'

'Don't they know it was you who fired the shot?'

'I haven't said anything to them about it.'

'Who took the rifle down to the stable?'

This time he blushed, looked around him in evident embarrassment, avoided meeting Maigret's eyes.

'You can hardly have gone downstairs and across the yard with that plaster on your leg,' insisted the chief-inspector. 'So what?'

'I asked Marcel . . .'

He stopped short.

'No. That's not true,' he admitted. 'It was Father. You'd find out sooner or later, anyway.'

'You asked him to take down the gun?'

'Yes. I didn't explain why.'

'When?'

'On Wednesday morning.'

'He didn't ask you any questions?'

'He only looked at me, kind of worried.'

'Didn't he tell your mother about it?'

'If he had done, she'd have been up here at once to drag the whole story out of me.'

'Does she usually drag stories out of you?'

'She always guesses when I try to tell lies.'

'Was it you who asked Marcel to say he'd seen the schoolmaster coming out of the tool-shed?'

'No. I didn't even know he'd be questioned.'

'Why did he do that?'

'I expect it was because he'd seen me at the window.'

'With the gun. You were holding the gun?'

Joseph was getting hot, but he went on valiantly, doing his best not to contradict himself and not to be seen hesitating.

Although Maigret was still speaking in a colourless voice, without emphasis, as though his words had no importance, the boy was intelligent enough to realize that he was slowly and steadily nearing the truth.

'I don't remember exactly. Perhaps I hadn't picked up the rifle yet.'

'But when he looked through the other window and saw the postwoman fall down, he guessed it was you who'd shot her?'

'He's never said so to me.'

'Haven't you talked it over together?'

'Not until today.'

'And then he simply announced that if he was questioned he'd have to own up?'

'Yes.'

'Was he upset?'

'Yes.'

'And you?'

'I'd like to get it over.'

'But you'd rather go to prison?'

'Perhaps.'

'Why?'

'No special reason. Just to see.'

He refrained from adding that prison would probably be more fun than his home.

Maigret stood up with a sigh.

'Would you have let the schoolmaster be found guilty?'

'I don't think so.'

'You're not sure?'

The answer to this was no. Joseph was not sure. It didn't seem to have occurred to him that he was doing any harm to Gastin. Had it occurred to the rest of the village?

'Are you going away?' he asked in surprise, as he saw the chief-inspector turn towards the door.

Maigret paused on the threshold.

'What else can I do?'

'You're going to tell everything to the lieutenant?'

'Except about your accident, perhaps.'

'Thank you.'

He did not seem overjoyed at being left.

'You've nothing more to tell me, I suppose?'

He shook his head.

'You're sure you've told me the truth?'

He nodded again, and then, instead of opening the door, Maigret sat down on the edge of the bed.

'Now suppose you tell me *exactly* what you saw in the yard.'

'In what yard?'

The little boy had blushed hotly and his ears were scarlet.

Before replying, Maigret, without having to get up, half-opened the door and said to Marcellin's wife, who was standing at the top of the stairs:

'Please be good enough to go down.'

He waited till she was down below, then shut the door again.

'In this yard.'

'Our yard?'

'Yes.'

'What could I have seen there?'

'That's for you to say, not for me.'

The boy had withdrawn to the far side of his bed close to the wall and was staring aghast at Maigret.

'What do you mean?'

'You were at the window and the old woman was showing you the horse-shoe.'

'That's what 1 told you already.'

'Only, the gun wasn't in your room.'

'How do you know?'

'Your father was down there, in the yard, with the stable door open. What was he doing?'

'He was quartering a lamb.'

'From where he was he could see you at your window, and he could see Léonie Birard too.'

'Nobody can have told you all that,' murmured the little boy, more astonished than distressed. 'Did you just guess it?'

'He was quite as much at loggerheads with the old woman as you were. She used to shout at him whenever he went past her house.'

'She used to call him a good-for-nothing and a beggar.'

'Used she to put out her tongue at him?'

'She had a craze for doing it.'

'Then your father went into the stable?'

'Yes.'

'When he came out, he was carrying your gun?'

'What will they do to him?'

'That depends. Have you decided to stop telling me lies?'

'I'll tell you the truth.'

'Could your father still see you then?'

'I don't think so. I'd stepped back.'

'So he shouldn't know you were watching?'

'Perhaps. I don't remember. It happened very quickly.'

'What happened very quickly?'

'He looked around him, and then fired. I heard him growl:
' "There's one for you, you louse!" '

'Did he aim carefully?'

'No. He just lifted the gun to his shoulder and fired.'

'Is he a good shot?'

'He can't hit a sparrow at ten yards.'

'Did he see Léonie Birard fall down?'

'Yes. He stood quite still for a moment, as though he was thunder-struck. Then he rushed into the stable to put away the gun.'

'And after that?'

'He looked up at my window, then went indoors. Later on I heard him go out.'

'Where was he going?'

'To Louis's, to drink.'

'How do you know?'

'Because he came home tight.'

'Was Théo in his garden?'

'He'd just come out of his wine-cellar.'

'Did he see your father fire the shot?'

'He couldn't have, from where he was standing.'

'But he saw you at the window?'

'I think so.'

'He heard the shot?'

'He must have heard it.'

'Your father hasn't said anything to you about it since?'

'No.'

'Nor you to him?'

'I didn't dare.'

'Marcel thought it was you who'd fired?'

'Surely.'

'And that's why he told a lie?'

'We're friends.'

Maigret patted the boy's head with a mechanical gesture.

'That's all, my lad!' he said, standing up.

He was on the verge of adding:

'Some people have to grow up quicker than others.'

What would be the point? Joseph wasn't taking the thing over-tragically. He was so accustomed to little everyday dramas that this one hardly struck him as exceptionally serious.

'Will he go to prison?'

'Not for long. Unless they prove that he was aiming at Léonie Birard and meant to hit her.'

'He only wanted to give her a fright.'

'I know.'

'The whole village will stand up for him.'

After a moment's thought, the boy nodded.

'Yes, I think they will. They're fond of him, in spite of everything. It isn't his fault.'

'What isn't his fault?'

'Everything.'

Maigret was half-way downstairs when the little boy called him back.

'Won't you take the plaster off my leg?'

'It'll be better for me to send the doctor along.'

'Will you send him at once?'

'If he's at home.'

'Don't forget.'

As Maigret reached the bottom of the stairs, he heard a soft:

'Thank you.'

He did not go into the kitchen. The sun was sinking behind the houses, and mist was rising from the ground. The three women were still there, motionless, and watched him in silence as he went past the window.

Outside the church, the *curé* was talking to an elderly woman, and it looked to Maigret as though he felt an impulse to come across the road and speak to him. He, too, must know the truth. He knew about Marcel's lie, from his confession. But he was the only person who had the right to say nothing.

Maigret raised his hat, and the priest seemed rather surprised. Then the chief-inspector went into the *mairie*, where he found Daniélou waiting, smoking a cigar; the lieutenant looked inquiringly at him.

'You can release the schoolmaster,' said Maigret.

'Was it Joseph?'

Maigret shook his head.

'Who?'

'His father, Marcellin.'

'So all I have to do is arrest him?'

'I'd like a word with him first.'

'Hasn't he confessed?'

'He's in no condition to confess anything whatever. If you'll come with me . . .'

The two men walked over to the inn, but as they were about to enter, Maigret remembered a promise he had made, and went along to ring Bresselles's door-bell.

The sister opened the door.

'The doctor isn't here?'

'He's just gone off to deliver a baby.'

'When he gets back, will you ask him to go and take the plaster off Joseph's leg?'

She, too, would be imagining that Joseph was the criminal. The lieutenant was waiting at Louis's door. There was no one standing about outside, now. Ten or a dozen drinkers were still lolling in the tap-room, one of them asleep with his head on a table.

'Where did they put Marcellin?' Maigret asked Thérèse.

He had spoken loud enough for Théo to hear. And now it was the chief-inspector's turn to throw the deputy-mayor a sparkling, mischievous glance. Théo, however, proved himself a good loser. Instead of scowling, he merely shrugged, as though saying:

'Well, that's that! It's not my fault . . .'

'The room to the left of the stairs, Monsieur Maigret.'

He went up alone; as he opened the door, the butcher, startled by the sound, sat up and stared at him, wide-eyed.

'Whaddye want, you?' he queried thickly. 'What's time?'

'Five o'clock.'

He swung his feet to the ground, rubbed his eyes, looked round for something to drink. His breath smelt so strongly of alcohol that the chief-inspector felt slightly sick, and the floor was spattered with vomit.

'The lieutenant's waiting for you downstairs, Marcellin.'

'Me? Why? What have I done?'

'He'll tell you that.'

'Have you been to my house?'

Maigret made no reply.

'You've been pestering the kid?' the butcher persisted, in a toneless voice.

'Get up, Marcellin.'

'I'll do as I please.'

His hair was tousled, his eyes glassy.

'Clever chap, aren't you! Must be proud of yourself! Pestering children! That's what you came here for! . . . And the government pays you to do it!'

'Come down.'

'Don't you touch me.'

He stood up, swaying, and growled:

'All this because the other fellow's a schoolmaster, an educated man, who takes the taxpayers' money too . . .'

He emphasized his contempt by spitting on the floor, staggered out, nearly fell downstairs.

'A *pernod*, Louis!' he ordered, holding tight to the bar.

He wanted to make a handsome exit, was staring round at the others, a forced sneer on his face.

Louis glanced at Maigret as though asking whether he should serve the requested drink, and the chief-inspector made a gesture of indifference.

Marcellin emptied the glass at one gulp, wiped his mouth, turned to face Théo and declared:

'I got her all the same, the louse!'

'Don't brag about!' the deputy-mayor muttered, looking at the cards in his hand.

'Well, didn't I get her?'

'Not on purpose. You couldn't hit a bullock at thirty yards.'

'Did I get her or did I not?'

'You got her, all right! Now shut up.'

The lieutenant intervened, saying:

'Please come with me quietly, so I don't have to handcuff you.'

'And suppose I want to be handcuffed?'

He was defiant to the last.

'As you like.'

There was a glint of metal, the sound of the handcuffs snapping round the butcher's wrists.

'See that, you chaps?'

He bumped against the doorpost as he went out, and a few seconds afterwards, they heard the slamming of a car door.

Silence fell. The air was saturated with the smell of wine and spirits; thick smoke hovered round the lamp which had just been lit, though it was still daylight outside. In half an hour it would be quite dark and the village would have vanished except for a few spots of light, two or three ill-lit shop windows, an occasional shadowy figure gliding past the house-fronts.

'I'd like my bill, please,' said Maigret, who was the first to speak.

'Are you leaving at once?'

'I'm catching the evening train.'

The others still remained silent, as though in suspense.

'How can I send for a taxi?'

'Just ask Marchandon. He'll take you in his van. He always takes people to the station.'

Théo spoke suddenly:

'Are we playing or are we not? I said spades were trumps. And I'm declaring a *tierce*.'

'With what?'

'The queen.'

'Good.'

'I'm playing the knave.'

Maigret seemed slightly depressed, or tired, as he nearly always did at the end of a case. He had come here to eat oysters, washed down with the local white wine.

'What will you have on me, Inspector?'

He hesitated. The smell of wine-dregs was sickening him. But because of what he had intended before leaving Paris, he said:

'A *chopine* of white wine.'

The light was on in the ironmonger's. One could see past the hanging buckets and pans in the shop to the kitchen at the back, where Marcel Sellier was sitting with a book in front of him, his head between his hands.

'Your health!'

'Yours!'

'You must have a queer opinion of this place?'

He made no reply, and a little later Thérèse brought down his suit-case, which she had packed for him.

'I hope your wife will find everything tidy,' she said.

Actually, it was pleasant to be suddenly reminded of Madame Maigret, of their flat in the Boulevard Richard-Lenoir, and of the brightly lit Grands Boulevards, where he would take her to their usual cinema, the very first evening.

When, sitting in the front of the van, he was driven past the *mairie*, he saw a light in the Gastins' house. In an hour or two the schoolmaster would be home, and the three of them would be together again, as like as three peas, trying to hide away, as it were, on a lost island.

Further on he failed to notice the masts swaying in the darkness to his right, and at the station he bought a whole sheaf of Paris newspapers.

*Shadow Rock Farm,*
*Lakeville (Connecticut),*
*8 December, 1953.*